Saving Faith

and

Absolute Power

David Baldacci is the author of seventeen *New York Times* bestsellers. With his books published in over forty languages in more than eighty countries, and with nearly seventy million copies in print, he is one of the world's favourite storytellers. David Baldacci is also the cofounder, along with his wife, of the Wish You Well Foundation, a nonprofit organization dedicated to supporting literacy efforts across America. Still a resident of his native Virginia, he invites you to visit him at www.DavidBaldacci.com, and his foundation at www.WishYouWellFoundation.org, and to look into its program to spread books across America at www.FeedingBodyandMind.com.

D1355423

Also by David Baldacci

DAVID BALDACCI

Saving Faith

and

Absolute Power

PAN BOOKS

Saving Faith first published 1999 by Warner Books USA
First published in Great Britain 1999 by Simon and Schuster UK
First published in paperback 2003 by Pan Books

Absolute Power first published 1996 by Warner Books USA
First published in Great Britain 1996 by Simon and Schuster UK
First published in paperback 2003 by Pan Books

This omnibus first published 2009 by Pan Books
an imprint of Pan Macmillan, a division of Macmillan Publishers Limited
Pan Macmillan, 20 New Wharf Road, London N1 9RR
Basingstoke and Oxford
Associated companies throughout the world
www.panmacmillan.com

ISBN 978-0-330-51748-5

1 3 5 7 9 8 6 4 2

A CIP catalogue record for this book is available from
the British Library.

Printed in the UK by CPI Mackays, Chatham ME5 8TD

Saving Faith

To Aaron Priest,
my friend

ONE

The somber group of men sat in a large room that rested far belowground, accessed by only a single, high-speed elevator. The chamber had been secretly built during the early 1960s under the guise of renovating the private building that squatted over it. The original plan, of course, was to use this "super-bunker" as a refuge during a nuclear attack. This facility was not for the top leaders of American government, it was for those whose level of relative "unimportance" dictated that they probably wouldn't be able to get out in time but who still rated protection afforded no ordinary citizen. Politically, even in the context of total destruction, there must be order.

The bunker was built at a time when people believed it possible to survive a direct nuclear hit by burrowing into the earth inside a steel cocoon. After the holocaust that would annihilate the rest of the country, leaders would emerge from the rubble with absolutely nothing left to lead, unless you counted vapor.

The original, aboveground building had been leveled long ago, but the subterranean room remained under what was now a small strip mall that had been vacant for years. Forgotten by virtually all, the chamber was now used as a meeting place for certain people in the country's primary intelligence-gathering agency. There was some risk involved, since the meetings were not related to the men's official duties. The matters discussed at these gatherings were illegal, and tonight even murderous. Thus additional precautions had been necessary.

The super-thick steel walls had been supplemented by a copper coating. That measure, along with tons of dirt overhead, protected against prying electronic ears lurking in space and elsewhere. These men didn't particularly like coming to this underground room. It was inconvenient, and ironically, it seemed a little too James Bondish even for their admittedly cloak-and-dagger tastes. However, the truth was the earth was now encircled with so much advanced surveillance technology that virtually no conversation taking place on its surface was safe from interception. One had to dig into the dirt to escape his enemies, and if there was a place where people could meet with reasonable confidence that their conversations would not be overheard even in their world of ultrasophisticated peekaboo, this was it.

The gray-headed people present at the meeting were all white males, and most were nearing their agency's mandatory retirement age of sixty. Dressed quietly and professionally, they could have been doctors, lawyers or investment bankers. One would probably not remember any of the group a day after seeing them. This anonymity was their stock-in-trade. These sorts of people lived and died, sometimes violently, over such details.

Collectively, this cabal possessed thousands of secrets that could never be known by the general public because the public would certainly condemn rather than applaud the actions giving rise to these secrets. However, America often demanded results – economic, political, social and otherwise – that could be obtained only by smashing certain parts of the world to a bloody pulp. It was the job of these men to figure out how to do so in a clandestine manner that would not reflect poorly on the United States, yet would still keep the country safe from the pesky, international terrorists and other foreigners unhappy with these global developments.

The purpose of tonight's gathering was to plot the killing of Faith Lockhart. Technically, the CIA was prohibited by presidential executive order from engaging in assassination. However, these men, though employed by the Agency, were not representing the CIA tonight. This was their private agenda, and there was little disagreement that the woman had to die, and soon; it was critical for the well-being of the country. These men knew this, even if American presidents did not. However, because of another life that was involved, the meeting had become acrimonious, the group resembling a cadre of posturing members fighting on Capitol Hill over billion-dollar slices of pork.

"What you're saying, then," one of the white-haired men said as he poked the smoke-filled air with a slender finger, "is that along with Lockhart we have to kill a federal agent." This man shook his head incredulously. "Why kill one of our own? It can only lead to disaster."

The gentleman at the head of the table nodded thoughtfully. Robert Thornhill was the CIA's most distinguished Cold War soldier, a man whose status at the Agency was unique. His reputation was unassailable, his compilation of professional victories unmatched. As associate deputy director of Operations, he was the Agency's ultimate free safety. The DDO, or deputy director of operations, was responsible for running the field operations that undertook the secret collection of foreign intelligence. The operations directorate of the CIA was also unofficially known as the "spy shop," and the deputy director was still not even publicly identified. It was the perfect place to get meaningful work done.

Thornhill had organized this select group, who were as upset as he about the state of affairs at the CIA. It was he who had remembered that this bloated underground time capsule existed. And it was Thornhill who had found the money to secretly bring the chamber back to working condition and upgrade its facilities. There were thousands of little taxpayer-funded toys like that sprinkled around the country, many of them gone to complete waste. Thornhill joked to himself, *Well, if governments didn't waste their citizens' hard-earned money, then what would be left for governments to do?*

Even now, as he ran his hand over the stainless steel console with its quaint built-in ashtrays, sniffed the filtered air and felt the protective coolness of the earth all around, Thornhill's mind wandered back for a moment to the Cold War period. At least there was a measure of certainty with the hammer and sickle. In truth, Thornhill would take the lumbering Russian bull over the agile sand snake that you never knew was out there until it flung its venom into you. There were many who wanted nothing more in life than to topple the United States. It was his job to ensure that never happened.

Gazing around the table, Thornhill gauged each man's devotion to his country and was satisfied. He had wanted to serve America for as long as he could remember. His father had been with the OSS, the World War II-era predecessor to the CIA. He had known little of what his father did at the time, but the man had instilled in his son the philosophy that there was no greater thing to do with one's life than to serve one's country. Thornhill had joined the Agency right out of Yale. Right up until the day he died, his father had been proud of his son. But no prouder than the son had been of the old man.

Thornhill's hair was a shining silver, which lent him a distinguished air. His eyes were gray and active, the angle of his chin blunt. His voice was deep, cultured; technical jargon and the poetry of Longfellow flowed from his mouth with equal ease. The man still wore three-piece suits and favored pipe smoking over cigarettes. The fifty-eight-year-old Thornhill could have quietly finished out his time at the CIA and led the pleasant life of a former public servant, well traveled, erudite. He had no thought of going out quietly, and the reason was very clear.

For the last ten years, the CIA's responsibilities and budgets had been decimated. It was a disastrous development, for the firestorms that were popping up across the world now often involved fanatical minds accountable to no political body and possessing the capability to obtain weapons of mass destruction. And while just about everyone thought high-tech was the answer for all the ills of the world, the best satellites in the world couldn't stroll down alleys in Baghdad, Seoul or Belgrade and take the emotional temperature of the people there. Computers in space could never capture what people were thinking, what devilish thoughts were lurking in their hearts. Thornhill would always choose a smart field operative willing to risk his or her life over the best hardware money could buy.

Thornhill had just such a small group of skilled operatives within the CIA, completely loyal to him and his private agenda. They had all worked hard to regain for the Agency its former prominence. Now Thornhill finally had the vehicle to do that. He would very soon have under his thumb powerful congressmen, senators, even the vice president

5

himself, and enough high-ranking bureaucrats to choke an independent counsel. Thornhill would see his budgets revive, his manpower skyrocket, his agency's scope of responsibility in the world return to its rightful place.

The strategy had worked for J. Edgar Hoover and the FBI. It was no coincidence, Thornhill believed, that the Bureau's budget and influence had flourished under the late director and his allegedly "secret" files on powerful politicians. If there was one organization in the world that Robert Thornhill hated with all his soul, it was the FBI. But he would use whatever tactics he could to bring his agency back to the forefront, even if it meant stealing a page from his most bitter foe. *Well, watch me do you one better, Ed.*

Thornhill focused again on the men clustered around him. "Not having to kill one of our own would, of course, be ideal," he said. "However, the fact is, the FBI have her under 'round-the-clock stealth security. The only time she's truly vulnerable is when she goes to the cottage. They may place her in Witness Protection without warning, so we have to hit them at the cottage."

Another man spoke up. "Okay, we kill Lockhart, but let the FBI agent live, for God's sake, Bob."

Thornhill shook his head. "The risk is too great. I know that killing a fellow agent is deplorable. But to shirk our duty now would be a catastrophic mistake. You know what we've invested in this operation. We cannot fail."

"Dammit, Bob," the first man to protest said, "do you know what will happen if the FBI learns we took out one of their people?"

"If we can't keep a secret like that, we have no business doing what we do," Thornhill snapped. "This is not the first time lives have been sacrificed."

Another member of the group leaned forward in his chair. He was the youngest of them. He had, however, earned the respect of the group with his intelligence and his ability to exercise extreme, focused ruthlessness.

"We've only really looked at the scenario of killing Lockhart to forestall the FBI's investigation into Buchanan. Why not appeal to the FBI director and have him order his team to give up the investigation? Then no one has to die."

Thornhill gave his younger colleague a disappointed look. "And how would you propose going about explaining to the FBI director why we wish him to do so?"

"How about some semblance of the truth?" the younger man said. "Even in the intelligence business there's sometimes room for that, isn't there?"

Thornhill smiled warmly. "So I should say to the FBI director – who, by the way, would love to see us all permanently interred in a museum – that we wish him to call off his potentially blockbuster investigation so that the CIA can use illegal means to trump his agency. Brilliant. Why didn't I think of that? And where would you like to serve *your* prison term?"

"For chrissakes, Bob, we *work* with the FBI now. This isn't 1960 anymore. Don't forget about CTC."

CTC stood for the Counter Terrorism Center, a cooperative effort between the CIA and the FBI to fight terrorism by sharing intelligence and resources. It had been generally deemed a success by those involved. To Thornhill, it was simply another way for the FBI to stick its greedy fingers into his business.

"I happen to be involved in CTC in a modest way," Thornhill said. "I find it an ideal perch on which to keep tabs on the Bureau and what they're up to, which is usually no good, as far as we're concerned."

"Come on, we're all on the same team, Bob."

Thornhill's eyes focused on the younger man in such a way that everyone in the room froze. "I request that you never say those words in my presence again," Thornhill said.

The man paled and sat back in his chair.

Thornhill clenched his pipe between his teeth. "Would you like me to give you concrete examples of the FBI taking the credit, the glory for work done by our agency? For the blood spilled by our field agents? For the countless times we've saved the world from annihilation? How they manipulate investigations in order to crush everyone else, to beef up their already bloated budget? Would you like me to give you instances in my thirty-six-year career where the FBI did all it could to discredit our mission, our people? Would you?" The man slowly shook his head as Thornhill's gaze bored into him. "I don't give a damn if the FBI director himself came down here and kissed my shoes and swore his undying allegiance to me – I will not be swayed. Ever! Have I made my position clear?"

"I understand." As he said this, the younger man managed not to shake his head in bewilderment. Everyone in this room other than Robert Thornhill knew that the FBI and CIA actually got along well. Though they could be ham-handed at times in joint investigations because they had more resources than anyone else, the FBI was not on a witch hunt to bring down the Agency. But the men in this room also understood quite clearly that Robert Thornhill believed the FBI was their worst enemy. And they also knew that Thornhill had, decades ago, orchestrated a number of Agency-authorized assassinations with cunning and zeal. Why cross such a man?

Another colleague said, "But if we kill the agent, don't you think the FBI will go on a crusade to find out the truth? They have the resources to scorch the earth. No matter how good we are, we can't match their strength. Then where are we?"

Some grumbling rose from the others. Thornhill looked around warily. The collection of men here represented an uneasy alliance. They were paranoid, inscrutable fellows long used to keeping their own counsel. It had truly been a miracle to forge them together in the first place.

"The FBI *will* do everything they can to solve the murder of one of their agents and the chief witness to one of their most ambitious investigations ever. So what I would propose doing is to give them the solution we desire them to have." They looked curiously at him. He sipped water from his glass and then took a minute to prime his pipe.

"After years of helping Buchanan run his operation, Faith Lockhart's conscience or good sense or paranoia got the better of her. She went to the FBI and has now begun telling them everything she knows. Through a little foresight on my part, we were able to discover this development. Buchanan, however, is completely unaware that his partner has turned against him. He also doesn't know that we intend to kill her. Only we know." Thornhill inwardly congratulated himself for this last remark. It felt good, omniscience; it was the business he was in, after all.

"The FBI, however, may suspect that he does know about her betrayal or may find out at some point. Thus, to the outside observer, no one in the world has greater motivation to kill Faith Lockhart than Danny Buchanan."

"And your point?" the questioner persisted.

"My point," said Thornhill tersely, "is quite

simple. Instead of allowing Buchanan to disappear, we tip off the FBI that he and his clients discovered Lockhart's duplicity and had her and the agent murdered."

"But once they get hold of Buchanan, he'll tell them everything," the man quickly responded.

Thornhill looked at him as a disappointed teacher to pupil. Over the last year, Buchanan had given them everything they needed; he was now officially expendable.

The truth slowly dawned on the group. "So we tip the FBI about Buchanan *posthumously*. Three deaths. Correction, three murders," another man said.

Thornhill looked around the room, silently gauging the reaction of the others to this exchange, to his plan. Despite their protestations about killing an FBI agent he knew that three deaths meant nothing to these men. They were from the old school, which quite clearly understood that sacrifices of that nature were sometimes necessary. Certainly what they did for a living sometimes cost people their lives; however, their operations had also avoided open war. Kill three to save three million, who could possibly argue with that? Even if the victims were relatively innocent. Every soldier who ever died in battle was innocent too. Covert action, quaintly referred to as the "third option" in intelligence circles, the one between diplomacy and open war, was where the CIA could really prove its worth, Thornhill believed. Although it was also at the heart of some of the Agency's worst disasters. Well, without risk there was never the possibility for glory. That epitaph could be put on his tombstone.

No formal vote was taken by Thornhill; none was needed.

"Thank you, gentlemen," Thornhill said. "I'll take care of everything." He adjourned the meeting.

10

TWO

The small, wood-shingled cottage stood alone at the end of a short, hard-packed gravel road, its dirt shoulders laced with the tangled sprawl of dandelion, curly dock and chickweed. The ramshackle structure rested on an acre of cleared flat land, but was surrounded on three sides by woods where each tree struggled to find sunlight at the expense of its neighbor. Because of wetlands and other development problems, the eighty-year-old home had never had any neighbors. The nearest community was about three miles away by car, but less than half that distance if one had the backbone to challenge the dense woods.

For much of the last twenty years the rustic cottage had been used for impromptu teen parties, and on occasion by the wandering homeless looking for the comfort and relative safety of four walls and a roof, however porous. The cottage's discouraged current owner, who had recently inherited the beast, had finally opted to rent it out. He had found a willing tenant who had paid the full year's rent in advance, in cash.

Tonight the calf-high grass in the front yard was pushed low and then straightened in the face of a strengthening wind. Behind the house a line of thick oaks seemed to mimic the movements of the grass as they swayed back and forth. It hardly seemed possible, yet except for the wind, there were no other sounds.

Save one.

In the woods, several hundred yards directly behind the house, a pair of feet splashed through a shallow creek bed. The man's dirty trousers and soaked boots attested to the difficulty with which he had navigated the congested terrain in the dark, even with the aid of a three-quarters-full moon. He paused to scrape his muddy boots against the trunk of a fallen tree.

Lee Adams was both sweaty and chilled after the punishing trek. At forty-one years of age, his six-foot-two body was exceptionally strong. He worked out regularly, and his biceps and delts showed it. Keeping in reasonably good shape was a necessity in his line of work. While he was often required to sit in a car for days on end, or in a library or courthouse reviewing microfiche records, he also, on occasion, had to climb trees, subdue men even larger than he was or, like now, slog through gully-filled woods in the dead of night. A little extra muscle never hurt. However, he wasn't twenty anymore either, and his body was letting him know it.

Lee had thick, wavy brown hair that seemed perpetually in his face, a quick, infectious smile, pronounced cheekbones and an engaging set of blue eyes that had caused female hearts spontaneously to flutter from fifth grade onward. He had suffered enough broken bones during his career, though, and other assorted injuries, that his body felt far older than it looked. And that's what hit him every morning when he rose. The creaks, the little pains. Cancerous tumor or merely arthritis? he sometimes wondered. What the hell did it really matter? When God punched your ticket, He did so with authority. A good diet and messing around with weights or pitter-pattering on the treadmill wasn't going to change the Man's decision to pull your string.

Lee looked up ahead. He couldn't see the cottage just yet; the forest clutter was too thick. He fussed with the controls of the camera he had pulled from his knapsack while he took a series of replenishing breaths. Lee had made this same trek several times before but had never gone inside the cottage. He had seen things, though – peculiar things. That's why he was back. It was time to learn the secret of this place.

His wind having returned, Lee trudged on, his only companions the scurrying wildlife. Deer, rabbit, squirrel and even beaver were plentiful in this still-rural part of northern Virginia. As he walked along, Lee listened to the flit of flying creatures. All he could envision were rabid, foaming bats blindly cleaving the air around his head. And it seemed that every few steps he would run straight into a twister of mosquitoes. Though he had been paid a large amount of cash up front, he was seriously considering increasing his daily fee on this one.

When he approached the edge of the woods, Lee stopped. He had a great deal of experience spying on the haunts of people and their activities. Slow and methodical was the best way, like a pilot's checklist. You just had to hope nothing happened to make you improvise.

Lee's bent nose was a permanent badge of honor from his time as an amateur boxer in the Navy, where he had taken out his youthful aggression in a square of roped canvas against an opponent of like weight and ability. A pair of stout gloves, quick hands and nimble feet, cagey mind and a strong heart had constituted his arsenal of weapons. The majority of the time, they had been enough for victory.

After his military stint, things had worked out mostly okay for him. Never rich, never actually poor despite being mostly self-employed over the years, usually free; never quite alone, though he had been divorced for almost fifteen years. The only good thing from that marriage had just turned twenty. His daughter was tall, blond and brainy, as well as the proud bearer of a full academic scholarship to the University of Virginia and a star on the women's soccer team. And for the last ten years, Renee Adams had no interest whatsoever in having anything to do with her old man. A decision that had her mother's full blessing, if not her insistence, Lee well knew. And his ex had seemed so kind on those first few dates, so infatuated with his Navy uniform, so enthusiastic in tearing up his bed.

His ex-wife, a former stripper named Trish Bardoe, had married on the rebound a fellow by the name of Eddie Stipowicz, an unemployed engineer with a drinking problem. Lee thought she was heading for disaster and had tried to get custody of Renee on the grounds that her mom and stepfather could not provide for her. Well, about that time, Eddie, a sneaky runt Lee despised, invented, mostly by accident, some microchip piece of crap that had made him a gazillionaire. Lee's custody battle had lost its juice after that. To add insult to injury, there had been stories on Eddie in the *Wall Street Journal*, *Time*, *Newsweek* and a number of other publications. He was famous. Their house had even been featured in *Architectural Digest*.

Lee had gotten that issue of the *Digest*. Trish's new home was grossly huge, mostly crimson red or eggplant so dark it made Lee think of the inside of a coffin. The windows were cathedral-size, the furniture large enough to become lost in and there were enough wood moldings, paneling and staircases to heat a typical midwestern town for an entire year. There were also stone fountains sculpted with naked people. What a kicker! A photo of the happy couple was included in the spread. In Lee's opinion they might as well have captioned it "The Nerd and the Bombshell strike it rich in poor taste."

One photo had captured Lee's complete attention, however. Renee had been poised on the most magnificent stallion Lee had ever seen, on a field of grass that was so green and perfectly trimmed that it looked like a pond of sea glass. Lee had carefully cut that photo out and put it away in a safe spot – his family album of sorts. The article, of course, made no mention of him; no reason that it should. The one thing that had ticked him off, though, was the reference to Renee as Ed's daughter.

"Stepdaughter," Lee had said out loud when he read that line. "Stepdaughter. That one you can't take away, Trish." Most of the time he felt no envy for the wealth his ex-wife now had, for it meant that his daughter would never want. But it still hurt.

When you had something for all those years, something you had made with a part of yourself, and loved more than it was probably good to love anything, and then lost it – well, Lee tried never to dwell for long on that loss. Big tough guy that he was, when he did let himself think about the massive hole dead center in his chest, he ended up blubbering like a baby.

Life was so funny sometimes. Funny like when you get a clean bill of health one day and drop dead the next.

Lee looked down at his muddy pants and worked a painful cramp out of his weary leg at the same time he swatted a mosquito out of his eye. Hotel-size house. Servants. Fountains. Big horses. Sleek private jet. . . . Probably all a real pain in the ass.

Lee hugged the camera to his chest. It was loaded with 400-speed film that Lee was "turbocharging" by setting the camera's ISO speed to 1600. Fast film required less light, and with the shutter opening for shorter periods of time, there was far less likelihood that camera wobble or vibration would distort any photos. He slipped on a 600mm telephoto lens and flipped down the lens' attached tripod.

Peering between the branches of a wild dogwood, Lee focused on the rear of the cottage. Scattered clouds drifted past the moon and deepened the darkness around him. He took a series of shots and then put the camera away.

As he stared at the house, the problem was he couldn't tell from here if the place was occupied or not. It was true he couldn't see a light on, but the place might have an interior room not visible from here. Added to that, he couldn't see the front of the house, and there might be a car parked there, for all he knew. He had observed the traffic and foot patterns on his other trips here. There hadn't been much to see. Few cars came down this road, and no walkers or joggers did. All the cars he had seen had turned around, obviously having made a wrong turn. All, that is, except one.

He glanced up at the sky. The wind had died down. Lee roughly calculated that the clouds would obscure the moonlight for a few minutes more. He slung the pack across his back, tensed for a moment, as though marshaling all of his energy, and then slid out of the woods.

Lee glided noiselessly until he reached a spot where he could squat behind a copse of overgrown bushes and still observe the front and back of the house. While he watched the house, the shades of darkness grew lighter as the moon reappeared. It seemed to be lazily watching him, curious as to what he was doing here.

Though isolated, the cottage was only a forty-minute drive from downtown D.C. That made it very convenient for any number of things. Lee had made inquiries about the owner and found him to be squeaky clean. The renter, however, had been a little tougher to pin down.

Lee pulled out a device that looked like a cassette recorder but was actually a battery-powered lock-pick gun, along with a zippered case, which he opened. He felt the different lock picks inside, then selected the one he wanted. Using an Allen wrench, he secured the pick into the machine. Lee's fingers moved quickly, confidently, even as another bank of cloud passed over, deepening the darkness once more. Lee had done this so many times that he could have closed his eyes and his fingers would carry on, manipulating his tools of felony with enviable precision.

Lee had already checked out the locks on the cottage with his spotting scope during daylight. That had also disturbed him. Deadbolt locks on all the exterior doors. Sash locks on both the first- *and* second-story windows. All the hardware looked new too. On a falling-down rental in the middle of nowhere.

Despite the cool weather, a bead of nervous sweat surfaced on Lee's forehead as he thought about this. He touched the 9mm in his belt clip holster; the metal was comforting. He took a moment to put the single-action pistol in a cocked-and-locked position – a round in the firing chamber, the hammer cocked and the safety set.

The cottage also had a security system. That had been a real stunner. If he was smart, Lee would pack his tools of criminality and go home, reporting failure to his employer. However, he took pride in his work. He would see it through at least until something happened to make him change his mind. And Lee could run very fast when he needed to.

Getting into the house wouldn't be all that difficult, particularly since Lee had the pass-code. He'd managed to get it the third time he'd been there, when the two people had come to the cottage. He had already confirmed the place was wired, so he had come prepared. He had beat the couple here and waited while they did whatever they were doing inside. When they had come out, the woman had entered the pass-code to arm the system. Lee, hiding in the same copse he was in now, just happened to have a bit of electronic wizardry that snatched that code right out of the air like a fly ball neatly falling into a glove. All electrical current produces a magnetic field, like a little transmitter. When the tall woman had punched in the numbers, the security system had thrown off a discrete signal for each digit, right into Lee's electronic mitt.

Lee checked the cloud cover once more, slapped on a pair of latex gloves with reinforced fingertip and palm pads, readied his flashlight and took another deep breath. A minute later he moved out from the cover of the bushes and made it quietly to the back door. He slipped off his muddy boots and set them next to the door. He didn't want to leave traces of his visit. Good private investigators were invisible. Lee held the light under his arm while he inserted the pick in the door lock and activated the device.

He used the pick gun partly for speed and partly because he didn't crack enough locks to be that proficient at it. A pick and tension tool required constant use to allow the fingers the level of sensitivity required to detect the proximity of the shear line, the subtle descent of the tension tool as the lock's tumblers began to do their little jig. Using a pick and tension tool, an experienced locksmith could pick the lock faster than Lee could with his pick gun. It was a true art and Lee knew his limitations. Soon, he felt the dead bolt sliding back.

When he eased open the door, the silence was broken by the low beeping sound of the security system. He quickly found the control pad, punched in six numbers and the beeping sound immediately stopped. As Lee closed the door softly behind him, he knew he was now a felon.

The man lowered his rifle and the red dot emanating from the weapon's laser scope disappeared from the wide back of an unsuspecting Lee Adams. The man holding the rifle was Leonid Serov, a former KGB officer specializing in assassination. Serov had found himself without gainful employment after the breakup of the Soviet Union. However, his ability to efficiently kill human beings was much in demand in the "civilized" world. Fairly well pampered as a communist for many years, with his own apartment and car, Serov had grown wealthy literally over-night as a capitalist. If he had only known.

Serov didn't know Lee Adams and had no idea why he was here. He had not noticed him until Lee had made his break for the bushes near the house, because Lee had come through the woods on the side farthest from the Russian. The sounds of his presence, Serov correctly surmised, had been covered by the wind.

Serov checked his watch. They would be coming soon. He inspected the elongated suppressor attached to the rifle. He rubbed its long snout gently, like a favorite pet, as though bestowing the notion of infallibility on to the polished metal. The rifle's stock was a special composite of Kevlar, fiberglass and graphite that provided remarkable stability. And the weapon's bore was not rifled in the conventional way. Instead it had a rounded rectangular profile, known as polygonal boring, with a right-hand twist. This type of rifling was supposed to increase muzzle velocity by upward of eight percent, and, more important, a ballistics match on a bullet fired from this gun was virtually impossible because there were no lands or grooves in the barrel that would make distinctive markings on the bullet as it exploded from the weapon. Success really was all in the details. Serov had built his entire career on that one philosophy.

The place was so isolated that Serov had mulled over perhaps removing the suppressor and relying on his skill as a marksman, his high-tech scope and his well-conceived exit plan. His confidence was justified, he believed. Just like the tree falling, when you kill someone in the middle of nowhere, who can hear him die? And he had known some suppressors to greatly distort the flight path of a bullet, with the unacceptable result that no one had died, except for the would-be assassin once his client had learned of the failure. Still, Serov had personally supervised this device's construction and was confident it would perform as designed.

The Russian shifted quietly, working out a cramp in his shoulder. He had been here since nightfall but was used to lengthy vigils. He never tired during these assignments. He took life seriously enough that preparing to extinguish another's kept his adrenaline high. With risk always came invigoration, it seemed. Whether you were mountain climbing or contemplating murder, it ironically made you feel more alive to have the possibility of death so close.

His escape route through the woods would take him to a quiet road where a car would be waiting to whisk him to nearby Dulles Airport. He would go on to other assignments, other places probably far more exotic than this. However, for his particular purpose, this setting had its virtues.

Killing someone in the city was the most difficult. Setting up where you would shoot, pulling the trigger and then escaping, all were vastly complicated by the fact that witnesses and the police were only a few anxious steps away in any direction. Give him the country, the isolation of the rural life, the cover of trees, the separation of homes, and like a tiger in a cattle pen he would kill with numbing efficiency every day of the week.

Serov sat on a stump a few feet from the tree line and only about thirty yards from the house. Despite the thickness of the woods, this spot allowed a clear field of fire: A bullet only needed an inch or so of free space. The man and woman, he had been told, would enter the house from the rear door. Only they would never make it that far. Whatever the laser touched, the bullet would destroy. He was confident he could hit a lightning bug from twice the distance he was confronted with here.

Things were set up so perfectly that Serov's instincts told him to be on high alert. Now he had an excellent reason not to fall into that trap: the man in the house. He was not the police. Law enforcement types didn't slink through the bushes and break into people's homes. Since he had not been made aware beforehand of the man's presence tonight, he concluded that the man was not on his side. However, Serov did not like to deviate from an established plan. He decided that if the man remained in the house after the bodies fell, he would follow through on his original plan and escape through the woods. If the man interfered in any way or came outside after the shots were fired – well, Serov had plenty of ammo, and the result would be three bodies instead of two.

THREE

Daniel Buchanan sat in his darkened office and sipped black coffee of such strength that he could almost feel his pulse rise with each swallow. After another long day of trying to convince legislators that his causes were worthy of their attention, the level of exhaustion was intense, and enormous amounts of caffeine were increasingly becoming the only remedy. A full night of sleep was not typically an option. A catnap here or there, closing his eyes while being driven around to the next meeting, the next flight, occasionally blanking out during an interminably long congressional hearing, even an hour or two in his bed at home – that was his official rest. Otherwise, he was working the Hill in all its near-mystical facets.

Sitting in the chambers of various congressmen, Buchanan would hear the voting buzzer go off and watch the TV every member had in his or her office. The monitor gave them the current bill up for vote, the tally for and against and the time they had left to scurry like ants to the floor and cast their ballot. With about five minutes remaining on a vote, Buchanan would conclude his meeting and hurry down the corridors looking for other members he needed to talk to, the Whip Wind-up Report clutched in his hand. It gave the daily voting schedules, which helped Buchanan determine where certain members might be – critical information when you were tracking dozens of moving targets who probably didn't want to talk to you.

Today Buchanan had managed to grab the ear of an important senator by riding the private underground subway to the Capitol for a floor vote. Buchanan left the man feeling fairly confident of help. He wasn't one of Buchanan's "special" people, but Buchanan was aware that you never knew where help could come from. He didn't care that his clients weren't popular or that they lacked a constituency that would hook a member's attention. He would just keep hammering away. The cause was a virtuous one; the means were therefore susceptible to a lower standard of conduct.

Buchanan's office was sparsely furnished and lacked many of the normal accoutrements of a busy lobbyist. Danny, as he liked to be called, kept no computer, no diskettes, no files, no records of anything of importance here. Paper files could be stolen, computers could be hacked into. Telephone conversations were bugged all the time. Spies were listening with everything from drinking glasses pressed to walls, to the latest gadgets that a year before hadn't even been invented but that could suck up streams of valuable information right out of the air. A typical organization bled confidential information the way a torpedoed ship shed its sailors. And Buchanan had a lot to hide.

For over two decades Buchanan had been the top influence peddler of them all. In some important ways he had laid the groundwork for lobbying in Washington. It had evolved from highly paid lawyers dozing at congressional hearings to a world of numbing complexity where the stakes couldn't possibly be higher. As a Capitol Hill hired gun, he had successfully represented environmental polluters in battles with the EPA, allowing them to spread death to an unsuspecting public; he had been the lead political strategist for pharmaceutical giants who had killed moms and their kids; next a passionate advocate for gun makers who didn't care if their weapons were safe; then a behind-the-scenes player for automobile manufacturers who would rather fight than admit they were wrong on safety issues; and finally, in the mother of all cash cows, he had spearheaded the efforts of tobacco companies in bloody wars with everyone. Back then Washington could not afford to ignore him or his clients. And Buchanan had earned an enormous fortune.

Many of the strategies he had concocted during that time had become staples of current legislative manipulation. He had had congressmen float bills on the House floor he knew would be defeated, in order to rip away platforms for change later. Buchanan's clients hated change. He had constantly fought rearguard actions as those who wanted what his clients had nipped at his heels. How many times had he avoided outright political disaster by flooding members' offices with letters, propaganda, thinly veiled threats to drop financial support. "My client will support you for reelection, Senator, because we know you'll do right by us. And, by the way, the contribution check is already in your campaign account." How many times had he said those words.

Ironically, it was the spoils of lobbying for the powerful that had led to a dramatic change in Buchanan's life over ten years ago. His original plan had been to build his career first and then settle down with a wife and raise a family. Deciding to see the world before he took on the responsibilities of marriage and family, Buchanan had driven through western Africa in a sixty-thousand-dollar Range Rover on a photography safari. In addition to the

24

beautiful animals, he had seen squalor and human suffering of unmatched depth. On another trip, to a remote region of the Sudan, he had witnessed a mass burial of children. An epidemic had swept the village earlier, he was told. It was one of the devastating diseases that routinely afflicted the area, killing off the young and elderly. What was the disease? Buchanan had asked. Something like measles, he was told.

Another trip he had watched as billions of American-produced cigarettes were unloaded on Chinese docks, to be consumed by people who already spent their lives wearing masks because of abysmal air pollution. He was witness to birth-control devices that had been banned in the United States being dumped by the hundreds of thousands in South America with one set of instructions written only in English. He had viewed shacks next to skyscrapers in Mexico City, starvation next to crooked capitalists in Russia. Though he had never been able to go there, North Korea, he knew, was a certified gangster state where it was believed that ten percent of the population had starved to death in the last five years. Every country had its schizophrenic story to tell.

After two years of this "pilgrimage," Buchanan's passion for marriage, having a family of his own, had evaporated. All the dying children he had seen became his children, his family. Fresh graves would still come by the millions for the young, the old, the starving of the world, but not without a fight that had become his. And he brought to it all that he had, more than he had ever given to the tobacco, chemical and gun behemoths. To this day he recalled in precise detail how this revelation of sorts had come: returning from a trip to South America, an airplane lavatory, him on his knees, his stomach sickened. It was as though he had personally murdered every dying child he had seen on that continent.

With eyes freshly opened, Buchanan started marching to these places to see precisely how he could help. He had personally brought a shipment of food and medicine to one country, only to discover there was no way to transport it to the interior regions. He had watched, helpless, as looters stripped his "care" package clean. Then he started working as an unpaid fund-raiser for humanitarian organizations ranging from CARE to Catholic Relief Services. He had done well, but the dollars amounted to a drip into a bottomless bucket. The numbers were not in their favor; the problem was only getting worse.

That's when Buchanan turned to his mastery of Washington. He had left the firm he had founded, taking only one person with him: Faith Lockhart. For the last decade his clients, his wards, were the most impoverished countries in the world. In truth, it was difficult for Buchanan to regard them as geopolitical units; he saw them as fragile clusters of devastated people under various flags who had no voice. He had dedicated the remainder of his life to solving the unsolvable problem of the global have-nots.

He had used all of his immense lobbying skills and contacts in Washington, only to find that these new causes paled in popularity to those he had represented before. When he had gone to Capitol Hill as an advocate of the powerful, the politicians had greeted him with smiles, no doubt with visions of campaign contributions and PAC dollars dancing in their heads. Now they gave him nothing. Some members of Congress bragged that they didn't even have passports, that the United States already spent far too much on foreign aid. Charity starts at home, they had said, and let's damn well keep it there.

But by far the most common retort was, "Where's the constituency, Danny? How does feeding the Ethiopians get me reelected in Illinois?" As he was quickly ushered from office after office, he sensed that they all looked at him with pity: Danny Buchanan, perhaps the greatest lobbyist ever, was now muddled, senile. It was so sad. Sure, it was a good cause and all, who can doubt that, but get real. Africa? Starving babies in Latin America? I've got my own problems right here.

"Look, if it ain't trade, troops or oil, Danny, why the hell are you here wasting my time?" one highly regarded senator had told him. That could be the quintessential statement on America foreign policy.

Could they be that blind? Buchanan had asked himself over and over. Or was he the utter fool?

Finally, Buchanan decided he had only one option. It was completely illegal, but a man pushed to the precipice could not afford allegiance to pristine ethics. Using the fortune he had amassed over the years, he had taken to bribing, in very special ways, certain key politicians for their assistance. It had worked wonderfully. The aid to his clients had grown, in so many different ways. Even as his own wealth was dissipated, things were looking up, Buchanan believed. Or at least things were not getting worse; he would count holding of precious, hard-won ground as a success. It had all worked well, until about a year ago.

As if on cue, the knock on his office door startled him from his reverie. The building was closed, supposedly secure, the cleaning crews long since departed. He didn't get up from his desk. He simply watched as the door swung inward, the silhouette of a tall man framed against the opening. The man's hand reached out and flicked on the light.

Buchanan squinted as the glare of the overheads

hit him. When his eyes adjusted to the brightness, he watched as Robert Thornhill took off his trench coat, smoothed down his jacket and shirt and sat down across from him. The man's movements were graceful, unhurried, as though he had plopped down for a leisurely drink at his country club.

"How did you get in here?" Buchanan asked sharply. "The building is supposed to be secure." For some reason Buchanan could sense that others lurked right outside the door.

"And it is, Danny. It is. For *most* people."

"I don't like you coming here, Thornhill."

"I'm courteous enough to use your given name. I'd appreciate reciprocity on that point. A small thing, to be sure, but at least I'm not demanding that you address me as *Mister* Thornhill. That's the norm between master and servant, isn't it, Danny? You see, I'm not so bad to work for."

The man's smug look was designed, Buchanan knew, to drive him to such distraction that he couldn't think clearly. Instead he leaned back in his chair and settled his hands across his middle.

"To what do I owe the pleasure of your visit, *Bob*?"

"Your meeting with Senator Milstead."

"I could easily have met him in town. I'm not sure why you insisted that I go to Pennsylvania."

"But this way you get one more opportunity to make your pitch for all those starving masses. You see, I do have a heart."

"Does it even make a dent in whatever you call a conscience that you're using the plight of millions of men, women and children who consider it a miracle to see the sun rise, to further your own selfish agenda?"

"I'm not paid to have a conscience. I'm paid to protect the interests of this country. *Your* interests. Besides, if having a conscience were the criteria,

28

there would be no one left in this town. In fact, I applaud your efforts. I have nothing against the poor and helpless. Good for you, Danny!"

"Sorry if I don't buy that."

Thornhill smiled. "Every country in the world has people like me. That is, they do if they're smart. We get the results everybody wants, because most 'everybody' lacks the courage to do it himself."

"So you play God? Interesting line of work."

"God is conceptual. I deal in facts. Speaking of which, you powered your agenda by illegal means; who are you to deny me the same right?"

In truth, Buchanan had no response to this statement. And Thornhill's intractably calm demeanor only reinforced the helplessness he felt.

"Any questions about the meeting with Milstead?" Thornhill asked.

"You have enough on Harvey Milstead to put him away for three lives. What are you really after?"

Thornhill chuckled. "I hope you're not accusing me of having a hidden agenda."

"You can tell me, Bob, we're partners."

"Maybe it's as simple as wanting you to jump when I snap my fingers."

"Fine, but a year from now, if you pop up like this, you may not leave under your own power."

"Threats from a solitary lobbyist to *me*." Thornhill sighed. "But not so solitary. You have an army of one. How is Faith? Doing well?"

"Faith is not a part of this. Faith will never be a part of this."

Thornhill nodded. "You're the only one in the crosshairs. You and your fine group of felonious politicians. America's best and brightest."

Buchanan stared coldly at his antagonist and said nothing.

"Things are coming to a head, Danny. As you said,

the show will be coming to a close soon. I hope you're ready to exit cleanly."

"When I leave, my trail will be so clean, not even your spy satellites will be able to pick it up."

"Confidence is inspiring. Yet so often misplaced."

"Is that all you wanted to tell me? Be prepared to escape? I've been ready to do that since the first minute I met you."

Thornhill stood. "You focus on Senator Milstead. Get us some good, juicy stuff. Get him to talk about the income he'll have when he retires, the nominal tasks he'll have to perform as window dressing. The more specific, the better."

"It heartens me to see you enjoying this so much. Probably a lot more fun than the Bay of Pigs."

"Before my time."

"Well, I'm sure you've made your mark in other ways."

Thornhill bristled for a moment and then his calm returned. "You'd make a fine poker player, Danny. But try to remember that a bluff when one is holding no face cards is still a bluff." Thornhill put on his trench coat. "Don't trouble yourself, I can find my way out."

In the next instant Thornhill was gone. The man appeared and disappeared at will, it seemed. Buchanan leaned back in his chair and let out a quick breath. His hands were trembling and he pressed them hard against the desk until the quivering stopped.

Thornhill had thundered into his life like an exploding torpedo. Buchanan had become, essentially, a lackey, now spying on those he had been bribing for years with his own money, now collecting a wealth of material for this ogre to use as blackmail. And Buchanan was powerless to stop the man.

Ironically, this decline in his material assets and now his work in the service of another had brought Buchanan directly back from whence he had come. He had grown up on the illustrious Philadelphia Main Line. He had lived on one of the most magnificent estates in that area. Stacked fieldstone walls – like thick gray brushstrokes of paint – outlined the grass perimeters of the vast, perfect lawns, on which was situated a sprawling twelve-thousand-square-foot house with broad, covered porches, and a detached quadruple-car garage with an apartment overhead. The house had more bedrooms than a dormitory, and lavish baths with costly tile and the luster of gold on something as commonplace as a faucet.

It was the world of the American blue bloods, where pampered lifestyles and crushing ex-pectations existed side by side. Buchanan had observed this complex universe from an intimate perspective, yet he was not one of its privileged inhabitants. Buchanan's family had been the chauffeurs and maids and gardeners, the handy-men, nannies and cooks to these blue bloods. Having survived the Canadian border winters, the Buchanans had migrated south, en masse, to a gentler climate, to less demanding work than that required by ax and spade, boat and hook. Up there they had hunted for food and cut wood for warmth, only to watch helplessly as nature mercilessly culled their ranks in a natural process that had made the survivors stronger, their descendants stronger still. And Danny Buchanan was perhaps the strongest of them all.

Young Danny Buchanan had watered the lawn and cleaned the pool, swept and repainted the tennis court, picked the flowers and vegetables and played, in a properly respectful manner, with the children.

As he had gotten older, Buchanan had huddled with the younger generation of the spoiled rich, deep in the privacy of the complex flower gardens, smoking, drinking and exploring each other sexually. Buchanan had even acted as pallbearer, weeping sincerely as he bore two of the young and the rich who had wasted their privileged lives, mixing too much whisky with a racing sports car, driving too fast for impaired motor skills. When you lived life that fast, often you died fast as well. Right now Buchanan could see his own end rushing headlong at him.

Buchanan had never felt comfortable in either group – the rich or the poor – since then. The rich he would never be a part of, no matter how much his bank account swelled. He had played with the wealthy heirs, but when mealtime came, they went to the formal dining room while he trudged to the kitchen to break his bread with the other servants. The baby blues had attended Harvard, Yale and Princeton; he had worked his way through night school at an institution his betters would openly mock.

Buchanan's own family was now equally foreign to him. He sent his relatives money. They sent it back. When he went to visit, he had found they had nothing to talk about. They neither understood nor cared about what he did. However, they made him feel that there was nothing honest about his life's occupation; he could see that in their tightly drawn faces, their mumbled words. Washington was as foreign as hell itself to all that they believed in. He lied for money, large sums of it. Better he had followed in their tread; honest if simple work. By rising above them, he had fallen far below what they represented: fairness, integrity, character.

The path he had chosen during the last ten years

had only deepened this solitary confinement. He had few friends. Nevertheless, he did have millions of strangers across the world who deeply depended on him for something as basic as survival. Even Buchanan had to admit, it was a bizarre existence.

And now, with the coming of Thornhill, Buchanan's foothold had dropped another rung on the ladder leading to the abyss. Now he could no longer even confide in his one indisputable soul mate, Faith Lockhart. She knew nothing about Thornhill, and she never would know of the man from the CIA; this was all that was keeping her safe. It had cost him his last thread of real human contact.

Danny Buchanan was now truly alone.

He stepped to the window of his office and looked out at majestic monuments known around the world. Some might argue that their beautiful facades were just that: Like the magician's hand, they were designed to guide the eyes away from the truly important business of this city, transacted usually for the benefit of a select few.

Buchanan had learned that effective, long-term power came essentially from the gentle force of rule of the few over the many, for most people were not political beasts. A delicate balance was called for, the few over the many, *gently*, civilly; and Buchanan knew that the most perfect example of it in the history of the world existed right here.

Closing his eyes, he let the darkness envelop him, let new energy spill into his body for the fight tomorrow. It promised to be a very long night, however, for in truth, his life had now become one long tunnel to nowhere. If he could only ensure Thornhill's destruction as well, it would all be worth it. One small crack in the darkness, that would be all Buchanan needed. If only it could be so.

FOUR

The car moved down the highway at precisely the speed limit. The man was driving, the woman next to him. Both sat rigidly, as though one feared a sudden attack from the other.

As a jet, landing gear down, roared over them like a swooping hawk on its way in to Dulles Airport, Faith Lockhart closed her eyes and pretended for a moment that she was on that plane, and instead of landing, it was beginning some far-flung journey. As she slowly opened her eyes, the car took an exit off the highway and they left the unsettling glare of sodium lights behind. They were soon sailing past jagged rows of trees on both sides of the road, the wide, grassy ditches deep and soggy; the dull pulse of flat-looking stars was now their only source of light other than the car's twin beams stabbing the darkness.

"I don't understand why Agent Reynolds couldn't come tonight," she said.

"The simple answer is, you're not the only investigation she has going, Faith," Special Agent Ken Newman replied. "But I'm not exactly a stranger, am I? We're just going to talk, like the other times. Pretend I'm Brooke Reynolds. We're all on the same team."

The car turned on to another, even more isolated road. On this stretch the trees were replaced by denuded fields awaiting the final scrape of the bulldozers. In a year's time there would be almost as many homes here as there had been trees before, as suburban sprawl continued its push. Now the land simply looked ravaged, naked. And bleak, perhaps because of what was to come. In that regard, the land and Faith Lockhart were as one.

Newman glanced over at her. Although he didn't like to admit it, he felt uneasy around Faith Lockhart, as though he were seated next to a ball of wired C-4 with no idea when it might explode. He shifted in his seat. His skin was a little raw where the leather of his shoulder holster usually rubbed against his skin. Most people developed a callus at that spot, but his skin just kept blistering and then peeling off. Ironically, he felt that the twinge of pain gave him an edge because he never relaxed; it was a clear warning that if he let down his guard, that small discomfort could become a fatal one. Tonight, however, because he was wearing body armor, the holster wasn't scraping his skin; the pain and heightened sense of awareness were not nearly as strong.

Faith could feel the blood rush through her ears, all senses elevated, the way they were when you were lying in bed late at night and hearing a strange, troubling sound. When you were a child and that happened, you raced to your parents' bed and climbed in, to be wrapped up, consoled by loving, understanding arms. Her parents were dead and she was now thirty-six years old. Who was out there for Faith Lockhart?

"And after tonight, it'll be Agent Reynolds instead of me," Newman said. "You're comfortable with her, aren't you?"

"I'm not sure 'comfort' applies to situations like this."

"Sure it does. It's very important, in fact. Reynolds is a straight shooter. Believe me, if it weren't for her, this thing would be going nowhere. You haven't exactly given us much to go on. But she believes in you. So long as you don't do anything to destroy that confidence, you have a powerful ally in Brooke Reynolds. She cares about you."

Faith crossed her legs and folded her arms across her chest. She was about five-five, and her torso was short. Her bosom was flatter than she would have liked, but her legs were long and well shaped. If nothing else, she could always count on her legs to get attention. The defined muscles in her calves and thighs, visible through her sheer stockings, were enough to cause Newman's gaze to flicker over them several times with what appeared to be mild interest, she noted.

Faith swatted her long auburn hair out of her face and rested her hand on the bridge of her nose. A few white strands of hair floated among the darker. They were not yet noticeable, but that would change with time. In fact, the pressure she was under would undoubtedly accelerate the aging process. Besides her hard work, agile wits and poise, Faith's good looks, she knew, had helped her career. It was shallow to believe that one's features made a difference. Yet the truth was they did, particularly when one dealt with an overwhelmingly male audience, as she had for her entire career.

The broad smiles she received when entering a senator's office were not so much due to her gray matter, she knew, as to the above-the-knee skirts she favored. Sometimes it was as simple as dangling a shoe. She was talking about children dying, families living in sewers in far-off lands, and these men were fixated on toe cleavage. God, testosterone was a man's greatest weakness and a woman's most powerful advantage. At least it helped to level a playing field that had always been tilted in favor of the males.

"It's nice to be so well loved," said Faith. "But picking me up in an alley. Coming out here in the middle of nowhere in the dead of night. That's a little much, don't you think?"

"Your walking into the Washington Field Office just wasn't an option. You're the star witness in what could be a very important investigation. This place is safe."

"You mean it's perfect for an ambush. How do you know we haven't been followed?"

"We've been followed, all right. By our people. If anyone else had been around, believe me, our people would've noticed it before sending us on. We had a tail car until we turned off the highway. There's nobody back there."

"So your people are infallible. I wish I had that kind of people working for me. Where do you find them?"

"Look, we know what we're doing, okay? Relax." Even as he said this, though, he checked the mirror again.

He glanced at the cell phone lying on the front seat, and Faith could easily read his thoughts. "Suddenly wanting backup?" Newman glanced sharply at her but said nothing. "Okay, so let's get to the principal terms," she said. "What do I really get out of all this? We've never quite nailed it down." When Newman still didn't respond, she studied his profile for a minute, sizing up his nerve. She reached over and touched his arm.

"I took a lot of risk to do what I'm doing," she said. She felt him tense through his suit jacket where her fingers rested. She kept her fingers there, applied slightly more pressure. Her fingertips could now distinguish the material of his jacket from that of his shirt. As he turned slightly toward her, Faith was able to see the bulletproof vest he was wearing. The

37

saliva in her mouth suddenly evaporated, along with her composure.

Newman glanced at her. "I'll give it to you straight. What exactly your deal will be, that's not up to me. So far, you haven't really given us anything. But play by the rules and everything will be okay. You'll cut your deal, you'll give us what we need and pretty soon you'll have a new identity selling seashells on Fiji, while your partner and his play-mates become long-term guests of the government. Don't revel in it, don't think too much about it, just try to survive it. Remember, we're on your side here. We're the only friends you have."

Faith sat back, finally drawing her gaze from the body armor. She decided it was time to drop her bombshell. She may as well try it out on Newman instead of Reynolds. In some ways, Reynolds and she had hit it off. Two women in a sea of men. In many subtle ways, the female agent had understood things a man never would have. In other ways, however, they had been like two alley cats circling around fish bones.

"I want to bring in Buchanan. I know I can get him to do it. If we work together, your case will be much stronger." She said all of this quickly, vastly relieved to have it finally out.

Newman's face betrayed his astonishment. "Faith, we're pretty flexible, but we're not cutting a deal with the guy who, according to you, masterminded this whole thing."

"You don't understand all the facts. Why he did it. He's not the bad person in all this. He's a good guy."

"He broke the law. According to you, he corrupted government officials. That's enough for me."

"When you understand why he did it, you won't think that way."

"Don't pin your hopes on that strategy, Faith. Don't do that to yourself."

"What if I say it's both or none?"

"Then you're making the biggest mistake of your life."

"So it's either me or him?"

"And it shouldn't be that tough a choice."

"I'll just have to talk to Reynolds, then."

"She'll tell you the same thing I just did."

"Don't be so sure. I can be pretty persuasive. And I also happen to be right."

"Faith, you have no idea what's involved here. FBI agents don't decide who to prosecute. The U.S. Attorney's Office does. Even if Reynolds sided with you, and I doubt she will, I can tell you there's no way in hell the lawyers will go along. If they try to take down all these powerful politicos and cut a sweetheart deal with the guy who got them into it in the first place, they're gonna lose their asses, and then their jobs. This is Washington, these are eight-hundred-pound gorillas we're dealing with here. There'll be phones ringing off the hook, a media frenzy, behind-the-scenes deals going a mile a minute, and at the end of the day, we'll all be toast. Trust me, I've been doing this for twenty years. It's Buchanan or nothing."

Faith sat back and stared at the sky. For a moment, amid the clouds, she envisioned Danny Buchanan slumped over in a dark, hopeless prison cell. She could never let it come to that. She would have to talk to Reynolds and the attorneys, make them see that Buchanan had to be given immunity too. That was the only way it could work. But Newman sounded so sure of himself. What he had just said made perfect sense. This was Washington. As suddenly as the strike of a match, her confidence completely deserted her. Had she, the consummate lobbyist, who had been tallying political scorecards for God knew how long, failed to account for the political situation here?

"I need a bathroom," Faith said.

"We'll be at the cottage in about fifteen minutes."

"Actually, if you take the next left, there's a twenty-four-hour gas station about a mile down the road."

He looked at her in surprise. "How do you know that?"

She looked back with a look of confidence that masked a rising panic. "I like to know what I'm getting into. That includes the people and the geography."

He didn't answer, but hung the left, and they were soon at the well-lit Exxon, which had a convenience store component. The highway had to be nearby, despite the isolation of the surroundings, because semis were parked up and down the lot. The Exxon obviously catered to open-road truckers. Men in boots and cowboy hats, Wrangler jeans and wind-breakers, with trucking- and automotive-parts' logos stenciled across them, strode across the lot. Some patiently filled their rigs with fuel; others sipped hot coffee, tiny wisps of steam heat rising past tired, leathery faces. No one paid attention to the sedan as it pulled up next to the rest room located on the far side of the building.

Faith locked the bathroom door behind her, put the toilet lid down and sat on it. She didn't need to use the facilities; she needed time to think, to control the panic hitting her from all sides. She looked around, her eyes absently taking in the handwritten scribbles on the chipping yellow paint covering the block walls. Some of the obscene language almost made her blush. Some of the writings were witty – belly-rocking funny, even – in their crudeness. They probably surpassed anything the men had composed to decorate their rest room next door, although most males would never concede this possibility. Men were always underestimating women.

She stood, splashed cold tap water on her face and dried it with a paper towel. About that time her knees decided to give, and she locked them, her fingers curling tightly around the stained porcelain of the sink. She had had nightmares about doing that at her wedding: locking her knees and then passing out because of it. Well, one less thing to worry about now. She'd never had a lasting relationship in her life, unless one counted a certain young man in fifth grade whose name she couldn't remember but whose sky-blue eyes she would never forget.

Danny Buchanan had given her lasting friendship. He'd been her mentor and substitute father for the last fifteen years. He had seen potential in her where no one else had. He had given her a chance when she so desperately needed one. She had come to Washington with boundless ambition and enthusiasm and absolutely no focus. Lobbying? She knew nothing about it, but it sounded exciting. And lucrative. Her father had been a good-natured if aimless wanderer, dragging his wife and daughter from one get-rich scheme to the next. He was one of nature's cruelest concoctions: a visionary lacking the skills to implement that vision. He measured gainful employment in days instead of years. They all lived one nervous week to the next. When his plans went awry and he was losing other people's money, he would pack up Faith and her mother and flee. They'd been homeless on occasion, hungry more often than not; still, her father had always gotten back on his feet, however totteringly. Until the day he died. Poverty was a lasting, powerful memory for her.

Faith wanted a good, stable life, and she wanted to be dependent on no one for it. Buchanan had given her the opportunity, the skills to accomplish her dream, and much more than that. He had not only vision, but also the tools to execute his sweeping ideas. She could never betray him. She was in breathless awe of what he had done and was still trying so hard to do. He was the rock she needed at that stage of her life. In the last year their relationship had changed. Ever more reclusive, he had stopped talking to her. Danny was irritable, snapping for little reason. When she pressed him to tell her what was troubling him, he withdrew even more. Their relationship had been so close that the change had been even harder for her to accept. He became stealthy, stopped inviting her to travel with him; they no longer even engaged in their lengthy strategy sessions.

And then he had done something entirely original and personally devastating: He had lied to her. The matter had been purely trivial, but the implications were serious. If he spun lies in small areas, what was he holding from her of importance? They had one final confrontation and Buchanan had told her that no possible good could come from him sharing what troubled him. And then he dropped the real stunner.

If she wanted to leave his employ, she was free to do so, and maybe it was time she did, he had strongly intimated. His employ! The father telling his precocious daughter to get the hell out of the house was more the effect upon her.

Why did he want her to go away? And then it finally dawned on her. How could she have been so blind? They were on to Danny. Somebody was on to him, and he didn't want her to share his fate. She had point-blank confronted him on that issue. And he had point-blank denied it. And then insisted that she leave. Noble to the end.

And yet if he wouldn't confide in her, she would map a separate course for them. After much deliberation she had gone to the FBI. She knew there was a chance it was the FBI that had somehow discovered Danny's secret, but this might make it easier, Faith had thought. Now a thousand doubts assailed her for the decision to approach the Bureau. Did she really believe the Bureau would just fall all over themselves inviting Buchanan into the prosecution's fold? She cursed herself for giving them Danny's name, although he was very famous in a town of famous people; the FBI would not have failed to make the connection. They wanted Danny to go to prison. Her for Danny. That was supposed to be her choice? She had never felt more alone.

She looked at herself in the cracked mirror. The bones of her face seemed to be pushing through her skin, her eye sockets hollowing right in front of her. A centimeter of skin between her and nothing. Her grand vision, the way out for them both, had suddenly become a free fall of insane, dizzying proportion. Her father would have just packed up and fled into the night. What was his daughter supposed to do?

FIVE

L ee pulled out his pistol and pointed it ahead of
    him as he moved through the hallway. With
    his other hand he swung the flashlight in slow,
steady arcs.

The first room he peered into was the kitchen,
containing a small 1950s-era refrigerator, GE electric
range and tattered black-and-yellow-checked linoleum flooring. The walls were discolored in places
by water damage. The ceiling was unfinished, the
joists and the subfloor above clearly visible. Lee
gazed at the old copper pipes and the newer grafts of
PVC as they made a series of right angles through
the exposed, darkened wall studs.

There was no aroma of food here, only a smell of
grease, presumably hardened in the stove-top
burners and in the bowels of the vent, along with
probably a few trillion bacteria. A chipped Formica
table and four bent-metal, vinyl-backed chairs stood
in the center of the kitchen. The counters were
barren, no dishes visible. There were also no towels,
coffeemaker or condiment canisters, nor any other
item or personal touch that might have suggested
the kitchen had been used in the last decade or so. It
was as though he had stepped back in time, or
happened upon a bomb shelter put into service
during the hysteria of the fifties.

The small dining room was across the hallway
from the kitchen. Lee looked at the waist-high wood
paneling, darkened and cracked over the years. He

had a sudden chill, though the air was stale and oppressive inside. The house apparently had no central heating, nor had Lee seen any wall-mounted air conditioners. There had been no heating oil tank outside either, at least aboveground. Lee eyed the chill-chasers bolted along the bottom of the walls, their power cords plugged into electrical outlets. As in the kitchen, the ceiling here was unfinished. The electrical line to the dust-ridden chandelier ran through holes bored in the exposed joists. Electricity, Lee deduced, must have come to the home after it was first built.

As he moved down the hallway toward the front of the house, Lee was unable to see the invisible trip beam, positioned at knee height, that stretched across the hall. He pierced this security perimeter, and from somewhere in the house a barely audible click was heard. Lee jerked for a moment, pointing his gun in wide circles, and then relaxed. It was an old house, and old houses made lots of noises. He was just being jumpy, yet he had a right to be. The cottage and its location were right the hell out of a *Friday the 13th* movie.

Lee entered one of the front rooms. There, under the sweep of his flashlight, he saw that the furniture had been moved up against the walls, and there were footprints and drag patterns in the layers of dust on the floor. In the center of the room were a number of folding chairs and a rectangular-shaped table. A stack of Styrofoam coffee cups rested at one end of the table next to a coffeemaker. Packets of coffee, creamer and sugar lay next to the coffeemaker.

Lee took all this in and jerked when he saw the windows. Not only were the heavy drapes drawn tight, but also the windows had been boarded over with big sheets of plywood, the drapes dangling from underneath the wood.

"Shit," Lee muttered. He quickly discovered that the small square windows set in the front door had been covered over with cardboard. He pulled out his camera and snapped some shots of all these puzzling items.

Wanting to complete his search as soon as possible, Lee hurried up the stairs to the second floor. He cautiously opened the door to the first bedroom and peered in. The bed was small and made, and its smell of mildew hit him immediately. The walls here were unfinished as well. Lee put his hand against the exposed wall and immediately felt air from the outside coming through the cracks. He was startled for a moment when he saw a slender line of light coming from the top of the wall. Then he realized it was the moonlight coming through a gap where wall was supposed to meet roof.

Lee carefully nudged open the closet door. It still let out a prolonged squeak that made him catch a breath. No clothes, not even a single hanger. He shook his head and went into the small connecting bathroom. Here, there was a more modern, drop-down ceiling, linoleum floor with pebble design and plasterboard walls covered with peeling flower-patterned wallpaper. The shower was a one-piece fiberglass unit. However, there were no towels, toilet paper or soap. No way to shower or even freshen up.

He went through into the other, adjoining bedroom. Here, the smell of mildew on the bedcovers was so strong he almost had to hold his nose. The closet here was empty as well.

None of this was making sense. He stood in the pool of moonlight coming through the window, felt his neck tickled by the drafts of air pushing through the cracks in the walls and shook his head. What was Faith Lockhart doing here if not using it as some kind of love nest? That was what his initial conclusion had been, even though he had only seen her with the tall woman. People swung lots of ways. But not even with concrete up their noses could they have been having sex on these sheets.

Returning downstairs, he went across the hallway and into the other front space, which Lee assumed was the living room. The windows here had been boarded over as well. There was a bookshelf notched into one of the walls, although no books were on it. As in the kitchen, the ceiling was unfinished. As Lee swung his light upward, he spied the short pieces of wood tacked between the joists at forty-five-degree angles, forming a line of X's across the ceiling. The wood was clearly different from that used for the original construction; it was lighter and of a different grain. Additional support? Why had that been necessary?

He shook his head in the manner of a man resigned to his fate. Now added to Lee's list of worries was the possibility that the damn second floor would collapse at any minute on his head. He envisioned his obit headlined something like: LUCKLESS PI FELLED BY BATHTUB/SHOWER COMBO; WEALTHY EX-WIFE REFUSES COMMENT.

As Lee shone his light around, he froze. Set into one wall was a door. A closet, most likely. Nothing unusual about that, except that this door was secured by a deadbolt. He went over and examined the lock more closely, glancing at the small pile of wood dust on the floor directly under the lock. Lee knew it had been left over when the person installing the lock had drilled the hole through the wooden door. Exterior deadbolts. A security system. A deadbolt recently installed on an *interior* closet door in a crappy rental in the boonies. What could be so valuable here to go to all this trouble?

"Shit," Lee said again. He wanted to leave this

place, but he could not take his eyes off the lock. If Lee Adams had one fault – and it could hardly be considered a fault for someone in his line of work – it was that he was a very curious man. Secrets plagued him. People attempting to hide things came close to infuriating him. As a "lunch pail" kind of guy utterly convinced that great monied forces stalked the earth creating all kinds of havoc for ordinary folk like him, Lee believed in the principle of full and fair disclosure with all his substantial heart. Putting action to that belief, he wedged the flashlight under his armpit, holstered his gun and pulled out his lock-pick kit. His fingers worked nimbly as he slipped a fresh pick into the lock-pick gun. He took a deep breath, inserted the pick in the lock and turned on the machine.

When the deadbolt slid back, Lee took another deep breath, pulled his pistol and pointed it at the door as he turned the knob. He didn't really believe that anyone had locked himself in a closet and was about to jump him, but then again, he had seen stranger things happen. Someone might be on the other side of this door.

When he saw what was in the closet, a part of him wished the problem were as simple as someone preparing to ambush him. He swore under his breath, holstered his pistol and ran.

In the closet the blink of red lights from the stacks of electronic equipment shone forth now in the open doorway.

Lee raced into the other front room and shone his light around the walls in even patterns, moving higher and higher. Then he saw it. There was a camera lens in the wall next to the molding. Probably a pinhole lens, designed specifically for covert surveillance. It was impossible to see in the poor lighting, but the beam from the flashlight was reflecting off it. As he moved the beam around, he hit a total of four camera lenses.

Holy shit. The sound he had heard earlier. He must have tripped some device that had triggered the cameras. He raced back to the living room closet, flashed his light on the front of the video machine.

Eject! Where the hell was eject? He found the button, hit it and nothing happened. He punched it again and again. He hit the other buttons. Nothing. Then Lee's gaze closed on the *second* small infrared portal in the front of the machine, and the answer hit him. The machine was controlled by a special remote, its function buttons overridden. His blood ran cold with the possibilities this sort of arrangement suggested. He thought about putting a bullet into the thing, to make it cough up the precious tape. But for all he knew, the damn thing was armored and he'd end up eating his own slug off the ricochet. And what if it had a real-time satellite link and the tape was only a backup? Was there a camera in here? People could be looking at him right now. For one ridiculous second, he thought about giving them the finger.

Lee was about to run again but then had a sudden inspiration. He fumbled in his knapsack, his usually steady fingers now not quite so dexterous. His hands closed around the small case. He whipped it out, fought with the lid for an instant and then managed to pull out the small but powerful magnet.

Magnets were a popular burglary tool because they were ideal for locating and popping window pins once you had cut through the glass. Otherwise, the pins would defeat the most accomplished burglar. Now the magnet would play the reverse role: not helping him break in, but rather assisting him in making what he hoped would be an invisible exit.

He palmed the magnet and then ran it in front of the video machine and then over the top. He did it as many times as he could in the one minute he had allowed himself before fleeing for his life. He prayed that the magnetic field would obliterate the images on the tape. *His* images.

He threw the magnet back in his bag, turned and ran for the door. God only knew who might be on their way here. Lee suddenly stopped. Should he go back to the closet, rip the VCR out and take it with him? The next sound Lee heard drove all thoughts of the VCR from his mind.

A car was coming.

"Sonofabitch!" hissed Lee. Was it Lockhart and her escort? They had come here every *other* evening. So much for a pattern. He raced back down the hall, threw open the back door, burst through and hurdled the concrete stoop. He landed heavily in the slick grass, his shoeless feet slipped and he fell hard. The impact knocked the breath out of him and he felt a sharp pain where his elbow had struck at an odd angle. But fear was a great painkiller. Within a few seconds he was up and chugging for the tree line.

He was halfway to the woods when the car pulled into the driveway, its light beams bouncing a little as the car moved from flat road to uneven ground. Lee took another few strides, hit the tree line and dove under cover.

The red dot had lingered for a few moments on Lee's chest. Serov could have taken the man so easily. But that would warn the people in the car. The former KGB man aimed the rifle at the driver's-side door. He hoped the man who had now made it to the woods would not be stupid enough to try anything. He had been very lucky up until now. He had escaped death not once, but twice. One should not waste that much luck. It would be in such poor taste, Serov thought as he once more sighted through the laser scope.

Lee should have kept running, but he stopped, his chest heaving, and crept back to the tree line. His curiosity had always been his strongest trait, sometimes too strong. Besides, the people behind all the electronic equipment probably had already identified him. Hell, they probably knew the dentist he used and his preference for Coke over Pepsi, so he might as well stick around and see what was coming next. If the people in the car started for the woods, he would do his best impersonation of an Olympic marathoner, shoeless feet and all, and dare anyone to catch him.

He crouched down and took out his night-vision monocular. It utilized forward-looking infrared, or FLIR, technology, which was a vast improvement over the ambient light intensifier, or I-squareds, Lee had used in the past. FLIR worked by detecting, in essence, heat. It needed no light to operate, and unlike the I-squareds, it could distinguish dark images against dark backgrounds, with the heat transferred into crystal-clear video images.

As Lee focused the contraption, his field of vision was now a green screen with red images. The car appeared so close that Lee had the sense that he could reach out and touch it. The engine area glowed particularly brightly, since it was still very hot. He watched the man as he climbed out of the driver's side. Lee didn't recognize him, but the private investigator tensed as he watched Faith Lockhart climb out of the car and join the man. They were side by side at this point. The man hesitated as though he had forgotten something.

"Damn," Lee hissed between clenched teeth. "The

door." Lee focused for a moment on the back door to the cottage. It was standing wide open.

The man had obviously seen this. He turned, facing the woman, and reached inside his coat.

*

In the woods, Serov fixed his laser point on the base of the man's neck. He smiled contentedly. The man and woman were lined up nicely. The ammo the Russian was chambering was highly customized, military-style ordnance with full metal jackets. Serov was a careful student of both weapons and the wounds they caused. With its high velocity, the bullet would have minimal projectile deformity as it passed through its target. However, it would still cause devastating injury when the kinetic energy the bullet carried was released and then rapidly lost in the body. The initial wound track and cavity would be many times larger than the size of the bullet before it partially closed. And the destruction to tissue and bone would occur radially, akin to the epicenter of an earthquake, with terrible damage resulting a great distance away. It was quite beautiful, in its own way, Serov felt.

Velocity was the key to kinetic energy levels – the Russian was well aware – which, in turn, determined damage force on the target. Double the weight of a bullet and it doubled the kinetic energy. However, Serov had long ago learned that when you doubled the velocity at which the bullet was fired, the kinetic energy was *quadrupled*. And Serov's weapon and ammo were at the top end of the scale on velocity. Yes, beautiful indeed.

However, because of its full metal jacket, the bullet could also easily pass through one person and then strike and kill another. This was not an unpopular result for soldiers who were going at it in combat. And for hired killers with two targets.

52

However, if another bullet was required to kill the woman, so be it. Ammo was relatively cheap. Consequently, so were humans.

Serov took a slight breath, became absolutely still and lightly squeezed the trigger.

"Omigod!" Lee shouted as he watched the man's body twist and then pitch violently against the woman. They both dropped to the ground as though sewn together.

Lee instinctively started to race out of the woods to help. A shot hit the tree right next to his head. Lee instantly dropped to the ground and sought cover as another shot hit near him. Lying on his back, his body shaking so hard he could barely focus the damn monocular, Lee scanned the area where he thought the shots had come from.

Another shot hit close to him, kicking up wet dirt in his face, stinging his eyes. Whoever was out there knew what he was doing and was loaded for dinosaur. Lee could sense the shooter methodically closing in on him grid by grid.

Lee could tell that the shooter was using a suppressor, because each shot sounded like someone slapping a wall hard with the palm of his hand. *Splat. Splat. Splat.* They could have been balloons exploding at a children's party, not cone-shaped pieces of metal flying at a million Mach seeking to wipe out a certain PI.

Other than the hand holding his monocular, Lee tried not to move, tried not to breathe. For one terrifying instant he saw the red line of the laser dart near his leg like a curious snake, and then it was gone. He didn't have much time. If he just stayed here, he was a dead man.

Laying his gun on his chest, Lee stretched his fingers out and carefully groped for a moment in the dirt until his hand closed around a stone. Using just the flick of his wrist, he tossed the stone about five feet away, waited; and when it hit a tree, a bullet struck the same spot a few seconds later.

With his infrared eye, Lee instantly zeroed in on the heat of this last muzzle flash, as oxygen-deprived, super-hot gas escaping from the rifle barrel collided with the outside air. This simple reaction of physical elements had cost many a soldier his life as it revealed his position. Lee could only hope for the same result now.

Lee used the muzzle flash to fix on the man's thermal image amid the cover of trees. The shooter wasn't that far away, well within range of Lee's SIG. Realizing he would probably get only one attempt, Lee slowly gripped his gun and raised his arm, trying to locate a clear line of fire. Keeping his gaze on his target through the monocular, Lee clicked off the safety, said a silent prayer and fired eight shots from his fifteen-round mag. They were all aimed fairly close together, increasing his chances of a hit. His pistol shots were much louder than the rifle's suppressed ones. On all sides of him wildlife fled the human conflict.

One of Lee's shots miraculously found its mark, mainly because Serov had moved right into the path of the shot as he was attempting to shift to a closer position. The Russian grunted in pain as the bullet entered his left forearm. For a split second it stung, then the dull throbbing came as the bullet ripped through soft tissue and veins, shattered his humerus and finally came to rest in his clavicle. His left arm immediately became heavy and useless. After killing a dozen people in his career, always with a gun, Leonid Serov finally knew what it felt like to be shot. Clutching the rifle in his good hand, the ex-KGB agent took the professional way out. He turned and ran, blood splattering on the ground with each step.

Through the FLIR, Lee watched him run for a few moments. From the way the man was retreating, Lee was pretty certain that at least one of his shots had scored a hit. He decided it would be both stupid and unnecessary to chase an armed and wounded man. Besides, he had something else to do. He grabbed his bag and ran toward the cottage.

SIX

While Lee and Serov were exchanging fire, Faith struggled to get her breath back. The collision with Newman had taken most of her wind and left a throbbing pain in her shoulder. With convulsive strength she was able to roll him off. She felt a warm and sticky substance on her dress. For a terrifying moment she thought she had been shot. Faith couldn't have known it, but the agent's Glock had acted as a mini-shield, deflecting the bullet as it left his body. It was the only reason she was still alive. For a moment she stared at what was left of Newman's face and felt herself growing sick.

Pulling her gaze away, Faith managed to squat low in the driveway and slide her hand into Newman's pocket, then pulled out his car keys. Faith's heart was pumping so frantically that it was difficult for her mind to focus. She could barely hold the damn car keys. Still crouching, she eased open the driver's-side door.

Her body was shaking so hard she didn't even know if she could drive the car once she got in it. Then she was inside, slammed the door shut and locked it. When the engine caught, she put the car in gear, hit the gas and the engine flooded and died on her. Swearing loudly, she turned the key again; the engine caught. She made a more cautious movement on the gas pedal and the engine remained purring.

She was about to hit the gas when her breath

caught in her throat. A man stood at the driver's-side window. He was breathing heavily and looked as scared as she felt. What really held her attention, though, was the gun pointed directly at her. He motioned for her to roll the window down. She contemplated hitting the gas.

"Don't try it," he said, seemingly reading her thoughts. "I'm not the one who shot at you," he said through the glass. He added, "If I were, you'd already be dead."

Finally Faith edged down the window.

"Unlock the door," he said, "and move over."

"Who are you?"

"Let's go, lady. I don't know about you, but I don't want to be here when someone else shows up. They might be a better shot."

Faith unlocked the door and slid over. Lee holstered his gun, threw his bag in the back, got in, slammed the door shut and backed out. Right at that instant the cell phone rang, causing them to both jump. He stopped the car and they looked down at the phone and then at each other.

"It's not my phone," he said.

"It's not mine either," replied Faith.

When the ringing stopped, he asked, "Who's the dead guy?"

"I'm not telling you anything."

The car hit the road and he shifted to drive and punched the gas. "You might regret that decision."

"I don't think so."

He appeared confused by her confident tone.

She slipped her seat belt on as he took a curve a little fast. "If you shot that man back there, then you'll shoot me regardless of what I tell you or not. If you're telling the truth and you didn't shoot him, then I don't think you'll kill me simply because I won't talk."

"You have a very naive perspective of good and bad. Even good guys have to kill on occasion," he said.

"Are you speaking from experience?" Faith edged closer against the door.

He hit the auto door lock. "Now, don't go and throw yourself out the car. I just want to know what's going on. Starting with who's the dead guy."

Faith stared at him, her nerves completely shattered. When she finally spoke, her voice was very weak. "Do you mind if we just go somewhere, anywhere, so I can just sit and think for a bit?" She curled her fingers and added hoarsely, "I've never seen anyone killed before. I've never almost been . . ." Her voice rose as she said this last part and she started to tremble. "Please pull over. For God's sake, pull over! I'm going to be sick."

He skidded the car to a stop on the shoulder and hit the auto unlock button. Faith threw open the door, leaned out and vomited.

He reached across and put his hand on her shoulder, squeezing tightly until she stopped shaking. He spoke in a slow, steady tone. "You're gonna be okay." He paused and waited until she was able to sit back up and close the door before continuing. "First we need to ditch this car. Mine's on the other side of the woods. It'll only take a few minutes to get there. Then I know a place where you can be safe. Okay?"

"Okay," Faith managed to say.

SEVEN

Barely twenty minutes later, a sedan pulled into the cottage's driveway and a man and woman got out. The metal of their weapons reflected off the light thrown from the car's headlights. Approaching the dead man, the woman knelt down and looked at the body. If she hadn't known Ken Newman very well, she might not have recognized him. She had seen human death before, yet she still felt something rising from her stomach to her throat. She quickly stood and turned away. The pair searched the cottage thoroughly and then did a quick sweep of the tree line before coming back to the body.

The large, barrel-chested fellow looked down at Ken Newman's body and uttered a curse. Howard Constantinople was "Connie" to all who knew him. A veteran FBI agent, he had seen just about everything in his career. However, tonight was new territory even for him. Ken Newman was a good friend of his. Connie looked as though he might burst into sobs.

The woman stood next to him. At six feet one, she matched Connie's height. Her brunette hair was cut very short, curving over her ears. Her face was long, narrow and intelligent, and she was dressed in a stylishly fitting pantsuit. Both the years and the stress of her occupation had hammered fine lines around her mouth and around her dark, sad eyes. Her gaze swept the surrounding area with the ease of someone accustomed not only to observing but also to making accurate deductions from what she observed. There was an edge to her features that clearly demonstrated a powerful internal anger.

At age thirty-nine, Brooke Reynolds's attractive features and tall, lean physique would make her appealing to men for as long as she desired the attention. However, immersed as she was in the middle of a bitter divorce that had wreaked havoc on her two young children, she questioned whether she would ever again want the companionship of a man.

Reynolds had been christened, over the objections of her mother, Brooklyn Dodgers Reynolds by her overzealous baseball-fan father. Her old man had never been the same when his beloved ball club went to California. Almost from day one, her mother had insisted she be called Brooke.

"My God," Reynolds finally said, her gaze fixed on her dead colleague.

Connie looked over at her. "So what do we do now?"

She shook off the net of despair that had settled over her. Action was called for, swift but methodical. "We have a crime scene, Connie. We don't have much choice."

"Locals?"

"This is an AFO," she said, referring to an assault on a federal officer, "so the Bureau will be in the lead." She found she couldn't take her gaze from the body. "But we'll still have to work with the county and state people. I have contacts with them, so I'm reasonably sure we can control the information flow."

"With an AFO we have the Bureau's Violent Crime Unit. That breaks our Chinese wall."

Reynolds took a deep breath to quell the tears she felt rising to her eyes. "We'll do the best we can. The first thing we have to do is secure the crime scene, not that it's going to be too difficult out here. I'll call Paul Fisher at HQ and fill him in." Reynolds mentally went up her chain of command at the Bureau's Washington Field Office, or WFO. The ASAC, SAC and ADIC would have to be notified; the ADIC, or assistant director in charge, was the head of the WFO, really only a notch below the director of the FBI himself. Soon, she thought, there would be enough abbreviations here to sink a battleship.

"Dollars to donuts the director himself will be out here too," Connie added.

The walls of Reynolds's stomach started to burn. An agent being killed was a shock. An agent losing his life on her watch was a nightmare she would never wake up from.

An hour later, forces had converged on the scene, fortunately without any media. The state medical examiner verified what everyone who had even remotely seen the devastating wound already knew: namely, that Special Agent Ken Newman had died from a distant gunshot entry wound to the upper neck, exiting from his face. While the local police stood guard, the VCU, or Violent Crime Unit, agents methodically collected evidence.

Reynolds, Connie and their superiors gathered around her car. The ADIC was Fred Massey, the ranking agent at the scene. He was a small, humorless man who kept shaking his head in exaggerated motions. His white shirt collar was loose around a skinny neck, his bald head seeming to glow under the moonlight.

A VCU agent appeared with a videotape from the cottage and a pair of muddy boots. Reynolds and

Connie had noted the boots when they had searched the cottage, but had wisely opted against disturbing any evidence.

"Someone was in the house," he reported. "These boots were on the back stoop. No forced entry. The alarm was deactivated and the equipment closet was open. Looks like we maybe got the person on tape. They tripped the laser."

He handed the tape to Massey, who promptly handed it over to Reynolds. The act was far from subtle. All this was her responsibility. She would either get the credit or take the fall. The VCU agent put the boots in an evidence bag and went back into the house to continue searching.

Massey said, "Give me your observations, Agent Reynolds." His tone was curt, and everyone understood why.

Some of the other agents had openly shed tears and cursed loudly when they saw their colleague's body. As the only woman here, and Newman's squad supervisor to boot, Reynolds didn't feel she had the luxury of dissolving into tears in front of them. The vast majority of FBI agents went through their entire careers without ever even drawing their sidearms except for weapons recertification. Reynolds had sometimes wondered how she would react if such a catastrophe ever hit home. Now she knew: Not very well.

This was probably the most important case Reynolds would ever handle. A while back, she had been assigned to the Bureau's Public Corruption Unit, a component of the illustrious Criminal Investigation Division. After receiving a phone call from Faith Lockhart one night and secretly meeting the woman on several occasions, Reynolds had been named the squad supervisor of a unit detailed to a special. That "special" had the opportunity, if

Lockhart was telling the truth, to topple some of the biggest names in the United States government. Most agents would die for such a case during their careers. Well, one had tonight.

Reynolds held up the tape. "I'm hoping this tape will tell us something of what happened here. And what happened to Faith Lockhart."

"You think it's likely she shot Ken? If so, a nationwide APB goes out in about two seconds," Massey said.

Reynolds shook her head. "My gut tells me she had nothing to do with it. But the fact is we don't know enough. We'll check the blood type and other residue. If it only matches Ken's, then we know she wasn't hit as well. We know Ken hadn't fired his gun. And he had on his vest. Something took a chunk out of his Glock, though."

Connie nodded. "The bullet that killed him. Through the back of the neck and out the front. He had his weapon out, probably eye-height, the slug hit and deflected off it." Connie swallowed with difficulty. "The residue on Ken's pistol supports that conclusion."

Reynolds stared sadly at the man and continued the analysis. "So Ken might have been between Lockhart and the shooter?"

Connie slowly shook her head. "Human shield. I thought only the Secret Service did that crap."

Reynolds said, "I spoke with the ME. We won't know anything until the post and we can see the wound track, but I think it was most likely a rifle shot. Not the sort of weapon a woman ordinarily carries in her purse."

"So another person waiting for them?" Massey ventured.

"And why would that person kill and then go inside the house?" Connie asked.

"Maybe it was Newman and Lockhart who went in the house," Massey surmised.

Reynolds knew it had been years since Massey had worked a field investigation, but he was still her ADIC and she couldn't very well ignore him. She didn't have to agree with him, though.

Reynolds shook her head decisively. "If they had gone in the house, Ken wouldn't have been killed in the driveway. They'd still be in the house. We interview Lockhart for at least two hours each time. We got here a half hour after they would have, tops. And those weren't Ken's boots. But they are men's boots, about a size twelve. Odds are a big guy."

"If Newman and Lockhart didn't go in the house, and there are no signs of forced entry, then this third party had the passcode to the alarm." Massey's tone was clearly accusatory.

Reynolds looked miserable, but she had to keep going. "From where Ken fell, it looked like he had just gotten out of the car. Then something must have spooked Ken. He pulls his Glock and then takes the round."

Reynolds led them over to the driveway. "Look at the rut marks here. The ground around here is reasonably dry, but the tires really gouged the dirt. I think somebody was getting out of here in a hurry. Hell, fast enough that he ran out of his boots."

"And Lockhart?"

"Maybe the shooter took her with him," Connie said.

Reynolds thought about this. "It's possible, but I don't see why. They'd want her dead too."

"In the first place, how would a shooter know to come here?" Massey asked, and then answered his own question. "A leak?"

Reynolds had been considering this possibility from the moment she had seen Newman's body.

"With all due respect, sir, I don't see how that could be the case."

Massey coldly ticked off the points on his fingers. "We've got one dead man, a missing woman and a pair of boots. Put it all together and I'm looking at a third party being involved. Tell me how that third party got here without inside information."

Reynolds spoke in a very low tone. "It could be a random thing. Lonely place, possible armed robbery. It happens." She took a quick breath. "But if you're right and there is a leak, it's not complete." They all looked at her curiously. "The shooter obviously didn't know about our last-second change of plan. That Connie and I would be here tonight," Reynolds explained. "Ordinarily, I would've been with Faith, but I was working another case. It didn't pan out and I decided at the last minute to hook up with Connie and come out here."

Connie glanced over at the van. "You're right, no one could have known about that. Ken didn't even know."

"I *tried* to call Ken about twenty minutes before we got here. I didn't want to just suddenly appear. If he heard a car pull up to the safe house without prior warning, he might have gotten spooked, shot first and asked questions later. He must have already been dead when I tried to reach him."

Massey stepped toward her. "Agent Reynolds, I know you've been handling this investigation from the beginning. I know that your use of this safe house and the closed-circuit TV surveillance of Ms. Lockhart were all approved by the appropriate parties. I understand your difficulties in pursuing this case and gaining this witness's trust." Massey paused for a moment, seeming to select his words with great care. Newman's death had stunned them all, although agents were often in harm's way. Still, there would be definite blame assessed in this case, and everyone knew it.

Massey continued, "However, your approach was hardly textbook. And the fact is, an agent is dead."

Reynolds plunged right in. "We had to do this very quietly. We couldn't exactly have surrounded Lockhart with agents. Buchanan would've been gone before we had enough evidence for prosecution." She took a long breath. "Sir, you asked for my observations. Here they are. I don't think Lockhart killed Ken. I think Buchanan is behind it. We have to find her. But we have to do it quietly. If we put out an APB, then Ken Newman has probably died in vain. And if Lockhart is alive, she won't be for long if we go public."

Reynolds looked over at the van just as its doors closed on Newman's body. If she had been escorting Faith Lockhart instead of Ken, the odds were that she would have lost her life tonight. For any FBI agent, death was always a possibility, however remote. If she were killed, would Brooklyn Dodgers Reynolds fade in her children's memory? She was certain her six-year-old daughter would always remember "Mommy." She had doubts about three-year-old David, though. If she were killed, would David, years from now, only refer to Reynolds as his "birth" mother? The thought itself was nearly paralyzing.

One day she had actually taken the ridiculous step of having her palm read. The palm reader had warmly welcomed Reynolds, given her a cup of herbal tea, and chatted with her, asking her questions that tried to sound casual. These queries, Reynolds knew, were designed to gather background information to which the woman could add appropriate mumbo-jumbo as she "saw" into Reynolds's past, as well as her future.

After examining Reynolds's hand, the palm reader had told her that her life line was short. Significantly so, in fact. The worst she'd ever seen. The woman said this as she stared at what appeared to be a scar on Reynolds's palm. Reynolds knew it was the result of falling on a broken Coke bottle in her backyard when she was eight.

The reader had picked up her cup of tea, apparently waiting for Reynolds to plead for more information, presumably at an appropriate premium over the initial fee. Reynolds had informed her that she was strong as a horse with years in between even a simple bout of flu.

Death needn't be by natural causes, the palm reader had replied, her painted eyebrows rising to emphasize the obvious point.

On that, Reynolds had paid her five dollars and walked out the door.

Now she wondered.

Connie scuffed the dirt with his toe. "If Buchanan is behind this, he's probably long gone by now anyway."

"I don't think so," Reynolds replied. "If he runs right after this, then he's as good as admitting guilt. No, he'll play it cool."

"I don't like this," Massey said. "I say we APB Lockhart and bring her in, assuming she's still living."

"Sir," Reynolds said, her voice tight, edgy, "we can't name her as a subject in a homicide when we have reason to believe she wasn't involved in the murder, but may well be a victim herself. That opens the Bureau to a whole civil-action can of worms if she does turn up. You know that."

"Material witness, then. She damn well qualifies for that," said Massey.

Reynolds looked directly at him. "An APB is not

the answer. It's going to do more harm than good. For everybody involved."

"Buchanan has no reason to keep her alive."

"Lockhart is a smart woman," Reynolds said. "I spent time with her, got to know her. She's a survivor. If she can hang on for a few days, we have a shot. Buchanan can't possibly know what she's been telling us. But we do an APB naming her as a material witness, we just sign her death notice."

. They were all silent for a bit. "All right, I see your point," Massey finally said. "You really think you can find her on the Q.T.?"

"Yes." What else could she say?

"Is that your gut talking, or your brain?"

"Both."

Massey studied her for a long moment. "For now, Agent Reynolds, you focus on finding Lockhart. The VCU people will investigate Newman's murder."

"I'd have them lockstep the yard looking for the slug that killed Ken. Then I'd search the woods," Reynolds said.

"Why the woods? The boots were on the stoop."

She glanced over at the tree line. "If I were here to ambush someone, that" – she pointed toward the woods – "would be my first tactical choice. Good cover, excellent line of fire and a hidden escape route. Car waiting, gun disposed of, a quick trip to Dulles Airport. In an hour the shooter's in another time zone. The shot that killed Ken entered the back of his neck. He's facing away from the woods. Ken must not have seen his attacker, or else he wouldn't have turned his back." She eyed the thick woods. "It all points there."

Another car pulled up and the director of the FBI himself climbed out. Massey and his aides hurried over, leaving Connie and Reynolds alone.

"So what's our plan of action?" Connie asked.

"Maybe I'll try to match those boots to my Cinderella," Reynolds said as she watched Massey talking to the director. The director was a former field agent who, Reynolds knew, would take this catastrophe extremely personally. Everybody and everything associated with it would be subject to intense scrutiny.

"We'll cover all the usual bases." She tapped her finger against the tape. "But this is really all we have. Whoever's on this tape we hit hard, like there's no tomorrow."

"Depending on how this turns out, we might not have many tomorrows left, Brooke," said Connie.

EIGHT

L ee gripped the steering wheel so hard his fingers were turning white. As the police car, lights blazing, raced past him going in the opposite direction, he let out an enormous breath and then pushed hard on the accelerator. They were in Lee's car after having ditched the other. He had scrubbed down the inside of the dead man's car, but he could have easily missed something. And nowadays equipment existed that could find things completely invisible to the naked eye. Not good.

As she watched the swirling lights disappear into the darkness, Faith wondered if the police were heading to the cottage. Did Ken Newman have a wife and kids? she wondered. There had been no wedding band on his finger. Like many women, Faith had the habit of making that quick observation. Yet he'd seemed like the fatherly type.

As Lee maneuvered the car through the back roads, Faith's hand moved up, down and then drew a vertical line across her chest as she finished crossing herself. The near-automatic movement conveyed a subtle sense of surprise to her. She added a silent prayer for the dead man. She whispered another prayer for any family he might have. "I'm so sorry you're dead," she said out loud, to help assuage her mounting feelings of guilt for simply having survived.

Lee looked over at her. "Friend of yours?"

She shook her head. "He was killed because of me. Isn't that enough?"

Faith was surprised at how easily the words of prayer and remorse had come back to her. Because of her nomadic father, her attendance at mass over the years had been sporadic. But her mother had insisted on Catholic schools wherever the family happened to venture, and her father had followed this rule after his wife had died. Catholic school must have ingrained something in her other than the constant bite of the ruler on her knuckles from Sister Something-or-other. The summer before her senior year, she had become an orphan, her travels with her father abruptly cut short by a heart attack. She was sent to live with a relative who did not want her and who took pains to show no attention to her. Faith had rebelled however she could. She smoked, she drank, she ceased to become virgin Faith long before it was fashionable to do so. At school the daily tugging down of her skirt to below her knees by the nuns only made her want to pull the damn thing up to her crotch. All in all, it was a truly forgettable year in her life, followed by several more as she struggled through college, tried to gain some direction in her life. Then for the past fifteen years she had thought her rudder was flawless, the grand movements of her life fluid. Now she was floundering, speeding toward the rocks.

Faith looked at Lee. "We need to call the police, tell somebody that he's back there."

Lee shook his head. "That opens a whole other can of worms. That is definitely not a good idea."

"We can't just leave him back there. It's not right."

"Do you suggest we go to the local precinct and try to explain this thing? They'll put us in strait-jackets."

"Dammit! If you won't do it, I will. I am *not* leaving him back there for the squirrels."

"All right, all right. Calm down." He sighed. "I guess we could place an anonymous call in a little while, get the cops to check it out."

"Fine," said Faith.

A few minutes later, Lee noticed that Faith was fidgeting.

"I have another request," she said.

The woman's demanding style was really starting to annoy him. Lee tried not to think about the hurt in his elbow, the irritating specks of cold dirt in his eyes, the unknown dangers that lay ahead.

"Like what?" he said wearily.

"There's a gas station near her. I'd like to wash up." She added quietly, "If that's okay."

Lee looked down at the stains on her clothes and his expression softened. "No problem," he said.

"It's down this road—"

"I know where it is," Lee said. "I like to get the lay of the land where I'm working."

Faith simply stared at him.

In the bathroom Faith tried not to focus on what she was doing as she painstakingly cleaned the blood off her clothing. Still, every couple of minutes she felt like ripping off all her clothes and scrubbing herself down using the soap from the dispenser and the stack of paper towels on the dirty sink.

When she climbed back in the car, her companion's look said what his mouth didn't.

"I'll make it, for now," she said.

"By the way, my name's Lee. Lee Adams."

Faith said nothing. He started the car and they left the gas station.

"You don't have to tell me your name," he said. "I

was hired to follow you, Ms. Lockhart."

She eyed him suspiciously. "Who hired you to do that?"

"Don't know."

"How could you possibly not know who hired you?"

"I admit it's a little unusual, but it happens, on occasion. Some people are embarrassed about hiring a private detective."

"So that's what you are, a private eye?" Her tone was one of contempt.

"It can be a very legit way of earning a buck. And I'm as legit as they come."

"And how did this person come to hire you?"

"Other than the fact that I've got a killer Yellow Pages ad, I don't have a clue."

"Do you have any idea what you're mixed up in, Mr. Adams?"

"Let's just say I have a better idea now than I did a little bit ago. Getting shot at is the one thing that has always captured my undivided attention."

"And who shot at you?"

"The same guy who nailed your friend. I think I winged him, but he got away."

Faith rubbed her temples and looked out into the darkness. His next words startled her.

"What are you, Witness Protection?" Lee waited. When she didn't answer, he continued. "I did a ten-second down-and-dirty on your friend while you were busy choking out the car. He had a Glock nine-millimeter and a Kevlar vest, for all the good it did him. The shield on his belt said FBI. I didn't have time to check for ID. So what was his name?"

"Does it matter?"

"It might."

"Why Witness Protection?" she asked.

"The cottage. Special locks, security system. It's a

73

safe house, of sorts. Nobody's living there, that's for sure."

"So you've been inside."

He nodded. "At first I thought you were having an affair. A couple minutes inside told me it wasn't a love nest. Strange house, though. Hidden cameras, tape-recording system. Did you know you were on stage, by the way?"

The astonished look on her face answered his question.

"If you didn't know who hired you, how were you engaged to follow me?"

"Easy enough. Phone message said a packet of information on you and an advance on my fee would be delivered to my office. They were. A file on you, and a big chunk of cash. It said to follow your movements, and I did."

"I was told I wasn't being followed."

"I've gotten pretty good at it."

"Apparently."

"Once I knew where you were going, I just got here ahead of you. Pretty simple."

"Was the voice a man's or woman's?"

"Couldn't tell; it was scrambled."

"Didn't that make you suspicious?"

"Everything makes me suspicious. One thing's for sure, whoever's after you, they ain't playing around. The ammo the guy was using back there could have wasted an elephant. I got to see it up close and personal."

He fell silent and Faith could not bring herself to say anything else. She had several credit cards in her purse, all with virtually limitless spending power. And they were all useless to her, because as soon as one went through the swipe machine, they would know where she was. She put her hand in her purse and touched the Tiffany pewter ring holding the keys to her beautiful home and her luxury car. Useless as well. In her wallet was the grand sum of fifty-five dollars and a few pennies. She had been stripped bare except for this cash and the clothes on her back. Her impoverished childhood had come roaring back in all its tarnished, hopeless memory.

She did have a large sum of cash, but it was in a safe-deposit box at her bank in D.C. The bank would not be open until tomorrow morning. And there were two other items she kept in that box that were even more critical to her: a driver's license and another credit card. They were both under a fake name. They had been relatively easy to set up, but she had hoped she would never have to use them. So much so that she had kept them in her bank instead of a more accessible place. Now she shook her head at such stupidity.

With those two cards she could go just about anywhere. If everything collapsed on top of her, she had often reminded herself, this would be her way out. *Well*, she thought now, *the roof's gone, the walls are creaking, the killer tornado's at the window and the fat lady is in the limo on the way back to the hotel. It's time to pull the tent and call it a life.*

She looked at Lee. What would she do with him? Faith knew that her most pressing challenge was surviving the rest of the night. Maybe he could help her do that. He seemed to know what he was doing, and he had a gun. If she could just get in and out of her bank without too much trouble, she would be okay. There were about seven hours between now and the bank's opening. They might as well have been seven years.

NINE

Thornhill sat in the small study of his lovely ivy-draped old home in a much-sought-after neighborhood in McLean, Virginia. His wife's family had money, and he enjoyed the luxuries that money could buy, as well as the freedom it gave him to be a public servant his entire career. Right now, though, he was not feeling much comfort.

The message he had just received was unbelievable to him, and yet all the plans had the potential for failure. He looked at the man sitting across from him. This person was also a veteran at the Agency, and a member of Thornhill's secret group. Philip Winslow shared Thornhill's ideals and concerns. They had spent many a night in Thornhill's study, both reminiscing about past glories and devising plans that would ensure there would be many future triumphs as well. They were both Yale graduates, two of the best and brightest. They had come along at a time when it was considered honorable to serve one's country. And the CIA had gotten its share of the Ivy League's best back then. They had also come from a generation in which a man did whatever it took to protect his country's interests. A man with vision, Thornhill believed with all his heart, had to be willing to take risks to achieve that vision.

"The FBI agent was killed," Thornhill said to his friend and colleague.

"And Lockhart?" Winslow asked.

Thornhill gave one brief shake of his head. "She's disappeared."

Winslow summed it up. "So we take out one of the Bureau's finest and let the real target get away." He clinked the ice in his drink. "Not good, Bob. The others won't be happy to hear that."

"Just to get all the good news out, our man was also shot in the process."

"By the agent?"

Thornhill shook his head. "No. There was some-one else there tonight. Unknown as yet. Serov has been debriefed. He gave a description of the man who was at the cottage. We're doing computer generations of him right now. We should know his identity shortly."

"Could he tell us anything else?"

"Not at present. Mr. Serov is being detained, for now, in safe quarters."

"You know the Bureau will go after this tooth and nail, Bob."

"More precisely," Thornhill said, "they will do everything in their power to find Faith Lockhart."

"Who do they suspect?"

"Buchanan, of course. It's logical," Thornhill replied.

"So what do we do with Buchanan?"

"For now, nothing. We'll keep him informed. Of at least our version of the truth, that is. We'll keep him busy at the same time we keep close tabs on the FBI. He has a trip out of town this morning, so we're covered there. However, if the FBI's investigation gets too close to Buchanan, we'll provide him with an early death and provide our professional brethren with all the sordid facts of how Buchanan tried to have Lockhart murdered."

"And Lockhart?" Winslow asked.

"Oh, the FBI will find her. They're quite good at that sort of thing, in their limited way."

"I don't see how that helps us. She talks, and Buchanan goes down and takes us with him."

"I hardly think that," Thornhill said. "When the FBI finds her, we will be there as well, if we don't find her first. And this time we won't miss her. With Lockhart gone, Buchanan will soon follow. Then we can move forward with our original plan."

"God, if it could only work."

"Oh, it will work," said Thornhill with his usual optimism. To last as long as he had in this business, one had to have a positive attitude.

TEN

Lee pulled the car into the alleyway and stopped. His gaze swept over the darkened landscape. They had driven around for over two hours until he felt reasonably sure they had not been followed, and then he had made the phone call to the police from a pay phone. Although they seemed relatively safe now, Lee still kept one hand resting on the grip of his pistol, ready to pull it in an instant, to terminate their enemies with the salvos from his deadly SIG. That was a joke.

These days you could kill from a sky away, with a bomb smarter than a man, taking the most important thing men had without so much as a "Hello, you're dead." Lee wondered if, during the millisecond it took to cremate the poor bastards, the brain moved fast enough to spark the thought that the Hand of God had struck them down instead of something manufactured by man, the idiot. For a crazy moment, Lee scanned the sky looking for a guided missile. And depending on who was involved in all this, maybe it wasn't so crazy after all.

"What did you tell the police?" Faith asked.

"Short and sweet. The location of the place and what happened."

"And?"

"And the dispatcher was skeptical but did his best to keep me on the line."

Faith looked around the alley. "Is *this* the safe

place you mentioned?" She took in the darkness, the hidden crevices, the garbage can and the distant tap of footsteps on pavement.

"No, we leave the car here and walk to the safe place. Which, by the way, is my apartment."

"Where are we?"

"North Arlington. It's being yuppified, but it can still be dangerous, especially this time of night."

She stayed right next to him as they made their way down the alley and out on to the next street, which was an avenue of old but nicely kept-up attached rowhouses.

"Which one's yours?"

"The big one at the end there. Owner's retired, lives in Florida. He's got a couple of other properties. I troubleshoot for him, and he gives me a break on the rent."

Faith started to walk out of the alley, but Lee stopped her. "Give me a sec, I want to check things first."

She clutched his jacket. "You are not leaving me here alone."

"I'm just making sure there's nobody there waiting to throw us a surprise party. Anything looks weird, give a shout and I'm back in two shakes."

He disappeared and Faith edged into the crevice of the alley. Her heart was beating so loud, she half expected a window to open and a shoe to come sailing out at her. When she thought she could not take being alone anymore, Lee reappeared.

"Okay, it looks good. Let's go."

The outer door to the building was locked, but Lee opened it with his key. Faith noted the video camera bolted to the wall above her head.

Lee looked at her. "My idea. I like to know who's coming to see me."

They went up four flights of stairs to the top floor

and down the hallway to the last door on the right. Faith eyed the three locks on the door. Lee opened each of them with the same special key.

When the door opened, she heard a beeping sound. They went inside the apartment. On the wall was an alarm panel. Screwed into the wall above it was a piece of shiny copper on a hinge. Lee flipped the copper shield down so that it covered the alarm panel. He reached his hand underneath the copper plate and hit some buttons on the panel and the beeping sound stopped.

He looked over at Faith, who was watching him closely.

"Van Eck radiation. You probably wouldn't understand."

She hiked her eyebrows. "You're probably right."

Next to the alarm panel was a small video screen built into the wall. On the screen Faith could see the front stoop of the building. It was obviously the video link to the surveillance camera outside.

Lee locked the front door and then put his hand on it. "It's steel, set in a special metal frame I built myself. It doesn't matter how strong the lock is. What usually gives is the frame. A lousy two-by-four if you're lucky. A crook's Christmas present handed out by the building industry. I've also got pick-proof window locks, outside motion detectors, piggyback cellular on the alarm system's phone link. We'll be okay."

"I take it you're somewhat security-minded?" she said.

"No, I'm paranoid."

Faith heard something approaching from down the hall. She flinched, but relaxed when she saw Lee smile and move toward the sound. A second later an old German shepherd wandered around the corner. Lee squatted and played with the big dog, who rolled over on his back. Lee accommodated the animal with a belly rub.

"Hey, Max, how you doing, boy?" Lee patted Max's head and the dog affectionately licked his owner's hand.

"Now, this thing is the best security device ever invented. Don't have to worry about electrical outages, batteries going dead or somebody turning his loyalties."

"So your plan is that we stay here?"

Lee looked up at her. "You want something to eat or drink? We might as well work on this over a full stomach."

"Hot tea would be nice. I couldn't really look at food right now."

A few minutes later they were sitting at the kitchen table. Faith sipped on herbal tea while Lee worked on a cup of coffee. Max dozed under the table.

"We have a problem," Lee began. "When I went in the cottage I tripped something. So I'm on the videotape."

Faith looked stricken. "My God, they could be on their way here right now."

"Maybe that's a good thing." Lee looked at her sharply.

"And why is that?"

"I'm not into helping criminals."

"So you think I'm a criminal?"

"Are you?"

Faith fingered her teacup. "I was working with the FBI, not against them."

"Okay, what were they doing with you?"

"I can't answer that."

"Then I can't help you. Come on, I'll give you a ride to your place." Lee started to rise from his chair.

She gripped his arm. "Wait, please wait." The thought of being left alone now was paralyzing.

He sat back down and waited expectantly.

"How much do I have to tell you before you'll help me?"

"Depends on what sort of help you want. I'm not doing anything against the law."

"I wouldn't ask you to."

"Then you've got no problem, other than somebody wanting to kill you."

Faith took a nervous sip of her tea while Lee watched her.

"If they know who you are from the video, should we be just sitting here?" she asked.

"I messed with the tape. Ran my magnet over it."

Faith looked at him, a glint of hope in her eyes. "You think you were able to erase it?"

"I can't tell for sure. I'm not an expert in that stuff."

"But at the very least it might take some time for them to reconstruct it?"

"That's what I'm hoping. But we're not exactly dealing with the Campfire Girls here. The recording equipment also had a security system built in. Chances are if the police try to force the tape out, it might self-destruct. Personally, I'd give the forty-seven bucks I have in the bank if that did happen. I'm a man who likes his privacy. But you still need to fill me in."

Faith didn't say anything. She just stared at him, like he had just made an unwanted pass at her.

Lee cocked his head at her. "I tell you what. I'm the detective, okay? I'll make some deductions and you tell me if I'm right or not, how's that?" When Faith still said nothing, he continued. "The cameras I saw were only in the living room. And the table, chairs, coffee and stuff were set up in the living room only. Now, I tripped the laser or whatever it was going in. That apparently set off the cameras."

"I guess that would make sense," Faith said.

"No, it doesn't. I had the access code to the alarm system," said Lee.

"So?"

"So I put in the code and disarmed the security system. So why have the trip device still operating? The way it was set up, even when the guy you were with disarmed the security system, he would still have engaged the cameras. Why would he want to record himself?"

Faith looked deeply confused. "I don't know."

"Hello, so they'd have you on film without you knowing it. Now the out-of-the-way place with the CIA-level security in place, the Feds, the cameras and taping equipment, all point to one thing." Lee paused as he thought about exactly how he was going to phrase this. "They brought you there to interrogate you. But maybe they're not sure of your level of cooperation, or they think somebody might try to pop you, so they film the interrogations just in case you turn up missing later on."

Faith looked at him with a resigned smile. "Terribly prescient of them, don't you think? The 'turning up missing' thing."

Lee stood and stared out the window as he thought things through. Something very important had just occurred to him. Something that he should have thought about a lot sooner. And even though he didn't know the woman, he was feeling kind of crappy about what he had to say. "I've got some bad news for you."

Faith looked startled. "What do you mean?"

"You're under interrogation by the FBI. Presumably you're also in their protective custody. One of their guys gets popped protecting you and I probably wounded the guy who killed him. The Feds have my face on their tape." He paused for a moment. "I've got to turn you in."

Faith jumped up. "You can't do that! You can't! You said you'd help me."

"If I don't, then I'm looking at some serious time in a place where guys get way too friendly with other guys. At the very least I lose my PI license. I'm sure if I knew you better I'd feel even worse about doing this, but at the end of the day I'm not sure even my grandma would be worth that much trouble." He slipped on his jacket. "Who's your principal handler?"

"I don't know his name," Faith said coldly.

"Do you have a phone number?"

"It wouldn't do any good. I doubt he'd be able to take the call now."

Lee eyed her dubiously. "Are you telling me the dead guy back there is your only contact?"

"That's it." Faith told this lie with a completely straight face.

"The guy was your handler and he never bothered to tell you his name? That's not exactly textbook FBI."

"Sorry, that's all I know."

"Is that right? Well, let me tell you what I know. I saw you at that cottage three other times with a woman. A tall brunette. What, did you sit around calling her Agent X?" He leaned right into her face. "Bullshit Rule Number One: Make damn sure the person you're lying to can't prove same." He hooked an arm around hers. "Let's go."

"You know, Mr. Adams, *you* have a problem you may not have thought about."

"Is that right? Care to share it?"

"What exactly are you going to tell the FBI when you bring me in?"

"I don't know, how about the truth?"

"Okay. Let's look at the truth. You were following

85

me because someone you don't know and can't identify instructed you to. Which means we only have your word for that. You were able to follow me even though the FBI assured me no one could. You were in that house tonight. Your face is on the tape. An FBI agent is dead. You fired your gun. You say you shot the other man, but you have no way to prove another man was even there. So the proven facts are we have you at the house and me at the house. You fired your gun and an FBI agent is dead."

"The ammo that killed that guy is not something my pistol happens to chamber," he said angrily, releasing her arm.

"So you threw the other gun away."

"Why would I snatch you from the place, then? If I was the shooter, why wouldn't I have killed you back there?"

"I'm not saying what *I* think, Mr. Adams. I'm just suggesting to you that the FBI might suspect you. I suppose if there's nothing in your past to make them suspicious, the FBI might believe you." She added offhandedly. "They'll probably just investigate you for a year and then drop it if nothing turns up."

Lee scowled at her. His recent past was squeaky clean. Going back a little further, the waters got a little murkier. When he was first starting out as a PI, he had done some things he would never even consider doing now. Not illegal, but still hard to explain to straightlaced federal agents.

And then there was the restraining order his ex had gotten right before Lucky Eddie had struck patent gold. Claimed Lee was stalking her, was perhaps violent. Lee would have become violent if he had gotten hold of the little shit. Every time Lee thought about the bruises on his daughter's arms and cheek when he had made an unexpected visit to their rat-trap apartment he almost had a stroke. Trish claimed Renee had fallen down the stairs. Stood there and lied to his face, when Lee could see the imprint of what he knew was a knuckle against his daughter's soft skin. He had taken a crowbar to Eddie's car and would've taken one to Eddie if the guy hadn't locked himself in the bathroom and called the cops.

So did he really want the FBI snooping around his life for the next twelve months? On the other hand, if he let the woman walk away and the Feds tracked him down, then where would he be? Everywhere he turned, he ran into a nest of snakes.

Faith spoke in a pleasant tone. "Do you want to drop me at the Washington Field Office? They're at Fourth and F Streets."

"Okay, okay, you've made your point," Lee said hotly. "But I didn't ask for this crap to be dropped in my lap."

"And I didn't ask for you to become involved in this either. But . . ."

"But what?"

"But if you weren't there tonight, I wouldn't be alive right now. I'm sorry I haven't thanked you before. I'm thanking you now."

Despite his suspicions, Lee felt his anger slowly receding. Either the woman was sincere or she was one of the slickest operators he'd come across. Or maybe it was a little slice of both. This was Washington, after all.

"Always glad to help a lady," he said dryly. "Okay, supposing I decide not to turn you in. What do you have in mind to pass the night away?"

"I need to get away from here. I need some time to think things through."

"The FBI is not going to just let you walk away. I'm assuming you've cut some sort of deal."

"Not yet. And even if I had, don't you think I have good grounds to declare them in default?"

"What about the people who tried to kill you?"

"Once I have some space, I can decide what to do. I'll probably end up just going back to the FBI. But I don't want to die. I don't want anyone else associated with me to die." She stared very deliberately at him.

"I appreciate your concern, but I can take care of myself. So where do you plan to run, and how do you plan to get there?"

Faith started to say something and then stopped. She looked down, suddenly wary.

"If you don't trust me, Faith, none of this works," Lee prodded gently. "If I let you walk, that means I'm going to bat for you big-time. But I haven't made that decision yet. A lot depends on what you're thinking. If the Feds need you to bring down some powerful people – and what I've seen so far clearly rules out this being shoplifting material – then I'm going to have to side with the Feds."

"What if I agreed to come back as long as they could give guarantees as to my safety?"

"I guess that sounds reasonable. But what guarantee is there that you'll come back at all?"

"What if you come with me?" she said quickly.

Lee stiffened so much that he accidentally kicked Max, who came out from under the table and looked at him pitifully.

Faith rushed on. "You said yourself that it's only a matter of time before they identify you on the tape. The person you shot, what if he identifies you to whoever hired him? It's obvious that you're in danger too."

"I'm not sure—"

"Lee," Faith said excitedly, "did it ever occur to you that the person who hired you to follow me had you trailed as well? You could very well have been used to set up the shooting."

"Well, if they could follow me, they could follow you," he countered.

"But what if they wanted to frame you for all this somehow?"

Lee blew the air from his cheeks as the hopelessness of his situation set in. Sonofabitch, what a night. How the hell hadn't he seen it coming? Anonymous client. Bag full of cash. Mystery target. Lonely cottage. Had he been in a frigging coma or what? "I'm listening."

"I have a safe-deposit box in a bank in D.C. In that box I have cash, and some pieces of plastic with another name on them that'll let us go about as far as we need to. The only problem is they might be watching my bank. I need your help."

"*I* can't access your safe-deposit box."

"But you can help me scope the place out, see if anyone's watching. You're obviously better at that than I am. I go in, clean out the box and get out as fast as possible while you cover me. Anything looks suspicious, we run like hell."

"It sounds like we're planning to rob the place," he said angrily.

"I swear to God all the things in that box are mine."

Lee put a hand through his hair. "Okay, maybe that works. Then what?"

"Then we head south."

"South where?"

"The Carolina shore. Outer Banks. I have a place there."

"Are you listed as the owner? They can check that."

"I bought it in the name of a corporation and signed the papers under my other name, as an officer. But what about you? You can't travel under your own name."

"Don't worry about me. I've been more people in my life than Shirley MacLaine, and I've got the papers to prove it."

"Then we're all set."

Lee looked down at Max, who had settled his big head in his lap. Lee gently stroked the dog's nose.

"How long?"

Faith shook her head. "I don't know. A week, maybe."

Lee sighed. "I guess I can have the lady downstairs take care of Max."

"Then you'll do it?"

"Just so long as you understand that while I don't mind helping somebody who needs it, I'm not playing the world's greatest sucker either."

"You don't strike me as someone who would ever play that role."

"If you really want a laugh, tell my ex-wife that."

ELEVEN

Old Town Alexandria was located in northern Virginia next to the Potomac River, about a fifteen-minute drive south of Washington, D.C. The waters had been the primary reason the city had been established, and it had flourished as a seaport for a very long time. It was still an affluent and desirable place to live, although the river no longer played a prominent role in the town's economic future.

It was a setting of both old wealth and freshly monied families nestled within the graceful brick, stone and wood-frame structures of late eighteenth and early nineteenth century architecture. A few of the streets were covered in the very same rolling cobblestone that had supported the treads of Washington and Jefferson. And of the young Robert E. Lee at his two boyhood homes, which were set across from each other on Oronoco Street, itself named after a particular brand of long-ago Virginia-grown tobacco. Many of the town's sidewalks were brick and had buckled up around the numerous trees that had shaded the homes, streets and inhabitants for so long. A number of the wrought-iron fences that encircled the courtyards and gardens of the homes were painted the color of gold on their European-inspired spikes and finials.

At this early hour the streets of Old Town were quiet except for the drizzle of rain and the rush of wind among the branches of the aged, knobby trees whose shallow roots clutched at the hard Virginia clay. The street names reflected the colonial origins of the place. Driving through town, one would pass King, Queen, Duke and Prince Streets. Off-road parking was scarce here, so the narrow avenues were lined with virtually every make and model of vehicle. Placed against the two-hundred-year-old homes, the chrome, rubber and metal hulls seemed oddly out of place, as though a time warp had whisked the automobile back to the era of horse and buggy.

The narrow four-story brick townhouse that was wedged among a line of others along Duke Street was by no means the grandest in the area. There was a lone, tilting maple in the small front yard, its split trunk covered with leafy suckers. The wrought-iron fencing was in good but not superb condition. The home had a garden and courtyard out back, yet the plantings, dripping fountain and brickwork there were unremarkable when compared with others located but a few steps away.

Inside the home, the furnishings were far more elegant than the outside of the place would have led the observer to expect. There was a simple reason for this: The outside of the home was something Danny Buchanan could not hide from curious eyes.

The first traces of the pink dawn were just starting to nudge at the edges of the horizon as Buchanan sat, fully dressed, in the small oval-shaped library off the dining room. A car was waiting to take him to Reagan National Airport.

The senator he was meeting with was on the Appropriations Committee, arguably the Senate's most important committee, since it (and its subcommittees) controlled the government's purse strings. More importantly for Buchanan's purposes, the man also chaired the Subcommittee on Foreign

Operations, which determined where most foreign aid dollars went. The tall, distinguished senator with the smooth manners and confident tones was a longtime associate of Buchanan's. The man had always enjoyed the power that came with his position and he had consistently lived beyond his means. The retirement package he had waiting from Buchanan would be almost impossible for a human being to exhaust.

Buchanan's bribery scheme had started out cautiously at first. He had analyzed all the players in Washington who even remotely might further his goals, and whether they could be bribed. Many members of Congress were wealthy, but many others were not. It was often both a financial and familial nightmare for people to serve in Congress. Members had to maintain two residences, and the Washington metro area was not cheap. And their families often did not come with them. Buchanan approached the ones he figured he could corrupt and began a long process of feeling them out on possible involvement. The carrots he dangled were small at first but quickly grew in size if the targets showed any enthusiasm. Buchanan had selected well, because he had never had a target not agree to exchange votes and influence for rewards down the road. Perhaps they felt that the difference between what he proposed and what occurred in Washington every day was marginal at best. He didn't know if they cared that the goal was a worthy one. However, they hadn't gone out of their way to increase foreign aid to any of Buchanan's clients on their own.

And they had all seen colleagues leave office and grab the gold of lobbydom. But who wanted to work that hard then? Buchanan's experience was that ex-members made terrible lobbyists anyway. Going back hat in hand to lobby former colleagues over whom you no longer had any leverage was not appealing to these overly proud folk. Much smarter to use them when they were the most powerful they would ever be. Work them hard first. And then pay them grandly later. What could be better?

Buchanan wondered if he could really hold it together during the meeting with a man he had already betrayed. But then, betrayal was doled out in large doses in this town. Everyone was constantly scrambling for a chair before the music stopped. The senator would be understandably upset. Well, he would have to stand in line with the rest.

Buchanan suddenly felt tired. He didn't want to get in the car or climb on another plane, but he had no say in the matter. *Still a member of the Philadelphia servant class?*

The lobbyist focused his attention on the man who was standing before him.

"He sends his compliments," the burly man said. To the outside world he was Buchanan's driver. In reality he was one of Thornhill's men keeping close tabs on their most important charge.

"And please send Mr. Thornhill my sincerest wishes that God should decree he not grow one day older," said Buchanan.

"There have been important developments of which he would like you to be aware," the man said impassively.

"Such as?"

"Lockhart is working with the FBI to bring you down."

For a brief, dizzying moment Buchanan thought he would vomit all over himself. "What in the hell are you talking about?"

"This information was just discovered by our operative inside the Bureau."

"You mean they entrapped her? Made her work

for them?" *Just like you did to me.*

"She voluntarily went to them."

Buchanan slowly regained his composure. "Tell me everything," he said.

The man responded with a series of truths, half-truths and outright lies. He told them all with equal, practiced sincerity.

"Where is Faith now?"

"She's gone underground. The FBI is looking for her."

"How much has she told them? Should I be making plans to leave the country?"

"No. It's very early in the game. What she's told them thus far would not warrant prosecution of any kind. She's told them more of the process of how it was done, but not who was involved. However, that's not to say they can't follow up what she's told them. But they have to be careful. The targets aren't exactly flipping burgers at McDonald's."

"And the vaunted Mr. Thornhill doesn't know where Faith is? I hope his omniscience isn't failing him now."

"I have no information about that," said the man.

"A poor state of affairs for an intelligence-gathering agency," Buchanan said, even managing a smile. A log in the fireplace let out a loud pop, and a fat wad of sap shot out and hit the screen. Buchanan watched it dripping down the mesh face, its escape halted, its existence over. Why did he suddenly feel the remainder of his life had just been symbolically played out?

"Perhaps I should try to find her."

"It's really not your concern."

Buchanan stared at him. Had the idiot really said that? *"You* won't be the one going to prison."

"It'll work out. You just continue right on."

"I want to be kept informed. Clear?" Buchanan

turned to the window. In its reflection he studied the man's reaction to his sharply spoken words. But what were they really worth? Buchanan had clearly lost this round; he had no way of winning it, actually.

The street was dark, no visible movement, just the familiar sounds of squirrels corkscrewing up the trees and then leaping from branch to branch in their never-ending game of survival. Buchanan was engaged in a similar contest, but even more dangerous than hopping across the slippery bark of thirty-foot-tall trees. The wind had picked up some; the beginnings of a low howling sound could be heard in the chimney. A bit of smoke from the fire drifted into the room with the backdraft of air.

The man looked at his watch. "We need to leave in fifteen minutes to make your flight." He picked up Buchanan's briefcase, turned and left.

Robert Thornhill had always been careful in how he contacted Buchanan. No phone calls to the house or office. Face-to-face meetings only under conditions such as these where it would not raise suspicions, where surveillance by others could not be maintained. The first meeting between the two had been one of the few times in Buchanan's life that he had felt inadequate in the face of an opponent. Thornhill had calmly presented stark evidence of Buchanan's illegal dealings with members of Congress, high-ranking bureaucrats, even reaching inside the White House. Tapes of them going over voting schemes, strategies to defeat legislation, frank discussions of what their fake duties would be once they left office, how the payoffs would occur. The CIA man had uncovered Buchanan's web of slush funds and corporations designed to funnel money to his public officials.

"You now work for me," Thornhill had said

bluntly. "And you will go right on doing what you are doing until my net is as strong as steel. And then you will stand clear, and I will take over."

Buchanan had refused. "I'll go to prison," he had said. "I'll take that over indentured servitude."

Thornhill, Buchanan recalled, had looked slightly impatient. "I'm sorry if I wasn't clear. Prison isn't an option. You either work for me or you cease to live."

Buchanan had paled in the face of this threat, but still held firm. "A public servant embroiled in murder?"

"I'm a special type of public servant. I work in extremes. It tends to justify what I do."

"My answer's the same."

"Do you also speak for Faith Lockhart? Or should I consult her personally on the matter?"

That remark had struck Buchanan like a bullet to the brain. It was quite clear to Buchanan that Robert Thornhill was no bully. There was not a hint of bluster in the man. If he said something as innocuous as, "I'm sorry it's come to this," you would probably be dead the next day. Thornhill was a careful, deliberate, focused person, Buchanan had thought at the time. Not unlike himself. Buchanan had gone along. To save Faith.

Now Buchanan understood the relevance of Thornhill's safeguards. The FBI was watching him. Well, they had their work cut out for them, for Buchanan doubted they were in Thornhill's league when it came to clandestine operations. But everyone had an Achilles' heel. Thornhill had easily found his in Faith Lockhart. Buchanan had long wondered what Thornhill's weakness was.

Buchanan slumped in a chair and studied the painting hanging on the library wall. It was a portrait of a mother and child. It had hung in a private museum for almost eighty years. It was by one of the acknowledged – but lesser known – masters of the Renaissance period. The mother was clearly the protector, the infant boy unable to defend himself. The wondrous colors, the exquisitely painted profiles, the subtle brilliance of the hand that had invented this image so clearly evident in every brushstroke, never failed to enrapture anyone who saw it. The gentle curl of finger, the luminosity of the eyes, each detail still so vibrant almost four hundred years after the paint had hardened.

It was perfect love on both sides, uncomplicated by silent, corrosive agendas. As one level it was the simple thread of biological function. At another it was a phenomenon enhanced by the touch of God. This painting was his most prized possession. Unfortunately, it would soon have to be sold, and perhaps his home as well. He was running out of money to fund the "retirements" of his people. Indeed, he felt guilty for still owning the painting. The funds it could generate, the help it could bring to so many. And yet just to sit and gaze at it was so soothing, so uplifting. It was the height of selfishness, and brought him more pleasure than just about anything else.

But maybe it was all moot at this point. The end was coming for Buchanan. He knew that Thornhill would never let him walk away from all of this. And he had no illusions that he would let Buchanan's people enjoy any retirement whatsoever. They were his slaves-in-waiting. The CIA man, despite his refinement and pedigree, was a spy. What were spies but living lies? However, Buchanan would honor his agreement with his politicians. What he had promised them in return for helping him would be there, whether they would be able to enjoy it or not.

As the light of the fire played over the painting,

the woman's face, it seemed to Buchanan, took on the characteristics of Faith Lockhart – not the first time he had observed this. His gaze traced the set of full lips that could turn petulant or sensual without warning. As his eye ran down the long, gracefully formed face, the hair golden, not auburn, in just the right splash of angled light, he always thought of Faith. She had a pair of eyes that held you; the left pupil slightly off center added depth to make Faith's countenance truly remarkable. And it was as though this flaw of nature had empowered her to see right through anyone.

He remembered every detail of their very first meeting. Fresh out of college, she had bounded into his life with the enthusiasm of a newly minted missionary, ready to take on the world. She was raw, immature at certain levels, largely ignorant of the ways of Washington, astonishingly naive in various respects. And yet she could also command a room like a movie star. She could be funny and then turn serious on a dime. She could stroke egos with the best of them and still get her message across, without overtly pushing the issue. After five minutes talking to her, Buchanan knew she had what it took to flourish in his world. After her first month on the job, his intuition proved correct. She did her homework, worked tirelessly, learned the issues, dissected the players down to the level needed to do the job and then went deeper. She understood what everyone needed in order to walk away a winner. Burning bridges in this town meant you didn't survive. Sooner or later, you needed help from everyone, and memories were exceptionally long in the capital city. As tenacious as a wolverine, she had endured defeat after defeat on a number of fronts, but continued to pound away until she was victorious. He had never met anyone like her before or since. They had been through more together in fifteen years than couples married a lifetime. She was really all the family he had. The precocious daughter he was destined never to have. And now? How did he protect his little girl?

As the rain drifted across the roof and the wind strummed its peculiar sounds down the aged firebrick of his Old Town chimney, Buchanan forgot about his car and his flight and the dilemmas confronting him. The man continued to stare at the painting in the soft glow of the quietly crackling fire. And it was clearly not the work of the grand master that fascinated him so.

Faith had not betrayed him. Nothing Thornhill could ever tell him would change that belief. But now she was in Thornhill's way, which meant she was in mortal danger. He stared at the painting. "Run, Faith, run just as fast as you can," he said under his breath, with all the anguish of a desperate father seeing violent death racing after his child. In the face of the protector mother in the painting, Buchanan felt even more powerless.

TWELVE

Brooke Reynolds sat in rented office space about ten blocks from the Washington Field Office. The Bureau sometimes took off-site space for agents engaged in sensitive investigations, where something overheard even in the cafeteria or hallway could have disastrous effects. Virtually everything the Public Corruption Unit did was of a sensitive nature. The usual targets of the unit's investigation were not bank robbers wearing masks and waving guns. They were often people one read about on the front pages of the newspapers or saw being interviewed on the TV news.

Reynolds leaned forward and slipped out of her flats, rubbing her aching feet against the legs of her chair. Everything about her was tight, raw and hurting: Her sinuses were almost completely closed, her skin feverish, her throat scratchy. But at least she was alive. Unlike Ken Newman. She had driven straight to his home after first calling ahead to let his wife know she had to see her. Reynolds hadn't said why, but Anne Newman had known that her husband was dead. Reynolds had heard it in the tone of the few words the woman had managed to speak.

Normally, a person of a higher level than Reynolds would accompany her to the home of a bereaved spouse, to show that the Bureau did care, from top to bottom, when it lost one of its own. However, Reynolds had not waited for anyone else to volunteer to come with her. Ken was her responsibility, including telling his family that he was dead.

When she had arrived at the house, Reynolds had gotten right down to it, figuring a drawn-out monologue would only prolong the woman's obvious agony. Reynolds's compassion and empathy for the bereaved woman had been unhurried, however, and sincere. She had held Anne, consoled her as best she could, broken down in tears with her. Anne had taken the absence of information well, Reynolds had thought, far better than she probably would were the roles reversed.

Anne would be allowed to see her husband's body. Then it would be autopsied by the state's chief medical examiner. Connie and Reynolds would attend the post along with representatives from the Virginia State Police and the commonwealth's attorney office, all of whom were under strict confidentiality orders.

They would also have to count on Anne Newman to help keep angry and confused family members under control. It was a potentially weak link in the chain, expecting a woman in personal agony to help a government agency that couldn't even tell her all the circumstances of her husband's death. But it was all they had.

As she had left the stricken woman's home – the kids had been away with friends – Reynolds had the distinct feeling that Anne blamed her for Ken's death. And as Reynolds had walked back to her car she couldn't really disagree with that. The guilt Reynolds was feeling right now was like a crusty barnacle sunk into her skin, a free radical roaming inside her body, seeking a place to nest, grow and eventually kill her.

Outside the Newmans' home she had run into the

director of the FBI as he had come to offer his own condolences. He conveyed heartfelt sympathy to Reynolds for the loss of one of her men. He told her that he had been briefed on her conversation with Massey and that he concurred in her judgment. However, he made it clear that results had better be both quick and substantial.

As Reynolds now eyed the considerable clutter of her office, it occurred to her that the mess well symbolized the disorganization, some would say dysfunction, of her personal life. Matters of importance from many open cases lay across her desk and small conference table. They were wedged on to her shelves, had mutated into piles on her floor and even found their way on to the couch where she often slept, far away from her children.

But for her live-in nanny and the nanny's teenage daughter, Reynolds didn't know how should could possibly keep a halfway normal life for her kids. Rosemary, a wonderful woman from Central America who loved the children nearly as much as Reynolds did and was fanatical about keeping the house clean, the meals cooked and the clothes laundered, was costing Reynolds over a quarter of her entire salary and was more than worth every penny. But after the divorce was final it would be very tight. And Reynolds's ex would not be paying any alimony. His work as a fashion photographer, though lucrative, came in quick bursts followed by long periods of deliberate inactivity. Reynolds would be lucky if she didn't end up paying *him* alimony. And child support from him, while she would seek it, would be a joke. The man may as well have had "dead-beat dad" engraved on his forehead.

She looked at her watch. The FBI lab was working on the videotape right now. Because the existence of her "special" was unknown within the FBI except for very select personnel, any lab work that was required was supposed to be sent over under a dummy case name and file number. It would be nice to have separate laboratory facilities and personnel, but that would entail enormous expense that just didn't figure in the Bureau's budget. Even elite crime fighters had to live within the allowance Uncle Sam gave them. Normally a liaison agent at the main agency would work with Reynolds's team to coordinate any lab submissions and findings with Reynolds. However, Reynolds didn't have time for normal channels. She had personally delivered the tape to the lab and with her superior's blessing it had received a very high priority.

After meeting with Anne Newman she had gone home, cuddled for as long as she could with her sleeping kids, showered, changed and driven right back to work. All the time she had been thinking of that damn tape. As if in response to her thoughts, the phone rang.

"Yes?"

"You better come over," said the man. "And just so you know, it's not good news."

THIRTEEN

Faith awoke with a start. She looked at her watch. It was nearly seven. Lee had insisted that she get some rest, but she hadn't expected to be out so long. She sat up, feeling thickheaded. Her body was aching and when she swung her legs over the side of the bed, she felt a little sick to her stomach. She still had her suit on, but she had slipped off her shoes and pantyhose before lying down.

She got off the bed, padded into the adjoining bathroom and looked at herself in the mirror. "God," was all she could manage to say. Her hair was matted flat, her face a mess, her clothes filthy and her brain felt like cement. Such a pleasant way to begin the day.

She turned on the shower and stepped back into the bedroom to undress. She had taken off her clothes and was standing naked in the middle of the bedroom when Lee knocked on the door.

"Yes?" she said anxiously.

"Before you get in the shower, we need to do something," Lee said through the door.

"Is that right?" The odd tone of his words sent a chill up her spine. She quickly put her clothes back on and stood rigidly in the middle of the room.

"Can I come in?" He sounded impatient.

She went over and edged open the door. "What is—" Faith almost screamed when she saw him.

The man looking at her was not Lee Adams. This

man had a buzz cut, the hair dyed blond and damp, a matching short beard and mustache, and he wore glasses. And instead of dazzling blue, his eyes were brown.

The man smiled as he watched her reaction. "Good, it passed the test."

"Lee?"

"We can't exactly walk past the FBI as ourselves."

Lee held out his hands. Faith saw the scissors and a box of hair coloring.

"Short hair is easier to take care of, and personally I think it's a myth that blondes have more fun."

She looked at him dully. "You want me to cut my hair? And then color it?"

"No, I'll cut it. And if you want, I can color it for you too."

"I can't do that."

"You have to do that."

"I know it seems silly under the circumstances—"

"You're right, it does seem silly under the circumstances. Hair grows back, but once you're dead, you're dead," he said bluntly.

She started to protest but then realized he was right.

"How short?"

He cocked his head, examining her hair from different angles. "How about a short, Joan of Arc do? Boyish, but cute."

Faith just stared at him. "Wonderful. Boyish, but cute – my lifetime ambitions realized with a few snips and a bottle of hair color."

They went into the bathroom. Lee sat her down on the toilet and began to cut while Faith kept her eyes tightly shut.

"Want me to do the color too?" Lee asked when he was done.

"Please. I'm not sure I can look at it right now."

It took some time under the sink, and the smell of chemicals contained in the coloring mix was tough to take on an empty stomach, but when Faith finally managed to look in the mirror she was pleasantly surprised. It didn't look as bad as she would have thought. The outline of her head, now more fully revealed, was actually a nice shape. And the dark color went well with her skin tones.

"Now grab a shower," Lee said. "You can get your hair wet. Blow dryer's under the sink. There'll be some clean clothes on the bed."

She eyed his big frame. "I'm not your size."

"Not to worry. I run a full-service resort."

Thirty minutes later, Faith emerged from the bedroom in jeans and a flannel shirt, jacket and low-heeled boots that Lee had left for her. From power suit to college student. She felt years younger. The short black hair encircled her face, which she left au naturel. Faith had decided to forgo her usual makeup routine. Fresh start all around.

Lee sat at the kitchen table. He studied her new appearance. "Looks good," he said approvingly.

"You did it." She looked at his wet hair and a thought struck her. "Do you have a second bathroom?"

"Nope, just the one. I showered while you were sleeping. I didn't use the hair dryer because I was afraid it would wake you. You'll find I'm a very considerate soul."

She recoiled slightly. It was a creepy revelation, that he had been lurking around while she was asleep in his bed. She got this sudden image of a maniacal, scissors-toting Lee Adams leering while she lay there tied to the bed, naked and helpless.

"God, I must have really been out," she said as casually as she could.

"You were. I actually grabbed some shut-eye too."

He continued to study her appearance. "You know, you look better without makeup."

Faith smiled. "Your lies are very much appreciated." She smoothed down her shirt. "By the way, do you always keep women's clothes around your apartment?"

Lee pulled on a pair of socks and then some tennis shoes. He wore jeans and a white T-shirt that was spread taut across his chest. The veins in his biceps and smooth forearms rippled, and Faith hadn't really noticed before how thick his neck was. His torso narrowed dramatically at his waist, the pants slightly loose there, giving him a hard V-shape. His thighs looked ready to burst through the denim. He caught her staring and Faith quickly looked away.

"My niece Rachel," he said. "She goes to law school at Michigan. She clerked at the law firm here last year and stayed with me, rent-free. Only she earned more money in one summer than I do in about a year. She left some of her stuff. Lucky you're about the same size. She'll probably be back next summer."

"Tell her to be careful. This town has a way of destroying people."

"I don't think she'll have your problems. She wants to be a judge one day. No felons need apply."

Faith's face flushed. She took a mug from the sink rack and poured a cup of coffee.

Lee stood. "Look, that was out of line. I'm sorry."

"I deserve a lot worse than that, actually."

"Fine, I'll let other people do the honors."

Faith poured a cup of coffee for him and sat down at the table. Max came into the kitchen and nudged her hand. She smiled and petted the dog's broad head.

"Max taken care of?"

"All set." He checked his watch. "The bank opens

shortly. We'll have just enough time to pack. We'll get your stuff, head to the airport, get our tickets and fly, fly away."

"I can call down and arrange for the house from the airport. Or should I try from here?"

"No. Phone logs can be checked."

"I didn't think of that."

"You're going to have to start to." He took a sip of coffee. "Hope the place is available."

"It will be. I happen to own it. Or at least my other identity does."

"Small place?"

"Depends on what you call small. I think you'll be comfortable."

"I'm easy." He carried his coffee into the bedroom and came out a few minutes later wearing a navy blue sweater over his T-shirt. His mustache and beard were gone and he had a baseball cap on. He was carrying a small plastic bag.

"The evidence of our makeovers," he explained.

"And no disguise?"

"Mrs. Carter's used to me keeping odd hours, but if I barge in looking like somebody else, it'll be a little much for her this early in the morning. And I don't want her being able to give anyone a description later on."

"You are good at this," said Faith. "That's reassuring."

He called Max. The big dog obediently padded from the small living room into the kitchen, stretched his body and then sat next to Lee. "If the phone rings, don't answer it. And stay away from the windows."

Faith nodded and then he and Max were gone. She took her coffee and walked around the small apartment. It was a curious cross between a messy college dorm and a more mature person's home. In what should have been the dining room, Faith found a home gym. Nothing fancy, no high-dollar, high-tech machines, just barbells, a weight bench and squat rack that were set up throughout the space. In one corner was a heavy punching bag and next to it a speed bag. Boxing and weight gloves, hand wraps and towels were neatly arranged on a small wooden table next to a box of white powder. A medicine ball sat in another corner.

On the walls were some photos of men in Navy whites. Faith picked out Lee quite easily. He looked pretty much the same at eighteen as he did now. However, the years had weathered his face, cut in lines and angles that made him even more attractive, even more seductive. Why was aging so damn tilted in favor of men? There were black and white photos of Lee in the boxing ring, and one of him with his hand raised in victory, a medal resting against his wide chest. His expression was calm, as though he had expected to win; in fact, as though he would not accept losing.

Faith gave the heavy bag a small punch with a loosely made fist, and her hand and wrist instantly throbbed. In that moment she recalled how big and thick Lee's hands were, the knuckles resembling a miniature mountain range. A very strong, resourceful, tough man. A man who could take punishment. She just hoped he would remain on her side.

She went into the bedroom. On the nightstand next to his bed was a cell phone and next to that a portable panic-button device. Faith had been too exhausted to notice them last night. She wondered if he slept with his pistol under his pillow. Was he really just paranoid or did he know something the rest of the world didn't?

It suddenly occurred to her: Wasn't he afraid she might make a run for it? She went back into the hallway. The front was covered; he would see her leave that way. But there was a back door off the kitchen that went down a fire escape. She went over to the door and tried to open it. It was locked. Deadbolted. The kind you could only open with a key even from inside. The windows also had key locks. It angered Faith, being trapped like this, but the truth was she had been trapped long before Lee Adams popped up in her life.

She continued looking through the apartment. Faith smiled at the collection of record albums housed in their original covers, and a framed poster from the movie *The Sting*. She doubted if the man had a CD player or even cable TV. She opened another door and went into the room. She started to turn on the light and then paused as a sound caught her attention. She stepped to the window, inched back the blinds and looked out. It was fully light outside now, although the sky was still gray and gloomy. She didn't see anyone, but that meant nothing. She could be encircled by an army and she'd never know it.

She turned the light on and looked around, surprised. A desk, file cabinets, a sophisticated phone system and shelves filled with manuals surrounded her. There were large pegboards on the wall with memo cards tacked to them. On the desk were neatly arranged files, a calendar and the usual desktop accessories. Apparently, Lee's home also served as his place of business.

If this was his office, maybe the file on her was here. Lee would probably be gone for a few more minutes. She started to sift carefully through the papers on his desk. Then she went through the desk drawers and then moved on to the file cabinets. Lee was very organized and he had a lot of clients – mostly business and law firms, from the file labels

111

she was seeing. Defense lawyers, she assumed, since prosecutors had their own detective force.

The ringing phone made her almost leap out of her shoes. Trembling, she went over to it. The base unit had an LCD readout. Lee obviously had caller ID, because the number of the person calling him was displayed on the readout. It was long distance, with a 215 area code. Philadelphia, she recalled. Lee's voice came on and told the caller to leave a message after the beep. When that person started talking, Faith froze.

"Where is Faith Lockhart?" asked the voice of Danny Buchanan. Danny sounded very distressed as he fired more questions: What had Lee found out? He wanted answers and he wanted them immediately. Buchanan left a phone number, then hung up. Faith felt herself backing away from the phone. She stopped and stood still, transfixed by what she had just heard. A full minute passed as numbing thoughts of betrayal swirled through her mind like confetti in a parade. Then she heard a sound behind her and whirled around. Her scream was short, sharp, leaving her momentarily breathless. Lee was staring at her.

FOURTEEN

Buchanan looked around the crowded airport. He had taken a risk in calling Lee Adams directly, but his options now were few. As his eyes roamed the area, he wondered which of the people it was. The old lady in the corner with her big purse and hair in a bun? She had been on Buchanan's flight. A tall, middle-aged man had been pacing the aisle while Buchanan had been on the phone. He too had been on the flight from National.

The truth was Thornhill's people could be anywhere, anyone. It was like being attacked by nerve gas. You never saw the enemy. A sense of profound hopelessness gripped Buchanan.

Buchanan's greatest fear had been that Thornhill would either try to get Faith involved in his scheme, or suddenly find her a liability. He might have pushed Faith away, but would never abandon her. This was why he had hired Adams to follow her. As the end drew near, he had to make sure she remained safe.

Buchanan had looked in the phone book, of all places, and used the simplest logic he could think of. Lee Adams had been the first person listed under private investigators. Buchanan almost laughed out loud now at what he had done. But unlike Thornhill, he didn't have an army at his beck and call. For all he knew, Adams hadn't reported in because he was dead.

He paused for a moment. Should he just flee to the

ticket counter, book the first flight available to anywhere remote and then lose himself? Easy to fantasize about, quite another thing to implement. He envisioned trying to escape: Thornhill's heretofore invisible army would suddenly materialize and descend upon him from the shadows, displaying official-looking badges to anyone bold enough to intervene. Then Buchanan would be taken to a quiet room in the bowels of the Philadelphia airport. There Robert Thornhill would be calmly waiting with his pipe and his three-piece suit and his casual arrogance. He would calmly ask Buchanan, did he want to die right this very minute? Because Thornhill would certainly accommodate him if he did. And Buchanan would have absolutely no response.

Finally Danny Buchanan did the only thing he could do. He left the airport, climbed in his waiting car and drove to see his friend the senator, to put another nail in the man's coffin with his smiling, disarming manner and the listening device he was wearing, which looked exactly like skin and hair follicles and was so advanced that it wouldn't set off the most sophisticated of metal detectors. A surveillance van would follow him to his destination and record every word said by Buchanan and the senator.

As a backup, in case the transmission from his listening device was somehow interfered with, Buchanan's briefcase had a tape recorder built in to its frame. A slight twist on the briefcase handle activated the recorder. It too was undetectable by even the most sophisticated airport security. Thornhill really had thought of everything. *Damn the man.*

On the drive over, Buchanan comforted himself with a deliriously inspiring fantasy involving a pleading, broken Thornhill, an assortment of poisonous snakes, boiling oil and a rusted machete.

If only dreams could come true.

The person sitting in the airport was clean-cut, mid-thirties, dressed in a dark, conservatively cut suit and working on a laptop computer – meaning he mirrored about a thousand other business travelers all around him. He seemed busy and focused, even talking to himself at times. He gave the appearance, to the casual passersby, of a man preparing for a sales pitch or compiling a marketing report. He was actually quietly talking into the tiny microphone embedded in his necktie. What looked like infrared data ports on the backside of his computer were really sensors. One was designed to capture electronic signals. The other was a sound wand that collected words and posted them on to the screen. The first sensor quite easily snagged the phone number Buchanan had just called and automatically transmitted it to the screen. The voice sensor had been a little garbled, what with so many conversations going on at the airport; but enough had come through to make the man excited. The words "Where is Faith Lockhart?" stared back at him from the screen.

The man conveyed the telephone number and other information to his colleagues back in Washington. Within seconds a computer at Langley had produced the account holder of the phone and the address to which the phone number was registered. Within minutes a very experienced team of professionals completely in the allegiance of Robert Thornhill – who had been waiting for just such a mission – was dispatched to Lee Adams's apartment.

Thornhill's instructions were simple. If Faith

Lockhart was there, they were to "terminate" her, as it was so benignly termed in official espionage parlance, as though she would simply be fired and asked to collect her personal belongings and leave the building, instead of a bullet fired into her head. Anyone with her would suffer the same fate. For the good of the country.

FIFTEEN

"You scared the hell out of me." Faith couldn't stop trembling.

Lee moved into the room and looked around. "What are you doing in my office?"

"Nothing! I was just wandering. I didn't even know you had your office here."

"That's because you didn't need to know that."

"I thought I heard a sound outside the window when I came in here."

"You did hear a sound, but it didn't come from the window." He pointed to the doorjamb.

Faith noted the rectangular piece of white plastic attached to the wood there.

"It's a sensor. Anybody opens the door to my office, it trips the sensor and triggers my beeper." He took the device out of his pocket. "If I hadn't had Max to calm down at Mrs. Carter's, I would've been up here a lot sooner." He scowled at her. "I don't appreciate this, Faith."

"Hey, I was just looking around, killing time."

"Interesting choice of words: 'killing.'"

"Lee, I'm not plotting against you. I swear it."

"Let's finish packing. Don't want to keep your bankers waiting."

Faith avoided looking at the phone again. Lee must not have heard the message. He had been hired by Buchanan to follow her. Had he killed the agent last night? When they got on the plane, would he somehow manage to push her out at thirty thousand feet and laugh riotously while she plummeted screaming through the clouds?

But he could have killed her at any point from last night to now. Leaving her dead at the cottage would have been the easiest move. That's when it hit her: It would have been the easiest move unless Danny wanted to know how much she had told the FBI. That would explain why she was still alive. And also why Lee was so eager to get her to talk. Once she did, then he would kill her. And here they were flying off together to a North Carolina beach community that would be largely deserted this time of year. She slowly walked out of the room, a condemned woman on the way to her execution.

Twenty minutes later, Faith closed the small travel bag and slid her purse strap over her head and on to her shoulder. Lee came into the bedroom. He had put back on the mustache and beard, and the baseball cap was gone. In his right hand was his pistol, two boxes of ammo and his belt holster.

Faith watched as he loaded the items into a special hard-sided container. "You can't take a gun on a plane," she said.

"You're kidding, really? When did they start that shit?" He closed the container and locked it, pocketing the keys before looking at her. "You *can* take a gun on a plane if you disclose the weapon when you check in and fill out a declaration form. They ensure that the weapon is unloaded and in an approved case." He rapped his knuckles against the hard-sided aluminum case. "Which it is. They check that the ammo is a hundred rounds or fewer and is in the manufacturer's original or otherwise FAA-approved packaging. Again, I'm cool. Then they mark the bag with a special tag and it goes to the cargo bay, where it would be real hard for me to get to if I was thinking about skyjacking the plane, wouldn't you agree?"

"Thanks for the explanation," Faith said curtly.

"I'm not a damn amateur," he said hotly.

"I never said you were."

"Right."

"Okay, I'm sorry." She hesitated, intensely desiring to establish some sort of truce, for a number of reasons, her survival being chief among them. "Would you do me a favor?"

He looked at her suspiciously.

"Call me Faith."

The door buzzer startled them both.

Lee checked his watch. "Little early for visitors."

Faith watched in amazement as his hands moved like a machine. Within twenty seconds the pistol was out of the container and fully loaded. He put the container and the ammo boxes in his small travel bag and hoisted it over his shoulder. "Get your bag."

"Who do you think it is?" Faith felt her pulse throbbing in her ears.

"Let's go find out."

They stepped quietly into the hallway and Faith followed Lee to the front door.

He checked the TV screen. They both saw the man standing there on the front stoop of the building, a couple of packages in his arms. The familiar brown uniform was clearly visible. As they watched, he hit the buzzer once more.

"It's just the UPS man," Faith said, letting out a relieved breath.

Lee didn't take his eyes off the screen. "Is that right?" He hit a button on the screen that obviously moved the camera, as Faith found herself now staring at the street in front of the building. Something that should have been there wasn't.

"Where's his truck?" she said, her fear abruptly returning.

"Excellent question. And the fact is I know the UPS guy on this route real well, and that's not him."

"Maybe he's on vacation."

"Actually, he just got back from a week in the islands with his new bride. And he never comes at this time of the morning. Which means we've got a big problem."

"Maybe we can get out through the back."

"Yeah, I'm sure they forgot to cover the rear."

"There's only the one man."

"No, he's the only one we can see. He's got the front. They probably want to flush us out the back right into their arms."

"So we're trapped," she managed to whisper.

The buzzer rang again and Lee reached out his finger to hit the intercom button.

Faith grabbed his hand. "What the hell are you doing?"

"I'm going to ask what he wants: He'll say UPS and I'm going to let him in."

"You're going to let him in," Faith repeated dully. She glanced at his pistol. "What, and have a shoot-out in your apartment building?"

Lee's face hardened. "When I tell you to move, you move your ass like a T-Rex is breathing down your neck."

"Move? Move where?"

"Just follow me. And no more questions."

Lee hit the intercom button, the man identified himself and Lee touched the door release. As soon as he did, he activated the apartment's alarm system, whipped open the front door, grabbed Faith by the arm and pulled her out into the hallway. There was a door across from Lee's apartment. It had no apartment number on it. As Faith listened to the UPS man's footsteps echoing in the building down below, Lee already had unlocked the door. They were through it in an instant and he quietly closed and locked the door behind them. The place was very dark, but Lee obviously knew his way around here. He led her to the back, through another door that opened up into what looked like a back bedroom, from the little Faith could see.

Lee opened another door in the room and motioned Faith in. She stepped through and almost immediately felt a wall against her. When Lee joined her, it was a very tight fit, like a telephone booth. He closed the door and the darkness became blacker than anything Faith had ever experienced before.

He startled her when he spoke, his breath tickling her ear. "Right in front of you there's a ladder. Here are the rungs." He gripped her hand and guided it until her fingers touched the rungs. "Okay?" She nodded. Lee continued whispering. "Give me your bag and start climbing. Take it slow. I'll sacrifice speed for silence right now. I'll be right behind you. When you get to the top, just stop. I'll take it from there."

As she began to climb, Faith started feeling severely claustrophobic. And, because she had lost her bearings, she was becoming queasy. Now would be such a perfect time to lose the contents of her stomach, little though it was.

She moved her hands and feet slowly as she went up. Then, gaining confidence, she started to pick up her pace. That was a mistake because her foot missed a rung, she slipped and her chin painfully clipped one of the rungs. But then Lee's strong arm was round her in an instant, holding her up. She took a moment to steady herself, tried to ignore the pain in her chin and kept climbing until she felt the ceiling above her head and then stopped.

Lee was still on the rung right below her. Then he

suddenly moved up on the same rung she was on, his legs on either side of hers so that her legs were pinched between his. He leaned against her with increasing force, and she wasn't sure what he was trying to do. It was becoming painful to breathe with her chest pushed up hard against the ladder rungs. For one terrifying moment she thought he had lured her in here to rape her. Suddenly a blast of light hit her from above and he moved away from her. She looked up, blinking rapidly. The view of the blue sky was so wonderful after the terror of the darkness that she felt like screaming in relief.

"Go up and on to the roof, but keep low. As low as you can," Lee whispered urgently into her ear.

She went up and through, dropping to her belly and looking around. The roof of the old building was flat, with a gravel and tar base. Bulky old heating units and newer air-conditioning machinery dotted the roof in various places. They made for good hiding places and Faith slid over and squatted next to the nearest one.

Lee was still on the ladder. He listened intently and then checked his watch. The guy would be at his door right about now. He would buzz, wait for Lee to answer. They had thirty seconds at most before the guy realized no one was coming to the door. It would be nice to have a little more time than that, and also a way to draw in the other forces Lee knew were out there. He pulled his cell phone from his pocket and hit a speed-dial number.

When the person answered, he said, "Mrs. Carter, it's Lee Adams. Listen to me, I want you to let Max out in the hallway. Right, I know I just dropped him off. I know he'll head up to my apartment. That's what I want. I, uh, I forgot to give him a shot he needs. Please hurry, I really need to get out of here."

He pocketed the phone and pushed the bags up

and out, then he hoisted himself through the opening and closed the hatch behind him. He scanned the roof and spotted Faith. Grabbing the bags, he slid over to her.

"Okay, we got a little time."

Down below they heard a dog start to bark loudly and Lee smiled. "Follow me." Squatting low, they made their way to the edge of the roof. The building attached to Lee's was a little shorter so that the roof was about five feet lower. Lee motioned for Faith to take his hands. She did so and he lowered her over the edge, holding tightly until her feet touched the roof. As soon as Lee joined her, they both heard shouts coming from Lee's building.

"Okay, they've made their all-out assault. They'll go through the door and that'll trip the alarm. I don't have a call-back option with the alarm company, so there's no delay in sending the cops. A few minutes and it'll be a big mess."

"What do we do in the meantime?" Faith asked.

"Three more buildings and then down the fire escape. Move!"

Five minutes later they were running through a back alley and then out on to another quiet suburban street flanked by a number of low-rise apartment buildings. The street was lined on both sides with parked cars. In the background Faith could hear the thump of a tennis ball being hit. She could make out a tennis court surrounded by several tall pine trees in a small park across from the apartment building.

She watched as Lee eyed a line of cars parked at the curb. Then he jogged across to the park area and bent down. When he straightened up, he was holding a tennis ball – one of many that had landed there from years of errant shots on the court. He walked back over to Faith. She could see that he was working a hole in the tennis ball with his pocketknife.

"What are you doing?" she asked.

"Go up on the sidewalk and walk as calmly as you can. And keep your eyes open."

"Lee—"

"Just do it, Faith!"

She spun around and went up on the sidewalk, paralleling his movements as he walked on the other side of the parked cars, his eyes scanning each of the vehicles. He finally stopped at a new-looking luxury model.

"See anybody watching us?" Lee asked.

Faith shook her head.

He walked over to the car and held the tennis ball against the key lock, the hole in the ball facing the lock's opening.

Faith looked at him as if he were insane. "What are you doing?"

In response, he slammed his fist against the tennis ball, driving all the air out of the ball and into the key lock. Faith watched in amazement as all four door locks popped open.

"How did you do that?"

"Get in."

Lee slid into the car, and Faith did the same.

He poked his head under the steering column and found the wires he needed.

"You can't hot-wire these new cars. The technology—" Faith stopped talking when the car started.

Lee sat up, put the car in gear and pulled away from the curb. He looked at Faith. "What?"

"All right, so how did the tennis ball unlock the car?"

"I've got my professional secrets."

Faith stared forward while he drove.

While Lee waited in the car with his eyes sharply on

the lookout, Faith entered her bank, explained what she wanted to the assistant manager and managed to sign her name, all without falling over in a dead faint. *Steady girl, one step at a time.* Fortunately, she knew the man.

The assistant manager looked curiously at her new appearance.

"Midlife crisis," she said, responding to his stare. "Decided to go for the youthful, streamlined look."

"It's very becoming, Ms. Lockhart," he said gallantly.

She closely watched him as he took her key, inserted it and the bank's duplicate key into the lock and pulled out her box. They left the vault and he set the box inside the private booth across from the vault reserved for safe-deposit box tenants. As he walked away, Faith continued to watch him.

Was he one of them? Was he going to slip away and call the police or the FBI or whoever was running around killing people? Instead he sat down at his desk, opened a white bag, extracted a glazed donut and proceeded to devour it.

Satisfied for the moment, Faith closed and locked the door. She opened the box and stared at the contents for a moment. Then she swept it all into her bag and closed the box. The young man put the safe-deposit box back in the vault and Faith walked out as calmly as she could.

Back in the car, Faith and Lee headed down Interstate 395, where they exited on to the GW Parkway and headed south to Reagan National Airport. Going against the morning rush hour, they made good time.

Faith looked over at Lee, who stared straight ahead, lost in thought.

"You did really well back there," she said.

"Actually, we cut it closer than I would have

liked." He paused and shook his head. "I'm really worried about Max, as stupid as that sounds under the circumstances."

"It doesn't sound stupid."

"Max and I have been together a long time. For years it's been only me and that old dog."

"I doubt they would have done anything to him with all those people around."

"Yeah, you'd like to think so, wouldn't you? But the fact is if they'll kill a man, a dog doesn't stand a chance."

"I'm sorry you had to do that for me."

He sat up straight. "Well, a dog is still a dog, Faith. And we've got other things to worry about, don't we?"

Faith found herself nodding. "Yes."

"I guess my magnet trick didn't work so well. They must have identified me through the video. Still, that was awfully fast." He shook his head, his expression a mix of admiration and fear. "Like scary fast."

Faith felt her spirits sink. If Lee was scared, at what level of sheer terror should she be operating? "Not very encouraging, is it?" she said.

"I might be a little better prepared if you tell me what's going on."

After the man's heroics, Faith found herself wanting to confide in him. But then the phone call from Buchanan came flashing back, ringing in her ears, like the shots last night.

"When we get to North Carolina, we'll have it all out. *Both* sides," Faith said.

SIXTEEN

Thornhill replaced the phone receiver and looked around his office, a disturbed expression on his face. His men had found the nest empty, and one of them had even been bitten by a dog. There had been reports of a man and woman running down the street. This was all just a little too much. Thornhill was a patient man, used to working on projects for many years, but still, there were limits to what he could tolerate. His men had listened to the message Buchanan had left on Lee's answering machine. They had taken the tape and played it back for Thornhill over his secure phone line.

"So you've hired a private investigator, Danny," Thornhill muttered to himself. "You'll pay for that one." He nodded thoughtfully. "I'll make you pay."

The police had responded to the burglar alarm, but when Thornhill's men had flashed official-looking IDs they had quickly backed off. Legally, the CIA had no authority to operate within the United States. Thus, Thornhill's team routinely carried several types of identification and would select one depending on who confronted them.

The patrolmen had been sent off with instructions to bury deeply all that they had seen. Still, Thornhill didn't like it. It was all too close to the edge. There were holes there, ways for people to gain an advantage over him.

He went to the window and looked outside. It was

a beautiful fall day, the colors starting to turn. As he studied the pleasing foliage, he primed his pipe, but unfortunately that was all he could do. CIA headquarters was a nonsmoking building. The deputy director had a balcony outside his office where Thornhill could sit and smoke, but it was not the same. During the Cold War, the CIA offices had been as foggy as steam baths. Tobacco helped one think, Thornhill believed. It was a minor thing, yet it symbolized all that had gone wrong with the place.

In Thornhill's opinion, the CIA's downfall had accelerated in 1994 with the Aldrich Ames' debacle. Thornhill still winced every time he thought of the former CIA counterintelligence officer being arrested for spying for the Soviets and later the Russians. And of course, as fate would have it, the FBI had broken the case. After that, the president had issued a directive ordering an FBI agent to be made a permanent employee of the CIA. From then on, this FBI agent oversaw the agency's counter-espionage efforts and had access to all CIA files. An FBI agent on the premises! His nose in all their secrets! Not to be outdone by the executive branch, the idiotic Congress had followed with a law requiring all government agencies, including the CIA, to notify the FBI whenever there was evidence that classified information might have been improperly disclosed to foreign powers. The result: The CIA took all the risk and gave the prize to the FBI. Thornhill seethed. It was a direct usurpation of the CIA's mission.

Thornhill's rage was building. The CIA could no longer even put people under surveillance or wire-tap. If it had suspicions of someone, it had to go to the FBI and request surveillance, electronic or other-wise. If electronic surveillance was desired, then the FBI had to go to FISC, the Foreign Intelligence

Surveillance Court, and obtain authorization. The CIA couldn't even approach FISC on its own. It had to have its hand held by Big Brother. Everything was stacked in the FBI's favor.

Thornhill's thoughts went into a tailspin as he reminded himself that the shackles on the CIA weren't just domestic; the Agency had to get authorization from the president before commencing any covert operations overseas. The congressional oversight committees had to be told of any such operations in a timely fashion. And with the world of espionage becoming more and more complicated, the CIA and FBI found themselves continually running into each other over jurisdictional squabbles, use of witnesses and informants and the like. Though it was supposed to be a domestic agency only, the FBI, in reality, did considerable work abroad, where it focused on antiterrorism and anti-drug operations, including the collection and analysis of information. Again, that hit right at the CIA's home turf.

Was it any wonder Thornhill hated his federal counterparts? Like a cancer, the bastards were everywhere. And to drive the nail a little farther into the CIA's coffin, a former FBI agent now headed up the Center for CIA Security, which conducted internal background checks on all current and prospective personnel. And all CIA employees had to file annual financial disclosure forms that were damn well exhaustive in their current requirements.

Before he suffered a stroke thinking any more on this sore subject, Thornhill forced himself to turn his attention to other matters. If Buchanan had hired this PI person to follow Lockhart, then he very well could have been the man at the cottage last night and the person who had shot Serov. There had been permanent nerve damage to the man's arm from the gunshot wound, and Thornhill had ordered the Russian to be finished off. A hired killer who could no longer hold a weapon steady enough to kill would look for other ways to make money and could pose a small threat. It was Serov's own fault, and if there was one thing Thornhill demanded from his people, it was accountability.

So this Lee Adams was now in the mix of things, he mused. Thornhill had already ordered a complete background search on the man. In these days of computerized files, he would have a full dossier in half an hour, if not sooner. Thornhill did have Adams's file on Faith Lockhart; his men had taken that from the apartment. The notes showed that the man was thorough, logical in his approach to investigation. That was both good and bad for Thornhill's purposes. Adams had also given Thornhill's men the slip. That was not an easy thing to do. On the good side, if Adams was logical, he should be amenable to a reasonable offer, meaning one that would allow him to live.

Presumably Adams had also escaped from the cottage with Faith Lockhart. He had not reported in to Buchanan about this, which was why Buchanan had left that phone message. Buchanan was obviously unaware of what had happened last night. Thornhill would do all he could to make sure this state of affairs continued.

How would they run? A train? Thornhill doubted it. Trains were slow. And you couldn't take a train overseas. Now, a train to an airport was a more intriguing possibility. Or a cab. That seemed certainly more likely.

Thornhill eased back into his chair as an assistant entered with some files he had requested. While everything at the CIA was computerized these days, Thornhill still liked the feel of paper in his hand. He could think much more clearly with paper than when he was simply staring at the pixeled screen.

So all the usual bases were covered. What about the unusual? With the added element of a professional investigator, Adams and Lockhart might be fleeing under false identities, even disguises. He had men at all three airports and the train stations. That would only go so far. The pair could easily rent a car and drive to New York and take a plane there. Or they could go south and do the same thing. It certainly was problematic.

Thornhill hated these sorts of chases. There were too many places to cover and he had limited manpower for these "extracurricular" activities of his. At least he had the advantage of operating more or less autonomously. No one from the director of central intelligence on down really questioned him as to what he was up to. Or if they did, he was able to dance around any issue they threw at him. He got results that made them all look good, and that was his biggest weapon.

It was much better to coax the runners out, bring them to you, which was certainly possible with the right sort of bait. Thornhill just had to come up with that bait. That would take some thinking. Lockhart had no family, no elderly parents or young children. He didn't know enough about Adams yet, but he would. If the man had just hooked up with the woman, he couldn't possibly be willing to sacrifice everything for her. Not just yet. Other things being equal, Adams was the one to focus on. And they had a communication link to him by virtue of knowing where he lived. If they needed to get a discreet message to him, they could.

Now Thornhill's thoughts turned to Buchanan. He was currently in Philadelphia meeting with a prominent senator on how best to further the agenda of one of Buchanan's clients. They had this particular fellow on enough felonious activity to make the man literally break down and plead for his miserable life. He had been a special pain in the ass to the CIA, nickle-and-diming them to death from the high perch of his Appropriations Committee seat. The payback would be so gratifying.

Thornhill envisioned walking into all these mighty politicians' offices and showing them the videos, the audiotapes, the paper trails. Of them and Buchanan plotting their little conspiracies, all the details of the future payoffs; they so eager to do Buchanan's bidding in return for all that money. How greedy they looked!

Good Senator, would you mind very much licking my boots, you whiny, squealing excuse for a human being. And then you will do exactly as I say, no more, no less, or I will crush you underfoot faster than you can say "vote for me."

Of course, Thornhill would never say that. These men demanded your respect even if they didn't deserve it. He would tell them that Danny Buchanan had disappeared and left these tapes with them. They weren't quite sure what to do with the evidence, but it appeared that the tapes should be turned over to the FBI. It seemed an awful thing to do; these fine men couldn't possibly be guilty of these sorts of things, but once the FBI started its feeding frenzy, they all knew where that would end: prison. And how could that possibly help the country? The world would laugh at us. Terrorists would be emboldened in the face of a supposedly weakened foe. And resources were so tight. Why, the CIA itself was understaffed and underfunded, it's responsibility unfairly curtailed. And could you fine people perhaps do something to change that? And would you please do so at the expense of the

FBI, the very bastards who would love to get their hands on these tapes so they could destroy you? Starting with getting them the hell off our backs? And we thank you very much, you fine public leaders. We knew you'd understand.

The first move in Thornhill's grand plan would be to have his new allies find a way to completely remove the FBI presence from the Agency. Next, the operations budget for the CIA would be increased by fifty percent. To start. In the next fiscal year he would get serious about the dollars. In the future, the CIA would only report to a joint intelligence committee instead of the separate House and Senate committees it was confronted with now. It was far easier to co-opt one committee. Then the hierarchy of the U.S. intelligence-gathering agencies needed to be straightened out once and for all. And the director of Central Intelligence would be at the very top of that pyramid. The FBI would be as far down the totem pole as Thornhill could bury it. And the tools of the CIA would be considerably strengthened. Domestic surveillance, the covert funding and arming of insurgency groups to overthrow enemies of the United States, even selective assassination, all would come back as weapons of choice for him and his colleagues. Right that minute Thornhill could think of five heads of state whose immediate deaths would leave the world a better, safer, more humane place. It was time to take the shackles off the best and brightest and let them do their jobs again. God, he was so close.

"Keep up the good work, Danny," Thornhill said out loud. "Pour it on until the end. That's a good man. Let them almost taste victory right before I take their lives away."

Grim-faced, he looked at his watch and rose from behind his desk. Thornhill was a man who loathed the press. He had, of course, never granted an interview in all his years at the Agency. But as senior as he was now, he occasionally had to undertake another sort of appearance, one that he equally detested. He had to testify before the House and Senate Select Committees on Intelligence on a series of matters involving the Agency.

In these "enlightened" times, CIA personnel gave more than one thousand substantive reports to Congress in a year's time. So much for covert operations. Thornhill was able to get through these briefings only by focusing on how easily he could manipulate the idiots who were supposed to be overseeing his agency. With their smug looks, they posed to him questions formulated by their very diligent staffs, who were more knowledgeable about most intelligence matters than the elected officials they served.

At least the hearing would be in camera, no public or press allowed. To Thornhill the First Amendment's rights to an unfettered press had been the biggest mistake the Founding Fathers had ever made. You had to be damn careful around the scribes; they looked for every advantage, any chance to put words in your mouth, trip you up, make the Agency look bad. It deeply hurt Thornhill that no one seemed to really trust them. Of course they lied about things; that was their job.

In Thornhill's mind the CIA was clearly the Hill's favorite whipping boy. The members loved to look tough in facing down the super-secret organization. That really played well back home: FARMER-TURNED-CONGRESSMAN STARES DOWN SPOOKS. By now Thornhill could write the headlines himself.

However, today's hearing actually promised to be positive because the Agency had scored some serious PR points lately in the most recent Middle

East peace talks. Indeed, largely through Thornhill's behind-the-scenes work, the Agency had overall fashioned a more benign, upstanding image, an image he would seek to bolster today.

Thornhill snapped his briefcase shut and put his pipe in his pocket. *Off to lie to a bunch of liars, and we both know it and we both win*, he thought. *Only in America.*

SEVENTEEN

"Senator," Buchanan said, shaking hands with the tall, elegant-looking gentleman. Senator Harvey Milstead was a proven leader with high morals and strong political instincts who offered thoughtful insight on the issues. A true statesman. That was the public perception. The reality was that Milstead was a womanizer of the first order and was addicted to painkillers for a chronically bad back, medications that sometimes left him incoherent. He also had a worsening drinking problem. It was years since he had sponsored any meaningful legislation of his own, although in his prime he had helped enact laws from which every American now benefited. These days when he spoke, it was in gobbledygook that no one ever bothered to check up on because he said it with such authority. Besides, the press loved the charming guy with such genteel manners, and he held a very powerful leadership position. He also fed the media machine with a flow of appropriately timed juicy leaks, and he was quotable to a fault. They loved him, Buchanan knew. How could they not?

There were five hundred and thirty-five members of Congress – a hundred senators plus the representatives in the House. Well over three-quarters of them, Buchanan estimated perhaps a little generously, were decent, hardworking, genuinely caring men and women who believed strongly in what they were doing both in Washington and for the people. Buchanan termed them, collectively, the "Believers." Buchanan stayed away from the Believers. Touching those folk would only have earned him a quick trip to prison.

The rest of the Washington leadership were like Harvey Milstead. Most were not drunks or womanizers or shells of their former selves, but, for various reasons, they were ripe for manipulation, easy targets for the lures Buchanan was tossing overboard.

There were two such groups that Buchanan had successfully recruited over the years. Forget Republicans and Democrats. The parties Buchanan was interested in were the members of the venerable "Townies," and the group Buchanan had labeled, only somewhat tongue-in-cheek, the "Zombies."

The Townies knew the system better than anyone. They *were* the system. Washington was their town, hence the nickname. They had all been here longer than God. If you cut them, their blood would run red, white and blue, or so they liked to tell you. There was another color Buchanan had added to that mix: green.

By contrast, the Zombies had come to Congress with nary a stitch of moral fiber or whiff of a political philosophy. They had won their place of leadership with the finest campaigns that media dollars could buy. They were fabulous on sound bite TV and in the confines of tightly controlled debates. They were, at best, mediocre in intellect and ability and yet delivered the sales pitch with the verve and enthusiasm of a JFK at his oratorical best. And when they were elected, they arrived in Washington with absolutely no idea what to do. Their only goal had already been achieved: They had won their campaign.

However, despite this, the Zombies tended to stay in Congress because they loved the power and access that came with being an incumbent. And with the cost of elections going through the stratosphere, it was still possible to defeat an entrenched incumbent . . . in the same way that it was still theoretically possible to climb Mount Everest without oxygen. One only had to hold his breath for several days.

Buchanan and Milstead sat down on a comfortable leather couch in the senator's spacious office. The shelves were filled with the usual spoils of a longtime politician: plaques and medals of appreciation, silver cups, awards made of crystal, hundreds of photographs of the senator standing with people even more famous than he; inscribed ceremonial gavels and bronzed miniature shovels symbolizing political pork brought to his state. As Buchanan looked around, it occurred to him that he had spent his entire professional life coming to places such as this, hat in hand, essentially begging.

It was early yet, but the man's staff was busy in the outer suite preparing for a hectic day with Keystone State constituents, a day laced with lunches, speeches, appearances and pop-in-and-out dinners, meet-and-greets, drinks and parties. The senator was not up for reelection, but it was always nice to put on a good show for the people back home.

"I appreciate your meeting with me on such short notice, Harvey."

"Hard to refuse you, Danny."

"I'll get right to it. Pickens's bill is looking to knock out my funding, along with about twenty other aid packages. We can't let that happen. The results speak for themselves. The infant mortality rate has been cut seventy percent. My God, the wonders of vaccine and antibiotics. Jobs are being created, the economy is moving from thuggery to legitimate business. Exports are up by a third, and imports from us are up twenty percent. So you see it's creating jobs here too. We can't let the plug be pulled now. Not only is it morally wrong, it's stupid from our side. If we can get countries like this on their feet, we won't have a trade imbalance. But you need reliable sources of electricity first. You need an educated population."

"AID has accomplished a lot," the senator pointed out.

Buchanan was intimately familiar with AID, or the Agency for International Development. Formerly an independent agency, it now reported to the Secretary of State, who also more or less controlled its very substantial budget. AID was the flagship of American foreign aid, with the vast majority of funds flowing through its long-standing programs. Every year it was like musical chairs to see where AID's limited budget dollars would end up. Buchanan had been caught without a seat many times, and he was so weary of it. The grant process was intensive and highly competitive, and unless you fit the template set up by AID for the programs it wanted to sponsor, you were out of luck.

"AID can't do it all. And my clients are too small a bite for IMF and the World Bank. Besides, now all I hear is 'sustainable development.' No dollars unless it goes for sustainable development. Hell, last time I looked, food and medicine were necessary for life. Doesn't that qualify?"

"You're preaching to the choir, Danny. But people count pennies around here too. The days of fat are over," Milstead said solemnly.

"My clients will take gristle. Just don't cut them off."

"Look, I just won't schedule the bill."

In the Senate, if a chairman didn't want a bill to get out of committee, he simply didn't schedule it for hearing, as Milstead was now suggesting. Buchanan had played that game many times before.

"But Pickens could end-run you on that," Buchanan said. "Word is he's dead set on getting this thing heard one way or another. And he might get a more sympathetic audience on the floor than he would in committee. Why not put a hold on the bill and run it out of session?" Buchanan suggested.

Danny Buchanan was the master at this technique. A hold was simply one senator objecting to a pending bill. The legislation would be in complete limbo until the hold was removed. Years ago, Buchanan and his allies on the Hill had used it to stunning effect in representing the most powerful special interests in the country. It took real power in Washington to make things not happen. And for Buchanan, that had always been the most fascinating aspect of the city. Why health care reform legislation or the tobacco settlement bills, propelled by intense media coverage and public clamor, simply disappeared into the yawning gulf of the Congress. And it was very often the case that special interests wanted to maintain the status quo they had worked so hard to erect. For them change was not good. Hence, a good deal of Buchanan's previous lobbying work had focused on burying any legislation that would harm his powerful clients.

The hold maneuver was also known as the "blind rolling" hold because, like the passing of the baton on a relay team, a different senator could place a new hold when the previous one had been released, and only the leadership knew who had placed the restriction. There was a lot more to it, but at the end of the day the blind rolling hold was an enormous waste of time, and hugely effective, which explained much of politics in a nutshell, Buchanan well knew.

The senator shook his head. "I found out Pickens has holds on two of my pieces, and I'm close to cutting a deal that'll make him let go. I hit him with another hold and the sonofabitch'll clamp down on my ass like a ferret on a cobra."

Buchanan sat back and sipped his coffee as a number of potential strategies rolled through his mind. "Look, let's go back to square one. If you have the votes to knock it out, schedule it and let the committee vote on it and kill the bastard for good. Then if he takes it to the floor I can't believe he'll have the support to carry it. Hell, once it's on the floor we can hold it up forever, ask for amendments, hit it in the cloak room, cut the crap out of it pretending to want to deal for some juice on one of your bills. In fact, we're so close to the elections now we can even play the quorum call game until he yells uncle."

Milstead nodded thoughtfully. "You know Archer and Simms are giving me a little trouble."

"Harvey, you've sent enough highway construction dollars to both those bastards' states to choke every man and woman and child there. Call them on it! They don't give a damn about this bill. They probably haven't even read the staff briefing materials."

Milstead looked suddenly confident. "One way or another, we'll get it done for you. In a one-point-seven-trillion-dollar budget, it's not that big a deal."

"It is for my client. A lot of people are counting on this one, Harvey. And most of them can't even walk yet."

"I hear you."

"You should take a fact-finding trip over there. I'll go with you. It's really beautiful country, you just can't use the land for shit. God might have blessed

America, but he forgot about a lot of the rest of the world. But they keep going. If you ever think you're having a bad day, it's a good memory to have."

Milstead coughed. "My schedule is really full, Danny. And you know I'm not running for re-election. Two more years and I'm out of here."

Okay, shop talk and humanitarian plea time is over, Buchanan thought. *Now let's play traitor*.

He leaned forward and casually moved his briefcase out of the way. One twist on the handle activated the recording device secreted inside. *This one's for you, Thornhill, you smug bastard*.

Buchanan cleared his throat. "Well, I guess it's never too early to talk about replacements. I need some people on Foreign Aid and Ops who'll participate in my little retirement program. I can promise them as good as I'll be paying you. They'll want for nothing. They just have to get my agenda done. I'm at the point now where I can't afford defeat on anything. They have to come through for me. That's the only way I can guarantee the payoff at the end. Just like you. You always come through for me, Harvey. Almost ten years and counting, and you always get it done. By hook or crook."

Milstead glanced at the door and then spoke in a very low voice, as though that made it all better. "I do have some people you might want to talk to." He looked nervous, uncomfortable. "About taking over some of my *duties*. I haven't broached the issue with them directly, of course, but I'd be surprised if they weren't amenable to some sort of arrangement."

"That's real good to hear."

"And you're right to plan ahead. The two years will go quickly."

"Hell, in two years I might not be here, Harvey."

The senator smiled warmly. "I didn't think you'd ever retire." He paused. "But I guess you have your

142

heir apparent. How is Faith, by the way? Vivacious as ever, I'm sure."

"Faith is Faith. You know that."

"Lucky to have someone like her backing you up."

"Very lucky," Buchanan said, frowning slightly.

"Give her my best when you see her. Tell her to come up and see old Harvey. Best mind and legs in the place," he added with a wink.

To this, Buchanan said nothing.

The senator sat back against the couch. "I've been in public service half my life. The pay is ridiculous – chickenshit, really, for somebody of my ability and stature. You know what I could earn on the outside. That's the trade-off when you serve your country."

"Absolutely, Harvey. Of course it is." *The bribe money is only your due. You earned it.*

"But I don't regret it. Any of it."

"No reason you should."

Milstead smiled wearily. "The dollars I've spent over the years rebuilding this country, shaping it for the future, for the next generation. And the next."

Now it was *his* money. *He* saved the country. "People never appreciate that," said Buchanan. "The media only goes after the dirt."

"Guess I'm just making up for it in my golden years."

After all these years a little humility, a little guilt remain. "You deserve it. You served your country well. It's all waiting for you. Just like we discussed. Better than we discussed. You and Louise will want for nothing. You'll live like a king and queen. You did your job, and you'll reap the rewards. The American way."

"I'm tired, Danny. Weary to the bones. Between you and me, I'm not sure I can last two more minutes, much less two more years. This place has sucked the life right out of me."

"You're a true statesman. A hero to us all."

Buchanan took a deep breath and wondered if Thornhill's boys parked in the van outside were enjoying this sappy exchange. In truth, Buchanan too was looking forward to getting out. He looked at his old friend. An expression of giddiness was on the man's features as he no doubt thought of a truly glorious retirement with his wife of thirty-five years, a woman he had cheated on many times, who had always allowed him back. And kept silent about it. The psychology of political wives would be a worthy college course, Buchanan believed.

In truth, Buchanan had a soft spot for his Townies. They actually had accomplished a lot, and in their own way were some of the most honorable people Buchanan had ever met. And yet the senator had no problem being bought.

Very soon Harvey Milstead would have a new master. The Thirteenth Amendment to the Constitution had outlawed slavery, but apparently no one had bothered telling Robert Thornhill that. He was turning his friends over to the Devil. That's what troubled Buchanan most of all. Thornhill, always Thornhill.

The men rose and Buchanan and the senator shook hands. "Thank you, Danny. Thank you for everything."

"Please, don't mention it," Buchanan said. "Please don't." He grabbed his spy briefcase and fled the room.

144

EIGHTEEN

"**D**egaussed?" Reynolds stared at the two technicians.

"My tape has been degaussed? Will someone please explain that to me?" She had watched the video twenty times now. From every angle possible. Or rather, she had watched jagged lines and dots swarm across the screen like a World War I aerial dogfight with heavy doses of ground flack thrown in. She had been sitting here for a very long time and knew no more than when she had first walked in.

"Without getting too technical—" one of the men started to say.

"Please don't," Reynolds interjected. Her head was pounding. If the tape was useless? Good God, it can't be.

"'Degaussing' is the reference term used for the erasure of a magnetic media. It's done for many reasons, some of the most common being so that the media can be used again, or to eliminate confidential information that was recorded on the media. A video-tape is a form of magnetic media. What happened to the tape you gave us was an unwanted intrusional influence that has distorted and/or corrupted the media, preventing its proper utilization."

Reynolds stared in wonder at the man. What the hell would his technical answer have been?

"So you're saying someone intentionally screwed with the tape?" she said.

"That's right."

"But couldn't it be a problem with the tape itself? How can you be sure someone 'intruded' upon it?"

The other technician spoke up. "The level of corruption we've seen in the images so far would preclude that conclusion. We can't be one hundred percent sure, of course, but it really does look like third party interference. From what I understand, the surveillance system used was very sophisticated. A multiplexer with three or four cameras on line, so there was no dwell time gap. How were the units activated? Motion or trip?"

"Trip."

"Motion is better. The systems these days are so sensitive they can pick up a hand reaching for something on a desk in a one-foot-square-zone. Trips are obsolete."

"Thanks, I'll keep that in mind," she said dryly.

"We did a pixel zoom for detail enhancement, but still nothing. Definitely interference."

Reynolds remembered that the closet at the cottage containing the video equipment had been found open.

"Okay, how could they have done it?"

"Well, there's a wide variety of specialized equipment available."

Reynolds shook her head. "No, we're not talking a lab setting. We're looking at doing it on site, where the equipment was set up. And maybe whoever did it wouldn't have even known there was video recording equipment there. So assume that whatever they happened to have with them would have been what they used."

The techs thought for a moment. "Well," one of them said, "if the person had a powerful magnet and passed it over the recorder a number of times, that could distort the tape by rearranging the metallic particles, which would, in turn, remove the previously recorded signals."

Reynolds took a deep, troubled breath. A simple magnet could have blown away her only clue. "Is there any way to get it back, the images on the tape?"

"It's possible, but it will take some time. We can't make any guarantees until we get in there."

"Do it. But let me make this real clear." She stood, towering over the two men. "I need to be able to see what's on that tape. I need to be able to see who was in that house. You have no higher priority than that. Check with the AD if you have a conflict, but whatever it takes, twenty-four hours a day. I need it. Understand?"

The men looked at each other briefly before nodding.

When Reynolds got back to her office, a man was waiting to see her.

"Paul." She nodded at him as she sat down.

Paul Fisher rose and closed the door to Reynolds's office. He was her liaison at Headquarters. He stepped over a pile of documents as he sat back down. "You look like you're overworked, Brooke. You always look like you're overworked. I guess that's what I love about you."

He smiled and Brooke caught herself smiling back.

Fisher was one of the few people at the FBI whom Reynolds looked up to, literally, as he was easily six-foot-five. They were about the same age, although Fisher was her superior in the chain of command and had been at the Bureau two years longer. He was competent and assured. He was also handsome, having retained the tousled blond hair and trim figure of his California days at UCLA. After her marriage had started to disintegrate, Reynolds had imagined having an affair with the divorced Fisher.

Even now, his unexpected visit made Reynolds feel fortunate she'd had the opportunity to go home, shower and change her clothes.

Fisher's jacket was off, his shirt draped gracefully over his long torso. He had just come on duty, she knew, although he tended to be around at all hours.

"I'm sorry about Ken," he said. "I was out of town, or I would've been there last night."

Reynolds played with a letter opener on her desk. "Not as sorry as I am. And neither of us is anywhere near where Anne Newman is on the sorry meter."

"I've talked to the SAC," Fisher said, referring to the special agent in charge, "but I want you to tell me about it."

After she told him what she knew, he rubbed his chin. "Obviously the targets know you're on to them."

"It would seem so."

"You're not that far along in the investigation, are you?"

"Nowhere near referring it to the U.S. attorney for indictment, if that's what you mean."

"So Ken's dead and your chief and only witness is MIA. Tell me about Faith Lockhart."

She glanced up sharply, being equally disturbed by his choice of words and the blunt tone he had used to say them.

He stared back at her, his hazel eyes holding a definable measure of unfriendliness, Reynolds concluded. But right now, she knew, he was not supposed to be her friend. He represented Headquarters.

"Is there something you want to tell *me*, Paul?"

"Brooke, we've always shot straight with each other." He paused and tapped his fingers against the arm of the chair as though trying to communicate with her in Morse code. "I know Massey authorized some leeway for you last night, but they're all very concerned about you. You need to know that."

"I know that in light of recent developments—"

"They were concerned *before* this. Recent developments have only heightened that level of concern."

"Do they want me to just drop it? Christ, it could implicate people who have government buildings named after them."

"It's a question of proof. Without Lockhart what do you have?"

"It's there, Paul."

"What names has she given you, other than Buchanan?"

Reynolds looked momentarily flustered. The problem was Lockhart hadn't given them any names. Yet. She had been too smart for that. She was saving that for when her deal was completed.

"Nothing specific yet. But we'll get it. Buchanan didn't do business with local school board members. And she told us some of his scheme. They work for him while in power, and when they leave office he lines up jobs for them with no real duties and mega-dollars in compensation and other perks. It's simple. Simply brilliant. The level of detail she's provided us could not be made up."

"I'm not disputing her credibility. But again, can you prove your case? Right now?"

"We're doing everything we can to prove it. I was going to ask her to wear a wire for us when all this happened, but you can't rush these things, you know that. If I pushed too hard, or lost her confidence, we'd end up with nothing."

"Do you want my coldly reasoned analysis?" Fisher took her silence as assent. "You've got all these nameless but very powerful people, many of whom may have things lined up in the future or currently have nice post-public service careers. What's so unusual about that? It happens all the time. They get on the phone, have lunches, whisper in ears, call in some favors. That's America. So where are we?"

"This is more than that, Paul. A lot more."

"Are you saying you can trace the actual illegal activity, how the legislation was manipulated?"

"Not exactly."

"'Not exactly' is right. It's really like trying to prove a negative."

Reynolds knew he was right on that point. How did you prove someone *didn't* do something? Many of the tools Buchanan's people would have used to further his agenda were probably tools every politician used, legitimately. They were talking motivation here. *Why* somebody was doing something, not *how* they were doing it. The why was illegal, the how wasn't. Like a basketball player not trying his best because he'd been paid off.

"Is Buchanan a director in these unknown firms where the former, unknown politicians get jobs? A stockholder? Did he put up the money? Does he have any ongoing business with any of them?"

"You sound like a defense lawyer," she said hotly.

"That's exactly my intent. Because those are the sort of questions you'll need answers for."

"We have not been able to uncover evidence directly tying Buchanan to any of it."

"Then what are you basing your conclusion on? What's your evidence that there is a connection at all?"

Reynolds started to speak and then stopped. Her face flushed and in her agitation she broke in half the pencil she was holding.

"Let me answer that for you," said Fisher. "Faith Lockhart, your missing witness."

"We'll find her, Paul. And then we're back in business."

"And if you don't find her? What then?"

"We'll find another way."

"Can you determine the identities of the bribed officials independently?"

Reynolds desperately wanted to say yes to that question, but she couldn't. Buchanan had been in Washington for decades. He'd probably had dealings with just about every politician and bureaucrat in the city. It would be impossible to narrow down the list without Lockhart.

"Anything's possible," she said gamely.

He shook his head. "Actually, it's not, Brooke."

Reynolds erupted. "Buchanan and his cronies have broken the law. Doesn't that count for anything?"

"In a court of law it counts for zero without proof," he shot back.

She slammed her fist down on the desk. "I damn well refuse to believe that. Besides, the evidence is there; we just have to keep digging."

"You see, that's the problem. It would be one thing if you could do it in complete secrecy. But an investigation of this magnitude, with the sort of important targets we're talking about, can never remain completely secret. And now we have a homicide investigation to deal with as well."

"Meaning there will be leaks," Reynolds said, wondering if Fisher suspected that those leaks might have already occurred.

"Meaning that when you go after important people, you better be damn sure of your case before any leaks do occur. You can't target people like that unless you're loaded for bear. Right now, your gun's empty and I'm not sure where you go to reload. It pretty much says in the Bureau manual, you can't hunt down public officials based on rumor and innuendo."

She looked at him coolly when he finished saying this. "Okay, Paul, would you like to tell me exactly what it is you want me to do?"

"The Violent Crime Unit will keep you informed on its investigation. You have to find Lockhart. Since the two cases are inextricably connected, I suggest cooperation."

"I can't tell them anything about our investigation."

"I'm not asking you to. Just work with them to help clear Newman's murder. And find Lockhart."

"And beyond that? If we can't find her? What happens to my investigation?"

"I don't know, Brooke. The tea leaves are very hard to read right now."

Reynolds stood and looked out the window. Thick, dark clouds had turned day almost into night. She could see both her reflection and Fisher's in the window. He never took his eyes off her, and she doubted if he was all that interested at the moment in how her backside and long legs looked in the black knee-length skirt and matching stockings she was wearing.

As she stood there her ears picked up on a sound they usually didn't: the "white noise." At sensitive government facilities windows were potential outlets for valuable information, namely speech. To plug this leak, speakers were mounted at the windows in these facilities to filter out the sound of voices such that anyone lurking outside with the fanciest in surveillance equipment would end up with zip. The speakers accomplished this by emitting a sound akin to a small waterfall, hence the term "white noise." Reynolds, like most employees in such buildings, had tuned out the background noise; it was such a daily part of her life. Now she noticed it with stunning clarity. Was that a signal to her to notice other things as well? Things, people she saw every day and then thought no more of, accepting them for what they proclaimed to be? She turned to face Fisher.

"Thanks for the ringing vote of confidence, Paul."

"Your career has been nothing short of spectacular. But the public sector is often like the private in one regard: It's the 'what have you done for me lately?' syndrome. I'm not going to sugarcoat this, Brooke. I've already started to hear the rumblings."

She folded her arms across her chest. "I appreciate your complete bluntness," she said coldly. "If you'll excuse me, I'll see what I can do for you lately, Agent Fisher."

As Fisher rose to leave, he moved next to her, touching her lightly on the shoulder. Reynolds recoiled slightly from this, the bite of his words still weighing heavily upon her.

"I've always supported you, and I will continue to support you, Brooke. Don't read this as though I'm throwing you to the wolves. I'm not. I respect the hell out of you. I just didn't want you to be blindsided on this. You don't deserve that. This messenger is friendly."

"That's good to know, Paul," she said unenthusiastically.

When he reached the door, he turned back. "We're handling the media relations from WFO. We've already had inquiries from the press. For now, an agent was killed during an undercover operation. No other details were provided, including his identity. That won't last long. And when the dam breaks, I'm not sure who can keep dry."

As soon as the door closed behind him, a cold shudder hit Reynolds. She felt as though she were being suspended over a vat of boiling something. Was it her old paranoia kicking in? Or was it simply her reasoned judgment? She kicked her shoes off and paced her office, stepping over the paper land mines as she did so. She rocked on the balls of her feet, trying to guide the massive tension she was feeling throughout her body toward the floor. It didn't come close to working.

NINETEEN

The recently named Ronald Reagan Washington National Airport, which everyone in the area still simply called "National," was very busy this morning. It was loved for its convenience to the city and its numerous daily flights, and hated for its congestion, short runways and stomach-jolting tight left turns to avoid restricted airspace. However, the airport's new sparkling terminal with its row of Jeffersonian-inspired domes and hulking, multi-tiered parking garages with skywalks to the terminal were very welcome to the hassled air traveler.

Lee and Faith entered the new terminal, where Lee eyed a police officer patrolling the corridor. They had left the car in one of the parking lots.

Faith watched the policeman's movements too. She was wearing "eyeglasses" that Lee had given her. The lenses were ordinary glass, but they helped to further change her look. She touched Lee's arm. "Nervous?"

"Always. It kind of gives me an edge. Makes up for a serious lack of formal schooling." He put their bags over his shoulder. "Let's grab a cup of coffee and let the line at the ticket counter die down a little, scope the place out." As they looked for a coffee shop, he asked, "Any idea of when we can get a flight out of here?"

"We fly through Norfolk and then take a commuter to Pine Island, off the Outer Banks of North

Carolina. Flights to Norfolk are pretty frequent. The commuter to Pine Island you have to call ahead and schedule. Once we get the Norfolk flight scheduled, I'll call down and arrange that. They only fly during daylight."

"Why's that?"

"Because we won't be landing on a regular runway; it's more like a little road. No lights or tower or anything. Just a wind sock."

"That's comforting."

"Let me call down and check on the house."

They went over to the phone bank and Lee listened while Faith confirmed their arrival. She hung up. "All set. We can get a rental car once we get down there."

"So far, so good."

"It's a nice place to relax. You don't need to see or talk to anybody else if you don't want to."

"I don't want to," said Lee firmly.

"I'd like to ask you a question," Faith said as they walked toward a café.

"Shoot."

"How long had you been following me?"

"Six days," he promptly answered, "during which you made three trips to the cottage, including last night."

Last night, Faith thought. Was that all it had been? "And you haven't reported back to your employer yet?"

"No."

"Why not?"

"I like to do weekly reports, unless something really extraordinary happens. Believe me, if I'd had time, last night would have qualified for the mother of all reports."

"How were you to make these reports if you don't know who hired you?"

"I was given a phone number."

"And you never checked up on it?"

He looked at her with annoyance. "Nah, why should I care? Take the money and run."

She looked chastened. "I didn't mean it like that."

"Uh-huh, sure." He shifted the bags slightly and continued, "There's a special crisscross directory that'll give you the corresponding address if you have the phone number."

"And?"

"And in these days of satellite phones and nationwide cell networks and crap like that, nothing came up. I called the number. It must have been set up just to receive calls from me because it told Mr. Adams to leave any information on the tape. It also gave a P.O. box in D.C. Being the ever curious type I checked that out too, but it was listed in the name of a corporation I'd never heard of, with an address that turned out to be phony. Dead end." He looked down at her. "I take my work seriously, Faith. I don't like walking into traps. Famous last words, right?"

They stopped at the small café, bought their coffee and a couple of bagels and sat down in a vacant corner of the place.

Faith took a troubled breath as she sipped her coffee and nibbled on a poppyseed bagel oozing butter. Maybe he was being straight with her, but he still had a connection to Danny Buchanan. It was such a strange feeling suddenly being fearful of a man she had idolized. If things had not changed so much between them the last year, she would have been tempted to call Danny. But she was confused now, the horror of last night so crystal clear in her mind. Besides, what was she supposed to ask him: *Danny, did you try and have me killed last night? If you did, please stop, I'm working with the FBI to help you,*

157

really. And why did you hire Lee to follow me, Danny?
Yes, she had to part company with Lee, and soon.

"The report you were given, tell me what it said about me," Faith said.

"You're a lobbyist. You used to be with a big outfit, represented Fortune 500s. About ten years ago, you and a man named Daniel Buchanan started your own firm."

"Did it mention any of our current clients?"

He cocked his head. "No, is that important?"

"What do you know about Buchanan?"

"The report didn't say much about him, but I did some digging on my own, nothing you won't know. Buchanan is a legend on the Hill. Knows everybody and everybody knows him. Fought all the big battles, made a ton of money doing it. I assume you didn't do so badly yourself."

"I did well. What else?"

He stared at her strangely. "Why do you want to hear something you already know? Is Buchanan somehow mixed up in all this?"

Now it was Faith's turn to scrutinize Lee. If he was playing dumb, he was doing an exceptional job, she thought.

"Danny Buchanan is an honorable man. I owe him everything I have."

"Sounds like a good friend. But you didn't answer my question."

"People like Danny are rare. A true visionary."

"And you?"

"Me? I just help implement his vision. People like me are a dime a dozen."

"You don't strike me as so ordinary." Faith took a sip of coffee and didn't respond. "So how does one become a lobbyist?"

Faith stifled a yawn and sipped her coffee again. Her head was starting to pound. She had never

158

needed much rest, galloping the globe, catching only plane catnaps. But right now she felt like curling up under the table and sleeping for the next ten years. Maybe her body was reacting to the last twelve hours of horror by shutting itself down, throwing in the towel. *Please don't hurt me.*

"I could lie and say I wanted to change the world. That's what everyone says, isn't it?" She pulled a bottle of aspirin from her bag, popped two and washed them down with coffee. "Actually, I remember watching the Watergate hearings when I was a kid. All those very serious people in that room. All these middle-aged men with wide ugly ties, puffy faces, over-easy hair, talking into these clunky microphones, and all the lawyers whispering into their ears. All the media, the whole world focused right there. What the rest of the country apparently found appalling, I found extremely cool. All that power!" She smiled weakly into her coffee cup. "My demented soul. The nuns were right about me. One in particular, Sister Audrey Ann, truly believed my name was a blasphemy. 'Dear Faith,' she would say, 'live up to your Christian name, not down to your devilish urges.'"

"So you were a rabble rouser?"

"It's like if I saw a habit coming my way I just turned evil. My dad moved us around a lot, but I did well enough in school, even if I raised hell outside it. I went to a good college, ended up in Washington with all those memories of absolute power dancing in my head. I didn't have the faintest idea what to do with myself, but I knew desperately I wanted to get into the game. I did a stint on Capitol Hill for a freshman congressman and caught the eye of Danny Buchanan. He snatched me up, saw something in me, I guess. I think he liked my spirit – I was running the office with all of two months' experience behind me. The way I sort of refused to back down from anyone, even the Speaker of the House."

"I guess that is impressive for somebody right out of college."

"My philosophy was, after the nuns, politicians weren't much of a challenge."

Lee cracked a smile. "Makes me glad I went to public school." He glanced away for a second. "Don't look now, but the FBI is circling."

"What?" She whipped her head around, looking everywhere.

Lee rolled his eyes. "Oh, that was good."

"Where are they?"

He lightly smacked the tabletop. "They're nowhere. And they're everywhere. The Feds don't walk around with their badges pinned to their foreheads. You won't see them."

"So why the hell did you say they were circling?"

"It was a little test. And you failed. *I* can spot the Feds, sometimes, not always. If I ever say that to you again, I won't be kidding. They will be there. And you can't react the way you just did. Normal, slow movements. Just a pretty woman on a holiday with her boyfriend. Understand?"

"Okay, fine. But just don't pull that crap on me again. My nerves aren't well rested."

"How are you paying for the tickets?"

"How should I pay for them?"

"Your credit card. Under your other name. Don't want to flash a bunch of cash around. You buy a one-way ticket with cash leaving today, that might be a red flag for the airline. Right now, the less attention, the better. What is it, by the way? Your other name?"

"Suzanne Blake."

"Nice name."

"Suzanne was my mother's name."

"Was? Passed on?"

160

"Both my parents. My mother when I was eleven. My dad six years later. No brothers or sisters. I was a seventeen-year-old orphan."

"That must've been tough."

Faith didn't say anything for a long moment. Talking about her past was always hard, so she rarely did so. And she really didn't know this man. Still, there was something about Lee Adams that was comforting, solid. "I really loved my mother," she began. "She was a good woman, and long-suffering, because of my dad. He was a good person too, but one of those souls who always have an angle, a way to make a quick buck with these crazy ideas. And when his plan blew up, and it always did, we'd have to pack up and move on."

"Why was that?"

"Because other people always lost their money with my dad's grand schemes too. And they were understandably upset about it. We moved four times before my mother died. Five more times after that. We prayed for my dad every day, my mom and I. Right before she died, she told me to take care of him, and me all of eleven."

Lee shook his head. "I can't even relate to that. My parents have lived in the same house for fifty years. How did you manage to keep it together after your mother died?"

The words somehow came easier for Faith now. "It wasn't as tough as you'd think. Mom loved my dad, hated how he lived, his schemes, all the moving. But he wasn't going to change, so they weren't the happiest couple to live with. There were times I really thought she was going to kill him. When she died, it sort of became my dad and me against the world. He'd dress me up in the one nice outfit I had and show me off to all his prospective partners. I guess people would think, how can this guy be so bad, what with his little girl right there and all? When I got to be sixteen I'd even help him pitch his deals. I grew up fast. I guess that's where I got my motor mouth and my backbone. I learned to think on my feet."

"Quite an alternative education," Lee commented. "But I can see how it would serve you well as a lobbyist."

Her eyes grew moist. "On the way to every meeting, he'd say, 'This is the one, Faith, darling. I can feel it right here,' and he'd put his hand over his heart. 'It's all for you, baby girl. Daddy loves his Faith.' And I believed him every single damn time."

"Sounds like he really ended up hurting you," Lee said quietly.

Faith shook her head stubbornly. "It wasn't like he was trying to rip people off. We're not talking Ponzi schemes or anything. He sincerely believed his ideas would work. But they never did and we'd move on. And it wasn't like we ever made any money. God, we slept in our car enough times. How many times do I remember my dad strolling into the back door of restaurants and walking out a little later with dinner he had talked them into giving him. We'd sit in the backseat and eat. He'd stare at the sky, pointing out the constellations to me. He never even finished high school, but he knew all about the stars. Said he'd been chasing enough of them his whole life. We'd just sit there far into the night, and my dad would tell me things would get better. Just down the road."

"Sounds like a man who could talk his way into anywhere. Probably would've made a good PI."

Faith smiled as she thought back. "I'd walk into a bank with him, and within five minutes he'd know everybody by name, drinking coffee, talking with the bank manager like he'd known him all his whole life. And we'd walk out with a letter of recommendation and a list of local high-net-worth individuals for my dad to solicit. He just had that way about him. Everyone liked him. Until they lost their money. And we always lost what little we had too. Dad was a stickler about that. His money went in too. He was actually very honest."

"You sound like you still miss him."

"I do," she said proudly. "He named me Faith because he said with Faith beside him, how could he ever fail?" On this Faith closed her eyes, tears trickling down her cheeks.

Lee pulled a napkin out of the holder and slipped it into her hand. She wiped her eyes.

"I'm sorry," she said. "I've never really talked about this with anyone before."

"It's okay, Faith. I'm a good listener."

"I found my dad again in Danny," she said, clearing her throat, her eyes wide. "He has the same way about him. The pluck of the Irishman. He can talk his way into seeing anybody. Knows every angle, every issue. Refuses to back down from anyone. He's taught me a lot. And not just about lobbying. About life. He didn't have it easy growing up either. We had a lot in common."

Lee smiled. "So from scams with your dad to lobbying in D.C.?"

"And some would say my job description hasn't changed." Faith smiled at her own remark.

"And some would say that the nut didn't fall far from the tree."

She bit into her bagel. "Since we're into true confessions, how about your family?"

Lee settled back. "Four of each. I'm number six."

"God! Eight kids. Your mother must be a saint."

"We gave them both enough heartache to last ten lifetimes."

"So they're both still around."

"Going strong. We're all pretty close now, although we had some rough times growing up. Good support groups when things go haywire. Help's only a phone call away. Usually, that is. Not this time, though."

"That sounds nice. Real nice." Faith looked away.

Lee eyed her keenly, easily reading her thoughts. "Families have their problems too, Faith. Divorces, serious illnesses, depression, hard times, we've seen it all. I have to say sometimes I'd rather be an only child."

"No, you wouldn't," she said with authority. "You might think you would, but trust me, you wouldn't."

"I do."

She looked confused. "You do what?"

"Trust you."

She said slowly, "You know, for a paranoid PI, you sure make friends fast. I could be a mass murderer, for all you know."

"If you were really bad, the Feds would've had you in custody."

She put down her coffee and leaned toward him, her expression very serious. "I appreciate the observation. But just so we're very clear on this, I've never physically harmed even an ant in my entire life, and I still don't consider myself a criminal, but I guess if the FBI wanted to put me in jail, they could. Just so we're clear," she said again. "Now, you still want to get on that plane with me?"

"Absolutely. You've really got my curiosity up now."

She sighed and sat back, glancing down the terminal's corridor. "Don't look now, but here come a pair who look an awful lot like the FBI."

"Seriously?"

"Unlike you, I wouldn't even attempt to joke about something like that." She bent over and fiddled with something in her bag. After a few anxious moments, she sat back up as the pair passed by without looking at them.

"Lee, depending on what they've found out, they may be looking for a man and a woman. Why don't you stay here while I go buy the tickets? I'll meet you at the security gate."

Lee looked uncertain. "Let me think about that."

"I thought you said you trusted me."

"I do." For a moment he envisioned Faith's dad standing in front of him, asking for money. And damn if Lee wasn't reaching in his pocket for his wallet.

"But even trust has its limits, right? I tell you what, you keep the bags. I need to take my purse. If you're really worried, you have a clear view of the security entrance from here. If I try to give you the slip, you've got me dead on. And I'm sure you can run much faster than I can." She stood. "And you know I can't call in the FBI, now, can I?"

She eyed him for a moment longer, apparently daring him to challenge her logic.

"Okay."

"What's your new name? I'll need it for your ticket."

"Charles Wright."

She winked at him. "And your friends call you Chuck?"

He gave her an uneasy smile and then Faith turned and disappeared into the crowd.

As soon as she was gone, Lee regretted his decision. Sure she had left her bag, but it only had a few clothes in it, the ones he had given her! She had her purse with her, which meant she had what she really needed: her fake ID and her money. Yes, he could see the security gate from here, but what if she just walked out the front door? What if that's what she was doing right now? Without her, he had nothing. Except some really dangerous people who now knew where he lived. People who would take great pleasure in breaking his bones one by one until he told them what he knew, which was nothing. They wouldn't be thrilled to hear that. Next stop: your standard landfill burial. That did it. Lee jumped up, grabbed the bags and headed after her.

TWENTY

There was a knock on Reynolds's door. Connie popped his head in. Reynolds was on the phone but she waved him in.

Connie had two cups of coffee. He put one in front of Reynolds, together with two cream packets, a sugar and a swizzle stick. She thanked him with an appreciative smile. He sat down and sipped on his coffee while she finished her call.

Reynolds put down the phone and started mixing her coffee. "I would absolutely love some good news, Connie." She noted that he also had gone home, showered and changed. Rambling through the woods in the dark had probably done a real number on his suit, she assumed. His hair was still damp and the wetness made it seem more gray than usual. Reynolds kept forgetting that he was in his fifties. Connie just never seemed to change, always big, always craggy, the weatherbeaten rock upon which she clung when the riptide came calling. As it was right now.

"Do you want lies or the truth?"

Reynolds took a sip of the coffee, sighed and leaned back in her chair. "Right now, I'm not sure."

He sat forward, perching his coffee on her desk. "I worked the scene with the VCU boys. That's where I started at the Bureau, you know. Just like old times." He put his palms flat on his knees and flexed his thick neck to work out a kink. "Damn, my back feels like Reggie White's been doing jumping jacks on it. I'm getting too old for this kind of work."

"You can't retire. I can't function without you."

Connie picked up his coffee cup. "The hell you say." It was obvious, though, that the remark had pleased him. He sat back, unbuttoned his jacket and let his belly push through. He let a minute or so pass as he presumably collected his thoughts.

Reynolds waited patiently. She knew Connie had not come down here to shoot the breeze with her. He rarely did that with anyone. Reynolds had learned that just about everything the man did had a specific purpose. Connie was a true veteran of the ways of bureaucracy and, consequently, he carried an agenda with him everywhere. While she thoroughly relied on him for his field expertise and his instincts, Reynolds never quite lost sight of the fact that she was younger, less experienced, yet was still his boss; it had to be a sore point with the man. And she was a woman, to boot, in a field that still didn't have many at her level of responsibility. She could not really blame Connie if he felt resentment toward her. And yet he had never said a negative word about her, nor had he ever dragged his feet on an assignment in order to make her look bad. On the contrary, he was methodical to a fault, and reliable as the sunrise. Still, she had to watch herself.

"I saw Anne Newman this morning. She appreciated your coming over last night. She said you were a real comfort."

This surprised Reynolds. Maybe the woman *didn't* blame her. "She took it about as well as anyone could."

"I understand the director went too. That was good of him. You know Ken and I go way back." The look on Connie's face was easily read. If the man caught up to the killer before the VCU did, there might not be any need for a trial.

"I know. I never stopped to think how hard this must be for you."

"You have enough on your mind. Besides, I'm the last person you need to worry about." Connie took a swallow of coffee. "The shooter was hit. Least it looks that way."

Reynolds immediately sat forward. "Let me have everything."

Connie momentarily smiled. "Don't want to wait for the written report from VCU?" He crossed one thick leg over the other, hitching up his cuffed trousers as he did so. "You were right about the shooter's location. We found blood, a fair amount of it in the woods behind the house. Did a rough trajectory. The location jells with where the shot probably came from. We followed the trail as best we could, but lost it in the woods after a few hundred feet."

"Exactly how much blood? Life-threatening?"

"Hard to say. It was dark. A team's over there right now continuing the search. They're lock-stepping the lawn, looking for the slug that killed Ken. They're also canvassing the neighborhood, but the place was so isolated, I'm not sure that'll pay off."

Reynolds took a deep breath. "If we find a body, that would both simplify and complicate things."

Connie nodded thoughtfully. "I see where you're going with that."

"You got a blood sample?"

"Lab's running it as we speak. Don't know what it'll be worth."

"At the very least it'll confirm whether it's human or not."

"That's true. Maybe all we'll find is a deer carcass. But I don't think so." Reynolds perked up. "Nothing

169

concrete," he said in response to her look, "just call it my gut."

"If the guy's wounded, that should make it a little easier to track him down."

"Maybe. If he required medical attention, he wouldn't be so stupid as to go to the local emergency room. They have to report gunshot wounds. And we don't know how badly he was hurt. Might have just been a flesh wound that bled like a bitch. If so, he bandages it up, gets on a plane and poof. Gone. I mean we've got all the bases covered, but if the guy was leaving on a private plane, then we got problems. The truth is he's probably already long gone."

"Or maybe dead. Apparently he missed his primary target. Whoever hired him won't be happy about that."

"Right."

Reynolds folded her hands in front of her as she thought of the next topic she wanted to discuss. "Connie, Ken's gun was unfired."

Connie had obviously given this line of inquiry some thought because he said, "Which means, if the blood is confirmed as human, we definitely have a *fourth* person at the cottage last night. And that party shot the shooter." He shook his head wearily. "Shit, listen to us, it all sounds crazy."

"Crazy but apparently true under the facts as we know them. Think about this: Could this fourth person have killed Ken? And not the guy who was wounded?"

"Don't think so. The VCUs are looking for shell cartridges in the woods where we think the other shot came from, as confirmation. If there was a gun battle between two unknown parties, then maybe we'll find another set of ejected shells as well."

"Well, this fourth person being present may

explain the door being unlocked and the cameras being tripped."

He sat up straight. "Anything on the tape yet? We had to get some faces or something."

"To put it simply, we have been degaussed."

"What?"

"Don't ask. For right now we can't count on the tape."

"Well, shit. That doesn't leave us with much."

"Specifically, it leaves us with Faith Lockhart."

"We've got all the airports, train and bus stations, rental car agencies covered. Her firm too, although I can't believe she'd go there."

"Agreed. Actually, that may be where the bullet came from," Reynolds said slowly.

"Buchanan?"

"Wish we could prove it."

"If we find Lockhart, we still may be able to. We'll have some leverage there."

"Don't count on it. Almost getting your head blown off can make you rethink loyalties," Reynolds said dryly.

"If Buchanan and his people are on to Lockhart, then they must be on to us as well."

"You said that before. A leak? From here?"

"A leak from somewhere. Here or at Lockhart's end. Maybe she did something to make Buchanan suspicious. From all accounts, the guy's cagey as hell. He had her followed somehow. They saw her meeting with you at the house. He dug a little more, hit the truth and contracted to take her out."

"I'd like to believe *that* more than someone here selling us down the river."

"So would I. But the fact is every law enforcement agency has some bad apples."

Reynolds briefly wondered for a moment if Connie was suspicious of her. Everyone who worked at the FBI, from special agents to support staff, had top-secret security clearance. When you applied for a job at the Bureau, teams of agents would show up investigating every single piece of your past, no matter how insignificant, talking to everyone who ever knew you. Every five years a full field investigation was conducted on on-board Bureau employees. In the interim any suspicious activity involving a bureau employee or any complaints of persons asking suspicious questions of an employee were to be reported to the security officer in the employee's division. That had never happened to Reynolds, thank God. Her record was clean.

If there were suspicions of a leak or other type of security breach, it might very well be investigated by the Office of Professional Responsibility, and a polygraph exam might be ordered for the suspect employee. Other than that, the Bureau was always on the lookout for any signs that an employee was having undue personal or professional problems that might make him or her susceptible to bribes or influence by third parties.

Reynolds knew Connie was doing okay financially. His wife had died years ago from a lengthy illness that had sapped their resources, but he lived in a nice house that was worth a lot more than he had paid for it. His kids' college educations were done, and he had his pension locked in. All in all, he had a nice retirement to look forward to.

On the other hand, Reynolds knew her personal life and finances were in abysmal shape. College funds? Hell, she'd be lucky if she could continue to afford the private school tuition for first grade. And pretty soon, she wouldn't have a house to call her own. That was being sold as part of the divorce. The condo she was eyeing was about the size of the one she had rented when she had finished college. It had seemed cozy with one person. An adult and two energetic kids would quickly turn cozy into cramped. And could she afford to keep her nanny? With her hours, how could she not? She couldn't leave the kids alone at night.

In any other occupation she would probably be on the top ten soon-to-crash-and-burn list. But in the FBI, the divorce rate was such that her mess of a marriage would not create a blip on the Bureau radar. A career in the FBI was often simply not conducive to a happy personal life.

She blinked for a moment as she found Connie's gaze still upon her. Did he really suspect her of being the leak? Of causing Ken Newman to die? She knew it looked bad. On the very night when she'd had Newman substitute for her with Lockhart, he was killed. She knew Paul Fisher had been thinking that, and she was reasonably sure Connie was right now.

She composed herself and said, "There's really nothing we can do about this theory of a leak right now. Let's concentrate on what we can do."

"Fine. So what's our next move?"

"Hit all our lines of investigation as hard as we can. Find Lockhart. Let's hope she uses a credit card for plane or train tickets. If she does that, we've got her. We need to at least make an effort to find the shooter. Shadow Buchanan. Unscramble that tape and see who was in the house. I want you to act as liaison with the VCU. We have a lot of threads, if we can only grab one or two of them and hold on."

"Hey, isn't that always the case?"

"We're in a *really* tight spot here, Connie."

He nodded thoughtfully. "I heard Fisher was here. Figured he'd been by to see you."

Reynolds didn't respond to this, and Connie plunged on.

"Thirteen years ago, I was heading up a joint undercover drug operation with the DEA in Brownsville, Texas." He paused for a moment as if deciding whether to go forward or not. "Our official goal was to disrupt the flow of cocaine over the Mexican border. Our unofficial goal was to accomplish our mission without making the Mexican government look bad. For that reason, we had open lines of communication with our counterparts in Mexico City. Perhaps too open, since there was rampant corruption south of the border at all levels. But it was done that way so the Mexican authorities could share in the glory after we did all the work and scored the perps heading up the cartel. After two years of work, a huge bust was planned. But our plans got leaked and my guys walked into an ambush that left two of them dead."

"Omigod. I heard about that case, but I didn't know you were involved in it."

"Hell, you were probably still cutting your teeth at Quantico."

Reynolds didn't know if this was a backdoor barb or not, but she chose not to respond.

"Anyway, after all that went down, I got a visit from one of the young ladder climbers at HQ who wouldn't know which end of his pistol to hold, and who politely informed me that if I didn't make things right, my ass was cooked. But there was one stipulation. If I found out our friends in Mexico sent us down the river, I couldn't use that as an excuse. International relations, I was told. I'd just have to fall on the sword for the good of the world." Connie's voice trembled a little as he said this last part.

Reynolds found she was holding her breath. It was not like Connie to talk this much. In the dictionary, the man's picture could well be found next to the word "taciturn."

He took a gulp of coffee and took a moment to wipe his lips with the back of his hand. "Well, you know what? I traced the leak right to the top of the Mexican police department and I put a big X on the bastards' foreheads and walked away from it. If my superiors didn't want to do anything about it, fine. But damn if I was going to take the fall for somebody else's shit." He eyed her steadily. "'International relations,'" he said, a bitter smile spreading across his lips as he did so. He rested his elbows on her desk.

Was this a challenge he was laying before her? Reynolds wondered. Was he expecting to leave an X on her forehead, or daring her to pin one on his?

"That's been my official motto ever since," he said.

"What's that?"

"Screw 'international relations.'"

TWENTY-ONE

Through the airport terminal drifted members of both the FBI and Central Intelligence, with the former group completely unaware of the latter's presence. Thornhill's men had the advantage of knowing that Lee Adams was probably traveling with Faith Lockhart. The FBI agents were only looking for the woman.

Lee unknowingly passed a couple of the FBI agents dressed as businessmen with briefcases and *Wall Street Journals*. They were equally oblivious to him. Faith had passed by the agents a moment earlier.

Lee slowed when he got near to the main ticket counter. Faith was up there speaking with a clerk. This was starting to look okay. He had a sudden feeling of guilt for not having trusted her. He edged over to a corner and waited.

At the counter, Faith displayed her new ID and purchased three tickets. Two tickets were in the name of Suzanne Blake and Charles Wright. The woman barely looked at her photo. Thank God for that, although Faith supposed people rarely looked like their ID photos anyway. The flight to Norfolk International left in about forty-five minutes. The third ticket she purchased was in the name of Faith Lockhart. It was a flight heading to San Francisco with a stopover in Chicago. It left in forty minutes. She had spotted it on the monitors. West Coast, big

176

city. She could lose herself, drive down the coast, maybe even sneak into Mexico. She wasn't sure how she would accomplish that, but she just had to take it one step at a time.

Faith had explained that she was buying the ticket to San Francisco for her boss, who would arrive shortly.

"She'll have to hurry," the clerk said. "She still has to check in. And they're going to begin boarding in about ten minutes."

"It won't be a problem," Faith assured her. "She doesn't have any luggage, so she can check in at the gate."

The clerk handed her the ticket. Faith figured she was safe using her real name on the ticket because she paid for all of them with her Suzanne Blake credit card. And the only other ID she had to check in with was her real one. It was Faith Lockhart or nothing. Everything would be okay.

She could not have been any more wrong.

As Lee watched Faith, a thought jolted him. His gun! He had to check it before going through security or all hell would break lose. He shot across to the counter and next to a startled Faith.

He put his arm around her and gave her a quick kiss on the cheek. "Hey, babe. Sorry, the phone call took longer than I thought." He looked at the ticket agent and said casually, "I have a pistol I need to check."

The ticket agent raised her eyes slightly at this.

"You're Mr. Wright?"

Lee nodded. She went about processing the necessary documents. He showed her his fake ID and she stamped his passenger ticket appropriately and entered the information in the computer. He turned over the gun and ammo, and filled out the declaration form. The agent tagged the container and they left the ticket counter.

"Sorry, I forgot about the gun." Lee looked up ahead to the security gate. "Okay, they're going to have people posted at the gate. We'll go through separately. Be cool; you don't look anything like Faith Lockhart."

Although Faith felt her heart in her throat the entire time, they went through the security gate without incident.

As they passed the flight information monitors, Lee spotted their gate. "Down this way."

Faith nodded as she noted how the gates were configured here. The departure gate for the San Francisco flight was close enough to easily get to, but far enough away from the Norfolk gate. She hid a smile. Perfect.

As they walked along, she looked over at Lee. He had done a lot for her. She wasn't feeling good about what she was about to do, but had convinced herself it was for the best. For both of them.

They reached the gate for the flight to Norfolk. The plane would be boarding in about ten minutes, they were told. There was a good crowd waiting.

Lee looked at her. "You better call that commuter service for the flight to Pine Island."

Lee and Faith walked over to the phone bank and she made that call.

"All set," Faith said. "Now we can relax."

"Right," Lee said dryly.

Faith looked around. "I need to use the rest room."

"Better hurry."

She hustled off while Lee looked after her thoughtfully.

TWENTY-TWO

"**B**ingo!" The man sitting in front of the computer screen said. He was in a van outside of the airport. The FBI had a designated liaison with the airlines to monitor the travel of persons the Bureau was looking for. With more than one airline sharing reservation systems and data and the advent of code-sharing, the FBI's job had been made a little easier. The Bureau had requested that the name Faith Lockhart be marked with a tag in the major airlines' reservation systems. That request had just paid an enormous dividend.

"She just made a reservation for a flight to San Francisco that leaves in about half an hour," he said into his headset microphone. "United Airlines." He passed along the flight number and gate information. "Hit it," he ordered the men inside the terminal. He picked up the phone to notify Brooke Reynolds.

Lee was leafing through a magazine someone had left on the seat next to his when two men dressed in suits flew past. A few moments later, a pair of gents in jeans and windbreakers hurried past, heading in the same direction.

Lee immediately jumped up, looked around for anyone else hustling by, saw no one moving fast and then followed after the group.

The FBI agents, followed by the men in jeans, hurried past the women's room a minute before

Faith came out. The men had disappeared into the crowds by the time she emerged.

Lee slowed as he saw Faith come out from the women's room. Another false alarm? When she turned away from him and went in the opposite direction, he knew his fears were justified. As he kept his gaze on her, she looked at her watch and picked up her pace. Shit, he knew exactly what she was doing: going for another flight. And from the way she had checked her watch and started walking faster, it must be close to leaving. As he pushed through the crowds, he scanned the aisle ahead. There were ten gates remaining down here. He stopped for a second at the monitors, his gaze flying down the listings, checking the gates off one by one until he stopped at the flashing "boarding" message for a United flight to San Francisco. As his eye drifted farther, he saw that a flight to Toledo was also boarding. Which one was it? Well, there was one definite way to find out.

He sprinted ahead, cut through a waiting area and managed to get past Faith without her seeing him. He abruptly stopped within sight of the gate for the San Francisco flight. The men in suits who had sprinted past him were standing at the departure door talking to a nervous-looking United employee. Then the stone-faced men moved off and stood behind a partition, their gaze fixed on the crowd and departure area. FBI for sure. The San Francisco flight had to be the one Faith was going for.

But something didn't make sense. If Faith had used her phony name, how . . .? Then it hit Lee. She couldn't use her phony name for both tickets for flights leaving a few minutes apart. That would have been a big red flag for the ticket agent. She had used her real name because she needed ID to get on the flight. Shit! She was heading right for them. She'd show her ticket, the agent would signal the FBI and then it would be over.

Just as he was about to turn, he spotted the two men in windbreakers and jeans who had rushed past him earlier. To Lee's experienced eyes, they were watching the Feds intently, without seeming to do so. He edged closer, and with the gloomy weather outside he managed to catch their reflection in the window. One man held something in his hand. A chill went down Lee's back as he maneuvered some more and managed to spot what it was. Or what he thought it was. This case suddenly took on a whole other dimension.

Lee fought his way back down the aisle; seemingly everyone who lived in the Washington metropolitan area had decided to fly today. He saw Faith across the aisle. In another moment she'd be past him. He made a lunge across the wall of people and tripped over a garment bag someone had set down. He fell to the floor hard, his knee taking the brunt of the collision. When he sprang up, Faith was past him. He had a few seconds, if that.

"Suzanne? Suzanne Blake?" he called out.

At first it didn't register. But then she stopped, looked around. If she saw him, Lee knew she might run. But her stopping had given him the few seconds he needed. He circled and came up behind her.

Faith almost collapsed when he gripped her arm. "Turn around and walk with me," he said.

She pulled at his fingers. "Lee, you don't understand. Please, let me go."

"No, *you* don't understand. The FBI is waiting for you at the San Francisco gate."

The words made her freeze.

"You messed up bad. You made the second reservation in your name. They monitor stuff like that, Faith. They know you're here now."

181

They headed as quickly as they could back down the aisle to the original departure gate. The plane was boarding. Lee grabbed their bags, but instead of getting on the plane, Lee veered off, pulling Faith along with him. They went back through security and headed toward the elevator.

"Where are we going?" Faith said. "The plane to Norfolk is leaving."

"We're getting the hell out of here before they shut the whole terminal down looking for us."

They took the elevator down to the lower level, went outside and Lee signaled for a taxi. They got in one, Lee gave the man an address in Virginia and the cab pulled off. Only then did Lee look at her.

"We couldn't get on the plane to Norfolk."

"Why not? That ticket was in my other name."

Lee glanced at the driver, an old guy slumped down in his seat listening to country western on the radio.

Satisfied, Lee still spoke in low tones. "Because the first thing they'll do is check at the ticket counter to see who purchased the ticket for Faith Lockhart. Then they'll know Suzanne Blake did. And they'll know Charles Wright is traveling with you. And they'll be given descriptions of us both. And they'll check the reservations for Blake and Wright and the FBI will be waiting for us when we get off the plane in Norfolk."

Faith paled. "They move that fast?"

Lee trembled with rage. "Who the hell do you think you're dealing with here? Larry, Moe and Curly Joe?" He slapped his thigh in sudden anger. "Sonofabitch!"

"What?" Faith said frantically. "What?"

"They have my gun. It's registered in my name. My *real* name. Dammit! Now I've aided and abetted, and the Feds right on our ass." In his despair he rested his head in his hands. "This must be my birthday, things are going so good for me."

Faith started to touch him on the shoulder, but pulled her hand back. She looked out the window instead. "I'm sorry. I'm really, really sorry." She put a hand against the car window, letting the cold from the glass seep into her skin. "Look, just take me to the FBI. I'll tell them the truth."

"That would be great except the FBI's not going to take your word for it. And there's another thing."

"What?" Faith wondered if he was going to tell her about working for Buchanan.

"Not now." Lee was actually thinking of the other men at the gate, what he had seen in one of the men's hands. "Right now I'd like you to tell me what that was all about back there."

She stared out the window at the choppy gray Potomac. "I'm not sure I can," she said so softly he could barely hear her.

"Well, I'd like you to try," he said very firmly. "I'd like you to try very, very hard."

"I don't think you'd understand."

"I can understand with the best of them."

She finally turned to him, her face flushed, her gaze refusing to catch his. She nervously played with the edge of her jacket. "I just thought it would be better if you weren't with me. You see, I thought you'd be safer that way."

Lee looked away in disgust. "Bullshit!"

"It's true!"

He whirled back around and clutched her shoulder so tightly she winced in pain. "Listen, Faith, they were at my apartment, whoever *they* are. They know I'm involved. Whether I'm with you or not, the danger level really doesn't change for me, it actually gets worse. And you running around trying to ditch me isn't damn well helping."

"But they knew you were involved. Remember back at your apartment."

Lee shook his head. "Those weren't the Feds."

She looked stunned. "Who, then?"

"I don't know. But the Feds don't show up disguised as UPS men. FBI Rule Number One: Overwhelming force trumps all. They would've come with about a hundred guys and the Hostage Rescue Team and the dogs and body armor and shit like that. And they just come in and take your ass, case closed." Lee's voice grew calmer as he thought things through. "Now, the guys waiting for you at the gate were FBI." He nodded thoughtfully. "They weren't trying to hide who they were." The other two men at the departure gate? All bets were off. But he knew Faith was very lucky to be alive.

"Oh, and by the way, you're welcome for me saving your butt again. Another few seconds and you're back in FBI land with more questions than you have answers for. Maybe I should've just let them take you," he added wearily.

"Why didn't you?" she asked quietly.

Lee almost felt like laughing. The whole experience was like a dream. *But where do I go to wake up?*

"Right now, lunacy seems to be at the top of the list."

Faith attempted a smile. "Thank God for lunatics."

Lee didn't smile back. "From now on, we are Siamese twins. You better get used to seeing a man take a piss because, lady, we are inseparable from here on."

"Lee—"

"I don't want to hear it! Just don't say a damn thing." His voice was trembling. "I'm so close to punching the shit out of you, I swear to God." He made a big show of reaching over and clamping one

184

big hand over her wrist, as though a living handcuff. Then he sat back, staring at nothing.

Faith didn't try to pull her hand away, not that she could have. And she was really terrified he might take a swing at her. This was probably about as angry as Lee Adams had ever gotten in his entire life, she thought. She finally sat back and tried to calm down. Her heart was beating so fast it seemed impossible for her blood vessels to survive the pressure. Maybe she'd save everyone a lot of trouble and just drop from a coronary.

In Washington you could lie about sex, money, power, loyalties. You could spin falsehoods into truths and simple facts into lies. She had seen it all. It was one of the most frustrating and cruelest places on earth, where one relied on old alliances and quick feet for survival and where every new day, every fresh relationship, could be the one that made you or destroyed you. And Faith had thrived in that world, loved it, in fact. Until now.

Faith could not look at Lee Adams, for fear of what she would see in his eyes. He was all she had. Although she barely knew the man, for some reason she craved his respect, his understanding. She knew she would get neither. She didn't deserve them.

Out of the car window she stared at a plane quickly gaining altitude. In another few seconds it would disappear into the clouds. Soon the passengers would only be able to see that layer of puffy cumulus beneath them, as though the world below had suddenly disappeared. Why couldn't she be on that plane and just keep climbing, to a place where she could start over? Why couldn't a place like that exist? Why?

TWENTY-THREE

Brooke Reynolds sat glumly at the small table, chin resting on her palm, and wondered if anything ever was going to go right on this case. They had found Ken Newman's car. It had been professionally cleansed such that her team of "experts" were unable to provide her with any real clues. She had just checked with the lab. They were still messing around with the tape. Worst of all, Faith Lockhart had slipped right through her fingers. At this rate she'd be FBI director in no time. She was certain there would be a stream of messages from the ADIC on down when she returned to her office, and none of them complimentary, she imagined.

Reynolds and Connie were in a private area at Reagan National. They had thoroughly questioned the airline employee who had sold Faith Lockhart her tickets. They had reviewed all the surveillance tapes and the agent had readily picked out Lockhart. Reynolds assumed the woman was Faith Lockhart. The ticket agent had been shown a picture of Lockhart and was reasonably sure she was the same woman.

If it was Lockhart, she had changed her appearance considerably: a haircut and dye job, from what Reynolds had seen on the airport surveillance tape. And now Lockhart had help. For also captured on the video was a tall, well-built man leaving with Lockhart. Reynolds had initiated the obvious inquiries including checking taxi pickups at the airport during that time. They also had colleagues checking in Norfolk in case the pair had made additional travel arrangements there. So far nothing had turned up. They did, however, have one very promising lead.

Reynolds opened the metal gun case and looked at the SIG-Sauer 9mm while Connie leaned against the wall and scowled at nothing. The gun had already been checked for prints, and they were running the results through the Bureau's databases, but they had something even better: The gun was registered. They had quickly gotten the name and address of the owner from the Virginia State Police.

Reynolds said, "Okay, so the gun's registered to this Lee Adams. We're getting a photo of the guy from DMV. I'm assuming he's the one with Lockhart. What do we know about him so far?"

Connie took a mouthful of Coke from the cup he was holding and popped two Advil. "PI. Been around awhile. Seems very legit. Some of the guys at the Bureau know him in fact. Say he's a good guy. We'll get his picture to the ticket agent. See if she can positive-ID him. That's all for right now. We'll have more soon." He glanced at the gun. "We found shell casings in the woods behind the cottage. They'd been fired from a pistol. Nine-millimeter. From the number we found, the person emptied half his mag at something."

"Think this is the pistol?"

"We haven't found any slugs to match it to, but ballistics will tell us if the pinprick on the shell casings we found match ones fired from that gun," Connie said, referring to the indentation a gun's firing pin makes on the bottom of the shell casing, a mark about as unique as a fingerprint. "And since we've got his ammo, we can test-fire from the source, which is ideal, you know. And we're

187

running a print check on the casings. That won't definitely confirm if Adams was there, since he could've loaded the pistol earlier and someone else could have fired it at the cottage, but it's still something."

They both knew that shell casings were much better surfaces for getting usable prints than a pistol grip.

"It'd be nice if we could get his prints inside the cottage."

"VCU found nothing. Adams obviously knows how to do this stuff. Had to be wearing gloves."

"If ballistics does match, then Adams looks to be the one who wounded the shooter."

"He didn't fire all those times at Ken, that's for sure, and a SIG is for shit long-distance. If Adams was able to hit Ken with a pistol shot from that distance in the dark, then we've got to get him a job at Quantico on the firing range."

Reynolds looked unconvinced.

Connie went on. "And the lab confirmed that the blood in the woods is definitely human. We also found a slug near the spot where all the pistol shell casings were. Struck a tree and stayed there. We also turned up a number of shell casings near the blood. Rifle ordnance. Full metal jacket, heavy-caliber stuff. And customized, no manufacturer's code or caliber stamp on the casings. But the lab did say the ammo used a Berdan primer instead of an American Boxer."

Reynolds looked at him sharply. "Berdan? So European manufacture?"

"There are so many freaky variations these days, but it looks that way."

Reynolds was very familiar with the Berdan primer. It differed from the American version principally in that it had no integral anvil. The anvil was constructed right into the cartridge case, forming a miniature T-shaped projection in the primer pocket with two flash holes to allow the exploded primer to get to the powder. It was a clever, efficient design, Reynolds thought.

When you pulled the trigger of a weapon, Brooke had learned when she joined the Bureau, the firing pin hit the primer cup, compressing the primer between the cup and anvil and causing the primer to explode. This mini-explosion, in turn, shot through the flash holes and ignited the powder to temperatures in excess of five thousand degrees. A millisecond later the bullet went roaring down the gun barrel, and before you could blink, a human being was probably dead. Guns were by far the weapon of choice for murder in America, and Brooke knew that homicide events happened at the rate of fifty-five times a day in the United States. Consequently, Reynolds and her colleagues would never lack for work.

"European-manufactured shells might tie in to the foreign interest angle Lockhart was telling us about," Reynolds said almost to herself. "So Adams and the shooter were going at it and Adams gets the better of it." Reynolds stared thoughtfully at her partner. "Any connection between Adams and Lockhart?"

"None that we can see right now, but we've just started digging."

"Here's another theory, Connie: Adams came out of the woods, killed Ken and then went back through the woods. He could've fallen on something and cut himself. That would account for the blood. I know that doesn't explain the rifle slug, but it's a possibility we can't ignore. For all we know, he was carrying a rifle as well. Or it could have been from a hunter's gun. They hunt in those woods, I bet."

"Come on, Brooke. The guy can't have a gun battle with himself. Remember the two separate piles of different shell casings. And no hunter I know is going to stand there and pump shot after shot at something. They'll kill their buddy or maybe themselves. Most states require plugs in a rifle's magazine to limit shots for that very reason. And those shell casings hadn't been there very long."

"Okay, okay, but I'm just not willing to trust Adams at this point."

"And you think I am? I don't trust my own mother, God rest her soul. But I can't ignore facts either. Lockhart drives away in Ken's car? And Adams just leaves his boots behind before he takes his jaunt through the woods? Come on, you don't believe that."

"Look, Connie, I'm just pointing out the possibilities. I'm not saying I'm sold on any of them. The thing that keeps bugging me is, what spooked Ken? If the shooter's in the woods, it wasn't *him*."

Connie rubbed his jaw. "Now, that's true."

Reynolds suddenly snapped her fingers. "Dammit, the door. How could I have been so blind? When we got to the cottage the screen door was wide open. I remember it clearly. It opens out, so Ken would have seen it when he turned that way. What would he have done? Pull his gun."

"And he might have seen the boots too. It was dark, but the cottage's back porch isn't that big." Connie took another swallow of Coke and rubbed his left temple. "Come on, Advil, do your magic. Well, we'll know for certain if Adams was even there when the lab guys unscramble the video."

"*If* they unscramble it. But why would Adams have been at the cottage in the first place?"

"Maybe someone hired him to shadow Lockhart."

"Buchanan?"

"Probably first on my list."

"But if Buchanan hired the shooter to take out Lockhart, why have Adams there to witness it?"

Connie bunched up his thick shoulders and then let them collapse, like a bear scratching itself against a tree. "That for sure doesn't make a helluva lot of sense."

"Well, let me complicate things further for you. Two tickets were purchased by Lockhart for a trip to Norfolk. But only *one* in her real name for the trip to San Francisco."

"And you got Adams running after our guys on the airport surveillance video."

"Think Lockhart tried to give him the slip?"

"Ticket agent said Adams didn't come up to the counter until after Lockhart had purchased the tickets. And the video shows Adams leading her back from the vicinity of the San Francisco gate."

"So maybe an involuntary partnership of sorts," Reynolds said. She had a sudden thought as she looked at Connie. *Like ours, perhaps?* "You know what I'd really like?" Reynolds said. Connie raised his eyebrows. "I'd like to return Mr. Adams's boots. We have his home address?"

"North Arlington. Twenty minutes from here, tops."

Reynolds rose. "Let's go."

TWENTY-FOUR

While Connie parked the car at the curb, Reynolds stared up at the old brownstone. "Adams must do pretty well. This isn't a cheap area."

Connie looked around and said, "Maybe I should sell my house and buy an apartment around here. Stroll around the street, sit in the park, enjoy life."

"Thoughts of retirement creeping in?"

"Seeing Ken in a body bag isn't making me want to do this forever."

They walked up to the front door. Each of them noted the video camera, and then Connie rang the door buzzer.

"Who is it?" a voice fiercely demanded.

"FBI," Reynolds said. "Agents Reynolds and Constantinople."

The door didn't buzz open as they had expected.

"Show me your badges," the elderly voice proclaimed. "Hold them up to the camera."

The two agents looked at each other.

Reynolds smiled. "Let's play nice and do as we're told, Connie."

The pair held up their credentials, or "creds," to the camera. They both carried them the same way: gold badge pinned to the outside of the ID case, so you got the shield first and the picture ID card last. It was intended to be intimidating. And it was. A minute later they heard a door open from inside the building and a woman's face appeared at the glass of the old-fashioned double doors.

"Let me see them again," she said. "My eyes aren't all that good anymore."

"Ma'am—" Connie began hotly until Reynolds elbowed him. They held up their creds again.

The woman scrutinized them and then opened the door.

"I'm sorry," she said as they came in. "But after all the goings-on this morning, I'm about ready to pack my bags and leave for good. And this has been my home for twenty years."

"What goings-on?" Reynolds asked sharply.

The woman eyed her warily. "Who did you come here to see?"

"Lee Adams," Reynolds said.

"I thought so. Well, he's not here."

"Any idea where he might be, Mrs. . . .?"

"Carter. Angie Carter. And no, I don't have any idea where he's got to. Left this morning and I haven't seen him since."

"So what happened this morning?" Connie said. "It was this morning, right?"

Carter nodded. "Fairly early. Just having my coffee when Lee called down and said he wanted me to watch Max because he was going away." They looked at her curiously. "Max is Lee's German shepherd." Her mouth quivered for a moment. "Poor animal."

Reynolds said, "What happened to the dog?"

"They hit him. He'll be okay, but they hurt him."

Connie edged closer to the old woman. "Who hurt him?"

"Ms. Carter, why don't we go into your apartment and sit down?" Reynolds suggested.

The apartment contained old, comfortable furniture, tiny shelves with odd knickknacks placed just so and the aroma of burnt kale and onions.

After they were seated, Reynolds said, "Maybe it would be better if you just started at the beginning, and we'll ask questions along the way."

Carter told of how she had agreed to keep Lee's dog. "I do it a lot, Lee's gone a lot. He's a private investigator, you know."

"We know. So he didn't say where he was going? Nothing at all?" Connie prompted.

"Never does. *Private* investigator is just what it means, and Lee was a stickler for that."

"Does he have a separate office somewhere?"

"No, he uses his spare bedroom for an office. He also looks after the building. He's the one who put in the camera outside, sturdy locks on the doors, things like that. Never accepted one penny for it either. Anybody has a problem in the building – the tenants are mostly old, like me – they go to Lee, and he takes care of it."

Reynolds smiled warmly. "Sounds like a nice guy. Go on with your story."

"Well, I had just gotten Max settled when the UPS man came. Saw him out the window. And then Lee called me and said to let Max out."

Reynolds interrupted. "Did he call from the building?"

"Don't know. The connection was a little scratchy, like one of those cellular phones, maybe. But the thing is, I didn't see him leave the building. Guess he could have gone out the back and down the fire escape, though."

"How did he sound?"

Mrs. Carter patted her hands together while she thought. "Well, I guess I have to say he was agitated about something. I was surprised he wanted me to let Max back out. I mean, I had just gotten him settled, like I told you. Lee said he needed to give the dog a shot or something. Now that didn't make any sense to me, but I did what Lee told me and then all hell broke loose after that."

"This UPS man, did you see him?"

Mrs. Carter snorted. "He wasn't the UPS man. I mean, he had on the uniform and everything, but he wasn't our regular UPS person."

"Maybe a replacement. A substitute."

"I've never seen a UPS man carrying a gun before, have you?"

"So you saw a gun?"

She nodded. "When he came running back down the steps. He had a gun in one hand, and his other hand was bleeding. But I'm getting ahead of myself. Before that I heard Max barking like I've never heard him bark before. Then there was a scuffle, could hear it clear as day. Feet stomping, a man yelling, Max's claws on the wood floor. Then I heard a thud and then I heard poor old Max howl. Then somebody started beating on Lee's door. The next thing I know, I hear a bunch of feet going up the fire escape. I looked out the window of my kitchen and saw all these men running up the fire escape. It was like I was watching a TV show. I went back to the front door and looked out my peephole. That's when I saw the UPS man go out the front door. Guess he went around back and joined the others. I'm not sure."

Connie leaned forward in his chair. "Did these other men have any type of uniforms on?"

Mrs. Carter looked at him strangely. "Well, you of all people should know."

Reynolds looked at her, confused. "What do you mean?"

But Mrs. Carter hurried on with her story. "When they knocked the back door in, the alarm went off. The police came right off."

"What happened when the police came?"

"The men were still here. At least some of them were."

"Did the police arrest them?"

"Of course not. The police took Max away and let them keep searching the place."

Reynolds exclaimed, "Do you have any idea why the police let them stay?"

"Same reason I let you in the door."

Reynolds looked in shock at Connie and then back at Carter and said, "You mean—"

"I mean," Carter broke in testily, "they were the FBI."

TWENTY-FIVE

"What exactly are we doing here, Lee?" Faith asked. They had taken two other cabs after the one from the airport. The last taxi had dropped them off in what seemed like the middle of nowhere, and they had been walking along back streets now for what seemed like several miles.

Lee glanced at her. "Rule number one when running from the law: Assume they'll find the cabbie or cabbies who dropped you off. So you never let a cabbie drop you off at your real destination." He pointed up ahead. "We're almost there." As he walked along, Lee put his hands up to his eyes and popped out the contact lenses, returning his eyes to their normal blue. He put the lenses away in a special case in his bag. "Those suckers kill my eyes."

Faith stared ahead but saw nothing other than run-down homes, cracked sidewalks and sickly-looking trees and lawns. They were traveling parallel to U.S. Route 1 in Virginia, also known as Jefferson Davis Highway after the president of the Confederacy. It was ironic they were here, Faith thought, since Davis himself knew very well about being chased. In fact he had been chased all over the South after the war until the boys in blue had finally caught up with him and Davis had served a long prison term. Faith knew the history, she just didn't want the same result.

She didn't ordinarily come to this part of northern

Virginia. It was heavily industrialized, speckled with on-the-fringe small businesses, truck and boat repair shops, shady-looking car dealerships working out of rusted trailers, and a flea market housed in a decrepit building one failing support beam from condemnation. She was a little surprised when Lee turned and headed for Jeff Davis. She hurried to stay up with him.

"Shouldn't we be getting out of town? I mean, according to you, the FBI can do anything. And then there's the other people you refused to name who are on our track. I'm sure they're incredibly deadly in their own right. And here we are strolling through the suburbs." Lee said nothing and she finally grabbed his arm. "Lee, will you please tell me what's going on?"

He stopped so abruptly she bumped into him. It was like hitting a wall.

Lee glared at her. "Call me stupid, but I just can't shake the feeling that the more information you have, the more likely you'll get another harebrained idea in your head that'll end up getting us both checked into coffins."

"Look, I'm sorry about the airport. You're right, it was stupid. But I had my reasons."

"Your reasons are bullshit. Your whole life is bullshit," he said angrily, and started walking again.

She hurried up next to him, jerked on his arm and they squared off.

"Okay, if you really feel like that, what do you say we just go our separate ways? Here and now. Each take our chances."

He put his hands on his hips. "Because of you I can't go home and I can't use my credit card. I don't have my gun, the Feds are right on my butt and I've got four bucks in my wallet. Let me just jump right on that offer, lady."

"You can have half my cash."

"And where exactly are you going to go?"

"My whole life might be bullshit, and this may shock you, but I *can* take care of myself."

He shook his head. "We stick together. For a lot of reasons. Number one being when and if the Feds pick us up, I want you right there next to me swearing on your mother's grave that yours truly is just an innocent babe stuck in the middle of *your* nightmare."

"Lee!"

"Discussion closed."

He started walking fast and Faith decided against saying anything else. The truth was she didn't *want* to go it alone. She jogged up to him as they turned on to Route 1. At the light they hurried across the street.

"I want you to wait here," Lee said, putting the bags down. "There's a chance I might get recognized where I'm going, and I don't want you with me."

Faith looked around. Behind her was an eight-foot-high chain-link fence with barbed wire on the top. It housed a boat repair facility. Inside the fence a Doberman patrolled the area. Did boats really require that much security? she wondered. Maybe in this area everything did. The business on the next corner was located inside an ugly cinder-block building with big red banners across the windows proclaiming the best deals in town on new and used motorcycles. The parking lot was filled with the two-wheeled machines.

"Do I *have* to stay here by myself?" she said.

Lee pulled out a baseball cap from his bag and put on his sunglasses. "Yes," he said curtly. "Or was that a ghost back there telling me she can take care of herself?"

With no snappy reply coming to mind, Faith had to content herself with angrily watching as Lee hurried across the street and into the motorcycle shop. As she waited, she suddenly sensed a presence behind her. When she turned, she was staring directly at the large Doberman. It had wandered out of the yard. Apparently the boat yard's tight security didn't include closing the damn gate! When the animal showed its teeth and uttered a low, terrifying growl, Faith slowly reached down and gripped the bags. Holding them in front of her, she backed across the street and into the parking lot of the motorcycle shop. The Dobie lost interest in her and went back inside the boat yard.

Faith breathed a sigh of relief and put down the bags. She noted a couple of fleshy teenagers sporting sparse goatees checking out a used Yamaha at the same time they were ogling her. She pulled her baseball cap down farther, turned away and pretended to examine a shiny red Kawasaki that was, surprise, on sale. Across Jeff Davis was a business that leased heavy construction equipment. She looked at a crane that rose a good thirty feet in the air. Dangling from its cable was a small forklift that had a sign painted across it that read, RENT ME. Everywhere she looked was a world she no longer knew much about. She had traveled a much different circuit: capital cities of the world, high political stakes, demanding clients, enormous amounts of power and money, all perpetually shifting like the continental plates. Things got crushed in between these masses all the time, and no one even knew it. She suddenly realized that the *real* world was a two-ton forklift dangling like a guppy on a string. Rent me. Employ people. Build something.

But Danny had given her a shot at redemption. She was a dime a dozen, yet she had been doing some good in the world. For ten years now she had been helping people who desperately needed it. Perhaps also these ten years she'd been atoning for the vicarious guilt she'd felt growing up, watching her father's shenanigans, however well intentioned, and all the pain they had caused. She had actually been afraid to ever analyze that part of her life too deeply.

Faith heard footsteps behind her and turned around. The man was dressed in jeans, black boots and a sweatshirt with the logo of the motorcycle shop printed across it. He was young, early twenties, big, sleepy eyes, tall, slender and good-looking. And he knew it, she could readily tell, by his cocky manner. His expression clearly evidenced that his interest in Faith was deeper than her choice in two-wheeled transportation.

"Can I help you with anything, ma'am? Anything at all?"

"Just browsing. I'm waiting for my boyfriend."

"Hey, this is a pretty machine over here." He pointed to a BMW cycle that just reeked, even to Faith's untrained eye, of money. Wasted money, in her opinion. But then again, wasn't she the proud owner of a big BMW sedan, which sat in the garage of her very expensive digs in McLean?

He rubbed one hand slowly across the Beemer's gas tank. "Purrs like a kitten. You take care of beautiful things, they take good care of you. Real good." A big smile broke across his features as he said this. He looked her over and winked.

Faith wondered if this was his best pickup line.

"I don't drive them, I just ride on them," she said casually, and then regretted her choice of words.

He smiled broadly. "Well, that's the best news I've heard all day. In fact, you just made my whole year. Just ride 'em, huh?" The young man laughed and clapped his hands together. "Well, how about we go for a spin, sweet thing? You can check out *my* equipment. Just climb on."

Her face flashed. "I don't appreciate your—"

"Now, don't go getting mad. If you need anything, my name's Rick." He held out his card and winked at her again. He added in a low voice, "Home phone's on the back, babe."

She looked at the card in his hand with distaste. "Okay, Rick, but I like full disclosure. My boyfriend is inside. Are you man enough to meet him?"

Rick didn't look so comfortable now. "I'm man enough for anything, babe."

"Good to hear. My boyfriend is inside. He's about your height, but he's got a real man's body."

The hand holding the card dropped to Rick's side as he scowled at her. Faith easily sensed that his pat lines had been forgotten and his mind was too slow to think of new ones.

Faith eyed him closely. "Yeah, his shoulders are about the size of Nebraska, and did I mention he's an ex-Navy boxing champ?"

"Is that right?" Rick pocketed his card.

"Don't take my word for it; he's right there. Go ahead and ask him." She pointed behind him.

Rick whirled around and watched as Lee came out of the building carrying two helmets and two one-piece riding suits. A map was stuffed into his front jacket pocket. Even under the bulky clothes he was wearing, Lee's impressive build was very apparent. He glared suspiciously at Rick.

"Do I know you?" Lee asked him gruffly.

Rick smiled uneasily and then swallowed with difficulty as he looked Lee over. "N-no, sir," he stammered.

"Then what the hell do you want, kid?"

Faith piped in, "Oh, he was just asking me the sorts of things I liked in my riding equipment, right,

Ricky?" She smiled at the young salesman.

"That's right. Yep. Well, see ya." Rick practically ran toward the shop.

"Bye-bye, sweet thing," Faith called after him.

Lee scowled at her. "I told you to wait across the street. Can I not leave you alone for one damn minute?"

"I had an encounter with a Dobie. Retreat seemed the wisest course."

"Right. What, were you negotiating with the guy to jump me so you can get away?"

"Don't get crazy on me, Lee."

"I kind of wished you had. It'd give me an excuse to kick the shit out of somebody. What'd he really want?"

"Junior wanted to sell me something, and it wasn't a motorcycle. What's that?" she asked, pointing at what he was carrying.

"Necessary equipment for motorcycle riders this time of year. At sixty miles an hour, there's a tiny bite in the air."

"We don't have a motorcycle."

"We do now."

She followed him around back to where an enormous Honda Gold Wing SE road bike sat. With its slick chrome and futuristic design, high-tech equipment and full windshield, the motorcycle looked like something Batman might tool around on. It was painted pearl-gray-green with dark gray green trim and had a king and queen seat with a padded backrest. The passenger would fit snugly there, like a ball in a glove. It was so big and elaborately equipped that it looked like an open-air recreational vehicle.

Lee stuck a key in the ignition and started putting on his suit. He handed the other outfit to Faith.

"Just where are we going on this thing?"

Lee zipped up his suit. "*We* are going to your little place in North Carolina."

"All that way on a motorcycle?"

"We can't rent a car without a credit card and ID. Your car and mine are useless. We can't take a train, plane or bus. They'll cover all those places. Unless you can sprout wings, this is it."

"I've never even been on a motorcycle."

He took off his shades. "You don't have to drive it. That's what I'm here for. So what do you say? Want to go for a ride?" He flashed a grin at her.

Faith felt as though a brick had hit her in the head when he said those words. Her skin was afire as she looked at him perched on that machine. And at that exact moment, as though by the will of God, the sun broke through the gloom. A shaft of light came down and ignited those already dazzling blue eyes into flame-filled sapphires. She found she couldn't move. Lord, she could barely breathe; her knees began to quiver.

It was fifth grade, recess. The boy with the man-size eyes the exact color of Lee's had ridden his bike with the banana seat up to where she sat on the swing reading a book.

"Want to go for a ride?" he had asked her. "No," she had said, and then immediately dropped her book and climbed on back. They were an "item" for two months, planning their lives together, vowing their undying love for each other, even though they never exchanged so much as a peck on the lips. Then her mother died, and Faith's father moved them away. She briefly wondered if Lee and he could be one and the same. She had banished the memory so completely from her subconscious that she couldn't even remember the boy's name. It could be Lee, couldn't it? She thought this because the only other time in her entire life when her knees had gone weak

204

was on that playground. The boy had said what Lee had just said, and the sun had hit those eyes just as it had smacked Lee's, and her heart felt as though it would explode if she didn't do exactly as he said. Just how it felt right now.

"Are you okay?" Lee asked.

Faith gripped one of the handlebars to steady herself, and said as calmly as she could, "And they're just going to let you drive off with it?"

"My brother runs the place. It's a demo. We're officially taking it for an extended test drive."

"I can't believe I'm doing this." Just like fifth grade, there was no way she could not get on that bike.

"Consider the alternative, and then the idea of your butt on this Honda starts looking beautiful." He slid his shades on and flipped his helmet's shield down as though putting an exclamation point on this statement.

Faith slipped on the suit, and with Lee's help managed to get the helmet on snugly. He loaded their bags into the Honda's spacious trunk and saddle pouches, and Faith climbed on behind him. He started the engine, gunned it for a moment or so and then hit the gas. When he released the clutch, the power of the Honda threw Faith back against the padded bar and she found herself clamping her arms and legs around Lee and the eight-hundred-pound motorcycle, respectively, as they rocketed on to Jeff Davis heading south.

She almost jumped off the bike when she heard the voice in her ear.

"Okay, calm down, it's a Chatterbox helmet-to-helmet audio link," Lee's voice said. He'd obviously felt her shock. "You ever driven down to your beach house?"

"No, I always flew."

"That's okay. I've got a map. We'll take 95 down and pick up Interstate 64 at Richmond. That'll get us to Norfolk. We'll figure out the best way from there. We'll grab something to eat on the way. We should make it before it gets too dark. Okay?"

She found herself nodding and then remembered to say, "Okay."

"Now, just sit back and relax. You're in good hands."

Instead, she leaned into him, circled her arms around his waist and held tightly. She was suddenly immersed in the recollection of those divine two months in fifth grade. This had to be an omen. Maybe they could drive off and never come back. Start at the Outer Banks, hire a boat and end up on a patch of soil somewhere in the Caribbean no one had ever been before, a place no one would ever see except for them. She could learn to keep a hut, cook with coconut milk or whatever they had there, be a good little homemaker while Lee was off catching fish. They could make love every night under the moonlight and there would be no one to complain. Or watch. She leaned farther into him. None of that sounded bad. Or too far-fetched, under the circumstances. None of it.

"Oh, and Faith?" Lee said into her ear.

She touched her helmet to his, felt the solid breadth of his torso against her breasts. She was twenty again, the wind was delicious, the warmth of the sun inspiring, her greatest worry a midterm exam. A sudden vision of them lying naked under the sky, skin brown, hair wet, limbs intertwined, made her wish they weren't in body suits with thick zippers, going sixty miles an hour over hard pavement.

"Yes?"

"If you even think about trying to pull another

206

stunt on me like at the airport, I'll use those good hands to wring your neck. Understand?"

She leaned away from him and rested her back against the sissy bar, pushing herself deep into the leather. And away from him. Her shining white knight with the bedeviling blue eyes.

So much for memories. So much for dreams.

TWENTY-SIX

The event was typical of Washington: A political fund-raising dinner at a downtown hotel. The chicken was stringy and cold, the wine cheap, the conversation high-powered, the stakes enormous, the protocol tricky, the egos often impossible. The attendees were either wealthy and/or well connected, or underpaid political staffers who worked long, frantic hours during the day and were rewarded for these prodigious efforts by being compelled to work these sorts of events at night. The Secretary of the Treasury was supposed to have attended, along with some other political heavy-weights; even since he had become engaged to a well-known Hollywood actress with a thing about exhibiting her cleavage at the drop of an intern, the secretary had been more in demand than the keeper of the cash normally was. Then, at the last minute, he had gotten a better offer to speak at another event, which was often the case in the endless game of "where is the political grass greener?" An underling had been sent in his place, a gawky, nervous person no one really knew or cared about.

The event was another opportunity to see and be seen, to check the ever-changing pecking order of a certain subgroup of the political hierarchy. Most never even sat down to eat. They just dropped off their check and then it was off to another fund-raiser. Networking flowed through the room as though from a well-fed spring. Or open wound, depending on how one looked at it.

Danny Buchanan surveyed the room. How many of these events had he attended over the years? During the frenzy of key fund-raising periods when he used to represent Big Business, Buchanan would attend breakfasts, luncheons, dinners and assorted parties nonstop for weeks. Exhausted, he had sometimes shown up at the wrong event – a reception for the senator from North Dakota instead of a dinner for the South Dakota congressman. After taking over for the world's poor, he had no such problems, for the simple fact that he now had no money to give members. However, Buchanan was well aware that if there was one truism in political fund-raising, it was that there was never enough money. And that meant that there would *always* be the opportunity for influence peddling. Always.

After he got back from Philly, his day had really started. He had met with half a dozen different members on the Hill and their staff on a myriad of matters, and set up appointments for future meetings. Staffs were important, particularly committee staff, especially appropriations committee staff. Members came and went. The staff tended to stay forever; they knew the issues and process cold. And Danny knew that you never wanted to surprise a member by trying to dodge the staff. You might be successful once, but you were dead after that, as the angry aides took their revenge by shutting you completely out.

A late luncheon followed, with a paying client whom Faith had typically taken care of. Buchanan had had to make excuses for her absence, and he did so with his usual aplomb and humor. "Sorry, you get the second string today," he told the client. "But I'll try not to mess things up too badly for you."

Though there was no need to bolster Faith's

excellent reputation, Buchanan had recounted to this client the story of how Faith had once personally hand-delivered – in a gift box with a big red ribbon, no less – to all five hundred and thirty-five members of Congress detailed polling data that showed the American public was fully in support of funding for global vaccination of all children. She'd included in the gift box accompanying briefing materials and before-and-after photos of vaccinated children from distant lands. Sometimes pictures were the most important weapons Danny and she had. Then she had worked the phone for thirty-six hours straight enlisting support here and overseas and made exhaustive presentations with several of the larger international relief organizations over a two-week period on three continents to show just how such a thing could be accomplished. How important it was. The result: passage of a bill in Congress that supported a study to determine if such an endeavor could work. Now consultants would rack up millions of dollars in fees and kill several forests of trees for the mountains of paper the study would generate (to justify the enormous consulting fees, of course), with no assurances that a single child would receive a single dose of vaccine.

"A small success, to be sure, but a step forward," Buchanan had told the client. "When Faith goes after something, stay out of her way." The client already knew this about Faith, Buchanan was aware. Perhaps he was just saying it to bolster his own spirits. Perhaps he just wanted to talk about Faith. He had been hard on her the last year, very hard. Terrified that she would be drawn into his Thornhillian nightmare, he had outright pushed her away. Well, he had succeeded in driving her right into the arms of the FBI, it seemed. *I'm sorry, Faith.*

After the luncheon it was back to the Hill, where

Buchanan waited with a handful of Rolaids on a series of floor votes. He sent in his cards to the floor asking for time from some of the members. He would buttonhole others as they came off the elevator.

"Foreign debt relief is essential, Senator," he individually told more than a dozen members, hustling along beside them and their overly protective entourage. "They're spending more on debt payments than on health and education," Danny would plead. "What good is a strong balance sheet when the population is dying at the rate of ten percent a year? They'll have great credit and not a damn person left to use it. Let's spread the wealth here."

"Right, right, Danny, we'll get back to you. Send me some materials." Like the petals of a flower closing up for the night, the entourage would close ranks around the member, and Danny the bee would be off to gather other nectar.

Congress was an ecosystem just as complicated as the one existing in the oceans. As Danny trolled the corridors, he looked at the activity swirling all around. True to their titles, whips were everywhere prodding members to follow party line. Back in the whip's chamber, Buchanan knew the phones were constantly being worked with the same goal in mind. Gofers scurried down the corridors in search of people more important than themselves. Small groups of people huddled in pockets of the broad hallways, discussing matters of importance with solemn, downcast expressions. Men and women pushed on to crowded elevators with the hope of snaring a few precious seconds with a member whose support they desperately needed. Members talked with each other, laying the groundwork for future deals or reaffirming agreements already struck. It was all chaotic and yet possessed a certain

211

order, as people coupled and uncoupled like robotic arms around hunks of metal on an assembly line. Give a touch here and on to the next one. Danny dared to think that his work might be as exhausting as childbirth; and he would swear it was more exhilarating than skydiving. Buchanan was thoroughly addicted to it. As crazy as it sounded, he would miss it.

"Get back to me?" was his typical closing to each member's aide.

"Of course, you can count on it," would be each aide's typical response.

And, of course, he'd never hear back. But they would hear from him. Again and again, until they got it. You just fired your shotgun pellets and hoped one stuck somewhere.

Next, Buchanan had spent a few minutes with one of his "chosen few," going over the language Buchanan wanted to insert in a line amendment in a bill's report. Almost no one ever read the report language, but it was in the monotonous details that important actions were accomplished. In this case, the language would tell the managers at AID precisely how funding approved by the underlying bill was to be spent.

With the verbiage in good shape, Buchanan mentally checked that off his list and went prowling again for other members. From years of practice, Buchanan navigated with ease the labyrinths of the Senate and House office buildings where even veterans of the Hill sometimes became lost. The only other place where he spent as much time was the Capitol itself. His eyes darted left and right, picking up on everyone he saw, staff members or other lobbyists, swiftly making a calculation as to whether a particular person could help the cause or not. And when you went into chambers with members or caught them in the halls, you had better be ready to roll. They were busy, often harassed, and thinking of five hundred things at once.

Fortunately, Buchanan could summarize the most complex issues in a matter of sentences, a talent for which he was legendary; members, besieged on all sides by special interests of every kind, absolutely demanded this skill. And he could pitch his client's position with passion. All in two minutes while walking down a crowded corridor or while packed inside an elevator or, if he was very lucky, on a long plane flight. Catching the really powerful members was important. If he could get the Speaker of the House to voice support for one of his bills, even informally, Buchanan would use that to leverage other members on the fence. Sometimes that was enough.

"He in, Doris?" Buchanan asked as he popped his head into a member's chambers and eyed the matronly appointments secretary, a veteran of the place.

"He's leaving in five minutes to catch a flight, Danny."

"That's great because I only need two minutes. I can use the other three to catch up with you. I like talking to you better anyway. And God bless Steve, but you're far easier on the eye, my dear."

Doris's heavy face crinkled into a smile. "You smoothie, you."

And he got his two minutes with Congressman Steve.

Buchanan next had stopped at the cloakroom and found out which Senate committees had been assigned to a series of bills he was interested in. There were committees of primary and sequential and, in rare cases, concurrent jurisdiction, depending on what was in a particular bill. Simply

213

determining who had what bill and in what priority of importance was a huge, ever-changing jigsaw puzzle that lobbyists had to constantly figure out. It was often a maddening challenge, and there was no one better at it than Danny Buchanan.

In the course of this day Buchanan had, as always, plied members' offices with his "leave behinds," information and summaries the staff would need to educate their members on the issues. If they had a question or concern, he would find an answer or an expert, promptly. And Buchanan had concluded every single meeting with the all-important question: "When can I follow up?" Without getting a date certain, he would never hear back from any of them. He would be forgotten, his place taken by a hundred others clamoring just as passionately for their clients.

Then he had spent the late afternoon covering other clients normally handled by Faith. He gave apologies and vague explanations for her absence. What else could he do?

After that he gave remarks at a think-tank-sponsored seminar on world hunger, and then it was back to his office to make phone calls ranging from reminding members' staffs of a variety of issues coming up for vote, to drumming up coalition support from other charitable organizations. A couple of dinners were arranged, future overseas travel booked, along with a visit in January to the White House, where he would personally introduce the President to the new head of an international children's right organization. It was a real coup that Buchanan and the organizations he supported hoped would generate some good publicity. They were constantly on the lookout for celebrity support. Faith had been particularly good at that. Journalists were rarely interested in the poor from faraway lands, but throw in a Hollywood superstar and the media room would be bustling with scribes. Such was life.

Then Buchanan had spent some time doing his FARA – or Foreign Agent Registration Act – quarterly reports, which were a real pain in the ass, particularly since you had to stamp every page filed with Congress with the ominous label "foreign propaganda," as if you were Tokyo Rose calling for the overthrow of the U.S. government, instead of, in Danny's case, selling his soul to get crop seeds and powdered milk.

After bending a few more ears on the phone, then studying a few hundred pages of briefing materials, he had decided to call it a day. A glamorous day in the life of a typical Washington lobbyist, which usually ended with him collapsing into bed, except that today he did not have that luxury. Instead, he was here in this downtown hotel, attending yet another political fund-raiser, and the reason was standing in the far corner of the room sipping a glass of white wine and looking extremely bored. Buchanan headed over.

"You look like you could use something stronger than white wine."

Senator Russell Ward turned and a smile broke across his face as he looked at Buchanan. "It's good to see an honest face in this sea of iniquity, Danny."

"How about we trade this place for the Monocle?"

Ward put his glass down on a table. "Best offer I've had all day."

TWENTY-SEVEN

The Monocle was a restaurant of longstanding on Capitol Hill's Senate side. The restaurant, and the U.S. Capitol Police building, which itself used to be an Immigration and Naturalization building, were the only two structures left in this location that formerly housed a long row of buildings. The Monocle was a favorite place for politicians, lobbyists and VIPs to gather for lunch, dinner and drinks.

The maître d' welcomed Buchanan and Ward by name and ushered the pair to a private corner table. The decor was conservative, the walls adorned with enough photographs of past and present politicians to fill the Washington Monument. The food was good, yet people didn't come for the delights of the menus; they came to be seen, do business and talk shop. Ward and Buchanan were regulars here.

They ordered drinks and perused the menu for a moment.

As Ward studied his menu, Buchanan studied him.

Russell Ward had been called Rusty for as long as Buchanan could remember. And that was a long time, since the two had grown up together. As chairman of the Senate Select Committee on Intelligence, Ward was a powerful influence on the well-being – or not – of all the country's intelligence agencies. He was smart, politically savvy, honest, hard-working, and he came from a very wealthy northeast family that had lost its fortune when Ward was a young man. He had gone south to Raleigh and methodically built himself a career in public service. He was North Carolina's senior senator and worshipped by the entire state. Under Buchanan's classification system, Rusty Ward would be absolutely labeled a "Believer." He was familiar with every political game ever played. Ward knew all the inside stories on everyone in this town. He knew people's strengths and, more important, their weaknesses. Physically, the man was a wreck, Buchanan knew, with problems ranging from diabetes to the prostate. Yet mentally, Ward was sharp as ever. Those who underestimated the man's massive intellect because of the physical ailments had all lived to regret it.

Ward looked up from his menu. "Anything interesting on your plate these days, Danny?"

Ward's voice was deep and sonorous, and so wonderfully southern, all traces of clipped Yankee long gone. Buchanan could sit and listen to the man for hours. And he had done so on many occasions.

Buchanan replied, "Same old, same old. You?"

"Had an interesting hearing this morning. Senate Intelligence. CIA."

"Is that right?"

"You ever hear of a gentleman by the name of Thornhill? Robert Thornhill?"

Buchanan's features were impassive. "Can't say that I know the man at all. Tell me about him."

"He's one of the old powers there. Associate DDO. Smart, cunning, lies his ass off with the best of them. I don't trust him."

"Doesn't sound like you should."

"I have to give the man his due though. He's done terrific work, outlasted numerous CIA directors. Really served his country extraordinarily well. He's actually a legend over there. They let him do more or less what he wants because of that. Such a policy, however, is dangerous."

"Really? He sounds like a real patriot."

"That's what worries me. People who believe themselves to be true patriots tend to be zealots. Zealots, in my opinion, are one short step from lunatics. History has given us enough examples of that." Ward grinned. "I remember this one time he came in to deliver the usual bullshit. He looked so smug I decided I had to tweak him a little."

Buchanan looked very interested. "How'd you do that?"

"I asked him about death squads." Ward paused and looked around for a moment. "We've had problems with the CIA over that in the past. They fund these little insurgency groups, outfit and train 'em, then turn 'em loose, like an old coon dog. Then, unlike a good coon dog, they go and do things they weren't supposed to be doing. At least according to the official agency rules."

"What'd he say to that?"

"Well, it wasn't part of his little script. He looked through his briefing book like he was attempting to shake out a small band of armed men." Ward laughed deeply. "Then he threw me some gobbledy-gook that really amounted to nothing. Said that the 'new' CIA was merely a collector and analyzer of information. When I asked him if he was conceding that there was something wrong with the 'old' CIA, I thought he might come over the table at me." Ward laughed again. "Same old, same old."

"So what's he up to now that's got you ticked off?"

Ward smiled. "Trying to get me to reveal confidences?"

"Of course."

Ward glanced around again and then leaned

218

forward and spoke quietly. "He was withholding information, what else? You know the spooks, Danny, they want more and more funding but when you start to ask questions about what they're doing with that money, Jesus, it's like you killed their mother. But what else am I going to do when I'm presented with reports from the CIA's inspector general that have so many damn redactions the paper looks black? So I brought that fact to Mr. Thornhill's attention."

"How did he react to that? Pissed off? Cool and collected?"

"Why are you so curious about him?"

"You started it, Rusty. Don't blame me if I find your work fascinating."

"Well, he said those reports had to be censored to protect the identities of intelligence sources. That it was a very fine line and that the CIA walked it the best it could. I told him that it was kind of like my granddaughter playing hopscotch. She can't hit all the squares just right, so she misses some of them on purpose. I told him it was damn cute. When *little kids* did it.

"Now, I have to give the man his due. He made some sense. He said that it's a delusion that we're going to knock out entrenched dictators with simple satellite photos and high-speed modems. We need old-fashioned assets on the ground. We need people inside their organizations, within their inner circles. That's the only way we win. I understand that well enough. But the arrogance of the man, well, it gets to me. And I'm convinced that even if Robert Thornhill had no reason to lie, the man still wouldn't tell the truth. Hell, he has this little system where he taps his pen against the table and one of his aides pretends to whisper in his ear so he'll have a couple extra breaths to think of some lie. He's been using that same code all these years. I guess he thinks I'm some kind of horse's ass and wouldn't ever catch on."

"I'd like to think this Thornhill fellow knows better than to underestimate you."

"Oh, he's good. I have to admit he got the better of today's jousting. I mean, the man can say absolutely nothing and make it sound as strong and noble as the Ten Commandments. And when he got backed into a corner, he pulled out his national security bullshit counting on the fact that it would scare everybody to death. Bottom line: He promised me all these answers. And I told him I looked forward to working with him." Ward sipped his water. "Yep, he won today. But there's always tomorrow."

The waiter returned with their drinks and they gave their orders. Buchanan worked on a glass of Scotch and water while Ward nuzzled a bourbon, neat.

"So how's your better half? Faith burning the midnight oil for another client looking to ravage us poor, defenseless elected officials?"

"Actually, right now I believe she's out of town. Personal reasons."

"Nothing serious, I hope."

Buchanan shrugged. "Jury's still out on that. I'm sure she'll pull through."

"I guess we're all survivors. I don't know how much longer this tired old carcass of mine will hold out, though."

Buchanan raised his drink. "Outlive us all, word of Danny Buchanan."

"God, I hope not." Ward looked at him keenly. "It's hard to believe that it's been forty years since we left Bryn Mawr. You know, sometimes I envy you having grown up in that apartment over our garage."

Buchanan smiled. "Funny, I was jealous of you for

220

growing up in the mansion with all that money while my family waited on yours. Now which of us sounds drunk?"

"You're the best friend I ever had."

"And you know that sentiment is reciprocated, Senator."

"It's even more remarkable that you've never asked me for a damn thing. You damn well know I sit on a couple committees that could help your causes."

"I like to avoid the appearance of impropriety."

"You must be the only one in this town." Ward chuckled.

"Let's just say our friendship is more important to me than even that."

Ward spoke softly. "I never told you, but what you said at my mother's funeral touched me deeply. I swear, I think you knew the woman better than I did."

"She was a class act. Taught me all I ever needed to know about everything. She deserved a grand sendoff. What I said didn't come close by half."

Ward stared into his glass. "If my stepfather could have only lived off my family's inheritance and not tried to play businessman we might have kept the estate, and he wouldn't have taken his head off with a shotgun. But then maybe I wouldn't have gotten to play senator all these years if I'd had a trust fund to blow."

"If more people played the game the way you do, Rusty, the country would be far better off."

"I wasn't fishing for a compliment, but I appreciate you saying it."

Buchanan drummed his fingers against the table. "I drove out to the old place the other day."

Ward looked up, surprised. "Why?"

Buchanan shrugged. "Not really sure. I was close

by, I had some time. It hasn't changed much. Still beautiful."

"I haven't been there since I left for college. Don't even know who owns it now."

"A young couple. I saw the wife and kids through the gate, playing on the front lawn. Investment banker or Internet mogul, probably. An idea and ten bucks in his pocket yesterday, a red-hot company and a hundred million in stock today."

Ward lifted his glass. "God bless America."

"If I had had the money back then, your mother wouldn't have lost that house."

"I know that, Danny."

"But everything happens for a reason, Rusty. Like you said, you might not have gone into politics. You've had a grand career. You're a Believer."

Ward smiled. "Your little classification system has always intrigued me. You have it all written down somewhere? I'd like to compare it with my own conclusions about my distinguished colleagues."

Buchanan tapped his forehead. "It's all up here."

"All that gold, stored in one man's brain. What a pity."

"You know everything about everybody in this town too." Buchanan paused and then added quietly, "So what do you know about me?"

Ward seemed surprised by the question.

"Don't tell me the world's greatest lobbyist is having self-doubt? I thought the book on Daniel J. Buchanan was unshakable confidence, encyclopedic mind and a keen insight into the psychology of windbag politicians and their innate weaknesses, which could fill the Pacific, by the way."

"Everybody has doubts, Rusty, even people like you and me. That's why we last so long. One inch from the edge. Death at any minute if you let down your guard."

The way he said this made Ward drop his amused look. "You got something you'd like to talk about?"

"Not in a million years," Buchanan said with a sudden smile. "If I start telling the sorry likes of you all my secrets, then I'll have to take my lemonade stand somewhere else and start over. And I'm way too old for that."

Ward leaned back against the soft cushion and looked his friend over. "What makes you do it, Danny? Not money, surely."

Buchanan slowly nodded in agreement. "If I did it solely for the dollars, I would've been gone ten years ago." He swallowed the rest of his drink and looked over at the doorway, where the ambassador from Italy and his substantial entourage stood, along with several senior Hill staffers, a couple of senators and three women in short black dresses who looked like they had been rented for the evening, and very well might have been. The Monocle was filling up with so many VIPs now you could hardly spit without nailing some leader of something. And they all wanted the world. And they all wanted you to get it for them. Eat you up and leave nothing and then call you a friend. Buchanan knew all the lyrics to that song.

He looked up at an old photograph on the wall. A bald-headed man with a beak nose, dour look and ferocious eyes peered down at him. Long dead now, he had once been one of the most powerful men in Washington for decades. And most feared. Power and fear seemed to go hand in hand here. Now Buchanan couldn't even remember the man's name. Didn't that speak volumes.

Ward put down his glass. "I think I know. Your causes have become much more benevolent over the years. You're out to save a world few even care about. You're really the only lobbyist I know who does it."

Buchanan shook his head. "A poor Irish lad who brought himself up by the bootstraps and made a fortune sees the light and then uses his golden years helping the less fortunate? Hell, Rusty, I'm driven more by fear than altruism."

Ward looked at him curiously. "How's that?"

Buchanan sat up very straight, put his palms together and cleared his throat. He had never told anyone this. Not even Faith. Maybe it was time. He would look insane, of course, but at least Rusty would keep it to himself.

"I have this recurring dream, you see. In my dream America keeps getting richer and richer, fatter and fatter. Where an athlete gets a hundred million dollars to bounce a ball, a movie star earns twenty million to act in trash and a model gets ten million to walk around in her underwear. Where a nineteen-year-old can make a billion dollars in stock options by using the Internet to sell us more things we don't need faster than ever." Buchanan stopped and smiled grimly at his bread plate. "And where a lobbyist can earn enough to buy his own plane. We keep hoarding the wealth of the world. Anybody gets in the way, we crush them, in a hundred different ways, while selling them the message of America the Beautiful. The world's remaining superpower, right?

"Then, little by little, the rest of the world wakes up and sees us for what we are: a fraud. And they start coming for us. In log boats and propeller planes and God knows how else. First by the thousands, then by the millions and then by the billions. And they wipe us out. Stuff us all down some pipe and flush us for good. You, me, the ballplayers, the movie stars, the supermodels, Wall Street,

Hollywood and Washington. The true land of make believe."

Ward stared at him wide eyed. "My God, a dream or a nightmare?"

Buchanan shot him a stern glance. "You tell me."

"Your country, love it or leave it, Danny. There's an element of truth in that slogan. We're not so bad."

"We also suck up a disproportionate share of the wealth and energy in the world. We pollute more than any other country. We trash foreign economies and never look back. But still, for a lot of big and small reasons that I really can't explain, I do love my country. That's why this nightmare disturbs me so much. *I don't want it to happen.* But it's getting harder and harder to feel any hope."

"If that's the case, why *do* you do it?"

Buchanan stared at the old photograph again and said, "Do you want something pithy or philosophical?"

"How about the truth?"

Buchanan looked at his old friend. "I deeply regret never having children," he began slowly, then paused. "A good friend of mine has a dozen grandchildren. He was telling me about a PTA meeting he had attended at his granddaughter's elementary school. I asked him why he was bothering with doing that. Wasn't that the parents' job? I said. You know what he told me? He said that with the way the world is now, we all have to think about things beyond our lifetime. Beyond our children's lifetime, in fact. It's our right. It's our duty, my good friend told me."

Buchanan smoothed out his napkin. "So maybe I do what I do because the sum of the world's tragedies outweighs its happiness.

"Other than that, I haven't the faintest idea."

TWENTY-EIGHT

Brooke Reynolds was just finished saying grace, and they all started on their meals. She had burst through the door ten minutes earlier, determined to eat dinner with her family. Her regular hours at the Bureau were eight-fifteen A.M. to five P.M. That was the funniest joke at the Bureau: regular hours. She had changed into jeans and a sweatshirt and exchanged her suede flats for Reeboks. Reynolds took much pleasure in scooping out spoonfuls of peas and mashed potatoes for all their plates. Rosemary poured out milk for the kids while her teenage daughter Theresa helped three-year-old David cut up his meat. It was a nice, quiet family gathering, which Reynolds had come to cherish and which she did everything possible to make each evening, even if it meant going back to work later.

Reynolds rose from the table and poured herself a glass of white wine. While half her brain focused on finding Faith Lockhart and her new confederate, Lee Adams, the other part was looking ahead with much anticipation to Halloween, less than a week away. Sydney, her six-year-old daughter, was dead set on being Eeyore, for the second year in a row. David would be the bouncy Tigger, a character that fit the perpetual-motion child perfectly. After that, Thanksgiving, perhaps a trip to her parents' in Florida, if she could find the time. Then Christmas. This year Reynolds was taking the kids to see Santa

Claus. She had missed last year because of – what else? – Bureau business. This year she would pull her 9mm on anyone who tried to stop her appointment with Kris Kringle. All in all, a good plan, if she could just make it work. Conception was easy; execution was the key that so often fell out of the lock.

As she put the cork back in the bottle, she looked sadly around a home that would not be hers much longer. Her son and daughter sensed that the change was coming. David hadn't slept through the night in over a week. Reynolds, home after working fifteen-hour days, would hold the quivering, wailing little boy, trying to calm him, rock him back to sleep. She tried to tell him that things would be just fine, when she was as uncertain as anyone whether they would be. It was sometimes terrifying being a parent, particularly in the midst of a divorce and all the pain it caused, which you saw every day etched into the faces of your children. More than once Reynolds had thought about calling off the divorce for that reason alone. But hanging on for the sake of the children wasn't the answer, she felt. At least not for her. They would have a better life without the man than they'd had with him. And her ex, she thought, might be a better father after the divorce than he had been before. Well, at least she could hope. Reynolds simply did not want to let her children down.

When Reynolds caught her daughter Sydney looking apprehensively at her, she smiled as naturally as she could. Sydney was six going on sixteen, so mature beyond her years that it scared Reynolds to death. She picked up on everything, missed nothing of significance. Reynolds had never in her career interrogated a suspect as thoroughly as Sydney did her mother nearly every day. The child dug deep, trying to understand what was going on, what their future would hold, and Reynolds had no ready answers for any of it.

More than once, she had found Sydney holding her crying brother in his bed late at night, attempting to soothe him, relieve his fears. Reynolds had recently told her daughter that she didn't need to assume the responsibility too, that her mother would always be there. Her statement had a hollow ring, and Sydney's face plainly showed a lack of belief. The fact that her daughter had not accepted this statement as dead, solid truth had aged Reynolds several years in several seconds. The memory of the palm reader and her predictions of premature death had come back to roost with a vengeance.

"Rosemary's chicken is awesome, isn't it, honey?" Reynolds said to Sydney.

The little girl nodded.

"Thank you, ma'am," Rosemary said, pleased.

"Are you okay, Mom?" Sydney asked. At the same time, she moved her little brother's milk away from the edge of the table. David had a propensity for spilling any liquid within his reach.

That subtle act of motherhood and her daughter's earnest question moved Reynolds almost to tears. She had been on such an emotional roller coaster of late that it didn't take much to set her off. She took a sip of wine, hoping it would prevent her from actually collapsing into a crying fit. It was like being pregnant again. The littlest thing affected her as if it were life or death. But then her common sense kicked in. She was a mom, things would work out. She had the luxury of a devoted live-in nanny. Sitting around whining, feeling sorry for yourself, wasn't the answer. So their life wasn't perfect. Whose was? She thought of what Anne Newman was going through right now. Suddenly Reynolds's problems didn't seem so bad.

"Everything's really good, Syd. Really good. Congratulations on your spelling test. Ms. Betack said you were the star of the day."

"I like school a lot."

"And it shows, young lady."

Reynolds was about to sit back down when the phone rang. She had caller ID and checked the readout screen. The ID screen came up blank. The caller must have ID block or his number was unlisted. She debated whether to answer it or not. The problem was that every FBI agent she knew had unlisted numbers. Ordinarily, though, anyone from the Bureau would call her on her pager or cell phone, both of which numbers she closely guarded; and calls to those two she would always answer. It was probably a random computer dialer and she would be told to wait until a real person came on and tried to sell her a time-share in Disney World. Still, something made her reach out and pick up the phone.

"Hello?"

"Brooke?"

Anne Newman sounded distressed. And as she listened to the woman, Reynolds sensed that there was something in addition to her husband's violent death – poor Anne, what worse could there be?

"I'll be there in thirty minutes," Reynolds said.

She grabbed her coat and car keys, took a bite out of a slice of the bread on her plate and kissed her children.

"Will you be back in time to read us a story, Mom?" Sydney asked.

"Three bears, three pigs, three goats." David promptly recited his favorite nighttime storytelling ritual to Brooke, his favorite story reader. His sister Sydney favored reading the stories herself, every night, sounding out each word along the way. Little David now took a big gulp of milk, loudly burped and then excused himself in a fit of laughter.

Reynolds smiled. Sometimes when she was tired she would tell the stories so fast they almost blurred together. The pigs built their houses, the bears went for their walk while Goldilocks burglarized the joint and the three billy goats gruff trounced the evil troll and lived happily ever after in their new pasture of grass. Sounded nice. Where could she buy some? And then, undressing for bed, Reynolds would endure spasms of crushing guilt. The reality was that her kids would be grown and gone before she blinked her eyes twice, and she routinely short-changed them on three short fairy tales because she wanted to do something so unimportant as sleep. Sometimes it was better not to think too much. Reynolds was a classic over-achiever and a perfectionist, to boot, while a "perfect parent" was the world's greatest oxymoron.

"I'll try my best. I promise."

The disappointed look on her daughter's face made Reynolds turn and flee the room. She stopped at the small room on the first floor that served as her study. From the top of a cabinet she removed a squat, heavy metal box, which she unlocked. Removing her SIG 9mm, she loaded in a fresh mag, pulled the slide back to chamber a round, clicked the safety on, slid the weapon in her clip holster and was out the door before she could think any more about another interrupted meal in a long string of disappointments for her children. Superwoman: career, kids, she had it all. Now, if she could only clone herself. Twice.

TWENTY-NINE

Lee and Faith had made two stops on the way to North Carolina, once for a late lunch at a Cracker Barrel and another at a large strip mall in southern Virginia. Lee had seen a billboard off the highway advertising a week-long gun show. The parking lot was packed with pickup trucks, RVs and cars with fat tires and engines erupting through their hoods. Some of the men were dressed in Polo and Chaps, and others in Grateful Dead T-shirts and ragged jeans. Americans of all backgrounds apparently loved their guns.

"Why here?" Faith asked as Lee got off the bike.

"Virginia law requires that licensed gun dealers conduct on-the-spot background checks on people trying to buy weapons," he explained. "You have to fill out a form, have your gun permit and two forms of identification. But the law doesn't apply to gun shows. All they want is your money. Which, by the way, I need."

"Do you *really* have to have a gun?"

He stared at her as though she had just hatched from an egg. "Everybody coming after *us* has them."

Unable to dispute this devastating logic, she said nothing more, gave him the cash and huddled on the bike as he went inside. Leave it to the man to say something that would paralyze her very soul.

Inside, Lee purchased a Smith & Wesson double-action autopistol with a fifteen-round mag, chambering 9mm Parabellums. The autopistol tag was misleading. You had to pull the trigger each time to fire. The "auto" term referred to the fact that the pistol automatically loaded a new round with each pull of the trigger. He also bought a box of ammo and a cleaning kit and then returned to the parking lot.

Faith watched closely as he packed the gun and ammo away in the motorcycle's storage compartment.

"Feel safer now?" she asked dryly.

"Right now I wouldn't feel safe sitting in the Hoover Building with a hundred FBI agents staring at me. Gee, I wonder why."

They made Duck, North Carolina, by nightfall, and Faith gave Lee directions to the house in the Pine Island community.

When they pulled up in front, Lee stared at the immense structure, tugged off his helmet and turned to her. "I thought you said it was small."

"Actually, I think you referred to it as small. I said it was comfortable."

She climbed off the Honda and stretched out her body. Every bit of her, especially her butt, was one solid knot.

"It must be at least six thousand square feet." Lee continued to stare at the three-story, wooden-shingle-siding house that had dual stone chimneys and a cedar shake roof. Two broad veranda-style porches ran across the second and third floors, which gave it a plantation feel. There were gabled turrets and walls of lattice and glass; and immense displays of fountain grass erupted from the ground. Lee watched as the automatic sprinklers came on, along with the exterior landscape lighting. Behind the house he could hear the pounding surf. The house was situated at the end of a quiet cul-de-sac, although there were similar monster homes painted yellow, blue, green and gray lined up on the beach side in both directions as far as the eye could see. Although the air was warm and slightly humid, they were approaching November, and virtually all the other homes were dark.

Faith said, "I've never really bothered to add up the square footage. I rent it out April through September. It covers the mortgage and nets me about thirty thousand a year – just in case you're interested." Taking off her helmet and running her hands through her sweaty hair, she said, "I need a shower and some food. The kitchen should be stocked. You can put the bike in the carport."

Faith unlocked the front door and went inside while Lee parked the Honda in one of two bays of the carport and then carried in the bags. The inside of the house was even more beautiful than the outside. Lee was also grateful to see that the place had a security system. As he looked around, he took in the soaring ceilings, pickled wood beams and paneling, an enormous kitchen, Italian tile floors in some places, high-dollar Berber carpeting elsewhere. He counted six bedrooms, seven bathrooms and discovered an outdoor Jacuzzi on the back porch big enough for at least six drunken adults to flop around in. There were also three fireplaces, including a gas one in the master suite. The furniture was overstuffed rattan and wicker, all seemingly designed to beckon one to catnap.

Lee opened a set of French doors off the kitchen, stepped on to the deck and looked down into the enclosed courtyard. A kidney-shaped pool was situated down there. The chlorinated water sparkled under the glow of the pool lights. A Creepy Crawly made its way through the water, sucking up bugs and debris.

Faith joined him on the deck. "I had the people

come out this morning and get everything going. They maintain the pool all year 'round anyway. I've skinny-dipped down here in December. It's gloriously peaceful."

"There doesn't seem to be anybody else in the other houses."

"Certain parts of the Outer Banks are pretty full about nine or even ten months out of the year now, what with the nice weather. But you always have the chance of hurricanes this time of year, and this area is pretty expensive. The houses rent out for a small fortune, even in the off season. Unless you can get a big group together to rent them, your average family isn't going to be staying here. Mostly, you see the owners come down this time of year. But with kids in school, it's tough to do that during the week. So empty we have."

"Empty I like."

"The pool's heated, if you want to take a dip."

"I didn't bring my trunks."

"Not into skinny-dipping, huh?" She smiled and was very relieved that it was too dark for her to really see his eyes. If his baby blues had hit her just right, she might have pushed him in the pool, dived after him and everything else be damned.

"There are plenty of places in town to get some swimming stuff. I keep clothes down here, so I'm okay. We'll buy you some things tomorrow."

"I think I'm fine with what I brought."

"You don't want to stick out here, do you?"

"I'm not sure we'll be here long enough for that."

Faith looked out toward the wooden walkways leading past the sand dunes to where the Atlantic Ocean pitched and bellowed. "You never know. I don't think there's a better place to sleep than at the beach. There's nothing like the sound of waves crashing in your ears to drive you into unconsciousness. Back in D.C. I never sleep well. Too many things to worry about."

"Funny, I sleep just fine there."

She glared at him. "To each his own."

"What's for dinner?"

"First, a shower. You can have the master suite."

"It's your place. I'm fine on a couch."

"With six bedrooms, I don't think that would make much sense. Take the one at the end of the hall upstairs. It opens out on to the back porch. The Jacuzzi's out there. Feel free. Even without trunks. Don't worry, I won't peek."

They went inside. Lee grabbed his bag and followed her upstairs. He showered and put on a clean pair of khakis, a sweatshirt and sneakers without socks, since he had forgotten to bring the latter. He didn't bother to dry his new buzz cut. He caught himself looking in the mirror. The haircut didn't look so bad on him. In fact, it had taken a few years off. He slapped his hard gut, even did an exaggerated flex in the mirror.

"Yeah, right," he said to his reflection. "Even if she were your type, which she sure as hell ain't." He left his room and was about to head downstairs when he stopped in the hallway.

Faith's bedroom was at the other end of the corridor. He could still hear her shower running. She was probably taking her time under the hot water after the long ride. She had held up well, he had to admit, hadn't complained too much. He was edging down the hallway the whole time he was thinking this, because it just occurred to him that Faith might at this very minute be escaping out the back door while using the running shower as a ruse. For all he knew, she had arranged for a rental car that was parked down the street, and she was about to drive off, leaving him with not much of a life. Was she just like her old man? Running away into the night when things got tough?

He knocked on her door. "Faith?" There was no answer, so he knocked louder. "Faith? Faith!" The water was still running. "Faith!" he yelled. He tried the door. It was locked. He pounded on the door again and yelled her name.

Lee was about to hustle down the stairs when he heard footsteps and the door was flung open. Faith stood there, her hair soaked and hanging in her face, water dripping down her legs, a towel covering, barely, the front of her.

"What?" she demanded. "What's wrong?"

Lee found himself staring at the elegant bone development of her shoulders, the now fully revealed Audrey Hepburn neck, the tightness of her arms. Then his gaze slid down to her upper thighs and he quickly concluded that her arms had nothing on her legs.

"What the hell is it, Lee?" she said loudly.

He snapped back. "Oh. I was just wondering, um, how about I make dinner?" He smiled weakly.

She stared incredulously at him as a puddle of water collected on the carpet at her feet. As she wrapped the mostly wet towel around her, Faith's small, firm breasts were now fully outlined against the thin wet fabric. That's when Lee began thinking seriously about taking another shower, only this time with water cold enough to turn certain parts of his anatomy the same color as his eyes.

"Fine." She slammed the door in his face.

"Very fine," Lee said quietly to the door.

He went downstairs and examined the contents of the refrigerator. He decided on a menu and started pulling food and pans. He had been living alone for so long that he had finally decided, after years of

Golden Arches food, that he had better learn how to cook properly. He actually found it therapeutic, and he fully expected to live an extra twenty years now that he had cleaned his arteries of all the grease. At least until he met Faith Lockhart. Now all bets on a long life were off.

Lee laid out talapia on a baking sheet, brushed the fish with butter he had melted in a pan and let it soak in. Then he added garlic, lemon juice and some other secret spices handed down to him through generations of Adamses and put the fish in the wall oven to broil. He sliced up tomatoes and a slab of mozzarella, arranged them nicely on a serving plate and doused them with olive oil and seasoning. Next he prepared a salad and then slit a length of French bread, buttered it, added garlic and placed it in the lower oven. He got out two plates, silverware and cloth napkins he found in a drawer and set the table. There were candles on the table, but lighting them seemed like a cheesy idea. This wasn't a honeymoon, and they still had that nationwide manhunt thing to consider.

He opened a small, built-in wine cooler next to the fridge and selected a chilled bottle of white. As he was pouring out two glasses of wine, Faith came down the stairs. She wore an unbuttoned blue denim shirt with a white T-shirt underneath, a pair of loose-fitting white slacks and red sandals. He noted she still wore no makeup, at least that he could detect. A silver bangle bracelet dangled at her wrist. She also wore turquoise earrings done in a loopy southwestern design.

She looked surprised at the kitchen activity. "A man who can shoot a gun, lose the Feds and cook too. You just never cease to amaze me."

He handed her a wine glass. "A good meal, a quiet evening and then we get down to serious business."

237

She glanced coolly at him as he clinked his glass against hers. "You clean up well," she said.

"Another one of my talents." He went to check the fish while Faith went over to the wall of windows and stared out.

They ate quietly, both of them apparently feeling a little awkward now that they had arrived at their destination. Getting here, ironically enough, seemed to be the easy part.

Faith insisted on cleaning up the kitchen while Lee turned on the TV.

"Did we make the news?" Faith asked.

"Not that I can see. But there must have been reports of the FBI agent being found. A murdered Fed is still pretty damn rare even in this day and age, thank God. I'll get a newspaper tomorrow."

Faith finished cleaning up, poured herself another glass of wine and joined him.

"Okay, our bellies are full, the booze has us about as mellow as we're ever going to get, so now's the time to talk," Lee said. "I need to hear the whole story, Faith. As sweet and simple as that."

"So you feed a girl a nice meal, fill her with wine and you think she's yours for the asking?" She smiled coyly.

He frowned. "I'm serious, Faith."

Her smile disappeared, along with her coyness. "Let's go for a walk on the beach."

Lee started to protest but then stopped. "Okay. It's your turf, home rules apply." He headed up the stairs.

"Where are you going?"

"Be right back."

When Lee came back down, he had on a wind-breaker.

"You didn't need a jacket, it's still pretty warm."

He spread open the front of the jacket, revealing

the clip holster and the Smith & Wesson in it. "Didn't want to spook any sand crabs we come across."

"Guns frighten me to death."

"Guns also prevent death, when *properly* used. Usually sudden, violent death."

"No one could have followed us. No one knows we're here."

His reply chilled her to the bone.

"I hope to God you're right."

THIRTY

Reynolds didn't use her bubble light but would have if a patrol car had tried to pull her over, as she was exceeding the speed limit by more than twenty miles per hour on the few open stretches of the Beltway before having to slow down in a sea of red brake lights. She checked her watch: seven-thirty. When wasn't there a rush hour in this damn area? People got up earlier and earlier to go to work, or stayed later and later before going home to avoid the traffic. Pretty soon the two groups would smack right into each other and the twenty-four-hour-a-day highway parking lot would officially begin. Luckily Anne Newman's house was only a few exits down from hers.

As she drove, Reynolds thought about her visit to Adams's apartment building. Reynolds had thought she had seen and heard everything by now, but Angie Carter's statement about the FBI had stunned her, and the shock of it had moved her and Connie into hyperspeed. They'd notified their superiors at the Bureau and quickly determined that no FBI operations had been conducted at Adams's address. Then the shit had really hit the fan. The impersonation of FBI agents got the attention of the director himself, and he had personally issued orders on the case. Even though the back door to Adams's apartment had been knocked off its hinges and they could have walked right in, a search warrant was fast-tracked and executed, again with the director's personal blessing. Reynolds was actually relieved about that because she didn't want to have any slip-ups on this one. Any mistakes would come home to roost right on her head.

The apartment was thoroughly searched by one of the Bureau's crack forensics teams, pulled off another high-profile case. In the end they didn't find much. There was no tape in the answering machine. That had really ticked Reynolds off. If the phony FBI people had taken the tape, there must have been something important on it. Her search team had continued to strike out. There were no travel documents, maps consulted, nothing that would hint as to where Adams and Lockhart were going. They had found fingerprints matching Faith Lockhart's, so that was something. They were checking into Adams's background. He had family in the area; maybe they knew something.

They had discovered the roof hatch in the empty apartment next door to Adams's. Clever. Reynolds had also noted the extra locks, video surveillance, steel door and frame and the copper shield over the alarm panel. Lee Adams knew what he was doing.

They had retrieved the bag of hair and hair coloring from one of the trash cans behind the apartment. That, together with the snips they had seen of the airport surveillance tapes, showed that Adams was now a blond, Lockhart a brunette. Not that this helped much. They were checking into whether either of them had other residences listed in their names elsewhere in the country. That was a needle in a haystack, she knew, even if they had used their real names. She doubted they would be that stupid. And even if they had used their aliases, the names Suzanne Blake and Charles Wright were too common to aid Reynolds very much.

The police officers who responded to the call at

Adams's apartment were pulled in and questioned. The men posing as FBI agents had fed them a story that Lee Adams was wanted in connection with a kidnapping ring across state lines. The FBI posers' credentials looked real, both police officers were quick to point out. And they carried the firepower and the professional swagger one normally associated with federal law enforcement. They were searching the place expertly and had made no move to run when the cruiser had shown up. The imposters talked the talk and walked the walk in all respects, said the two police officers, who were both veterans on the street. They had been given the name of the supposed special agent in charge. It was run through the FBI personnel database and came up negative. No surprise there. The police officers had given descriptions of the men they had seen, and a Bureau technician was creating computer images of them. Still, all in all, it was a dead end, with frightening implications. Implications that struck very close to home for Reynolds.

She had received another visit from Paul Fisher. He came with orders right from Massey, as he was quick to point out. Reynolds was to proceed with all due speed, but with the utmost caution, to find Faith Lockhart, and she could be assured of all the support she needed.

"Just don't make any more mistakes," he had said.

"I wasn't aware I had made any mistakes, Paul."

"An agent killed. Faith Lockhart falls into your lap and you let her get away. What would you call those?"

"Leaked information caused Ken to die," she had fired back. "I fail to see how that was my fault."

"Brooke," Fisher had said, "if you really believe that, then you might want to request reassignment right now. The buck stops with you. As far as the

Bureau is concerned, if there is a leak, every member of your squad, including you, is at the top of the list. And that's how the Bureau's following that up."

As soon as he left her office, Reynolds had thrown her shoe against the closed door. Then she had thrown the other one, just to be sure he was aware of her extreme displeasure. Paul Fisher was officially off her sexual fantasy list.

Reynolds raced down the exit ramp, hung a left on Braddock Road and fought through some late traffic backup until she turned off and entered the quiet residential neighborhood of the slain FBI agent. She slowed when she reached the Newmans' street. The house was dark, a single car in the driveway. Reynolds parked her government-issue sedan at the curb, got out and hustled up to the door.

Anne Newman must have been watching for her, because the door opened before Reynolds could ring the bell.

Anne Newman didn't attempt to make small talk or ask Reynolds if she wanted anything to drink. She led the FBI agent directly to a small back room that had been set up as an office with a desk, metal file cabinet, computer and fax machine. On the wall were framed baseball cards and other sports memorabilia. On the desk were stacks of silver dollars encased in hard plastic and neatly labeled.

"I was looking through Ken's office. I don't know why. It just seemed . . ."

"You don't have to explain, Anne. There are no set rules for what you're going through."

Anne Newman wiped away a tear as Reynolds studied her. Clearly the woman was near the breaking point, on all fronts. She was dressed in an old robe, her hair unwashed, eyes red and puffy. Yesterday afternoon, the most pressing decision she probably had to make was what to have for dinner,

Reynolds assumed. God, it could all turn on a dime. Ken Newman wasn't the only one being buried. Anne was right there beside him. The only catch was she still had to go on living.

"I found these photo albums. I didn't even know they were back here. They were in a box with some other things. I know this might look bad, but . . . but if it helps in finding out what happened to Ken . . ." She faded out for a moment as more tears plunked down on to the photo album with its tattered, seventies-style psychedelic cover.

"Calling you was the right thing to do," Anne finally said with a bluntness that was both painful and gratifying for Reynolds to hear.

"I know this is terribly difficult for you." Reynolds eyed the album, not wanting to prolong this any more than absolutely necessary. "Can I see what you found?"

Anne Newman sat down on a small sofa and opened the album and pulled up the clear plastic sheet that kept the photos securely inside. On the page she had opened to was an eight-by-ten photo of a group of men in hunting garb holding rifles. Ken Newman was one of the men. She pulled out the photo, revealing a piece of paper and a small key pressed into the album page. She handed Reynolds both and watched her closely as the FBI agent examined them.

The piece of paper was an account statement for a safe-deposit box at a local bank. The key, presumably, fit that box.

Reynolds looked at her. "You didn't know about this?"

Anne Newman shook her head. "We have a safe-deposit box. But not at that bank. And of course that's not all."

Reynolds looked back at the bank statement and

she jerked involuntarily. The name of the boxholder was not Ken Newman. Nor was the billing address for the house she was in. "Who's Frank Andrews?"

Anne Newman looked like she would burst into tears again. "God, I have no idea."

"Did Ken ever mention that name to you?" Newman shook her head.

Reynolds took a deep breath. If Newman had a safe-deposit box under a false name, he would have needed one thing to set up the account.

She sat on the sofa next to Anne and took her hand. "Have you found any identification around here that might match the name Frank Andrews?"

The tears welled in the stricken woman's eyes and Reynolds truly felt for her.

"You mean with Ken's picture on it? Showing that he was this Frank Andrews person?"

"Yes, that's what I mean," Reynolds said softly.

Anne Newman put her hand in her robe and pulled out a Virginia driver's license. The name on it was Frank Andrews. The license number, which in Virginia was the person's Social Security number, was on there. And in the small accompanying photo Ken Newman was staring back at her.

"I thought about going to open the safe-deposit box myself, but then I realized they wouldn't let me. I'm not on the account. And I wouldn't be able to explain that it was my husband, but just under a false name."

"I know, Anne. I know. You were right to bring me in. Now, where exactly did you find the fake ID?"

"In another one of the photo albums. They weren't family albums, of course. I keep those, been through them a zillion times. These albums were pictures of Ken and his hunting and fishing buddies. They took trips every year. Ken was good about taking pictures. I never knew he kept them in albums. I wasn't all that interested in looking at those pictures, you see." She stared wistfully at the far wall. "Sometimes it seemed Ken was happier with his buddies shooting at ducks or at his coin and card shows than he was at home." She caught a quick breath, put a hand over her mouth and looked down.

Reynolds could sense Anne had never meant to share that personal bit of information with her, a semi-stranger. She said nothing. Experience told her to allow Anne Newman to work her way through this. A minute later the woman started speaking again.

"I never would have found it, I suppose, unless . . . what happened to Ken . . . you know. I guess life is funny sometimes."

Or terribly cruel. "Anne, I need to check this out. I'm going to take these items, and I don't want you to mention it to anyone. Not friends, family . . ." She paused, choosing her words as carefully as she could. "Or anyone else at the Bureau. Not until I dig a little bit."

Anne Newman looked up at her with frightened eyes. "What do you think Ken was involved in, Brooke?"

"I don't know yet. Let's not jump to conclusions on this. The safe-deposit box might be empty. Ken might have leased it a long time ago and then forgotten about it."

"And the fake ID?"

Reynolds licked her dry lips. "Ken worked some undercover over the years. This might be a souvenir of those days." Reynolds knew this was a lie, and Anne Newman probably did too, she thought. The license had a recent issue date on it. And those working undercover in the FBI didn't usually take

246

home the props with their secret identities on them once their tasks were completed. The fake license, she was fairly certain, was unrelated to his FBI duties. It was her job to discover what it *was* connected to.

"Anne, not a word to anyone. It's for your own safety as much as anything."

Anne Newman clutched her arm as Reynolds stood. "Brooke, I've got three kids. If Ken was mixed up in something . . ."

"I'll put the house under twenty-four-hour surveillance. Anything remotely suspicious catches your eye, you call me." She handed her a card with her direct-dial numbers on it. "Day or night."

"I didn't know where else to turn. Ken thought a lot of you, he really did."

"He was a damn good agent and he had a terrific career." If she discovered that Ken Newman had been a sell-out, however, the Bureau would crush his memory, his reputation, everything about his professional life. That would, of course, destroy his private side as well, including the woman Reynolds was looking at, and her children. But that was life. Reynolds didn't make the rules, didn't always agree with the rules, but she lived by them. However, she would check out the safe-deposit box by herself. If there was nothing suspicious in there, she would tell no one. She would continue to investigate why Newman was using an alias, but that would be done on her own time. She wasn't going to destroy his memory without a very compelling reason. She owed the man that.

She left Anne Newman sitting on the sofa, the photo album open in her lap. The ironic thing was, if Newman was the leak on the Lockhart case, he had probably helped himself to an early death. Now that Reynolds thought about it, whoever might have hired him had probably hoped to eliminate the mole and the main target in one efficient thrust. Only a slug deflecting off a pistol barrel had saved Faith Lockhart from joining Ken Newman on a slab. And perhaps the assistance of Lee Adams as well?

Whoever had orchestrated it clearly knew what he was doing. Which was bad for Reynolds. Contrary to popular fiction and film, most criminals weren't that accomplished and couldn't so easily out-maneuver the police at every turn. The majority of murderers, rapists, burglars, robbers, drug dealers and other felons were usually uneducated or scared; or drugged-out punks or drunks terrified of their own shadows when off the needle or bottle, yet demons when high. They left many clues behind and were usually caught, or turned themselves in, or were ratted on by their "friends." They were prosecuted and did jail time or, in rare cases, were executed. They were in no sense of the word professionals.

Reynolds knew that this was not the case here. Amateurs didn't find ways to pay off veteran FBI agents. They didn't hire hit men who lurked in the woods waiting for their prey. They didn't impersonate FBI agents with credentials so authentic they had scared off the cops. Sinister theories of conspiracy swirled in her head, sending a shiver of fear down her back. No matter how long you did this, the fear was always there. To be alive was to be afraid. To not be afraid was to be dead.

As she walked out, Reynolds passed under a blinking fire detector that was in the hallway. There were three other such devices in the house, including one in Ken Newman's office. While they were plugged into the home's electrical wiring and did function as designed, they all also housed sophisticated surveillance cameras with pinhole lenses. Two of the wall outlets on each level were similarly "modified." The modifications had taken place two weeks ago when the Newmans had taken a rare three-day vacation. This type of surveillance mode was based upon PLCs, power line carrier technology favored by the FBI. And the Central Intelligence Agency.

Robert Thornhill was on the prowl. And his attention would now turn to Brooke Reynolds.

As she climbed in her car, Reynolds understood very clearly that she was perhaps at the crossroads of her career. She would probably need every bit of ingenuity and inner strength she could muster to survive this. And yet the only thing she really wanted to do right now was drive home and tell her two beautiful children the story of the three pigs, just as slowly, accurately and colorfully as she possibly could.

THIRTY-ONE

The wind, it turned out, was blowing hard along the beach, and the temperature had dropped drastically. Faith buttoned her overshirt; then, despite the cold, she took off her sandals and held them in one hand.

"I like to feel the sand," she explained to Lee. The tide was low, so they had a broad beach on which to meander. The sky held scattered clouds, the moon almost full, the stars winks of light staring down upon them. Far out on the water they saw the blink of what was probably a ship's light or stationary buoy. Except for the wind, it was completely quiet. No cars, no blaring TVs, no planes, no other people.

"It's really nice out here," Lee finally said as he watched a sand crab do its funny sideways scuttle into its tiny home. Stuck in the sand was a piece of PVC pipe. Lee knew that fishermen would stick their poles in the hollow tube when they were fishing from the beach.

"I've thought of moving here permanently," said Faith. She broke ranks with him and ventured into the water up to her ankles. Lee slipped off his shoes, rolled up his pants legs and joined her.

"Colder than I thought it would be," he said. "No swimming out here."

"You wouldn't believe how invigorating a swim in cold water can be."

"You're right, I wouldn't."

"I'm sure you've been asked this a million times,

but how did you become a private investigator?"

He shrugged and looked out toward the ocean. "Sort of fell into it. My dad was an engineer and I was a gadget guy, like him. But I never had the book smarts he did. I was sort of a rebel too, like you. But I didn't go to college. I joined the Navy."

"Please tell me you were a Navy SEAL. I'd sleep better."

Lee smiled. "I can barely shoot straight. I can't build a nuclear device out of toothpicks and gum wrappers, and the last time I checked, I couldn't disable a man simply by pressing my thumb against his head."

"I guess I'll keep you anyway. Sorry to interrupt."

"Not much more to it. I studied telephony, communications, that sort of thing in the Navy. Got married, had a kid. Worked at the phone company as a repairman. Then I lost my daughter in a messy divorce. I quit my job, answered an ad at a private security firm for someone experienced in electronic surveillance. I figured with my technical background I could learn what I needed to know. The job really got into my blood. I started my own private investigation firm, got some decent clients, made mistakes along the way but then got a firm footing. Now you see me today as the head of a mighty empire."

"How long have you been divorced?"

"A long time." He looked at her. "Why?"

"Just curious. Ever gotten close to the altar since then?"

"No. I guess I'm terrified of making the same mistakes." He stuffed his hands into his pockets. "Quite honestly, the problems came from both ends. I'm not easy to live with." He smiled. "I think God makes two kinds of people: those who should marry and procreate and those who should remain alone

251

and have sex only for fun. I think I'm in the latter group."

Faith looked down. "Save some room for me."

"Not to worry. There's plenty of space left."

He touched her elbow. "Let's talk. We're running out of time."

Faith led him back up on to the beach and plopped down cross-legged on a patch of dry sand. He sat next to her.

"Where would you like to begin?" she asked.

"How about the beginnings?"

"No, I mean do you want me to tell you all first, or do you want to spill *your* secrets first?"

He looked startled. "*My* secrets? Sorry, I'm fresh out."

She picked up a stick, drew the letters *d* and *b* in the sand and then glanced at him. "Danny Buchanan. What do you really know about him?"

"Just what I told you. He's your partner."

"He's also the man who hired you."

Lee couldn't find his voice for a few seconds. "I told you I didn't know who had hired me."

"That's right. That's what you *told* me."

"How do you know he hired me?"

"While I was in your office, I listened to a message from Danny, and he sounded quite anxious to know where I was and what you had found out. He left his phone number for you to call him back. He was more distressed than I've ever heard him. I guess I would be too if someone I had arranged to have killed was still alive and kicking."

"You're sure it was him on the phone?"

"After fifteen years of working with him I think I know his voice. So you didn't know?"

"No, I didn't."

"You know that's really hard to believe."

"I guess it is," he agreed. "But it happens to be the

truth." He scooped up some sand and let it run through his fingers. "So I take it that phone call is why you tried to give me the slip at the airport? You don't trust me."

She licked her dry lips and glanced at the holstered gun, which was visible as the wind whipped Lee's jacket around. "I *do* trust you, Lee. Otherwise I wouldn't be sitting on a lonely beach in the dark with an armed man who's still pretty much a stranger to me."

Lee let his shoulders slump. "I was hired to follow you, Faith. That's all."

"Don't you first find out if the client or his intentions are legitimate?"

Lee started to say something and then stopped. That was a reasonable question. The fact was business had been slow recently and the assignment and cash had been timely. And the file he had been given had a photo of Faith. And then he had seen her in person. Well, what the hell could he say? Most of his targets weren't as attractive as Faith Lockhart. In the photo her face had suggested vulnerability. After meeting her, he knew that impression wasn't necessarily true. But it was a very potent combination for him. For any man.

"Normally, I like to meet with a client, get to know him and his agenda before I agree to accept a job."

"But not here?"

"It was a little difficult, since I didn't know who had hired me."

"So instead of returning the cash, you accepted the offer and started following me – blindly, as it were."

"I didn't see any harm in just following you."

"But they could have been using you to get to me."

"It's not exactly like you were in hiding. Like I said, I thought you might be having some sort of affair. When I went inside the cottage, I knew that wasn't the case. The rest of the night's events damn sure reinforced that conclusion. That's all I really know."

Faith stared out toward the ocean, to the horizon, where water met sky. It was a visual collision of sorts that happened every day and was comforting for some reason. It gave her hope when she probably had no other reason to feel it. Other than the man sitting beside her, perhaps.

"Let's go back to the house," she said.

THIRTY-TWO

They sat in the spacious family room. Faith picked up a remote control, hit a button and the flames in the gas fireplace crept to life. She poured another glass of wine, offered one to Lee, but he declined. They sat on the overstuffed couch.

Faith took a sip of wine and stared out the window, her eyes focusing on nothing. "Washington represents the richest, most enormous pie in the history of mankind. And everyone in the whole world wants a slice of it. There are certain people who hold the knife that portions out that pie. If you want a slice, you have to go through them."

"That's where you and Buchanan come in?"

"I lived, breathed and ate my career. Sometimes I worked more than twenty-four hours in a day because I'd cross the International Date Line. I can't tell you the hundreds of details, nuances, mind-reading, gut checks and sheer nerve and per-severance that lobbying on the scale we did requires." She put down her wine glass and focused on him. "I had a great teacher in Danny Buchanan. He almost never lost. That's remarkable, don't you think?"

"I guess never losing at anything is pretty re-markable. We can't all be Michael Jordan."

"In your line of work can you guarantee to your client that a certain result will occur?"

Lee smiled. "If I could foresee the future, I'd start playing the lottery."

"Danny Buchanan could guarantee the future."

Lee stopped smiling. "How?"

"He who controls the gatekeepers controls the future."

Lee slowly nodded in understanding. "So he was paying off people in government?"

"On a more sophisticated scale than anyone's done before."

"Congressmen on the payroll? That sort of thing?"

"Actually, they did it for free."

"What—"

"Until they left office. Then Danny had a whole world of goodies lined up for them. Lucrative do-nothing jobs in companies he had set up. Income from private portfolios of stocks and bonds, and cash funneled through legitimate businesses under the cover of services rendered. They could play golf all day, make a couple of sham phone calls to the Hill, take a few meetings and live like Kings. Hell, it's like a super 401(k). You know how Americans are so into their stocks. Danny worked them hard while they were on the Hill, but he would give them the best golden years money could buy."

"How many of them have 'retired'?"

"None, as yet. But everything is set up for when they do. Danny's been doing this only about ten years."

"He's been in D.C. a lot longer than ten years."

"I mean he's been bribing people for only ten years. Before then, he was a much more successful lobbyist. Since the start of his private company, he's made a lot less money."

"I thought guaranteeing results would bring him a lot *more* money."

"The last ten years have been pretty much a charitable decade for him."

"The man must have deep pockets."

256

"Danny has pretty much gone through his money. We started representing paying clients again so we could continue what we were doing. And the longer his people do what they are told, the more they will receive later. And by waiting until they're out of office to be paid, the chances any of them will be caught go down considerably."

"They must really trust Buchanan's word."

"I'm sure he's had to show them proof of what's waiting for them. But he's also an honorable man."

"All crooks are, aren't they? Who are some of the people on his retirement plan?"

She looked at him suspiciously. "Why?"

"Just humor me."

Faith named two of the men.

"Correct me if I'm mistaken, but aren't they the current vice president of the United States and the Speaker of the House?"

"Danny doesn't work with middle management. He actually started working with the vice president before he rose to that office, back when he was a House whip. But when Danny needs the man to pick up the phone and put the screws to someone, the man does."

"Holy shit, Faith. What the hell did you need that kind of firepower for? Are we talking military secrets?"

"Actually, something much more valuable." She picked up her wine glass. "We represent the poorest of the world's poor. African nations, in issues of humanitarian aid, food, medicine, clothing, farm equipment, crop seed, desalinization systems. In Latin America, money for vaccines and other medical supplies. The export of legal birth control devices, sterile needles and health information in the poorest countries."

Lee looked skeptical. "You're saying you were

bribing government officials to help third world countries?"

She set down her wine glass and looked directly at him. "Actually, the official lexicon has changed. The rich nations have developed very politically correct terminology for their destitute neighbors. The CIA publishes a manual on them, in fact. So instead of 'third world,' you have new categories: LDCs are 'less-developed countries,' meaning they're in the bottom group of the hierarchy of developed countries. There are officially one hundred and seventy-two LDCs, or the vast majority of countries in the world. Then there are the LLDCs. They're the 'least developed countries.' They're the bottom of the barrel, dead in the water. There are *only* forty-two of them. This may surprise you, but about half of the people on this planet live in abject poverty."

"And that makes it right?" Lee said. "That makes bribery and cheating right?"

"I'm not asking you to condone any of it. I don't really care if you agree with it or not. You wanted the facts, I'm giving them to you."

"America gives lots of foreign aid. And we don't *have* to give a dime."

She gave him a fierce look, one he had never seen from her before. "If you talk facts with me, you lose," she said sharply.

"Come again?"

"I've been researching this – hell, living this – for more than ten years! We pay farmers in this country more *not* to grow crops than we do on humanitarian relief overseas. Of the total federal budget, foreign aid represents about one percent, with the majority of that going to two countries, Egypt and Israel. Americans spend a hundred times as much money on makeup or fast food or video rentals in a year's time than we do on feeding starving children in third world countries in a decade. We could wipe out a dozen serious childhood diseases in undeveloped countries around the world with less money than we spend on Beanie Babies."

"You're naïve, Faith. You and Buchanan are probably just filling the lining of some dictator's pockets."

"No! That's an easy excuse, and one that I'm sick of. The money we do manage to get goes directly to legitimate humanitarian relief organizations, and never to the government directly. I've personally seen enough health ministers in African countries wearing Armani and driving a Mercedes while babies starve at their feet."

"And there aren't starving children in this country?"

"They get a lot of aid, and rightfully so. All I'm saying is that Danny and I had our agenda, and ours involved the *foreign* poor. Human beings are dying, Lee, by the millions. Children all over the world are perishing for no reason other than neglect. Every day, every hour, every minute."

"And do you really expect me to believe you two did this out of the goodness of your hearts?" He looked around the house. "This isn't exactly a soup kitchen, Faith."

"The first five years I worked with Danny I did my job, represented the big clients and I made a lot of money. A *lot* of money. I'll be the first to admit I'm one materialistic hardass. I like the money, and I loved what the money could buy."

"And then what happened? You found God?"

"No, he found me." Lee looked bewildered, and Faith quickly continued. "Danny had begun lobbying on behalf of the foreign poor. He was getting nowhere. No one cared, he kept telling me. The other partners at our firm were getting tired of

Danny's charitable endeavors. They wanted to represent IBM and Philip Morris, not Sudan's starving masses. Danny came to my office one day, said he was forming his own firm and wanted me to go with him. We weren't taking any clients, but Danny told me not to worry, that he'd take care of me."

Lee appeared mollified. "That much I can believe: You didn't know he was bribing people, or at least planning to."

"Of course I knew about it! He told me everything. He wanted me to go into this with eyes wide open. That's how he is. He's not some crook."

"Faith, do you know what you're saying? You *went along*, even though you knew you'd be breaking the law?"

She fixed a cold gaze upon him. "If I could fix it so that cigarette companies could keep selling cancer on a stick to anybody with a fresh set of lungs and gun manufacturers could roll out machine guns to anyone with a heartbeat, I guess I felt nothing was beneath me. And the goal here was something I could actually be proud of."

"Materialistic hardass goes soft?" Lee said with contempt.

"It's been known to happen," she shot back.

"How did you two work it?" Lee said in a baiting tone.

"I was Mister Outside, working all the people we didn't have in our back pockets. I was also good at getting celebrities to appear at some events, even travel to some of the countries. Photo ops, meet-and-greets with members." She sipped her wine. "Danny was Mister Inside. He worked all the people on the take while I pushed from the outside."

"And you kept this up for ten years?"

Faith nodded. "About a year ago Danny started

running out of money. A lot of our lobbying expenses he paid out of his own pocket. It wasn't like our clients could afford to pay us anything. And he had to invest a lot of his own money into these 'trust' funds, as he called them, for the members we were bribing. Danny took that part very seriously. He was their trustee. Every cent he promised would be there."

"Honor among thieves."

Faith ignored the barb. "That's when he told me to concentrate on paying clients while he carried the torch on the other matters. I offered to sell my house, and this house, to help raise money. He refused. He said I'd done enough." She shook her head. "Maybe I should still sell it – believe me, no one could ever do enough."

She fell silent for a bit and Lee chose not to break it. She stared across at him. "We really were accomplishing a lot of good."

"What do you want, Faith? You want me to break out in applause?"

Her eyes flashed at him. "Why don't you get on that stupid motorcycle and get the hell out of my life?"

"All right," Lee said calmly, "if you thought so highly of what you were doing, how did you turn out to be a witness for the FBI?"

Faith covered her face with her hands, as though she were about to start bawling. When Faith finally looked at him she seemed so distressed, Lee felt his anger slip away.

"For some time Danny had been acting strangely. I suspected that maybe someone was on to him. That scared the hell out of me. I didn't want to go to prison. I kept asking him what was wrong, but he wouldn't talk to me about it. He kept withdrawing, became more and more paranoid, finally even asking me to leave the firm. I felt so alone, for the first time in a long time. It was like I had lost my father again."

"So you went to the FBI, tried to cut a deal. You for Buchanan."

"No!" she exclaimed. "Never!"

"What, then?"

"About three months ago there was a lot of news coverage about the FBI breaking a major public corruption case, involving a defense contractor bribing several congressmen to help it win a large federal contract. A couple of employees at the defense contractor contacted the FBI and revealed what was going on. They were actually part of the conspiracy early on, but were granted immunity in exchange for their testimony and assistance. That sounded like a good deal to me. Maybe I could get a deal too. Since Danny wouldn't confide in me, I decided to go for it. The lead agent was named in the article: Brooke Reynolds. I called her.

"I didn't know what to expect from the FBI but I knew one thing: I wouldn't tell them much right away, no names or anything, not until I saw what the lay of the land was. And I had leverage. They needed a live witness with a head full of dates, times, names, meetings, records of votes and agendas to make this work."

"And Buchanan was ignorant of all this?"

"I guess not, considering he hired someone to kill me."

"We don't know that he did."

"Oh, come on, Lee, who else could it be?"

Lee thought back to the other men he had seen at the airport. The device in the man's hand was a high-tech blowgun of sorts. Lee had seen a demonstration of one at a seminar on counterterrorism. The gun and ammo were constructed solely from plastic to allow passage through metal detectors. You hit the palm trigger and the air compression fired a tiny needle either tipped or filled with a deadly toxin, like thallium or ricin, or the all-time favorite of assassins, curare, because it reacted so damn fast in the body that there was no known antidote. In a crowd, the act could be carried out and the assassin gone before the victim fell dead.

"Go on," he said.

"I offered to bring Danny into the fold."

"And how did they react to that?"

"They made it very clear that Danny was going down."

"I'm not following your logic. If you *and* Buchanan were going to turn witness, who were the Feds going to prosecute: the foreign countries?"

"No. Their representatives didn't know what we were doing. As I said, the money didn't go directly to the governments. And it's not like CARE or the Catholic Relief Services or UNICEF would ever condone bribery. Danny was their unofficial and unpaid lobbyist-in-residence but they had no idea what he was doing. He represented about fifteen such organizations. It was tough going. They all had their agendas, took a scattergun approach. They typically proposed hundreds of single-issue bills, instead of a few comprehensive ones. Danny got them organized, working together, sponsoring a small number of bills containing more comprehensive legislation. He taught them what they had to do to be more effective."

"So tell me exactly who were you going to testify against, then?"

"The politicians we paid off," she said simply. "They did it just for the money. It's not like they gave a damn about children with dead eyes living in Hepatitis Heaven. I saw it every day in their greedy faces. They just expected a rich reward – thought it was their due."

"Don't you think you're coming down a little heavy on these guys?"

"Why don't *you* stop being so naïve? How do you think people get elected in this country? They get elected by the groups who *organize* the voters, who shape citizens' decisions on who and what to vote for. And do you know who those groups are? They're big business and special interests, and the wealthy who fill the coffers of political candidates every year. Do you really think ordinary people attend five-thousand-dollar-a-plate dinners? And then do you really think these groups give all that money out of the goodness of *their* collective hearts? When the politicians get into office, you better believe they're expected to deliver."

"So you're saying all politicians in this country are corrupt. That still doesn't make what you did right."

"No? What congressman from the state of Michigan would vote to do anything to seriously hurt the automobile industry? How long do you think she'd be in office? Or high-tech in California? Or farmers in the Midwest? Or tobacco in the South? It's like a self-fulfilling prophecy in a way. Business and labor and other special interests have a lot at stake. They're focused, they have big dollars, they have PACs and lobbyists blasting their messages to Washington nonstop. Big and small business employ just about everybody. Those same people vote in elections. They vote their pocketbooks. Voilà, there's your big, dark conspiracy of American politics. I see Danny as the first visionary ever to outsmart greed and selfishness."

"But what about the foreign aid? If this story came out, wouldn't that kill the pipeline?"

"That's the thing! Can you imagine all the positive

attention it would get? The poorest countries on earth forced to bribe greedy American politicians to get the help they so desperately needed because it was unavailable any other way. You get stories like that in the media, then maybe some real, substantive changes would be made."

"That all sounds pretty far-fetched. I mean, come on."

"Maybe so, but my options weren't exactly flowing over. It's real damn easy to second-guess, Lee."

Lee sat back as he muddled this over. "Okay, okay. Do you *really* think Buchanan would try to kill you?"

"We were partners, friends. Actually, more than that. In many ways he was like a father to me. I . . . I just don't know. Maybe he found out I went to the FBI. He would think I betrayed him. That could have driven him over the edge."

"There's a major problem with the theory that Buchanan is behind all this."

She looked over at him curiously.

"I *hadn't reported back* to Buchanan, remember? So unless he has someone else working for him, he doesn't know you're dealing with the FBI. And it takes time to set up a professional-caliber hit. You can't just call your local shooter and ask him to pop somebody for you and charge it to your Visa."

"But he might have known a hired killer already, and then he planned to somehow set you up for the murder."

Lee was shaking his head before she finished. "He would have had no idea I would be there that night. And if you had been killed, he'd have the problem of me finding out about it and maybe going to the police with the result that everything gets traced back to him. Why bring all that misery on himself?

Think about it, Faith, if Buchanan was planning to kill you, he would not have hired me."

She slumped in a chair. "My God, what you're saying makes perfect sense." Terror seeped into Faith's eyes as she thought about what all this meant. "Then you're saying . . .?"

"I'm saying that somebody else wants you dead."

"Who? Who?" She almost shouted this at him.

"I don't know," he said.

Faith abruptly stood and stared into the fire. The shadows of the flames lapped against her face. When she spoke her voice was calm, almost resigned. "Do you see your daughter much?"

"Not much. Why?"

"I thought marriage and kids could wait. And then months turned to years and years to decades. And now this."

"You're not in your golden years yet."

She looked at him. "Can you tell me I'll be alive tomorrow, a week from tomorrow?"

"Nobody has that guarantee. We can always go to the FBI, and now maybe we should."

"I can't do that. Not after what you've just told me."

He stood and gripped her shoulder. "What are you talking about?"

She moved away from him. "The FBI won't let me bring Danny in. Either he goes to jail or I do. When I thought he was behind trying to have me killed, I probably would have gone back and testified. But I can't do that now. I can't be part of him going to prison."

"If there hadn't been an attempt on your life, what were you going to do?"

"I was going to give them an ultimatum. If they wanted my cooperation, then Danny would have to be given immunity."

"And if they turned you down, like they did?"

"Then Danny and I would have been long gone. Somehow." She stared directly at him. "I'm not going back. For a lot of reasons. Not wanting to die being right at the top."

"And exactly where the hell does that leave me?"

"This isn't such a bad place, is it?" Faith said weakly.

"Are you crazy? We can't stay here forever."

"Then we better think of another place to run to."

"And what about my home? My life? I *do* have a family. Do you expect me to just kiss it all good-bye?"

"Whoever wants me dead will assume you know everything I do. You won't be safe."

"That's *my* decision, not yours."

"I'm sorry, Lee. I never thought anyone else would be dragged into this. Especially not someone like you."

"There has to be another way."

She headed for the stairs. "I'm very, very tired. And what else is there to talk about?"

"Dammit, I can't just walk away and start over."

Faith was halfway up the stairs. She stopped, turned and looked down at him.

"Do you think things will look better in the morning?" she asked.

"No," said Lee frankly.

"Which is why there's nothing left for us to talk about. Good night."

"Why do I think you made your decision not to go back a long time ago? Like the minute you met me."

"Lee—"

"You sucker me into going with you, pull that stupid stunt at the airport and now I'm trapped too. Thanks a helluva lot, lady."

"I didn't plan it like this! You're wrong."

"And you really expect me to believe you?"

"What do you want me to say?"

Lee stared up at her. "Granted it's not much, but I like my life, Faith."

"I'm sorry." She fled upstairs.

THIRTY-THREE

Lee grabbed a six-pack of Red Dog from the refrigerator and slammed the side door on his way out. He stopped at the Honda, wondering whether he should just climb on the big machine and run until his gas, money or sanity were gone. Then another possibility occurred to him. He could go to the Feds alone. Turn Faith in and claim ignorance about all of this. And he *was* ignorant. He hadn't done anything wrong. And he owed the woman nothing. In fact, she had been a source of misery, terror and near-death experiences. Turning her in should be an easy decision. So why the hell wasn't it?

He went out the rear gate and on to the walkway leading past the dunes. Lee intended to go down to the sand, watch the ocean and drink beer until either his mind ceased to function or he came up with a brilliant plan that would save them both. Or at least him. For some reason, he turned to look back at the house for a moment. The light was on in Faith's bedroom. The mini-blinds were down but not closed.

As Faith came into view, Lee stiffened. She didn't close the blinds. She moved through the room, disappeared into the bathroom for a minute and then reappeared. As she started to undress, Lee looked around to see if anyone was watching him watching her. The police responding to a Peeping-Tom call would put the finishing touches on a spectacular day in the charmed life of Lee Adams. The other homes were dark, however; he could safely continue his voyeurism. Her shirt came off first, then her pants. She kept shedding clothes until all the window was filled with skin. And she didn't slip into any pajamas or even a T-shirt. Apparently this highly paid lobbyist-turned-Joan-of-Arc slept in the raw. Lee had a fairly clear view of things the towel had only hinted at. Maybe she knew he was out here and was putting on a peep show for him. What, as compensation for destroying his life? The bedroom light went out and Lee popped a beer, turned and headed for the beach. The show was over.

He had finished the first beer by the time he hit the sand. The tide was starting to roll in, and he didn't have to venture far to be in water past his ankles. He cracked another beer and went in farther, up to his knees. The water was freezing, but he went in farther still, almost to his crotch, and then stopped, for a practical reason: A wet pistol wasn't particularly useful.

He sloughed back to the sand, dropped the beer, slipped off his waterlogged sneakers and started to run. He was tired, but his legs moved seemingly of their own accord, his limbs scissoring, his breath coming in great chunks of foggy air. He did a quick mile, one of his fastest ever, it seemed to him. Then he dropped to the sand, sucking oxygen from the damp air. He felt hot and then chilled. He thought about his mother and father, his siblings. He envisioned his daughter Renee when she was young, falling off her great horse and calling for Daddy, her cries finally dying away to nothing when he did not come. It was as though his flow of blood had been reversed; it was all backing up, not knowing where to go. He felt the walls of his body giving way, unable to hold everything inside.

He stood on shaky legs, jogged unsteadily back to the beer and his shoes. He sat on the sand for a while, listened to the ocean scream at him and downed another two cans of Red Dog. He squinted into the darkness. It was funny. A few beers and he could see clearly the end of his life at the edge of the horizon. Always wondered when it was going to happen. Now he knew. Forty-one years, three months and fourteen days and the Man upstairs had pulled his ticket. He looked to the sky, waved. *Thanks a lot, God.*

He rose and moved on to the house but didn't go inside. Instead he went to the enclosed courtyard, put his pistol on the table, stripped off all his clothes and dived into the pool. The water temperature, he figured, hovered around eighty-five degrees. His chills quickly disappeared and he went under, touched bottom, did an awkward handstand, blowing freshly chlorinated water out his nostrils, and then floated on the surface, staring at a sky smeared with clouds. He swam some more, practiced his crawl and breast strokes and then drifted over to the side and downed another beer.

He crawled up on the pool deck and thought of his ruined life and of the woman who had done it to him. He dove back in, did another few laps and then climbed out of the pool for good. He looked down, surprised. That was a real kicker. He looked up at the dark window. Was she asleep? How could she be? How in hell could she be, after all this?

Lee decided he would find out for certain. No one could screw up his life and then fall into peaceful sleep. He looked down at himself again. Shit! He glanced at his soggy, sandy clothes and then up at the window. He finished another can of beer in quick gulps, his pulse seemingly spiking with each swallow. He wouldn't need the threads. He'd leave his pistol down here too. If things got out of hand, he didn't want lead to start flying. He pitched the last can of Red Dog over the fence, unopened. Let the birds pry it open and get a buzz. Why should he have all the fun?

He opened the side door quietly and took the stairs two at a time. He thought about kicking her bedroom door in but found it unlocked. He pushed the door open, peered in, letting his eyes adjust to the darkness here. He could make her out on the bed, one long hump. *One long hump.* To his alcohol-saturated mind, that phrase was immensely funny. He took three quick strides and was next to the bed.

Faith stared up at him. "Lee." It wasn't a question, how she said it. It was a simple statement that he didn't know the meaning of.

He knew she could see he was naked. Even in the darkness he trusted she could see he was fully aroused. With a sudden thrust of his arm he stripped the cover off her.

"Lee?" she said again, this time a question.

He looked down at the fine curves and softness of her naked body. His pulse rose, the blood rocketed through his veins, delivering a devilish potency to a man severely wronged. He roughly bulled between her legs, flopped down chest-to-chest. She made no move to resist, her body limp. He started to kiss her on the neck and then stopped. It was not that sort of thing. No tenderness. He clenched her wrists hard.

She just lay there, saying nothing, not telling him to stop. This angered him. He breathed heavily in her face. He wanted her to know it was the beer, not her. He wanted her to feel, to know this was not about her or how she looked or how he felt about her or anything else. He was a red-eyed drunken sonofabitch and she was easy meat. That was all. He loosened his grip. He wanted her to scream, to slug him as hard as she could. Then he would stop. But not before.

Her voice broke through the sounds of what he was doing. "I'd appreciate if you'd get your elbows off my chest."

He wouldn't stop, however, kept going. Hard elbow against soft tissue. The king and the peasant. *Give it to me, Faith. Clean my clock.*

"You don't have to do it like this."

"Whad'cha have in mind?" he slurred back. Navy shore leave in New York City was the last time he had even come close to being this drunk. Intense pain clacked against his temples. Five beers and a few glasses of wine and he was pretty damn well blitzed. God, he was getting old.

"Me on top. You're obviously too intoxicated to know what you're even doing." Her tone was blunt, reproachful.

"On top? Always the boss, even between the sheets? The hell with you." He squeezed her wrists so tightly his thumbs and index fingers touched together. To her credit she didn't even make a whimper, though he could sense the pain coursing through her in how her body tensed under him. He pawed her breasts and buttocks, roughly pummeled her legs and torso. He made no move, though, to enter her. And it wasn't because he was too drunk to accomplish the mechanics; it was because not even alcohol could make him do that to a woman. He kept his eyes closed, didn't want to look at her. But he dipped his face to hers. Lee wanted Faith to smell the stink of his sweat, to soak in the barley and hops base of his lust.

"I just thought you might enjoy it more, that's all," she said.

"Dammit!" he roared. "Are you just gonna let me do this?"

"Would you have me call the police?"

Her voice was like a twirling drill bit against his already throbbing skull. He hovered over her, arms locked, the cords of his triceps bulging.

He felt a tear escape his eye, touch his cheeks, like a single wandering snowflake – homeless, just like him. "Why aren't you kicking the shit out of me, Faith?"

"Because it's not your fault."

Lee started to feel sick to his stomach, his arms weakening. She moved her arm, and he let it go, releasing her without Faith having to say a word. She touched his face, very gently, like a feather dropped from the sky. With a simple motion she rubbed the single tear away. When she spoke, her voice was hoarse. "Because I took your life."

He nodded in understanding. "So if I run with you, do I get this every night? My little dog biscuit?"

"If that's what you want." She suddenly took her hand away, let it drop to the bedding.

He made no move to take it again.

He finally opened his eyes and stared down at the numbing sadness in her gaze, the lingering pain in the tightness of her neck and face; pain he had inflicted and she had taken, silently; the outline of her own hopeless tears against pale cheeks. They all were like searing heat that somehow flashed right past his skin, collided with his heart, vaporizing it.

He pulled himself off her, staggered into the bathroom. He barely made it to the toilet, where the beer and dinner came out much faster than it had gone in. Then Lee passed out on the very expensive Italian tile floor.

The tingle of the cold washcloth against his forehead brought him around. Faith was behind him, cradling him. She seemed to be wearing some kind of long-

274

sleeved T-shirt. He could make out her long, muscular calves and her skinny, curved toes. Lee felt a thick towel across his middle. He was still nauseous, and cold, his teeth chattering. She helped him sit up and then stand, her arm around his waist. He was wearing a pair of Jockeys. She must have done it; he wouldn't have been capable. As it was, he felt like he'd been hog-tied to a whirlybird for about two days. Together they made it back to the bed and she helped him in, covering him with the sheet and comforter.

"I'll sleep in another room," she said softly.

He said nothing, refusing to open his eyes once more.

He could hear her move to the door. Right before she left, he said, "I'm sorry, Faith." He swallowed; his tongue felt big as a damn pineapple.

Before she closed the door, he heard her say so very quietly, "You won't believe this, Lee, but I'm more sorry than you."

THIRTY-FOUR

B rooke Reynolds looked calmly around the interior of the bank. It had just opened and there were no other customers in the branch. In another life she might have been casing the place for future robbery. The thought actually brought a rare smile to her face. She had several scenarios she could have played out, but the very young man sitting behind the desk, with the title of assistant branch manager on a name plate in front of him, had decided the matter.

He looked up as she approached. "Can I help you?"

His eyes grew appreciably larger when the FBI creds came out, and he sat up much straighter, as though attempting to show her that he indeed had a backbone beneath the boyish facade. "Is there a problem?"

"I need your assistance, Mr. Sobel," Reynolds said, eyeing the name on the brass plate. "It has to do with an ongoing Bureau investigation."

"Of course, certainly, whatever I can do," he said.

Reynolds sat down across from him and spoke in a quiet, direct manner. "I have a key here that fits a safe-deposit box at this branch. It was obtained during the investigation. We think whatever's in the box might lead to serious consequences. I need to get inside that box."

"I see. Well, um—"

"I have the account statement with me, if that'll help."

Bankers loved paper, she knew; and the more numbers and statistics, the better. She handed it across to him.

He looked down at the statement.

"Do you recognize the name Frank Andrews?" she asked.

"No," he said. "But I've only been at this branch for a week. Bank consolidation, it never ends."

"I'm sure; even the government is cutting way back."

"I hope not with you people. Lot of crime out there."

"I guess, being in bank management, you see a lot."

The young man looked smug and sipped his coffee. "Oh, the stories I could tell you."

"I bet. Is there any way to tell how often Mr. Andrews visited the box?"

"Absolutely. We transfer those logs to the computer now." He punched in the account number on his computer and waited while it crunched the data. "Would you like some coffee, Agent Reynolds?"

"Thanks, no. How large a box is it?"

He glanced at the statement. "From the monthly fee, it's our deluxe, double width."

"I guess it can hold a lot."

"They're very roomy." He leaned forward and spoke in a low voice. "I bet this has to do with drugs, doesn't it? Laundering, that sort of thing? I've taken a class on the subject."

"I'm sorry, Mr. Sobel, it's an ongoing investigation, and I really can't comment. You understand."

He quickly leaned back. "Absolutely. Sure. We all have rules – you wouldn't believe what we have to deal with at this place."

"I'm sure. Anything come up on the computer?"

"Oh, right." Sobel looked at the screen. "He's actually been in here quite a bit. I can print the log out for you, if you'd like."

"That would be a big help."

As they walked toward the vault a minute later, Sobel started looking nervous. "I'm just wondering if I should check upstairs first. I mean, I'm sure they'd have no problem and all, but still, they're incredibly strict with safe-deposit box access."

"I understand, but I thought the assistant branch manager would have the authority. I won't be taking anything out, just reviewing the contents. And depending on what I find, the box may have to be impounded. It's not the first time the Bureau's had to do this. I'll take full responsibility. Don't worry."

That seemed to relieve the young man and they proceeded into the vault. He took Reynolds's key and his own master and pulled out the large box.

"We have a private room where you can look at it."

He showed her into the small room and Reynolds closed the door. She took a deep breath and noticed that her palms were sweaty. In this box might be something that could shatter any number of lives and perhaps careers. She slowly raised the lid. What she saw made her swear under her breath.

The cash was neatly bundled with thick rubber bands, old, not new bills. She did a quick count. Tens of thousands. She put the lid back down.

Sobel was standing outside the booth when she opened the door. He returned the box to the vault.

"Can I see the sign-in register for this box?"

He showed her the signature log. It was Ken Newman's handwriting; she knew it well. A murdered FBI agent and a box full of cash under an alias. God help them.

"Did you find anything helpful?" Sobel asked.

"I need this box impounded. Anyone shows up wanting to get inside, you're to call me immediately at these numbers." She handed him her card.

"This is serious, isn't it?" Sobel suddenly looked very unhappy that he had been assigned to this branch.

"I appreciate your help, Mr. Sobel. I'll be in touch."

Reynolds returned to her car and drove as quickly as possible toward Anne Newman's house. She called from her car and confirmed the woman would be home. The funeral was scheduled to take place in three days. It would be a big affair, with top officials from the Bureau as well as law enforcement agencies from across the country attending. The funeral motorcade would be especially long and would pass between columns of somber, respectful federal agents and men and women in blue. The FBI buried its agents who died in the line of duty with the great honor and dignity they deserved.

"What did you find out, Brooke?" Anne Newman wore a black dress, her hair was nicely styled, and there was a touch of makeup on her face. Reynolds could hear talk coming from the kitchen. There were two cars parked out front when she had arrived. Probably family or friends offering condolences. She also noted platters of food on the dining room table. Cooking and condolences seemed, ironically, to go hand in hand; grief was better digested on a full stomach, apparently.

"I need to see records of your and Ken's bank accounts. Do you know where they are?"

"Well, Ken always handled the finances, but I'm sure they're in his office." She led Reynolds down the hallway and they went into Ken Newman's home office.

"Do you have more than one bank you deal with?"

"No. That much I do know. I always get the mail. It's just the one bank. And we only have a checking account, no savings. Ken said the interest they paid was a joke. He was really good about money. We own some good stocks, and the kids have their college accounts."

While Anne looked for the records, Reynolds idly glanced around the room. Stacked on one bookshelf were numerous hard plastic containers in various colors. While she had noted the coins encased in clear plastic on her previous visit, she hadn't really focused on these.

"What's in those containers?"

Anne looked at where she was pointing. "Oh, those are Ken's sports cards. Coins too. He was really good at it. He even took a course and became certified to grade both cards and coins. Just about every weekend he was at some show or another." She pointed up to the ceiling. "That's why there's a fire detector in here. Ken was really afraid of fire, in this room especially. All that paper and plastic. It could go up in a minute."

"I'm surprised he found the time for collecting."

"Well, he made the time. He really loved it."

"Did you or the kids ever go with him?"

"No. He never asked us to."

Her tone made Reynolds drop that line of inquiry. "I hate to ask this, but did Ken have life insurance?"

"Yes. A lot."

"At least you won't have to worry about that. I know it's little enough consolation, but so many people never think about those things. Ken obviously wanted you all to be taken care of if anything happened to him. Acts of love often speak louder than words." Reynolds was sincere, yet that last statement had sounded so incredibly lame that she decided to shut her mouth on the subject.

Anne pulled out a three-inch red notebook and handed it to Reynolds.

"I think this is what you're looking for. There are more in the drawer. This is the most current one."

Reynolds looked down at the binder. There was a laminated label affixed to the front flap of the notebook indicating that it contained checking account statements for the current year. She flipped it open. The statements were neatly labeled and organized chronologically by month, the most recent month on top.

"The canceled checks are in the other drawer. Ken kept them divided by year."

Damn! Reynolds kept her financial records stuffed in an assortment of drawers in her bedroom and even in the garage. Tax time at the Reynolds household was an accountant's worst nightmare.

"Anne, I know you have company. I can look through these by myself."

"You can take them with you if you want."

"If you don't mind, I'll look at them here."

"Okay. Would you like something to drink or eat? Lord knows we've got plenty of food. And I just put on a fresh pot of coffee."

"Actually, coffee would be great, thanks. Just a little cream and sugar."

Anne suddenly looked nervous. "You still haven't told me if you found out anything."

"I want to make absolutely sure before I say anything. I don't want to be wrong." As Reynolds looked into the poor woman's face, she felt tremendous guilt. Here she was letting the man's wife unknowingly assist her in possibly tarnishing her husband's memory.

"How are the kids holding up?" Reynolds asked, doing her best to shake this traitorous feeling.

"How any children would be, I suppose. They're sixteen and seventeen, so they understand things better than a five-year-old would. But it's still hard. For all of us. Only reason I'm not still bawling is that I ran out of tears this morning. I sent them to school. I decided it couldn't be any worse than sitting around here while a parade of people came through talking about their dad."

"You're probably right."

"You can only do the best you can. I knew there was always the possibility. God, Ken was an agent for twenty years. The only time he ever got hurt on duty was when his car got a flat and he wrenched his back changing the tire." Anne smiled briefly at this memory. "He was even talking about retirement. Maybe moving away when the kids were both at college. His mother lives in South Carolina. She's getting to the age where she needs some family close by."

Anne looked like she might start crying again. If she did, Reynolds wasn't sure she wouldn't join her, given her own mental state right now.

"You have children?"

"Boy and girl. Three and six."

Anne smiled. "Oh, still babies."

"I understand it gets tougher as they get older."

"Well, let's put it this way, it gets more complex. You go from spitting, biting, potty-training, to battles over clothes, boys, money. About age thirteen they suddenly can't stand being around Mom and Dad. That one was tough, but they finally came back. Then you worry yourself sick over alcohol and cars and sex and drugs."

Reynolds managed a weak smile. "Gee, I can't wait."

"How long have you been with the Bureau?"

"Thirteen years. Joined after one incredibly boring

year as a corporate lawyer."

"It can be a dangerous business."

Reynolds stared at her. "It certainly can be."

"You're married?"

"Technically, yes, but in a couple of months, no."

"Sorry to hear that."

"Believe me, it's best all around."

"You're keeping the children?"

"Absolutely."

"That's good. Children belong with their mothers, I don't care what the politically correct folk say."

"In my case, I wonder – I work long, unpredictable hours. All I know is that my children belong with me."

"You say you have a law degree?"

"From Georgetown."

"Lawyers make good money. And it's not nearly as dangerous as being an FBI agent."

"I suppose not." Reynolds finally realized where this was going.

"You might want to think about a career change. Too many nuts out there now. And too many guns. When Ken started at the Bureau, there weren't kids just out of diapers running around with machine guns shooting people down like they were in some damn cartoon."

Reynolds had no answer for that. She just stood there hugging the notebook to her chest, thinking of her kids.

"I'll bring your coffee."

Anne closed the door behind her and Reynolds sank into the nearest chair. She was having a sudden vision of her body being put inside a black pouch while the palm reader delivered the bad news to her bereaved children. *I told your mother so.* Shit! She shook off these thoughts and opened the notebook. Anne returned with her coffee, and then, left to herself, Reynolds made considerable progress. What she found out was very disturbing.

For at least the last three years, Ken Newman had made deposits, all in cash, to his checking account. The amounts were small – a hundred dollars here, fifty there – and they were made at random times. She pulled out the log Sobel had given her and ran her eye down the dates Newman had visited the safe-deposit box. Most of them corresponded with the dates he had also deposited cash into his checking account. Visit the box, put fresh cash in, take some old cash out and deposit it in the family bank account, she surmised.

It all added up to a significant amount of money, yet not a vast fortune. The thing was, the total balance of the checking account was never very large because there were always checks written on the account that depleted this balance. Newman's FBI payroll checks were on direct deposit, she noted. And there were numerous checks written to a stock brokerage firm. Reynolds found those records in another drawer and quickly determined that while Newman was far from wealthy, he'd had a nice stock portfolio going, and the records showed he religiously added to it. With the long bull market still steaming along, his investments had grown considerably.

Except for the cash deposits, what she was looking at wasn't really that unusual. He had saved money and invested it well. He wasn't wealthy, but he was comfortable. Dividends from the investment account were also deposited to the Newmans' checking account, further muddling the income picture. Simply put, it would be difficult to conclude that there was anything suspicious about the agent's finances unless one really took a very close look. And unless one knew about the safe-deposit box cash, the amount of money seemingly at issue just didn't warrant that level of scrutiny.

The confusing thing was the amount of cash she had seen in the safe-deposit box. Why keep that much in the box where it was earning no interest? What puzzled her almost as much as the cash was what she *wasn't* finding. When Anne came to check on her, she decided to ask her directly.

"I'm not finding any mortgage or credit card payments recorded here."

"We don't have a mortgage. That is, we did, a thirty-year one, but Ken made extra payments and finally paid it off early."

"Good for him. When was that?"

"About three or four years ago, I think."

"What about credit cards?"

"Ken didn't believe in them. What we bought, we bought with cash. Appliances, clothes, even cars. We never bought new, only used."

"Well, that's smart. Saves a ton in finance charges."

"Like I said, Ken was really good with the money."

"If I'd known how good, I would've had him help me."

"Do you need to look at anything else?"

"One more thing, I'm afraid. Your tax returns for the last couple of years, if you have them."

The large amount of cash in the box made sense now to Reynolds. If Newman paid cash for everything, then he would have no need to deposit it in his checking account. Of course, for things like the mortgage, the utilities and the phone bill, he needed to write a check, so he would have to deposit cash to cover those checks. And this also meant that for the money he didn't deposit into his checking account there was no record that he ever had the money in

285

the box at all. Cash was cash, after all. And that meant that the IRS would have no way of knowing Newman ever had it either.

He wisely hadn't changed his lifestyle. Same house, no fancy cars, and he hadn't gone on insane shopping binges that had toppled so many thieves. And with no mortgage or credit card payments, he had a lot of free cash flow; on a cursory examination, this would seem to explain the ability to make the regular stock investments. Someone would have to really dig as Reynolds had to uncover the truth.

Anne found tax returns for the last six years in the metal filing cabinet standing against one wall. These were as well organized as the rest of the man's financial records. A quick look at the returns for the last three years confirmed Reynolds's suspicions. The only income listed was Newman's FBI salary and some miscellaneous investment interest and dividends and bank interest.

Reynolds put the files back and slipped on her coat. "Anne, I'm so sorry I had to come and do all this in the middle of everything you're having to deal with."

"I asked *you* for help, Brooke."

Reynolds felt another stab of guilt. "Well, I don't know how much help I've been."

Anne gripped her arm. "Now can you tell me what's going on? Has Ken done anything wrong?"

"All I can tell you right now is that I found some things I can't explain. I won't lie to you, they are very troubling."

Anne slowly took her hand away. "I guess you'll have to report what you've found."

Reynolds stared at the woman. Technically what she should do was go directly to OPR and tell them everything. The Office of Professional Responsibility was officially under the umbrella of the Bureau but

286

was actually run by the Department of Justice. OPR investigated allegations of misconduct by Bureau personnel. They had a reputation for being very thorough. An OPR investigation could put a scare into even the toughest FBI agent.

Yes, from a simple technical point of view, it was a no-brainer. If life could only be so simple. The devastated woman standing before Reynolds made her decision much less simple. In the end she went with her human side and put aside the Bureau manual for now. Ken Newman would be buried a hero. The man had been an agent for two decades; he at least deserved that.

"At some point, yes, I'll have to report my findings. But not right now." She paused and gripped the woman's hand. "I know when the funeral is. I'll be there with everyone else, paying our respects to Ken."

Reynolds gave Anne a reassuring hug and then walked out, her mind whirling so fast she felt a little dizzy.

If Ken Newman was on the take, he had been doing it for a while. Was he the leak on Reynolds's investigation? Had he sold out other investigations as well? Was he just a freelancing mole selling to the highest bidder? Or was he a regular snitch working for the same party? If so, why was such a party interested in Faith Lockhart? There were foreign interests involved. Lockhart had told them that much. Was that the key? Was Newman working for a foreign government all this time, a foreign government that was also coincidentally caught up in Buchanan's scheme?

She sighed. The whole thing was snowballing into something so big, she halfway felt like running home and pulling the covers over her head. Instead she would get in her car, drive to the office and continue chipping away at this case, as she had hundreds of others over the years. She had won more than she had lost. And that was the best anyone in her line of work could ever hope for.

THIRTY-FIVE

Lee had awoken very late with the mother of all hangovers and decided to run it off. At first, each of his strides on the sand sent lethal darts through his brain. Then, as he loosened up, breathed the chilly air, felt the salty wind on his face, at about the one-mile point in his run, the effects of his crushed grape and Red Dog shooters disappeared. When he got back to the beach house, he went around to the pool and retrieved his clothes and his gun. He sat in a sling chair for a while, letting the sun warm him. When he went back inside, he smelled coffee and eggs.

Faith was in the kitchen, pouring a cup of coffee. She had on jeans and a short-sleeved shirt and was barefoot. When she saw him come in, she pulled out another mug and filled it. For a moment, this simple act of companionship pleased him. And then his actions of the night before washed that feeling away, like ocean waves brutally wiping out sand castles.

"I figured you'd sleep all day," she said. Her tone was excessively casual, he thought, and she didn't look at him when she spoke.

This qualified for the most awkward moment in Lee's entire life. What was he supposed to say? *Hey, sorry about that little sexual assault thing last night.*

He came into the kitchen area, fingered the mug, half hoping the large lump in his throat would end up strangling him to death. "Sometimes the best remedy for doing something incredibly stupid and inexcusable is to run until you drop." He glanced at the eggs. "Smells good."

"Doesn't compare to the meal you made last night. But then again, I'm no whiz in the kitchen. I guess I'm a room-service kind of girl. But I'm sure you already figured that out." As she moved over to the stove, he noted she walked with a slight limp. He also couldn't fail to notice the bruises on her uncovered wrists. He laid the pistol down on the counter before he could impulsively use it to blow his brains out.

"Faith?"

She didn't turn around, just kept scrambling the eggs around in the pan.

"If you want me to leave, I'll leave," said Lee.

While she seemed to consider this, he decided to say what he had been thinking during his run. "What happened last night, what I *did* to you last night, there's no excuse for. I've never, ever done anything like that in my life. That's not who I am. I can't blame you if you don't believe that. But it's the truth."

She suddenly turned to him, her eyes glistening. "Well, I can't say I hadn't imagined something happening between us, even in the nightmare we're in. I just didn't think it would be like that. . . ." Her voice broke off and she just as quickly turned away from him.

He looked down and nodded slightly, her words doubly devastating to him. "You see, I'm in a bit of a dilemma here. My gut and my conscience tell me to get out of your life so you won't have to be reminded of what happened last night every time you see me. But I don't want to leave you alone with all this. Not when someone's out to kill you."

She turned the burner off and set out two plates, shoveled the eggs on them, buttered two pieces of toast and put everything on the table. Lee didn't move. He just watched her, moving slowly, her cheeks wet from her tears. The bruises on her wrists were like permanent shackles around his soul.

He sat down across from her and picked at his eggs.

"I could have stopped you last night," she said bluntly. The tears slid down her cheeks and she made no attempt to wipe them away.

Lee felt his own eyes begin to burn with the beginnings of tears. "I wish to God you had."

"You were drunk. I'm not saying that's an excuse for what you did, but I also know you wouldn't have done it if you had been sober. And you also didn't go all the way. I choose to believe you would never sink so low as that. In fact, if I weren't absolutely sure of that, I would've shot you with your gun when you passed out." She paused, seemed to be searching for the right combination of words. "But maybe what I've done to you is much more awful than what you could have done to me last night." She pushed her plate away and looked out the window at what was shaping up to be a beautiful day.

When she next spoke, it was in a wistful, faraway tone that was curiously both hopeful and tragic. "When I was a little girl, I had my whole life planned out. I was going to be a nurse. And then a doctor. And I was going to get married and have ten kids. Dr. Faith Lockhart was going to save lives during the day and then come home to a wonderful man who loved her and be the perfect mother to her perfect children. After moving around all those years with my father, I just wanted *one* home. I'd live there the rest of my life. My children would always, always know where to find me. It seemed so simple, so . . . achievable, when I was only eight years old." She finally used her paper napkin to dab at her eyes, only then seeming to feel the wetness on her face.

291

She looked back at Lee. "But I have this life instead." Her gaze roamed the lovely room. "I actually had a pretty good run. Made a lot of money. What do I have to complain about? That's the American dream, isn't it? Money? Power? Owning beautiful things? Hell, I even ended up doing a little good, even if I did it illegally. But then I went and ruined everything. The best of intentions, but I struck out in the end. Just like my father. You're right, the nut didn't fall far from the tree." She paused again, played with her silverware, precisely placing the fork and butter knife perpendicular to one another.

"I don't want you to leave." On this she rose, quickly crossed the room and then raced up the stairs.

Lee heard her bedroom door slam shut.

Lee took a deep breath, stood and was surprised to find his legs so rubbery. It wasn't from the run, he knew. He showered, changed and came back downstairs. Faith's door was still closed and he had no intention of interrupting whatever she was doing in there. With his nerves unraveling, he decided to spend an hour with the mundane task of thoroughly cleaning his gun. The downside to salt and water was that they were tough on weapons, and automatic pistols were notoriously finicky anyway. If the ammo wasn't of a very high quality, you could count on the thing misfiring and then jamming – or a little sand and grit could cause the same malfunction. And you couldn't clear a pistol by simply pulling the trigger and bringing up a clean cylinder, as you would a revolver. By the time you got your pistol all straightened out, you'd be dead. And with Lee's luck to date, it would happen right when he absolutely needed the thing to fire true and straight. However, on the plus side, the 9mm Parabellums fired by the compact Smith & Wesson had excellent stopping power. Whatever they hit would drop. He prayed he wouldn't have to use the gun, however. Because that would probably mean someone was shooting at him.

He reloaded the fifteen-shot magazine, inserted it in the grip and chambered a round. He clicked the safety on and holstered the gun. He thought about taking the Honda down to the store for a newspaper but decided he didn't quite have the energy or desire to undertake even such a simple task. He also didn't want to leave Faith alone. When she came downstairs, he wanted to be here.

When Lee went to get a drink of water at the kitchen sink, he glanced out the window and almost had a heart attack. Across the road, above a tall hedge that ran about as far as the eye could see, suddenly exploding into his line of vision was a small plane! That's when Lee remembered the runway Faith had told him about. It was across from the house and shielded by the tall hedge.

Lee hurried to the front door to watch the landing. By the time he got outside, the plane had already disappeared. Then whizzing above the top of the hedge was the tail of the plane. It flashed in front of him and then continued past at a fast clip.

He went up on the second-story front porch and watched as the plane taxied to a stop and the passengers deplaned. A car was waiting to pick them up. Bags were off-loaded and stored in the car, which left with the passengers. The pilot got out of the twin-prop plane, checked a few things and then climbed back in. A few minutes later the plane taxied to the other end of the runway and turned around. The pilot opened the throttle and came roaring down the runway in the same direction he had landed, and then lifted gracefully into the air.

The plane headed out toward the water, made a turn and quickly disappeared into the horizon.

Lee went back inside and tried to watch some TV, while at the same time listening for Faith. After roaming through about a thousand channels, he concluded there was absolutely nothing worth watching, and he played a game of solitaire. He enjoyed losing so much, he played another dozen games, with the same result. He wandered downstairs and shot some pool in the game room. When lunchtime came around, he fixed a tuna sandwich and some beef barley soup and ate out on the deck overlooking the pool. He watched the same plane land once more around one o'clock. It shed its passengers and soared once more. He thought about knocking on Faith's door to see if she was hungry and then decided against it. He went for a swim in the pool and then lay on the cool concrete and caught some rays from the intense sun. He felt guilty every minute for enjoying it.

The hours passed and when it started to grow dark, he began contemplating cooking dinner. He would go and get Faith this time, and make her eat. He was just about to head up the stairs when her door opened and she came out.

The first thing that caught his eye was what she was wearing: a white cotton dress, knee-length and clingy, paired with a light blue cotton sweater. Her legs were bare, and she wore simple sandals that managed to look very classy. Her hair was nicely styled; a touch of makeup highlighted her features and pale red lipstick completed the look. She held a small clutch purse. The sweater covered the bruises on her wrists. Probably why she had picked it, he thought. He was thankful that her limp seemed to be gone.

"Going out?" Lee asked.

"Dinner. I'm starving."

"I was going to make something."

"I'd rather eat out. I'm getting cabin fever."

"So where are you going?"

"Well, actually I thought *we* might go."

Lee looked down at his faded khakis, deck shoes and short-sleeved Polo shirt. "I look sort of ragged next to you."

"You look fine." She glanced at the holstered gun. "I'd leave the six-shooter behind, though."

He looked at her dress. "Faith, I'm not sure how comfortable you'll be on the Honda in that."

"The country club's only a half mile up the road. It has a public restaurant. I thought we could walk. Looks to be a beautiful evening."

Lee finally nodded, understanding that getting out made perfect sense, for a lot of reasons. "Sounds good. Give me a sec." He ran upstairs, slipped off his gun and put it in a drawer in his room. He splashed water on his face, wet down his hair a little, grabbed his jacket and joined Faith at the front door, where she was activating the alarm. They left the house and crossed the service road. Reaching the sidewalk, which ran parallel to the main road, they strolled along under a sky that had changed to pink from blue as the sun sank. Landscape lighting had come on in the common areas and so had the underground sprinklers. The sound of the pressurized water was soothing to Lee. The lighting lent a nice mood to the walk, he thought. The whole place seemed to possess almost an ethereal glow, as though they were in a perfectly lit scene from a movie.

Lee looked up in time to see the same twin-prop airplane coming in for a landing. He shook his head.

"Scared the hell out of me the first time I saw that thing this morning."

"It would have scared me too, except the first time

I came here I was flying on it. That's the last flight for the evening. It's getting too dark now."

They reached the restaurant, which was decorated with a distinctly nautical theme: a big ship's wheel at the front entrance, diving helmets hung on the wall, fish netting suspended from the ceiling, knotty pine walls, rope banisters and hand rails and an enormous aquarium filled with castles, plant life and an odd assortment of fish peeking out here and there. The servers were young, energetic and attired in cruise line uniforms. The one attending Faith and Lee's table was particularly bubbly. She took their drink orders. Lee opted for iced tea. Faith ordered a wine spritzer. That done, the waitress proceeded to sing the specials of the day in a pleasant if wavering alto. After she left, Faith and Lee looked at each other and had to laugh.

While they waited for their drinks, Faith looked around the room.

Lee shot her a glance. "See anybody you recognize?"

"No. I never really went out when I came down here. I was afraid I'd run into someone I knew."

"Stay cool. You look very different from Faith Lockhart." He looked her over. "And I should have said this before, but you look really . . . well, you really look pretty tonight. I mean really fine." He suddenly looked embarrassed. "Not that you don't look good all the time. I meant . . ." Thoroughly tongue-tied, Lee lapsed into silence, sat back and perused his menu.

Faith looked over at him, feeling just as awkward as he did, she was sure, but a smile still eased across her lips. "Thank you."

They were there for two pleasant stolen hours, discussing innocuous subjects, telling stories of times past and learning more about each other. Since it was the off-season and a weekday, there were few other patrons. They finished their meal, then had coffee and shared a thick slice of coconut cream pie. They paid in cash and left a very generous tip, which would probably make their waitress sing all the way home.

Faith and Lee walked slowly back, enjoying the crisp night air and digesting their meals. Instead of going to the house, though, Faith led Lee down to the beach after dropping her purse off by the back door of the beach house. She slipped off her sandals and they continued their stroll on the sand. It was completely dark now, the wind light and refreshing, and they had the beach entirely to themselves.

Lee looked over at her. "Going out was a good idea. I really enjoyed myself."

"You can be very charming when you want to be."

He looked annoyed for a moment until he realized she was kidding him. "I guess going out together made for a fresh start of sorts too."

"That did cross my mind." She stopped and sat down on the beach, sinking her feet into the sand. Lee remained standing, looking out to the ocean.

"So what do we do now, Lee?"

He sat next to her, slipped off his shoes and curled his toes under the sand. "It would be great if we could stay here, but I don't think we can."

"Then where? I'm fresh out of houses."

"I've been thinking about that. I've got some good buddies in San Diego. Private investigators like me. They know everybody. If I ask, I'm sure they'll help us slip across the border into Mexico."

Faith didn't look very enthusiastic about that idea. "Mexico? And from there?"

Lee shrugged. "I don't know. We can maybe get some fake documents and use them to get to South America."

"South America? And you work the cocaine fields while I labor in a brothel?"

"Look, I've been there. It's not just drugs and prostitutes. We'll have lots of options."

"Two fugitives from justice with God knows who else after them?" Faith looked down at the sand and shook her head doubtfully.

"If you have a better idea, I'm listening," said Lee.

"I've got money. A lot of it in a numbered account in Switzerland."

He looked skeptical. "They really have those things?"

"Oh, yes. And all those global conspiracies you've probably heard about? Secret organizations ruling the planet? Well, they're all true." She smiled and tossed sand on him.

"Well, if the Feds search your home or office, will they find records for it? If they know the account numbers, they can put a tag on it. Trace the money."

"The whole purpose of a Swiss numbered account is to ensure absolute confidentiality. If Swiss bankers ran around giving out that information to anyone who asked for it, their whole system sort of topples."

"The FBI isn't just anyone."

"Not to worry, I didn't keep any records. I have the access information with me."

Lee looked unconvinced. "So do you have to go to Switzerland to get the money? Because that would be, you know, sort of impossible."

"I went there to open the account. The bank appointed a fiduciary, a bank employee, with a power of attorney to handle the transaction in person. It's pretty elaborate. You have to show your access numbers, give positive ID, then provide your signature, which they compare with the one they have on file."

"So from then on you call the fiduciary and he

does all that for you?"

"Right. I've done small transactions in the past, just to make sure it works. It's the same guy. He knows me and my voice. I give him the numbers and where I want the money to go. And it happens."

"You know you can't deposit it in Faith Lockhart's checking account."

"No, but I have a bank account down here under the name of SLC Corporation."

"And you're a signatory as an officer?"

"Yes, as Suzanne Blake."

"The problem is, the Feds know that name. Remember, from the airport."

"Do you know how many Suzanne Blakes there are in this country?"

Lee shrugged. "That's true."

"So at least we'll have money to live off. It won't last us forever, but it's something."

"Something is good."

They fell silent for a bit. Faith alternated between nervously looking at him and then out toward the ocean.

He glanced at her, having noticed her scrutiny. "What is it? Do I have coconut pie on my chin?"

"Lee, when the money comes, you can take half and leave. You don't have to come with me."

"Faith, we've already been through this."

"No, we haven't. I practically ordered you to come with me. I know it would be difficult to go back without me, but at least you'll have the money to go somewhere. Look, I can even call the FBI. I'll tell them you had no involvement. You were just blindly helping me. And that I gave you the slip. Then you can go back home."

"Thanks, Faith, but let's take it one step at a time. And I can't leave until I know you're safe."

"Are you sure?"

"Yes, I'm really sure. I won't go unless you tell me to. And then even if you do, I'll still stalk you, to make sure you're okay."

She reached out and took his arm. "Lee, I can never thank you enough for all you've done for me."

"Just consider me the big brother you never had."

The look they shared, though, held more than sibling affection. He looked down at the sand, trying to get his head straight. Faith looked back out at the water. When Lee looked over at her a minute later, Faith was moving her head from side to side and smiling.

"What are you thinking?" he asked.

She stood and looked down at him. "I'm thinking that I'd like to dance."

He stared up at her in amazement. "Dancing? How much *did* you have to drink?"

"How many nights do we have left here? Two? Three? Then it's off to play fugitive for the rest of our lives? Come on, Lee, last chance to party." She slipped off her sweater and let it fall to the sand. The white dress had spaghetti straps. She slipped them off her shoulders, gave him a heart-stopping wink and held out her hands for Lee to take. "Let's go, big boy."

"You're crazy, you truly are." However, Lee gripped her hands and stood. "Fair warning, I haven't danced in a long time."

"You're a boxer, right? Your footwork is probably better than mine. I'll lead first, and then you take over."

Lee took a few halting steps and dropped his hands. "This is silly, Faith. What if somebody's watching? They'll think we're nuts."

She looked at him stubbornly. "I've spent the last fifteen years of my life worrying about what everybody thought about everything. So right now, I don't give a damn about what anybody thinks about anything."

"But we don't even have any music."

"Hum a tune. Listen to the wind, it'll come."

And surprisingly it did. They started slowly at first, Lee feeling clumsy and Faith unused to leading. Then, as they started to get more familiar with each other's movements, they began making wider circles in the sand. After about ten minutes, Lee's right hand was perched comfortably on Faith's hip, hers was around his waist, their other pair of hands were interlocked and held chest high.

Then they grew noticeably braver and started doing some spins and twirls and other moves reminiscent of Big Band swing and Lindy hop. It was difficult, even in the hard-packed sand, but they gave it an inspired effort. Anyone watching would have thought them either intoxicated or reliving their youth and having the time of their lives. And, in a way, both observations would have been true.

"I haven't done this since high school," Lee said, smiling. "Although Three Dog Night was the big thing back then, not Benny Goodman."

Faith said nothing as she twirled and dipped around him, her moves growing more and more daring, more and more seductive; a flamenco dancer in white flaming heat.

She hiked her skirt up to give herself more freedom of movement, and Lee felt his heart race at the sight of her pale thighs.

They even ventured out into the water, splashing mightily as they went about their increasingly intricate dance steps. They had some tumbles into the sand and even into the salty, chilly water, but they got back up and kept going. Occasionally a truly spectacular combination, perfectly executed, left them both breathless and grinning like school-kids at a prom.

They finally reached the point where they both grew silent, their smiles faded and they drew closer to each other. The spins and twirls stopped, their heavy breaths eased and they found their bodies touching as their dance circles grew smaller. Finally they stopped altogether and simply stood there rocking slightly side to side, the last dance of the evening, arms around each other, faces close, eyes directly on one another as the wind whistled around them, the waves pitched and crashed hard, the stars and the moon watched from above.

Faith finally stepped away from him, her eyelids heavy, her limbs starting to once again erotically move to a silent tune.

Lee reached out to take her back. "I don't feel like dancing anymore, Faith." His meaning was crystal clear.

She reached out to him too, and then, quick as the snap of a whip, she shoved him hard in the chest and he flopped backward into the sand. She turned and ran, her peals of laughter descending over him as he looked after her, stunned. He grinned, jumped up and raced after her, catching her at the stairs going up to the beach house. He slung her over his shoulder and carried her the rest of the way, her legs and arms flailing in mock protest. They had forgotten the house alarm was set and went in the back door. Faith had to race like mad to the front door to disarm it in time.

"God, that was close. Like we really want the police coming by," she said.

"I don't want anybody coming by."

Gripping his hand tightly, Faith led Lee up to her bedroom. They sat on the bed in the darkness for a few minutes holding one another, gently rocking back and forth as though extending their movements on the beach to this more intimate place.

Finally she eased back from him, cupped his chin with her hand. "It's been a while, Lee. It's been a long time, in fact." Her tone was almost one of embarrassment, and Faith did feel embarrassed at this admission. She didn't want to disappoint him.

He stroked her fingers gently, held her gaze with his as the sounds of the waves reached them through the open window. It was comforting, she thought, the water, the wind, the touches of skin; a moment she may not experience again for a very long time, if ever.

"It'll never be easier for you, Faith."

This surprised her. "Why do you say that?"

Even in the darkness the glow of his eyes surrounded her, held her – protectively, she felt. The fifth-grade romance finally consummated? And yet she was with a man, not a boy. A very unique man, in his own right. She looked him over. No, definitely not a boy.

"Because I can't believe you've ever been with a man who feels the way I do about you."

"Easy to say," she murmured, though in fact his words had touched her deeply.

"Not for me," Lee said.

These few words were spoken with such depth of sincerity, with not a trace of the glibness, the self-servedness of the world she had thrived in for the last fifteen years, that Faith honestly didn't know how to react. But the time for talk had passed. She found herself sliding Lee's clothes off, and then he disrobed her. He massaged her shoulders and neck as he did so. Lee's big fingers were surprisingly gentle. She would've expected them to be rough.

All of their movements were unhurried, natural, as though they had done this thousands of times over the course of a long, happy marriage, seeking just the right spots to work, to please the other.

They slid under the covers. Ten minutes later Lee slumped down, breathing heavy. Faith was under him, gasping for air as well. She kissed his face, his chest, his arms. Their sweat mingled, their limbs intertwined, they lay there talking and slowly kissing for another two hours, falling in and out of sleep as they did so. About three in the morning they made love again. And then both collapsed into deep, exhausted sleep.

THIRTY-SIX

Reynolds was sitting at her desk when the phone call came. It was Joyce Bennett, the lawyer representing Reynolds in her divorce.

"We have a problem, Brooke. Your husband's attorney just called, ranting and raving about you hiding assets."

Brooke's face collapsed in disbelief. "Are you serious? Well, tell him to let me in on it. I could use the extra money."

"This isn't a joke. He faxed me some account statements he says he just discovered. Under the children's names."

"For God's sake, Joyce, those are the kids' college accounts. Steve knew about those. That's why I didn't list them with my assets. Besides, they only have a few hundred dollars in them."

"Actually, the statements I'm looking at show a balance of fifty thousand dollars in each."

Reynolds's mouth went dry. "That's not possible. There must be some mistake."

"The other troubling thing is that the accounts are set up as Uniform Transfer to Minor's Act accounts. That means they're revocable at the discretion of the donor and trustee. You're the listed trustee, and I'm assuming you would be the donor of the funds as well. In essence, it's your money. You should have told me about these, Brooke."

"Joyce, there was nothing to tell. I have no idea

where that money came from. What do the statements show as the origin of funds?"

"Several wire transfers of roughly equal amounts. It doesn't show where they came from. Steve's attorney is threatening to go to court and claim fraud. Brooke, he also says he's called the Bureau."

Reynolds squeezed the phone and sat rigidly. "The Bureau?"

"You're sure you don't know where the money came from? How about your parents?"

"They don't have that kind of money. Can we trace the funds?"

"It's *your* account. I think you better do something. Keep me posted."

Reynolds hung up the phone and stared blankly at the papers on her desk, her mind reeling from this latest development. When the phone rang again a few minutes later, she almost didn't answer it. She knew who it was.

Paul Fisher spoke more coldly than ever to her. She was to come to the Hoover Building immediately. That was all he would tell her. As she walked down the stairs to the parking garage, her legs threatened to collapse under her several times. Every instinct she had told her she had just been summoned to her own professional execution.

The conference room at the Hoover Building was small and windowless. Paul Fisher was there, along with the ADIC, Fred Massey. Massey sat at the head of the table, twirling a pen between his fingers, his gaze locked on her. She recognized the two other people in the room: a Bureau lawyer and a senior investigator from OPR.

"Sit down, Agent Reynolds," Massey said firmly.

Reynolds sat. She wasn't guilty of anything, so why did she feel like Charlie Manson with a bloody knife in his sock?

"We have some things to discuss with you." He glanced at the Bureau lawyer. "I have to advise you, however, that you have the right to have counsel present, if you so wish."

She tried to act surprised, but couldn't really, not after the phone call from Joyce Bennett. Her forced reaction certainly increased her guilt in their eyes, she felt sure. She wondered about the timing of that phone call from Bennett. Not a big believer in conspiracies, Reynolds suddenly began to reconsider that stance.

"And why would I need counsel?"

Massey eyed Fisher, who turned to Reynolds. "We received a phone call from the attorney representing your husband in the divorce."

"I see. Well, I just received a call from my attorney, and I can assure you I'm as much in the dark as anyone else about how that money got into those accounts."

"Really?" Massey looked at her skeptically. "So you're saying it's a mistake that someone very recently dumped a hundred thousand dollars into accounts under your children's names, monies which are solely controlled by you?"

"I'm saying I don't know what to think. But I will find out, I can assure you."

"The timing, as you can understand, has us deeply troubled," Massey said.

"Not as troubled as me. It's my reputation at stake."

"Actually, it's the reputation of the Bureau we're concerned about," Fisher bluntly pointed out.

Reynolds gave him a cold stare and then looked back at Massey. "I don't know what's going on. Feel free to investigate; I've got nothing to hide."

Massey glanced down at a file in front of him. "Are you quite certain of that?"

Reynolds looked at the file. This was a classic interrogation technique. She had used it herself. Bluff the subject by suggesting you had incriminating evidence that would catch him in a lie and hope he'd cave. The only thing was, she didn't know if Massey was really bluffing or not. She suddenly knew what it was like to be on the other side of the interrogation. It wasn't fun.

"Am I quite certain of what?" she said, buying time.

"That you have nothing to hide?"

"I really resent that question, sir."

He tapped the file with his index finger. "You know what has deeply distressed me about Ken Newman's death? The fact that on the night he was murdered, he had taken your place. At your instruction. But for that order, he would be alive today. Would you?"

Reynolds's face turned red and she stood, towering over Massey. "Are you accusing me of being involved in Ken's murder?"

"Please sit down, Agent Reynolds."

"Are you?"

"I'm saying the coincidence, if it is one, has me concerned."

"It *was* a coincidence, since I didn't happen to know there was someone waiting there to kill him. If you recall, I showed up almost in time to stop it."

"Almost in time. That was convenient. Almost like a built-in alibi. A coincidence, or perfect timing? Perhaps too perfect timing?" Massey's gaze burned into her.

"I was working another case and finished sooner than I thought I would. Howard Constantinople can corroborate that."

"Oh, we plan to talk to Connie. You and he are friends, aren't you?"

"We're professional colleagues."

"I'm sure he wouldn't want to say anything that would implicate you in any way."

"I'm *sure* he'll tell you the truth if you just ask him."

"So you're saying there is no connection between Ken Newman's murder and the money showing up in your account?"

"Let me put it a little more strongly than that. I'm saying it's all bullshit! If I were guilty, why would I have anyone put a hundred grand into one of my accounts so close to the time Ken was killed? Don't you think that's a little obvious?"

"But it wasn't really your account, was it? It was in your children's names. And according to your personnel records, you're not due for a Bureau five-year check for another two years. I rather doubt the money would be in the account at that time, and by then I'm sure you'd have a good answer in case anyone did discover that money had once been there. The point is, if your husband's attorney hadn't dug it up, no one would know. That hardly qualifies as obvious."

"Okay, if it's not a mistake, then someone is setting me up."

"And who exactly would be doing that?"

"The person who killed Ken, and who tried to kill Faith Lockhart. Maybe he's afraid I'm getting too close."

"So Danny Buchanan is trying to set you up, is that what you're saying?"

Reynolds glanced at the Bureau lawyer and the representative from OPR. "Do they have clearance to hear this?"

"Your investigation has taken a backseat to these more recent charges," Fisher said.

Reynolds glared at him with rising anger. "Charges! They're unsubstantiated garbage."

Massey opened the file. "So are you saying that your *private* investigation into Ken Newman's finances is garbage?"

On this Reynolds froze and then abruptly sat down. She pressed sweaty palms against the table and tried to get her emotions under control. Her temper was not doing her any good. She was playing right into their hands. Indeed, Fisher and Massey exchanged what she saw as pleased glances at her obvious distress.

"We talked to Anne Newman. She told us everything you've done," Fisher said. "I can't even begin to tell you how many Bureau rules you've broken."

"I was trying to protect Ken and his family."

"Oh, please!" Fisher exclaimed.

"It's true! I was going to go to OPR, but not until after the funeral."

"That was so very considerate of you," Fisher said sarcastically.

"Why don't you go to hell, Paul."

"Agent Reynolds, keep a civil tongue in your head," Massey commanded.

Reynolds sat back and rubbed her forehead. "May I ask how you found out about what I was doing? Did Anne Newman come to you?"

"If you don't mind, we'll ask the questions." Massey leaned forward and made a pyramid with his fingers. "What exactly did you find in the safe-deposit box?"

"Cash. A lot. Thousands."

"And Newman's financial records?"

"A lot of unexplained income."

"We've also talked to the bank branch you visited. You told them not to allow access to the box to anyone except yourself. And you told Anne Newman not to tell anyone about it, not even anyone

310

at the Bureau."

"I didn't want anybody getting to that money. It was material evidence. And I told Anne to keep quiet until I had a chance to dig further. It was for her own protection, until I found out who was behind it."

"Or did you want the time to get the money for yourself? With Ken dead and Anne Newman apparently not even aware her husband had the safe-deposit box, you would be the only one who knew the money was there." Massey stared directly at her; his tiny eyes resembled twin bullets coming for her.

Fisher piped in: "It's curious that when Newman dies you access a box with thousands of dollars in it that he had under a fake name, and about the same time, accounts controlled by you fill up with a hundred thousand dollars."

"If you're somehow trying to say I had Ken killed because of the money in the box, you're way off base. Anne called and asked for my help. I never knew Ken had a safe-deposit box until she told me about it. I had no idea what was in the box until after Ken was already dead."

"So you say," Fisher said.

"So I know," Reynolds replied hotly. She looked at Massey. "Am I being formally charged with anything?"

Massey sat back and put his hands behind his head. "You must realize how very, very bad this all looks. If you were sitting in my chair, what would your conclusions be?"

"I can see how you might have your suspicions. But if you just give me the chance—"

Massey closed his file and stood. "You're suspended, Agent Reynolds, effective immediately."

Reynolds was stunned. "Suspended? I haven't

even been formally charged. You don't even have any specific evidence that I've done anything wrong. And you're suspending me?"

"You should be grateful it's not worse," Fisher said.

"Fred," Reynolds said, half rising from her chair, "I can understand your taking me off this assignment. You can transfer me somewhere else while you investigate, but don't suspend me. Everybody in the Bureau will assume I'm guilty. It's not right."

Massey's face did not soften at all. "Please turn in your credentials and sidearm to Agent Fisher. You are not to return to your office. And you are not to leave the area for any reason."

The blood drained from Reynolds's face and she fell back into her chair.

Massey went to the door. "Your highly suspicious actions, coupled with the murder of an agent and reports of unknown people impersonating FBI agents, does not allow me the option of merely reassigning you, Reynolds. If you're innocent as you claim, then you'll be reinstated with no loss in pay, seniority or responsibility. And I'll make absolutely certain there's no permanent damage to your reputation. If you're guilty, well, you know better than most what awaits you." Massey closed the door behind him.

Reynolds stood to leave, but Fisher blocked her way.

"Creds and gun. Now."

Reynolds slipped them out and handed them over. It was as though she were giving up one of her children. She looked at Fisher's triumphant features. "Gee, Paul, try not to enjoy it so much. You'll look like less of a fool when I'm exonerated."

"Exonerated? You'll be lucky if you're not under arrest by day's end. But we want this case to be airtight. And if you're thinking of running, we'll be watching. So don't even try."

"I wouldn't dream of it. I want to be here to see your face when I come and get my gun and badge back. Don't worry, I won't ask you to kiss my ass."

Reynolds walked down the hallway and out of the building, feeling as though every pair of eyes in the entire Bureau were fully upon her.

THIRTY-SEVEN

L ee got up before Faith, showered, changed his clothes and then stood next to the bed, watching her as she slept. For a few seconds he allowed himself to forget about everything except the wonderful night the two had spent together. He knew it had changed his life forever, and that thought scared him to death.

He went downstairs, moving a little slowly. Parts of him were aching that hadn't in a long time. And it wasn't just from the dancing. He went into the kitchen and made coffee. While it was brewing, he thought about last night. In his mind, Lee had made a very strong commitment to Faith Lockhart. Perhaps an old-fashioned sentiment to some, but sleeping with a woman meant you had deep feelings for her, at least as far as Lee was concerned.

He poured a cup of coffee and went out to sit on the deck off the kitchen. It was a warm day, sunny, but off in the distance, Lee could see darkening clouds approaching. Ahead of the storm was the twin-prop plane as it floated in for a landing with another load of passengers. Faith had told him that during the summer months, the planes might make ten or so trips a day. Now it was down to three; morning, noon and early evening. And so far none of the plane passengers had remained on this street. They had driven off to other places, which suited Lee just fine.

As he sipped his coffee, Lee concluded that he did

have such feelings for Faith, even though he had only known her a few days. Stranger things had happened. Did he love Faith Lockhart? He knew that right now he didn't want to be away from her. He wanted to protect her from harm. He wanted to hold her, spend every minute with her and, yes, have incredibly energetic sex with her as often as his body could manage. Did that constitute love?

On the other hand, she had participated in a bribery scheme involving government officials and was wanted by the FBI, among others. Yes, he thought with a sigh, things had gotten very complicated indeed. Right before they were taking off to God knew where. It wasn't like they could go to a church or even a justice of the peace and get married. *That's right, Father, we're the fugitive couple. Could you please hurry it up?*

Lee rolled his eyes and slapped his forehead hard. Marriage! Good God, was he nuts? Maybe that was how he felt, but what about Faith? Maybe she was into one-night stands, although everything he had observed about the woman argued against such a conclusion. Did she love him? Maybe she was infatuated, caught up in his role as her protector. Last night could be explained away by alcohol, the intoxication of the danger swirling around them or perhaps just simple lust. And he wasn't going to ask her how she felt. She had enough going on.

He focused on the immediate future. Was traveling cross-country on the Honda to San Diego the best plan? Mexico and then South America? He felt a pang of guilt when he thought of the family he would be leaving behind. Then he thought about something else: what everybody would think. His reputation. If he ran, he would be admitting guilt of sorts. And if they did get caught while running, who would believe them?

315

He slumped back in his chair and suddenly pondered a very different strategy. A few minutes before, flight seemed the wisest choice. Faith, understandably, didn't want to go back and help send Buchanan to prison. Lee really didn't have much interest in doing that either, not after hearing why the man had been bribing the politicians. Danny Buchanan probably should be sainted instead. That's when an idea started to form in his head.

Lee went back inside and picked up his cell phone from the coffee table. He had one of those mega-minute deals with no long distance or roaming charges, so that he rarely even used his hard-line phone anymore. It had voice mail, text mail, caller ID. It even had a news banner where you could check out late-breaking stories, or how your stocks were doing, not that he had any.

When he had first started out as a private investigator, Lee had used an IBM typewriter; touch-tone phones were cutting edge; and fax machines spit out curly thermal paper and were the domain of only the largest companies. That was less than fifteen years ago. Now he was holding a global communications command center in the palm of his hand. Change that fast just couldn't be healthy. But still, who could live without these damn things now?

He plopped down on the couch and stared at the slowly revolving ceiling fan's rattan blades, contemplating the pros and cons of what he was thinking about doing. Then he made up his mind, and slipped his wallet out of his back pocket. The piece of paper was in there with the number his client, Danny Buchanan, had originally given him. The one he had been unable to trace. Then doubt seized him. What if he was wrong about Buchanan's not being involved in the attempt on Faith's life? He stood and paced. When he looked out the window at the blue sky, he saw only possible disaster looming in the approaching storm clouds. Still, Buchanan had hired him. He was technically working for the man. Maybe it was time to report in. He said a silent prayer, picked up his cell phone and punched in the numbers from the piece of paper.

THIRTY-EIGHT

Connie did not look happy as Paul Fisher leaned toward him and addressed him in a conspiratorial tone.

"We have every reason to believe that she's in on it, Connie. Despite what you've told us."

Connie glared at the man. He hated everything about Fisher, from his perfect hair and rocky-ledge chin down to his ramrod-straight posture and wrinkle-free shirts. He had been sitting in here for half an hour. He had told Fisher and Massey his side of the story, and they had told him theirs. They were not going to find any middle ground.

"That's bullshit with a capital *B*, Paul."

Fisher sat back and looked at Massey. "You heard the facts. How can you sit there and defend her?"

"Because I know she's innocent, how about that?"

"Do you have any facts to back that up, Connie?" Massey wanted to know.

"I've been sitting here telling you the facts, Fred. We had a hot lead at Agriculture on another case. Brooke didn't even want Ken to go with Lockhart that night. She wanted to go."

"Or so she told you," Massey replied.

"Look, I've got twenty-five years' worth of experience that says Brooke Reynolds is as clean as they come."

"She investigated Ken Newman's finances without telling anyone."

"Come on, it's not the first time an agent's gone off

318

the manual. She gets a hot one and wants to follow it up. But she doesn't want to bury Ken's reputation along with the body. Not until she's sure."

"And the hundred thousand dollars in her kids' accounts?"

"Planted."

"By whom?"

"That's what we have to figure out."

Fisher shook his head in frustration. "We're going to have her followed. Every minute until we break this."

Connie leaned forward and did his best to keep his big hands from flying to Fisher's neck. "What you should be doing, Paul, is following up the leads from Ken's murder. And trying to track down Faith Lockhart."

"If you don't mind, Connie, we'll run the investigation."

Connie looked over at Fred Massey. "You want a tail on Reynolds, I'm your guy."

"You! No way!" Fisher protested.

"Hear me out, Fred," Connie said, his gaze locked on Massey. "I admit, things look bad for Brooke. But I also know there's not a finer agent in the Bureau. And I don't want to see a good agent's career go down the toilet because somebody made the wrong call. I've been down that road myself. Right, Fred?"

Massey looked intensely troubled at this last statement. He seemed to shrink in his chair under Connie's withering gaze.

"Fred," Fisher said, "we need an independent source—"

Connie interrupted, "*I* can be independent. If I'm wrong, then Brooke goes down, and I'll be the first one to break the news to her. But I'm betting she's going to come back and pick up her badge and gun.

In fact, in ten years I see her running this whole damn place."

"I don't know, Connie," Massey began.

"I think *somebody* owes me that opportunity, Fred," Connie said very quietly. "What do you think?"

There was a long moment of silence while Fisher looked back and forth between the two men.

"All right, Connie, you follow her," Massey said. "And you report back to me at regular intervals. Exactly what you see. No more. No less. I'm counting on you. For old times' sake."

Connie rose from the table and flicked a victorious glance at Fisher. "Thanks for the vote of confidence, gentlemen. I won't disappoint."

Fisher followed Connie out into the hallway.

"I don't know what you just pulled in there, but remember this: Your career already has one black mark against it, Connie. It can't afford another. And anything you report to Massey, I want to know about."

Connie crowded the much taller Fisher back against the wall.

"Listen up, Paul." He paused, ostensibly to pick a piece of lint off Fisher's shirt. "I understand that, technically, you're my superior here. Don't confuse that, though, with reality."

"You're treading a dangerous line, Connie."

"I like danger, Paul, that's why I joined the Bureau. That's why I carry a gun. I've killed somebody with mine. How about you?"

"You're not making sense. You're throwing your career away." Fisher felt the wall behind him; his face was growing red as Connie continued to lean into him like a listing oak against a picket fence.

"Is that right? Well, let me make some sense of this for you. Somebody is setting Brooke up. Now, who could that be? It's got to be the leak here at the Bureau. Somebody wants to discredit her, bring her down. And if you ask me, Paul, you're trying awfully hard to do just that."

"Me? You're accusing me of being the leak?"

"I'm not accusing anybody of anything. I'm just reminding you that until we do find that leak, nobody, and I mean nobody, from the director down to the guys who clean the johns here, is above suspicion in my book."

Connie moved away from Fisher. "Have a nice day, Paul. I'm off to catch some bad guys."

Fisher stared after him, slowly shaking his head, something close to fear in his eyes.

THIRTY-NINE

The phone number Lee called was linked to a pager, so that Buchanan would know the instant the number was called. When the pager went off, Buchanan was at home packing his briefcase for a meeting at a downtown law firm that was doing pro bono work for one of Buchanan's clients. He had given up hope of the damn beeper ever sounding. When it did, he thought he would suffer a stroke.

Now Buchanan's dilemma was apparent. How to check the message and call back without Thornhill knowing about it. Then he thought of a plan. He called his driver. It was Thornhill's man, of course. It always was. They drove downtown to the law firm.

"I'll be a couple of hours. I'll phone when I'm done," he told the driver.

Buchanan went into the building. He had been here before, knew the layout well. He didn't go to the elevator bank, but instead went through the main lobby and passed through a door in the back that also served as a rear entrance to the parking garage. He took the elevator down two levels and stepped off. He went through the underground lobby area and out into the parking level. Right next to the door leading out from the lobby was a pay phone. He put in his coins and dialed the number that would allow him to check the message. His reasoning was clear: If Thornhill could intercept a random hard-line call under a thousand tons of concrete, he was the devil himself and Buchanan had no chance of beating him anyway.

On the message Lee's voice was tight, his words few. And the impact on Buchanan was enormous. He had left a number. Buchanan dialed it. A man answered the phone immediately.

"Mr. Buchanan?" Lee asked.

"Is Faith all right?"

Lee gave a sigh of relief. He was hoping that would be the man's first question. That told him a lot. But still, he had to be cautious. "Just to verify it's really you: You sent me a package of information. How did you send it, and what was in it? And let me have the answers fast."

"Personal courier. I use Dash Services. The packet had a photo of Faith, five pages of background information on her and my firm, the contact phone number, a summary of my concerns and what I wanted you to do. It also had five thousand dollars in cash in denominations of fifties and twenties. I also called you three days ago at your office and left a message on your machine. Now please tell me that Faith is all right."

"She's fine, for now. But we have some problems."

"Yes, we do. For starters, how do I know you're Adams?"

Lee thought quickly. "I have a great Yellow Pages ad with a corny magnifying glass and everything. I have three brothers. The youngest works at a motorcycle shop in south Alexandria. He goes by Scotty, but his nickname in college was Scooter because he played football and could run so damn fast. If you want you can call him, check it out and call me back."

"Not necessary. I'm convinced. What happened? Why did you run?"

"Well, you would have too if someone tried to kill you."

"Tell me everything, Mr. Adams. Leave nothing out."

"Well, I know *who* you are, but I'm not sure I trust *you*. What can you do about that?"

"You tell me *why* Faith went to the FBI. That much I do know. And then I'll tell you who you're really up against. And it's not me. When I tell you who it is, you'll wish it were me."

Lee debated this for a moment. He could hear Faith getting up and heading probably to the shower. *Well, here goes.* "She was scared. She said you had been acting strangely, jumpy for a while. She had tried to talk to you about it, but you blew her off, even asked her to leave the firm. That made her even more fearful. She was afraid the authorities were on to you. She went to the FBI with the idea of bringing you in to testify too. Against the people you were bribing. You both cut a deal and walk."

"That would never have worked."

"Well, as she's fond of telling me, it's easy to second-guess."

"So she's told you everything?"

"Pretty much. She thought maybe you were the one who tried to kill her. But I put that notion to rest." *I hope I was right.*

"I had no idea Faith had even gone to the FBI until after she disappeared."

"It's not just the FBI after her. There are some other people too. They were at the airport. And they were carrying something I've only seen at a seminar on counterterrorism."

"Who sponsored the seminar?"

This question puzzled Lee. "The counterterrorism stuff was put on by the official spooks. You know, I guess the guys at CIA."

324

Buchanan said, "Well, at least you have encountered the enemy and you're still alive. That's good."

"What are you talking . . ." The blood suddenly seemed to pool over Lee's temples. "Are you saying what I think you're saying?"

"Let's just put it this way, Mr. Adams: Faith is not the only one working for a prominent federal agency. At least her involvement was voluntarily. Mine wasn't."

"Oh, shit."

"To put it mildly, yes. Where are you?"

"Why?"

"Because I need to get to you."

"And how can you do that without bringing the ACME assassin squad down on us? I assume you're under surveillance."

"Unbelievably, astonishingly tight surveillance."

"Okay, so you're not coming anywhere near us."

"Mr. Adams, the only chance we have is to work together. That can't be done from a distance. I have to come to you, because I don't think it wise for you to come here."

"You're not convincing me."

"I won't come if I can't lose them."

"Lose them? Look, who do you think you are, Houdini reincarnated? Well, let me tell you, not even Houdini could lose *both* the FBI *and* the CIA."

"I'm neither a spy nor a magician. I'm a humble lobbyist, but I owe one advantage: I know this city better than anyone alive. And I have friends in both high and low places. And right now, they are equally valuable to me. Rest assured, I will get to you alone. And then we might be able to survive this. Now I want to speak to Faith."

"I'm not sure that's a good idea, Mr. Buchanan."

"Yes, it is."

Lee whirled around and saw Faith standing on the stairs in a T-shirt. "It's time, Lee. In fact, it's way past time."

He took a deep breath and held out the phone.

"Hello, Danny," she said into the phone.

"God, Faith, I'm sorry. For all of this." Buchanan's voice cracked in midsentence.

"I should be apologizing. I started this whole nightmare by going to the FBI."

"Well, we have to finish it. We may as well do it together. How is Adams? Is he capable? We're going to need some support."

Faith glanced over at Lee, who was anxiously watching her. "In my informed opinion, we have no problems there. In fact, that's probably our one ace in the hole."

"Tell me where you are, and I'll be down as quickly as possible."

She did. She also told Buchanan everything she and Lee knew. When she hung up, she looked over at Lee.

He shrugged. "I figured it was our only shot. Either that or we spend the rest of our lives running."

She sat on his lap, curled her legs up and laid her head against his chest. "You did the right thing. Whoever's involved in this, they'll find a tough opponent in Danny."

Lee's hopes, however, had plummeted. The CIA. Hired assassins, legions of people expert in all sorts of nasty things: computers, satellites, covert operations, air guns with poisoned bullets, all coming for him. If he was smart, he'd throw Faith on the Honda and run like hell.

"I'm going to grab a shower," Faith said. "Danny said he'd be down as soon as he could."

"Right," Lee said, a faraway look in his eyes.

As Faith headed up the stairs, Lee picked up his phone, glanced at it and froze. Lee Adams had never been more stunned in his life. And with the events of the last few days, the bar on what surprised him had risen to about the level of the sun. The text message on the cell phone's screen was concise. And it came close to stopping even Lee's very strong heart.

Faith Lockhart for Renee Adams, it said. There was a phone number to call. They wanted Faith in exchange for his daughter.

FORTY

Reynolds sat in her living room cradling a cup of tea and staring into a fire that was slowly dying. The last time she could remember being home at this time of the day was when she had been on maternity leave with David. Her son had been as surprised to see her come through the door as Rosemary. David was now napping, and Rosemary was busy doing laundry. Just another normal day for them. Reynolds simply stared into the embers of the fire, wishing that something, anything about her life could be normal.

It had started to rain hard, which fit in perfectly with her deep depression. Suspended. She felt naked without her gun and credentials. All those years at the Bureau, never a blemish, and now she was a step away from a ruined career. Then what would she do? Where could she go? Without her job, would her husband try to take the kids? Could she stop him if he did?

She put her cup down, kicked off her shoes and sank back on the couch. The tears started to come fast and heavy, and she put an arm across her face both to soak them up and muffle her sobs. The ringing doorbell made her sit up, wipe at her face and head to the door. She looked through the peephole and found herself staring at Howard Constantinople.

Connie stood in front of the fire he had just stoked,

warming his hands. An embarrassed Reynolds quickly dabbed at her eyes with a tissue. He could not have missed her red eyes and splotchy cheeks, she knew, but he had tactfully said nothing.

"Did they talk to you?" she asked.

Connie turned and dropped into a chair, nodding as he did so. "And I came damn close to being suspended myself. I was about two seconds from punching out Fisher, that shit-faced excuse for an agent."

"Don't go and crater your career for me, Connie."

"If I had sugged the guy, believe me, it would've been for me, not you." He popped a big knuckle, as though emphasizing the point, and then looked across at her. "The thing that kills me is, they actually believe you're somehow involved in this. I told them the truth. Something came up, we were working another case. You wanted to go with Lockhart because you had the relationship with her, but we had this potential whistleblower over at Agriculture we were committed to. I told them you were fretting like all get-out because you didn't know if Ken going with Lockhart out there was the right thing to do."

"And?"

"And they weren't listening. They've already made up their minds."

"Because of the money? Did they tell you about that?"

Connie nodded slowly and suddenly hunched forward. For a big man his movements could be quick, agile. "I don't like kicking you while you're down, but why in hell did you go sniffing around Newman's accounts without telling somebody? Like me, for instance? You know detectives go in pairs for lots of reasons, not the least of which is to cover the other's ass. Now you've got nobody to corroborate shit for you, except Anne Newman. And as far as they're concerned, she doesn't count."

Reynolds threw up her hands. "I never in a million years thought this would happen. I was trying to do right by Ken and his family."

"Well, if he was being paid off, maybe Ken doesn't deserve that sort of consideration. And that's coming from a good friend of his."

"We don't know that he was bad yet."

"Cash in a safe-deposit box under a fake name? Yeah, I guess everybody does that, don't they?"

"Connie, how did they know I was investigating Ken's finances? I can't believe Anne would have called the Bureau. She asked me for help."

"I asked Massey, but he's a clam. Figures I'm the enemy too. I nosed around a bit, though, and I think they got a phone tip. Anonymous, of course. Massey told me you were screaming frame-up. And you know what, I think you're right, even if they don't."

The sight of Connie at the door had been welcome. The fact that he was still loyal meant a lot to her. And she wanted to do right by him too. Especially him. "Look, this isn't going to help your career, being seen with me, Connie. I'm sure Fisher has a tail on me."

"Actually, I'm your tail."

"You're kidding."

"No, the hell I am not. I talked the ADIC into it. Called in a few markers. For old times' sake, Massey said. In case you didn't know, Fred Massey was the guy who asked me to take the dive on the Brownsville case all those years ago. If he thinks this evens us up, he's brain-dead. But don't get all excited. They know I have every incentive to cover *my* ass on this. And that means if you fall, they don't have to go putting blame anywhere else.

Including on yours truly." Connie paused and made a mock show of surprise. "ADIC? Come to think of it, that acronym really fits. Massey's a little shit too."

"You don't have much respect for your chain of command." Reynolds smiled. "What do you think of me, Agent Constantinople?"

"I think you screwed up big-time, and you just gave the Bureau a face-saving scapegoat," he said bluntly.

Reynolds's face grew serious. "You don't sugar-coat."

"Do you want me to waste time doing that?" Connie stood. "Or do you want to clear your name?"

"I *have* to clear my name. If I don't, I could lose it all, Connie. My kids, my career. All of it." Reynolds could feel herself trembling again and she took several deep breaths to counteract the panic she was feeling. She felt like a high schooler who had just learned she was pregnant. "But I'm suspended. No creds, no gun. No authority."

In answer Connie pulled on his overcoat. "Well, you've got me. I've got creds, a gun and, while I'm only a humble field agent after two and a half decades of doing this crap, I can do authority with the best of them. So get your coat and let's try to track down Lockhart."

"Lockhart?"

"I figure we deliver her, the pieces start to fall into place. The more they do, the more the blame gets shifted off you. I've talked to the VCU boys. They're spinning their wheels waiting on lab results and crap like that. And now Massey has them going hot and heavy on your angle and to hell with Lockhart for now. You know nobody's even gone to her house looking for clues?"

Reynolds looked miserable. "We were so reactive

on the whole thing. Ken killed. Lockhart gone. The fiasco at the airport. Then people calling themselves the FBI at Adams's apartment. We never really had a chance to take the proper investigative steps."

"So I figure we follow up some leads while they're still hot. Like checking out Adams's family in the area. I've got the list of names and addresses. If he went on the run, he might have gotten one of them to help."

"You could get into deep trouble for this, Connie."

He shrugged. "Not for the first time. Besides, we don't have a squad supervisor anymore. I don't know if you heard, but she was suspended for being stupid."

They exchanged smiles.

Connie continued. "So, as second-in-command, I'm entitled to investigate an active case I happened to be assigned to. My instructions are to find Faith Lockhart, so that's what I'm going to do. They just don't know I'm doing it with you. And I talked to the VCU guys. They know what I'm up to, so we won't run into another team going through Adams's relatives."

"I need to tell Rosemary I might be gone overnight."

"Then go." He looked at his watch. "I guess Sydney's still in school. Where's your boy?"

"Sleeping."

"Whisper in his ear that Mommy's gonna kick some butt."

When Reynolds returned, she went straight to the closet and got her coat. She hustled toward her study and then stopped.

"What's wrong?" Connie asked.

She looked at him, slightly embarrassed. "I was going to get my gun. Old habits die hard."

"Not to worry. You'll get yours back soon enough.

But you have to make me a promise. When you go to get your gun and creds, take me with you. I want to see their faces."

She opened the door for him. "Deal."

FORTY-ONE

Buchanan made a number of other phone calls from the parking garage as he worked out his arrangements. He then went up to the law firm and spent time on an important matter he suddenly cared nothing about. He was driven home, his mind working the whole time as he devised his plan against Robert Thornhill. That was one area of his being that the CIA man could never penetrate or control: Buchanan's mind. That fact was enormously comforting. Buchanan was slowly regaining his confidence. Maybe he could give the man a run for his money.

Buchanan unlocked the front door to his home and went inside. He lay his briefcase down on a chair and passed the darkened library. He turned on the light to gaze at his beloved painting, to give him strength for what lay ahead. As the light came on, Buchanan stared in disbelief at the empty frame. He staggered over to it, put his hands through the frame and touched the wall. He had been robbed. Yet he had a very good security system, and it had not been tripped.

He raced across to the phone to call the police. As his hand touched the receiver, it rang. He picked it up.

"Your car will be around in a couple of minutes, sir. Going to the office?"

At first Buchanan's mind didn't register.

"To the office, sir?"

"Yes," Buchanan was finally able to say.

He put the phone down and stared over at where his painting had hung. First Faith, and now his painting. All Thornhill's doing. *All right, Bob, first point to you. Now it's my turn.*

He went upstairs, washed his face and changed his clothes, carefully selecting what he needed to wear. He had a custom-built entertainment system in his bedroom housing a TV, stereo, VCR and DVD player. It was relatively safe from burglars since one couldn't take the components out without un-screwing numerous wooden pieces, a very time-consuming process. Buchanan did not watch TV or movies. And when he wanted music, he put a 33 platter on his old phonograph.

Sticking his hand in the slot of the VCR, Buchanan pulled out his passport, credit card and ID, all under an alias, and a slim bundle of hundred-dollar bills and put it all in a zippered inner pocket of his coat. Coming back downstairs, he looked outside and saw his car waiting. He would let him wait for a few more minutes, just for the hell of it.

When that time had passed, Buchanan picked up his briefcase and walked out to the car. He climbed in and the car drove off.

"Hello, Bob," Buchanan said as calmly as he could.

Thornhill glanced down at the briefcase.

Buchanan nodded his head toward the tinted window.

"I'm going to the office. The FBI will expect me to take my briefcase. Unless you assume they haven't tapped my phone line by now."

Thornhill nodded. "You have the makings of a good field operative in you, Danny."

"Where is the painting?"

"In a very safe place, which is far more than you deserve under the circumstances."

"What exactly does that mean?"

"That exactly means Lee Adams, private investigator. Hired by you to follow Faith Lockhart."

Buchanan feigned being taken aback for a minute. As a young man he'd had notions of being an actor. Not in the movies, but on the stage. For him, lobbying was the next best thing. "I didn't know she had gone to the FBI when I did that. I was only concerned for her safety."

"And why was that?"

"I think you know the answer."

Thornhill looked offended. "Why in the world would I want to harm Faith Lockhart? I don't even know the woman."

"Do you have to know someone before you destroy her?"

Thornhill's tone was mocking. "You were wrong to have done it, Danny. The painting will probably be returned to you. But for now, learn to live without it."

"How did you get into my house, Thornhill? I have a security system."

Thornhill looked as though he might burst out laughing. "A *home* security system? Oh, dear."

It was all Buchanan could do not to fling himself on the man.

"You amuse me, Danny, you really do. Running around trying to save the have-nots. Don't you understand? That's what makes the world go 'round. The rich and the poor. The powerful and the powerless. We'll always have them, until the world ends. And nothing you do will change that. Just as people will always hate each other, will betray each other. If it weren't for the evil qualities in humanity, I wouldn't have a job."

"I was just thinking that you missed your calling as a psychiatrist," said Buchanan. "For the criminally insane. You'd have so much in common with your patients."

Thornhill smiled. "That's how I got on to you, you know. Someone you tried to help ended up betraying you. Jealous of your success, your wanting to do good, I suppose. He didn't know about your little scheme, but he aroused my curiosity. And when I focus on someone's life, well, kept secrets are not an option. I tapped your home, your office, even your clothing, and found myself a treasure trove. We so enjoyed listening to you."

"Fascinating. Now tell me where Faith is."

"I was hoping you could tell me that."

"What do you want with her?"

"I want her to come and work for me. There is a friendly competition between the two agencies, but between the FBI and my agency, I would have to say that we play much fairer with our people. I've been working on this project longer than the Bureau. I don't want all my efforts to be in vain."

Buchanan chose his words carefully. He knew he was in great personal danger here. "What can Faith possibly give you that I haven't already?"

"In my line of work, two is always better than one."

"Would your math include the FBI agent you had killed, Bob?"

Thornhill took out his pipe and fiddled with it.

"You know, Danny, you would be well advised to keep yourself focused on your part of this puzzle only."

"I consider *every* part my part. I read the newspapers. You told me Faith had gone to the FBI. An FBI agent is killed working on an undisclosed case. Faith disappears at the same time. You're right, I hired Lee Adams to find out what was going on. I haven't heard from him. Did you have him killed too?"

"I'm a public servant. I don't have people killed."

"The FBI got on to Faith somehow, and you couldn't allow that, because your whole plan goes down the tubes if they find out the truth. And did you really think I believed you'd let me walk away with a slap on the back for a job well done? I didn't survive this long in the business by being a damned idiot."

Thornhill put his pipe away. "Survival, interesting concept. You consider yourself a survivor, and yet you come to me and make all these sorts of unfounded accusations—"

Buchanan leaned forward and placed his face right next to Thornhill's. "I've forgotten more about the subject of survival than you ever knew. I don't have armies of people with guns running around doing my bidding while I sit safely behind the walls of Langley analyzing the field of battle like it was a chess game. The minute you came into my life, I made contingency plans that will absolutely *destroy* you if anything happens to me. Didn't you ever consider the possibility that someone might be half as agile as yourself? Or have all your successes really gone to your head?"

Thornhill simply stared at him, so Buchanan kept going. "Now, I consider myself a partner of sorts with you, no matter how loathsome that thought is. And I want to know if you killed the FBI agent, because I want to know exactly what I have to do to get out of this nightmare. And I want to know if you killed Faith and Adams as well. And if you don't tell me, the minute I leave this car, my next stop will be the FBI. And if you think yourself so invincible as to try and kill me while the Feds are back there, then go ahead. However, if I die, you go down too."

Buchanan leaned back and allowed himself a

smile. "You know the old story of the frog and the scorpion, don't you? The scorpion needs a ride across the water and tells the frog he won't sting it if the frog will provide that ride. And the frog knows that if the scorpion does sting it, that the scorpion will drown, so he gives it the ride. Halfway across the water, the scorpion, against all reason, does sting the frog. As it's dying, the frog cries out, 'Why did you do it? Now you'll die too.' And the scorpion simply tells him, 'It's my nature.'" Buchanan made a mock show of waving. "Hello, Mr. Frog."

The two men sat staring at each other for the next mile until Thornhill broke the silence.

"Lockhart needed to be eliminated. The FBI agent was with her. So he had to die too."

"But you missed Faith?"

"With your private investigator's help. But for your blunder, this crisis would never have happened."

"It never *occurred* to me that you would be planning to kill anyone. So you have no idea where she is?"

"It's only a matter of time. I have a number of irons in the fire. And where there's bait, there's always hope."

"Meaning what?"

"Meaning I'm done talking with you."

The next fifteen minutes passed in complete silence. The car drove into the underground parking garage of Buchanan's building. A gray sedan waited on the lower level, its engine running. Before Thornhill got out, he gripped Buchanan's arm.

"You claim to have the ability to destroy me if anything happens to you. Well, here's my side. If your colleague and her new 'friend' bring all that I've worked for crashing down, you will all be eliminated. Immediately." He removed his hand.

"Just so we understand one another, Mr. Scorpion," Thornhill added scornfully.

A minute later, the gray sedan pulled out of the parking garage. Thornhill was already on the phone.

"Buchanan is not to be out of sight for even one second." He clicked off and began to think of how to attack this new development.

FORTY-TWO

"This is the last place," Connie said as they pulled up to the motorcycle shop in his sedan.

They got out and Reynolds looked around. "His younger brother?"

Connie nodded as he checked his list. "Scott Adams. Manages the place."

"Well, let's hope he's a little more helpful than the others."

They had covered all of Lee's relatives in the area. None had seen or heard from him in the last week. Or at least that's what they said. Scott Adams might be their last chance. However, when they got inside they were told he was out of town for a friend's wedding and wouldn't be back for a couple of days.

Connie handed the young man behind the counter his card. "Tell him to call me when he gets in."

Rick, the salesman who had obnoxiously flirted with Faith, looked down at the card. "Does this have anything to do with his brother?"

Connie and Reynolds eyed him. "Do you know Lee Adams?" Reynolds asked.

"Can't say I know him. He don't know my name or nothing. But he's come by a few times. Just a couple of days ago, in fact."

The two agents looked Rick up and down, gauging his credibility.

"Was he alone?" Reynolds asked.

"No. He had some chick with him."

Reynolds took out a photo of Lockhart and handed it over to him. "Think short hair, not long, black, not auburn."

Rick nodded as he stared at the photograph. "Yep, that's her. And Lee's hair was different too. Short and blond. And he had a beard and mustache too, but I'm real good at noticing things."

Reynolds and Connie looked at each other, trying hard to hide their excitement.

"Any idea where they might have gone?" Connie asked.

"Maybe. But I sure know why they came here."

"Really? Why's that?"

"They needed wheels. Took a bike. One of the big Gold Wings."

"Gold Wing?" Reynolds repeated.

"Yeah." Rick rifled through a stack of color brochures on the counter and flipped one around so Reynolds could see. "This one here. The Honda Gold Wing SE. If you're going long distance, nothing beats this baby. Trust me."

"And you say Adams took one. Got a color, license plate number?"

"I can look the plate up. The color's the same as on the brochure. That was a demo. Scotty let him take it."

"You said you might have an idea where they went," Reynolds prompted.

"What do you want with Lee?"

"We want to talk with him. And the lady he's with," she said amiably.

"They do something wrong?"

"Won't know until we talk to them," Connie replied. He stepped forward a little. "It's an ongoing FBI investigation. You a friend of theirs or something?"

Rick paled at the suggestion. "Hell, no, that chick

342

is bad news. A real attitude. While Lee was inside, I went out to the sales lot and tried to help her. Real professional-like, and she jumped all over me. And Lee's no better. When he came out, he gave me some lip. I came close to kicking his ass, in fact."

As Connie looked at the beanpole Rick, he recalled the surveillance tape of the physically imposing Lee Adams. "Kick his ass? Is that right?"

Rick looked defensive. "He's got some weight on me, but he's an old guy. And I'm into tae kwon do."

Reynolds studied Rick closely. "So you're saying that Lee Adams was inside for a while, and the woman was out in the lot by herself?"

"That's right."

Reynolds and Connie traded a quick glance. "If you have information as to where they went, the Bureau would greatly appreciate it," Reynolds said, growing impatient. "That and the plate number on the bike. Like right now, if you don't mind. We're sort of in a hurry."

"Sure. Lee also got a map for North Carolina. We sell 'em here, but Scotty just gave it to him. That's what Shirley, the girl who usually works the desk, said."

"Is she in today?"

"Nope. Sick. I'm it."

"Can I get one of those Carolina maps?"

Rick pulled one out and handed it to her. "How much?"

He smiled. "Hey, it's on the house. Just being a good citizen. You know, I'm thinking about joining the FBI."

"Well, we could always use a good man," Connie said with a blank expression, his gaze averted.

Rick looked up the plate number on the demo and gave it to Connie. "You guys let me know what happens," Rick said as they started to leave.

"You'll be the first," Connie called back over his shoulder.

The two agents settled back in the car.

Reynolds looked at her partner. "Well, Lockhart isn't being held by Adams against her will. He left her outside by herself. She could've taken off."

"They sure look to be a team of sorts. At least right now."

"North Carolina," Reynolds said almost to herself.

"Big state," Connie said back.

Reynolds looked at him with a wry expression. "Well, let's see if we can cut it down some. At the airport, Lockhart bought two tickets for a flight to Norfolk International."

"So why the map for North Carolina?"

"They couldn't take the plane. We'd have been waiting for them in Norfolk. At least Adams seemed to know that. He was probably aware we have an arrangement with the airlines, and that's how we scored Lockhart at the airport."

"Lockhart screwed up by using her real name for the second ticket. But that was probably all she could do, unless she had a third fake ID," Connie added.

"So no plane. Can't use a credit card, so no rental car. Adams figures we have the bus and railroad terminals covered. So they get the Honda from his brother and a map for their true destination: North Carolina."

"Meaning that when they got to Norfolk by plane they were either going to drive or hop another plane to someplace in Carolina."

Reynolds shook her head. "But that doesn't make sense. If they were going to North Carolina, why not just take a plane directly there? There are tons of flights to Raleigh and Charlotte out of National. Why go through Norfolk?"

"Well, maybe you'd go through Norfolk if you

weren't going to Charlotte or Raleigh or anyplace near them," Connie ventured, "but still wanted to go to someplace in North Carolina."

"But why not still go through one of those two major airports?"

"Well, what if Norfolk is a lot closer to where they wanted to go than Charlotte or Raleigh are?"

Reynolds thought a moment. "Raleigh's roughly in the middle of the state. Charlotte is west."

Connie snapped his fingers. "East! The coast. The Outer Banks?"

Reynolds found herself nodding in agreement. "Maybe. The Outer Banks has thousands of beach houses where one could hide."

Connie suddenly looked less hopeful. "Thousands of beach houses," he muttered.

"Well, the first thing you can do is call the Bureau's airline liaison and find out what flights run out of Norfolk for the Outer Banks. And we have some times to work with. Their flight was scheduled to get into Norfolk at noon. I don't see them cooling their heels any longer than necessary at a public place, so the flight out had to be relatively close to noon or so. Maybe one of the commuters has regular service. We already checked with the major airlines. They didn't reserve with any of them out of Norfolk."

Connie picked up the car phone and placed the call. It didn't take long before they got an answer.

Connie's features looked hopeful again. "You're not going to believe this, but there's only one commuter service to the Outer Banks from Norfolk International."

Reynolds smiled broadly and shook her head. "Finally, some luck in this damn case. Talk to me."

"Tarheel Airways. They fly out of Norfolk to five places in Carolina: Kill Devil Hills, Manteo,

Ocracoke, Hatteras and a place called Pine Island, near Duck. There're no regular departures. You call ahead and the plane is waiting for you."

Reynolds spread open the map and scanned it. "Okay, there are Hatteras and Ocracoke. They're the farthest south." She put a finger on the map. "Kill Devil Hills is here. Manteo south of that. And Duck is here, to the north."

Connie looked at where she was pointing. "I've been down there on vacation. You cross the bridge over the sound and head north for Duck. South for Kill Devil. They're fairly equidistant from each other at that point."

"So what do you think? North or south?"

"Well, if they were going to North Carolina, it was probably at Lockhart's prompting." Reynolds looked at him curiously. "Because Adams took the map," Connie explained. "If he knew the area, he wouldn't have done that."

"Nice, Sherlock, what else?"

"Well, Lockhart has some serious money. One look at her house in McLean will tell you that. If I were her, I'd have a safe house under my phony name in case the roof caved in."

"But we're still at square one: north or south?"

They sat there stewing over this until Reynolds suddenly slapped her forehead. "God, how stupid. Connie, if you have to call Tarheel to arrange for a flight, our answer's right there."

Connie's eyes grew wide. "Damn, talk about blind." He picked up the phone, got the number for Tarheel and placed the call, relaying the date and approximate time and the name Suzanne Blake.

He hung up and looked at her. "A reservation for two people with Tarheel was made by our Ms. Blake two days ago to fly out of Norfolk around two P.M. They were pissed because she never showed. They

346

normally take a credit card, but she'd flown with them before, and so they just took her on her word."

"And their destination?"

"Pine Island."

Reynolds couldn't help but smile. "God, Connie, we might actually pull this off."

Connie put the car in gear. "Only bad thing is, I don't rate one of the Bureau's planes. We're stuck with the old Crown Vic here. I figure six hours or so, not counting stops." He checked his watch. "With stops, that'll put us there about one in the morning."

"I'm not supposed to leave the area."

"Bureau Rule Number One: You can go anywhere so long as you have your guardian angel along."

Reynolds looked troubled. "What do you think about calling in reinforcements?"

He eyed her quizzically. "Well, I guess we could call Massey and Fisher and let them take all the credit."

Reynolds suddenly smiled. "Like you said, screw international relations. Give me a minute to call home and then let's roll."

FORTY-THREE

It had taken Lee several agonizing hours, but he had finally tracked down Renee. Her mother had flatly refused to give him her phone number at college, but in a series of calls to the admissions office, among others, Lee had lied, begged and threatened until the number had been given up. It figured. He hadn't called his daughter for a long time, and when he did, it had to be for something like this. Boy, she was really going to cherish her old man now.

Renee's roommate at UVA swore on her grave that Renee had left for class accompanied by two members of the football team, one of whom she was dating. After telling the young woman who he was and leaving a number for Renee to call, Lee had hung up the phone and then gotten the telephone number for the Albermarle County Sheriff's office. He talked his way to a deputy sheriff and told the woman that someone had made threats against Renee Adams, a student at UVA. Would they please send someone to check on her? The woman asked questions that Lee could not answer, including wanting to know who the hell he was. *Just check the latest most-wanted list*, he wanted to tell her. Sick with worry, he tried his best to impress upon her the sincerity of what he was saying. Then he hung up and stared down at the digital missive once more: "Renee for Faith," he slowly said to himself.

"What?"

He jerked around and stared at Faith, there on the stairs, her eyes wide, her mouth open.

"Lee, what is it?"

Lee was out of ideas at the moment. He simply held up the phone for Faith, his face an anguished mess.

She looked at the message and then stared at him. "We have to call the police."

"She's okay, I just talked to her roommate. And I called the police. Somebody's blowing smoke at us. Trying to spook us."

"You don't know that."

"You're right, I don't," he said miserably.

"Are you going to call the number back?"

"That's probably what they want me to do."

"You mean so they can trace the call? Can you trace a cellular call?"

"It's possible, if you have the right equipment. Phone carriers have to be able to trace a cell call to determine the location of a 911 caller. It uses a time difference of arrival method by measuring signal distances between cell towers and kicks out a string of possible locations. . . . Shit, my daughter's head might be in the guillotine and I sound like a damn walking science magazine."

"But not an exact location."

"No, at least I don't think so. It's not as precise as satellite positioning, that's for certain. But who the hell really knows? Some geeky asshole invents some new piece of shit every second that rips away a little bit more of your privacy. I know, my ex-wife married one."

"You should call, Lee."

"And what the hell am I supposed to say? They want to trade you for her."

She put one hand on his shoulder, rubbed his neck and then leaned against him. "Call them. And then we'll see what we can do. Nothing is going to happen to your daughter."

He looked at her. "You can't guarantee that."

"I *can* guarantee that I will do everything I can to make sure she's not harmed."

"Including walking into their hands?"

"If it comes to that, yes. I'm not going to let an innocent person get hurt because of me."

Lee slumped back against the couch. "I'm supposed to be so good under pressure too and I can't even think straight."

"Call them," Faith said very firmly.

Lee took a long breath and punched in the numbers. With Faith sitting beside him and listening in, they waited as the phone rang once and then was answered.

"Mr. Adams?" Neither of them recognized the voice. It had a mechanical quality to it, making them both think it was being altered somehow. It sounded inhuman enough to make their skin tingle with absolute dread.

"This is Lee Adams."

"Nice of you to leave your cell phone number at your apartment. It made contacting you much more convenient."

"I just checked on my daughter. She's fine. And the cops are on the scene. So your little kidnapping plan—"

"I have no need to kidnap your daughter, Mr. Adams."

"Then I'm not sure why I'm talking to you."

"You needn't abduct someone to kill her. Your daughter can be eliminated today, tomorrow, next month, next year. While going to class, lacrosse practice, driving on holiday, even while she's sleeping. Her bed is right next to a window, first floor. She often stays late at the library. It couldn't be easier, really."

"You sick bastard! You sonofabitch!" Lee looked like he wanted to break the phone in two.

Faith gripped his shoulders, trying to calm him down.

The voice continued with irritating calm. "Histrionics won't help your daughter. Where is Faith Lockhart, Mr. Adams? That's all we want. Give her up and all your problems go away."

"And I'm supposed to just accept that as gospel?"

"You really don't have a choice."

"How do you know I've even got the woman?"

"Do you want your daughter to die?"

"I'm telling the truth, Lockhart got away."

"Fine, next week you can bury Renee."

Faith jerked at Lee's arm and pointed at the phone.

"Wait, wait!" Lee said. "Okay, okay, if I have Faith, what do you propose?"

"A meeting."

"She's not going to come voluntarily."

"I don't really care how you get her there. That's your responsibility. We'll be waiting."

"And you'll just let me walk away?"

"Drop her off and drive away. We'll take care of the rest. You don't interest us."

"Where?"

Lee was given an address outside of Washington D.C., on the Maryland side. He knew it well: very isolated.

"I have to drive it. And the cops are everywhere. I need a few days."

"Tomorrow night. Twelve sharp."

"Dammit, that's not a lot of time."

"Then I suggest you start right now."

"Listen, if you lay a hand on my daughter, I'll find you, somehow I will. I swear it. First I'll break every bone in your body, and then I'll really hurt you."

351

"Mr. Adams, consider yourself the luckiest human being on the face of the earth that we don't see you as a threat. And do yourself a favor. When you walk away don't ever, ever look back. You won't turn to salt, but it still won't be pretty." The line went dead.

Lee put the phone down. For a few minutes he and Faith just sat there without speaking. "Now what do we do?" Lee finally managed to say.

"Danny said he'd be here as soon as he could."

"Great. I've got a deadline: tomorrow, midnight."

"If Danny's not here in time we'll drive to the place they gave you. But first we'll call in some reinforcements."

"Like who, the FBI?" Faith nodded. "Faith, I'm not sure we could explain all this to the Feds in one year, much less one day."

"It's all we have, Lee. If Danny gets here in time and has a better plan, so be it. Otherwise I'll call Agent Reynolds. She'll help us. I'll make it work." She squeezed his arm. "Nothing is going to happen to your daughter. I promise."

Lee gripped her hand, hoping with all his heart that the woman was right.

FORTY-FOUR

Buchanan had a number of meetings on Capitol Hill scheduled for the early evening, pitching to an audience that didn't want to hear him. It was like throwing a ball at a wave. It would either be kicked back in your face or lost at sea. Well, today was the end. No more.

His car dropped him off near the Capitol. He went up the front steps and over to the Senate side of the building, where he climbed the broad staircase to the second floor, which was mostly restricted space, and continued to the third floor, where people could freely wander.

Buchanan knew he was being followed by more people now. While there were lots of dark suits around, he had trekked these halls long enough to sense who should be here as opposed to those who looked out of place. He assumed they were the FBI and Thornhill's men. After the encounter in the car, the Frog would have deployed more resources. Good. Buchanan smiled. He would, from now on, refer to the CIA man as the Frog. Spies liked code names. And he couldn't think of a more appropriate one for Thornhill. Buchanan just hoped that his stinger was ready, filled to the hilt with poison, and that the Frog's shiny, inviting back wouldn't prove too slippery.

The door was the first one a person would come to upon reaching the third floor and turning left. A middle-aged man in a suit stood next to it. There was no brass plate to identify whose office this was. Right next door was the office of Franklin Graham, the Senate sergeant-at-arms. The sergeant-at-arms was the Senate's principal law enforcement, administrative support and protocol officer. Graham was a good friend of Buchanan's.

"Good to see you, Danny," the man in the suit said.

"Hello, Phil, how's that back of yours?"

"Doc says I should have the surgery."

"Listen to me, don't let them cut you. When you're feeling the pain, have a nice, pleasing shot of Scotch, sing a song at the top of your lungs and then make love to your wife."

"Drinking, dancing and loving – sounds like good advice to me," Phil said.

"What'd you expect from an Irishman?"

Phil laughed. "You're a good man, Danny Buchanan."

"You know why I'm here?"

Phil nodded. "Mr. Graham told me. You can go right in."

He unlocked the door and Buchanan passed through, and then Phil closed the door and stood guard. He didn't notice the two pairs of people who had idly watched this exchange.

The agents reasonably figured they could wait for Buchanan to come out and then take up their surveillance once more. They were on the third floor, after all. It wasn't like the man could fly away.

Inside the room, Buchanan grabbed a raincoat off the hook on the wall. Lucky for him it was drizzly outside. There was also a yellow hard hat on another wall hook. He slipped this on as well. Then he pulled Coke-bottle glasses and work gloves from his briefcase. At least from a distance, with his briefcase under the raincoat, he would change from lobbyist to laborer.

Going to another door at the end of the room, Buchanan removed the chain locking this door and opened it. He went up the stairs and then opened a hatchlike door, which revealed a ladder leading up. Buchanan put his feet on the rungs and started climbing. At the top, he popped another hatch and found himself on the roof of the Capitol.

The attic room was how the pages accessed the roof to change the flags that flew over the Capitol. The inside joke was that the flags were constantly changed, some flying only for seconds, so that members could send generous constituents back home a continuous supply of Stars and Stripes that had "flown" over the Capitol. Buchanan rubbed his brow. God, what a town.

Buchanan looked down at the front grounds of the Capitol. People were scurrying here and there, running for meetings with people they desperately needed help from. And with all the egos, factions, agendas, crisis upon crisis and stakes greater than anything that had come before in the world's history, everything somehow seemed to work out. A large anthill came to mind as Buchanan looked down upon this well-oiled machine of democracy. At least the ants did it for survival. But maybe in a way, we did too, he thought.

He looked up at Lady Liberty on her century-and-a-half perch atop the Capitol's dome. She had recently been removed via helicopter and stout cable, and the grime of a hundred fifty years had been thoroughly cleaned away. Too bad the sins of people weren't as easy to scrape off.

For one insane moment, Buchanan contemplated jumping. He might have, too, except the desire to beat Thornhill was simply too strong. And that would be the coward's way out anyway. Buchanan was many things, but a coward was not one of them.

There was a catwalk that ran across the roof of the Capitol, and it would take Buchanan to the second part of his journey. Or, more accurately, his escape. The House wing of the Capitol building had a similar attic room, which its pages used to raise and lower its flags. Buchanan quickly went across the catwalk and through the hatch on the House side. He climbed down the ladder and into the attic room, where he removed the hard hat and gloves, but kept on the glasses. He pulled a snap-brim hat from his briefcase and put it on. Pulling up the collar on the raincoat, he took a deep breath, opened the door to the attic room and passed through. People milled here and there, but no one really gave him a second glance.

In another minute he had left the Capitol through a rear doorway known only to the few veterans of the place. A car was waiting for him there. A half hour later he was at National Airport, where a private plane, its twin engines revving, awaited its sole passenger. Here was where the friend in *high* places earned his money. The plane received clearance for takeoff a few minutes later. Soon thereafter Buchanan looked out the window of the plane as the capital city slowly disappeared from view. How many times had he seen that sight from the air?

"Good riddance," he said under his breath.

FORTY-FIVE

Thornhill was heading home early after a very productive day. With Adams now in the fold, they would soon have Faith Lockhart. The man might try to dupe them, but Thornhill didn't think so. He had heard the very real fear in Adams's voice. Thank God for families. Yes, all in all, a productive day. The ringing phone would soon change all that.

"Yes?" Thornhill's confident look vanished as the man reported to him that somehow, some way, Danny Buchanan had utterly vanished, from the very top floor of the Capitol, no less.

"Find him!" Thornhill roared into the phone before slamming it down. What could the man's game be? Had he decided to begin his escape a little early? Or was it for another reason? Had he contacted Lockhart somehow? That was intensely troubling. Shared information between the two was not good for Thornhill. He thought back to their meeting in the car. Buchanan had displayed his usual temper, his little word games – empty bluster, really – but had otherwise been fairly subdued. What could have precipitated this latest development?

In his agitation, Thornhill drummed his fingers on the briefcase, he had in his lap. As he looked down at the hard leather, his mouth dropped open. The briefcase! The damn briefcase! He had provided one for Buchanan. It had a backup recorder in it. The conversation in the car. Thornhill admitting he had

had the FBI agent killed. Buchanan had tricked him into betraying himself and then taped him. Taped him with CIA-issue equipment. That two-faced sonofabitch!

Thornhill grabbed the phone; his fingers were shaking so badly he misdialed twice. "His briefcase, the tape in it. Find it. And him. You must get it. You *have* to get it."

He dropped the phone and slumped back in the seat. The master strategist of over a thousand clandestine operations spanning nearly four decades was absolutely stunned by this development. Buchanan could take him down with this. He was running loose with the evidence to crush him. But Buchanan would go down too, had to, there was no way around it.

Wait. The scorpion! The frog! Now it all made sense. Buchanan was going to go down and take Thornhill with him. The CIA man loosened his tie, wedged himself into the seat and fought the panic he felt flooding his body.

This is not how it will end, Robert, he told himself. *After thirty-five years this is not damn well how it's going to end. Calm down. Now is when you need to think. Now is where you earn your place in history. This man will not beat you.* Slowly, steadily, Thornhill's breathing returned to normal.

It could be that Buchanan would simply use the tape as insurance. Why spend the rest of his life in prison when he could quietly disappear? No, it made no sense that he would take the tape to the authorities. He had as much to lose as Thornhill, and he couldn't possibly be that vindictive. Thornhill had a sudden thought: Perhaps it was the painting, the idiotic painting. Maybe that was what had started this whole thing. Thornhill should never have taken the damned thing. He would leave a message on Buchanan's machine at once, telling him his precious object had been returned. Thornhill left the message and arranged for the painting to be returned.

As Thornhill sat back and looked out the window, his confidence returned. He had one ace in the hole. A good commander always held something in reserve. Thornhill made another phone call and received some positive news, a piece of intelligence that had just come in. His face brightened, the visions of doom receding. It would be all right after all. His mouth eased into a smile. The snatch of victory from the jaws of defeat; it could either age a man several decades overnight or give him bronze balls. Or sometimes both.

In another few minutes Thornhill was getting out of his car and walking up the sidewalk to his lovely house. His impeccably dressed wife met him at the door and gave him a perfunctory peck on the cheek. She had just come back from a country club function. In fact, she was always coming back from a country club function, he thought, muttering to himself. While he agonized over terrorists sneaking into the country with nuclear-bomb-making materials, she lounged at fashion shows where young, vacuous women with legs stretching to their inflated bosoms pranced about in outfits that didn't even bother to cover their derrieres. He was out every day saving the world, and his spouse ate finger sandwiches and drank champagne in the afternoon with other ladies of considerable means. The idle rich were as stupid as the uneducated poor – more brainless than cows, in fact, was Thornhill's opinion. At least cows had a reasonable understanding that they were the slaves. *I'm an underpaid civil servant*, Thornhill mused, *and if I ever let my defenses down, the only thing left of the wealthy and powerful in this country would be the echoes of their screams.* It was a powerful, mesmerizing thought.

He barely heard his wife's inconsequential ramblings on "her day" as he put down his briefcase, mixed a drink and escaped to his study and closed the door. He never told the woman about *his* day. She'd chat about it to her one-name, oh-so-chic glorified barber, who would tell another client, who would let it slip to someone else and the world would stop tomorrow. No, he never talked shop with the wife. But he did indulge her in just about everything else. But finger sandwiches indeed!

Ironically, Thornhill's home office was much like Buchanan's. There were no plaques, testimonials or souvenirs of his long career on display. He was a spy, after all. Was he supposed to act like the idiotic FBI and wear T-shirts and hats emblazoned with CIA? He almost choked on his whiskey at the thought. No, his career had been invisible to the public, but highly visible to those who mattered. The country was far better off because of him, though the ordinary folk would never know it. That was all right. To seek accolades from the great and ignorant public was the vice of a fool. He did what he did because of pride. Pride in himself, in his devotion to his country.

Thornhill thought back to his beloved father, a patriot who carried his secrets, his distinguished triumphs to the grave. Service and honor. That was what it was all about.

Soon, with a little luck, the son would notch another triumph in his own career. When Faith showed up, she would be dead within an hour. And Adams? Well, he would have to die too. Certainly Thornhill had lied to the man on the phone. Thornhill understood quite clearly that deceit was nothing more nor less than a highly effective tool of the trade. One just had to make sure that lies at work didn't interfere with one's personal life. But Thornhill had always been good with compartmentalization. Just ask his country club wife. He could initiate a covert action in Central America in the morning and play, and win, at bridge at the Congressional Country Club in the evening. Now, dammit, *that* was compartmentalization!

And whatever anyone said about him within the confines of the Agency, he had always been good with his people. He pulled them out of situations when they needed to be pulled. He had never left an agent or case officer spinning in the wind, helpless. But he also kept them in the field when he knew they could carry it home. He had developed an instinct for such things, and it had hardly ever proved wrong. He also didn't play political games with intelligence collection. He had never told the politicians simply what they wanted to hear, as others at the Agency had – sometimes with disastrous consequences. Well, he could only do what he could. In two years it would be someone else's problem. He would leave the organization in as strong a state as he could. His parting gift. There was no need to thank him. Service and honor. He lifted his drink in memory of his late father.

FORTY-SIX

"Stay low, Faith," Lee said as he edged close to a window overlooking the street. He had his gun out and was watching a car drop a man off out front. "Is that Buchanan?" he asked.

Faith anxiously peered over the windowsill and then immediately relaxed.

"Yes."

"Okay, answer the front door. I'll cover you."

"I told you it was Danny."

"Great, then go let *Danny* in. I'm not taking any unnecessary chances."

Frowning at this remark, Faith went to the front door and opened it. Buchanan slipped through and she closed and locked the door behind him. They exchanged a prolonged hug as Lee watched from the stairs, his gun in plain sight in his belt clip. He felt a pang of jealousy at this embrace. It quickly passed, though, as he sensed the exchange of affection was clearly that of a father and his daughter.

"You must be Lee Adams," Buchanan said, extending his hand. "I'm sure you regret the day you ever took on this assignment."

Lee came down and shook his hand. "Nah. This one's been a piece of cake. I'm actually thinking about specializing in this area, especially considering no one else would be stupid enough to do it."

"I thank God you were there to protect Faith."

"Actually, I've gotten pretty good at saving Faith." Lee and Faith exchanged smiles, then Lee looked back at Buchanan. "But the fact is we have one additional complication. A very important one," Lee added. "Let's go to the kitchen. You might want to hear it over a drink."

As they sat at the kitchen table, Lee filled Buchanan in on the situation with his daughter.

Buchanan looked furious. "That bastard."

Lee eyed him keenly. "This bastard have a name? I'd love to know it, for future reference."

Buchanan eyed him keenly and then shook his head. "Trust me, you don't want to go down that route."

"Who is behind all this, Danny?" Faith touched his arm. "I think I have a right to know."

Buchanan looked at Lee.

"Sorry," Lee said, putting up his hands, "that's your call."

Buchanan gripped Faith's arm. "They're very powerful people and they happen to work for this country. That's all I can really say without endangering you even more."

Faith sat back astonished. "*Our* own government is trying to kill us?"

"The gentleman I've been dealing with tends to go his own way. But he does have resources, lots of them."

"So Lee's daughter is in real danger?"

"Yes. This man will usually say rather less than what he actually intends."

"Why'd you come here, Buchanan?" Lee wanted to know. "You got away from the guy. At least for our sakes I hope you did. You could've lost yourself in a million different places. Why come here?"

"I got you both into this. I intend to get you out."

"Well, whatever plan you have better include

saving my daughter or else you can count me out. I'll park myself inside her skin for the next twenty years if I have to."

Faith said, "I thought I could call the FBI agent I was working with, Brooke Reynolds. We can tell her what's going on. She could place Lee's daughter in protective custody."

"For the rest of her life?" Buchanan shook his head. "No, that won't work. We have to cut the hydra's head off and then burn the stub. Otherwise we're just wasting time."

"And exactly how do we do that?" Lee asked.

Buchanan opened his briefcase and pulled out the tiny cassette tape from a hidden crevice. "With this. I was able to record the gentleman I've been talking about. On this tape he admits that he had the FBI agent killed, among other incriminating things."

For the first time Lee looked hopeful. "Are you serious?"

"Trust me, I would never joke about this man."

"So we use this tape to keep the hound at bay. He hurts us, we destroy him? He knows that. Then we've pulled his fangs."

Buchanan slowly nodded. "Exactly."

"And you know how to contact him?" asked Lee.

Buchanan nodded. "I'm sure that he's figured out what I did and is right now trying to deduce what my intention is."

"Well, *my* intention is that you call up this asshole right this second and tell him to stay the hell away from my daughter. I want it in blood. And I don't trust the sonofabitch, so I still want something like a company of SEALs outside her dorm room for good measure. And I still plan on heading up there myself. Just in case. They want Renee? They go through me."

"I'm not sure that's a good idea," Buchanan said.

"I don't remember asking for your permission," Lee fired back.

"Lee, please," Faith said. "Danny's just trying to help."

"I wouldn't be in this nightmare if this guy had been straight with me up front. So excuse the hell out of me if I don't treat him like he's my best buddy."

"I don't blame you for feeling that way," Buchanan said. "But you called me for help, and I'll do whatever I can to help you. And your daughter. That I swear."

Lee's guarded manner relaxed somewhat in the face of this seemingly frank declaration.

"Okay," he said grudgingly. "I admit you get points for coming here. You'll get more points when you call off the assassins. And then after that we should get the hell out of here. I've already called this psycho once on my cell phone. I'm assuming that at some point he'll be able to narrow our location down from that. When you call him, it'll give them even more info to work with."

"Understood. I have a plane at my disposal at a private airstrip not too far from here."

"Your friends in high places?"

"*Friend*. Senior senator from this state, Russell Ward."

"Good old Rusty," Faith said, smiling.

"You're sure you weren't followed?" Lee glanced at the front door.

"No one could have followed me. I'm not sure of much anymore, but I am certain of that."

"If this guy is as good as you seem to think he is, I wouldn't feel too certain of anything." Lee held out his cell phone. "Now please make the call."

FORTY-SEVEN

Thornhill was in his study at home when Buchanan's phone call came in. His communication link was such that the call was not traceable to Thornhill, if Buchanan was perhaps sitting at FBI headquarters. And Thornhill's phone also had a voice scrambler that would make voice ID impossible. On the other hand, Thornhill's people were working on tracing Buchanan's location, but as yet they hadn't been successful. Even the CIA had its limits, what with the explosion in the field of communications technology. There were so many electronic signals flying through the air, it made it damn near impossible to trace a wireless call to a precise location.

The National Security Agency would be able to trace the call with its stadium-size circular antennas. The super-secret NSA possessed technological might that made anything the CIA had pale by comparison, Thornhill well knew. It was said that the intelligence the NSA perpetually swept out of the air could fill the Library of Congress every *three* hours, gobbling up information in avalanche-byte mouthfuls. Thornhill had availed himself of the NSA's services before. However, the NSA (the inside joke was that the acronym stood for "no such agency") was often difficult for anyone to control. Thus Thornhill didn't want to involve them in this highly sensitive matter. He would handle it himself.

"You know why I'm calling?" Buchanan said.

"A tape. A highly personal one."

"It's good doing business with someone who considers himself omniscient."

"I would appreciate some small bit of evidence, if it's not too much trouble," Thornhill said placidly.

Buchanan played a snatch of the earlier conversation between the two men.

"Thank you, Danny. Now, your terms?"

"Point one, you don't go near Lee Adams's daughter. That is called off. Now and forever."

"Do you happen to be with Mr. Adams and Ms. Lockhart right now?"

"Second, all three of us are off limits as well. If anything remotely suspicious happens, then the tape goes directly to the FBI."

"During our last conversation you said you already had the means to destroy me."

"I lied."

"Do Adams and Lockhart know of my involvement?"

"No."

"How can I trust you?"

"It would only have put them in more danger to tell them. All they want to do is survive. It seems a common enough goal these days. And I'm afraid you'll just have to take my word for it."

"Even though you just admitted lying to me?"

"Exactly. Tell me, how does it feel?"

"And my long-term plan?"

"I really don't give a damn at this point."

"Why did you run?"

"Put yourself in my place; what would you have done?"

"I would never have allowed myself to be put in your place," said Thornhill.

"Thank God we can't all be like you. Do we have an agreement?"

"I don't have much choice, do I?"

"Join the club," said Buchanan. "However, you can be absolutely certain that if anything happens to any of us, it's over for you. But if you play fair, you accomplish your goal. Everyone lives to celebrate."

"Good doing business with you too, Danny."

Thornhill clicked off and sat there seething for a few moments. Then he made another call but came away disappointed. The trace had not been made. Well, that was all right. He hardly expected it to be so easy. He still had his ace in the hole. He made one more phone call and this time the information brought a broad smile to his lips. As Danny had said, Thornhill did know all there was to know, and he thanked God for his omniscience. When you planned for every possible contingency you were difficult to beat.

Buchanan was with Lockhart, of that he was almost certain. His two golden birds were occupying the same nest. That made his task infinitely simpler. Buchanan had outsmarted himself.

He was just about to refill his scotch when his wife popped her head in. Would he like to go to the club with her? There was a bridge tournament going on. She had just gotten a call. A couple had canceled and wanted to know if the Thornhills could take their place.

"Actually," he said, "I'm very much engaged in a game of chess." His wife looked around the empty room. "Oh, it's long-distance, dear," Thornhill explained, nodding at his desktop computer. "You know the things one can do with technology these days. You can do battle and never even see your opponent."

"Well, don't stay up too late," she said. "You've

been working very hard and you're not a young man anymore."

"I see light at the end of the tunnel," Thornhill replied. And this time he was telling the absolute truth.

FORTY-EIGHT

Reynolds and Connie reached Duck, North Carolina, around one in the morning after only a single stop for fuel and food and reached Pine Island a short while later. The streets were dark, the businesses closed. They were fortunate in finding an all-night gas station, however. While Reynolds got two coffees and some pastries, Connie found out from the clerk on duty where the airplane runway was located. They sat in the gas station lot, ate, and mulled things over.

"I checked in at WFO," Connie told Reynolds as he stirred sugar into his coffee. "Interesting twist. Buchanan's disappeared."

She swallowed a bite of her pastry and stared at him. "How the hell did that happen?"

"Nobody knows. That's why so many people are catching grief over it."

"Well, at least they can't blame that one on us."

"Don't be too sure of that. Laying blame is a fine art in D.C., and the Bureau ain't no exception."

Reynolds had a sudden thought. "Connie, do you think Buchanan could be trying to rendezvous with Lockhart? That may be why he disappeared."

"If we could nail them both at the same time, you might get appointed director."

Reynolds smiled. "I'll settle for having my suspension lifted. But Buchanan might be on his way here. What time did they say they lost the tail?"

"Late this afternoon."

370

"Then he could already be here, if he took a plane."

Connie sipped his coffee, while he thought this over. "Why would Buchanan and Lockhart be doing anything together?" he asked slowly.

"Don't forget, if we're right about Buchanan hiring Adams, then maybe Adams called Buchanan and they hooked up that way."

"*If* Adams is innocent in all this. But he sure as hell wouldn't call Buchanan if he thought the guy had anything to do with trying to knock off Lockhart. After all we've found out, I'm gauging the guy as her protector, of sorts."

"I think you're right about that. But maybe Adams found out something that made him believe Buchanan didn't order the hit. If that was the case, he might try to team with Buchanan to figure out together what the hell was going on and who else was out there trying to kill Lockhart."

"Somebody else behind this? One of the foreign governments Buchanan was working with, maybe? If the truth came out, they'd be sitting out there with world-class egg on their face. That's plenty of incentive to kill somebody," Connie said.

"I wonder," Reynolds began, as Connie watched her closely. "There's just been something about this case that's never added up," she said. "We've got somebody impersonating FBI agents. Somebody who seems to know our every move."

"Ken Newman?"

"Maybe. But that doesn't seem to make sense either. Ken's had cash coming in for a long time. Has he been somebody's mole for that long a period of time? Or is it somebody else?"

"And don't forget about whoever's trying to frame you. Moving money around accounts like that takes some expertise."

"Exactly. But I just don't see operatives of a

foreign government being able to do all that, and no one the wiser."

"Brooke, countries conduct industrial espionage against us every day. Shit, our staunchest allies even do it, ripping off our technology because they're not smart enough to do it on their own. And our borders are so open it doesn't take much to get in. You know that."

Reynolds let out a deep sigh as she stared into the darkness lying right outside the gas station's harsh ring of lights. "I suppose you're right. I guess instead of trying to figure out who's behind this, we should try to find Lockhart and company and just ask them."

"Now, that's a plan I can relate to." Connie put the car in gear and they sped off into the darkness.

After locating the runway, Reynolds and Connie cruised the dark streets looking for the Honda Gold Wing. Virtually all of the beach houses appeared vacant now, which made their search both easier and more difficult. It cut down the number of places they had to focus on, but it also made the agents stand out more.

Connie finally spotted the Honda in the carport of one of the beach houses. Reynolds eased out of the car and got a close enough look to confirm that the license tag matched the bike Lee Adams had borrowed from his brother's shop. Then they drove to the other end of the street, hit the lights and talked it over.

"Maybe it's as simple as me going in the front and you going in the back," Reynolds said as she studied the dark house. Her skin was tingling with the thought that a bare fifty feet away were two or possibly the three key people in this whole investigation.

Connie shook his head. "I don't like that. The Honda being there means Adams is in there too."

372

"We've got his gun."

"A guy like that, first thing he would've done is get another one. And we go in, even if we surprise him, he knows the lay of the land better than we do. He might get one of us." He added, "And you don't even have a gun, so we're not splitting up."

"You're the one who said you thought Adams wasn't a bad guy."

"Thinking something and being absolutely certain of it are two different things. And that difference is not something I'm willing to risk anybody's life over. And rushing in on anybody, good or bad, in the middle of the night, mistakes can happen. I intend on getting you back to your kids in one piece. And I wouldn't mind doing the same."

"So how do we play it? Wait for daylight and call in reinforcements?"

"Calling in the locals will probably mean every TV station down here will be on the block an hour after we do. That won't earn us many points at HQ."

"Well, I guess we can wait for them to ride off on the Honda and then pull them."

"Other things being equal, I'm inclined to watch the place and see what happens. If they come out, we move in. If we get real lucky, Lockhart will surface without Adams and we can take her. After that, I'm figuring we can bait Adams out pretty easy."

"And if they don't come out, together or singly?"

"Then we'll cross that bridge when we come to it."

"I don't want to lose them again, Connie."

"It's not like they can just take off down the beach or swim to England. Adams went to a lot of trouble to get those wheels. He's not going to abandon the bike because he doesn't have another way to replace it. Where he goes, that Honda goes. And that Honda ain't going anywhere without us seeing it."

They settled down and waited.

FORTY-NINE

His pistol resting on his belly, Lee had spent a few fitful hours on the couch downstairs. Every few minutes he thought he heard someone breaking in, and each time it proved to be nothing more than his very tired imagination doing its best to drive him crazy. Since he couldn't sleep, he had finally decided to get ready to leave for Charlottesville. He grabbed a quick shower and changed his clothes. He was packing his bag when a soft knock came on his door.

Faith was dressed in a long white robe; her puffy cheeks and tired-looking eyes were stark testaments to her inability to sleep.

"Where's Buchanan?" he asked.

"Actually dozing, I think. I never came close."

"Tell me about it." He finished packing and closed his bag.

"Are you sure you don't want me to come with you?" she asked.

He shook his head. "I don't want you anywhere near this guy and his goons if they show up. I got through to Renee last night. First time I've talked to her in I don't know how long and I have to tell her she might be the target of some psycho because of something her stupid dad did."

"How did she take it?"

On this Lee brightened. "Actually, she seemed happy to hear from me. I didn't tell her everything that was going on. I didn't want to panic her, but I

374

think she's looking forward to seeing me."

"I'm glad to hear that. I'm really happy for you, Lee."

"The cops at least took my call seriously. Renee said a patrolman came by and a marked car's been cruising the area."

He put his bag down, took her hand. "I don't feel good about leaving you."

"It's your daughter. We'll be fine. You heard Danny. He's got this person over a barrel."

Lee looked unconvinced. "The last thing you should do right now is let down your guard. The car will be here at eight to take you and Buchanan to the plane. You head back to D.C."

"And then what?"

"Go to a motel in the suburbs. Register under a false name and then call me on my cell phone. As soon as things are okay with Renee I'll head back. I already talked it over with Buchanan. He's in agreement."

"And then?" Faith persisted.

"Let's just take it a step at a time. I told you there are no guarantees in this."

"I was actually talking about *us*."

Lee played with the strap on his bag. "Oh," was all that came out, and it sounded idiotic.

"I see."

"You see what?" Lee demanded.

"Wham, bam, thank you, ma'am."

"Where do you get off thinking like that? Don't you know what kind of a man I am by now?"

"Actually, I thought I did. But I guess I forgot. You're in the loner group: sex only for fun. Right?"

"Why are we doing this? Like we don't have enough going on. We can talk about it later. It's not like I'm not coming back."

Lee didn't mean to put her off, but – hell, why

couldn't she see there was no time for this right now?

Faith sat down on the bed.

"Like you said, no guarantees," she said.

He put a hand on her shoulder. "I am coming back, Faith. I didn't come this far to desert you now."

"Okay," was all she said. She stood, wiped her face and gave him a quick hug. "Please, please, be careful."

Faith let him out the rear door. As she turned to go back in, Lee's gaze was riveted on her. He took in everything, from the bare feet to the short dark hair and all points in between. For one troubling moment, he wondered if this was the last time he would ever see her.

Lee climbed on the Honda and quickly started up the bike.

As Lee roared out the driveway and hit the street, Brooke Reynolds raced back to the Crown Vic and threw open the door. Breathless, she looked inside.

"Shit, I knew the minute I left the car to get a closer look at the house this would happen. He must have come out a rear door. He didn't even turn on the carport light. I never saw him until the bike cranked up. So what do we do? House or the bike?"

Connie looked down the road. "Adams is already out of sight. And that bike is a lot more agile than this tank."

"I guess that leaves the house and Lockhart."

Connie suddenly looked worried. "We're presuming she's still inside. In fact, we don't even know if she was ever inside."

"Shit, I knew you were going to say that. She damn well better be. If we just let Adams go and Lockhart isn't in that house, *I* will swim to England. And you're going to have to be right beside me.

Come on, Connie, we have to go in the house."

Connie climbed out of the car, pulled his gun and looked around nervously. "Shit, I don't like this. It could be a setup. We could be walking right into an ambush. And we've got no backup."

"We don't have much choice, do we?"

"All right, but dammit, stay behind me."

They headed for the house.

FIFTY

D ressed in black sweats and tennis shoes, the three men raced along the beach, keeping low to the sand. Although the dawn was fast approaching, they were virtually invisible in their dark clothing against the backdrop of the ocean, and the pounding surf covered all sounds of their movements.

They had arrived in the area barely an hour ago and had just received some very disturbing news. Lee Adams had left the house. Lockhart wasn't with him. She must still be in the house. Or at least they hoped she was. Buchanan, they had been told, might be there as well. They would take those two over Adams. He could wait. They would eventually get him. In fact, they would not stop until they got him.

Each team member was equipped with an automatic pistol and a knife specially designed to take out the carotid in one efficient stroke. Each man was well skilled in exactly how to execute just such a lethal blow. Their orders were clear. Everyone in the house had to die. Perfectly executed, it could be a clean operation. They could be back in Washington by late morning.

They were proud men, professionals in their own right and long in the service of Robert Thornhill. As a team they had survived some dangerous times in the last twenty years with their wit, skill, physical strength and stamina. They had saved lives, made certain parts of the world safer, helped to ensure that the United States would become the world's sole remaining superpower. This would mean a fairer, more just world for many. Like Robert Thornhill, they had joined the Agency to perform a service, to engage in a public trust. To them, there was no higher calling.

All three men were also part of the group Lee and Faith had eluded at Adams's apartment. The episode had embarrassed them, tarnishing their reputation for near perfection. They had been hoping for a shot at redemption, and now they did not intend to waste it.

One man stayed near the top of the stairs to keep watch, while the other two hurried down the boardwalk to the rear of the house. The plan was simple, direct, unencumbered by layers of detail. They would hit the house hard and fast, starting on the ground floor and moving up. When they ran into anyone, they wouldn't ask questions or seek identification. Their suppressor-equipped pistols would fire one time for each victim, and then they would move on until every living thing in the house no longer was. Yes, it was definitely conceivable they could be back in Washington before lunch.

FIFTY-ONE

Lee slowed down the Honda and then stopped in the middle of the road, his feet coming down lightly on the asphalt. He looked back over his shoulder. The street was long, black and empty. The dawn would be coming soon, though. He could see it in the softening edges of the sky, like the streaked edges of a Polaroid slowly lapping to vibrancy.

So why couldn't he have waited? He could have waited until the car came to take Faith and Buchanan to the airstrip. It would only delay his trip to Charlottesville by a couple of hours at most. And it would certainly increase his peace of mind. Why the hell was he running away so fast? Renee was protected. What about Faith?

His gloved hand tapped against the Honda's throttle. It would also give him a chance to talk to the woman, to let Faith know that he cared very much for her.

He turned the Honda around and headed back. When he reached the street, he slowed the bike. The car was parked at the far end of the street. It was a big sedan that just screamed federal government. True, it was at the opposite end of the street and he wouldn't have passed it heading to the main road, but how the hell had his "expert" eyes missed that? God, was he really getting that old?

He drove directly at the car, figuring that if it was the Feds, he could cut off easily enough and lose them. As he drew closer, however, it was clear the car was empty. Starting to panic, he swung the Honda around, drove up into the driveway of the beach house two lots down from Faith's and jumped off. Throwing down his helmet and pulling his pistol, Lee raced around to the rear courtyard of the house and then on to the boardwalk that criss-crossed the rear common areas connecting all the houses to the main steps going to the beach, like human veins leading to the heart's arteries. His own heart was pumping at a feverishly high pace.

He jumped off the boardwalk, squatted low behind some sawgrass and peered at the back of Faith's beach house. What he saw chilled him to the bone. The two men were dressed all in black and were sliding over the rear wall of Faith's courtyard. Were they the Feds? Or were they the men who had been prepared to assassinate Faith at the airport? *Please, God, don't let it be them.* The two men had already disappeared over the wall. In seconds they would be in the house. Had Faith reset the alarm system after she let him out? No, he thought, she probably hadn't.

Lee jumped up and dashed toward the house. As he crossed the boardwalk, he sensed something coming at him from the left as the darkness began to lift even more. That sensation was probably the only thing that saved his life.

The knife plunged into his arm instead of his neck as he ducked and rolled. He came up bleeding, but the rigid material of the bike suit had absorbed a good deal of the blow. His attacker didn't hesitate but leaped straight at him.

However, Lee timed it just right, managed to raise his good arm, pushed hard, levered the man over him, throwing him into the sawgrass, which was about as unpleasant as having a sharp knife driven into your flesh. Lee lunged for his gun, which he had lost when the guy had slammed into him. Lee had no qualms about shooting the guy down and raising a ruckus. Right now he would welcome any assistance the local police cared to provide.

His opponent made a stunning recovery, however, bursting out of the sawgrass with startling velocity and colliding with Lee before he could retrieve his pistol. The two men landed at the edge of the steps. Lee saw the knife thrust coming again but was able to grip the man's wrist before the blade hit him. The guy was strong; Lee could feel the steely tendons in the man's forearm and in the rocklike triceps as he grabbed the man's upper arm in an attempt to force the knife out of his hand. But Lee wasn't exactly a weakling either. He hadn't shoved tons of barbells around for years for nothing.

The guy he was battling was an experienced fighter as well because he had managed to get in two or three efficient gut punches with his free hand. After the first one, though, Lee tightened his abdominals and obliques and felt little pain from the other jabs. He had spent over two decades doing stomach crunches and having medicine balls slammed into his belly. After that punishment, the human fist offered very little difficulty for him, no matter how hard it was thrown.

Thinking that two could play at that game, Lee let go of the man's upper arm and landed a body uppercut to the diaphragm. He felt the wind go out of the guy, but the grip on the knife remained unbroken. Then Lee landed three successful kidney punches, about the most painful ones you could throw and still leave your opponent conscious. The knife fell from the man's hand, clattering down the steps.

Then both men rose to their feet, breathing hard, still clinging one to the other. Like a burst of wind, the man executed a nifty loopkick that knocked Lee's legs from under him. He went down with a grunt but popped right back up when he saw the guy go for his pistol. Being seconds from death gave Lee's body resiliency he could never summon in less dangerous times. He hit the guy low and hard, linebacker to running back in a textbook impact, and they both went over the edge of the steps, bouncing painfully down each pressure-treated plank and landing in a pile of twisted arms, legs and torsos in the sand and then eating mouthfuls of salty water as they rolled into the water, the rising tide being almost up to the steps.

Lee had seen the pistol tumble away during the fall, so he kicked himself free and stood in ankle-deep water. The guy rose too, but not as swiftly. Lee, however, was tightly on guard. The guy knew karate; Lee had felt it in the kick at the top of the stairs; he was seeing it in the defensive posture the man now assumed, making himself into a little ball, leaving no angles, nothing of much width to hit. His brain working faster than conscious thought, Lee figured he had about four inches and fifty pounds on the guy, but if the man nailed him with a lethal foot to the head, Lee would go down. And then he and Faith and Buchanan were all dead. But if he didn't finish the guy within the next minute, Faith and Buchanan would be dead anyway.

The man aimed a crushing side kick to Lee's torso; however, his having to slosh through water to deliver the kick gave Lee the little extra time he needed. Lee had to get in close, grab what he could and not give Chuck Norris Jr. enough space to do his martial arts magic. Lee was a boxer; in-close fighting, where whipping legs couldn't do much damage, was where he could be absolutely devastating. Lee braced himself and absorbed the rib-rattling leg shot to the body but then held on to the limb with his bloodied arm, clinching it to his side in a viselike grip. With his free hand, he landed a cartilage-shattering blow to the guy's knee, driving it backward to a degree knees were not designed to go. The man screamed. Then Lee delivered a crunching straight jab to the guy's face, feeling the nose flatten under the impact. Finally, in a flash of almost choreographed movement, Lee dropped the leg, curled low and then erupted out of that position with a cannonball left hook that carried all two hundred and twenty pounds of his bulk plus whatever multiplying factor pure fury brought to the table. When his fist hit facial bone, which promptly yielded under the terrible impact, Lee knew he had won. Nobody short of a professional heavyweight had a jaw that hard.

The man went down as though shot through the head. Lee instantly flipped him on his stomach and pushed his head under the water. He didn't have time to actually drown the guy, so he brought his elbow down with all his might dead center on the back of the man's neck. The resulting sound was unmistakable, even with the water lapping all over them, as though God wanted Lee to damn well know what he'd done, and didn't want him to ever forget it.

The body went limp and Lee rose over the dead man. Lee had been in more than his share of fights both in and out of the boxing ring, but he had never killed anyone before. As he looked down at the body, he knew it was nothing to be proud of. Lee was just grateful it wasn't him lying dead.

Sick to his stomach, suddenly feeling the full force of the pain in his wounded arm, Lee looked up the steps leading to the beach houses. He had only two other beasts to conquer and then he could call it a day. And it was clear they weren't the FBI. FBI agents didn't run around trying to kill people with fancy knives and karate kicks; they pulled their shield and guns and told you to stop right in your tracks. And if you were smart, you did.

No, they were the other guys. The CIA robokillers. He raced up the steps, found his pistol and hustled as fast as he could to the beach house, hoping with every labored breath that he was not too late.

FIFTY-TWO

Faith had changed into jeans and a sweatshirt and now sat on her bed staring at her bare feet. The sounds of the motorcycle had disappeared as though into an enormous vacuum. As she looked around the room, it was as though Lee Adams had never even been here, had never been real. She had spent so much time and energy trying to lose the man, and now that he was gone, all of her spirit seemed to have been swept into the void Lee had left behind.

At first she thought the sound she heard in the stillness of the house was Buchanan stirring. Then she thought it might actually be Lee returning. It had sounded like the back door. As she rose from the bed, it suddenly occurred to her that it couldn't be Lee because she hadn't heard the motorcycle pull into the carport; as this thought hit her, her heartbeat went through the roof.

Had she locked the door? She couldn't remember. She knew she hadn't set the alarm. Could it be just Danny stumbling around? For some reason Faith knew it wasn't.

She eased over to the doorway and peered out, her ears straining to hear any sound. She knew she hadn't imagined the noise. Someone had come in the house, she was sure of it. Someone was in the house right now. She looked down the hallway. There was another alarm control panel in the bedroom Lee had used. Could she reach it, activate the system, the motion detector? She dropped to her knees and crawled out into the hallway.

Connie and Reynolds had gone in the side door and made their way down the lower-floor hallway. Connie had his gun pointed ahead. Reynolds was behind him, feeling naked and useless without her own pistol. They eased open each door on the lower level and found each room empty.

"They must be upstairs," Reynolds whispered into Connie's ear.

"I hope there's somebody here," he whispered back, his voice carrying an ominous tone.

They both froze when a sound came from somewhere within the house. Connie motioned upstairs with his finger and Reynolds nodded in agreement. They approached the stairs and headed up. Fortunately, the stairs were carpeted and absorbed the sounds of their footsteps. They reached the first landing and paused, listening intently. Silence. They moved forward again.

The family area was empty, as far as they could see. They moved along one wall, their heads swiveling in near-synchronized motion.

Right above them, in the upstairs hallway, Faith was flat on her stomach on the floor. She peered over the edge and relaxed slightly as she saw that it was Agents Reynolds and Constantinople. When she saw the two other men moving up the stairs from the lower level, her fear instantly returned.

"Look out," Faith yelled.

Connie and Reynolds turned back to look at her and saw where she was pointing. Connie swung his gun in the direction of the two men, who also had their guns out, pointed directly at the two agents.

"FBI," Reynolds barked out to the men in black.

"Drop your weapons." Usually when she said that, she felt fairly confident of the response. Now, with two guns against one, she was not nearly as confident.

The two men didn't drop their weapons. They moved forward as Connie swung his gun back and forth between the two.

One of the men looked up at Faith. "Come down here, Ms. Lockhart."

"Stay up there, Faith," Reynolds called out, her gaze finding Faith's and holding on it. "Go to your room and lock the door."

"Faith?" Buchanan appeared in the hallway, his hair disheveled, his eyes blinking.

"You too, Buchanan. Now," the same man commanded. "Down here."

"No!" Reynolds said, moving forward. "Listen up, an HRT unit is on its way here right now. We're looking at an ETA of about two minutes. If you won't put your weapons down, then I suggest you run like hell unless you want to go up against those guys."

The man looked at her and smiled. "There's no HRT unit coming, Agent Reynolds."

Reynolds could not hide her astonishment. That astonishment immeasurably increased with the man's next words.

"Agent Constantinople," the man said, looking over at Connie, "you can leave now. We have it under control, but we appreciate your assistance."

Slowly, Reynolds turned and looked at her partner, her mouth open in absolute shock.

Connie stared back at her, both extreme discomfort and a profound sense of resignation on his features.

"Connie?" Reynolds took a quick breath. "It can't be, Connie. Please tell me it's not."

Connie fingered his pistol and he shrugged. Gradually his taut posture relaxed. "My plan was to get you out of this alive *and* get your suspension lifted." He looked over at the two men. One of them shook his head decisively.

"You're the leak?" Reynolds said. "Not Ken?"

"Ken was no leak," Connie said.

"But the money in the safe-deposit box?"

"That came from his card and coin trading. He operated all in cash. I actually did some shows with him. I knew. He was cheating the tax guys. So who the hell cared? More power to him. Most of it was going to college funds for his kids anyway."

"You let me think he was the leak."

"Well, I didn't want you to think it was me. Obviously, that would not have been good."

One of the men ran upstairs and disappeared into one of the bedrooms. A minute later he emerged carrying Buchanan's briefcase. He escorted Faith and Buchanan down the stairs. The man popped open the briefcase and took out the cassette. He played a little of the tape to confirm what was on it. Then he cracked open the cassette, pulled out the tape and threw the long strands into the gas fireplace and hit the remote switch. They all watched in silence as the tape was quickly reduced to a gooey mess.

As Reynolds watched the tape disappear, she couldn't help but think she was being shown the next few minutes of her life. The *last* few minutes of her life.

Reynolds looked at the two men and then at Connie. "So they just tailed us all the way down? I didn't see anybody," she said bitterly.

Connie shook his head. "There was a transmitter in my car. They've been listening in. They let us find the right house and then followed."

"Why, Connie? Why turn traitor?"

Connie's tone was reflective. "I put in twenty-five years at the Bureau. Twenty-five damn good years, and I'm still at square one, still a grunt in the field. I got a dozen years on you and you're my boss. Because I wouldn't play the political game south of the border. Because I wouldn't lie and just go along, they tanked my career." He shook his head and looked down. When he stared back up at her, he looked apologetic. "Understand, I got nothing against you, Brooke. Nothing. You're a damn fine agent. I didn't want it to end like this. The plan was for us to stay outside and let these guys do their thing. When I got the all-clear, we'd go in and find the bodies. Your name would be cleared, everything would work out fine. Adams taking off like that blew our plan apart." Connie stared with unfriendly eyes at the man in black who had identified him by name. "But if this guy hadn't said anything, maybe I still could have figured out a way for you to walk away with me."

The man shrugged. "Sorry, I didn't know that was important to you. But you'd better get going. It's getting light outside. Give us half an hour. Then you can call the cops. Make up any cover story you want."

Reynolds never took her eyes off Connie. "Let me make up a cover story for you, Connie. It goes like this: We found the house. I go in the front while you cover the rear. I don't come out. You hear shots, you go in. Find us all dead." Reynolds's voice broke as she thought of her children, of never seeing them again. "You see someone leaving, empty your pistol at him. But you miss, give chase, are almost killed, but luckily barely survive. You call the cops. They get here. You call HQ, fill them in. They send people down. You get bitched at a little for coming down here with me, but you were just standing by your boss. Loyalty. Who could really blame you? They investigate and never reach a satisfactory answer. Probably think I'm the leak for sure, came down for a payoff. You can tell them it was my idea to come here, that I knew exactly where to go. I go in the house, get popped. And you, a poor innocent dupe, almost lost your life too. Case closed. How's that sound, Agent Constantinople?" She almost spat this last part out.

One of Thornhill's men looked over at Connie and smiled. "Sounds good to me."

Connie never took his eyes off Reynolds. "I'm sorry, Brooke, I really am."

Reynolds's eyes filled with tears and her voice cracked again when she spoke. "Tell Anne Newman that. Tell *my* kids that, you bastard!"

His eyes downcast, Connie moved past them and started to head down the stairs.

"We'll do them here, one by one," the first man said.

He looked at Buchanan. "You first."

"I take it that was a special request from your boss," Buchanan said.

"Who? I want a name," Reynolds demanded.

"What does it matter?" the second man said. "It's not like you're going to be around to testify—"

The instant he said this, the bullet hit him in the back of the head and he went down instantly.

The other man whirled, trying to aim his gun, but was too late and took a blast right in the face. He dropped, dead, next to his partner.

Connie came back up the stairs, a wisp of smoke still trailing from his pistol's muzzle. He looked down at the two dead men. "That was for Ken Newman, you assholes." He looked up at Reynolds. "I didn't know they were going to kill Ken, Brooke. I swear that on a stack of Bibles. But after it happened, there was nothing I could do but bide my time and see what happened."

"And let me chase a wild goose? Watch me get suspended. My career ruined."

"There wasn't much I could do about that. Like I said, my intent was to get you out of this, get you reinstated. Let you be the hero. Let Ken take the charge as snitch. He was dead, what did it matter?"

"It would matter to his family, Connie."

Connie's features turned angry. "Look, I don't have to stand here and explain shit to you or anybody else. I'm not proud of what I did, but I had my reasons. You don't have to agree with them, and I'm not asking you to, but don't stand there and lecture me about something you know nothing about, lady. You want'a talk pain and bitterness? I got about fifteen years of it on you."

Reynolds blinked and stepped back, eyeing the pistol.

"Okay, Connie, you just saved our lives. That'll count for a lot."

"You think so, do you?"

She pulled out her cell phone. "I'm going to call Massey and get a team down here."

"Put the phone away, Brooke."

"Connie—"

"Put the damn phone down. Now!"

Reynolds let the phone drop to the floor. "Connie, it's over."

"It's never over, Brooke, you know that. Stuff that happened years ago will always come back to bite you in the ass. People find out stuff and look you up and suddenly your life is over."

"Is that why you're involved in this? Somebody was blackmailing you?"

He slowly gazed about. "What the hell does it matter?"

"It matters to me!" said Reynolds.

Connie let out a deep sigh. "When my wife got cancer, our insurance wouldn't cover all the specialized treatments. The doctors thought the treatments might give her a chance, a few more months. I mortgaged the house to the hilt. I cleaned out our bank accounts. It still wasn't enough. What was I supposed to do? Just let her die?" Connie angrily shook his head. "So some coke and other stuff turned up missing from the Bureau evidence room. Some people found out about it later. And suddenly I had a new employer." He paused and looked down for a moment. "And the most damnable thing is June died anyway."

"I can help you, Connie. You can end this right now."

Connie smiled grimly. "Nobody can help me, Brooke. I made my deal with the devil."

"Connie, let them go. It's over."

He shook his head. "I came here to do a job. And you know me well enough to know that I always finish what I start."

"Then what? How will you talk yourself out of these?" She looked at the two dead men. "And now you're going to kill three *more* people? That's crazy. Please."

"Not as crazy as giving up and spending the rest of my life in prison. Or maybe getting the chair." He shrugged his big shoulders. "I'll think of something."

"Please, Connie. Don't do this. You can't do this. I know you. You can't."

Connie looked at his pistol and then knelt down and picked up one of the dead men's guns that had a suppressor attached. "I've got to. And I am sorry, Brooke."

They all heard the click. Connie and Reynolds

instantly recognized it as the cock of a semi-automatic pistol.

Lee barked, "Drop the pistol. Now! Or I put a tunnel in your head."

Connie froze and let the gun fall to the floor.

Lee came up the stairs and put the muzzle of his pistol against the agent's head. "I'm real tempted to shoot you anyway, but you did save me the trouble of tangling with two more gorillas." Lee looked at Reynolds. "Agent Reynolds, I'd appreciate if you'd pick up the pistol and keep it trained on your boy here."

Reynolds did so, her eyes burning into her partner's. "Sit down, Connie. Now!" she ordered.

Lee went over and put his arms around Faith.

"Lee," was all she said, leaning into him.

"Thank God I decided to come back."

"Can someone tell me what the hell this is all about?" Reynolds said.

Buchanan stepped forward. "I can, but it may not do any good. The proof I had was on that tape. I was planning on making copies, but I didn't have the chance to before I left Washington."

Reynolds looked down at Connie. "You obviously know what's going on. If you cooperate, it'll help your sentencing."

"I might as well strap myself in the chair," Connie said.

"Who? Dammit, who is behind this that everybody's so scared to death of?"

"Agent Reynolds," Buchanan said, "I'm sure that particular gentleman is waiting to hear the outcome of all this. If he doesn't get it soon, he'll send out more men. I suggest we stop that from happening."

Reynolds looked at him. "Why should I trust you? What I should do is call the cops."

Faith said, "The night Agent Newman was killed,

I told him I wanted Danny to come in and testify with me. Newman told me that would never happen."

"Well, he told you right."

"But I think if you know all the facts, you won't think that way. What we did was wrong, but there was *no other way. . . .*"

"Well, that makes it all perfectly clear," Reynolds replied.

"That can wait," Buchanan said with urgency. "Right now we have to take care of the man behind these people." He looked down at the dead men.

"You can add one more to that count," Lee said. "He's outside taking a dip in the ocean."

Reynolds looked exasperated. "Everybody except for me seems to know everything." She turned to Buchanan with a scowl. "Okay, I'm listening. What's your suggestion?"

Buchanan started to answer when they all heard the sound of a plane coming in. Their eyes went to the window, where the dawn had broken.

"It's just the commuter service. It's daylight. First flight in. The runway's across the street," Faith explained.

"That I *do* know," Reynolds said.

"I suggest we use your friend there," Buchanan said, nodding at Connie, "to communicate with this person."

"And tell him what?"

"That his operation was a total success, except that his men were killed in the ensuing battle. He'll understand that, of course. Losses happen. But that Faith and I were killed and the tape was destroyed. That way he'll feel safe."

"And me?" Lee said.

Buchanan glanced at him. "We'll let you be our wild card."

"And why exactly should I do that?" Reynolds wanted to know. "When I could take you and Faith, and him" – she flicked her pistol at Connie – "to the WFO, get my job back and walk away a hero."

"Because if you do that, the man who has caused all of this will go free. Free to do something like this again."

Reynolds looked confused and troubled.

Buchanan watched her closely. "It's up to you."

Reynolds looked at each of them and then her gaze came to rest on Lee. She noted the blood on his sleeve, the cuts and bruises on his face.

"You saved all of our lives. You're probably the most innocent person in this room. What do you think?"

Lee looked at Faith and then at Buchanan before coming back to Reynolds. "I don't think I can give you a great reason to do it, but if you want my gut, I'd say to go along with them."

Reynolds sighed and looked over at Connie. "You have a way of contacting this monster?" Connie said nothing. "Connie, you work with us on this, it'll help you. I know you were just prepared to kill all of us, and I shouldn't give a damn about what happens to you." She paused and looked down for a moment. "But I do. Last chance, Connie, what do you say?"

Connie's big hands clenched and unclenched nervously. He looked at Buchanan. "What exactly do you want me to say?"

Buchanan told him precisely, and Connie sat down on the couch, picked up the phone and dialed. When the line was answered, he said, "This is . . ." – Connie looked embarrassed for a moment – "this is Ace-in-the-Hole." Ten minutes later Connie put down the phone and looked at each of them. "Okay, it's done."

"Did he seem to buy it?" Lee asked.

"Yes, but you can never be sure with these guys."

"Good, enough; that gives us some time," Buchanan said.

"Well, right now we have some things to tend to," Reynolds said. "Like a number of dead bodies. And I've got to report in. And get you" – she looked at Connie – "into a cell."

Connie glared at her. "So much for loyalty," he said.

She glared back. "You made your choices. What you did for us *will* help you. But you're going to be in prison a long time, Connie. At least you get to live. That's more of a choice than Ken had."

She looked at Buchanan. "Now what?"

"I suggest we leave here immediately. Once we're out of the area, you can call the police. When we get back to Washington, Faith and I will meet with the FBI, tell them what we know. We must keep everything completely secret. If he knows we're working with the FBI, we'll never get the proof we need."

"This guy had Ken killed?"

"Yes."

"Is he with a foreign interest?"

"Actually, you both have the same employer."

Reynolds looked at him, stunned. "Uncle Sam?" she said slowly.

Buchanan nodded. "If you trust me, I will do my best to bring him to you. I have my own personal score to settle with him."

"And what exactly do you expect in return?"

"For me? Nothing. If I go to prison, I go to prison. But Faith goes free. Unless you can guarantee me that, you can just call the police right now."

Faith grabbed his arm. "Danny, you're not taking the fall for this."

"Why not? It was my doing."

"But your reasons—"

"Reasons are no defense. I knew I was taking a chance when I broke the law."

"Well, so did I, dammit!"

Buchanan turned back to Reynolds. "Do we have a deal? Faith does not go to prison."

"I'm really not in a position to offer you anything." She pondered the issue for a moment. "But I can promise you this: If you are shooting straight with me, I'll do everything in my power to see that Faith goes free."

Connie stood up, suddenly looking pale. "Brooke, I need to hit the john, like quick." He was wobbly on his feet; one hand slid to his chest.

She glanced at him suspiciously. "What's the matter?" She scrutinized his pallid features. "Are you all right?"

"To tell the truth, I've been better," he mumbled, his head rolling to one side, his left side drooping.

"I'll go with him," Lee said.

As the pair started to the stairs, Connie seemed to lose his balance and he pressed his hand hard against the center of his chest, his face contorted in pain. "Shit. Oh, God!" He dropped to one knee, moaning, saliva dripping out of his mouth; he started gurgling.

"Connie!" Reynolds started toward him.

"He's having a heart attack," Faith cried out.

"Connie!" Reynolds said again as she stared at her stricken partner, who was fast sinking to the floor, his body twitching uncontrollably.

The movement was fast. It seemed too fast for a man in his fifties, but then again, desperation could mix with adrenaline in a flash.

Connie's hand dipped to his ankle. A compact pistol was in a holster there. The gun was out and aimed before anyone could react. Connie had multiple targets, but he chose Danny Buchanan and fired.

The only one who reacted as fast as Connie did was Faith Lockhart.

From where she was standing next to Buchanan, she saw the pistol come out before anyone else. She saw the barrel pointed at her friend. In her mind she could hear the explosion that would launch the bullet that would kill Buchanan. How she moved that fast was inexplicable.

The bullet hit Faith in the chest; she gasped once and then dropped at Buchanan's feet.

"Faith!" Lee screamed. Instead of tackling Connie, he lunged for her.

Reynolds's gun was trained on Connie. As he swung the pistol around in her direction, the image of the palm reader flashed through her mind. That all-too-short life line. MOTHER OF TWO, FEDERAL AGENT DEAD. She saw the headline fully and boldly in her mind. The whole thing was almost paralyzing. Almost.

She and Connie locked gazes. He was bringing up his pistol, lining it up with her. He would pull the trigger, she had no doubt. He clearly had the nerve, the balls to kill. Did she? Her finger tightened on her own trigger as the entire world seemed to slow to the pace of an underwater world, where gravity was either suspended or magnified. Her partner. An FBI agent. A traitor. Her children. Her own life. Now or never.

Reynolds pulled the trigger once and then a second time. The recoil was short, her aim perfect. As the bullets entered Connie's body, his bulk quivered, his mind perhaps still sending messages, not yet realizing that it was dead.

Reynolds thought she saw Connie stare searchingly at her as he started to go down, the gun falling from his hand. That image would haunt her forever. Only when Agent Howard Constantinople hit the floor and didn't move again did Brooke Reynolds take a breath.

"Faith, Faith!" Lee was tearing at her shirt, exposing the horribly bloody wound in her chest. "Omigod. Faith." She was unconscious, her breathing barely detectable.

Buchanan stared down in blank horror.

Reynolds knelt beside Lee. "How bad?"

Lee looked up in anguish. He couldn't speak.

Reynolds assessed the wound. "Bad," she said. "Slug's still in her. The hole's right near her heart."

Lee looked at Faith. Her skin was already beginning to pale. He could feel the warmth of life spilling out from her with each shallow breath she took. "Oh, God. No. Please!" he cried out.

"We've got to get her to a hospital. Fast," Reynolds said. She had no idea where the closest hospital was, let alone a trauma center, which was what Faith really needed. And searching the local area by car would be akin to signing the woman's death warrant. She could call the paramedics, but who knew how long it would take for them to get here? The roar of the plane engine outside made Reynolds glance at the window. The plan formed in her head within seconds. She raced back to Connie and lifted his FBI credentials from his body. For one brief moment she gazed at her former colleague. She shouldn't feel bad for what she had done. He had been well prepared to kill her. So why did she feel crushed by remorse? But Connie was dead. Faith Lockhart wasn't. At least not yet. Reynolds hustled back over to where Faith lay. "Lee, we're taking the plane. Hurry!"

The group raced outside, Reynolds in the lead. They could hear the plane's engines revving up as it prepared to take off. Reynolds sprinted ahead, tore her way through the hedge and found herself on the runway. She looked down at the opposite end. The plane was turning, getting ready to roar down the tarmac, lift into the air; their only hope would be gone in seconds. She ran down the asphalt, directly at the aircraft, waving the pistol, the badge, screaming, "FBI!" at the top of her lungs. The plane came racing at her, as Buchanan, holding clear an opening in the hedge, helped Lee carry Faith through. They burst on to the runway.

The pilot finally focused on the woman waving a pistol and coming at him. He pulled back on the throttle and the aircraft stopped its roll, the engines whined down.

Reynolds reached the plane, held up the badge and the pilot slid open his window.

"FBI," she said hoarsely. "I have a badly wounded person. I need your aircraft. You're going to fly us to the nearest hospital. Now."

The pilot looked at the badge, the gun and nodded dumbly. "Okay."

They all climbed on the plane, Lee cradling Faith against his chest. The pilot turned the aircraft around again, went back to the end of the runway and started his takeoff roll once more. A minute later the plane lifted into the air and rushed toward the embrace of the quickly lightening sky.

FIFTY-THREE

The pilot radioed ahead and a life-support ambulance was waiting on the tarmac at the airstrip in Manteo, which was thankfully only a few minutes of flight time away. Reynolds and Lee had used some bandages from the first-aid kit on the plane to try to stop the bleeding, and Lee had given Faith oxygen from the small canister on board, but none of it seemed to have any effect. She had not yet regained consciousness; they could barely get a pulse now. Her limbs were beginning to grow cold, even as Lee clung to her, tried to give her heat from his own body, as though that would do any good.

Lee rode in the ambulance with Faith over to Beach Medical Center, which had an emergency and trauma center. Reynolds and Buchanan were driven there in a car. On the way to the hospital, Reynolds called Fred Massey in Washington. She told him just enough that he was already running to catch a Bureau plane. Just him, Reynolds had insisted; no one else could come. Massey had accepted this condition without comment. Perhaps it had been the tone of her voice, or simply the stunning content of her very few words.

Faith was immediately taken to the emergency room, where doctors labored over her for almost two hours, trying to get her vitals up, her heart regulated, the internal bleeding stopped. None of it looked good. Once, the crash cart even had to be called.

Through the doors Lee had watched in the

numbest horror as Faith repeatedly jerked under the impact of the electrical current surging through the paddles. Only when he saw the heart monitor go from flat line to its regular peaks and valleys did he find he could even move.

Barely two hours later they had to cut her chest open, spread her ribs wide and massage her heart to get it going. Every hour seemed to bring a new crisis as she barely clung to life.

Lee paced the floor incessantly, hands shoved in his pockets, head down, talking to no one. He had said every prayer he could remember. He had made up some new ones. He was helpless to do anything for the woman, and that's what tore at him. How could he have let this happen? How could Connie, that old, bulky sonofabitch, have gotten that shot off? And him right beside the guy? And Faith, why had she taken the round? Why? Buchanan should be the guy lying on that gurney with people swarming over him, trying desperately to push life back into his wrecked body.

Lee slumped against the wall and slid down to the floor, covering his face with both hands as his big body shook.

In a private room, Reynolds waited with Buchanan, who had barely spoken a word since Faith had been shot. He just sat there and stared at the wall. To look at Buchanan, no one would have guessed that anger was building in him: the absolute hatred he was holding for Robert Thornhill, a man who had destroyed everything he had cared about.

About the time Fred Massey arrived, Faith was taken to the ICU. She was stabilized for the time being, the doctor told them. The bullet was one of those vicious dum-dums, he said. It had tumbled

403

through her body like a runaway bowling ball, doing considerable damage to organs, and the internal hemorrhaging had been severe. She was strong and for now she was alive. She had a chance, that was all, he cautioned. They would know more soon.

As the doctor walked away, Reynolds put a hand on Lee's shoulder and handed him a fresh cup of coffee.

"Lee, if she survived until now, I have to believe she's going to make it."

"No guarantees," he mumbled to himself, unable to look at the woman.

They went to the private room, where Reynolds introduced Buchanan and Lee to Fred Massey.

"I think Mr. Buchanan should start telling you his story," Reynolds said to Massey.

"And he's willing to do that?" Massey asked skeptically.

At this Buchanan perked up. "Something more than willing. But before I do, tell me one thing. What's more important to you? What I did, or arresting the person who killed your agent?"

Massey leaned forward. "I'm not sure I'm prepared to discuss any sort of deal with you."

Buchanan put his elbows on the table. "When I tell you my story, you will be. But I'll do so on only one condition. You let me deal with this man. In my own way."

"Agent Reynolds informed me this person works for the federal government."

"That's right."

"Well, that's pretty damn unbelievable. Do you have proof?"

"You let me do this my way, and you'll have your proof."

Massey looked over at Reynolds. "The bodies at

the house. Do we know who they are yet?"

She shook her head. "I just checked in. The police and agents from D.C., Raleigh and Norfolk are on the scene. But it's too early yet to have that info. But everything's on the QT. The locals have been told nothing. We're controlling all flows of information. You won't see anything on the news about the bodies or about Faith being alive and in this hospital."

Massey nodded. "Good work." As though suddenly remembering something, he opened his briefcase, pulled out two objects and handed them to her.

Reynolds looked down at her pistol and creds.

"I'm sorry any of this happened, Brooke," Massey said. "I should have trusted you and I didn't. Maybe I've been out of the field too damn long. Pushing too many papers and not listening to my instincts anymore."

Reynolds holstered her gun and put the creds in her purse. She once more felt complete. "Maybe I wouldn't have either, in your position. But it's in the past, Fred, let's move on. We don't have much time."

"Rest assured, Mr. Massey," Buchanan said, "you'll never identify those men. Or if you do, they'll have no ties to the person I'm talking about."

"How can you be so sure of that?" Massey demanded.

"Trust me, I know how this man operates."

"Look, why don't you just tell me who it is and I'll handle it from there?"

"No," Buchanan said firmly.

"What do you mean no? We're the FBI, mister, we do this for a living. If you want any sort of deal—"

"You will listen to me." Buchanan hardly raised his voice, but his eyes bored into Massey with such overwhelming force that the ADIC lost his train of thought and fell silent. "We have one chance to bring him in. One! He's already infiltrated the FBI. Constantinople may not be the only mole. There may be others."

"I highly doubt that—" Massey began.

Now Buchanan raised his voice. "Can you guarantee me that there aren't? Can you?"

Massey sat back, looking uncomfortable. He glanced at Reynolds, who shrugged.

"If they could turn Connie, they could turn anybody," she said.

Massey looked miserable, shaking his head slowly. "Connie . . . I still can't believe it."

Buchanan tapped the tabletop. "And if there is another spy in your ranks and you try to trap this man on your own, you will absolutely fail. And your chance will be gone. Forever. Do you really want to risk that?"

Massey rubbed his smooth chin, thinking it over. When he looked up at Buchanan, his expression was wary but interested.

"Do you really think you can nail this guy?"

"I'm prepared to die trying. And I need to work the phones. Call in some very special help." Buchanan smiled to himself. A lobbyist to the very end. He turned to Lee. "And I need your help, Lee. If you're willing."

Lee looked surprised. "Me? What can I do to help anybody?"

"I spoke with Faith about you last night. She told me about your 'special' abilities. She said you were a good man to have in a bad situation."

"I guess she was wrong about that. Otherwise she wouldn't be lying up there with a hole in her chest."

Buchanan put a hand on Lee's arm. "I can barely function with the guilt I have, for her having stepped in front of that bullet. But I can't change that now.

406

What I can do is try to make sure she didn't risk her life for nothing. There's great danger for you. Even if we get this man, he has many at his back. There'll always be some out there."

Buchanan settled back in his chair and watched Lee closely. Massey and Reynolds stared at the PI too. Lee's muscular arms and broad shoulders were in stark contrast to the fragility of the look deep within his eyes.

Lee Adams took a deep breath. What he really wanted to do was stand next to Faith's bed and never leave until she woke up, saw him, smiled, said she'd be okay. And then, so would he. But, Lee knew, one rarely got what one wished for in this life. So instead, he looked at Buchanan and said, "I guess I'm your man."

FIFTY-FOUR

The black sedan pulled up to the front of the house. Robert Thornhill and his wife, dressed in formal evening clothes, came out the front door. Thornhill locked the house, then the two got in the car and were driven away. The Thornhills were attending an official dinner at the White House.

The sedan passed the phone-line control pedestal belonging to the community where the Thornhills lived. The metal box was large, bulky and painted light green. It had been placed there about two years ago when the phone company had upgraded the communications lines for this old neighborhood. The metal box had been a sudden eyesore in an area that prided itself on splendid homes and high-dollar landscaping. Thus, the residents had paid for a number of large bushes to be planted around the aboveground pedestal. These bushes now hid the box completely from the road, which meant that the telephone servicemen had to approach it from the rear side, which faced the woods. Aesthetically pleasing, the bushes were also very welcome to the man who had watched the sedan pass by and then had opened the box and begun delicately picking his way through its electronic guts.

Lee Adams identified the line going to the Thornhills' residence with a special piece of his own customized equipment. His background in communications hardware was serving him well. The Thornhills' home had a good security system.

However, every security system had an Achilles' heel: the phone line. Always the phone line. Thank you, Mr Bell.

Lee went through the steps in his head. When an intruder broke into someone's home, the alarm went off and the computer dialed the central monitoring station to inform them of the break-in. Then the security person at the monitoring station called the home to see if everything was okay. If the owner answered, he had to give his special code or else the police would be sent. If no one answered the phone, the police would be sent automatically.

Simply put, Lee was making sure that the home's computer would never reach the monitoring station, yet would let it think that it had. He was accomplishing this by building an in-line component or phone simulator. He had dropped the Thornhill home from the landline feed, effectively severing outside phone communication. Now he had to trick the alarm computer into thinking it had phone service. To do this, he installed the in-line component and threw the switch, effectively giving the Thornhills' home a dial tone and phone line that went absolutely nowhere.

He had also found out that the Thornhills' alarm system had no cellular backup, just the regular landline. That was a big hole. A cellular backup was incapable of being fooled, since it was a wireless system with no way for Lee to access its feed line. Virtually all alarm systems in the country had the very same backbone land- and data-lines. And, thus, they all had back doors in. Lee had just completed his.

He packed up his tools and made his way through the woods to the rear of the Thornhills' home. He located a window that was not visible from the street. He had a copy of the Thornhills' floor plan and alarm layout. It had been provided to him by Fred Massey. By accessing this window, he could reach the upstairs alarm panel without passing any motion detector points.

He pulled a stun gun from his backpack and held it flush against the window. The windows were all wired, even the second-floor ones, he knew. And both top and bottom window components had contacts. Most homes only had contacts at the bottom window casement; if that had been the case here, Lee would have simply picked the window lock and slid down the top window, without breaking any contacts.

He pulled the trigger on the stun gun and then moved it to another position on the window where he thought the contact elements were probably located. In all, he fired eight shots into the window frame from the stun gun. The electrical charge from the gun would melt the contacts, fusing them together and rendering them inoperable.

He picked the sash lock, held his breath and slid the window up. No alarm sounded. He quickly climbed through the window and closed it. Pulling a small flashlight from his pocket, he found the stairs and headed up. The Thornhills, he quickly observed, lived in extremely comfortable luxury. The furnishings were mostly antique; real oil paintings hung on the walls; and his feet melted into the thick and, he assumed, expensive carpet.

The alarm panel was where all such alarm panels were located; on the upper floor in the master bedroom. He unscrewed the plate and found the wire for the sound cannon. Two snips and the alarm system had suddenly developed laryngitis. Now he was free to roam. He went downstairs and passed in front of the motion detector, waving his arms in defiance, even giving it the finger, pretending it was

Thornhill there scowling at him, helpless to do anything about the intrusion. The red light came on and the alarm system was activated, although the system no longer could scream its warning. The computer would soon be dialing the central station, only its call would never get there. It would dial the number eight times, get no answer and then it would stop trying and go back to sleep. At the central station, everything would seem perfectly normal: a burglar's dream.

Lee watched as the red light on the motion detector disappeared. Each time he passed in front of it, though, it would go through the same routine, with the same result. Call eight times and then stop. Lee smiled. So far, so good. Before the Thornhills came home he would reattach the wires for the sound cannons: Thornhill would be suspicious if the normal beeping sound didn't occur when he opened the door. But for now, Lee had work to do.

FIFTY-FIVE

The White House dinner was very memorable for Mrs. Thornhill. Her husband, on the other hand, was working. He sat at the long table and made inconsequential conversation when called upon, but spent most of his time listening intently to the guests. There were a number of foreign visitors tonight, and Thornhill knew that good intelligence might come from unusual sources, even a White House dinner. Whether the foreign guests knew he was with the CIA, he wasn't sure. That was certainly not public knowledge. The guest list that would be printed in the *Washington Post* the next morning would identify them only as Mr. and Mrs. Robert Thornhill.

Ironically, the invitation to the dinner had not come because of Thornhill's position at the Agency. Who was invited to White House functions such as this, and why, were the greatest of mysteries in the capital city. However, the Thornhills' invitation had been extended because of his wife's well-known philanthropic work for the District of Columbia poor – a charitable endeavor in which the first lady herself was much involved as well. And Thornhill had to admit, his wife was dedicated to this cause. When she wasn't at the country club, of course.

The ride home was uneventful; the couple talked of mundane things while most of Thornhill's mind was focused on the phone call from Howard Constantinople. Losing his men had been a blow to

Thornhill, both personally and professionally. He had worked with them for years. How all three had been killed was beyond his comprehension. He had people down in North Carolina right now finding out as much as possible.

He had not heard anything further from Constantinople. Whether the man had run was unknown. But Faith and Buchanan were dead. And so was the other FBI agent, Reynolds. At least he was almost certain they were dead. The fact that no newspaper reports had come out regarding at least six dead bodies at a beach house in an affluent area in the Outer Banks was particularly troubling. It had been over a week, and nothing. It might be the Bureau's doing, covering up what was quickly building to a PR nightmare for them. Yes, he could see them doing that. Unfortunately, without Constantinople he had lost his eyes and ears at the Bureau. He would have to do something about that soon. It would take time to cultivate a new mole, yet nothing was impossible.

Well, the trail could never lead back to him. His three operatives had cover buried so deeply that the authorities would be incredibly fortunate if they managed to dig through even the surface layer. They would find nothing after that. Well, the three had died heroes. He and his colleagues had toasted their memory in the underground chamber upon learning of their deaths.

There was one more troubling loose end: Lee Adams. He had gone off on his motorcycle, presumably to Charlottesville to make sure his daughter was safe. He had never arrived in Charlottesville, that Thornhill knew for a fact. So where was he? Had he come back and managed to kill Thornhill's men? And yet one man taking out all three of them was incomprehensible. But

Constantinople had not mentioned Adams in the call.

As the car drove along, Thornhill felt much less confident than he had at the beginning of the evening. He would have to watch the situation very carefully. Perhaps there would be some message waiting for him at home.

As the car pulled into their driveway, Thornhill glanced at his watch. It was late, and he had an early morning. He had to testify tomorrow before Rusty Ward's committee. He had finally tracked down the answers the senator wanted, meaning he was prepared to throw out so much bullshit that the room would have to be fumigated after he had finished.

Thornhill disarmed the security system, kissed his wife good night and watched as she went up the stairs to her bedroom. She was still a very attractive woman, slender, fine-boned. Retirement would be coming soon. Perhaps it wouldn't be so bad. He'd had nightmares about it; his sitting in agony at interminable bridge games, country club dinners, fund-raisers; or hacking his way through infinite rounds of golf, his insufferably perky wife at his side for all of it.

However, as he watched the woman's nicely shaped backside gliding up the stairs, Thornhill suddenly saw more enticing possibilities for his golden years. They were relatively young, wealthy; they could travel the world. He even thought he might turn in early tonight, and take advantage of the physical urges he was suddenly feeling as he watched Mrs. Thornhill gracefully ascend the stairs to their bedroom. He liked the way she slid her high heels off, exposing black-hosed feet; moved a hand along her curvy hip; let her hair down her back, her shoulder muscles tensing with each movement.

Those hours at the country club certainly hadn't all been wasted. He would just pop in his study to check his messages and then head upstairs.

He clicked on the light in his study and went over to his desk. He was about to check for any messages on his secure phone when he heard a noise. He turned to the French doors that opened out on to the garden. The doors were opening and a man was stepping through.

Lee put a finger to his lips and smiled, his gun pointed directly at Thornhill. The CIA man stiffened, his eyes darting left and right, looking for escape, but there was none to be had. If he ran or screamed, he would be dead; he could see that in the man's eyes. Lee crossed the room and closed, then locked the door to the study. Thornhill watched him silently.

Thornhill received a second shock when another man stepped through the French doors, closing and locking them too.

Danny Buchanan looked so calm as to be almost asleep, yet a high level of energy danced behind his eyes.

"Who are you? What are you doing in my house?" Thornhill demanded.

"I expected something a little more original, Bob," said Buchanan. "How often is it that you see a ghost from the very recent past?"

"Sit," Lee ordered Thornhill.

Thornhill eyed the gun one more time, then went over and sat on the leather couch facing the two men. He undid his bow tie and dropped it on the couch, trying, with some difficulty, to assess the situation and decide on a course of action.

"I thought we had a deal, Bob," Buchanan said. "Why did you send your team of killers down? A lot of people lost their lives unnecessarily. Why?"

Thornhill looked at him suspiciously and then at Lee.

"I don't know what you're talking about. I don't even know who the hell you are."

It was clear what Thornhill was thinking: Lee and Buchanan were wired. Perhaps they were working with the FBI. And they were in his house. His wife was upstairs undressing, and these two men were in his house asking him these sorts of questions. Well, they would get nothing for their troubles.

"I" – Buchanan stopped and glanced at Lee – "we came here, as the sole survivors, to see what sort of arrangement we can work out. I don't want to keep looking over my shoulder for the rest of my life."

"Arrangement? How about I yell up to my wife to call the police? You like that arrangement?" Thornhill eyed Buchanan closely and then pretended recognition. "I know I've seen you somewhere before. In the newspapers?"

Buchanan smiled. "That certain tape Agent Constantinople told you was destroyed?" He slid his hand in his coat pocket and pulled out a cassette. "Well, he didn't get it exactly right."

Thornhill stared at the cassette as if it were plutonium about to be shoved down his throat. He reached into his own jacket.

Lee raised the pistol.

Thornhill gave him a disappointed look and slowly edged out his pipe and lighter, taking a moment to light it. Several soothing puffs later, he eyed Buchanan.

"Since I don't even know what you're talking about, why don't you play the tape? I'd be interested to know what's on it. It might explain why two complete strangers have broken into my house." *And if that tape had me talking about killing an FBI agent, neither of you would be here, and I'd already be under*

416

arrest. Bluff, bluff, bluff, Danny.

Buchanan slowly tapped the cassette against his palm, while Lee looked nervous.

"Come now, don't tease me with something and then pull it away," said Thornhill.

Buchanan dropped the cassette on the desk. "Maybe later. Right now I want to know what you're going to do for us. Something that will make us not go to the FBI and tell them what we know."

"And what might that be? You talked about people getting killed. Are you insinuating that I might have killed somebody? I'm assuming that you know I'm employed by the CIA. Are you foreign agents attempting some sort of bizarre blackmail scheme? The problem with that is, you need to have something to blackmail me with."

Lee said, "We know enough to bury you."

"Well, then I suggest you go get your shovel and start digging, Mr. . . . ?"

"Adams, Lee Adams," Lee said with a fierce scowl.

"Faith is dead, you know, Bob," Buchanan said. As he said this, Lee looked down. "She almost made it. Constantinople killed her. He also killed two of your men. Payback for your killing the FBI agent."

Thornhill looked suitably bewildered. "Faith? Constantinople? What the hell are you talking about?"

Lee came and stood directly in front of Thornhill. "You bastard! You kill people like stepping on ants. A game. That's all it is to you."

"Please put the gun away and leave my house. Now!"

"Damn you!" Lee aimed his pistol directly at Thornhill's head.

Buchanan was next to him in an instant. "Lee, please don't. That won't do any good."

417

"I would listen to your friend if I were you," Thornhill said as calmly as he could. He had had a gun pulled on him once before, when his cover had been blown in Istanbul many years ago. He had been lucky to get out alive. He wondered if his luck would hold tonight.

"Why should I listen to anybody?" Lee growled.

"Lee, please," Buchanan said.

Lee's finger hovered on the trigger for an instant, his gaze locked with Thornhill's. Finally, he lowered the gun, slowly.

"Well, I guess we'll have to go to the Feds with what we have," Lee said.

"I just want you out of my house."

"And all I want," Buchanan said, "is your personal assurances that no one else will be killed. You've got what you want. You don't have to harm anyone else."

"Right. Right, whatever you say. I won't kill anybody else," Thornhill said sarcastically. "Now if you'll please leave my house. I don't want to upset my wife. She has no idea she's married to a mass murderer."

"This is no joke," Buchanan said angrily.

"No, it really isn't, and I hope you get the help you so obviously need," said Thornhill. "And please take care that your gun-toting friend doesn't hurt anyone." *That should sound very nice on the tape. I am actually caring about others.*

Buchanan picked up the cassette.

"Not leaving the evidence of my crimes?"

Buchanan swiveled around and eyed him severely. "Under the circumstances, I don't think it will be necessary."

He looks like he wants to kill me, Thornhill thought. *Good, very good.*

Thornhill watched as the two men hurried down

418

his driveway and disappeared on to the darkened street. A minute later he heard a car start up. He raced to the phone and then stopped. Was it tapped? Was this whole thing a charade to trick him into a mistake? He stared at the window. Yes, they could be out there right now. He hit a button under his desk. All the drapes in the room descended and then a small whooshing sound commenced at each of the windows: white noise. He slid open his drawer and pulled out his secure phone. It had so many security and scrambling features that not even the NSA jocks could lift it from the air. Like the technology used on military aircraft, the phone threw out electronic chaff that jammed attempts to intercept its signal. *So much for electronic eavesdropping, you amateurs.*

"Buchanan and Lee Adams were in my study," he said into the phone. "Yes. In my home, dammit! They just left. I want all the men we can spare. We're only minutes from Langley. You should be able to find them." He paused to relight his pipe. "They sang some bullshit song about the cassette tape where I admitted to having the FBI agent killed. But Buchanan was just bluffing. The tape is gone. I figured they were wired, and I played dumb with everything. It almost cost me my life. That idiot Adams was two seconds away from blowing my head off. Buchanan said Lockhart was dead, which is good for us, if it's true. But I don't know if they're somehow working with the FBI. But without that tape they've got no evidence of what we've done. What? No, Buchanan was begging for us to leave him alone. We could go ahead with the blackmail plan, just let him live. It was pitiful, actually. When I first saw them, I thought they had come to kill me. That Adams is dangerous. And they told me Constantinople killed two of our men. Constantinople must be dead, so we need to get another

419

spy at the FBI. But whatever you do, you find them. And this time no mistakes. They are dead. And after that, it's time to execute the plan. I can't wait to see those pitiful faces on Capitol Hill when I hit them with this."

Thornhill clicked off and sat at his desk. It was funny, their coming here that way. A desperate act. From desperate men. Did they really think they could bluff a man such as himself? It was rather insulting. But he had won in the end. The reality was that tomorrow or soon thereafter they would be dead and he wouldn't be.

He rose from behind the desk. Having survived that little scare had actually made him feel quite invigorated. He had been brave, cool under pressure. It was rather intoxicating, primal. He bounded up the stairs. To see Mrs. Thornhill. To demonstrate for her quite clearly who the man of the house was.

FIFTY-SIX

The Dirksen Senate Office Building was bustling as usual on this crisp morning. Robert Thornhill walked with special purpose down the long hallway, swinging his briefcase cavalierly at his side. Last night had been quite something, a success in many ways. The only downside was that they had failed to find Buchanan and Adams.

The rest of the night had been simply marvelous. Mrs. Thornhill had been impressed with his animalistic zeal. The woman had even gotten up early and made him breakfast, dressed in a sheer, clingy black outfit. That hadn't happened in years: making his breakfast or the clingy number.

The hearing room was at the far end of the hallway. Rusty Ward's little fiefdom, Thornhill thought with a snort. He ruled with a Southern fist, meaning velvet-gloved, yet with granite knuckles underneath. Ward would lull you to sleep with his ridiculously syrupy drawl and when you least expected it, he would pounce and shred you, his intense gaze and oh-so-precise words melting the unsuspecting foe right in his uncomfortable, government-issue hot seat.

Everything about Rusty Ward painfully assaulted Thornhill's old-school, Ivy-League sensibilities. But this morning he was ready. He would talk death squads and redactions until the cows came home, to borrow one of Ward's favorite lines; and the senator would be left with no more information at the end of the day than when he had started.

Before entering the hearing room, Thornhill took one energizing deep breath. He envisioned the setting that he was about to confront: Ward and company behind their little bench, the chairman pulling at his suspenders, his fat face looking here and there as he rustled through his briefing papers, missing nothing in the confines of his pathetic kingdom. When Thornhill entered, Ward would look at him, smile, nod, give him some little innocent greeting intended to disarm Thornhill's defenses, as if that were even a possibility. *But I guess he has to go through the motions. Teaching an old dog new tricks indeed.* That was another of Ward's stupid little sayings. How dreary.

Thornhill pulled open the door and strode confidently down the aisle of the hearing room. About halfway down, he realized that the room held many more people than usual. The small space was literally bursting with bodies. And as he looked around, he noted numerous faces he did not recognize. As he approached the witness table, he received another shock. There were already people sitting there, their backs to him.

He looked up at the committee. Ward stared back at him. There was no smile, no inane greeting from the portly chairman.

"Mr. Thornhill, take a seat in the front row, will you? We have one person testifying before you."

Thornhill looked dazed. "Excuse me?"

"Just sit down, Mr. Thornhill," Ward said again.

Thornhill looked at his watch. "I'm afraid I have limited time today, Mr. Chairman. And I wasn't told about anyone else testifying." Thornhill glanced at the witness table. He didn't recognize the men sitting there. "Perhaps we should just reschedule."

Ward looked past Thornhill. The latter turned and followed his gaze. The uniformed Capitol Hill police officer ceremoniously closed the door to the hearing room and then stood with his broad back against it, as though daring anyone to try to get past him.

Thornhill looked back around at Ward. "Am I missing something here?"

"If you are, it will be made crystal clear in a minute," Ward replied ominously. Then he looked over at one of his aides and nodded.

The aide disappeared through a small doorway behind the committee. He was back in a few seconds. And then Thornhill received what amounted to the greatest shock of his life, as Danny Buchanan walked through the doorway and made his way to the witness table. He never even looked at Thornhill, who just stood there in the middle of the aisle, his briefcase now resting motionless against his leg. The men rose from the witness table and took seats in the audience.

Buchanan stood in front of the witness table, raised his right hand, was sworn in and then sat down.

Ward glanced over at Thornhill, who still hadn't moved.

"Mr. Thornhill, will you please sit down so we can get started here?"

Thornhill couldn't take his eyes off Buchanan. He shuffled sideways toward the one remaining empty seat in the front row. The large man sitting at the end of the row moved aside so Thornhill could pass by. As Thornhill sat, he glanced over at the man and found himself staring at Lee Adams.

"Good to see you again," Lee said with a smile before settling back in his chair and turning his attention toward the front of the room.

"Mr. Buchanan," Ward began. "Can you tell us why you're here today, sir?"

"To provide testimony regarding a shocking conspiracy at the Central Intelligence Agency," Buchanan replied in a calm, assured tone. Over the years he had testified before more committees than all the Watergate folk combined. He was on familiar ground, his best friend in the world doing the questioning. This was his time. Finally.

"Then I guess you should start at the beginning, sir."

Buchanan placed his hands neatly in front of him, leaned forward and spoke into the microphone.

"Approximately fifteen months ago I was approached by a high-level official at the CIA. The gentleman was quite familiar with my lobbying practice. He was aware that I knew many of the members on the Hill intimately. He wanted me to help him with a very special project."

"What sort of project?" Ward prompted.

"He wanted me to help him gather evidence against congressmen that could be used to blackmail them."

"Blackmail? How?"

"He knew of my efforts to lobby on behalf of impoverished countries and world humanitarian organizations."

"We all are aware of your efforts in that regard," Ward said magnanimously.

"As you can imagine, it's a tough sell up here. I've used most of my own money in that crusade. The man knew that too. He felt I was desperate. An easy mark, I believe is what he said."

"Precisely how would this blackmail scheme work?"

"I would approach certain congressmen and bureaucrats who could help influence foreign-aid

424

dollars and other overseas relief. I would only approach those who needed money. I would tell them that in return for their help, they would be compensated after they left office. They didn't know it, of course, but the CIA would finance these 'retirement' packages. If they agreed to help, then I would wear a wire provided by the CIA and record incriminating conversations with these men and women. They would also be placed under surveillance by the CIA. All this 'illegal' activity would be captured and subsequently used against them by the man at the CIA."

"How so?"

"Many of the people I was supposed to bribe for foreign aid also serve on committees overseeing the CIA. For example, two of the members of this very committee, Senators Johnson and McNamara, also sit on the appropriations committee for foreign operations. The gentleman from CIA gave me a list of names of all the people he wanted to target. Senators Johnson and McNamara were on that list. The plan was to blackmail them and others into using their committee positions to help the CIA. Increased budgets for the CIA, greater responsibilities, less congressional oversight. That sort of thing. In return, I would be paid a large sum of money."

Buchanan looked at Johnson and McNamara, men he had recruited so easily ten years ago. They stared back at him with exactly the proper look of shock and anger. Over the last week Buchanan had met with every single one of his bribees and had explained what was happening. If they wanted to survive, they would back up every word of the lie he was now telling. What choice did they have? They would also continue to support Buchanan's causes, and they wouldn't be getting a dime from him for doing so. Their efforts would really turn out to be "charitable." Praise God.

And he had confided in Ward as well. His friend had taken it better than Buchanan had thought possible. He had not condemned Buchanan's actions, but he had decided to stand by his old friend. There were greater crimes to punish.

"This is all the truth, Mr. Buchanan?"

"Yes sir," Buchanan said, with the look of a saint.

Thornhill sat impassively in his seat. The man's expression was akin to the condemned walking alone to the gas chamber – a mixture of bitterness, terror and disbelief. Buchanan had obviously cut a deal. The politicians were backing his story. He could see it in Johnson's and McNamara's faces. How could Thornhill attack their claims without revealing his own participation? He could hardly jump up and say, "That's not how it happened. Buchanan was already bribing them, I just caught him and used him for my own blackmail purposes." His Achilles' heel. It had never occurred to him. The frog and the scorpion, only the scorpion was going to survive.

"What did you do?" Ward asked Buchanan.

"I immediately went to the people on the list and told them what had happened, including Senators Johnson and McNamara. I'm sorry we were unable to bring you into the loop at the time, Mr. Chairman, but absolute confidentiality was the key. We collectively decided to set up a sting of sorts. I would pretend to go along with the CIA's plan, and the targets would pretend to be part of the plan. Then, while the CIA was gathering its blackmail material, I would secretly gather evidence against the CIA. When we felt the case was strong enough, we planned to go to the FBI with what we had."

Ward took off his glasses and dangled them in

front of his face. "Damn risky business, Mr. Buchanan. Was this blackmail operation officially sanctioned by the CIA, do you know?"

Buchanan shook his head. "It was clearly the work of one official there, and not the CIA."

"What happened then?"

"I gathered my evidence, but then my associate, Faith Lockhart, who was unaware of any of this, became suspicious of me. She thought, I suppose, that I was actually involved in a blackmail scheme. I, of course, couldn't confide in her. She went to the FBI with her story. They commenced an investigation. The man from the CIA found out about this development and arranged to have Ms. Lockhart killed. Thankfully, she escaped, but an FBI agent was killed."

The entire room began buzzing at this.

Ward looked pointedly at Buchanan. "Are you telling me that an official from the CIA was responsible for the murder of an FBI agent?"

Buchanan nodded. "Several other deaths have also occurred, including" – Buchanan looked down for a moment, his lips trembling – "Faith Lockhart. That is what has prompted my appearance here today. To stop the killing."

"Who is this man, Mr. Buchanan?" Ward said with as much indignity and curiosity as he could feign.

Buchanan turned and pointed directly at Robert Thornhill.

"Associate Deputy Director of Operations Robert Thornhill."

Thornhill erupted from his chair, waving an angry fist in the air, and roared, "This is a damnable lie! This entire event is a circus, an abomination the likes of which I have never witnessed in all my years in government. You bring me here under false pretenses and then subject me to the preposterous, outrageous accusations of this person. They – they were in my home last night. This Buchanan person, and this man!" Thornhill pointed an angry finger at Lee. "This man held a gun to my head. They threatened me with this same insane story. They claimed to have evidence of this nonsense, but when I called their bluff, they ran off. I demand that you place them under immediate arrest. I intend to press full charges. And now, if you'll excuse me, I have legitimate business elsewhere."

Thornhill tried to get past Lee, but the PI stood up and blocked his way.

Thornhill looked at Ward. "Unless you do something right this instant, Mr. Chairman, I will be forced to call the police on my portable phone. I doubt if it would look very good on the evening news."

"I have proof of all that I've said," Buchanan said.

"What," Thornhill cried out, "the silly tape you threatened me with last night? If you have it, produce it. But whatever's on it is obviously forged."

Buchanan opened a briefcase, which rested on the table in front of him. Instead of an audiocassette, he took out a videocassette and handed it to an aide of Ward's.

Everyone in the room watched as another aide wheeled a television, with a VCR attached, out into a corner of the room where everyone could see the screen. The aide took the tape and inserted it in the VCR, hit the remote, stepped back. Everyone in the room watched breathlessly as the screen came to life.

On the TV Lee and Buchanan were just leaving Thornhill's study. Then Thornhill was at his desk, picking up his phone. He spoke into it anxiously. His conversation of the night before was played out before the entire room. His blackmail scheme, the killing of the FBI agent, his ordering the murders of Buchanan and Lee Adams. The look of triumph on his face as he put down the phone was in monumental contrast to the look the man wore now.

As the screen went to black, Thornhill continued to stare at the TV, his mouth slightly open, his lips moving but no words coming out. His briefcase, with all its important papers, fell to the floor, forgotten.

Ward tapped his pen against the microphone, his eyes squarely on Thornhill. There was some satisfaction in the Senator's features, but it could not overcome the horror there as well. Ward was sickened by what he had just seen; he was ready to pitch his political career and go sit on his back porch and watch his grandchildren play games of complete innocence. He didn't want to do this anymore.

"I suppose that since you've admitted that these men were in your home last night, then you won't claim this piece of evidence is a forgery, Mr. Thornhill?" Ward said.

Danny Buchanan sat quietly at the table, his eyes downcast. On his features were relief, sadness, hope; and uneasiness for what lay ahead. He too had clearly had enough.

Lee watched Thornhill intently. The other task he had performed at the Thornhill residence last night had been a relatively simple one. The underlying technology was known as PLC, or power line carrier technology. It was a wireless system with a 2.4-gigahertz transmitter, covert camera and antenna installed in a device that looked just like the smoke alarm in Thornhill's study and actually performed the functions of a smoke detector while it simultaneously conducted surveillance. It was powered by the home's regular electrical current and produced clear, crisp video and audio of everything in its range. Thornhill had stopped his incriminating conversation from leaving his house, but it had never occurred to him that there was a miniature Trojan horse *inside* his house.

"I will be available to testify at the trial," said Danny Buchanan. He rose, turned and started to walk up the aisle.

Lee put a hand on Thornhill's shoulder. "Excuse me," he said politely. He made his way past the frozen Thornhill and joined Buchanan. The two men quietly walked out together.

FIFTY-SEVEN

One month to the day after Buchanan's testimony to Ward's committee, Robert Thornhill bounded down the steps of the federal courthouse in Washington, leaving his lawyers in his liberated, if anxious, wake. The car was waiting for him. He slid inside. He had been granted bail, after four weeks of sitting behind bars. Now it was time to get to work. Now it was damn well time for revenge.

"Have they all been contacted?" Thornhill asked the driver.

The man nodded. "They're already there. Waiting for you."

"Buchanan and Adams? Status?"

"Buchanan is in Witness Protection, but we have some leads. Adams is right out in the open. Available anytime to take out."

"Lockhart?"

"Dead."

"You're certain?"

"We haven't actually dug up her body, but everything else points to her having died from her wounds at the hospital in North Carolina."

Thornhill leaned back against his seat with a sigh. "Lucky her."

The car entered a public garage, where Thornhill left the vehicle. He stepped directly into a van waiting there for him, which then pulled out from the garage and headed in the opposite direction. So much for any tail the FBI had.

Within forty-five minutes he was at the small abandoned strip mall. He stepped into the elevator and was zipping several hundred feet down into the earth. The lower he was carried, the better Thornhill felt. This thought deeply amused him.

The doors parted and he literally burst out of the confines of the elevator. The men, his colleagues, were all there. His chair at the head of the table was empty. His trusty comrade Phil Winslow was in the seat to the immediate right. Thornhill allowed himself a grateful smile. Back in business, ready to go.

He sat down, looked around.

"Congratulations on getting bail, Bob," Winslow said.

"Four weeks later," Thornhill said bitterly. "I think the Agency needs to upgrade its legal counsel."

"Well, that video was very damaging," said Aaron Royce, the younger man who had butted heads with Thornhill at the previous meeting here. "I'm actually surprised you were able to get bail at all. And, quite frankly, I'm a little stunned that the Agency even saw fit to provide counsel."

"Of course it was damaging," Thornhill said scornfully. "And the Agency provided counsel because of loyalty. It doesn't forget its people. Unfortunately, however, it means I have to disappear. The lawyers think we have a shot at suppressing the video, but I think all would agree that, despite having technical legal deficiencies, the subject matter of the tape was a little too detailed to allow me to continue in my present capacity." Thornhill looked saddened for a moment. His career over, and not in the way he had planned. But then his features reassumed their usual steeliness; his resolve flooded back into him like an oil gusher. He looked around the room in triumph. "But I will lead the battle from a distance. And we will win the war. Now, I understand Buchanan went underground. But Adams didn't. We'll go the path of least resistance. Adams first. Then Buchanan. I want someone at the U.S. marshal's service. We have people there. We locate good old Danny and make his life disappear. Next, I want to make damn *sure* Faith Lockhart is no more." He looked at Winslow. "Are my travel documents ready, Phil?"

"Actually, no, Bob," Winslow said slowly.

Royce stared at Thornhill. "This operation has cost us too much," he said. "Three operatives dead. You indicted. The Agency's turned upside down. The FBI is all over us. It's a total and complete disaster. This makes Aldrich Ames seem like a bounced check."

Thornhill noticed that every man in the room, Winslow included, was looking at him with a very unfriendly face. "We will survive this, make no mistake about that," Thornhill said in an encouraging tone.

"I'm quite sure *we* will survive it," Royce said forcefully.

Royce was definitely beginning to bother Thornhill. He was showing backbone in a way that had to be quickly quashed. But for now Thornhill decided to ignore him. "The damn FBI," complained Thornhill. "Bugging my house. Is the Constitution not applicable to them?"

"Thank God you didn't mention my name during the phone call that night," Winslow said.

Thornhill looked at him again, struck by the curious tone in his friend's voice. "About my documents . . . I should prepare to leave the country as soon as possible."

"That won't be necessary, Bob," Royce said. "And

frankly, despite your constant outbursts to the contrary, until you screwed everything up, we had quite a good working relationship with the FBI. Cooperation is the key these days. Turf battles make losers of everyone. You made us into dinosaurs and you're dragging us down into the mud with you."

Thornhill gave him an exasperated look and then glanced at Winslow. "Phil, I don't have time for this. You deal with him."

Winslow coughed nervously. "I'm afraid he's right, Bob."

Thornhill froze for a moment and then looked around the table before settling back on Winslow. "Phil, I want my documents and my cover, and I want them right now."

Winslow looked at Royce and gave a slight nod of the head.

Aaron Royce rose from his chair. He didn't smile; he showed no signs of triumph. Just as he had been trained.

"Bob," he said, "there's been a change in plan. We won't be needing your assistance in this matter any further."

Thornhill's face flushed with anger. "What the hell are you talking about? I'm running this operation. And I want Buchanan and Adams dead. Now!"

"There will be no more killing," Winslow said fiercely. "No more killing of innocent people," he added quietly.

He stood. "I'm sorry, Bob. I truly am."

Thornhill stared at him, the first tremors of the truth hitting him. Phil Winslow had been his classmate at Yale, his fraternity brother. The two men were members of Skull & Bones. Winslow had been his best man. They'd been lifelong friends. Lifelong.

"Phil?" Thornhill said cautiously.

Winslow motioned to the other men, who rose too. They all headed for the elevator.

"Phil?" Thornhill said again, his mouth going dry.

When the group reached the elevator, Winslow looked back. "We can't let this matter go any further. We can't let it go to trial. And we can't let you steal away. They'll never stop looking for you. We need closure, Bob."

Thornhill half rose from his chair. "Then we can fake my death. My suicide."

"I'm sorry, Bob. We need complete and *honest* closure."

"Phil!" Thornhill screamed out. "Please!"

When all the men were inside the elevator, Winslow looked at his friend one last time. "Sacrifices are sometimes necessary, Bob. You know that better than anyone. For the good of the country."

The elevator doors closed.

FIFTY-EIGHT

Lee carefully held the basket of flowers in both hands as he walked down the hospital corridor. Once she'd regained enough strength, Faith had been transferred to a hospital outside of Richmond, Virginia. There she was listed under an alias, though, and an armed guard was stationed outside her room at all times. The hospital was considered far enough away from Washington to maintain absolute secrecy on her whereabouts, yet close enough for Brooke Reynolds to keep a close watch on her.

This was the first time Lee had been allowed in to see her, despite his frantic pleas to Reynolds. At least she was alive. And getting better every day, he had been told.

Thus he was very surprised when he approached her room and there was no guard outside. He knocked on the door, waited, then pushed it open. The room was empty, the bed stripped. He walked around the room in a daze for a few seconds and then ran back out into the hallway where he nearly collided with a nurse. He grabbed the woman's arm.

"The patient in 212? Where is she?" he asked.

The nurse glanced at the empty room and then back at him, her expression a sad one. "Are you family?"

"Yes," he lied.

She looked at the flowers and her expression grew even more distressed. "Didn't anyone call you?"

"Call me? About what?"

"She passed away last night."

Lee's face paled. "Passed away," he said numbly. "But she was out of danger. She was going to make it. What the hell are you talking about – passing away?"

"Please, sir, there are other patients here." She took his arm and steered him away from the room. "I don't know the exact details. I wasn't on duty. I can refer you to someone here who can answer your questions."

Lee pulled his arm free. "Look, she can't be dead, okay? That was just a story. To keep her safe."

"What?" The woman looked puzzled.

"I'll take it from here," a voice said.

They both turned and looked at Brooke Reynolds standing there. She held out her badge for the nurse to see. "I'll take it from here," she said again. The nurse nodded and walked quickly away.

"What the hell is going on?" Lee demanded.

"Let's go to a quiet place and talk this over."

"Where is Faith?"

"Lee, not here! Dammit, do you want to ruin everything?" She pulled on his arm, but he wasn't budging, and she knew she couldn't physically make him.

"Why should I go with you?"

"Because I'm going to tell you the truth."

They got in Reynolds's car and she pulled out of the parking lot.

"I knew you were coming today, and I was planning on being at the hospital ahead of you, waiting. I didn't quite make it. I'm sorry you had to hear about it from a nurse: that's not what I intended." Reynolds looked down at the flowers he still held tightly, and her heart went out to him. She wasn't an FBI agent for this moment – she was simply a fellow human being sitting next to someone whose heart, she knew, was being torn apart. And what she had to tell him would only make it worse.

"Faith has been placed in Witness Protection. Buchanan too."

"What? Buchanan I can understand! But Faith isn't a witness to anything!" Lee's relief was matched only by his outrage. This was all wrong.

"But she is in need of protection. If certain people knew she was still alive – well, you know what could happen."

"When's the damn trial?"

"Actually, there isn't going to be a trial."

He stared over at her. "Don't tell me that sonofabitch Thornhill copped some sort of sweetheart deal. Don't tell me that."

"He didn't."

"So why no trial?"

"A trial needs a defendant." Reynolds tapped her fingers against the steering wheel and then slid on a pair of sunglasses. She proceeded to fiddle with the heating control.

"I'm waiting," Lee said. "Or don't I qualify for an explanation?"

Reynolds sighed and straightened up. "Thornhill is dead. He was found in his car on a back-country road with a single gunshot wound to the head. Suicide."

Lee was stunned into silence. After a minute he was able to mutter, "The coward's way out."

"I think everyone's relieved, actually. I know the people at CIA are. To say this whole thing rocked them to their super-secretive bones is an understatement. I guess for the good of the country, it's better to be spared a lengthy, embarrassing trial."

"Right, dirty laundry and all," Lee said acidly.

"Hooray for the country." Lee gave a mock salute to a flag flying in front of a post office they passed. "So if Thornhill's out of the way, why does Faith need Witness Protection?"

"You know the answer to that. When Thornhill died, he took the identity of everyone else involved in this with him to the grave. But they're out there, we know they are. Remember the videotape you orchestrated? Thornhill was talking to somebody on that phone, and that somebody is still out there. The CIA is doing an internal investigation to try to ferret them out, but I'm not holding my breath. And you know these people will do their best to get to Faith and Buchanan. For pure revenge, if nothing else." She touched his arm. "And you too, Lee."

He glanced over at her, read her mind. "No. There is no way I'm going into Witness Protection. I can't deal with a new name. I have a hard enough time remembering my real one. Might as well wait for Thornhill's sidekicks. Least I'll have some fun before I die."

"Lee, this is no joke. If you don't go underground, you'll be in great danger. And we can't follow you around twenty-four hours a day."

"No? After all I did for the Bureau? Does this also mean I don't get the FBI decoder ring and free T-shirt?"

"Why are you being such a smartass about this?"

"Maybe I don't give a shit anymore, Brooke. You're a smart lady, didn't that one ever occur to you?"

Neither said a word for the next couple of miles.

"If it were up to me, you'd get anything you wanted, including your own island somewhere with servants, but it's not up to me," Reynolds finally said.

He shrugged. "I'll take my chances. If they want to

come after me, so be it. They'll find me a little tougher bite than they think."

"Isn't there anything I can say to change your mind?"

He held up the flowers. "You can tell me where Faith is."

"I can't do that. You know I can't do that."

"Oh, come on, sure you can. You just have to *say* it."

"Lee, please—"

He smashed his big fist against the dashboard, cracking it. "Dammit, Brooke, you don't understand. I have to see Faith. I have to!"

"You're wrong, Lee, I do understand. And that's why this is so hard for me. But if I tell you and you go to her, that puts her in danger. And you too. You know that. That breaks all the rules. And I'm not going to do that. I'm sorry. You don't know how terrible I feel about all this."

Lee laid his head against the back of the seat and the two remained silent for another several minutes as Reynolds drove aimlessly.

"How is she?" he finally asked quietly.

"I won't lie to you. That bullet did a lot of damage. She's recovering, but slowly. They almost lost her a couple more times along the way."

Lee put his hand over his face, slowly shook his head.

"If it's any consolation, she was as upset as you are about this arrangement."

"Boy," Lee said, "that just makes everything wonderful. I'm the friggin' king of the world."

"That's not how I meant it."

"You're really not going to let me see her, are you?"

"No, I'm really not."

"Then you can drop me at the corner."

440

"But your car's back at the hospital."

He opened the car door before she came to a stop. "I'll walk."

"It's miles," Reynolds said, her voice strained. "And it's freezing outside. Lee, let me drive you. Let's go get some coffee. Talk about this some more."

"I need the fresh air. And what's there to talk about? I'm all talked out. I may never talk again." He climbed out and then leaned back in. "You *can* do something for me."

"Just name it."

He handed her the flowers. "Could you see that Faith gets these? I'd appreciate it." Lee shut the door and walked off.

Reynolds gripped the flowers and looked at Lee as he trudged away, head down, hands stuffed in his pockets. She saw his shoulders quiver. And then Brooke Reynolds lay back against the seat as the tears trickled down her face.

FIFTY-NINE

Nine months later Lee was staking out the hideaway townhouse of a man soon to be involved in an acrimonious divorce proceeding with his many-times-cheated-on wife. Lee had been hired by the very suspicious spouse to collect dirt on her hubby, and it hadn't taken him long to fill up bag after bag, as Lee watched a parade of pretty young things flounce through the premises. The wife wanted a nice-size financial settlement from the guy, who had about five hundred million bucks worth of stock options at some high-tech Internet outfit he had cofounded. And Lee was very happy to help her get it. The adulterous husband reminded him of Eddie Stipowicz, his ex-wife's billion-dollar man. Collecting evidence on this guy was a little bit like hurling rocks at little Eddie's bloated head.

Lee took out his camera and shot some pictures of a tall, blond, miniskirted number sauntering up to the townhouse. The photo of the bare-chested guy standing at the door awaiting her, beer can in hand, a goofy, lascivious smile on his fat face, would be exhibit numero uno for the wife's lawyers. No-fault divorce laws had seriously depressed the business of PIs running around digging up dirt, but when it came time to split the marriage loot, the slimy ooze still carried weight. Nobody liked being embarrassed with that stuff. Especially when there were kids involved, as there were here.

442

The long-legged blond couldn't have been more than twenty, about his daughter Renee's age, while the hubby was pushing fifty. God, those stock options. Must be nice. Or maybe it was the man's bald head, diminutive stature and soft pooch. You couldn't figure some women. *Nah, must be the dough*, Lee told himself. He put the camera away.

It was August in Washington, which meant just about everybody, other than cheating husbands and their bimbos, and PIs who spied on them, was out of town. It was hot, muggy, miserable. Lee had his window rolled down, praying for even the slightest movement of air, as he munched on trail mix and bottled water. The hardest thing with this type of surveillance was the lack of pee-pee breaks. That's why he preferred bottled water. The empty plastic containers had come in handy more than once for him.

He checked his watch; it was close on midnight. Most lights in the apartments and townhouses in the area had long since gone out. He was thinking about heading on, himself. He had gotten enough stuff in the last few days, including some embarrassing shots of a late-night romp in the townhouse's outdoor hot tub, to make the guy easily fork up half his net worth. Two naked girls who looked young enough to be thinking about the senior prom, frolicking in the bubbly water with a guy old enough to know better – this probably wouldn't sit too well with the upstanding stockholders of the husband's nice little high-tech concern, Lee imagined.

His own life had taken on a routine bordering on obsessive monotony, or so he had dubbed it. He got up early, worked out hard, pounding the bag, crunching the stomach and hoisting the weights until he thought his body would raise the white flag and then present him with an aneurysm. Then he went to work and kept at it nonstop until he barely made it to dinner at the McDonald's late-night drive-through near his apartment. Then he went home, alone, and tried to sleep, but found that he was never able to actually accomplish total unconsciousness. So he would prowl the apartment, look out the window, wonder about a whole bunch of things he couldn't do a damn thing about. His life's "what if" book was filled up. He'd have to go buy another one.

There had been some positives. Brooke Reynolds had made it her mission to send as much business his way as possible, and it had been quality, good-paying stuff. She had also had a number of ex-FBI agent buddies now in corporate security offer him full-time employment with, of course, stock options. He had turned them all down. The gesture was appreciated, he had told Reynolds, but he worked alone. He was not a suit type. He didn't like eating the kinds of lunches that required silverware. Traditional elements of success would undoubtedly be hazardous to his health.

He had seen Renee a great deal, and each time, things had gotten better between them. For about a month after everything had shaken out, he had barely left her side, making sure that nothing would happen to her because of Robert Thornhill and company. After Thornhill had killed himself his concerns had faded, although he was always on her to stay alert. She was going to come and visit him before school started up again. Maybe he'd drop Trish and Eddie a postcard, telling them what a fabulous job they'd done raising her. Or maybe he wouldn't.

Life was good, he kept telling himself. Business was good, he was in good health, his daughter was back in his life. He wasn't six feet under helping to fertilize grass. And he had served his country. All good shit. Which made him wonder why he was so unhappy, so out-and-out miserable. Actually, he knew, but there was absolutely nothing he could do about it. Wasn't that a kicker? Story of his life. Know the blues, but just can't change them.

A car's headlights flicked across his side mirror. His gaze immediately went to the car that had just pulled up behind him. It wasn't a cop wondering why he had parked here for several hours. He frowned and looked over at the townhouse. He wondered if his naughty tech mogul had noticed him and called in some reinforcements to help teach the curious PI a little lesson. Lee hoped that was the case. He had his crowbar in the seat next to him. This might actually be fun. Kicking the crap out of somebody might be the depression antidote he needed; get those endorphins going. At least it might get him through the night.

He was surprised when only one person emerged from the passenger side and headed his way. The person was small, slender, hidden inside an ankle-length coat with a hood, not exactly your recommended attire for a ninety-degree thermometer and one hundred percent humidity. His hand tightened on the crowbar. As the figure came up to his passenger door, he hit the door lock. The next moment, his lungs had locked up and he was gasping for air.

The face looking in at him was very pale and very thin. And very Faith Lockhart. He unlocked the door and she slid in.

He looked at her, finally found his voice down near his knees. "God, is it really you?"

She smiled, and suddenly she didn't seem so pale, so drawn, so frail. She slid off her long, hooded coat. Underneath she had on a short-sleeved shirt and khaki shorts. Her feet were in sandals. Her legs were

445

very pale and thinner than he remembered; all of her was. Months in a hospital had decimated her, he realized. Her hair had grown out and was longer, though far from its original length. She looked better with her real hair color, he thought. Actually, he would have taken the woman bald.

"It's me," she said quietly. "At least, what's left."

"Is that Reynolds back there?"

"Nervous and upset that I talked her into it."

"You look beautiful, Faith."

She smiled in a resigned fashion. "Liar. I look like hell. I can't even bear to look at my chest. God!" She said the words in a joking manner, but Lee could sense the anguish behind the light tone.

He very gently touched her face with his hand. "I'm not lying, and you know it."

She put her hand around his and gripped it with amazing strength. "Thank you."

"How are you really doing? I want facts, nothing but."

She stretched her arm slowly, the pain in her face so evident from such a simple movement. "I'm officially retired from the aerobics circuit, but I'm hanging in there. Actually, each day it gets better. The doctors expect a full recovery. Well, in the ninety percentile anyway."

"I never thought I'd see you again."

"I couldn't let that happen."

He slid over to her, put his arm around her. She winced a little as he did this, and he quickly backed off.

"I'm sorry, Faith, I'm sorry."

She smiled and put his arm back around her, patting his hand as she did so. "I'm not that fragile. And the day you can't put your arm around me is the day I call it a life."

"I'd ask you where you're living, but I don't want

to do anything that could put you in danger."

"Helluva way to have to live, don't you think?" Faith asked.

"Yes."

She leaned against him, resting her head against his chest. "I saw Danny right after I got out of the hospital. When they told us Thornhill had killed himself, I didn't think he was ever going to stop smiling."

"Can't say I felt any different."

She looked at him. "How are *you*, Lee?"

"Me! Nothing happened to me. Nobody shot me. Nobody tells me where I have to live. I'm doing fine. I got the best deal of all."

"Lie or the truth?"

"Lie," he said softly.

They exchanged a quick kiss and then a longer one. The movements were so easy, Lee thought, their heads turning at just the right angle, their arms going around each other with no wasted motion, like pieces in a puzzle someone was sliding together. They could be waking up at the beach house, the morning after. The nightmare never having occurred. How was it possible that one could know another person for such a short period of time and have it feel like several lifetimes? God would only let that happen once, if ever. And in Lee's case, he had taken it away. It wasn't fair, it wasn't right. He pressed his face into her hair, soaking up every particle of her scent.

"How long are you here?" he asked.

"What did you have in mind?"

"Nothing fancy. Dinner at my place, a quiet talk. Letting me hold you all night."

"As wonderful as that sounds, I'm not sure I'm up to that last part just yet."

He looked at her. "I'm being literal, Faith. I just

447

want to hold you. That's all. That's all I've been thinking about all these months. Just holding you."

Faith looked as though she might start crying. Instead she brushed away the lone tear that had tumbled down Lee's face.

Lee glanced in the rearview mirror. "But I guess that's not in Reynolds's agenda, is it?"

"I doubt it."

He looked back at her. "Faith," he said softly, "why did you step in front of that bullet? I know you care for Buchanan and all, but why?"

She took a shallow breath. "Like I said, he's unique, I'm ordinary. I couldn't let him die."

"I wouldn't have done it."

"Would you have done it for me?" she asked.

"Yes."

"You sacrifice for people you care about. And I care a great deal about Danny."

"I guess the fact that you had all the means to disappear – fake ID, Swiss bank account, safe house – and instead went to the FBI to try and save Buchanan should have clued me in on that."

She clutched his arm. "But I survived. I made it. Maybe that makes me just a little extraordinary, in a way?"

He cupped her face with his hand. "Now that you're here, I really don't want you to go, Faith. Like I would give everything I have, do anything I can, if you wouldn't leave me."

She traced his mouth with her fingers, kissed his lips, stared at his eyes, which even in the darkness seemed to have the blinding heat of the sun behind them. She never thought she would ever see those eyes again; maybe the fact that she might, if she were to survive, had been the only thing that had saved her, had not let her die. Right now she wasn't sure what else she had to live for. Other than the apparently depthless love of this man.

"Start the car," she said.

Puzzled, he looked at her but said nothing. He turned the key in the ignition, put the car in gear.

"Go ahead," Faith said.

He pulled the car away from the curb and the vehicle behind them immediately did the same.

They drove along, the car following them.

"Reynolds must be pulling her hair out," Lee said.

"She'll get over it."

"Where to?" he said.

"How much gas do you have in the car?" Faith asked.

He looked surprised. "I was on a stakeout. Full tank."

She was settled against him, her arm curling around his middle, her hair tickling his nose; she smelled so wonderful he felt dizzy.

"Let's go get some takeout Chinese. We can drive to the lookout spot off the GW Parkway." She looked at the star-filled sky. "I can show you the constellations."

He looked at her. "Been chasing stars lately?"

She smiled at him. "Always."

"And after that?"

"They can't keep me in Witness Protection against my will, can they?"

"No. But you'd be in danger."

"How about *we'd* be in danger?"

"In a second, Faith. In a second. But what happens when we run out of gas?"

"For now, just drive."

And that's exactly what he did.

ACKNOWLEDGMENTS

To my dear friend Jennifer Steinberg, for tracking down so much information for me. You'd make a great PI!

To my wife, Michelle, for always telling me the truth about the books.

To Neal Schiff at the FBI for his continued help and cooperation with my novels.

A very special thanks to FBI Special Agent Shawn Henry, who was very generous with his time, expertise, and enthusiasm, and who helped me avoid some serious gaffes in the story. Shawn, your comments made the book much better.

To Martha Pope for her valuable, insightful knowledge on Capitol Hill matters, and her patience with a political neophyte. Martha, you'd make a great teacher!

To Bobby Rosen, Diane Dewhirst, and Marty Paone for sharing their experiences and institutional memories with me.

To Tom DePont, Dawn Bailey, and Charles Nelson of NationsBank for assistance on financial and tax matters.

To Joe Duffy for enlightening me on foreign aid policy and procedures. And to his wife, Anne Wexler, for sharing her valuable time and insight with me.

A very, very special thanks to my friend Bob Schule for going above and beyond the call of duty in helping me on this book, by not only providing fascinating details about his long and distinguished career in Washington, but also for casting a wide net among his friends and colleagues in order to help me better understand politics, lobbying, and how Washington really works. Bob, you're a wonderful friend and a true professional.

To Congressman Rod Blagojevich (D. Ill) for allowing me a glimpse into the life of a member of Congress.

To Congressman Tony Hall (D. Ohio) for helping me better understand the plight of the world's poor, and how that issue plays out (or doesn't) in Washington.

To my good friend and family member Congressman John Baldacci (D. Maine) for his support and assistance with this project. If everyone in Washington were like John, the plot of this book would seem totally implausible.

To Larry Benoit and Bob Beene for their help on everything from lobbying to the nuts and bolts of governing, to all the little nooks and crannies in the U.S. Capitol building. To them I owe one of the best scenes in the book.

To John Deutch for his generous assistance in helping me to better understand the Central Intelligence Agency.

To Mark Jordan of Baldino's Lock and Key for educating me on the ways of security and phone systems and how to crack them. Mark, you're the best.

To Steve Jennings for reading every word as usual and helping to make them better.

To my dear friends David and Catherine Broome for exposing me to the North Carolina settings and for their continued encouragement and support.

To all those other people who contributed to this novel but for various reasons wish to remain anonymous. I couldn't have done it without all of you.

To my editor and my friend Frances Jalet-Miller. Her skill, encouragement, and gentle persuasion are all that any writer could ever want in an editor. To many more books together, Francie.

Last, but absolutely not least, to Larry, Maureen, Jamie, Tina, Emi, Jonathan, Karen Torres, Martha Otis, Jackie Joiner, and Jackie Meyer, Bruce Paonessa and Peter Mauceri, and all the rest of the Warner Books family. It takes *all* of us to make this happen. Friends for life.

All the people listed above gave me the knowledge and help I needed to write this novel. How I used all of that assistance to conjure up all sorts of shenanigans, misdeeds, outright crimes, and depictions of felonious and conspiratorial souls in *Saving Faith*, however, is my responsibility alone.

Absolute Power

To Michelle,
my dearest friend, my loving wife, my partner in crime,
without you this dream would have remained a feeble
glint in a weary eye

To my mother and father,
no parents could have done any more

To my brother and sister,
for putting up with a lot from their younger sibling and
still always being there for me

"Absolute power corrupts absolutely."
—LORD ACTON

ONE

He gripped the steering wheel loosely as the car, its lights out, drifted slowly to a stop. A few last scraps of gravel kicked out of the tire treads and then silence enveloped him. He took a moment to adjust to the surroundings and then pulled out a pair of worn but still effective night-vision binoculars. The house slowly came into focus. He shifted easily, confidently in his seat. A duffel bag lay on the front seat beside him. The car's interior was faded but clean.

The car was also stolen. And from a very unlikely source.

A pair of miniature palm trees hung from the rear-view mirror. He smiled grimly as he looked at them. Soon he might be going to the land of palms. Quiet, blue, see-through water, powdery salmon-colored sunsets and late mornings. He had to get out. It was time. For all the occasions he had said that to himself, this time he felt sure.

Sixty-six years old, Luther Whitney was eligible to collect Social Security, and was a card-carrying member of AARP. At that age most men had settled down into second careers as grandfathers, part-time raisers of their children's children, when weary joints were eased down into familiar recliners and arteries finished closing up with the clutter of a lifetime.

Luther had had only one career his entire life. It involved breaking and entering into other people's homes and places of business, usually in the nighttime, as now, and taking away as much of their property as he could feasibly carry.

Though clearly on the wrong side of the law, Luther had never fired a gun or hurled a knife in anger or fear, except for his part in a largely confusing war fought where South and North Korea were joined at the hip. And the only punches he had ever thrown were in bars, and those only in self-defense as the suds made men braver than they should have been.

Luther only had one criterion in choosing his targets: he took only from those who could well afford to lose it. He considered himself no different from the armies of people who routinely coddled the wealthy, constantly persuading them to buy things they did not need.

A good many of his sixty-odd years had been spent in assorted medium- and then maximum-security correctional facilities along the East Coast. Like blocks of granite around his neck, three prior felony convictions stood to his credit in three different states. Years had been carved out of his life. Important years. But he could do nothing to change that now.

He had refined his skills to where he had high hopes that a fourth conviction would never materialize. There was absolutely nothing mysterious about the ramifications of another bust: he would be looking at the full twenty years. And at his age, twenty years was a death penalty. They might as well fry him, which was the way the Commonwealth of Virginia used to handle its particularly bad people. The citizens of this vastly historic state were by and large a God-fearing people, and religion premised upon the notion of equal retribution consistently demanded the ultimate payback. The common-wealth succeeded in disposing of more death row criminals than all but two states, and the leaders, Texas and Florida, shared the moral sentiments of their Southern sister. But not for simple burglary; even the good Virginians had their limits.

Yet with all that at risk he couldn't take his eyes off the home — mansion, of course, one would be compelled to call it. It had engrossed him for several months now. Tonight that fascination would end.

Middleton, Virginia. A forty-five-minute drive west on a slingshot path from Washington, D.C. Home to vast estates, obligatory Jaguars, and horses whose price tags could feed the residents of an entire inner-city apartment building for a year. Homes in this area sprawled across enough earth with enough splendor to qualify for their own appellation. The irony of his target's name, the Coppers, was not lost upon him.

The adrenaline rush that accompanied each job was absolutely unique. He imagined it was somewhat like how the batter felt as he nonchalantly trotted the bases, taking all the time in the world, after newly bruised leather had landed somewhere in the street. The crowd on its feet, fifty thousand pairs of eyes on one human being, all the air in the world seemingly sucked into one space, and then suddenly displaced by the arc of one man's glorious swing of the wood.

Luther took a long sweep of the area with his still sharp eyes. An occasional firefly winked back at him. Otherwise he was alone. He listened for a moment to the rise and fall of the cicadas and then that chorus faded into the background, so omnipresent was it to every person who had lived long in the area.

He pulled the car further down the blacktop road and backed onto a short dirt road that ended in a mass of thick trees. His iron-gray hair was covered with a black ski hat. His leathery face was smeared black with camouflage cream; calm, green eyes hovered

3

above a cinder block jaw. The flesh carried on his spare frame was as tight as ever. He looked like the Army Ranger he had once been. Luther got out of the car.

Crouching behind a tree, Luther surveyed his target. The Coppers, like many country estates that were not true working farms or stables, had a huge and ornate wrought iron gate set on twin brick columns but had no fencing. The grounds were accessible directly from the road or the nearby woods. Luther entered from the woods.

It took Luther two minutes to reach the edge of the cornfield adjacent to the house. The owner obviously had no need for home-grown vegetables but had apparently taken the country squire role to heart. Luther wasn't complaining, since it afforded him a hidden path almost to the front door.

He waited a few moments and then disappeared into the embracing thickness of the corn stalks.

The ground was mostly clear of debris and his tennis shoes made no sound, which was important, for any noise carried easily here. He kept his eyes straight ahead; his feet, after much practice, carefully picked their way through the slender rows, compensating for the slight unevenness of the ground. The night air was cool after the debilitating heat of another stagnant summer, but not nearly cool enough for breath to be transformed into the tiny clouds that could be seen from a distance by restless or insomniac eyes.

Luther had timed this operation several times over the past month, always stopping at the edge of the field before stepping into the front grounds and past no-man's-land. In his head, every detail had been worked and reworked hundreds of times until a precise script of movement, waiting, followed by more movement was firmly entrenched in his mind.

He crouched down at the edge of the front grounds and took one more long look around; no need to rush. No dogs to worry about, which was good. A human, no matter how young and fleet, simply could not outrun a dog. But it was the noise they made that stopped men like Luther cold. There was also no perimeter security system, probably because of the innumerable false alarms that would be caused by the large populations of deer, squirrel and raccoon roaming over the area. However, Luther would shortly be faced with a highly sophisticated defense package that he would have thirty-three seconds to disarm – and that included the ten seconds it would take him to remove the control panel.

The private security patrol had passed through the area thirty minutes earlier. The cop clones were supposed to vary their routines, making sweeps through their surveillance sectors every hour. But after a month of observations, Luther had easily discerned a pattern. He had at least three hours before another pass would be made. He wouldn't need nearly that long.

The grounds were pitch black, and thick shrubs, the lifeblood of the burglary class, clung to the brick entryway like a caterpillar nest to a tree branch. He checked each window of the house: all black, all silent. He had watched the caravan carrying the home's occupants parade out two days ago to points south, and carefully took inventory of all owners and personnel. The nearest estate was a good two miles away.

He took a deep breath. He had planned everything out, but in this business, the simple fact was that you could never account for everything.

He loosened the grips on his backpack and then glided out from the field in long, smooth strides across the lawn, and in ten seconds was facing the thick, solid-wood front door with reinforced steel framing together with a locking system that was rated at the top of the charts for holding force. None of which concerned Luther in the least.

He slipped a facsimile front-door key out of his jacket pocket and inserted it into the keyhole without, however, turning it.

He listened for another few seconds. Then he slipped off his backpack and changed his shoes so there would be no traces of mud. He readied his battery-operated screwdriver, which could reveal the circuitry he needed to fool ten times faster than he could by hand.

The next piece of equipment he carefully pulled from his backpack weighed exactly six ounces, was slightly bigger than a pocket calculator and other than his daughter was the best investment he had ever made in his life. Nicknamed "Wit" by its owner, the tiny device had assisted Luther in his last three jobs without a hitch.

The five digits comprising this home's security code had already been supplied to Luther and pro-grammed into his computer. Their proper sequence was still a mystery to him, but that obstacle would have to be eradicated by his tiny metal, wire and microchip companion if he wanted to avoid the ear-piercing shriek that would instantly emit from the four sound cannons planted at each corner of the ten-thousand-square-foot fortress he was invading. Then would follow the police call dialed by the nameless computer he would battle in a few moments. The home also had pressure-sensitive windows and floor plates, in addition to tamperproof door magnets. All of which would mean nothing if Wit could tear the correct code sequence from the alarm system's grasp.

He eyed the key in the door and with a practiced motion hooked Wit to his harness belt so that it hung easily against his side. The key turned effortlessly in the lock and Luther prepared to block out the next sound that he would hear, the low beep of the security system that warned of impending doom for the intruder if the correct answer was not fed into it in the allotted time and not a millisecond later.

He replaced his black leather gloves with a pair of more nimble plastic ones that had a second layer of padding on the fingertips and palms. It was not his practice to leave any evidence behind. Luther took one deep breath, then opened the portal. The shrill beep of the security system met him instantly. He quickly moved into the enormous foyer and confronted the alarm panel.

The automatic screwdriver whirled noiselessly; the six metal pieces dropped into Luther's hands and then were deposited in a carrier on his belt. Slender wires attached to Wit flashed against the sliver of moonlight seeping through the window beside the door, and then Luther, probing momentarily like a surgeon through a patient's chest cavity, found the correct spot, clipped the strands into place and then flipped on the power source to his companion.

From across the foyer, a slash of crimson stared down at him. The infrared detector had already locked on Luther's thermal offset. As the seconds ticked down, it patiently waited for the security system's "brain" to pronounce the intruder friend or foe.

Faster than the eye could follow, the numbers flashed across Wit's digital screen in neon amber; the allotted time blinked down in a small box at the top-right-hand corner of the same screen.

Five seconds elapsed and then the numbers 5, 13, 9, 3 and 11 appeared on Wit's tiny glass face and locked.

The beep stopped on cue as the security system was

disarmed, the red light flashed off and was replaced with the friendly green, and Luther was in business. He removed the wires, screwed the plate back on and repacked his equipment, then carefully locked the front door.

The master bedroom was on the third floor, which could be reached by an elevator down the main first-floor hallway to the right, but Luther chose the stairs instead. The less dependent he was on anything he did not have complete control over the better. Getting stuck in an elevator for several weeks was not part of his battle plan.

He looked at the detector in the corner of the ceiling as its rectangular mouth smiled at him, its surveillance arc asleep for now. Then he headed up the staircase.

The master bedroom door was not locked. In a few seconds he had his low-power, nonglare work lamp set up and took a moment to look around. The green glow from a second control panel mounted next to the bedroom door broke the darkness.

The house itself had been built within the last five years; Luther had checked the records at the court-house and had even managed to gain access to a set of blueprints of the place from the planning commissioner's office, it being large enough to require special blessing from the local government as though they would ever actually deny the rich their wishes.

There were no surprises in the building plans. It was a big, solid house more than worth the multi-million-dollar price tag that had been paid in cash by its owner.

Indeed, Luther had visited this home once before, in broad daylight, with people everywhere. He had been in this very room and he had seen what he needed to see. And that was why he was here tonight.

Six-inch crown molding peered down at him as he

knelt next to the gigantic, canopied bed. Next to the bed was a nightstand. On it were a small silver clock, the newest romance novel of the day and an antique silver-plated letter opener with a thick leather handle.

Everything about the place was big and expensive. There were three walk-in closets in the room, each about the size of Luther's living room. Two were occupied by women's clothes and shoes and purses and every other female accoutrement one could rationally or irrationally spend money on. Luther glanced at the framed prints on the nightstand and wryly observed the twenty-something "little woman" next to the seventy-something husband.

There were many types of lotteries in the world and not all of them state-run.

Several of the photos showed off the lady of the house's proportions to almost maximum degree, and his quick examination of the closet revealed that her dressing pleasures leaned to the downright sleazy.

He looked up at the full-length mirror, studying the ornate carvings around its edges. He next surveyed the sides. It was a heavy, nifty bit of work, built right into the wall, or so it seemed, but Luther knew that hinges were carefully hidden into the slight recess six inches from the top and bottom.

Luther looked back at the mirror. He had the distinct advantage of having seen a target like this full-length model a couple of years ago although he hadn't planned to crack it. But you didn't ignore a second golden egg just because you had the first in hand, and that second golden egg had been worth about fifty thou'. The prize on the other side of this private looking glass he figured would be about ten times that.

Using brute force and the aid of a crowbar he could overcome the locking system built into the mirror's carvings but that would take precious time. And, more than that, it would leave behind obvious signs of the place having been violated. And although the house was supposed to be empty for the next several weeks, one never knew. When he left the Coppers there would be no obvious evidence he had ever been there. Even upon their return the owners might not check the vault for some time. In any event, he did not have to take the hard route.

He walked quickly over to the large-screen TV located against one wall of the vast chamber. The area was set up as a sitting room with matching chintz-covered chairs and a large coffee table. Luther looked at the three remotes lying there. One to work the TV, one for the VCR and one that would cut his night's work by ninety percent. Each had a brand name on it, each looked pretty much like the other, but a quick experiment showed that two worked their appropriate apparatus and one did not.

He walked back across the room, pointed the control at the mirror and pushed the lone red button located at the bottom of the hardware. Ordinarily that action meant the VCR was recording. Tonight, in this room, it meant the bank was opening for business for its one fortunate customer.

Luther watched the door swing open easily, silently on the now-revealed no-maintenance hinges. From long habit, he replaced the control exactly where it had been, pulled a collapsible duffel bag out of his backpack and entered the vault.

As his light swept through the darkness he was surprised to see an upholstered chair sitting in the middle of the room, which looked to be about six feet by six feet. On the chair's arm rested an identical remote, obviously a safeguard against being locked in by accident. Then his eyes took in the shelves down each side.

The cash, bundled neatly, went in first, then the

contents of the slender boxes that were definitely not costume jewelry. Luther counted about two hundred thousand dollars' worth of negotiable bonds and other securities, and two small boxes of antique coins and another of stamps, including one of an inverted figure that made Luther swallow hard. He ignored the blank checks and the boxes full of legal documents, which were worthless to him. His quick assessment ended at almost two million dollars, probably more.

He took one more look around, taking care not to miss any stray nook. The walls were thick – he figured they had to be fireproof, or as fireproof as man could make something. The place wasn't hermetically sealed; the air was fresh, not stale. Somebody could stay in here for days.

The limo moved quickly down the road followed by the van, each driver expert enough to accomplish this feat without the benefit of headlights.

Inside the spacious back seat of the limo were a man and two women, one of whom was close to being drunk and who was doing her best to undress the man and herself right there, despite the gentle defensive efforts of her victim.

The other woman sat across from them tight-lipped, ostensibly trying to ignore the ridiculous spectacle, which included girlish giggling and much panting, but in reality she closely observed every detail of the pair's efforts. Her focus was on a large book that sat open in her lap where appointments and notes battled each other for space and the attention of the male sitting across from her, who took the oppor- tunity of his companion wrenching off her spike heels to pour himself another drink. His capacity for alcohol was enormous. He could drink twice the amount he had already consumed tonight and there would be no outward signs, no slurring of speech or impeded motor functions – which would have been deadly for a man in his position.

She had to admire him, his obsessions, his truly raw edges, while at the same time his being able to project an image to the world that cried out purity and strength, normalcy but, at the same time, greatness. Every woman in America was in love with him, enamored with his classic good looks, immense self-assurance and also what he represented, for all of them. And he returned that universal admiration with a passion, however misplaced, that astonished her.

Unfortunately, that passion had never pointed itself in her direction despite her subtle messages, the touches that lingered a shade too long; how she maneuvered to see him first thing in the morning when she looked her best, the sexual references used in their strategy sessions. But until that time came – and it would come, she kept telling herself – she would be patient.

She looked out the window. This was taking too long; it threw everything else off. Her mouth curled up in displeasure.

Luther heard the vehicles enter the front drive. He flitted to a window and followed the mini-caravan as it went around back, where it would be hidden from view from the front drive. He counted four people alighting from the limo, one from the van. His mind scrolled swiftly through possible identities. Too small a party for it to be the owners of the house. Too many for it to be someone simply checking on the place. He could not make out any faces. For one ironic instant Luther debated whether the home was destined to be burgled twice on the same night. But that was too enormous a coincidence. In this business, like a lot of others, you played the percentages. Besides, criminals did not march up to their targets wearing clothing more suitable for a night on the town.

He thought quickly as noises filtered up to him, presumably from outside the rear of the house. It took him a second to realize that his retreat was cut off and to calculate what his plan of action would be.

Grabbing his bag, he raced to the alarm panel next to the bedroom door and activated the home's security system, silently thanking his memory for numbers. Then Luther slipped across to the vault and entered it, carefully closing the door behind him. He pushed himself as far back into the little room as he could. Now he had to wait.

He cursed his misfortune; everything had been going so smoothly. Then he shook his head clear, forced himself to breathe regularly. It was like flying. The longer you did it, the greater your chance of something bad happening. He would just have to hope that the house's most recent arrivals would have no need to make a deposit in the private bank he was now occupying.

A burst of laughter and then the drum of voices filtered up to him, together with the loud beep from the alarm system, which sounded like a jet plane screeching directly over his head. Apparently there was slight confusion about the security code. A bead of sweat appeared on Luther's forehead as he envisioned the alarm exploding and the police wanting to examine every inch of the house just in case, starting with his little roost.

He wondered how he would react as he listened to the mirrored door being opened, a light blazing in, without the slightest possibility of missing him. The strange faces peering in, the drawn guns, the reading of his rights. He almost laughed. Trapped like a fucking rat, nowhere to go. He hadn't had a cigarette

13

in almost thirty years, but now he desperately craved a smoke. He put his bag down quietly and slowly let his legs out straight so they wouldn't go to sleep.

Heavy steps on the oak plank staircase. Whoever they were they didn't care who knew they were there. Luther counted four, possibly five. They turned left and headed his way.

The door to the bedroom opened with a slight squeak. Luther searched his mind. Everything had been picked up or put back in its place. He'd only touched the remote, and he had replaced it right in line with the slight dust pattern. Now Luther could only hear three voices, a man and two women. One of the females sounded drunk, the other was all business. Then Ms. Business disappeared, the door closed but wasn't locked, and Ms. Drunk and the man were alone. Where were the others? Where had Ms. Business gone? The giggles continued. Footsteps came closer to the mirror. Luther scrunched down in the corner as far as he could, hoping that the chair would shield him from view but knowing that it couldn't possibly.

Then a burst of light hit him right in the eyes and he almost gasped at the suddenness of his little world going from inky black to broad daylight. He blinked rapidly to adjust to the new level of brightness, his pupils going from almost full dilation to pinpoints in seconds. But there were no screams, no faces, no guns.

Finally, after a full minute had passed, Luther peered around the corner of the chair and received another shock. The vault door seemed to have disappeared; he was staring right into the goddamned room. He almost fell backward but caught himself. Luther suddenly understood what the chair was for.

He recognized both of the people in the room. The woman he had seen tonight already, in the photos: the little wife with the hooker taste in clothes.

The man he knew for an altogether different reason; he certainly wasn't the master of this house. Luther slowly shook his head in amazement and let out his breath. His hands shook and a queasiness crept over him. He fought back the grip of nausea and stared into the bedroom.

The vault door also served as a one-way mirror. With the light on outside and darkness in his little space, it was as though he were watching a giant TV screen.

Then he saw it and a fist of breath kicked out of his lungs: the diamond necklace on the woman's neck. Two hundred thou' to his practiced eye, maybe more. And just the sort of bauble one would routinely put away in a home vault before retiring for the evening. Then his lungs relaxed as he watched her take the piece off and casually drop it on the floor.

His fear receded enough to where he rose and inched over to the chair and slowly eased himself into it. So the old man sat here and watched his little woman get her brains screwed out by a procession of men. From the looks of her, Luther figured that some members of that procession included young guys making minimum wage or hanging on to freedom by the width of a green card. But her gentleman caller tonight was in an altogether different class.

He looked around, his ears focused for any sound of the other inhabitants of the house. But what could he really do? In over thirty years of active larceny, he had never encountered anything like this, so he decided to do the only thing he could. With only an inch of glass separating him from absolute destruction, he settled down quietly into the deep leather and waited.

TWO

Three blocks from the broad white bulk of the United States Capitol, Jack Graham opened the front door of his apartment, threw his overcoat on the floor and went straight to the fridge. Beer in hand he flopped down on the threadbare couch in his living room. His eyes quickly perused the tiny room as he took a drink. Quite a difference from where he'd just been. He let the beer stand in his mouth and then swallowed. The muscles of his square jaw tensed and then relaxed. The nagging prickles of doubt slowly drained away, but they would reappear; they always did.

Another important dinner party with Jennifer, his soon-to-be wife, and her family and circle of social and business acquaintances. People at that level of sophistication apparently didn't have mere friends they hung with. Everyone served a particular function, the whole being greater than the sum of the parts. Or at least that was the intent, although Jack had his own opinion on the matter.

Industry and finance had been well represented, brandishing names Jack read about in the *Wall Street Journal* before he chucked it for the sports pages to see how the 'Skins or Bullets were doing. The politicos had been out in full force, scrounging future votes and current dollars. The group was rounded out by the ubiquitous lawyers of which Jack was one, the occasional doctor to show ties to the old ways and a couple of public-interest types to demonstrate that the powers that be had sympathy for the plight of the ordinary.

He finished the beer and flipped on the TV. His shoes came off, and the forty-dollar patterned socks his fiancée had bought for him were carelessly flung over the back of the lamp shade. Given time she'd have him in two-hundred-dollar braces with matching hand-painted ties. Shit! Rubbing his toes, he seriously considered a second beer. The TV tried but failed to hold his interest. He pushed his thick, dark hair out of his eyes and focused for the thousandth time on where his life was hurtling, seemingly with the speed of the space shuttle.

Jennifer's company limo had driven the two of them to her Northwest Washington townhouse where Jack would probably move after the wedding; she detested his place. The wedding was barely six months off, apparently no time at all by a bride's standards, and he was sitting here having severe second thoughts.

Jennifer Ryce Baldwin possessed instant head-turning beauty to such a degree that the women stared as often as the men. She was also smart and accomplished, came from serious money and was intent on marrying Jack. Her father ran one of the largest development companies in the country. Shopping centers, office buildings, radio stations, entire subdivisions, you name it, he was in it, and doing better than just about anyone else. Her paternal great-grandfather was one of the original Midwest manufacturing tycoons, and her mother's family had once owned a large chunk of downtown Boston. The gods had smiled early and often on Jennifer Baldwin. There wasn't one guy Jack knew who wasn't jealous as hell of him.

He squirmed in his chair and tried to rub a kink out of his shoulder. He hadn't worked out in a week. His six-foot-one body, even at thirty-two, had the same hard edge it had enjoyed all through high school where he was a man among boys in virtually every sport offered, and in college where the competition was a lot rougher but where he still managed to make first-string varsity as a heavyweight wrestler and first-team All-Academic. That combination had gotten him into the University of Virginia School of Law, where he made *Law Review*, graduated near the top of his class and promptly settled down as a public defender in the District of Columbia's criminal justice system.

His classmates had all grabbed the big-firm option out of law school. They had routinely called with phone numbers of psychiatrists who could help coax him out of his insanity. He smiled and then went and grabbed that second beer. The fridge was now empty.

Jack's first year as a PD had been rough as he learned the ropes, losing more than he won. As time went on, he graduated to the more serious crimes. And as he poured every ounce of youthful energy, raw talent and common sense he had into each of those cases, the tide began to turn.

And then he started kicking some serious ass in court.

He discovered he was a natural at the role, as talented at cross-examination as he had been at throwing men much bigger than he across a two-inch-thick mat. He was respected, liked as an attorney if you could believe that.

Then he had met Jennifer at a Bar function. She was vice president of development and marketing at Baldwin Enterprises. Dynamic in presence, she had the added skill of making whomever she was talking to feel important; their opinions were listened to if not necessarily followed. She was a beauty who had no need to rely solely on that asset.

When you got past the eye-catching looks, there was a lot more there. Or seemed to be. Jack would have been less than human had he not been attracted to her. And she had made it clear, early on, that the attraction was mutual. While being ostensibly impressed at his dedication in defending the rights of those accused of crimes in the Capital City, little by little Jennifer had convinced Jack that he had done his bit for the poor, dumb and unfortunate, and that maybe he should start thinking about himself and his future, and that maybe she wanted to be a part of that future. When he finally left PD, the U.S. Attorney's office had given him quite a send-off party, and good riddance. That should have told him then and there that there were a lot more of the poor, dumb and unfortunate who needed his help. He didn't expect to ever top the thrill he had felt being a PD; he figured times like that came around once in life and then they were gone. It was time to move on; even little boys like Jack Graham had to grow up someday. Maybe it was just his time.

He turned off the TV, grabbed a bag of corn chips and went to his bedroom, stepping over the piles of dirty laundry strewn in front of the doorway. He couldn't blame Jennifer for not liking his place; he was a slob. But what bothered him was the dead certainty, that, even spotless, Jennifer would not consent to live here. For one thing it was in the wrong neighborhood; Capitol Hill to be sure, but not a gentrified part of Capitol Hill, actually not even close.

Then there was the size. Her townhouse must have run five thousand square feet, not counting the live-in maid's quarters and the two-car garage that housed her Jag and brand new Range Rover, as if anybody living in D.C., with its traffic-strangled roads, needed a vehicle capable of driving up the vertical side of a twenty-thousand-foot-high mountain.

He had four rooms if you counted the bathroom. He reached his bedroom, stripped off his clothes and dropped into bed. Across the room, on a small plaque that had once hung in his office at work until he had grown embarrassed looking at it, was the announcement of his joining Patton, Shaw & Lord. PS&L was the Capital City's number-one corporate firm. Legal caterer to hundreds of blue-chip companies, including his soon-to-be father-in-law's, representing a multimillion-dollar account that he was credited with bringing to the firm and that, in turn, guaranteed him a partnership at the next review. Partnerships at Patton, Shaw were worth, on average, at least half a million dollars a year. That was tip money for the Baldwins, but then he wasn't a Baldwin. At least not yet.

He pulled the blanket over him. The building's insulation left a lot to be desired. He popped a couple of aspirin and washed them down with the rest of a Coke that was sitting on his nightstand, then looked around the cramped, messy bedroom. It reminded him of his room growing up. It was a warm, friendly memory. Homes should look lived in; they should always give way to the screams of kids as they dashed from room to room in search of new adventures, of fresh objects to break.

That was the other thing with Jennifer: she had made it clear that the sound of little feet was a distant project that was far from certain. Her career at her father's company was first and foremost in her mind and heart – maybe more so, Jack felt, than he was.

He rolled over and tried to close his eyes. The wind pushed against the window and he glanced in that direction. He looked away, but then with a resigned air, his eyes drifted back over to the box.

It held part of his collection of old trophies and awards from high school and college. But those items were not the object of his focus. In the semidarkness he reached out a long arm for the framed photo, decided against it, and then changed his mind again.

He pulled it out. This had almost become a ritual. He never had to worry about his fiancée stumbling onto this particular possession of his because she absolutely refused to enter his bedroom for longer than a minute. Whenever they slid between the sheets it was either at her place, where Jack would lie on the bed staring up at the twelve-foot ceiling where a mural of ancient horsemen and young maidens shared space while Jennifer amused herself until she collapsed and then rolled over for him to finish on top of her. Or at her parents' place in the country where the ceilings were even higher and the murals had been taken from some thirteenth-century church in Rome, all of which made Jack feel that God was watching him being ridden by the beautiful and absolutely naked Jennifer Ryce Baldwin and that he would languish in eternal hell for those few moments of visceral pleasure.

The woman in the photo had silky brown hair that curled slightly at the ends. Her smile looked up at Jack and he remembered the day he had taken the picture.

A bike ride far into the countryside of Albemarle County. He was just starting law school; she was in her second year of college at Mr. Jefferson's university. It was only their third date but it was like they had never lived without each other.

Kate Whitney.

He said the name slowly; his hand instinctively traced the curves of her smile, the lone dimple right above the left cheek that gave her face a slightly lopsided look. The almond-shaped cheekbones bordered a dainty nose that sloped toward a pair of sensual lips. The chin was sharp and screamed out "stubborn." Jack moved back up the face and stopped at the large teardrop-shaped eyes that always seemed full of mischief.

Jack rolled back over and lay the photo on his chest so that she stared directly at him. He could never think of Kate without seeing an image of her father, with his quick wit and crooked smile.

Jack had often visited Luther Whitney at his little row house in an Arlington neighborhood that had seen better days. They spent hours drinking beer and telling stories, mostly Luther telling and Jack listening.

Kate never visited her father, and he never attempted to contact her. Jack had found his identity almost by accident, and despite Kate's objections, Jack had wanted to get to know the man. It was a rare thing for her face to hold anything but a smile, but that was one thing she never smiled about.

After he graduated they moved to D.C. and she enrolled in law school at Georgetown. Life seemed idyllic. She came to his first few trials as he worked the butterflies from his stomach and the squeak from his throat and tried to remember which counsel table to sit at. But as the seriousness of the crimes his clients were accused of committing grew, her enthusiasm diminished.

They had split up his first year in practice.

The reasons were simple: she couldn't understand why he had chosen to represent people who broke the law, and she could not tolerate that he liked her father.

At the very last breath of their lives together he remembered sitting with her in this very room and asking, pleading, for her not to leave. But she had and that was four years ago, and he hadn't seen or heard from her since.

He knew that she had taken a job with the

Commonwealth Attorney's office in Alexandria, Virginia, where she was no doubt busily putting former clients of his behind bars for stomping on the laws of her adopted state. Other than that Kate Whitney was a stranger to him.

But lying there with her staring at him with a smile that told him a million things that he had never learned from the woman he was supposed to marry in six months, Jack wondered if Kate would remain a stranger to him; whether his life was destined to become far more complicated than he ever intended. He grabbed the phone and dialed.

Four rings and he heard the voice. It had an edge that he didn't remember, or maybe it was new. The beep came and he started to leave a message, something funny, right out of the blue, but then right on cue he got nervous and quickly hung up, his hands shaking, his breathing accelerated. He shook his head. Jesus Christ! He had done five murder one cases and he was shaking like a goddamned sixteen-year-old sucking up the courage to call his first date.

Jack put the picture away and imagined what Kate was doing right that very minute. Probably still in her office pondering over how many years to take off somebody's life.

Then Jack wondered about Luther. Was he at this very minute on the wrong side of someone's door-step? Or leaving with another bundle of financial joy slung over his back?

What a family, Luther and Kate Whitney. So different and so much the same. As focused a pair as he had ever encountered, but their respective focuses occupied different galaxies. That last night, after Kate had walked out of his life, he had gone around to Luther's to say good-bye and to drink a last beer. They had sat in the small well-tended garden, watching the clematis and ivy cling to the fence; the scent of lilacs and roses lay thick like a net over them.

The old man had taken it all right, asked few questions, and wished Jack well. Some things did not work out; Luther understood that as well as anyone. But as Jack left that night he had noticed the glistening in the old man's eyes – and then the door closed on that part of his life.

Jack finally put out the light and closed his eyes with the knowledge that another tomorrow was close upon him. His pot of gold, his once-in-a-lifetime payoff, was one day closer to reality. It did not make for easy sleep.

THREE

As Luther stared through the glass, the thought
struck him that the two made a very attractive
couple. It was an absurd opinion to have under
the circumstances, but that didn't make the conclusion any less valid. The man was tall, handsome, a
very distinguished mid-forties. The woman could
not have ventured far into her twenties; the hair was
full and golden, the face oval and lovely, with a pair
of enormous deep blue eyes that now looked up
lovingly into the man's elegant countenance. He
touched her smooth cheek; she nestled her lips
against his hand.

The man had two tumblers and filled them with
the contents of the bottle he had brought with him.
He handed the woman one. After a clink of glasses,
their eyes firmly set on each other, he finished his
drink in one swallow while she only managed a small
sip of hers. Glasses put down, they embraced in the
middle of the room. His hands slid down her backside
and then back up to the bare shoulders. Her arms and
shoulders were tanned and well-toned. He grasped
her limbs admiringly as he leaned down to kiss her
neck.

Luther averted his eyes, embarrassed to be viewing
this very personal encounter. A strange emotion to
have when he was still clearly in danger of being
caught. But he was not so old that he could not
appreciate the tenderness, the passion that was slowly
unfolding in front of him.

As he raised his eyes up, he had to smile. The couple was now engaged in a slow dance around the room. The man was obviously well-practiced at the endeavor; his partner was less so, but he gently led her through the simple paces until they again ended up beside the bed.

The man paused to fill his glass again and then quickly drained it. The bottle was now empty. As his arms encircled her once more, she leaned into him, pulled at his coat, started to undo his tie. The man's hands drifted to the zipper of her dress and slowly headed south. The black dress slid down and she slowly stepped out of it, revealing black panties and thigh-high stockings, but no bra.

She had the sort of body that made other women who didn't instantly jealous. Every curve was where it was supposed to be. Her waist Luther could have encircled with both hands touching. As she turned to the side to slide out of her stockings, Luther observed that the breasts were large, round and full. The legs were lean and defined, probably from hours of daily exercise under the watchful eyes of a personal trainer.

The man quickly undressed down to his boxers and sat on the side of the bed watching the woman as she took her time slipping out of her underwear. Her rear end was round and firm and creamy white against the backdrop of a flawless tan. With her last piece of clothing shed, a smile cut across the man's face. The white teeth were straight and thick. Despite the alcohol, his eyes seemed clear and focused.

She smiled at his attention and slowly advanced. As she drew within his reach, his long arms gripped her, pulled her to him. She rubbed up and down against his chest.

Again, Luther began to avert his eyes, wishing more than anything else that this spectacle would soon be over and that these people would leave. It would only take him a few minutes to return to his car, and this night would be filed away in his memory as a unique, if potentially disastrous, experience.

That's when he saw the man grip the woman's buttocks hard and then slap them, again and again. Luther winced in vicarious pain at the repeated blows; the white skin now glowed red. But either the woman was too drunk to feel the pain or she enjoyed this sort of treatment, because her smile didn't fade. Luther felt his gut clinch again as the man's fingers dug into the soft flesh.

The man's mouth danced across her chest; she ran her finger through his thick hair as she positioned her body inside his legs. She closed her eyes, her mouth gathered into a contented smile; she arched her head back. Then she opened her eyes and attacked his mouth with hers.

His strong fingers moved up from the abused buttocks and started to gently massage her back. Then he dug in hard until she winced and pulled back from him. She half-smiled and he stopped as she touched his fingers with hers. He turned his attention back to her breasts and suckled them. Her eyes closed once again, as her breathing turned perceptibly to a low moan. The man moved his attention again to her neck. His eyes were wide open, looking across at where Luther sat but with no idea of his presence.

Luther stared at the man, at those eyes, and didn't like what he saw. Pools of darkness surrounded by red, like some sinister planet seen through a telescope. The thought struck him that the naked woman was in the grip of something not so gentle, not so loving as she probably anticipated.

The woman finally grew impatient and pushed her lover down on the bed. Her legs straddled the man, giving Luther a view from behind that should have been reserved for her gynecologist and husband. She hoisted herself up, but then with a sudden burst of energy he roughly pushed her aside and went on top of her, grabbing her legs and lifting them up until they were perpendicular with the bed.

Luther stiffened in his chair at the man's next movement. He grabbed her by the neck and jerked her up, pulling her head between his legs. The suddenness of the act made her gasp, her mouth a bare inch from him there. Then he laughed and threw her back down. Dazed for a moment, she finally managed a weak smile and sat up on her elbows as he towered over her. He grabbed his erection with one hand, spreading her wide with the other. As she lay placidly back to accept him, he stared wildly at her.

But instead of plunging between her legs, he grabbed her breasts and squeezed, apparently a little too hard, because, finally, Luther heard a yelp of pain and the woman abruptly slapped the man. He let go and then slapped her back, viciously, and Luther saw a patch of blood emerge at the corner of her mouth and spill onto the thick, lipstick-coated lips.

"You fucking bastard." She rolled off the bed and sat on the floor rubbing her mouth, tasting her blood, her drunken brain momentarily lucid. The first words Luther had clearly heard spoken the entire night hit his brain like a sledgehammer. He stood up, inched toward the glass.

The man grinned. Luther froze when he saw it. It was more like the snarl of a wild animal close to a kill than a human being.

"Fucking bastard," she said again, a little more quietly, the words slurred. As she stood up he grabbed her arm, twisted it, and she fell hard to the floor. The man sat on the bed and looked down triumphantly.

His breathing accelerating, Luther stood before the

glass, his hands clenching and unclenching as he continued to watch and hoped that the other people would come back. He eyed the remote on the chair and then his eyes shot back to the bedroom. The woman had raised herself half off the floor, the wind slowly coming back to her. The romantic feelings she had been experiencing had vanished. Luther could see that in her body movements, wary and deliberate. Her companion apparently failed to notice the change in her movements and the flash of anger in the blue eyes, or else he would not have stood up and put out a hand for her to take, which she did.

The man's smile abruptly vanished as her knee caught him squarely between the legs, doubling him over and ending any arousal he had been experiencing. As he crumpled to the floor, no sound came from his lips, except for his labored breathing while she grabbed her panties and started to put them on.

He caught her ankle, threw her to the floor, her underwear halfway up her legs.

"You little cunt." The words came out in short gasps as he tried to get his breath back, all the time holding on to that ankle, drawing her closer to him.

She kicked at him, again and again. Her feet thudded against his rib cage, but still he hung on. "You fucking little whore," he said.

At the menace he heard in those words, Luther stepped toward the glass, one of his hands flying to its smooth surface as if to reach through it, to grab the man, make him let go.

The man painfully dragged himself up and his look made Luther's flesh turn cold.

The man's hands gripped the woman's throat.

Her brain, clouded by the alcohol, snapped back to high gear. Her eyes, now completely filled with fear, darted to the left and right as the pressure on her neck increased and her breath started to weaken. Her fingers clawed at his arms, scratching deeply.

Luther saw the blood rise to the man's skin where she attacked him but his grip did not loosen.

She kicked and jerked her body, but he was almost twice her weight; her attacker didn't budge.

Luther again looked at the remote. He could open the door. He could stop this. But his legs would not move. He stared helplessly through the glass, sweat poured from his forehead, every pore in his body seemed to be erupting; his breath came in short bursts as his chest heaved. He placed both hands against the glass.

Luther's breath stopped as the woman fixed on the nightstand for an instant. Then, with a frantic motion, she grabbed the letter opener, and with one blinding stroke she slashed the man's arm.

He grunted in pain, let go and grabbed his bloody arm. For one terrible instant he looked down at his wound, almost in disbelief that he had been damaged like that. Pierced by this woman.

When the man looked back up, Luther could almost feel the murderous snarl before it escaped from the man's lips.

And then the man hit her, harder than Luther had seen any man hit a woman. The hard fist connected with the soft flesh and blood flew from her nose and mouth.

Whether it was all the booze she had consumed or what, Luther didn't know, but the blow that ordinarily would have crippled a person merely incensed her. With convulsive strength she managed to stagger up. As she turned toward the mirror, Luther watched the horror in her face as she suddenly viewed the abrupt destruction of her beauty. Eyes widening in disbelief, she touched the swollen nose; one finger dropped down and probed the loosened teeth. She had become a smeared portrait, her major attribute had vanished.

She turned around to face the man, and Luther saw the muscles in her back tense so hard they looked like small pieces of wood. With lightning quickness, she again slammed her foot into the man's groin. Instantly the man was weak again, his limbs useless as nausea overcame him. He collapsed to the floor, rolled over onto his back, moaning. His knees curled upward, his hand protectively at his crotch.

With blood streaming down her face, with eyes that had gone from stark horror to homicidal in an instant, the woman dropped to her knees beside him and raised the letter opener high above her head.

Luther grabbed the remote, took a step toward the door, his finger almost on the button.

The man, seeing his life about to end as the letter opener plunged toward his chest, screamed with every bit of strength he had left. The call did not go unheeded.

His body frozen in place, Luther's eyes darted to the bedroom door as it flew open.

Two men, hair cropped short, crisp business suits not concealing impressive physiques, burst into the room, guns drawn. Before Luther could take another step they had assessed the situation and made their decision.

Both guns fired almost simultaneously.

Kate Whitney sat in her office going over the file one more time.

The guy had four priors, and had been arrested but ultimately not charged on six other occasions because witnesses had been too frightened to talk or had ended up in trash Dumpsters. He was a walking time bomb ready to explode on another victim, all of whom had been women.

The current charge was murder during the commission of robbery and rape, which met the criteria for capital murder under Virginia's laws. And this time she decided to go for the home run: death. She had never asked for it before, but if anybody deserved it, this guy did, and the commonwealth was not squeamish about authorizing it. Why allow him life when he had cruelly and savagely ended the one given to a nineteen-year-old college student who made the mistake of going to a shopping mall in broad daylight to pick up some nylons and a new pair of shoes?

Kate rubbed her eyes and, using a rubber band from the pile on her desk, pulled her hair back into a rough ponytail. She looked around her small, plain office; the case files were piled high around the room and for the millionth time she wondered if it would ever stop. Of course it wouldn't. If anything it would get worse, and she could only do what she could do to stem the flow of blood. She would start with the execution of Roger Simmons, Jr., twenty-two years old, and as hardened a criminal as she had ever confronted, and she had already faced an army of them in her as yet short career. She remembered the look he had given her that day in court. It was a countenance totally without remorse or caring or any other positive emotion. It was also a face without hope, an observation substantiated by his background history, which read like a horror story of a childhood. But that was not her problem. It seemed like the only one that wasn't.

She shook her head and checked her watch: well after midnight. She went to pour some more coffee; her focus was starting to wander. The last staff attorney had left five hours ago. The cleaning crew had been gone for three. She moved down the hallway in her stocking feet to the kitchen. If Charlie

Manson were out and doing his thing now, he'd be one of her milder cases; an amateur compared to the monsters roaming loose today.

Cup of coffee in hand, she walked back into her office and paused for a moment to look at her reflection in the window. With her job looks were really unimportant; hell, she hadn't been on a date in over a year. But she couldn't pull her eyes away. She was tall and slender, perhaps too skinny in certain areas, but her routine of running four miles every day had not changed while her caloric intake had steadily dwindled. Mostly she subsisted on bad coffee and crackers, although she limited herself to two cigarettes a day and was hoping with luck to quit altogether.

She felt guilty about the abuse her body was taking with the endless hours and stress of moving from one horrific case to another, but what was she supposed to do? Quit because she didn't look like the women on the cover of *Cosmopolitan*? She consoled herself with the fact that their job twenty-four hours a day was to make themselves look good. Hers was to ensure that people who broke the law, who hurt others, were punished. Under any criteria she reasoned she was doing far more productive things with her life.

She swiped at her own mane; it needed to be cut, but where was the time to do that? The face was still relatively unmarked by the burden she found increasingly difficult to carry. Her twenty-nine-year-old face, after four years of nineteen-hour days and countless trials, had held its own. She sighed as she realized that probably would not last. In college she had been the gracious recipient of turned heads, the cause of raised heartbeats and cold sweats. But as she got ready to enter her thirties, she realized that what she had taken for granted for so many years, that what she had, in fact, derided on so many occasions, would not be with her that much longer. And like so many things you took for granted or dismissed as unimportant, being able to quiet a room by your mere entrance was one she knew she was going to miss.

That her looks had remained strong over the last few years was remarkable considering she had done relatively little to preserve them. Good genes, that must be it; she was fortunate. But then she thought of her father and decided that she wasn't very lucky at all in the genes department. A man who stole from others and then pretended to live a normal life. A man who deceived everyone, including his wife and daughter. A man you could not depend on to be there.

She sat at her desk, took a quick sip of the hot coffee, poured in more sugar and looked at Mr. Simmons while she stirred the black depths of her nighttime stimulus.

She picked up the phone, called home to check messages. There were five, two from other lawyers, one from the policeman she would put on the stand against Mr. Simmons and one from a staff investigator who liked to call her at odd hours with mostly useless information. She should change her telephone number. The last message was a hang-up. But she could hear very low breathing on the end, she could almost make out a word or two. Something in the sound was familiar, but she couldn't place it. People with nothing better to do.

The coffee flowed through her veins, the file came back into focus. She glanced up at her little bookshelf. On top was an old photo of her deceased mother and ten-year-old Kate. Cut out from the picture was Luther Whitney. A big gap next to mother and daughter. A big nothing.

"Jesus fucking Christ!" The President of the United States sat up, one hand covering his limp and damaged privates, the other holding the letter opener that a moment before was to have been the instrument of his death. It had more than just his blood on it now. "Jesus fucking Christ, Bill, you fucking killed her!" The target of his barrage stooped to help him up while his companion checked the woman's condition: a perfunctory examination, considering two heavy-caliber bullets had blown through her brain.

"I'm sorry, sir, there wasn't time. I'm sorry, sir."

Bill Burton had been a Secret Service agent for twelve years, and a Maryland state trooper for eight years before that, and one of his rounds had just blown apart a beautiful young woman's head. Despite all his intense training, he was shaking like a pre-schooler just awakened from a nightmare.

He had killed before in the line of duty: a routine traffic stop gone wrong. But the deceased had been a four-time loser with a serious vendetta against uni-formed officers and wielding a Glock semiautomatic pistol in a sincere attempt to lift Burton's head from his shoulders.

He looked down at the small, naked body and thought he would be sick. His partner, Tim Collin, looked across at him, grabbed his arm. Burton swallowed hard and nodded his head. He would make it.

They carefully helped up Alan J. Richmond, President of the United States, a political hero and leader to young, middle-aged and old alike, but now simply naked and drunk. The President looked up at them, the initial horror finally passing as the alcohol worked its effects. "She's dead?" The words were a little slurred; the eyes seemed to roll back in the head like loose marbles.

"Yes, sir," Collin answered crisply. You didn't let a question from the President go unanswered, drunk or not.

Burton hung back now. He glanced at the woman again and then looked back at the President. That was their job, his job. Protect the goddamned President. Whatever it took, that life must not end, not like that. Not stuck like a pig by some drunken bitch.

The President's mouth curled up into what looked like a smile, although neither Collin nor Burton would remember it that way later. The President started to rise.

"Where are my clothes?" he demanded.

"Right here, sir." Burton, snapping back to attention, stooped to pick up the clothes. They were heavily spotted – everything in the room seemed to be – with her.

"Well, get me up, and get me ready, goddammit. I've got a speech to give for somebody, somewhere, don't I?" He laughed shrilly. Burton looked at Collin and Collin looked at Burton. They both watched as the President passed out on the bed.

At the sound of the explosions, Chief of Staff Gloria Russell had been in the bathroom on the first floor, as far away from that room as she could get.

She had accompanied the President on many of these assignations, but rather than growing used to them, they disgusted her more each time. To imagine her boss, the most powerful man on the face of the earth, bedding all these celebrity whores, these political groupies. It was beyond comprehension, and yet she had almost learned to ignore it. Almost.

She had pulled her pantyhose back up, grabbed her purse, flung open the door, run down the hallway and even in heels took the steps two at a time. When she reached the bedroom door Agent Burton stopped her.

"Ma'am, you don't want to see this, it's not pretty."

She pushed past him and then stopped. Her first thought was to run back out, down the stairs, into the limo, out of there, out of the state, out of the miserable country. She wasn't sorry for Christy Sullivan, who'd wanted to get screwed by the President. That had been her goal for the last two years. Well, sometimes you don't get what you want; sometimes you get a lot more.

Russell steadied herself and faced off with Agent Collin.

"What the hell happened?"

Tim Collin was young, tough and devoted to the man he was assigned to protect. He was trained to die defending the President, and there was no question in his mind that if the time came he would. Several years had passed since he had tackled an assailant in the parking lot of a shopping center where the then presidential candidate Alan Richmond had been making an appearance. Collin had had the potential assassin down on the asphalt and completely immobile before the guy had even gotten his gun fully out of his pocket, before anyone else had even reacted. To Collin, his only mission in life was to protect Alan Richmond.

It took Agent Collin one minute to report the facts to Russell in succinct, cohesive sentences. Burton solemnly confirmed the account.

"It was either him or her, Ms. Russell. There was no other way to cut it." Burton instinctively glanced at the President, who still lay on the bed oblivious to anything. They had covered the more strategic portion of his body with a sheet.

"Do you mean to tell me you heard nothing? No

sounds of violence before, before this?" She waved at the mess of the room.

The agents looked at each other. They had heard many sounds emanating from bedrooms where their boss happened to be. Some might be construed as violent, some not. But everybody had always come out okay before.

"Nothing unusual," Burton replied. "Then we heard the President scream and we went in. That knife was maybe three inches from going into his chest. Only thing fast enough was a bullet."

He stood as erect as he could and looked her right in the eye. He and Collin had done their job, and this woman wasn't going to tell them otherwise. No blame would be put on his shoulders.

"There was a goddamned knife in the room?" She looked at Burton incredulously.

"If it was up to me, the President wouldn't go out on these, these little excursions. Half the time he won't let us check anything out beforehand. We didn't get a chance to scope the room." He looked at her. "He's the President, ma'am," he added, for good measure, as if that justified everything. And for Russell it usually did, a fact Burton was well aware of.

Russell looked around the room, taking in everything. She had been a tenured professor of political science at Stanford with a national reputation before answering the call in Alan Richmond's quest for the presidency. He was such a powerful force, everybody wanted to jump on his bandwagon.

Currently Chief of Staff, with serious talk of becoming Secretary of State if Richmond won re-election, which everyone expected him to do with ease. Who knew? Maybe a Richmond-Russell ticket might be in the making. They made a brilliant combination. She was the strategist, he was the consummate campaigner. Their future grew brighter every day. But now? Now she had a corpse and a drunken President inside a home that was supposed to be vacant.

She felt the express train coming to a halt. Then her mind snapped back. Not over this little piece of human garbage. Not ever!

Burton stirred. "You want me to call the police now, ma'am?"

Russell looked at him like he had lost his mind. "Burton, let me remind you that our job is to protect the President's interests at all times and nothing – absolutely nothing – takes precedence over that. Is that clear?"

"Ma'am, the lady's dead. I think we—"

"That's right. You and Collin shot the woman, and she's dead." After exploding from Russell's mouth, the words hung in the air. Collin rubbed his fingers together; a hand went instinctively to his holstered weapon. He stared at the late Mrs. Sullivan as if he could will her back to life.

Burton flexed his burly shoulders, moved an inch closer to Russell so that the significant height difference was at its maximum.

"If we hadn't fired, the President would be dead. That's our job. To keep the President safe and sound."

"Right again, Burton. And now that you have prevented his death, how do you intend to explain to the police and the President's wife and your superiors, and the lawyers and the media and the Congress and the financial markets and the country and the rest of the goddamned world, why the President was here? What he was doing while he was here? And the circumstances that led up to you and Agent Collin having to shoot the wife of one of the wealthiest and most influential men in the United States? Because if you call the police, if you call

39

anybody, that is exactly what you will have to do. Now if you are prepared to accept full responsibility for that undertaking, then pick up that phone over there and make that call."

Burton's face changed color. He backed up a step, his superior size useless to him now. Collin was frozen, watching the two square off. He had never seen anyone talk that way to Bill Burton. The big man could have snapped Russell's neck with a lazy thrust of his arm.

Burton looked down at the corpse one more time. How could you explain that so that everybody came out all right? The answer was simple: you couldn't.

Russell watched his face carefully. Burton looked back at her. His eyes twitched perceptibly; they would not meet hers now. She had won. She smiled benignly and nodded. The show was hers to run.

"Go make some coffee, a whole pot," she ordered Burton, momentarily relishing this switching of roles. "And then stay by the front door just in case we get any late-night visitors.

"Collin, go to the van, and talk to Johnson and Varney. Don't tell them anything about this. For now just tell them there was an accident, but that the President's okay. That's all. And that they're to stay put. Understood? I'll call when I want you. I need to think this out."

Burton and Collin nodded and headed out. Neither had been trained to ignore orders so authoritatively given. And Burton didn't want to be calling the shots on this one. They couldn't pay him enough to do that.

Luther hadn't moved since the shots had blown apart the woman's head. He was afraid to. His feelings of shock had finally passed, but he found his eyes continually wandering to the floor and to what had once been a living, breathing human being. In all his years as a criminal he had only seen one other person killed. A thrice-convicted pedophile whose spinal cord had collided with a four-inch shiv wielded by an unsympathetic fellow inmate. The emotions sweeping over him now were totally different, as though he were the sole passenger on a ship that had sailed into a foreign harbor. Nothing looked or seemed familiar at all. Any sound now would do him no good, but he slowly sat back down before his trembling legs gave way.

He watched as Russell moved around the room, stooped next to the dead woman, but did not touch her. Next she picked up the letter opener, holding it by the end of the blade with a handkerchief she pulled from her pocket. She stared long and hard at the object that had almost ended her boss's life and had played a major role in ending someone else's. She carefully put the letter opener in her leather purse, which she had placed on the nightstand, and put the handkerchief back in her pocket. She glanced briefly at the contorted flesh that had recently been Christine Sullivan.

She had to admire the way Richmond accomplished his extracurricular activities. All his "companions" were women of wealth and social position, and all were married. This ensured that no exposé of his adulterous behavior would appear in any of the tabloids. The women he bedded had as much to lose if not more than he, and they understood that fact very well.

And the press. Russell smiled. In this day and age the President lived under a never-ending barrage of scrutiny. He couldn't pee, smoke a cigar or belch without the public knowing all of the most intimate details. Or so the public thought. And that was based largely on the overestimation of the press and their abilities to nudge out every morsel of a story from its hiding place. What they failed to understand was that while the office of the President might have lost some of its enormous power over the years as the problems of a troubled globe soared beyond the ability of any one person to confront them on an equal basis, the President was surrounded by absolutely loyal and supremely capable people. People whose skill level at covert activities were in another league from the polished, cookie-cutter journalists whose idea of trailing down a tough story was asking puffball questions of a congressman who was more than willing to talk for the benefit of the evening news coverage. It was a fact that, if he so desired, President Alan Richmond could move about without fear that anyone would be successful in tracking his where-abouts. He could even disappear from public view for as long as he wished, although that was the antithesis of what a successful politician hoped to accomplish in a day's work. And that privilege boiled down to one common denominator.

The Secret Service. They were the best of the best. This elite group had proved it time and again over the years, as they had in planning this most recent activity.

A little after noon, Christy Sullivan had walked out of her beauty salon in Upper Northwest. After walking one block she had stepped into the foyer of an apartment building and thirty seconds later she had walked out encased in a full-length hooded cloak pulled from her bag. Sunglasses covered her eyes. She had walked for several blocks, randomly window-shopping, then taken a redline Metro train to Metro Center. Exiting the Metro she had walked two more blocks and entered an alley between two buildings scheduled for demolition. Two minutes later, a car with tinted windows had emerged from the alley.

Collin had been driving. Christy Sullivan was in the back seat. She had been sequestered in a safe place with Bill Burton until the President had been able to join her later that night.

The Sullivan estate had been chosen as the perfect spot for the planned interlude because, ironically, her home in the country was the last place anyone would expect Christy Sullivan to be. And Russell knew it would also be perfectly empty, guarded by a security system that was no barrier to their plans.

Russell sat down in a chair and closed her eyes. Yes, she had two of the most capable members of the Secret Service in this house with her. And, for the first time, that fact troubled the Chief of Staff. The four agents with her and the President tonight had been handpicked, out of the approximately one hundred agents assigned to the presidential detail, by the President himself for these little activities. They were all loyal and highly skilled. They took care of the President and held their tongues, regardless of what was asked of them. Up until tonight President Richmond's fascination with married women had spawned no overwhelming dilemmas. But tonight's events clearly threatened all of that. Russell shook her head as she forced herself to think of a plan of action.

Luther studied the face. It was intelligent, attractive but also a very hard face. You could almost see the mental maneuvering as the forehead alternately wrinkled and then went lax. Time slipped by and she didn't budge. Then Gloria Russell's eyes opened and moved across the room, not missing any detail.

Luther involuntarily shrank back as her gaze swept by him like a searchlight across a prison-yard. Then her eyes came to the bed and stopped. For a long minute she stared at the sleeping man, and then she got a look on her face that Luther could not figure out. It was halfway between a smile and a grimace.

She got up, moved to the bed and looked down at the man. A Man of the People, or so the people thought. A Man for the Ages. He did not look so great right now. His body was half on the bed, legs spread, feet nearly touching the floor; an awkward position to say the least when one was wearing no clothes.

She ran her eyes up and down the President's body, lingering on some points, an activity that was amazing to Luther considering what was lying on the floor. Before Gloria Russell had entered the room and faced off with Burton, Luther had expected to hear sirens and to be sitting there watching policemen and detectives, medical examiners and even spin doctors swarming everywhere; with news trucks piling up in vast columns outside. Obviously, this woman had a different plan.

Luther had seen Gloria Russell on CNN and the major networks, and countless times in the papers. Her features were distinctive. A long, aquiline nose set between high cheekbones, the gift from a Cherokee ancestor. The hair was raven black and hung straight, stopping at her shoulders. The eyes were big and so dark a blue that they resembled the deepest of ocean water, twin pools of danger for the careless and unwary.

Luther carefully maneuvered in the chair. Watching the woman in front of a stately fireplace inside the White House pontificating on the latest political concerns was one thing. Watching her move through a room containing a corpse and examining a drunk, naked man who was the leader of the Free World was an entirely different matter. It was a spectacle Luther did not want to watch anymore but he could not pull his eyes away.

Russell glanced at the door, walked quickly across

the room, took out her handkerchief, and closed and locked it. She swiftly returned to again stare down at the President. Her hand went out and for a moment Luther cringed in anticipation, but she simply stroked the President's face. Luther relaxed, but then stiffened again as her hand moved down to his chest, lingering momentarily on the thick hair, and then dropped still lower to his flat stomach, which rose and fell evenly in his deep sleep.

Then her hand moved lower and she slowly pulled the sheet away and let it drop to the floor. Her hand reached down to his crotch and held there. Then she glanced at the door again and knelt down in front of the President. Now Luther had to close his eyes. He did not share the peculiar spectator interests of the house's owner.

Several long minutes passed, and then Luther opened his eyes.

Gloria Russell was now shedding her pantyhose, laying them neatly on a chair. Then she carefully climbed on top of the slumbering President.

Luther closed his eyes again. He wondered if they could hear the bed squeak downstairs. Probably not, as it was a very large house. And even if they did, what could they do?

Ten minutes later Luther heard a small, involuntary gasp from the man, and a low moan from the woman. But Luther kept his eyes closed. He wasn't sure why. It seemed to be from a combination of raw fear and disgust at the disrespect shown to the dead woman.

When Luther finally opened his eyes, Russell was staring directly at him. His heart stopped for a moment until his brain told him it was okay. She quickly slipped on her pantyhose. Then, in confident, even strokes, she reapplied her lipstick in the looking glass.

A smile clung to her face; the cheeks were flushed.

45

She looked younger. Luther glanced at the President. He had returned to a deep sleep, the last twenty minutes probably filed away by his mind as an especially realistic and pleasant dream. Luther looked back at Russell.

It was unnerving to see this woman smile directly at him, in this room of death, without knowing he was there. There was power in that woman's face. And a look Luther had already seen once in this room. This woman, too, was dangerous.

"I want this entire place sanitized, except for that." Russell pointed to the late Mrs. Sullivan. "Wait a minute. He was probably all over her. Burton, I want you to check every inch of her body, and anything that looks remotely like it doesn't belong there I want you to make disappear. Then put her clothes on."

Hands gloved, Burton moved forward to carry out this order.

Collin sat next to the President, forcing another cup of coffee down the man's throat. The caffeine would help clear away the grogginess, but only the passage of time would clean the slate completely. Russell sat down next to him. She took the President's hand in hers. He was fully clothed now although his hair was in disarray. His arm hurt, but they had bandaged it as best they could. He was in excellent health; it would heal quickly.

"Mr. President? Alan? *Alan*?" Russell gripped his face and pointed it toward her.

Had he sensed what she had done to him? She doubted it. He had so desperately wanted to get laid tonight. Wanted to be inside a woman. She had given him her body, no questions asked. Technically she had committed rape. Realistically she was confident she had fulfilled many a male's dream. It didn't matter if he had no recollection of the event, of her sacrifice.

But he would damn sure know what she was going to do for him now.

The President's eyes came in and out of focus. Collin rubbed his neck. He was coming around. Russell glanced at her watch. Two o'clock in the morning. They had to get back. She slapped his face, not hard, but enough to get his attention. She felt Collin stiffen. God, these guys had tunnel vision.

"Alan, did you have sex with her?"

"Wha . . ."

"Did you have sex with her?"

"Wha . . . No. Don't think so. Don't remem . . ."

"Give him some more coffee, pour it down his damned throat if you have to, but get him sober." Collin nodded and went to work. Russell walked over to Burton, whose gloved hands were dexterously examining every inch of the late Mrs. Sullivan.

Burton had been involved in numerous police investigations. He knew exactly what detectives looked for and where they looked for it. He never imagined himself using that specialized knowledge to inhibit an investigation, but then he had never imagined anything like this ever happening either.

He looked around the room, his mind calculating which areas would need to be gone over, what other rooms they had used. They could do nothing about the marks on the woman's throat and other microscopic physical evidence that was no doubt imbedded in her skin. The Medical Examiner would pick those up regardless of what they tried to do. However, none of those things could be realistically traced to the President unless the police identified the President as a suspect, which was pretty much beyond the realm of possibility.

The incongruity of attempted strangulation of a small woman with death caused by gunshot was something they would have to leave to the police's imagination.

Burton turned his attention back to the deceased and started to carefully slide her underwear up her legs. He felt a tap on his shoulder.

"Check her."

Burton looked up. He started to say something.

"Check her!" Russell's eyebrows were arched. Burton had seen her do that a million times with the White House staff. They were all terrified of her. He wasn't afraid of her, but he was smart enough to cover his ass whenever she was around. He slowly did as he was told. Then he positioned the body exactly as it had fallen. He reported back with a single shake of his head.

"Are you sure?" Russell looked unconvinced, although she knew from her interlude with the President that chances were he had not entered the woman, or that if he had he hadn't finished. But there might be traces. It was scary as hell, the things they could determine these days from the tiniest specimens.

"I'm not a goddamned ob-gyn. I didn't see anything and I think I would have, but I don't carry a microscope around with me."

Russell would have to let that one go. There was still a lot to do and not much time.

"Did Johnson and Varney say anything?"

Collin looked over from where the President was ingesting his fourth cup of coffee. "They're wondering what the hell's going on, if that's what you mean."

"You didn't te—"

"I told them what you said to tell them and that's all, ma'am." He looked at her. "They're good men, Ms. Russell. They've been with the President since the campaign. They're not going to do anything to mess things up, okay?"

Russell rewarded Collin with a smile. A good-looking kid and, more important, a loyal member of the President's personal guard; he would be very useful to her. Burton might be a problem. But she had a strong trump card: he and Collin had pulled the trigger, maybe in the line of duty, but who really knew? Bottom line: they too were in this all the way.

Luther watched the activity with an appreciation that he felt guilty about under the circumstances. These men were good: methodical, careful, thought things through, and didn't miss anything. Dedicated lawmen and professional criminals were not so different. The skills, the techniques were much the same, just the focus was different, but then the focus made all the difference, didn't it?

The woman was now completely dressed, lying exactly where she had fallen. Collin was finishing with her fingernails. A solution had been injected under each, and a small suction device had cleaned away traces of skin and other incriminating remnants.

The bed had been stripped and remade; the evidence-laden sheets were already packed in a duffel bag for their ultimate destination in a furnace. Collin had already scoped the downstairs area.

Everything any of them had touched, except for one item, had been wiped clean. Burton was now vacuuming parts of the carpet and he would be the last one to leave, backing out, as he painstakingly extinguished their trail.

Earlier Luther had watched the agents ransack the room. Their obvious goal made him smile in spite of himself. Burglary. The necklace had been deposited in a bag along with her plethora of rings. They would make it appear as if the woman had surprised a burglar in her house and he had killed her, not knowing that six feet away a real-life burglar was watching and listening to everything they were doing.

An eyewitness!

Luther had never been an eyewitness to a burglary other than those he had committed. Criminals hated eyewitnesses. These people would kill Luther if they knew he was there; there was no question about that. An elderly criminal, a three-time loser, was not much to sacrifice for the Man of the People.

The President, still groggy but with Burton's aid, slowly made his way out of the room. Russell watched them go. She did not notice Collin frantically searching the room. Finally, his sharp eyes fixed on Russell's purse on the nightstand. Poking out from the bag was about an inch of the letter opener's handle. Using a plastic bag, Collin quickly pulled out the letter opener and prepared to wipe it off. Luther involuntarily jerked as he watched Russell race over and grab Collin's hand.

"Don't do that, Collin."

Collin wasn't as sharp as Burton, and certainly wasn't in Russell's league. He looked puzzled.

"This has his prints all over it, ma'am. Hers too, plus some other stuff if you know what I mean – it's leather, it's soaked right in."

"Agent Collin, I was retained by the President as his strategic and tactical planner. What appears to you an obvious choice appears to me to require much more thought and deliberation. Until that analysis has been completed you will not wipe that object down. You will put it in a proper container, and then you will give it to me."

Collin started to protest but Russell's menacing stare cut him off. He dutifully bagged the letter opener and handed it to her.

"Please be careful with that, Ms. Russell."

"Tim, I am always careful."

50

She rewarded him with another smile. He smiled back. She had never called him by his first name before; he had been unsure if she even knew it. He also observed, and not for the first time, that the Chief of Staff was a very good-looking woman.

"Yes, ma'am." He began to pack up the equipment.

"Tim?"

He looked back at her. She moved toward him, looked down, and then her eyes caught his. She spoke in low tones; she almost seemed embarrassed, Collin felt.

"Tim, this is a very unique situation we're faced with. I need to feel my way a little bit. Do you understand?"

Collin nodded. "I'd call this a unique situation. Scared the hell out of me when I saw that blade about to go into the President's chest."

She touched his arm. Her fingernails were long and perfectly manicured. She held up the letter opener. "We need to keep this between us, Tim. Okay? Not the President. Not even Burton."

"I don't know—"

She gripped his hand. "Tim, I really need your support on this. The President has no idea what happened and I don't think Burton is looking at this too rationally right now. I need someone I can depend on. I need you, Tim. This is too important. You know that, don't you? I wouldn't ask you if I didn't think you could handle it."

He smiled at the compliment, then looked squarely at her.

"Okay, Ms. Russell. Whatever you say."

As Collin finished packing up, Russell looked at the bloody seven-inch piece of metal that had come so close to ending her political aspirations. If the President had been killed, there could have been no

51

cover-up. An ugly word – cover-up – but often necessary in the world of high politics. She shivered slightly at the thought of the headlines. "PRESIDENT FOUND DEAD IN BEDROOM OF CLOSE FRIEND'S HOME. WIFE ARRESTED IN SLAYING. CHIEF OF STAFF GLORIA RUSSELL HELD RESPONSIBLE BY PARTY LEADERS." But that had not happened. Would not happen.

This thing she held in her hand was worth more than a mountain of weapons-grade plutonium, more than the total oil production of Saudi Arabia.

With this in her possession, who knew? Perhaps even a *Russell*-Richmond ticket? The possibilities were absolutely infinite.

She smiled and put the plastic bag inside her purse.

The scream made Luther whip his head around. The pain shot through his neck and he almost cried out.

The President ran into the bedroom. He was wide-eyed, but still half-drunk. The memory of the last few hours had come back like a Boeing 747 landing on his head.

Burton ran up behind him. The President started toward the body; Russell dropped her purse on the nightstand, and she and Collin met him halfway.

"Goddammit! She's dead. I killed her. Oh sweet Jesus help me. I killed her!" He screamed and then cried and then screamed again. He tried to push through the wall in front of him but was still too weak. Burton pulled at the President from behind.

Then with convulsive strength, Richmond tore loose and launched himself across the room and slammed into the wall, rolling into the nightstand. And finally the President of the United States crumpled to the floor and curled up like a fetus, whimpering, next to the woman he had intended to have sex with that night.

Luther watched in disgust. He rubbed at his neck and slowly shook his head. The incredibility of the entire night's events was becoming too much to endure.

The President slowly sat up. Burton looked like Luther felt, but said nothing. Collin eyed Russell for instructions. Russell caught the look and smugly accepted this subtle changing of the guard.

"Gloria?"

"Yes, Alan?"

Luther had seen the way Russell had looked at the letter opener. He also knew something now that no one else in the room knew.

"Will it be okay? Make it okay, Gloria. Please. Oh God, Gloria!"

She rested her hand on his shoulder in her most reassuring manner, as she had done across hundreds of thousands of miles of campaign dust. "Everything's under control, Alan. I've got *everything* under control."

The President was far too intoxicated to catch the meaning, but she didn't really care.

Burton touched his radio earpiece, listening intently for a moment. He turned to Russell.

"We better get the hell out of here. Varney just scoped a patrol car coming down the road."

"The alarm . . . ?" Russell looked puzzled.

Burton shook his head. "It's probably just a rent-a-cop on routine, but if he sees something . . ." He didn't need to say anything else.

Leaving in a limo in this land of wealth was the best cover they could have. Russell thanked God for the routine she had developed for using rented limos without the regular drivers for these little adventures. The names on all the forms were dummies, the rental fee and deposit paid in cash, the car picked up and dropped off after hours. There were no faces

53

associated with the transaction. The car would be sterilized. That would be a dead end for the police if they ever snagged that line, which was highly doubtful.

"Let's go!" Russell was now slightly panicked.

The President was helped up. Russell went out with him. Collin grabbed the bags. Then stopped cold.

Luther swallowed hard.

Collin turned back, grabbed Russell's purse off the nightstand and headed out.

Burton started up the small vacuum, completed the room and then left, closing the door and turning off the light.

Luther's world returned to inky darkness.

This was the first time he had been alone in the room with the dead woman. The rest of them had apparently grown used to the bloody figure lying on the floor, unconsciously stepping over or around the now inanimate object. But Luther had not grown accustomed to the death barely eight feet away.

He could no longer see the pile of stained clothing and the lifeless body inside of them, but he knew it was there. "Sleazy rich bitch" would probably be her informal epitaph. And, yes, she had cheated on her husband, not that he seemed to care about that. But she hadn't deserved to die like that. He would've killed her, there was no question about that. Except for her swift counterattack, the President would've committed murder.

The Secret Service men he could not really fault. That was their job and they did it. She had picked the wrong man to attempt to kill in the heat of whatever she had been feeling. Maybe it was better. If her hand had been a little faster or the agents' response a little slower, she might be spending the rest of her life in jail. Or she'd probably get death for killing a President.

Luther sat down in the chair. His legs were almost numb. He forced himself to relax. Soon he would be getting the hell out of there. He needed to be ready to run.

He had a lot to think through, considering that they were unwittingly setting up Luther Whitney to be the number-one suspect in what would no doubt be deemed a heinous and gruesome crime. The wealth of the victim would demand that enormous law enforcement resources be expended in finding the perpetrator. But there was no way they would be looking to 1600 Pennsylvania Avenue for the answer. They would search elsewhere, and despite Luther's intense preparations, they might very well find him. He was good, very good, but then he had never faced the types of forces that would be unleashed to solve this crime.

He quickly thought back through his entire plan leading up to tonight. He could think of no obvious holes, but it was the not-so-obvious ones that usually did you in. He swallowed, curled and uncurled his fingers, stretched his legs to calm himself. One thing at a time. He still wasn't out of here. Many things could go wrong, and one or two undoubtedly would.

He would wait two more minutes. He ticked off the seconds in his head, visualized them loading the car. They would probably wait for any further sight or sound of the patrol car before heading out.

He carefully opened his bag. Inside were much of the contents of this room. He had almost forgotten that he had come here to steal and in fact had stolen. His car was a good quarter mile away. He thanked God he had quit smoking all those years ago. He would need every ounce of lung capacity he could muster. How many Secret Service Agents was he confronted with? At least four. Shit!

The mirrored door slowly opened and Luther stepped out into the room. He hit the remote one more time and then tossed it back onto the chair as the door swung closed.

He eyed the window. He had already planned an alternate escape through that aperture. A hundred-foot coil of extremely strong nylon rope, knotted every six inches, was in his bag.

He made a wide berth around the body, careful not to step in any of the crimson, the position of which he had programmed into his memory. He glanced only once at the remains of Christine Sullivan. Her life could not be brought back. Luther was now faced with keeping his own intact.

It took him a few seconds to reach the nightstand, and probe down behind it.

Luther's fingers clutched the plastic bag. The President's collision with the furniture had toppled Gloria Russell's purse on its side. The plastic bag and its immensely valuable occupant had fallen out and slid down behind the nightstand.

Luther's finger nudged the blade of the letter opener through the plastic before secreting it in his duffel bag. He went quickly over to the window and carefully peered out. The limo and van were still there. That wasn't good.

He went across to the other side of the room, took out his rope, secured it under the leg of the enormously heavy chest of drawers, and ran the line across to the other window, which would drop him at the opposite end of the house, hidden from the road. He carefully opened the window, praying for a well-oiled track, and was rewarded.

He played out the rope and watched it snake down the brick sides of the house.

Gloria Russell looked up at the massive face of the mansion. There was real money there. Money and position that Christine Sullivan did not deserve. She had won it with her boobs and artfully displayed ass and her trashy mouth that had somehow inspired the elderly Walter Sullivan, awakening some emotion buried deep within his complex depths. In six months he would not miss her anymore. His world of rock-solid wealth and power would hurtle on.

Then it struck her.

Russell was halfway out of the limo before Collin caught her arm. He held up the leather bag she had bought in Georgetown for a hundred bucks and was now worth incalculably more to her. She settled back down in her seat, her breath normalized. She smiled, almost blushed at Collin.

The President, slumped in a semicatatonic state, didn't notice the exchange.

Then Russell peeked inside her bag, just to be sure. Her mouth dropped open, her hands frantically tore through the few contents of the bag. It took all her willpower not to shriek out loud as she stared horror-stricken at the young agent. The letter opener was not there. It must still be in the house.

Collin tore back up the stairs, a thoroughly confused Burton racing after him.

Luther was halfway down the wall when he heard them coming.

Ten more feet.

They burst in the bedroom door.

Six more feet.

Stunned, the two Secret Service men spotted the rope; Burton dove for it.

Two more feet, and Luther let go, hitting the ground running.

Burton flew to the window. Collin threw the

nightstand aside: nothing. He joined Burton at the window. Luther had already disappeared around the corner. Burton started to head out the window. Collin stopped him. The way they had come would be faster.

They bolted out the door.

Luther crashed through the cornfield, no longer concerned with leaving a trail, now only worried about surviving. The bag slowed him down slightly, but he had worked too hard over the last several months to walk away empty-handed.

He exploded out from the friendly cover of the crops and hit the most dangerous phase of his flight: a hundred yards of open field. The moon had disappeared behind thickening clouds and there were no streetlights in the country; in his black clothing he would be almost impossible to spot. But the human eye was best at spotting movement in the darkness, and he was moving as fast as he could.

The two secret service agents stopped momentarily at the van. They emerged with Agent Varney and raced across the field.

Russell rolled down the window and watched them, shock on her face. Even the President was somewhat awake, but she quickly calmed him and he returned to his half-slumber.

Collin and Burton slipped on their night-vision goggles and their view instantly resembled a crude computer game. Thermal images registered in red, everything else was dark green.

Agent Travis Varney, tall and rangy, and only vaguely aware of what was going on, was ahead of them. He ran with the easy motion of the collegiate miler he used to be.

In the Service three years, Varney was single,

committed entirely to his profession, and looked to Burton as a father figure to replace the one killed in Vietnam. They were looking for someone who had done something in that house. Something that involved the President and that therefore involved him. Varney pitied whoever he was chasing if he caught up to him.

Luther could hear the sounds of the men behind him. They had recovered faster than he had thought. His head start had dwindled but it still should be enough. They had made a big mistake by not jumping in the van and running him down. They had to have known he would have transportation. It wasn't like he would have coptered in. But he was grateful that they weren't quite as smart as they probably should have been. If they had he would not be alive to see the sun come up.

He took a shortcut through a path in the woods, spotted on his last walk-through. It gained him about a minute. His breath came in quick bursts, like machine-gun fire. His clothes felt heavy on him; as in a child's dream, his legs seemed to move in slow motion.

Finally he broke free from the trees, and he could see his car and was again grateful for having taken the precaution to back in.

A hundred yards behind, a thermal figure other than Varney's finally came alive on Burton's and Collin's screens. A man running, and running hard. Their hands flew to their shoulder holsters. Neither weapon was effective long-range but they couldn't worry about that now.

Then an engine roared to life and Burton and Collin ran like a tornado was raging at their heels.

Varney was still ahead of them and to the left. He

would have a better line of fire, but would he shoot? Something told them he would not; that was not part of his training, to fire at a fleeing person who was no longer a danger to the man he was sworn to protect. However, Varney did not know that at stake here was more than a mere beating heart. There was an entire institution that would never be the same, in addition to two Secret Service agents who were certain they had done nothing wrong, but were intelligent enough to realize that the blame would fall heavily on their shoulders.

Burton was never much of a runner, but he picked up his pace as these thoughts flew through his head, and the younger Collin was hard-pressed to keep up with him. But Burton knew it was too late. His legs started to slow down as the car exploded out and turned away from them. In moments it was already two hundred yards down the road.

Burton stopped running, dropped to his knee, aimed his gun, but all he could see was the dust kicked up by the fleeing vehicle. Then the taillights went out and in a moment he lost the target entirely.

He turned to see Collin next to him, looking down at him, the reality of the whole event starting to set in. Burton slowly got up and put his gun away. He took off his goggles; Collin did likewise.

They looked at each other.

Burton sucked air in; his limbs shook. His body was finally reacting to the recent exertions now that the adrenaline had stopped flowing. It was over, wasn't it?

Then Varney came running up. Burton was not too distraught to note with an envious twinge and a small measure of pride that the younger man wasn't even out of breath. He would see to it that Varney and Johnson didn't suffer with them. They didn't deserve that.

He and Collin would go down, but that was all. He felt bad about Collin; however, there was nothing he could do about that. But when Varney spoke, Burton's thoughts of the future went from complete and absolute doom to a small glimmer of hope.

"I got the license plate number."

"Where the hell was he?" Russell looked incredulously around the bedroom. "What? Was he under the goddamned bed?"

She tried to stare Burton down. The guy hadn't been under the bed, not in any of the closets. Burton had examined all those spaces when he was sanitizing the room. He told her so in no uncertain terms.

Burton looked at the rope and then the open window. "Jesus, it was like the guy was watching us the whole time, knew right when we left the house." Burton looked around for other possible bogeymen hovering nearby. His eyes rested on the mirror, then moved on, stopped and went back.

He looked down at the carpet in front of the mirror.

He had gone over that area repeatedly with the vacuum until it was smooth; the carpet nape, already plush and expensive, had been a good quarter inch thicker by the time he was finished. No one had walked there since they had come back into the room.

And yet now as he stooped down, his eye discerned very rough traces of footprints. He hadn't noticed them before because now the whole section was matted down, as if something had swept out. . . . He slapped on his gloves, rushed to the mirror, pulling and prying around its edges. He yelled to Collin to get some tools while Russell looked on stunned.

Burton inserted the crowbar about midway down

the side of the mirror and he and Collin threw all their weight against the tool. The lock was not that strong, depending on deception rather than brute strength to safeguard its secrets.

There was a grinding sound and then a tear and a pop and the door swung open.

Burton plunged inside with Collin right behind. A light switch was on the wall. The room turned bright and the men looked around.

Russell peered in, saw the chair. As she looked around, her face froze on the inner side of the mirror door. She was staring right at the bed. The bed where a little while before . . . She rubbed her temples as a searing pain ripped through her skull.

A one-way mirror.

She turned to find Burton looking over her shoulder and through the mirror. His earlier remark about someone watching them had just proven itself prophetic.

Burton looked helplessly at Russell. "He must have been right here the whole time. The whole god-damned time. I can't fucking believe this." Burton looked at the empty shelves inside the vault. "Looks like he took a bunch of stuff. Probably cash and untraceables."

"Who cares about that!" Russell exploded, pointing at the mirror. "This guy saw and heard everything, and you let him get away."

"We got his license plate." Collin was hoping for another rewarding smile. He didn't get it.

"So what? You think he's going to wait around for us to run his tag and go knock on his door?"

Russell sat down on the bed. Her head was spinning. If the guy had been in there he had seen everything. She shook her head. A bad but controllable situation had suddenly become an incomprehensible disaster, and totally out of her control.

Particularly considering the information Collin had relayed to her when she had entered the bedroom.

The sonofabitch had the letter opener! Prints, blood, everything, straight to the White House.

She looked at the mirror and then at the bed, where a short time before she had been on top of the President. She instinctively pulled her jacket tighter around herself. She was suddenly sick to her stomach. She braced herself against the bedpost.

Collin emerged from the vault. "Don't forget he committed a crime being here. He can get in big-time trouble if he goes to the cops." That thought had struck the young agent while he peered around the vault.

He should have thought a little more.

Russell pushed back a strong urge to vomit. "He doesn't have to exactly go and turn himself in to cash in on this. Have you ever heard of the goddamned phone? He's probably calling the *Post* right now, *Dammit!* And then next the tabloids and by the end of the week we'll be watching him on Oprah and Sally being shot on remote from whatever little island he's retired to with his face blurred. And then comes the book and after that the movie. *Shit!*"

Russell envisioned a certain package arriving at the *Post* or the J. Edgar Hoover Building or the U.S. Attorney's office or the Senate Minority Leader's office, all possible depositories promising maximum political damage – not to mention the legal repercussions.

The note accompanying it would ask them to please match the prints on it and the blood with specimens of the President of the United States. It would sound like a joke, but they would do it. Of course they would do it. Richmond's prints were already on file. His DNA would be a match. Her body would be found, her blood would be checked

63

and they would be confronted with more questions than they could possibly have answers to.

They were dead, they were all dead. And that bastard had just been sitting in there, waiting for his chance. Not knowing that tonight would bring him the biggest payoff of his life. Nothing as simple as dollars. He would bring down a President, in flames and tatters, crashing to earth without a chance of survival. How often did someone get to do that? Woodward and Bernstein had become supermen, they could do no wrong. This topped the hell out of Watergate. This was too fucking much to deal with.

Russell barely made it to the bathroom. Burton looked over at the corpse and then back at Collin. They said nothing, their hearts pounding with increased frequency as the absolute enormity of the situation settled down on them like the stone lid of a crypt. Since they could think of nothing else to do, Burton and Collin dutifully retrieved the sanitizing equipment while Russell emptied the contents of her stomach. In an hour they were packed and gone.

The door closed quietly behind him.

Luther figured he had a couple of days at best, maybe less. He risked turning on a light and his eyes went quickly over the interior of the living room.

His life had gone from normal, or close to it, straight to horror land.

He took off the backpack, switched off the light, and stole over to the window.

Nothing – everything was quiet. Fleeing from that house had been the most nerve-racking experience of his life, worse than being overrun by screaming North Koreans. His hands still twitched. All the way back, every passing car seemed to bore its headlights into his face, searching out his guilty secret. Twice, police cars had passed him, and the sweat had poured off his forehead, his breathing constricted.

The car had been returned to the impoundment lot where Luther had "borrowed" it earlier that night. The plate would get them nowhere, but something else could.

He doubted they had gotten a look at him. Even if they had, they would only know generally his height and build. His age, race and facial features would still be a mystery, and without that they had nothing. And as fast as he had run, they probably figured him for a younger man. There was one open end, and he had thought about how to handle that on the ride back. For now, he packed up as much of the last thirty years as he could into two bags; he would not be coming back here.

He would clear out his accounts tomorrow morning; that would give him the resources to run far away from here. He had faced more than his share of danger during his long life. But the choice between going up against the President of the United States or disappearing was a no-brainer. The night's haul was safely hidden away. Three months of work for a prize that could end up getting him killed. He locked the door and disappeared into the night.

FOUR

At seven A.M. the gold-colored elevator doors opened, and Jack stepped into the meticulously decorated expanse that was Patton, Shaw's reception area.

Lucinda wasn't in yet, so the main reception desk, solid teakwood and weighing about a thousand pounds, and costing about twenty dollars for each of those pounds, was unmanned.

He walked down the broad hallways under the soft lights of the neoclassical wall sconces, turned right, and then left and in one minute opened the solid-oak door to his office. In the background, a smattering of ringing phones could be heard as the city woke up for business.

Six floors, well over one hundred thousand square feet in one of the best addresses downtown, housing over two hundred highly compensated attorneys, with a two-story library, fully equipped gymnasium, sauna, women's and men's showers and lockers, ten conference rooms, a supporting staff of several hundred and, most important, a client list coveted by every other major firm in the country, that was the empire of Patton, Shaw & Lord.

The firm had weathered the miserable end to the 1980s, and then picked up speed after the recession had finally subsided. Now it was going full-bore as many of its competitors had downsized. It was loaded with some of the best attorneys in virtually every field of law, or at least the fields that paid best. Many had been scooped from other leading firms, enticed by signing bonuses and promises that no dollar would be spared when chasing a new piece of business.

Three senior partners had been tapped by the current administration for top-level positions. The firm had awarded them severance pay in excess of two million dollars each, with the implicit understanding that after their government stint they would be back in harness, bringing with them tens of millions of dollars in legal business from their newly forged contacts.

The firm's unwritten, but strictly adhered to, rule was that no new client matter would be accepted unless the minimum billing would exceed one hundred thousand dollars. Anything less, the management committee had decided, would be a waste of the firm's time. And they had no problem sticking to that rule, and flourishing. In the nation's capital, people came for the best and they didn't mind paying for the privilege.

The firm had only made one exception to that rule, and ironically it had been for the only client Jack had other than Baldwin. He told himself he would test that rule with increasing frequency. If he was going to stick this out, he wanted it to be on his terms as much as that was possible. He knew his victories would be small at first, but that was okay.

He sat down at his desk, opened his cup of coffee and glanced over the *Post*. Patton, Shaw & Lord had five kitchens and three full-time housekeepers with their own computers. The firm probably consumed five hundred pots of coffee a day, but Jack picked up his morning brew at the little place on the corner because he couldn't stand the stuff they used here. It was a special imported blend and cost a fortune and tasted like dirt mixed in with seaweed.

He tipped back in his chair and glanced around his

67

office. It was a good size by big-firm associate standards, about fourteen by fourteen, with a nice view up Connecticut Avenue.

At the Public Defenders Service, Jack had shared an office with another attorney and there had been no window, only a giant poster of a Hawaiian beach Jack had tacked up one repulsively cold morning. Jack had liked the coffee at PD better.

When he made partner he would get a new office, twice this size – maybe not a corner just yet, but that was definitely in the cards. With the Baldwin account he was the fourth biggest rainmaker in the firm, and the top three were all in their fifties and sixties, looking more toward the golf courses than to the inside of an office. He glanced at his watch. Time to start the meter.

He was usually one of the first ones in, but the place would soon be stirring. Patton, Shaw matched top New York firm wages, and for the big bucks, they expected big-time efforts. The clients were enormous and their legal demands were of equal size. Making a mistake in this league might mean a four-billion-dollar defense contract went down the tubes or a city declared bankruptcy.

Every associate and junior partner he knew at the firm had stomach problems; a quarter of them were in therapy of one kind or another. Jack watched their pale faces and softening bodies as they marched daily through the pristine hallways of PS&L bearing yet another Herculean legal task. That was the trade-off for compensation levels that put them in the top five percent nationwide among all professionals.

He alone among them was safe from the partnership gauntlet. Control of clients was the great equalizer in law. He had been with Patton, Shaw about a year, was a novice corporate attorney, and was accorded the respect of the most senior and experienced members of the firm.

All of that should have made him feel guilty, undeserving – and it would have if he hadn't been so miserable about the rest of his life.

He popped the final miniature doughnut into his mouth, leaned forward in his chair and opened a file. Corporate work was often monotonous and his skill level was such that his tasks were not the most exciting in the world. Reviewing ground leases, preparing UCC filings, forming limited liability companies, drafting memorandums of understanding and private placement documents, it was all in a day's work, and the days were growing longer and longer, but he was learning fast; he had to in order to survive. His courtroom skills were virtually useless to him here.

The firm traditionally did no litigation work, preferring instead to handle the more lucrative and steady corporate and tax matters. When litigation did arise it was farmed out to select, elite litigation-only firms, who in turn would refer any nontrial work that came their way to Patton, Shaw. It was an arrangement that had worked well over the years.

By lunchtime he had moved two stacks of drift from his in to his out basket, dictated three closing checklists and a couple of letters, and received four calls from Jennifer reminding him about the White House dinner they would be attending that night.

Her father was being honored as Businessman of the Year by some organization or other. It spoke volumes about the President's close nexus to big business that such an event would be worthy of a White House function. But at least Jack would get to see the man up close. Getting to meet him was probably out of the question, but then you never knew.

"Got a minute?" Barry Alvis popped his balding

head in the door. He was a senior staff associate, meaning he had been passed over for partner more than three times and in fact would never successfully complete that next step. Hardworking and bright, he was an attorney any firm would be fortunate to have. His schmooz skills and hence his client-generating prospects, however, were nil. He made a hundred sixty thousand a year, and worked hard enough to earn another twenty in bonuses each year. His wife didn't work, his kids went to private schools, he drove a late-model Beemer, was not expected to generate business and had little to complain about.

A very experienced attorney with ten years of intense and high-level transactional work behind him, he should have resented the hell out of Jack Graham, and he did.

Jack waved him in. He knew Alvis didn't like him, understood why, and didn't push it. He could take his lumps with the best of them, but then he would only allow himself to be pushed so far.

"Jack, we've got to get cranking on the Bishop merger."

Jack looked blank. That deal, a real pain in the ass, had died, or at least he thought it had. He took out a legal pad, his hands twitching.

"I thought Raymond Bishop didn't want to get into bed with TCC."

Alvis sat down, placed the fourteen-inch file he was carrying on Jack's desk and leaned back.

"Deals die, then they come back to haunt you. We need your comments on the secondary financing documents by tomorrow afternoon."

Jack almost dropped his pen. "That's fourteen agreements and over five hundred pages, Barry. When did you find out about this?"

Alvis stood up and Jack caught the beginnings of a smile tugging at the other man's face.

"Fifteen agreements, and the official page count is six hundred and thirteen pages, single-spaced, not counting exhibits. Thanks, Jack. Patton, Shaw really appreciates it." He turned back. "Oh, have a great time with the President tonight, and say hello to Ms. Baldwin."

Alvis walked out.

Jack looked at the bundle in front of him and rubbed his temples. He wondered when the little sonofabitch had really learned the Bishop deal had been resurrected. Something told him it wasn't this morning.

He checked the time. He buzzed his secretary, managed to clear his schedule for the rest of the day, picked up the eight-pound file and headed for conference room number nine, the firm's smallest and most secluded, where he could hide and work. He could do six intense hours, go to the party, come back, work all night, hit the steam room, shower and shave here, finish up the comments and have them on Alvis's desk by three, four at the latest. The little shit.

Six agreements later, Jack ate the last of his chips, finished off his Coke, pulled on his jacket and ran the ten flights down to the lobby.

The cab dropped him at his apartment. He stopped cold.

The Jag was parked in front of his building. The vanity plate SUCCESS told him his soon-to-be date for life was up there waiting. She must be upset with him. She never condescended to come to his place unless she was upset with him about something and wanted to let him know it.

He checked his watch. He was running a little late, but he was still okay. He unlocked his front door, rubbing his jaw; maybe he could get by without shaving. She was sitting on the couch, having first draped a sheet across it. He had to admit, she looked stunning; a real blue blood, whatever that meant these days. Unsmiling, she stood up and looked at him.

"You're late."

"I'm not my own boss you know."

"That's no excuse. I work too."

"Yeah, but the difference is your boss has the same last name, and is wrapped around his daughter's pretty little finger."

"Mother and Dad went on ahead. The limo will be here in twenty minutes."

"Plenty of time." Jack undressed and jumped in the shower. He pulled the curtain aside. "Jenn, can you get out my blue double-breasted?"

She walked into the bathroom, looked around in ill-concealed disgust. "The invitation said black tie."

"Black tie optional," he corrected her, rubbing the soap out of his eyes.

"Jack, don't do this. It's the White House for godsakes, it's the President."

"They give you an option, black tie or not. I'm exercising my right to forgo the black tie. Besides, I don't have a tux." He grinned at her and pulled the curtain closed.

"You were supposed to get one."

"I forgot. C'mon, Jenn, for chrissakes. Nobody's going to be watching me, nobody cares what I'll be wearing."

"Thank you, thank you very much, Jack Graham. I ask you to do one little thing."

"Do you know how much those suckers cost?"

The soap was stinging his eyes. He thought of Barry Alvis and having to work all night and having to explain that fact to Jennifer and then to her father, and his voice got angrier. "And how many times am I going to wear the goddamned thing? Once or twice a year?"

"After we're married we'll be attending a lot of

functions where black tie isn't optional, it's mandatory. It's a good investment."

"I'd rather put my retirement funds into baseball cards." He poked his head out again to show her he was kidding, but she wasn't there.

He rubbed a towel through his hair, wrapped it around his middle and walked into the tiny bedroom where he found a new tux hanging on the door. Jennifer appeared, smiling.

"Compliments of Baldwin Enterprises. It's an Armani. It'll look wonderful on you."

"How'd you know my size?"

"You're a perfect forty-two long. You could be a model. Jennifer Baldwin's personal male model." She wrapped her perfumed arms around his shoulders and squeezed. He felt her considerable breasts push into his back and inwardly cursed that there wasn't time to take advantage of the moment. Just once without the goddamn murals, without the cherubs and chariots, maybe it would be different.

He looked longingly at the small, untidy bed. And he had to work all night. Goddamned Barry Alvis and the wishy-washy Raymond Bishop.

Why was it every time he saw Jennifer Baldwin he hoped that things could be different between them? Different meaning better. That she would change, or he would, or they both would meet somewhere in the middle? She was so beautiful, had everything in the world going for her. Jesus, what was wrong with him anyway?

The limo moved easily through the dregs of post-rush-hour traffic. Past seven o'clock on a weeknight, downtown D.C. was pretty much deserted.

Jack looked over at his fiancée. Her light but very expensive coat didn't conceal the plunging neckline. The perfectly chiseled features were covered by flawless skin that occasionally flashed a perfect smile. Her thick auburn hair was piled high on top of her head; she usually wore it down. She looked like one of those one-name supermodels.

He moved closer to her. She smiled at him, checked her makeup, which was immaculate, and patted his hand.

He stroked her leg, slid her dress up; she pushed him away.

"Later, maybe," she whispered so the driver wouldn't hear.

Jack smiled and mouthed that later he might have a headache. She laughed and then he remembered there would be no "later" tonight.

He slumped back in the thickly padded seat and stared out the window. He had never been to the White House; Jennifer had, twice before. She didn't look nervous; he was. He tugged at his bow tie, and smoothed his hair as they turned onto Executive Drive.

The White House guards checked them methodically; Jennifer as usual got second and third looks from all of the men and women present. When she bent down to adjust her high heel, she almost spilled out of her five-thousand-dollar dress and made several White House staffers far happier men for it. Jack got the usual envious looks from the guys. Then they moved into the building and presented their engraved invitations to the Marine sergeant who escorted them through the lower-level entry corridor and then up the stairs to the East Room.

"Dammit!" The President had bent down to pick up a copy of his speech for the night's event and the pain had shot up to his shoulder. "I think it nicked a tendon, Gloria."

Gloria Russell sat in one of the wide, plush chairs

with which the President's wife had decorated the Oval Office.

The First Lady had good taste if not a lot else. She was nice to look at, but a little light in the intellect department. No challenge to the President's power, and an asset in the polls.

Her family background was impeccable: old money, old ties. The President's connection to the conservative wealth and influence segment of the country had not hurt his standing with the liberal contingent in the least, however, owing mainly to his charisma and skills at consensus-building. And his good looks, which counted for a lot more than anyone cared to admit.

A successful President had to be able to talk a good game, and this President's batting average was up there with Ted Williams's.

"I think I need to see a doctor." The President was not in the best of moods, but then neither was Russell.

"Well, Alan, then exactly how would you explain a stab wound to the White House press?"

"What the hell ever happened to doctor-patient confidentiality?"

Russell rolled her eyes. He could be so stupid sometimes.

"You're like a Fortune 500 company, Alan, everything about you is public information."

"Well, not everything."

"That remains to be seen, doesn't it? This is far from over, Alan." Russell had smoked three packs of cigarettes, and drunk two pots of coffee since last night. At any moment their world, her career, could come crashing down. The police knocking on the door. It was all she could do to keep herself from running screaming from the room. As it was, nausea continuously swept over her in vast waves. She clenched her teeth, gripped the chair. The image of total destruction would not budge from her mind.

The President scanned the copy, memorizing some, the rest he would ad-lib; his memory was phenomenal, an asset that had served him well.

"That's why I have you, Gloria, isn't it? To make it all better?"

He looked at her.

For a moment she wondered if he knew. If he knew what she had done with him. Her body stiffened and then relaxed. He couldn't know, that was impossible. She remembered his drunken pleadings; oh how a bottle of Jack could change a person.

"Of course it is, Alan, but some decisions have to be made. Some alternative strategies have to be developed depending on what we find ourselves faced with."

"I can't exactly cancel my schedule. Besides, this guy can't do anything."

Russell shook her head. "We can't be sure of that."

"Think about it! He'll have to admit to burglary to even place himself there. Can you see him trying to get on the evening news with that story? They'll put him in a rubber room in a New York minute." The President shook his head. "I'm safe. This guy cannot touch me, Gloria. Not in a million years."

They had worked out a threshold strategy on the limo ride back to town. Their position would be simple: categorical denial. They would let the absurdity of the allegation, if it ever came, do their work for them. And it was an absurd story despite the fact that it was absolutely true. Sympathy from the White House for the poor, unbalanced and admitted felon and his shamefaced family.

There was, of course, another possibility, but Russell had chosen not to address that with the

President just yet. In fact she concluded it was the more likely scenario. It was really the only thing allowing her to function.

"Stranger things have happened." She looked at him.

"The place was cleaned, right? There's nothing left to find, right, except her?" There was a hint of nervousness in his voice.

"Right." Russell licked her lips. The President didn't know that the letter opener with his prints and blood on it was now in the possession of their felonious eyewitness.

She stood up and paced. "Of course I can't speak about certain traces of sexual contact. But that wouldn't be linked to you in any event."

"Jesus, I can't even remember if we did it or not. It seems like I did."

She couldn't help smiling at his remark.

The President turned and looked at her. "What about Burton and Collin?"

"What about them?"

"Have you talked to them?" His message was clear enough.

"They have as much to lose as you, don't they, Alan?"

"As *us*, Gloria, as us." He fixed his tie in the mirror. "Any clue to the Peeping Tom?"

"Not yet; they're running the plate."

"When do you think they'll realize she's missing?"

"As warm as it's been during the day, soon I hope."

"Real funny, Gloria."

"She'll be missed, inquiries will be made. Her husband will be called, they'll go to the house. The next day, maybe two, maybe three tops."

"And then the police will investigate."

"There's nothing we can do about that."

"But you'll keep on top of it?" A trace of concern

crossed the President's brow as he thought swiftly through various scenarios. *Had he fucked Christy Sullivan? He hoped that he had. At least the night wouldn't have been a total disaster.*

"As much as we can without arousing too much suspicion."

"That's easy enough. You can use the angle that Walter Sullivan is a close friend and political ally of mine. It would be natural for me to have a personal interest in the case. Think things through, Gloria, that's what I pay you for."

And you were sleeping with his wife, Russell thought. *Some friend.*

"That rationale had already occurred to me, Alan."

She lit a cigarette, blew the smoke out slowly. That felt good. She had to keep ahead of him on this. Just one small step ahead and she would be fine. It wouldn't be easy; he was sharp, but he was also arrogant. Arrogant people habitually overestimated their own abilities and underestimated everyone else's.

"And nobody knew she was meeting you?"

"I think we can assume she was discreet, Gloria. Christy didn't have too much upstairs, her gifts were slightly lower, but she understood economics with the best of them." The President winked at his Chief of Staff. "She had about eight hundred million to lose if her husband found out she was screwing around, even with the President."

Russell knew about Walter Sullivan's odd viewing habits from the mirror and chair, but then again, for the assignations he didn't know about, didn't get to watch, who knew what his reaction would've been? Thank God it hadn't been Sullivan sitting there in the dark.

"I warned you, Alan, that one day your little extracurricular activities would get us into trouble."

Richmond looked at her, disappointment on his features. "Listen, you think I'm the first guy to hold this office to catch a little action on the side? Don't be so goddamned naive, Gloria. At least I'm a helluva lot more discreet than some of my predecessors. I take the responsibilities of the job . . . and I take the perks. Understand?"

Russell nervously rubbed at her neck. "Completely, Mr. President."

"So it's just this one guy, who can't do anything."

"It only takes one to bring the house of cards tumbling down."

"Yeah? Well there are a lot of people living in that house. Just remember that."

"I do, Chief, every day."

There was a knock at the door. Russell's deputy assistant leaned in. "Five minutes, sir." The President nodded and waved him off.

"Great timing on this presentation."

"Ransome Baldwin contributed heavily to your campaign, as did all of his friends."

"You don't have to explain political paybacks to me, sweetheart."

Russell stood up and moved over to him. She took his good arm, looked intently at him. On his left cheek was a small scar. A souvenir from some shrapnel during a brief stint in the Army toward the end of the Vietnam War. As his political career had taken off, the female consensus was that the tiny imperfection greatly enhanced his attractiveness. Russell found herself staring at that scar.

"Alan, I will do whatever it takes to protect your interest. You will get through this, but we need to work together. We're a team, Alan, we're a helluva team. They can't take us down, not if we act together."

The President studied her face for a brief moment,

and then rewarded her with the smile that routinely accompanied front-page headlines. He pecked her on the cheek, squeezed her against him; she clung to him.

"I love you, Gloria. You're a trouper." He picked up his speech. "It's showtime." He turned and walked out. Russell stared after his broad back, carefully rubbed at her cheek and then followed him out.

Jack looked around the overstated elegance of the immense East Room. The place was full of some of the most powerful men and women in the country. Skillful networking was taking place all around him, and all he could do was stand and gawk. He looked across the room and spied his fiancée cornering a congressman from some state out West, no doubt plying Baldwin Enterprises's needy case for the good legislator's assistance on riparian rights.

His fiancée spent much of her time gaining access to holders of power at all levels. From county commissioners to Senate Committee chairmen, Jennifer stroked the right egos, fed the right hands, and made certain that all the important players were in place when Baldwin Enterprises wanted another mammoth deal orchestrated. The doubling of the assets of her father's company during the last five years was due in no small part to her excelling at that task. In truth, what man was really safe from her?

Ransome Baldwin, all six feet five inches, thick white hair and baritone voice, made his rounds, solidly shaking hands with politicians he already owned and rubbing elbows with the few he didn't as yet.

The award ceremony had been mercifully brief. Jack glanced at his watch. He would need to be getting back to the office soon. On the way over Jennifer had mentioned a private party at the Willard Hotel at eleven. He rubbed his face. Of all the friggin' luck.

He was about to pull Jennifer aside to explain his early exit, when the President walked up to her, was joined by her father, and a moment later all three headed his way.

Jack put his drink down and cleared his throat so he wouldn't sound like a complete fool when the words stumbled out of his mouth. Jennifer and her father were talking to the President like old friends. Laughing, chatting, touching elbows like he was Cousin Ned in from Oklahoma. But this wasn't Cousin Ned, this was the President of the United States for godsakes!

"So you're the lucky fellow?" The President's smile was immediate and pleasant. They shook hands. He was as tall as Jack, and Jack admired that he had kept trim and fit with a job like his.

"Jack Graham, Mr. President. It's an honor to meet you, sir."

"I feel like I already know you, Jack, Jennifer's told me so much about you. Most of it good." He grinned.

"Jack's a partner at Patton, Shaw & Lord." Jennifer still held on to the President's arm. She looked at Jack and smiled a cutesy smile.

"Well, not a partner yet, Jenn."

"Matter of time is all." Ransome Baldwin's voice boomed out. "With Baldwin Enterprises as a client, you could name your price at any firm in this country. Don't you forget that. Don't let Sandy Lord pull the wool over your eyes."

"Listen to him, Jack. The voice of experience." The President raised his glass and then involuntarily jerked it back. Jennifer stumbled, letting go of his arm.

81

"I'm sorry, Jennifer. Too much tennis. Damn arm's giving me problems again. Well, Ransome, you look like you've got yourself a fine protégé here."

"Hell, he'll have to fight my daughter for the empire. Maybe Jack can be queen and Jenn can be the king. How's that for equal rights?" Ransome laughed a big laugh that swept everybody up with it.

Jack felt himself redden. "I'm just a lawyer, Ransome; I'm not necessarily looking for an empty throne to occupy. There are other things to do in life."

Jack picked up his drink. This wasn't exactly going as well as he would have liked. He felt on the defensive. Jack crunched an ice cube. And what did Ransome Baldwin really think about his future son-in-law? Especially right now? The point was Jack didn't really care.

Ransome stopped laughing and eyed him steadily. Jennifer cocked her head the way she did when he said something she thought was inappropriate, which was most of the time. The President looked at all three of them, smiled quickly and excused himself. He went over to the corner where a woman was standing.

Jack watched him go. He had seen the woman on TV, defending the President's position on a myriad of issues. Gloria Russell did not look very happy right now, but with all the crises in the world, happiness was probably a rare commodity in her line of work.

That was an afterthought. Jack had met the President, had shaken hands with him. He hoped his arm got better. He pulled Jennifer aside and made his regrets. She was not pleased.

"This is totally unacceptable, Jack. Do you realize how special a night this is for Daddy?"

82

"Hey, I'm just a working stiff. You know? Billable hours?"

"That's ridiculous! And you know it. No one at that firm can make those demands of you, let alone some nothing associate."

"Jenn, it's not that big a deal. I had a great time. Your dad got his little award. Now it's time to go back to work. Alvis is okay. He's kicking my butt a little bit, but he works just as hard, if not harder than I do. Everybody has to take their lumps."

"This isn't fair, Jack. This is not convenient for me."

"Jenn, it's my job. I said don't worry about it, so don't worry about it. I'll see you tomorrow. I'm gonna grab a cab back."

"Daddy will be very disappointed."

"Daddy won't even miss me. Hey, hoist one for me. And remember what you said about later? I'll take a rain check on that. Maybe we can make it my place for a change?"

She allowed herself to be kissed. But when Jack was gone she stormed over to her father.

FIVE

Kate Whitney pulled into the parking lot of her building. The grocery bag clunked against one leg, her overflowing briefcase against the other as she jogged up the four flights of stairs. Buildings in her price range had elevators, just not ones that worked on a consistent basis.

She changed quickly into her running outfit, checked her messages, and headed back out. She stretched the cramps and kinks out of her long limbs in front of the Ulysses S. Grant statue and started her run.

She headed west, past the Air and Space Museum, and then by the Smithsonian castle that, with its towers and battlements and twelfth-century-style Italian architecture, looked more like a mad scientist's home than anything else. Her easy, methodical strides took her across the Mall at its widest point and she circled the Washington Monument twice.

Her breath was coming a little quicker now; the sweat began to seep through her T-shirt and blot the Georgetown Law sweatshirt she was wearing. As she made her way along the fringes of the Tidal Basin, the crowds of people grew thicker. The early fall brought plane-, bus- and carloads of people from across the country hoping to miss the summer crush of tourists and the infamous Washington heat.

As she swerved to avoid one errant child she collided with another runner coming the other way. They went down in a tangle of arms and legs.

"Shit." The man rolled over quickly and then sprang back up. She started to get up, looked at him, an apology on her lips, and then abruptly sat back down. A long moment went by as camera-toting clans of Arkansans and Iowans danced around them.

"Hello, Kate." Jack gave her a hand up and helped her to a spot under one of the now bare cherry blossom trees that encircled the Tidal Basin. The Jefferson Memorial sat big and imposing across the calm water, the tall silhouette of the country's third President clearly visible inside the rotunda.

Kate's ankle was starting to swell. She took off her shoe and sock and began to rub it out.

"I didn't think you'd have time to run anymore, Jack."

She looked over at him: no receding hairline, no paunch, no lines on the face. Time had stood still for Jack Graham. She had to admit it, he looked great. She, on the other hand, was an absolute and total disaster.

She silently cursed herself for not getting that haircut and then cursed herself again for even thinking that. A drop of sweat plunged down her nose, and she brushed it away with an irritable swipe of her hand.

"I was wondering the same thing about you. I didn't think they let prosecutors go home before midnight. Slacking off?"

"Right." She rubbed her ankle, which really hurt. He saw the pain, leaned over and took her foot in his hands. She flinched back. He looked at her.

"Remember I used to almost do this for a living and you were my best and only client. I have never seen a woman with such fragile ankles, and the rest of you looks so healthy."

She relaxed and let him work the ankle and then the foot, and she soon realized he had not lost his touch. Did he mean that about looking healthy? She frowned. After all, she had dumped him. And she had been absolutely right in doing so. Hadn't she?

"I heard about Patton, Shaw. Congratulations."

"Aw shucks. Any lawyer with millions in legal business could've done the same thing." He smiled.

"Yeah, I read about the engagement in the paper too. Congratulations twice." He didn't smile at that one. She wondered why not.

He quietly put her sock and shoe back on. He looked at her. "You're not going to be able to run for a day or two, it's pretty swollen. My car's right over there. I'll give you a lift."

"I'll just take a cab."

"You trust a D.C. cabbie over me?" He feigned offense. "Besides, I don't see any pockets. You going to negotiate a free ride? Good luck."

She looked down at her shorts. Her key was in her sock. He had already eyed the bulge. He smiled at her dilemma. Her lips pressed together, her tongue slid along the bottom one. He remembered that habit from long ago. Although he hadn't seen it for years, it suddenly seemed like he had never been away.

He stretched out his legs and stood up. "I'd float you a loan, but I'm busted too."

She got up, put an arm against his shoulder as she tested the ankle.

"I thought private practice paid better than that."

"It does, I've just never been able to handle money. You know that." That was true enough; she had always balanced the checkbook. Not that there was much to balance back then.

He held on to one of her arms as she limped to his car, a ten-year-old Subaru wagon. She looked at it amazed.

"You never got rid of this thing?"

"Hey, there's a lot of miles left on it. Besides, it's

full of history. See that stain right over there? Your Dairy Queen butterscotch-dipped ice cream cone, 1986, the night before my tax final. You couldn't sleep, and I wouldn't study anymore. You remember? You took that curve too fast."

"You have a bad case of selective memory. As I recall you poured your milkshake down my back because I was complaining about the heat."

"Oh, that too." They laughed and got in the car.

She examined the stain more closely, looked around the interior. So much coming back to her in big, lumpy waves. She glanced at the back seat. Her eyebrows went up. If that space could only talk. She turned back to see him looking at her, and found herself blushing.

They pulled off into the light traffic and headed east. Kate felt nervous, but not uncomfortable, as if it were four years ago and they had merely jumped in the car to get some coffee or the paper or have breakfast at the Corner in Charlottesville or at one of the cafés sprinkled around Capitol Hill. But that was years ago, she had to remind herself. That was not the present. The present was very different. She rolled the window down slightly.

Jack kept one eye on traffic, and one eye on her. Their meeting hadn't been accidental. She had run on the Mall, that very route in fact, since they had moved to D.C. and lived in that little walk-up in Southeast near Eastern Market.

That morning Jack had woken up with a desperation he had not felt since Kate had left him four years ago when it dawned on him about a week after she had gone that she wasn't coming back. Now with his wedding looming ahead, he had decided that he had to see Kate, somehow. He would not, could not, let that light die out, not yet. It was quite likely that he was the only one of the two who sensed any illumination left. And while he might not have the courage to leave a message on her answering machine, he had decided that if he was meant to find her out here on the Mall amidst all the tourists and locals, then he would. He had let it go at that.

Until their collision, he had been running for an hour, scanning the crowds, looking for the face in that framed photo. He had spotted her about five minutes before their abrupt meeting. If his heart rate hadn't already doubled because of the exercise, it would've hit that mark as soon as he saw her moving effortlessly along. He hadn't meant to sprain her ankle, but then that was why she was sitting in his car; it was the reason he was driving her home.

Kate pulled her hair back and tied it in a ponytail, using a braid that had been on her wrist. "So how's work going?"

"Okay." He did not want to talk about work. "How's your old man?"

"You'd know better than me." She did not want to talk about her father.

"I haven't seen him since . . ."

"Lucky you." She lapsed into silence.

Jack shook his head at the stupidity of bringing up Luther. He had hoped for a reconciliation between father and daughter over the years. That obviously had not happened.

"I hear great things about you over at the Commonwealth's Attorney."

"Right."

"I'm serious."

"Since when."

"Everyone grows up, Kate."

"Not Jack Graham. Please, God, no."

He turned right onto Constitution, and made his way toward Union Station. Then he caught himself.

He knew which direction to go, a fact he did not want to share with her. "I'm kind of rambling here, Kate. Which way?"

"I'm sorry. Around the Capitol, over to Maryland and left on 3rd Street."

"You like that area?"

"On my salary, I like it just fine. Let me guess. You're probably in Georgetown, right, one of those big federal townhouses with maid's quarters, right?"

He shrugged. "I haven't moved. I'm in the same place."

She stared at him. "Jack, what do you do with all of your money?"

"I buy what I want; I just don't want that much." He stared back. "Hey, how about a Dairy Queen butterscotch-dipped ice cream cone?"

"There's none to be had in this town, I've tried." He did a U-turn, grinned at the honkers, and roared off.

"Apparently, counselor, you didn't try hard enough."

Thirty minutes later he pulled into her parking lot. He ran around to help her out. The ankle had stiffened a little more. The butterscotch cone was almost gone.

"I'll help you up."

"You don't have to."

"I busted your ankle. Help me relieve some of my guilt."

"I've got it, Jack." That tone was very familiar to him, even after four years. He smiled wearily and stepped back. She was halfway up the stairs, moving slowly. He was getting back in his car when she turned around.

"Jack?" He looked up. "Thanks for the ice cream." She went into the building.

Driving off, Jack did not see the man standing near the little cluster of trees at the entrance to the parking lot.

Luther emerged from the shadows of the trees and looked up at the apartment building.

His appearance from two days ago had drastically changed. It was lucky his beard grew fast. His hair had been cut very short, and a hat covered what was left. Sunglasses obscured his intense eyes and a bulky overcoat concealed the lean body.

He had hoped to see her one more time before he left. He had been shocked to see Jack, but that was all right. He liked Jack.

He huddled in his coat. The wind was picking up, and the chill was more than Washington usually carried at this time of year. He stared up at his daughter's apartment window.

Apartment number fourteen. He knew it well; had even been inside it on a number of occasions, unbeknownst to his daughter, of course. The standard front-door lock was child's play for him. It would've taken longer for someone with a key to open it. He would sit in the chair in her living room and look around at a hundred different things, all of them carrying years of memories, some good times, but mostly disappointments.

Sometimes he would just close his eyes and examine all the different scents in the air. He knew what perfume she wore – very little and very non-descript. Her furniture was big, solid and well-worn. Her refrigerator was routinely empty. He cringed when he viewed the meager and unhealthy contents of her cabinets. She kept things neat, but not perfect; the place looked lived in as it should have.

And she got a lot of calls. He would listen to some of them leaving messages. They made him wish she had picked a different line of work. Being a criminal himself, he was well aware of the number of real crazy bastards out there. But it was too late for him to recommend a career change to his only child.

He knew that it was a strange relationship to have with one's offspring, but Luther figured that was about all he deserved. A vision of his wife entered his mind; a woman who had loved him and stood by him all those years and for what? For pain and misery. And then an early death after she had arrived at her senses and divorced him. He wondered again, for the hundredth time, why he had continued his criminal activities. It certainly wasn't the money. He had always lived simply; much of the proceeds of his burglaries had been simply given away. His choice in life had driven his wife mad with worry and forced his daughter from his life. And for the hundredth time he came away with no compelling answer to the question of why he continued to steal from the well-protected wealthy. Perhaps it was only to show that he could.

He looked up once again at his daughter's apartment. He hadn't been there for her, why should she be there for him? But he could not sever the bond entirely, even if she had. He would be there for her if she so desired, but he knew that she never would.

Luther moved quickly down the street, finally running to catch a Metro bus heading toward the subway at Union Station. He had always been the most independent of people, never relying to any significant degree on anyone else. He was a loner and had liked that. Now, Luther felt very alone, and the feeling this time was not so comforting.

The rain started and he stared out the back window of the bus as it meandered its way to the great rail terminus, which had been saved from extinction by an ambitious railway-shopping mall renovation. The water bubbled up on the smooth surface of the window and clouded his view of where he had just been. He wished he could, but he couldn't go back there now.

He turned back in his seat, pulled his hat down tighter, blew into his handkerchief. He picked up a discarded newspaper, glancing down its old headlines. He wondered when they would find her. When they did, he would know about it immediately; everyone in this town would know that Christine Sullivan was dead. When rich people got themselves killed, it was front-page news. Poor people and Joe Average were stuck in the Metro section. Christy Sullivan would most certainly be on page one, front and center.

He dropped the paper on the floor, hunched down in his seat. He needed to see a lawyer, and then he would be gone. The bus droned on, and his eyes finally closed, but he wasn't sleeping. He was, for the moment, sitting in his daughter's living room, and this time, she was there with him.

SIX

Luther sat at the small conference room table in the very plainly furnished room. The chairs and table were old and carried a thousand scrapes. The rug was just as ancient and not very clean. A card holder was the only thing on the table other than his file. He picked up one of the cards and thumbed it. "Legal Services, Inc." These people weren't the best in the business; they were far from the halls of power downtown. Graduates of third-rate law schools with no shot at the traditional firm practice, they eked out their professional existence hoping for some luck down the road. But their dreams of big offices, big clients and, most important, big money faded a little more with the passage of each year. But Luther did not require the best. He only required somebody with a law degree and the right forms.

"Everything is in order, Mr. Whitney." The kid looked about twenty-five, still full of hope and energy. This place was not his final destination. He still clearly believed that. The tired, pinched, flabby face of the older man behind him held out no such hope. "This is Jerry Burns, the managing attorney, he'll be the other witness to your will. We have a self-proving affidavit, so we won't have to appear in court as to whether or not we witnessed your will." A stern-looking, forty-something woman appeared with her pen and notary seal. "Phyllis here is our notary, Mr. Whitney." They all sat down. "Would you like me to read the terms of your will out to you?"

Jerry Burns had been sitting at the table looking bored to death, staring into space, dreaming of all the other places he would rather be. Jerry Burns, managing attorney. He looked like he would rather be shoveling cow manure on some farm in the Midwest. Now he glanced at his young colleague with disdain.

"I've read it," Luther replied.

"Fine," said Jerry Burns. "Why don't we get started?"

Fifteen minutes later Luther emerged from Legal Services, Inc., with two original copies of his last will and testament tucked in his coat pocket.

Fucking lawyers, couldn't piss, shit or die without them. That was because lawyers made all the laws. They had the rest of them by the balls. Then he thought of Jack and smiled. Jack was not like that. Jack was different. Then he thought of his daughter and his smile faded. Kate was not like that either. But then Kate hated him.

He stopped at a camera shop and purchased a Polaroid OneStep camera and a pack of film. He didn't plan to let anyone else develop the pictures he was going to be taking. He arrived back at the hotel. An hour later he had taken a total of ten photos. These were wrapped in paper and placed in a manila folder that was then secreted far down into his backpack.

He sat down and looked out the window. It was almost an hour before he finally moved, sliding over and then collapsing onto the bed. Some tough guy he was. Not so indifferent that he could not flinch at death, not be horrified by an event that had ripped the life out of someone who should've lived a lot longer. And on top of it all was the fact that the President of the United States was involved in all of it. A man Luther had respected, had voted for. A man who held the country's highest office had almost murdered a woman with his own drunken hands. If he had seen his closest relative bludgeon someone in cold blood, Luther would not have been any more sickened or shocked. It was as though Luther himself had been invaded, as though those murderous hands had been around his throat.

But something else gripped at him; something he could not confront. He turned his face to the pillow, closed his eyes in a futile effort to sleep.

"It's great, Jenn." Jack looked at the brick and stone mansion that stretched more than two hundred feet from end to end and had more rooms than a college dorm, and wondered why they were even there. The winding driveway ended in a four-car garage behind the massive structure. The lawns were groomed so perfectly that Jack felt he was staring at an enormous jade pool. The rear grounds were triple-terraced, with each terrace sporting its own pool. It had the standard accoutrements of the very wealthy: tennis courts and stables, and twenty acres – a veritable land empire by Northern Virginia standards – on which to roam.

The realtor waited by the front door, her late-model Mercedes parked by the large stone fountain covered with fist-size roses carved out of granite. Commission dollars were being swiftly calculated and recalculated. Weren't they a terrific young couple? She had said that enough to where Jack's temples throbbed.

Jennifer Baldwin took his arm and two hours later their tour was finished. Jack walked over to the edge of the broad lawn and admired the thick woods, where an eclectic grouping of elm, spruce, maple, pine and oak jostled for dominance. The leaves were beginning to turn and Jack observed the beginnings of reds, yellows and oranges dance across the face of the property they were considering.

"So how much?" He felt he was entitled to ask that question. But this had to be out of their ballpark. His ballpark anyway. He had to admit it was convenient. Only forty-five rush-hour minutes from his office. But they couldn't touch this place. He looked expectantly at his fiancée.

She looked nervous, played with her hair. "Three million eight."

Jack's face went gray. "Three million eight hundred thousand? Dollars?"

"Jack, it's worth three times that."

"Then why the hell are they selling it for three million eight? We can't afford it, Jenn. Forget it."

She answered him by rolling her eyes. She waved reassuringly to the realtor, who sat in her car writing up the contract.

"Jenn, I make a hundred twenty thou' a year. You make about the same, maybe a little more."

"When you make partner—"

"Right. My salary goes up, but not enough for this. We can't make the mortgage payments. I thought we were moving into your place, anyway."

"It's not right for a married couple."

"Not right? It's a friggin' palace." He walked over to a forest-green-painted garden bench and sat down.

She planted herself in front of him, arms crossed, a determined look on her face. Her summer tan was starting to fade. She wore a creamy brown fedora from under which her long hair tumbled across her shoulders. Her pants were perfectly tailored to her elegantly slender form. Polished leather boots encased her feet and disappeared under the pant legs.

"We won't be carrying a mortgage, Jack."

He looked up at her. "Really? What, are they

giving us the place because we're such a terrific young couple?"

She hesitated, then said, "Daddy is paying cash for it, and we're going to pay him back."

Jack had been waiting for that one.

"Pay him back? How the hell are we going to pay him back, Jenn?"

"He's suggested a very liberal repayment plan, which takes into account future earnings expectations. For godsakes, Jack, I could pay for this place out of accumulated interest on one of my trusts, but I knew you'd object to that." She sat down next to him. "I thought if we did it this way, you'd feel better about the whole thing. I know how you are about the Baldwin money. We *will* have to pay Daddy back. It's not a gift. It's a loan *with interest*. I'm going to sell my place. I'll net about eight from that. You're going to have to come up with some money too. This is not a free ride." She playfully stuck a long finger into his chest, driving home her point. She looked back at the house. "It's beautiful, isn't it, Jack? We'll be so happy here. We were meant to live here."

Jack looked over at the front of the house but without really seeing it. All he saw was Kate Whitney, in every window of the monolith.

Jennifer squeezed his arm, leaned against him. Jack's headache moved into the panic zone. His mind was refusing to function. His throat went dry and his limbs felt stiff. He gently disengaged his arm from his fiancée's, got up and walked quietly back to the car.

Jennifer sat there for several moments, disbelief chief among the emotions registering across her face, and then angrily followed him.

The realtor, who had intently watched the exchange between the two while seated in her

Mercedes, stopped writing up the contract, her mouth pursed in displeasure.

It was early morning when Luther emerged from the small hotel hidden in the cluttered residential neighborhoods of Northwest Washington. He hailed a cab to the Metro Center subway, asking the driver to take a circuitous route on the presumption of seeing various D.C. landmarks. The request did not surprise the cabbie and he automatically went through the motions to be replicated a thousand times before the tourist season was officially over, if it was ever truly over for the town.

The skies threatened rain but you never knew. The unpredictable weather systems swirled and whipped across the region either missing the city or falling hard on it before sliding into the Atlantic. Luther looked up at the darkness, which the newly risen sun could not penetrate.

Would he even be alive six months from now? Maybe not. They could conceivably find him, despite his precautions. But he planned to enjoy the time he had left.

The Metro took him to Washington National Airport, where he took a shuttle bus across to the Main Terminal. He had prechecked his luggage onto the American Airlines flight that would take him to Dallas/Fort Worth, where he would change airlines and then head to Miami. He would stay there overnight and then another plane would drop him in Puerto Rico and then a final flight would deposit him in Barbados. Everything was paid for in cash; his passport proclaimed him to be Arthur Lanis, age sixty-five, from Michigan. He had a half-dozen such identifying documents, all professionally crafted and official-looking and all absolutely phony. The passport was good for eight more years and showed him to be well-traveled.

He settled into the waiting area and pretended to scan a newspaper. The place was crowded and noisy, a typical weekday for the busy airport. Occasionally Luther's eyes would rise over the paper to see if anyone was paying more than casual attention to him, but nothing registered. And he had been doing this long enough that something would have clicked if he had anything to worry about. His flight was called, his boarding pass was handed over and he trudged down the ramp to the slender projectile that within three hours would deposit him in the heart of Texas.

The Dallas/Fort Worth run was a busy one for American, but surprisingly he had an empty seat next to him. He took his coat off and laid it across the seat daring anyone to trespass. He settled himself in and looked out the window.

As they began to taxi to the takeoff runway, he could make out the tip of the Washington Monument over the thick, swirling mist of the clammy morning. Barely a mile from that point his daughter would be getting up shortly to go to work while her father was ascending into the clouds to begin a new life somewhat ahead of schedule and not exactly easy in his mind.

As the plane accelerated through the air, he looked at the terrain far below, noted the snaking of the Potomac until it was left behind. His thoughts went briefly to his long-dead wife and then back to his very much alive daughter.

He glanced up at the smiling, efficient face of the flight attendant and ordered coffee and a minute later accepted the simple breakfast handed to him. He drank down the steaming liquid and then reached over and touched the surface of the window with its queer streaks and scratches. Wiping his glasses clean, he noted that his eyes were watering freely. He looked around quickly; most passengers were finishing up their breakfast or reclining for a short nap before they landed.

He pushed his tray up, undid his seat belt and made his way to the lavatory. He looked at himself in the mirror. The eyes were swollen, red-blotched. The bags hung heavy, he had perceptibly aged in the last thirty-six hours.

He ran water over his face, let the droplets gather around his mouth and then splashed on some more. He wiped his eyes again. They were painful. He leaned against the tiny basin, tried to get his twitching muscles under control.

Despite all his willpower, his mind wandered back to that room where he had seen a woman savagely beaten. The President of the United States was a drunk, an adulterer and a woman beater. He smiled to the press, kissed babies and flirted with enchanted old women, held important meetings, flew around the world as his country's leader, and he was a fucking asshole who screwed married women, then beat them up and then got them killed.

What a package.

It was more knowledge than one person should be carrying around.

Luther felt very alone. And very mad.

And the sorry thing was the bastard was going to get away with it.

Luther kept telling himself if he were thirty years younger he would take this battle on. But he wasn't. His nerves were still stronger than most, but, like river rock, they had eroded over the years; they were not what they were. At his age battles became someone else's to fight, and win or lose. His time had finally come. He wasn't up to it. Even he had to understand that, to accept that reality.

Luther looked at himself in the tiny mirror again.

A sob swelled in his throat before it reached the surface and filled the small room.

But no excuse would justify what he had not done. He had not opened that mirrored door. He had not flung that man off Christine Sullivan. He could have prevented the woman's death, that was the simple truth. She would still be alive if he had acted. He had traded his freedom, perhaps his life, for another's. For someone who could have used his help, who was fighting for her very life while Luther just watched. A human being who had barely lived a third of Luther's years. It had been a cowardly act, and that fact gripped him like some savage anaconda, threatening to explode every organ in his body.

He bent low over the sink as his legs began to fail him. He was grateful for the collapse. He could not look at his reflection anymore. As choppy air buffeted the plane he was sick to his stomach.

A few minutes elapsed and he wet a paper towel with cold water and wiped it across his face and the back of his neck. He finally managed to stumble back to his seat. As the plane thundered on his guilt grew with each passing mile.

The phone was ringing. Kate looked at the clock. Eleven o'clock. Normally she would screen her calls. But something made her hand dart out and pick it up before the machine engaged.

"Hello."

"Why aren't you still at work?"

"Jack?"

"How's your ankle?"

"Do you realize what time it is?"

"Just checking on my patient. Doctors never sleep."

"Your patient is fine. Thanks for the worry." She smiled in spite of herself.

"Butterscotch cone, that prescription has never failed me."

"Oh, so there were other patients?"

"I've been advised by my attorney not to answer that question."

"Smart counsel."

Jack could visualize her sitting there, one finger playing with the ends of her hair, the same way she had done when they studied together; he laboring through securities regulations, she through French.

"Your hair curls enough at the ends without you helping it."

She pulled her finger back, smiled, then frowned. That statement had brought a lot of memories back, not all good ones.

"It's late, Jack. I've got court tomorrow."

He stood up and paced with the cordless, thinking rapidly. Anything to hold her on the phone for a few more seconds. He felt guilty, as though he were sneaking around. He involuntarily looked over his shoulder. There was no one there, at least no one he could see.

"I'm sorry I called late."

"Okay."

"And I'm sorry I hurt your ankle."

"You already apologized for that."

"Yeah. So, how are you? I mean except for your ankle?"

"Jack, I really need to get some sleep."

He was hoping she would say that.

"Well tell me over lunch."

"I told you I've got court."

"After court."

"Jack, I'm not sure that's a good idea. In fact, I'm pretty sure it's a lousy idea."

He wondered what she meant by that. Reading

too much into her statements had always been a bad habit of his.

"Jesus, Kate. It's just lunch. I'm not asking you to marry me." He laughed, but knew he'd already blown it.

Kate was no longer fiddling with her hair. She too stood up. Her reflection caught in the hallway mirror. She pulled at the neck of her nightgown. The frown lines were prominent on her forehead.

"I'm sorry," he said quickly. "I'm sorry, I didn't mean that. Look, it'll be my treat. I have to spend all that money on something." He was met with silence. In fact, he wasn't sure if she was still on the line.

He had rehearsed this conversation for the last two hours. Every possible question, exchange, deviation. He'd be so smooth, she so understanding. They would hit it off so well. So far, absolutely nothing had gone according to plan. He fell back on his alternate plan. He decided to beg.

"Please, Kate. I'd really like to talk to you. Please."

She sat back down, curled her legs under her, rubbed at her long toes. She took a deep breath. The years hadn't changed her as much as she had thought. Was that good or bad? Right now she had no way to deal with that question.

"When and where?"

"Morton's?"

"For lunch?"

He could see her incredulous face at the thought of the ultra-expensive restaurant. Wondering what type of world he now lived in. "Okay, how about the deli in Old Town near Founder's Park around two? We'll miss the lunchtime crowd."

"Better. But I can't promise. I'll call if I can't make it."

He slowly let out his breath. "Thanks, Kate."

He hung up the phone and collapsed on the couch.

Now that his plan had worked, he wondered what the hell he was doing. What would he say? What would she say? He didn't want to fight. He hadn't been lying, he did just want to talk to her, and to see her. That was all. He kept telling himself that.

He went to the bathroom, plunged his head into a sink of cold water, grabbed a beer and went up to the rooftop pool and sat there in the darkness, watching the planes as they made their approach up the Potomac into National. The twin, bright red lights of the Washington Monument blinked consolingly at him. Eight stories down, the streets were quiet except for the occasional police or ambulance siren.

Jack looked at the calm surface of the pool, put his foot in the now cool water and watched as it rippled across. He drank his beer, went downstairs and fell asleep in a chair in the living room, the TV droning in front of him. He did not hear the phone ring, no message was left. Almost one thousand miles away, Luther Whitney hung up the phone and smoked his first cigarette in over thirty years.

The Federal Express truck pulled slowly down the isolated country road, the driver scanning the rusty and leaning mailboxes for the correct address. He had never made a delivery out here. His truck seemed to ride ditch to ditch on the narrow road.

He pulled into the driveway of the last house and started to back out. He just happened to look over and saw the address on the small piece of wood beside the door. He shook his head and smiled. Sometimes it was just luck.

The house was small, and not very well kept up. The weathered aluminum window awnings, popular about twenty years before the driver had been born, sagged down, as if they were tired and just wanted to rest.

104

The elderly woman who answered the door was dressed in a pullover flowered dress, a thick sweater wrapped around her shoulders. Her thick red ankles told of poor circulation and probably a host of other ailments. She seemed surprised by the delivery, but readily signed for it.

The driver glanced at the signature on his pad: Edwina Broome. Then he got in his truck and left. She watched him leave before shutting the door.

The walkie-talkie crackled.

Fred Barnes had been doing this job for seven years now. Driving around the neighborhoods of the rich, seeing the big houses, manicured grounds, the occasional expensive car with its mannequinlike occupants coming down the perfect asphalt drive and through the massive gates. He had never been inside any of the homes he was paid to guard, and never expected to be.

He looked up at the imposing structure. Four to five million dollars, he surmised. More money than he could make in five lifetimes. Sometimes it just didn't seem right.

He checked in on his walkie-talkie. He would take a look around the place. He didn't exactly know what was going on. Only that the owner had called and requested a patrol car check.

The cold air in his face made Barnes think about a hot cup of coffee and a danish, to be followed by eight hours of sleep until he had to venture out again in his Saturn for yet another night of protecting the possessions of the wealthy. The pay wasn't all that bad, although the benefits sucked. His wife worked full-time too, and with three kids, their combined incomes were barely enough. But then everybody had it tough. He looked at the five-car garage in back, the pool and the tennis courts. Well, maybe not everybody.

As he rounded the corner, he saw the dangling rope and thoughts of coffee and a creamy danish disappeared. He crouched down, his hand flying to his sidearm. He grabbed his mike and reported in, his voice cracking embarrassingly. The real police would be here in minutes. He could wait for them or investigate himself. For eight singles an hour he decided to stay right where he was.

Barnes's supervisor arrived first in the stark white station wagon with the company's logo on the door panel. Thirty seconds later the first of five patrol cars pulled down the asphalt drive until they were stacked like a waiting train in front of the house.

The window was covered by two officers. It was probable that the perps had long since exited the premises, but assumptions were dangerous in the police business.

Four officers went to the front, two more covered the back. Working in pairs, the four policemen proceeded to make their way in. They noted that the front door was unlocked, the alarm off. They satisfied themselves with the downstairs and cautiously moved up the broad staircase, their ears and eyes straining for any trace of sound or movement.

By the time they reached the second-floor landing, the nostrils of the sergeant in charge told him that this would not be a routine burglary.

Four minutes later they stood in a circle around what had recently been a young, beautiful woman. The healthy coloring of each of the men had faded to dull white.

The sergeant, fiftyish and a father of three, looked at the open window. Thank God, he thought to himself; even with the outside air the atmosphere inside the room was stupefying. He looked once more at the corpse, then strode quickly to the window and sucked in deep gulps of the crisp air.

He had a daughter about that age. For a moment he imagined her on that floor, her face a memory, her life brutally over. The matter was out of his bailiwick now, but he wished for one thing: he wished to be there when whoever had done this atrocious thing was caught.

SEVEN

Seth Frank was simultaneously munching a piece of toast and attempting to tie his six-year-old daughter's hair ribbons for school when the phone call came. His wife's look told him all he needed. She finished the ribbon. Seth cradled the phone while he finished knotting his tie, listening all the while to the calm, efficient tones of the dispatcher. Two minutes later he was in his car; the official bubble light needlessly stuck to the top of his department-issued Ford and aqua blue grille lights flashing ominously as he roared through the nearly deserted back roads of the county.

Frank's tall, big-boned frame was beginning its inevitable journey to softness, and his curly black hair had seen more affluent days. At forty-one years old, the father of three daughters who grew more complex and bewildering by the day, he had come to realize that not all that much in life made sense. But overall he was a happy man. Life had dealt him no knockout punches. Yet. He had been in law enforcement long enough to know how abruptly that could change.

Frank wadded up a piece of Juicy Fruit and slowly chewed it while compact rows of needle pines flew past his window. He had started his law enforcement career as a cop in some of the worst areas of New York City where the statement "the value of life" was an oxymoron and where he had seen virtually every way one person could kill another. He had eventually made detective, which had thrilled his wife. At least now he would arrive at crime scenes after the bad guys had departed. She slept better at night, knowing that the dreaded phone call would probably not come to destroy her life. That was as much as she could hope for being married to a cop.

Frank had finally been assigned to homicide, which was pretty much the ultimate challenge in his line of work. After a few years, he decided he liked the job and the challenge, but not at the rate of seven corpses a day. So he had made the trek south to Virginia.

He was senior homicide detective for the County of Middleton, which sounded better than it actually was, since he also happened to be the only homicide detective the county employed. But the relatively innocuous confines of the rustic Virginia county had not lent itself to much demanding work over that time. The per capita income levels in his jurisdiction were off the scale. People were murdered, but other than wives shooting husbands or vice versa or inheritance-minded kids popping off their parents, there hadn't been much excitement. The perps in those cases were pretty self-evident, less mental work than legwork. The dispatcher's phone call promised to change all that.

The road snaked past a wooded area and then opened out onto fenced, green fields where leggy thoroughbreds lazily faced the new morning. Behind impressive gates and long, winding driveways, were the residences of the fortunate few, who were actually very plentiful in Middleton. Frank concluded that he wasn't going to get any help from the neighbors on this one. Once inside their fortresses they probably saw or heard nothing on the outside. Which was undoubtedly the way they wanted it and paid dearly for that privilege.

As Frank approached the Sullivan estate he

straightened his tie in the rearview mirror and pushed back some stray wisps of hair. He had no particular affinity for the wealthy, nor did he dislike them. They were parts of the puzzle. A conundrum that was as far from a game as you could get. Which led to the most satisfying part of his job. For amidst all the twists, turns, red herrings and plain mistakes, there lurked an undeniable truism: if you killed another human being, you came within his domain and you would be ultimately punished. What that punishment was, Frank usually did not care. What he did care about was that someone stand trial and, if convicted, that someone receive the meted penalty. Rich, poor or in-between. His skills may be somewhat dulled, but the instincts were still there. In the long run, he'd always go with the latter.

As he pulled in the drive he noticed a small combine chewing under the adjacent cornfield, its driver watching the police activity with a keen eye. That information would soon be passing through the area in rapid movements. The man had no way to know he was destroying evidence, evidence of a flight. Neither did Seth Frank as he climbed out of his car, threw on his jacket and hustled through the front door.

Hands deep in his pockets, his eyes moved slowly around the room, taking in each detail of the floor, walls, and venturing to the ceiling before coming back to the mirrored door and then to the spot where the deceased had lain for the last several days.

Seth Frank said, "Take a lot of pics, Stu, looks like we'll need it."

The crime unit photographer paced through the room in discrete grids outward from the corpse in his effort to reproduce on film every aspect of the room including its lone occupant. This would be followed by a videotaping of the entire crime scene complete with a narrative. Not necessarily admissible in court, but it was invaluable to the investigation. As football players watched game films, detectives were more and more scrutinizing the videos for additional clues that might only be seized upon on the eighth, tenth or hundredth examination.

The rope was still tied to the bureau and still disappeared out the window. Only now it was covered with black fingerprint powder, but there wouldn't be much there. One usually wore gloves to climb down a rope, even a knotted one.

Sam Magruder, the officer in charge, approached, having just spent two minutes leaning out the window sucking in air. Fiftyish with a shock of red hair that topped a plump, hairless face, he was having a hard time keeping his breakfast down. A large portable fan had been brought in and the windows were fully open. All the CU personnel wore floater masks, but the stench was still oppressive. Nature's parting laugh to the living. Beautiful one minute, rotting the next.

Frank checked Magruder's notes, noted the greenish tint to the OIC's face.

"Sam, if you'd stay away from the window, your sense of smell would go dead in about four minutes. You're just making it worse."

"I know that, Seth. My brain tells me that, but my nose won't listen."

"When did the husband phone in?"

"This morning, seven-forty-five local time."

Frank tried to make out the cop's scribbles. "And he's where?"

"Barbados."

Frank's head inclined. "How long?"

"We're confirming it."

"Do that."

111

"How many calling cards they leave, Laura?" Frank looked over at his ident technician, Laura Simon.

She glanced up. "I'm not finding much, Seth."

Frank walked over to her. "Come on, Laura, she's gotta be all over the place. How about her husband? The maid? There's gotta be usables everywhere."

"Not that I'm finding."

"You're shitting me."

Simon, who took her work very seriously and was the best print lifter Frank had ever worked with, including at NYPD, looked almost apologetic. Carbon dusting powder was everywhere, and there was nothing? Contrary to popular belief, a lot of criminals left their prints at the scene of the crime. You just had to know where to look. Laura Simon knew where to look and she was getting zip. Hopefully they would get something after analysis back at the lab. Many latents just weren't visible no matter how many angles you hit them with the light. That's why they called them latents. You just powdered and taped everything you thought the perps might have touched. And you might get lucky.

"I've got a few things packaged to take back to the lab. After I use the ninhydrin and hit the rest with the Super Glue I might have something for you." Simon dutifully returned to her work.

Frank shook his head. Super Glue, a cyanoacrylate, was probably the best method of fuming and could pull prints off things you couldn't believe. The problem was the damn process took time to work its magic. Time they didn't have.

"Come on, Laura, from the looks of the body the bad guys have had enough of a head start."

She looked at him. "I've got another cyanoacrylate ester I've been wanting to use. That's faster. Or I can always speed-burn the Super Glue." She smiled.

The detective grimaced. "Right. The last time you

tried that we had to evacuate the building."

"I didn't say it was a perfect world, Seth."

Magruder cleared his throat. "Looks like we're dealing with some real professionals."

Seth looked at the OIC sternly. "They're not professionals, Sam, they're criminals, they're killers. It's not like they went to goddamned college to learn how to do this."

"No, sir."

"We sure it's the lady of the house?" Frank inquired.

Magruder pointed to the photo on the nightstand. "Christine Sullivan. Of course, we'll get a positive ID."

"Any witnesses?"

"No obvious ones. Haven't canvassed the neighbors yet. Gonna do that this morning."

Frank proceeded to make copious notes of the room and its occupant's condition and then made a detailed sketch of the room and its contents. A good defense attorney could make any unprepared prosecution witness look like a candidate for the Silly Putty factory. Being unprepared meant guilty people went free.

Frank had learned the only lesson he would ever need on the subject as a rookie cop and the first on the scene of a breaking and entering. He had never been more embarrassed or depressed in his life as he had when he had gotten off the witness stand, his testimony torn to shreds and actually used as the basis to get the defendant off. If he had been able to wear his .38 in court, the world would have had one fewer lawyer that day.

Frank crossed the room to where the Deputy Medical Examiner, a beefy, white-haired man who was perspiring heavily despite the morning chill outside, was lowering the skirt on the corpse. Frank knelt down and examined one of the small Baggieclad hands, then glanced at the woman's face. It looked like it had been beaten black and blue. The clothing was soaked through with her body fluids. With death comes an almost immediate relaxing of the sphincters. The resulting smell combination was not pleasant. Luckily the insect infestation was minimal, despite the open window. Even though a forensic entomologist could usually ascertain time of death more accurately than could a pathologist, no detective, despite the increased accuracy, ever relished the thought of examining a human body that had become an insect buffet.

"Got an approximate yet?" Frank asked the Medical Examiner.

"My rectal thermometer isn't going to be much use to me, not when body temperature drops one and a half degrees an hour. Seventy-two to eighty-four hours. I'll have a better number for you after I open her up." The ME straightened up. "Gunshot wounds to the head," he added, although there was no doubt about the woman's cause of death to anyone in the room.

"I noticed the marks on her neck."

The Medical Examiner looked at Frank keenly for a moment and then shrugged. "They're there. I don't know what they mean yet."

"I'd appreciate a quick turnaround on this one."

"You'll get it. Not many murders out this way. They usually get a priority, y'know."

The detective winced slightly at the remark.

The Medical Examiner looked at him. "Hope you enjoy dealing with the press. They'll be on this like a swarm of honeybees."

"More like yellowjackets."

The Medical Examiner shrugged. "Better you than me. I'm way too old for that crap. She's ready to go whenever."

114

The Medical Examiner finished packing up and left.

Frank held the small hand up to his face, looked at the professionally manicured nails. He noted several tears in two of the cuticles, which seemed likely enough if there was a struggle before she'd gotten popped. The body was grossly distended; bacteria raged everywhere as the putrefaction process raced on. Rigor had passed long ago, which meant she had been dead well over forty-eight hours. The limbs were supple as the body's soft tissue dissolved. Frank sighed. She had indeed been here awhile. That was good for the killer, bad for the cops.

It still amazed him how death changed a person. A bloated wreck barely recognizable as a human, when just days before . . . Had his sense of smell not already gone dead, he would have been unable to do what he was doing. But that came with being a homicide detective. All your clients were dead.

He carefully held the deceased's head up, turning each side to the light. Two small entry wounds on the right side, one large, ragged exit hole on the left. They were looking at heavy-caliber stuff. Stu had already gotten pictures of the wounds from several different angles, including from directly overhead. The circular abrasion collars and the absence of burns or tattooing on the skin's surface led Frank to conclude that the shots had been fired from over two feet away.

Small-caliber contact wounds, those fired muzzle to flesh, and near-contact wounds fired from a distance of less than two inches from the target, could duplicate the types of entry wounds present on the victim. But there would be powder residue deep in the tissues along the bullet track if they were looking at a contact wound. The autopsy would definitively answer that question.

Next Frank looked at the contusion on the left side of her jaw. It was partially hidden by the natural blistering of the body as it decomposed but Frank had seen enough corpses to tell the difference. The surface of the skin there was a curious amalgamation of green, brown and black. A big blow had done that. A man? That was confusing. He called Stu over to take pictures of the area with a color scale. Then he laid the head back down with the reverence the deceased deserved even under the largely clinical circumstances.

The medico-legal autopsy to follow would not be so deferential.

Frank slowly lifted the skirt. Underwear intact. The autopsy protocol would answer the obvious question.

Frank moved around the room as the CU members continued their work. One thing about living in a rich, although largely rural county, the tax base was more than enough to support a first-rate if relatively small crime scene unit complete with all the latest technology and devices that theoretically made catching bad people easier.

The victim had fallen on her left side, away from the door. Knees tucked partially under her, left arm stretched out, the other against her right hip. Her face was pointed east, perpendicular with the right side of the bed; she was almost in a fetal position. Frank rubbed his nose. From beginning to end, back to the beginning. Nobody ever knew how they were going to eventually exit this old world, did they?

With Simon's help he did the triangulation of the body's location; the tape measure made a screeching sound as it unwound. It sounded somehow unholy in this room of death. He looked at the doorway and the position of the body. He and Simon performed a preliminary trajectory path of the shots. That

116

indicated the shots most probably came from the doorway, which with a burglary you'd expect the other way around if the perp was caught in the act. However, there was another piece of evidence that would pretty much confirm which way the slugs had traveled.

Frank again kneeled next to the body. There were no drag marks across the carpet and the bloodstains and spray patterns indicated the deceased was shot at the spot she had fallen. Frank carefully turned to the body, again lifting up the skirt. Postmortem, blood settles to the lowest portions of the body, a condition called livor mortis. After four to six hours, the livor mortis remains fixed in position. Consequently, movement of the body does not lead to a change in distribution of blood. Frank laid the body back down. All indications were strong that Christine Sullivan had died right here.

The spray patterns also reinforced the conclusion that the deceased was probably facing toward the bed when she met her end. If so, what the hell had she been looking at? Normally a person about to be shot would look in the direction of the assailant, pleading for their life. Christine Sullivan would have begged, Frank was certain of that. The detective looked at the opulent surroundings. She had a lot to live for.

He eyed the carpet carefully, his face barely inches from its surface. The spray patterns were irregularly distributed as though something had been lying in front of or to the side of the deceased. That could prove to be important later on. Much had been written about spray patterns. Frank respected their usefulness, but tried not to read too much into them. But if something had partially shielded the carpet from the blood, he would want to know what that something was. Also the absence of spotting on her dress puzzled him. He would catalogue that one away; it might mean something too.

Simon opened her rape kit and with Frank's assistance swabbed the deceased's vagina. Next they combed through both the hair on her head and her pubic hair with nothing readily apparent in the way of foreign substances. Next they bagged the victim's clothing.

Frank looked over the body minutely. He glanced at Simon. She read his mind.

"There's not going to be any, Seth."

"Indulge me, Laurie."

Simon dutifully lugged her print kit over and applied powder to the corpse's wrists, breasts, neck and inside upper arms. After a few seconds she looked at Frank and slowly shook her head. She bagged what they did find.

He watched as the body was wrapped in a white sheet, deposited in a body pouch and taken outside where a silent ambulance would transport Christine Sullivan to a place everyone prayed they would never have to go.

He next viewed the vault, noted the chair and remote. Dust patterns on the floor of the vault had been disturbed. Simon had already covered the area. There was a smudge of dust on the chair seat. The vault had been forced though; the door and wall were heavily marked where the lock had been broken. They would cut out the levered piece of evidence, see if they could get a tool print. Frank looked back through the vault door and shook his head. One-way mirror. That was real nice. In the bedroom too. He couldn't wait to meet the man of the house.

He went back into the room, looked down at the picture on the nightstand. He looked over at Simon.

"I've already got it, Seth," she said. He nodded and picked up the picture. Nice-looking woman, he

118

thought to himself, real nice-looking in a come-fuck-me kind of way. The photo had been taken in this very room, the recently departed seated in the chair next to the bed. Then he noticed the mark on the wall. The place had real plaster walls instead of the usual drywall, but the mark was still deep. Frank noted the nightstand had been moved slightly; the thick carpet betrayed its original position. He turned to Magruder.

"Looks like somebody slammed into this."

"Probably during the struggle."

"Probably."

"Find the slug yet?"

"One's still in her, Seth."

"I mean the other one, Sam." Frank impatiently shook his head. Magruder pointed to the wall beside the bed where a small hole was barely visible.

Frank nodded. "Cut the section and let the lab boys pull it out. Don't screw with it yourself." Twice in the last year ballistics had been rendered useless because an overzealous uniform had scraped a bullet out of a wall, ruining the striations.

"Any brass?"

Magruder shook his head. "If the murder weapon ejected any spent shells, they've been picked up."

He turned to Simon. "Any treasures from the E-vac?" The evidence vacuum was a highly powerful machine that, utilizing a series of filters, was used to comb the carpet and other materials for fibers, hairs and other small objects that more often than not turned out big dividends because if the perps couldn't see 'em, they weren't going to try to remove 'em.

Magruder tried to joke. "My carpet should be that clean."

Frank looked at his CU team. "Did we find any trace, people?" They all looked at one another not knowing if Frank was kidding or not. They were still wondering when he walked out of the room and went downstairs.

A representative from the alarm company was talking with a uniformed officer at the front door. A CU member was packing the plate and wires in plastic evidence bags. Frank was shown where the paint had been slightly chipped and an almost microscopic metal shard indicated that the panel had been removed. On the wiring were small toothlike indentations. The security rep looked admiringly at the lawbreaker's handiwork. Magruder joined them, his color slowly returning.

The rep was nodding his head. "Yep, they probably used a counter. Looks that way anyway."

Seth looked at him. "What's that?"

"Computer-assisted method of ramming massive numbers of combinations into the system's recognition bank until they hit the right combo. You know, like they do to bust the ATMs.'

Frank looked at the gutted panel and then back at the man. "I'm surprised a place like this wouldn't have a more sophisticated system."

"It is a sophisticated system." The rep sounded defensive.

"Lotta crooks using computers these days."

"Yeah, but the thing is, this baby has a fifteen-digit base, not a ten, and a forty-three-second delay. You don't hit it, the gate comes crashing down."

Frank rubbed his nose. He would have to go home and shower. The stench of death warmed over several days in a hot room left its indelible mark on your clothes, hair and skin. And sinuses.

"So?" Frank asked.

"So, the portable models you'd most likely have to use on a job like this can't crunch enough combos through in thirty seconds or so. Shit, based on a fifteen-digit configuration you're looking at over a trillion-three in possibles. It's not like the guy's gonna be lugging around a PC."

The OIC piped in. "Why thirty seconds?"

Frank answered. "They needed some time to get the plate off, Sam." He turned back to the security man. "So what are you saying?"

"I'm saying that if he knocked this system over with a numbers cruncher then he had already eliminated some of the possible digits from the process. Maybe half, maybe more. I mean, maybe you got a system that'll do it all right, or they might've rigged something up that could pop this cage. But you're not talking cheap hardware and you're not talking some bozos off the street that walked into a Radio Shack and came out with a calculator. I mean, they're making computers faster and smaller every day but you gotta realize that the speed of *your* hardware doesn't solve the problem. You gotta factor in how fast the security system's computer will respond back to all the combos flowing in. It's probably gonna be a lot slower than your equipment. And then you gotta big problem. Bottom line if I were these guys I'd want a nice comfort zone, you know what I'm saying? In their line of work, you don't get second chances."

Frank looked at the man's uniform and then back at the panel. If the guy was right he knew what that meant. His line of thinking had already moved in that direction by virtue of the fact that the front door had not been forced or even nominally tampered with.

The security company rep continued, "I mean, we could eliminate the possibility entirely. We have systems that refuse to react to massive combos being forced down their throat. Computers would be jack-shit useless. Problem is, those systems are so sensitive to interference they were also routinely slamming down on owners who couldn't seem to remember their numbers on the first or second try. Hell, we were getting hit with so many false alarms the police departments were starting to fine us. Go fucking figure."

Frank thanked him and then moved through the rest of the house. Whoever had committed these crimes knew what they were doing. This was not going to be a quick one. Good pre-crime planning usually meant equally good post-planning. But they probably hadn't counted on blowing away the lady of the house.

Frank suddenly leaned against a doorway and pondered the word used by his friend the Medical Examiner: *wounds*.

EIGHT

Jack was early. His watch showed one-thirty-five. He had taken the day off, spending much of it deciding what to wear; something he had never concerned himself with before, but which now seemed vitally important.

He pulled at his gray tweed jacket, fingered a button on his white cotton shirt and adjusted the knot in his tie for the tenth time.

He walked down to the dock and watched the deck hands clean the *Cherry Blossom*, a tour ship built to resemble an old Mississippi riverboat. He and Kate had gone on it their first year in D.C. during a rare afternoon off from work. They had tried to hit all the touristy attractions. It had been a warm day like today, but clearer. Gray clouds were now rolling in from the west; afternoon thunderstorms were almost a given this time of year.

He sat on the weathered bench near the dock-master's small hut and followed the lazy drift of the sea gulls across the choppy water. The Capitol was visible from his vantage point. Lady Liberty, minus the collective filth of over a hundred and thirty years of residing outdoors thanks to a recent cleaning, stood imperiously on top of the famous dome. People in this town were encased in grime over time, Jack thought to himself. It just came with the territory.

Jack's musings turned to Sandy Lord, the firm's most prolific rainmaker, and the biggest ego Patton, Shaw had ever seen. Sandy was close to being an institution in the legal and political circles of D.C. The other partners dropped his name as though he had just that moment stepped down from Mount Sinai with his own version of the Ten Commandments, which would have commenced with "Thou Shalt Make Patton, Shaw and LORD Partners As Much Money As Possible."

Ironically, Sandy Lord was part of the attraction when Ransome Baldwin had mentioned the firm. Lord was one of the best, if not the best example of a power lawyer the city had to offer, and it had dozens in that league. The possibilities were limitless for Jack. Whether those possibilities included his personal happiness, he was far from certain.

He was also not certain what he expected from this lunch. What he was sure about was that he wanted to see Kate Whitney. He wanted that very much. It seemed as though the closer his marriage came, the more he was emotionally retreating. And where more likely a spot to retreat than to the woman he had asked to marry him over four years ago? He shuddered as that memory engulfed him. He was terrified of marrying Jennifer Baldwin. Terrified that his life would soon become unrecognizable to him.

Something made him turn, he wasn't sure what exactly. But she was standing there, at the edge of the pier, watching him. The wind whipped her long skirt around her legs, the sun battled the darkening clouds, but still provided enough light to sparkle across her face as she moved the long strands of hair from her eyes. The calves and ankles were summer brown. The loose blouse bared her shoulders, showing off the freckles, and the tiny half-moon birthmark Jack had the habit of tracing after they had finished making love, she asleep and he watching her.

He smiled as she walked toward him. She must have gone home to change. This was clearly not her courtroom armor; these clothes represented a far more feminine side to Kate Whitney than any of her legal opponents would ever witness.

They walked down the street to the small deli, ordered and spent the first few minutes alternately staring out the window watching the approaching rain as it whipped the trees around, and exchanging awkward glances, as if on a first date and afraid to make steady eye contact.

"I appreciate your making the time, Kate."

She shrugged. "I like it here. Haven't been for a while. It's nice to get out for a change. I usually eat at my desk."

"Crackers and coffee?" He smiled and stared at her teeth. The funny one that curved inwardly slightly, like it was giving a quick hug to its neighbor. He liked that tooth the best. It was the only flaw he had ever noticed about her.

"Crackers and coffee." She smiled back. "Down to two cigarettes a day."

"Congratulations." The rain came at the same time their orders did.

She looked up from her plate, her eyes swept over to the window and then abruptly to Jack's face. She caught him staring at her. Jack smiled awkwardly and took a quick gulp of his drink.

She put her napkin on the table.

"The Mall's a big place to accidentally run into someone."

He didn't look at her. "I've been having a run of good luck lately." Now he met her eye. She waited. His shoulders finally collapsed.

"Okay, so it was less of an accident and more premeditated. You can't argue with the results."

"What are the results? Lunch?"

"I'm not looking ahead. I'm just taking it one step at a time. New life resolution. Change is good."

She said with more than a little contempt, "Well, at least you're not defending rapists and murderers anymore."

"And burglars?" he shot back, and then instantly regretted it.

Kate's face turned gray.

"I'm sorry, Kate. I didn't mean that."

She pulled out a cigarette and matches, lit up and blew smoke in his face.

He waved the cloud away. "Your first or second of the day?"

"Third. For some reason you always make me feel daring." She stared at the window, crossed her legs. Her foot touched his knee and she quickly jerked it back. She stabbed out her cigarette and stood up, grabbing her purse.

"I have to get back to work. How much do I owe you?"

He stared at her. "I invited *you* to lunch. Which you haven't even eaten."

She pulled out a ten and tossed it down on the table and headed for the door.

Jack threw another ten down and raced after her.

"Kate!"

He caught up to her just outside the deli. The rain had stiffened and despite holding his jacket over their heads they were quickly soaked. She didn't seem to notice. She climbed in her car. He jumped in the passenger side. She looked at him.

"I really have to get back."

Jack took a deep breath, wiped the moisture off his face. The heavy rain drummed on the car's exterior. He felt it all slipping away. He was far from sure how to handle this situation. But he had to say something.

"Come on, Kate, we're dripping wet, it's almost three o'clock. Let's go get cleaned up and hit a

126

movie. No, we can drive out to the country. Remember the Windsor Inn?"

She looked at him, absolute astonishment on her features. "Jack, by any chance, have you discussed this with the woman you're engaged to marry?"

Jack looked down. What was he supposed to say? That he was not in love with Jennifer Baldwin despite having asked her to marry him? Right at that moment, he could not even recall asking her.

"I'd just like to spend some time with you, Kate. That's all. There's nothing wrong with that."

"There is everything wrong with that, Jack. *Everything!*" She started to put the key in the ignition but he held her hand back.

"I'm not looking to make this a battle."

"Jack, you've made your decision. It's a little late for this now."

His face curled into disbelief. "Excuse me? My decision? I made a decision to marry you over four years ago. That was my decision. It was your decision to end it."

She pushed wet hair out of her eyes. "Okay, it was my decision. Now what?"

He turned to face her, gripped both her shoulders.

"Look, it suddenly occurred to me last night. Oh what the hell! It's been every night since you left. I knew it was a mistake, goddammit! I'm not at PD anymore. You're right, I don't defend criminals anymore. I make a good, respectable living. I, we . . ." As he looked at her astonished face, his entire mind went blank. His hands were shaking. He let go of her, slumped back in the seat.

He stripped off his drenched tie, stuffed it in his pocket, and stared at the little clock on the dashboard. She checked out the motionless speedometer, then glanced at him. There was kindness in her tone, although the pain was evident in her eyes.

127

"Jack, lunch was very nice. It was good to see you. But that's as far as we can go. I'm sorry." She bit her lip, a movement he didn't see because he was getting out of the car.

He poked his head back in. "Have a good life, Kate. You ever need anything, call me."

She watched his thick shoulders as he walked through the steady rain, got in his car and drove off. She sat for several minutes. A tear traced its way down her cheek. She angrily flicked it away, put the car in gear and drove off in the opposite direction.

The next morning, Jack picked up the phone and then slowly put it back down. What was the point really? He had been in the office since six, wiped out his backlog of high-priority work and moved on to projects that had been on the back burner for weeks. He looked out the window. The sun ricocheted off the concrete and brick edifices. He rubbed the glare out of his eyes and pulled the blinds down.

Kate was not going to suddenly plunge back into his life and he had to adjust to that. He had spent the night turning every possible scenario over in his head, most wildly unrealistic. He shrugged. Things like this happened to men and women every day in every country in the world. Things sometimes did not work out. Even if you wanted them to more than anything else. You couldn't will someone to love you back. You had to move on. He had plenty to move on to. Maybe it was time for him to enjoy the future he knew he did have.

He sat down at his desk and methodically moved through two more projects, a joint venture for which he was doing low-level, no-brain grunt work, and a project for the only client he had other than Baldwin, Tarr Crimson.

Crimson owned a small audiovisual company, was

a genius with computer-generated graphics and images, and made a very good living running AV conferences for companies at area hotels. He also rode a motorcycle, dressed in cutoff jeans, smoked everything including an occasional cigarette, and looked like the biggest burnt-out druggie in the world.

Jack and he had met when a friend of Jack's had prosecuted Tarr for drunk and disorderly, and lost. Tarr had come in dressed in a three-piece suit, briefcase and neatly trimmed hair and beard, and argued persuasively that the officer's testimony was biased because the bust was outside a Grateful Dead concert, that the field test was inadmissible because the cop had not given the proper verbal warnings and lastly because an improperly functioning piece of equipment had been used to administer the test.

The judge, burdened with over a hundred D&Ds from the concert, had dismissed the case after admonishing the officer to adhere strictly to the rules in the future. Jack had watched the entire affair in amazement. Impressed, Jack walked out of the court-room with Tarr, had a beer with him that night, and they quickly became friends.

Except for occasional, relatively innocuous brushes with the law, Crimson was a good, if unwelcome, client to the halls of Patton, Shaw. It had been part of Jack's deal that Tarr, who had fired his last attorney, would be allowed to follow Jack to Patton, Shaw – as if the firm would have actually said no to their new four-million-dollar man.

He put down his pen and moved once again to the window as his thoughts drifted back to Kate Whitney. An idea lumbered across the forefront of his mind. When Kate had left him originally, Jack had gone to see Luther. The old man had had no words of wisdom, no instant solution to Jack's dilemma.

Indeed, Luther Whitney was the unlikeliest person in the world to have the answer that would reach to his daughter's heart. And yet Jack had always been able to talk to Luther. About anything. The man listened. He really listened. He didn't merely wait for you to pause with your own story so he could plunge in with his own troubles. Jack wasn't sure what he was going to say to the man. But whatever it was he was certain Luther would listen. And that was probably going to have to be good enough.

One hour later Jack's computerized calendar buzzed a warning. He checked the time and threw on his jacket.

Jack moved quickly down the hallway. Lunch with Sandy Lord in twenty minutes. Jack was uncomfortable about being with the man, alone. Legions had been spoken about Sandy Lord, mostly true, Jack assumed. He wanted lunch with Jack Graham, Jack's secretary had told him this morning. And what Sandy Lord wanted he got. Jack's secretary also reminded him of that in a hushed whisper that made Jack slightly repulsed.

Twenty minutes, but first Jack had to check with Alvis on the Bishop documents. Jack smiled as he remembered Barry's face when the drafts had been placed carefully on his desk, thirty minutes before the deadline. Alvis had scanned them, the astonishment clear on his features.

"This looks pretty good. I realize I gave you a tough deadline. I don't usually like to do that." His eyes were averted. "I really appreciate the hustle, Jack. I'm sorry if I screwed up your plans."

"No sweat, Barry, that's what they pay me for." Jack had turned to leave. Barry had risen from his desk.

"Jack, uh, we really haven't had a chance to talk since you've been here. Place is so damn big. Let's have lunch one day, soon."

130

"Sounds great, Barry, have your secretary give mine some dates."

At that moment Jack realized that Barry Alvis wasn't such a bad guy. He had dinged Jack, but so what? Compared to how the senior partners ran their underlings, Jack had gotten off easy. Besides, Barry was a first-rate corporate attorney and Jack could learn a lot from him.

Jack passed Barry's secretary's desk but Sheila was not there.

Then Jack noticed the boxes stacked against the wall. Barry's door was closed. Jack knocked, but there was no answer. He looked around and then opened the door. His eyes closed and reopened as he looked at the empty bookcases, at the rectangular patches of unfaded wallpaper where a slew of diplomas and certificates had hung.

What the hell? He closed the door, turned and bumped into Sheila.

Normally professional and precise in her manner, without a hair out of place and glasses set firmly on the bridge of her nose, Sheila was a wreck. She had been Barry's secretary for ten years. She stared at Jack, fire flashed through her pale blue eyes, and then was gone. She turned around, walked quickly back to her cubicle and started packing up boxes. Jack stared blankly at her.

"Sheila, what's going on? Where's Barry?" She did not respond. Her hands moved faster until she was literally throwing things into the box. Jack moved over next to her, looked down at the petite frame.

"Sheila? What the hell's going on? Sheila!" He grabbed her hand. She slapped him, which shocked her so badly she abruptly sat down. Her head slowly went down to her desk and stayed there. She began to quietly sob.

Jack looked around again. Was Barry dead? Had

there been a terrible accident and no one had bothered to tell him? Was the firm that big, that callous? Would he read about it in a firm memo? He looked at his hands. They were trembling.

He perched on the edge of the desk, gently touched Sheila's shoulder, trying to bring her out of it, but without success. Jack looked around helplessly as the sobs continued, rising higher and higher in their intensity. Finally, two secretaries from around the corner appeared and quietly led Sheila away. Each of them gave Jack a not very friendly glance.

What the hell had he done? He looked at his watch. He had to meet Lord in ten minutes. Suddenly he was very much looking forward to this lunch. Lord knew everything that happened at the firm, usually before it actually did happen. Then a thought tickled the back of his head, a truly horrible thought. His mind went back to the White House dinner and his irate fiancée. He had mentioned Barry Alvis by name to her. But she wouldn't have . . . ? Jack practically sprinted down the hallway, the back of his jacket flapping behind him.

Fillmore's was a Washington landmark of fairly recent vintage. The doors were solid mahogany and bedecked with thick, weighty brass; the carpets and drapes were handwoven and supremely costly. Each table area was a self-contained haven of intense meal-time productivity. Phone, fax and copier services were readily available and widely used. The ornately carved tables were surrounded by richly upholstered chairs in which sat the truly elite of Washington's business and political circles. The prices ensured that the clientele would remain that way.

While crowded, the pace of the restaurant was unhurried; its occupants unused to being dictated to, they moved at their own level of intensity. Sometimes their very presence at a particular table, a raised eyebrow, a stifled cough, a knowing look, was a full day's work for them, and would reap huge rewards for them personally or for those whom they represented. Money and raw power floated through the room in distinct patterns, coupling and uncoupling.

Waiters in stiff shirts and neat bow ties appeared and then disappeared at discreetly placed intervals. Patons were coddled and served and listened to or left alone as the particular occasion called for. And the gratuities reflected the clientele's appreciation.

Fillmore's was Sandy Lord's favorite lunch spot. He peered over his menu, briefly, but methodically surveyed with his intense, gray eyes the broad expanse of the dining room for potential business or perhaps something else. He moved his heavy bulk gracefully in his chair and carefully coaxed a few gray hairs back into place. The trouble was, familiar faces kept disappearing as time moved forward, stolen away by death or retirement to points south. He removed a fleck of dust from one of his monogrammed shirt cuffs and sighed. Lord had picked this establishment, maybe this town, clean.

He punched on his cellular phone and checked his messages. Walter Sullivan hadn't called. If Sullivan's deal came through, Lord could land a former Eastern Bloc country as a client.

A whole goddamned country! How much could you charge a country for legal work? Normally a lot. The problem was the ex-communists had no money, unless you counted rubles and coupons and kopecks and whatever else they were using these days, all of which might as well be used for toilet paper.

That reality did not trouble Lord. What the ex-commies had in abundance was raw materials that Sullivan was salivating to acquire. That was the reason Lord had spent three godforsaken months there. But it would be worth it if Sullivan came through.

Lord had learned to have his doubts about everyone. But if anyone could pull this deal off, Walter Sullivan could. Everything he had touched seemed to multiply to global proportions, and the droppings that went to his cohorts were truly awe-inspiring. And at almost eighty, the old man hadn't slowed a step. He worked fifteen-hour days, was married to a twenty-something babe right out of a drive-in movie. He was right this minute in Barbados where he had flown the three highest-ranking politicos for a little business and entertainment Western style. Sullivan would call. And Sandy's short but select client list would grow by one, but what a one it would be.

Lord took note of the young woman in the painfully short skirt and tiptoe heels strolling across the dining room.

She smiled at him; he returned the look with slightly elevated eyebrows, a favorite signal of his because of its ambiguity. She was a congressional liaison for one of the big 16th Street associations, not that he cared about her occupation. She was excellent in bed, that he did care about.

The view brought back a number of pleasant memories. He would have to call her soon. He jotted a note to that effect in his electronic notebook. Then he turned his attention, as did most of the ladies in the room, to the tall, angular figure of Jack Graham striding across the room, heading straight for him.

Lord rose and extended his hand. Jack didn't take it.

"What the hell happened to Barry Alvis?"

Lord introduced one of his blank stares to the confrontation and sat back down. A waiter appeared and then was dismissed by a short wave of Lord's hand. Lord eyed Jack, who remained standing.

"You don't give a person a chance to catch their breath, do you? Straight out the mouth and into the fire. Sometimes that strategy is smart, sometimes it isn't."

"I'm not kidding, Sandy, I want to know what is going on. Barry's office is empty, his secretary is looking at me like I personally ordered a hit on him. I want some answers." Jack's voice was rising, and with it the stares increased.

"Whatever you have on your mind, I am sure we can discuss it with a little more dignity than you're mustering right now. Why don't you have a seat and start acting like a partner at the best damned law firm in this city."

Their eyes stayed locked for a full five seconds until Jack slowly sat down.

"Drink?"

"Beer."

The waiter reappeared and went away with an order for beer and Sandy's potent gin and tonic. Sandy lit a Raleigh and casually looked out the window, then back at Jack.

"You know about Barry then."

"All I know is he's gone. Why he's gone is what I want you to tell me."

"Not much to tell. He was let go, effective today."

"Why?"

"What's it to you?"

"Barry and I were working together."

"But you weren't friends."

"We didn't have a chance to be friends yet."

"Why on God's earth would you want to be friends with Barry Alvis? Man was permanent associate material if ever I saw one, and I've seen plenty."

"He was a helluva lawyer."

"No, technically, he was a highly competent attorney, proficient in the area of corporate transactional matters and tax, with a sub-specialty in health care acquisitions. He's never generated a dime in business, and never would. Thus he was not a 'helluva lawyer.'"

"Goddammit, you know what I mean. He was a very valuable asset to the firm. You need somebody to do the friggin' work."

"We have roughly two hundred attorneys who are very well suited to do the friggin' work. On the other hand, we have only a dozen or so partners who bring in any material clients. That is not the proportion one should strive for. Plenty of soldiers, not enough chiefs. You see Barry Alvis as an asset, we saw him as a high-priced liability without the talent to leverage himself. He billed enough to keep himself very highly compensated. That is not how we, the partners, make the most money. Thus a decision was made to sever our relationship."

"And you're telling me you didn't get a little nudge from Baldwin?"

Lord's face contained genuine surprise. A lawyer with over thirty-five years' experience blowing smoke in people's faces, he was a consummate liar. "What the hell do the Baldwins care about Barry Alvis?"

Jack scrutinized the corpulent face for a full minute and then let his breath out slowly. He looked around the restaurant suddenly feeling silly and embarrassed. All this for nothing? But if Lord was lying? He glanced again at the man, but the face was impassive. But why would he lie? Jack could think of several reasons, but none of them made too much sense. Could he have been wrong? Had he just made a complete ass out of himself in front of the firm's most powerful partner?

Lord's voice was softer now, almost consoling. "Barry Alvis was let go as part of an ongoing effort to clear out the deadwood near the top. We want more attorneys who can do the work *and* produce the rain. Hell, like you. Simple as that. Barry wasn't the first and he won't be the last. We've been working on this for a long time, Jack. Long before you ever came to the firm." Lord paused and looked keenly at Jack. "Is there something you're not telling me? We're going to be partners soon, you can't keep things from your partners."

Lord chuckled inwardly. The list of secret deals he had had with clients was a long one.

Jack was close to biting, but decided not to.

"I'm not a partner yet, Sandy."

"Pure formality."

"Things don't happen till they happen."

Lord shifted uncomfortably in his chair, waved his cigarette smoke like a wand. So maybe the rumors that Jack was contemplating jumping ship were true. Those rumors were the reason Lord was sitting here with the young lawyer. They looked at each other. A smile tugged at Jack's mouth. Jack's four million in legal business was an irresistible carrot. Particularly because it meant another four hundred grand to Sandy Lord, not that he needed it, but not that he would turn it down either. He had the reputation of being a big spender. And lawyers didn't retire. They worked until they dropped. The best made a lot of money, but compared to CEOs, rock stars and actors they were strictly minor-league compensation-wise.

"I thought you liked our shop."

"I do."

"So?"

"So what?"

Sandy's eye roamed the dining room again. He spotted another female acquaintance encased in a

137

sleek and costly business suit under which Sandy had good reason to believe she wore absolutely nothing. He swallowed the rest of his gin and tonic, looked at Jack. Lord grew more and more irritated. The stupid, green sonofabitch.

"You ever been to this place before?"

Jack shook his head, surveyed the thick menu, searching for a burger and fries and not finding it. Then the menu was yanked out of his hand and Lord leaned into him, his breath heavy and saggy in Jack's face.

"Well, why don't you take a look around then?"

Lord lifted a finger for the waiter and ordered a Dewar's and water, which appeared a minute later. Jack leaned back in his chair, but Lord inched closer, almost straddling the ornately carved table.

"I've been in restaurants before, Sandy, believe it or not."

"Not this one though, right? You see that little lady over there?" Lord's surprisingly slender fingers sliced through the air. Jack's gaze fell on the congressional liaison. "I've fucked that woman five times in the past six months." Lord could not help but smile as Jack appraised the subject and came away duly impressed.

"Now ask yourself why a creature like that would condescend to sleep with a big old bag of fat like me."

"Maybe she feels sorry for you." Jack smiled.

Lord did not. "If you actually believe that, then you possess a naïveté that borders on incompetence. Do you really believe women in this town are any more pure than the men? Why should they be? Just because they have tits and a skirt doesn't mean they won't take what they want and use any means at their disposal to do so.

"You see, son, it's because I can give her what she wants, and I don't mean between the sheets. She knows that, I know that. I can open doors in this

138

town only a handful of men can. And the quid pro quo for that is she lets me fuck her. It's a straight commercial transaction entered into by intelligent, highly sophisticated parties. How about that?"

"How about it?"

Lord sat back in his chair, lit a fresh cigarette and blew precise rings to the ceiling. He picked at his lip and chuckled to himself.

"Something funny, Sandy?"

"I was just now thinking how you probably got a kick out of people like me when you were in law school. Thinking how you were never going to be like me. Gonna go defend illegal aliens wanting political asylum or do death row appeals for poor sonofabitches who've butchered a few too many people and blamed it on getting spanked by their momma when they were bad. Now come on, tell the truth, you did that, didn't you?"

Jack loosened his tie, took a sip of beer. He had seen Lord in action before. He smelled a setup.

"You're one of the best lawyers around, Sandy, everybody says so."

"Shit, I haven't practiced law in years."

"Whatever works for you."

"What works for you, Jack?"

Jack felt a slight but perceptible clinch in his gut as he heard his name pass through Lord's lips. It suggested a coming intimacy that had startled him, despite his knowledge of its inevitability. Partner? Jack took a breath and shrugged.

"Who knows what they want to be when they grow up?"

"But see you are grown up, Jack, and it's time to pay the man at the door. So what's it gonna be?"

"I'm not following this."

Lord leaned in again, hands clenched, like a heavyweight pressing the exchange, looking for the tiniest opening. Indeed, for a moment, an attack seemed imminent. Jack tensed.

"You think I'm an asshole, don't you?"

Jack picked up his menu again. "Recommend anything?"

"Come on, kid, you think I'm a greedy, ego-centric, power-happy asshole who doesn't give a shit about anything or anybody that can't do something for me. Ain't that right, Jack!" Lord's voice was rising, his thick body half out of his chair. He pushed Jack's menu back down to the table.

Jack nervously scanned the room, but no one seemed to be paying attention, which meant every word of the exchange was being carefully absorbed and dissected. Lord's red eyes focused directly on Jack's, pulling them to him.

"I am, you know. That's exactly what I am, Jack."

Lord settled back in his chair, triumphant. He grinned. Jack felt inclined to smile in spite of the repulsiveness.

Jack relaxed a notch. Almost as if sensing that slight release, Lord slid his chair over next to Jack's, crowding him. For a moment Jack seriously con-templated decking the older man – enough was enough.

"That's right, I'm all those things, Jack, all those things and more, much more. But you know what, Jack? That's who I am. I don't try to disguise it or explain it. Every sonofabitch that has ever met me has come away knowing exactly who and what I was. I believe in what I do. There's no bullshit there." Lord took a deep breath, and then slowly let it out. Jack shook his head, trying to clear it.

"What about you, Jack?"

"What about me?"

"Who are you, Jack? What do you believe in, if anything?"

"I've got twelve years of Catholic school, I've got to believe in something."

Lord shook his head wearily. "You're disappointing me. I heard you were a bright kid. Either my reports are wrong, or you've got that shit-eating grin on your face because you're afraid of what you might say."

Jack grasped Lord's wrist in a viselike grip.

"What the fuck do you want from me?"

Lord smiled and gently rapped Jack's hand until the grip was released.

"You like these kinds of places? With Baldwin as a client you'll be eating in places like this until your arteries are hard as drill bits. In about forty years, you'll keel over in some sand trap in the Caribbean and leave behind some young and suddenly rich third-time-around honey; but you'll die happy, believe me."

"One place is the same as another to me."

Lord's hand came down hard on the table. This time several heads did turn. The maitre d' glanced in their direction, trying to conceal his apprehension behind his thick mustache and quiet air of competence.

"That's my whole goddamned point, son, that goddamned ambivalence of yours." His voice lowered, but he continued to lean into Jack, crowding him. "One place is definitely not the same as another. You have the key to this place, you know. Your key is Baldwin and that nice-looking daughter of his. Now the question becomes: will you or won't you open that door? Which query interestingly enough leads us right back to my original question. What do you believe in, Jack? Because if you do not believe in this" – Lord spread his arms wide – "if you do not want to become the Sandy Lord of the next generation, if you wake up at night and laugh at or

141

curse my little idiosyncrasies, my assholeness if you will, if you really and truly believe you are above that, if you really hate whaling away at Ms. Baldwin and if you don't see one single item on that menu that you care for, then why don't you tell me to fuck off? And get up and walk out that door there, your head high, your conscience clear, and your beliefs intact? Because frankly this game is far too important and intensely played for the uncommitted."

Lord slumped back in his chair, his mass extrapolating outward until it fully engulfed the space.

Outside the restaurant a truly beautiful fall day was unfolding. Neither rain nor excessive humidity marred the blue sky's perfectness; the gentle breeze rustled discarded newspapers. The torrid pace of the city seemed to have momentarily slowed a notch. Down the street at LaFayette Park, sunseekers lay in the grass, hoping for a few more moments of tan before the really cold weather set in. Bike messengers on break prowled the area looking for unconcealed legs and blouses open just a peek.

Inside the restaurant Jack Graham and Sandy Lord were staring at each other.

"You don't pull any punches, do you?"

"I don't have time for that, Jack. Not for the last twenty years. If I didn't believe you could handle the direct approach, I would've just bullshit with you and let it go."

"What do you want me to say?"

"All I want to know is whether you're in or out. The truth is, with Baldwin, you could go to any other shop in town. You chose us, I'm presuming, because you like what you saw."

"Baldwin recommended you."

"He's a smart man. Lots of people would follow his lead. You've been with us one year. If you choose to stay, you'll be made a partner. Frankly, the twelve-month wait was purely a formality, to see if we were a good fit. After that you will never have any financial concerns, not counting your future wife's considerable monies. Your main occupation will be to keep Baldwin happy, and to expand that piece of business, and to bring in anybody else you can. Because let's face it, Jack, the only security any lawyer has are the clients he controls. They never tell you that in law school and it's the most important lesson you have to learn. Never, never lose sight of that fact. Even doing the work should take a back seat to that. There'll always be bodies to do the work. You will be given carte blanche to chase more business. You will have no one supervising you, except Baldwin. You will not have to monitor the legal work being done for Baldwin, we have others who will do that for you. All in all, not such a terrible life."

Jack looked down at his hands. Jennifer's face appeared there. So perfect. He felt guilty for having assumed she had had Barry Alvis fired. Then he thought of the numbing hours as a PD. His thoughts finally turned to Kate, and then quickly stopped. What was there? The answer was nothing. He looked up.

"Stupid question. Do I get to keep practicing law?"

"If that's what you want." Lord eyed him closely. "So do I take that as a yes?"

Jack glanced down at the menu. "The crab cakes look good."

Sandy exhaled smoke to the ceiling and smiled broadly. "I love 'em, Jack. I goddamn love 'em."

Two hours later, Sandy stood in the corner of his massive office suite staring out onto the busy street below, while a conference call plodded forward on the speaker phone.

Dan Kirksen walked in the door, his stiff bow tie

and crisp shirt concealing a slender jogger's body. Kirksen was the firm's managing partner. He had unwavering control over everyone in the place except Sandy Lord. And now perhaps Jack Graham.

Lord glanced at him with uninterested eyes. Kirksen sat down and waited patiently until the conference call participants said their good-byes. Lord clicked the phone off and sat down in his chair. Leaning back, he eyed the ceiling and lit up. Kirksen, a health fanatic, inched back from the desk.

"You want something?" Lord's eyes had finally come to rest on Kirksen's lean, hairless face. The man consistently controlled a shade under six hundred thousand in business, which guaranteed him a long, secure home at PS&L, but those numbers were chickenshit to Lord and he did nothing to hide his dislike of the firm's managing partner.

"We were wondering how the lunch went."

"You can handle the softballs. I don't have time to play fucking softball."

"We had heard unsettling rumors, and then with Alvis having to be terminated when Ms. Baldwin called."

Lord waved a hand through the air. "That's taken care of. He loves us, he's staying. And I wasted two hours."

"The amount of money at stake, Sandy, we all felt it would be better, it would convey the strongest possible impression if you—"

"Yeah. I understand the numbers, Kirksen, better than you, I understand the numbers. Okay? Now, Jacky boy is staying put. With luck he might double his fishing line in ten years, and we can all retire early." Lord looked over at Kirksen, who seemed to grow smaller and smaller under the big man's gaze. "He's got balls, you know. More balls than any of my other partners."

Kirksen winced.

"In fact, I kind of like the kid." Lord stood up and moved over to the window, where he watched a procession of preschoolers attached together with rope cross the street ten stories below.

"Then I can report a positive to the committee?"

"You can report any goddamn thing you like. Just remember one thing: don't you boys ever bother me with one of these things again, unless it's really, really important, you understand me?"

Lord glanced once more at Kirksen and then his eyes returned to the window. Sullivan still had not called. That was not good. He could see his country slipping away, like the little bodies disappearing around the corner. Gone.

"Thank you, Sandy."

"Yeah."

NINE

Walter Sullivan stared at the face, or what was left of it. The exposed foot showed the official morgue toe tag. While his entourage waited outside, he quietly sat alone with her. The identification had already been formally made. The police had gone off to update their records, the reporters to file their stories. But Walter Sullivan, one of the most powerful men of his era, who had made money from nearly everything he had touched since he was fourteen, now suddenly found himself bereft of energy, of any will whatsoever.

The press had had a field day with him and Christy after his marriage of forty-seven years had ended in the death of his first wife. But at almost eighty years old, he had just wanted something young and alive. After so much death, he had wanted something that would most certainly outlive him. With close friends and loved ones dying around him, he had passed his tolerance level as a mourner. Growing old was not easy, even for the very rich.

But Christy Sullivan had not survived him. And he was going to do something about that. It was fortunate that he was largely ignorant of what lay ahead for the remains of his late wife. It was a necessary process that was not in the least designed to comfort the victim's family.

As soon as Walter Sullivan left the room, a technician would enter and wheel the late Mrs. Sullivan into the autopsy room. There she would be weighed and have her height confirmed. She would be photographed, first fully clothed, and then in the nude. Then X-rayed and fingerprinted. A complete external exam would be conducted, with the intent of noting and obtaining as much usable evidence and as many clues as possible from the body. Fluids would be taken and sent to toxicology for drug and alcohol screens and other testing. A Y incision would split her body shoulder to shoulder, chest to genitals. A horrific chasm for even the veteran observer. Every organ would be analyzed and weighed, her genitalia checked for signs of sexual intercourse or damage. Every trace of semen, blood or foreign hair would be sent for DNA typing.

Her head would be examined, wound patterns traced. Then a saw would make an intermastoid incision over the top of the skull, cutting through the scalp and down to the bone. Next, the front quadrant of the skull would be cut away and the brain removed through the frontal craniotomy and examined. The one slug would be extracted, marked for chain-of-custody purposes and held for ballistics.

Once that process was completed, Walter Sullivan would be given back his wife.

Toxicology would verify the contents of her stomach and traces of foreign substances in her blood and urine.

The autopsy protocol would be prepared, listing the cause and mechanism of death and all relevant findings, and the official opinion of the Medical Examiner.

The autopsy protocol, together with all photographs, X-rays, fingerprints, toxicology reports and any other information constituting the entire case file would be deposited with the detective in charge.

Walter Sullivan finally rose, covered the remains of his deceased wife and left.

From behind yet another one-way mirror, the detective's eyes followed the bereaved husband as he left the room. Then Seth Frank put on his hat and quietly exited.

Conference room number one, the largest in the firm, held a prominent center position right behind the reception area. Now, behind the thick sliding doors, a meeting of the entire partnership had just convened.

Between Sandy Lord and another senior partner sat Jack Graham; his partnership not yet official, but protocol was not important today and Lord had insisted.

Coffee was poured by the housekeeping staff, danishes and muffins were distributed around, and then the help retreated, closing the doors behind them.

All heads turned to Dan Kirksen. He sipped his juice, tapped his mouth affectedly with his napkin and rose.

"As I'm sure you've heard by now, a terrible tragedy has befallen one of our most" – Kirksen glanced quickly at Lord – "or I should say, our most significant client." Jack looked around the sixty-foot marble-top table. Most heads remained trained on Kirksen, a few others were filled in on the events by whispers from their neighbor. Jack had seen the headlines. He had never worked on any of Sullivan's matters but he knew they were extensive enough to occupy forty attorneys at the firm on almost a full-time basis. He was, by far, Patton, Shaw's biggest client.

Kirksen continued, "The police are investigating the matter thoroughly. As yet there have been no developments in the case." Kirksen paused, glanced again at Lord, and then continued, "As one can imagine, this is a very distressing time for Walter. To make matters as easy as possible for him during this time, we are asking all attorneys to pay particular attention to any Sullivan-related matters, and, hopefully, to nip any potential problem in the bud before it escalates. Further, while we do not believe that this is anything other than a routine burglary with a very unfortunate result, and is in no way connected to any of Walter's business affairs, we are asking each of you to be alert for any unusual signs in any of the dealings in which you are engaged on Walter's behalf. Any suspicious activity is to be reported immediately to either myself or Sandy."

A number of heads turned toward Lord, who was looking at the ceiling in his customary fashion. Three cigarette butts lay in the ashtray in front of him, the remains of a Bloody Mary beside it.

Ron Day, from the international law section, spoke up. His neatly trimmed hair framed an owlish face partially obscured by slender oval spectacles. "This isn't a terrorist thing, is it? I've been putting together a string of Middle Eastern joint ventures for Sullivan's Kuwaiti subsidiary, and those people operate under their own rules, I can tell you that. Should I be worried for my personal safety? I'm on a flight this evening for Riyadh."

Lord swiveled his head around until his eyes fell on Day. Sometimes it surprised him how myopic if not downright idiotic many of his partners were. Day was a service partner whose main, and in Lord's mind only, strength was his ability to speak seven languages and politely kiss the ass of the Saudis.

"I wouldn't worry about that, Ron. If this is an international conspiracy, you're not important enough to dick around with, and if they do target you, you'll be dead before you ever see it coming."

Day fiddled with his necktie as an uneasy mirth quietly circled the table.

"Thank you for the clarification, Sandy."

"You're welcome, Ron."

Kirksen cleared his throat. "Rest assured that everything that can be done to solve this heinous crime is being done. There's even talk that the President himself will authorize a special investigative task force to look into the matter. As you know, Walter Sullivan has served in various capacities in several administrations, and is one of the President's closest friends. I think we can assume that the criminals will be in custody shortly." Kirksen sat down.

Lord looked around the table, elevated his eyebrows and crushed out his last cigarette. The table cleared.

Seth Frank swiveled around in his chair. His office was a six-by-six pen, the Sheriff warranting the only spacious area in the small headquarters building. The Medical Examiner's report was on his desk. It was only seven-thirty in the morning but Frank had already read every word of the report three times.

He had attended the autopsy. It was just something detectives had to do, for a lot of reasons. Although he had been present at literally hundreds of them, he had never grown comfortable with seeing the dead tinkered with like the animal remains every college biology student has sunk their digits into. And although he no longer became ill at the sight, it usually took him two or three hours of driving around aimlessly before he could attempt to settle back down to work.

The report was thick and neatly typed. Christy Sullivan had been dead at least seventy-two hours, probably longer. The swelling and blistering of the body, and the bacteria and gaseous onset in her organs, substantiated that time range with pretty good accuracy. However, the room had been very warm, which had accelerated the postmortem putrefaction of the body. That fact, in turn, made ascertaining the actual time of death increasingly difficult. But not less than three days, the Medical Examiner had been firm on that. Frank also had ancillary information that led him to believe that Christine Sullivan had met her death on Monday night, which would put them smack in the three-to-four-day range.

Frank felt himself frowning. A minimum of three days meant he was facing a very cold trail. Someone who knew what they were doing could disappear from the face of the earth in three or four days. Added to that was the fact that now Christine Sullivan had been dead a while now and his investigation was really no further along than when he started. He could not remember a case where the trail was so nonexistent.

As far as they could ascertain there were no witnesses to the incidents at the Sullivan estate, other than the decedent and whoever had murdered her. Notices had been placed in the papers, at banks and shopping centers. No one had come forward.

They had talked to every homeowner within a three-mile radius. They had all expressed shock, outrage and fear. Frank had seen the latter in the twitch of an eyebrow, hunched shoulders and the nervous rubbing of hands. Security would be even tighter than ever in the little county. All those emotions, however, yielded no usable information. The staffs of each of the neighbors had also been thoroughly questioned. There was nothing there. Telephone interviews had been conducted of Sullivan's household staff, who had accompanied him to Barbados, with nothing earth-shattering to report back. Besides, they all had ironclad alibis. Not that that was insurmountable. Frank filed that away in the back of his mind.

They also did not have a good snapshot of Christine Sullivan's last day of life. She was murdered in her house, presumably late at night. But if she had indeed been murdered on Monday night, what had she been doing during the day? Frank believed that information had to lend them something to go on.

At nine-thirty in the morning on that Monday, Christine Sullivan had been seen in downtown Washington at an upscale salon where it would cost Frank two weeks' pay to send his wife for a pampering. Whether the woman was gearing up for some late-night fun or this was something the rich did on a regular basis was something Frank would have to find out. Their inquiries had turned up nothing on Sullivan's whereabouts after she had left the salon around noon. She had not returned to her apartment in the city, nor had she taken a taxicab anywhere that they could determine.

If the little woman had stayed behind when everyone else went to the sunny south, she had to have a reason, he figured. If she had been with someone that night, that was someone Frank wanted to talk to, and maybe handcuff.

Ironically, murder in the commission of a burglary did not constitute capital murder in Virginia, although, interestingly enough, murder during the course of an armed robbery did. If you robbed and killed, you could be sentenced to death. If you burgled and killed, the most you'd be looking at was life, which wasn't that great a choice given the barbaric conditions of most state prisons. But Christine Sullivan had worn much jewelry. Every report the detective had received indicated she was a great lover of diamonds, emeralds, sapphires; you name it, she wore it. There was no jewelry on the body, although it was easy enough to see the marks on the skin the rings had made. Sullivan had also confirmed that his wife's diamond necklace was missing. The beauty salon owner also remembered seeing that particular piece on Monday.

A good prosecutor could make out a case of robbery on those facts, Frank was sure of it. The perps were lying in wait, premeditation the whole way. Why should the good people of Virginia have to pay thousands of dollars a year to feed, clothe and house a coldblooded killer? Burglary? Robbery? Who the fuck really cared? The woman was dead. Blown away by some sick goon. Legal distinctions like that did not sit well with Frank. Like many law enforcement people, he felt the criminal-justice system was weighted far too heavily in favor of the defendant. It often seemed to him that lost in the entire convoluted process with its intricate deals, technical traps and ultrasmooth defense attorneys was the fact that someone had actually broken the law. That someone had been hurt, raped or killed. That was just flat-out wrong. Frank had no way to change the system, but he could peck around its edges.

He pulled the report closer, fumbling with his reading glasses. He took another sip of the thick, black coffee. Cause of death: lateral gunshot wounds to the cephalic region caused by high-velocity, large-caliber firearm(s) firing one expanding, softnose bullet causing a perforating wound, and a second slug of unknown composition from an unidentified weapon source causing a penetrating wound. Which, in ordinary English, meant her brain had been blown apart by some heavy-duty hardware. The report also stated that the manner of death was homicide, which was the only clear element Frank could see in the entire case. He noted that he had been correct in his

153

conclusion of the distance from which the shots had come. There were no traces of powder in the wound track. The shots had come from over two feet away: Frank surmised that the distance was probably closer to six feet, but that was only his gut talking. Not that suicide had ever been a consideration. But murders for hire were usually of the barrel-to-flesh variety. That particular method cut down considerably on the margin of error.

Frank leaned closer to his desk. Why more than one shot? The woman most certainly was killed with the first round. Was the assailant a sadist, pumping round after round into a dead body? And yet they could account for only two entries into the body, hardly the lead barrage of some madman. Then there was the issue of the slugs. A dumdum and a mystery bullet.

He held up a bag with his mark on it. Only one round had been recovered from the body. It had entered below the right temple, flattened and expanded on impact, penetrated the skull and brain, causing a shock wave of the soft brain tissue, like rolling up a carpet.

He carefully nudged the caged creature or what was left of it. A gruesome projectile that was designed to flatten upon impact and then proceed to rip apart everything in its path, it had worked as designed on Christine Sullivan. Problem was dumdums were everywhere now. And the projectile deformity had been immense. Ballistics had been next to useless.

The second round had entered a half-inch above the other, traversed the entire brain, and exited the other side, leaving a gaping hole much larger than the entrance wound. The bone and tissue damage had been considerable.

This bullet's resting place had given them all a surprise. A half-inch hole in the wall against the bed.

Ordinarily after having cut out the piece of plaster, the lab personnel, using special tools, would have extracted the slug, being careful to preserve the grooving of the bullet, which would enable them to narrow down the make of gun from which it was fired and hopefully to eventually match it to a particular piece of ordnance. Fingerprints and ballistics identification were as close to certain as you got in this business.

Except in this case, while the hole was there, there was no slug in the hole, and no other slug in the room. When the lab had called him to report that finding, Seth Frank had gone down to see for himself. That was as angry as he had gotten in a long time.

Why go to the trouble of digging out a slug when you still had one in the corpse? What would the second slug show that the first wouldn't? There were possibilities.

Frank made some notes. The missing bullet could be a different caliber or type, which probably would show there were at least two assailants. Strong as his imagination was, Frank could not realistically envision one person wielding a gun in each hand and popping off at the woman. So now he had a probable two suspects. That would also explain the different entry, exit and internal wound patterns. The tumbling dumdum's entry hole was larger than the other slug's. So the second slug wasn't a hollow or softnose. It had blown right through her head, leaving a tunnel half the width of a pinkie in its wake. Projectile deformity had probably been minimal, which was meaningless since he didn't have the damn slug.

He looked over his initial scene notes. He was in the collection-of-information stage. He hoped he would not be stuck there forever. At least he didn't have to worry about the statute of limitations expiring on this one.

He looked at the report one more time, and his frown returned.

He picked up his phone and dialed. Ten minutes later he was sitting across from the Medical Examiner in the latter's office.

The big man pried at his cuticles with an old scalpel and finally glanced up at Frank.

"Strangulation marks. Or at least *attempted* strangulation. Understand, the trachea wasn't crushed, although there was some swelling and hemorrhaging in the tissue, and I found evidence of a slight fracture of the hyoid bone. Got traces of petechia in the conjunctiva of the eyelids too. Nonligature. It's all in the protocol."

Frank turned that over in his mind. Petechia, or tiny hemorrhages in the conjunctiva, or mucous membrane, of the eyes and eyelids, could be caused by strangulation and the resulting pressure on the brain.

Frank leaned forward in his chair, looked at the degrees lining the wall proclaiming the man opposite from him to be a long-dedicated student of forensic pathology.

"Man or woman?"

The Medical Examiner shrugged at the inquiry.

"Hard to tell. Human skin isn't a stellar surface for prints, as you know. In fact it's pretty impossible except in a few discrete areas, and after about half a day, if there was anything there, it won't be anymore. Hard to imagine, though, a woman trying to strangle another woman with her bare hands, but it's happened. Doesn't take much pressure to crush a trachea, but bare-handed strangling's usually a macho method of inflicting death. In a hundred strangling cases, I've never seen one where it was proved that a woman committed it. This was from the front too," he added. "*Mano a mano*. You'd have to be pretty damn confident of your strength advantage. My educated guess? It was a man, for what a guess is worth."

"The report also says there were contusions and bruises on the left side of her jaw, loosened teeth and cuts on the inside of her mouth?"

"Looks like somebody belted her a good one. One of the molars almost penetrated her cheek."

Frank glanced at his case file. "The second bullet?"

"The damage inflicted leads me to believe it's a large caliber, just like the first."

"Any guesses on the first?"

"That's all it would be. Maybe .357, .41. Could've been a 9mm too. Jesus, you saw the slug. Damn thing was flat as a pancake with half of it dispersed through her brain tissue and fluid. No lands, grooves, twists. Even if you find a probable firearm you're not going to get a match there."

"If we can find the other one, we might be in business."

"Maybe not. Whoever dug it out of that wall probably messed up the markings. Ballistics won't be happy with that."

"Yeah, but it might just have some of the deceased's hair, blood and skin imbedded in the nose. That's some trace I'd love to get my hands on."

The ME rubbed his chin thoughtfully. "That's true. But you've got to find it first."

"Which we probably won't." Frank smiled.

"You never know."

The two men looked at each other, knowing full well that there was no way in hell they were going to find the other slug. Even if they did, they couldn't place it at the murder scene unless it had trace evidence of the deceased on it, or they could find the gun that had fired it and placed the weapon at the murder scene. A potential double whammy.

157

"Find any brass?"

Frank shook his head.

"Then you got no pinprick either, Seth." The Medical Examiner was referring to the unique imprint left by the firing pin of a gun on the base of the shell casing.

"Never said it would be easy. By the way, state guys giving you room to breathe on this one?"

The Medical Examiner smiled. "Remarkably silent. Now if it had been Walter Sullivan getting whacked, who knows? I already filed my report in Richmond."

Then Frank said the question he had really come to ask.

"Why two shots?"

The Medical Examiner stopped picking his cuticle, put down his scalpel and looked at Frank.

"Why not?" His eyes crinkled. He was in the unenviable position of being more than competent for the opportunities presented him in the quiet county. One of approximately five hundred Deputy Medical Examiners in the commonwealth, he enjoyed a thriving general practice but had a personal fascination with both police investigations and forensic pathology. Before settling into a quiet life in Virginia he had served as a deputy coroner for Los Angeles County for almost twenty years. It didn't get much worse than L.A. for homicides. But this was one he could get his teeth into.

Frank looked at him intently and said, "Either shot would have obviously been fatal. No question. So why fire a second? You wouldn't for a lot of reasons. Number one being the noise. Number two, if you want to get the hell out of there, why take the time to pump another round into her? On top of that, why leave behind another slug that could ID you later on? Did Sullivan startle them? If so, why did the shot

158

come from the doorway into the room, and not the other way around? Why was the firing line descending? Was she on her knees? She probably was or else the shooter was off the scale height-wise. If she was on her knees, why? Execution-style? But there were no contact wounds. And then you have the marks on the neck. Why try to strangle her first, then stop, pick up a gun and blow her head off? And then blow it off again. One slug's taken. Why? A second gun? Why try to hide that? What's significant about that?"

Frank stood up and moved around the room, his hands stuck deep into his pockets, a habit of his when thinking intently. "And the crime scene was so fucking clean I couldn't believe it. There was nothing left. And I mean nothing. I'm surprised they didn't operate on her and pull out the other slug.

"I mean, come on, this guy was a burglar or maybe that's what he wants us to believe. But the vault *was* cleaned out. About four and a half million taken. And what was Mrs. Sullivan doing there? She was supposed to be sunning in the Caribbean. Did she know the guy? Was she screwing around on the side? If she was, are the two incidents related in any way? And why the hell would you waltz in the front door, knock out the security system, and then use a rope to climb out the window? Every time I ask myself one question another one pops up." Frank sat back down, looking slightly bewildered at his outpouring.

The Medical Examiner leaned back in his chair, twirled the case file around and took a minute to read over it. He took off his glasses and wiped them on his sleeve, tugged at a corner of his lip with his thumb and index finger.

Frank's nostrils quivered as he watched the ME. "What?"

"You mentioned nothing being left at the crime

159

scene. I've been thinking about that. You're right. It was *too* clean." The Medical Examiner took his time in lighting up a Pall Mall – unfiltered, Frank noted. Every pathologist he had ever worked with had smoked. The Medical Examiner blew rings in the air, obviously enjoying this mental exercise.

"Her fingernails were too clean."

Frank looked puzzled.

The Medical Examiner continued, "I mean, there was no dirt, nail polish – although she was wearing it, bright red stuff – none of the ordinary residues you'd expect to find. Nothing. It was like they had been scoped out, you know what I mean?" He paused and then continued, "I also found minute traces of a solution." He paused again. "Like a cleansing solution."

"She'd been to some fancy beauty salon that morning. For a nail job and all that."

The ME shook his head. "Then you'd expect to find more residue, not less, with all the chemicals they use."

"So what are you saying? That her nails were deliberately cleaned out?"

The Medical Examiner nodded. "Someone was real careful not to leave any ident material behind."

"Which means they were paranoid about being identified, somehow, by the physical evidence."

"Most perps are, Seth."

"To a degree. But squirting out fingernails and leaving a place so clean our E-vac came up basically empty is a little much."

Frank scanned the report. "You also found traces of oil on her palms?"

The ME nodded, looked closely at the detective. "A preservative/protective compound. You know, like you'd use on fabrics, leathers, stuff like that."

"So she may have been holding something and the residue was left there?"

160

"Yep. Although we can't be sure exactly when the oil came to be on her hands." The Medical Examiner put his glasses back on. "You think she knew the person, Seth?"

"None of the evidence points that way, unless she invited him over to burglarize the place."

The Medical Examiner had a sudden inspiration. "Maybe she set up the burglary. You know? Tired of the old man, brings in the new bedroom buddy to conveniently steal their nest egg and it's off to Fairy Tale Land?"

Frank considered the theory. "Except they have a falling out or there's a double cross all along, and she gets the business end of some serious lead?"

"It fits the facts, Seth."

Frank shook his head. "From all accounts the deceased loved *being* Mrs. Walter Sullivan. More than the money, if you know what I mean. She got to rub shoulders, and probably other parts of her anatomy, with famous people all over the world. Pretty heady for somebody who used to flip burgers at a Burger King."

The ME stared at him. "You're kidding?"

The detective smiled. "Eighty-year-old billionaires sometimes get strange ideas. It's like where does the eight-hundred-pound gorilla sit? Anywhere he damn well pleases."

The Medical Examiner grinned and shook his head. Billionaire? What would he do with a billion dollars? He looked down at the ink blotter on his desk. Then he put out his cigarette and looked back at the report, then at Frank. He cleared his throat.

"I think the second slug was a semi- or full-metal jacket."

Frank loosened his tie, put his elbows on the desk. "Okay."

The Medical Examiner went on. "It blew through

161

the right temporal bone of the cranium and burst through the left pareital bone, leaving an exit wound over twice the size of the entry."

"So you're saying definitely two guns."

"Not unless the guy was chambering different types of ammo in the same gun." He looked keenly at the detective. "That doesn't seem to surprise you, Seth."

"It would have an hour ago. It doesn't now."

"So we probably have two perps."

"Two perps with two guns. And a lady how big?"

The Medical Examiner didn't need to refer to his notes. "Sixty-two inches tall, one hundred and five pounds."

"So a little woman and two probable male perps with heavy-caliber hardware who try to strangle her, beat her up and then both open fire on her, killing her."

The Medical Examiner rubbed at his chin. The facts were more than a little puzzling.

Frank glanced at the report. "You're sure the strangulation marks and beating came before death?"

The Medical Examiner looked offended. "Positive. Pretty mess, isn't it?"

Frank flipped through the report, making notes as he went. "You could say that. No attempted rape. Nothing like that?"

The Medical Examiner didn't answer.

Finally Frank looked up at him, took off his glasses, put them down on the desk and leaned back, sipping the black coffee he had been offered earlier.

"The report doesn't say anything about a sexual assault," he reminded his friend.

The Medical Examiner finally stirred. "The report's correct. There was no sexual assault. No trace of seminal fluid, no evidence of penetration, no overt bruising. All that leads me to conclude,

162

officially, that no sexual assault occurred."

"So? You're not satisfied with that conclusion?" Frank looked at him expectantly.

The Medical Examiner took a sip of coffee, stretched out his long arms until he felt a comforting pop deep within the confines of his aging body and then leaned forward.

"Your wife ever go in for a gynecological exam?"

"Sure, doesn't every woman?"

"You'd be surprised," the Medical Examiner replied dryly, then continued. "Thing is, you go in for an exam, no matter how good the ob-gyn is, there's usually some slight swelling and small abrasions in the genitalia. It's the nature of the beast. To be thorough, you have to get in there and dig around."

Frank put down his coffee, shifted in his chair. "So what are you saying, she had her gynecologist visit her in the middle of the night right before she got popped?"

"The indications were slight, very slight, but they were there." The Medical Examiner paused, choosing his words carefully. "I've been thinking about it ever since I handed in the protocol. Understand, it could be nothing. She could have done it herself, you understand what I'm saying? To each their own. But from the looks of it, I don't think it was self-inflicted. I think somebody examined her shortly *after* her death. Maybe two hours after, maybe earlier."

"Checked her for what? To see if something had happened?" Frank did not try to hide his incredulity.

The Medical Examiner eyed him steadily. "Not much else to check a woman for down there in that particular situation, is there?"

Frank stared at the man for a long moment. This information merely added to his already increasing temple throbber. He shook his head. The balloon theory again. Push one side in and it bulges out somewhere else. He scribbled down some notes, his eyebrows bunched together, the coffee sipped unconsciously.

The Medical Examiner looked him over. This was not an easy one, but so far, the detective had punched all the right buttons, asked good questions. He was puzzled, but then that was a big part of the process. The good ones never solved them all. But then they also didn't remain puzzled forever. Eventually, if you were lucky and diligent, maybe more of some on one case than on another, you would break it open, and the pieces would come tumbling into place. The Medical Examiner hoped this was one of those cases. Right now, it didn't look all that good.

"She was pretty drunk when she bought it." Frank was examining the toxicology report.

"Point two-one. I haven't personally seen that number since my college frat days."

Frank smiled. "Well I'm wondering where she got that point two-one."

"Plenty of booze in a place like that."

"Yeah, except there were no dirty glasses, no open bottles, and no discards in the trash."

"So, maybe she got drunk somewhere else."

"So how'd she get home?"

The Medical Examiner thought for a moment, rubbed the sleep from his eyes. "Drove. I've seen people with higher percentages behind the wheel."

"You mean in the autopsy room, don't you?" Frank continued: "The problem with that theory is that none of the cars in the garage had been driven from the time the household left for the Caribbean."

"How do you know that? An engine isn't going to be warm after three days."

Frank perused the pages of his notebook, found what he wanted and slid it around to his friend.

"Sullivan has a full-time chauffeur. Old guy named Bernie Kopeti. Knows his cars, anal as a tax lawyer, and he keeps meticulous records on Sullivan's fleet of automobiles. Has the mileage for every one of them in a log book, updated daily, if you can believe it. At my request he checked the odometer on each of the cars in the garage, which presumably were the only ones the wife would have access to, and in fact were the only cars in the garage at the time of the discovery of the body. On top of that Kopeti confirmed that no vehicles were missing. There was no additional mileage on any of them. They hadn't been driven since everyone cleared out for the Caribbean. Christine Sullivan didn't drive home in one of those cars. So how did she get home?"

"Cab?"

Frank shook his head. "We've talked to every cab company that operates out here. No fare was dropped off at the Sullivan address on that night. It'd be pretty hard to forget the place, wouldn't you think?"

"Unless maybe the cabbie whacked her, and isn't talking."

"You're saying she invited a cabbie into her house?"

"I'm saying she was drunk and probably didn't know what the hell she was doing."

"That doesn't jibe with the fact that the alarm system was tampered with, or that there was a rope dangling outside her window. Or that we're probably talking about two perps. I've never seen a cab driven by two cabbies."

A thought struck Frank and he scribbled in his notebook. He was certain Christine Sullivan had been driven home by someone she knew. Since that person or persons had not come forward, Frank thought he had a pretty good idea why they hadn't. And exiting out the window via a rope instead of the way they'd entered – through the front door – meant that something had caused the killers to rush. The most obvious reason was the private security patrol, but the security guard on duty that night had not reported anything out of the ordinary. The perps didn't know that, however. The mere sight of the patrol car might have prompted such a hasty exit.

The Medical Examiner leaned back in his chair, unsure of what to say. He spread out his hands. "Any suspects?"

Frank finished writing. "Maybe."

The Medical Examiner looked sharply at him. "What's her husband's story? One of the richest guys in the country."

"The world." Frank put his notebook away, picked up the report, drained the last of his coffee. "She decided to opt out on the way to the airport. Her husband believes she went to stay at their Watergate apartment in town. That fact has been confirmed. Their jet was scheduled to pick her up in three days and take her down to the Sullivan estate outside of Bridgetown, Barbados. When she didn't show at the airport, Sullivan got worried and started calling. That's his story."

"She give him any reason for the change in plan?"

"Not that he's telling me."

"Rich guys can afford the best. Make it look like a burglary while they're four thousand miles away swinging in a hammock sipping island bug juice. Think he's one of them?"

Frank stared at the wall for a long moment. His thoughts went back to the memory of Walter Sullivan sitting quietly next to his wife at the morgue. How he looked when he had no reason to believe anyone was watching.

Frank looked at the Medical Examiner, then got up to leave.

"No. I don't."

TEN

Bill Burton was sitting in the White House Secret Service command post. He slowly put down the newspaper, his third of the morning. Each carried a follow-up account of the murder of Christine Sullivan. The facts were virtually the same as the initial stories. Apparently there were no new developments.

He had talked to Varney and Johnson. At a cookout over the weekend at his place. Just him, Collin and their two fellow agents. The guy had been in the vault, seen the President and the Mrs. The man had come out, knocked out the President, killed the lady and gotten away despite the best efforts of Burton and Collin. That story didn't exactly match the actual sequence of events that night but both men had unfailingly accepted Burton's version of the occurrence. Both men had also expressed anger, indignation that anyone had laid a hand on the man they were dedicated to protect. The perp deserved what was coming to him. No one would hear of the President's involvement from them.

After they had left, Burton had sat in his backyard sipping a beer. If they only knew. The trouble was, he did. An honest man his entire life, Bill Burton did not savor his new role as prevaricator.

Burton swallowed his second cup of coffee and checked his watch. He poured himself another cup and looked around the White House Secret Service quarters.

He had always wanted to be a member of an elite security force, protecting the most important individual on the planet: the quiet resourcefulness, strength and intelligence of the Secret Service agent, the close camaraderie. The knowledge that at any moment you would be expected to and in fact would sacrifice your life for that of another man, for the benefit of the common good, made for a supremely noble act in a world more and more devoid of anything remotely virtuous. All that had allowed Agent William James Burton to get up with a smile each morning and sleep soundly at night. Now that feeling was gone. He had simply done his job, and the feeling was gone. He shook his head, sneaked a quick smoke.

Sitting on a keg of dynamite. That's what they all were doing. The more Gloria Russell explained it to him, the more impossible he thought it was.

The car had been a disaster. Very discreet inquiries had traced it directly to the goddamned D.C. police impoundment lot. That was too dangerous to push. Russell had been pissed. But let her be. She said she had this under control. Bullshit.

He folded up the paper, placed it neatly away for the next agent.

Fuck Russell. The more Burton thought about it the madder he became. But it was too late to go back now. He touched the left side of his jacket. His .357, filled with cement, along with Collin's 9mm, was at the bottom of the Severn River at the most remote point they could find. To most perhaps an unnecessary precaution, but to Burton, no precaution was unnecessary. The police had one useless slug and would never find the other. Even if they could, the barrel on his new pistol would be squeaky clean. Burton wasn't worried about the ballistics department of the local Virginia police bringing him down.

Burton hung his head as the events of that night raced through his mind. The President of the United States was an adulterer who had roughed up his lay for the night so badly she had tried to kill him and Agents Burton and Collin had to blow her away.

And then they had covered it all up. That's what made Burton wince every time he looked in the mirror. The cover-up. They had lied. By their silence they had lied. But hadn't he lied all this time? All these late-night trysts? When he greeted the First Lady each morning? When he played with their two kids on the rear lawn? Not telling them that her husband and their father was not nearly so nice and kind and good as they probably believed he was. As the whole country believed he was.

The Secret Service. Burton grimaced. It was an apt title for an unlikely reason. The crap he had seen going on over the years. And Burton had looked the other way. Every agent had, at one time or another. They all joked or complained about it in private, but that was all. That particular, if unwelcome, function came with the job. Power made people crazy; it made them feel invincible. And when something bad happened it was the working staff of the Secret Service who were expected to clean up the mess.

Several times Burton had picked up the phone to call the Director of the Secret Service. Tell him the whole story, try to cut his losses. But each time he had put the phone back down, unable to say the words that would end his career and, in essence, his life. And with each passing day, Burton's hopes grew a little brighter that it might all blow over, even though his common sense told him that could not possibly happen. Now it was too late to tell the truth, he felt. Calling in a day or two later with the story might be explained away, but not now.

His thoughts turned back to the investigation of

Christine Sullivan's death. Burton had read with great interest the findings of the autopsy, courtesy of the local police at the request of the President, who was so, so distraught over the tragedy. Fuck him too.

A shattered jaw and strangulation marks. His and Collin's shots had not inflicted those injuries. She had good reason to want to kill him. But Burton couldn't let that happen, under no circumstances could he let that happen. There were few absolutes anymore, but that was sure as hell one of them.

He had done the right thing. Burton told himself that a thousand times. The very action he had trained virtually his entire adult life for. The ordinary person couldn't understand, could never possibly comprehend how an agent would think or feel if something bad went down on their watch.

He had talked to one of Kennedy's agents a long time ago. The man had never gotten over Dallas. Walking right beside the President's limo, nothing he could do. And the President had died. Right in front of his eyes, the President's head had been blown apart. Nothing he could do, but there was always something. Always another precaution you could have taken. Turned to the left instead of the right, watched one building more closely than you had. Scanned the crowd with a little more intensity. Kennedy's guy had never been the same. Quit the Service, divorced, finished his human existence in obscurity in some rat's hole in Mississippi, but still living in Dallas for the last twenty years of his life.

That would never happen to Bill Burton. That was why he had hurled his body in front of Alan Richmond's predecessor six years ago and caught twin .38 caliber steel jackets for his trouble despite his body armor; one through the shoulder, the other through the forearm. Miraculously, neither had struck any vital organs or arteries, leaving Burton only with a number of scars and the heartfelt gratitude of an entire country. And, more important, the adulation of his fellow agents.

And that was why he had fired upon Christine Sullivan. And he would do the same thing today. He would kill her, kill her as often as it took. Pull the trigger, watch the one-hundred-sixty-grain bullet slam into the side of the head at over twelve hundred feet per second, the young life over. Her choice, not his. Dead.

He went back to work. While he still could.

Chief of Staff Russell walked briskly down the corridor. She had just finished briefing the President's press secretary on the appropriate spin for the Russia-Ukraine conflict. The bare politics of the matter dictated backing Russia, but bare politics rarely controlled the decision-making process in the Richmond administration. The Russian Bear had all the intercontinental nuclear forces now, but Ukraine was in a much better position to become a major trade player with the Western countries. What had tipped the scales in Ukraine's favor was the fact that Walter Sullivan, the good and now grieving friend of the President, was homing in on a major deal with that country. Sullivan and friends, through various networks, had contributed approximately twelve million dollars to Richmond's campaign, and garnered him virtually every major endorsement he needed in his quest for the Oval Office. There was no way he could not make a significant payback on that kind of effect. Hence, the United States would back Ukraine.

Russell looked at her watch, counting her blessings that there were independent reasons for siding with Kiev over Moscow, although she felt sure Richmond would have come out the same way regardless. He

172

did not forget loyalty. Favors must be returned. A President just happened to be in a position to return them on a massive, global scale. One major problem out of the way, she settled down at the desk and turned her attention to a growing list of crises.

Fifteen minutes into her political juggling, Russell rose and slowly walked over to the window. Life went on in Washington, much like it had for two hundred years. Factions were scattered everywhere, pouring money, massive intellects and established heavyweights into the business of politics, which essentially meant screwing others before they got around to screwing you. Russell understood that game, better than most. She also loved and excelled at it. This was clearly her element, and she was as happy as she'd been in years. Being unmarried and childless had started to worry her. The piles of professional accolades had grown monotonous, and hollow. And then Alan Richmond had come into her life. Made her see the possibility of moving up to the next level. Perhaps to a level where no woman had ever gone. That thought weighed so powerfully inside her head that she sometimes shook with anticipation.

And then a goddamned hunk of metal exploded in her face. Where was he? Why hadn't he come forward? He must, had to know what he had in his possession. If it was money he wanted, she would pay it. The slush funds at her disposal were more than adequate for even the most unreasonable demands, and Russell expected the worst. That was one of the wonderful things about the White House. No one really knew how much money it actually took to run the place. That was because so many agencies contributed parts of their budget and personnel to help the White House function. With so much financial confusion, administrations rarely had to worry about finding money for even the most outrageous purchases. No, Russell thought to herself, money would be the least of her worries. She had many others to concern herself with, however.

Did the man know that the President was totally oblivious to the situation? That was what was tearing Russell's stomach apart. What if he tried to communicate with the President directly, and not with her? She started to shake, and plopped down in a chair by the window. Richmond would immediately recognize Russell's intentions, there was no question of that. He was arrogant but no fool. And then he would destroy her. Just like that. And she would be defenseless. There would be no good exposing him. She couldn't prove a thing. Her word against his. And she would be relegated to the political toxic waste dump, condemned and then, worst of all, forgotten.

She had to find him. Somehow get a message to him, that he must work through her. There was only one person who could help her do that. She sat back down at her desk, collected herself and resumed working. This was no time to panic. Right now she needed to be stronger than she had ever been in her life. She could still make it, still control the outcome if she just kept her nerves in check, used the first-rate mind God had bestowed upon her. She could get out of this mess. She knew where she had to start.

The mechanism that she had chosen to use would strike anyone who knew Gloria Russell as particularly odd. But there was a side to the Chief of Staff that would surprise those few who claimed to know her well. Her professional career had always come foremost to the detriment of every other facet of her life, including the personal, and the sexual relationships that were spawned from that area of one's life. But Gloria Russell considered herself a very desirable woman; indeed, she possessed a feminine side that was in the sharpest contrast to her official shroud. That the years were going by, and rapidly, only increased the apprehension she had been starting to feel regarding this imbalance in her life. Not that she was necessarily planning anything, especially in light of the potential catastrophe she was confronted with, but she believed she knew the best way to accomplish this mission. And confirm her desirability in the process. She could not escape her feelings, no more than she could her shadow. So why try? Anyway, she also felt that subtlety would be lost on her intended target.

Several hours later she clicked off her desk lamp and called for her car. Then she checked the Secret Service staffing for the day and picked up her phone. Three minutes later Agent Collin stood before her, his hands clasped in front of him in a pose standard to all the agents. She motioned for him to wait a moment. She checked her makeup, performing a perfect oval with her lips as she reapplied her lipstick. Out of the corner of her eye she studied the tall, lean man standing next to her desk. The magazine-cover looks would've been difficult for any woman to consciously ignore. That his profession also dictated that he lived on the brink of danger and could, indeed, be dangerous himself, only added favorably to the total package. Like the bad boys in high school girls always seemed to be drawn to, if only to escape, momentarily, the dullness of their own existence. Tim Collin, she surmised with reasonable confidence, must have broken many a female heart in his relatively short life.

Her calendar was clear tonight, a rarity. She pushed her chair back and slipped into her heels. She didn't see Agent Collin as his eyes shifted to her legs and then quickly back to stare straight ahead. Had she seen, she would have been pleased, not least of all for the obvious reason.

"The President will be giving a press conference next week at the Middleton Courthouse, Tim."

"Yes, ma'am, nine-thirty-five A.M. We're working on the preliminaries right now." His eyes stared straight ahead.

"Do you find that a little unusual?"

Collin looked at her. "How so, ma'am?"

"It's after working hours, you can call me Gloria."

Collin shifted uncomfortably from one foot to another. She smiled at him, at his obvious awkwardness.

"You understand what the press conference is for, don't you?"

"The President will be addressing the" – Collin swallowed perceptibly – "the killing of Mrs. Sullivan."

"That's right. A President conducting a press conference regarding the homicide of a private citizen. Don't you find that curious? I believe it's a first in presidential history, Tim."

"I wouldn't know about that, ma— Gloria."

"You've spent a lot of time with him lately. Have you noticed anything unusual about the President?"

"Like what?"

"Like has he appeared overly stressed or worried? More than the usual?"

Collin slowly shook his head, not knowing where this conversation was intended to go.

"I think we might have a slight problem, Tim. I think the President might need our help. You're ready to help him, aren't you?"

"He's the President, ma'am. That's my job, to take care of him."

Rummaging in her bag, she said, "Are you busy tonight, Tim? You're off at the regular time tonight,

176

aren't you? I know the President's staying in."

He nodded.

"You know where I live. Come over as soon as you're off duty. I'd like to talk to you privately, continue this discussion. Would you mind helping me, and the President?"

Collin's answer was immediate. "I'll be there, Gloria."

Jack knocked on the door again. No answer. The blinds were drawn and no light emitted from the house. He was either asleep or not home. He checked the time. Nine o'clock. He remembered Luther Whitney to rarely be in bed before two or three A.M. The old Ford was in the driveway. The tiny garage door was shut. Jack looked in the mailbox beside the door. It was overflowing. That didn't look good. Luther was what now, mid-sixties? Would he find his old friend on the floor, cold hands clutching at his chest? Jack looked around and then lifted up a corner on a terra-cotta planter next to the front door. The spare key was still there. He looked around once more, then put the key in the door and went in.

The living room was neat and spare. Everything was stacked where it should be.

"Luther?" He moved through the hallway, his memory steering him through the simple con-figurations of the house. Bedroom on the left, toilet on the right, kitchen at the rear of the house, small screened porch off that, garden in the back. Luther was in none of these rooms. Jack entered the small bedroom, which, like the rest of the house, was neat and orderly.

On the nightstand a number of picture frames containing various photos of Kate looked at him as he sat on the side of the bed. He turned quickly away and left the room.

The tiny rooms upstairs were mostly bare. He listened intently for a moment. Nothing.

He sat down in the small wire and plastic kitchen chair, looked around. He didn't turn on a light, but sat in the darkness. He leaned across and popped open the refrigerator. He grinned. Two six-packs of Bud looked back at him. You could always count on Luther for a cold brew. He took one and opened the back door to step outside.

The small garden looked beaten down. The hostas and ferns drooped even in the shade of a thick oak and the Nelly Moser clematis clinging to the board-on-board fence was painfully withered. Jack looked at Luther's prized annuals flowerbed and noted more victims than survivors of the Washington late-summer heat furnace.

He sat down, put the beer to his lips. Luther had clearly not been here for a while. So? He was an adult. He could go where he wanted, when he wanted. But something just felt wrong. But it had been several years. Habits change. He reflected a moment more. But Luther's habits would not have changed. The man was not like that. He was rock-solid, as dependable a person as Jack had ever met in his life. Stacked-up mail, dead flowers, car not in the garage, that was not how he would have voluntarily left things. *Voluntarily.*

Jack went back inside. The answering machine tape was blank. He went back into the small bed-room, the musty air hitting him again as he opened the door. He scanned the room once more, then started to feel a little silly. He wasn't a goddamned detective. Then he laughed to himself. Luther was probably living it up on some island for a couple of weeks, and here he was playing the nervous parent. Luther was one of the most capable men Jack had ever met. Besides, it was no business of his anymore.

The Whitney family were not his concern, father or daughter. In fact, why was he even here? Trying to relive old times? Trying to get to Kate through her old man? That was the most unlikely scenario one could imagine.

Jack locked the door on the way out, replaced the key under the planter. He glanced back at the house and then walked to his car.

Gloria Russell's home occupied a cul-de-sac in a quiet upper-brackets Bethesda suburb off River Road. Her consulting work on behalf of many of the country's largest corporations coupled with her sizable professorship, and now Chief of Staff salary and many years of careful investing, had left her with a deep purse, and she liked to be surrounded by beautiful things. The entrance was framed by an aged arbor interlaced with strong, thick ivy. The entire front yard was enclosed by a waist-high brick and mortar serpentine wall and set up as a private garden complete with tables and umbrellas. A small fountain bubbled and hissed in a darkness broken only by the shallow light thrown from the big bay window in the front of the house.

Gloria Russell was sitting at one of the garden tables when Agent Collin pulled up in his convertible, back ramrod straight, suit still crisp, tie knotted rigidly. The Chief of Staff had not changed either. She smiled at him and they walked up the front walk together and into the house.

"Drink? You look like a bourbon-and-water person." Russell looked at the young man and slowly drained her third glass of white wine. It had been a long time since she had a young man over. Maybe too long, she was thinking, although the alcohol guaranteed that she wasn't thinking that clearly.

"Beer, if you have it."

"Coming up." She stopped to kick off her heels and padded into the kitchen. Collin looked around the expanse of the living room with its billowy professionally done curtains, textured wallpaper and tasteful antiques and wondered what he was doing here. He hoped she hurried with the beer. A star athlete, he had been seduced by women before, from high school on up. But this was not high school and Gloria Russell was no cheerleader. He decided he would not be able to endure the night without a heavy buzz. He had wanted to tell Burton about it, but something had made him keep quiet. Burton had been acting aloof and moody. What they had done was not wrong. He knew the circumstances were awkward, and an action that would ordinarily have brought them praise from the entire country had to be kept secret. He had regretted killing the woman, but there were no other options. Death happened, tragedies occurred all the time. It was her time. Christine Sullivan's number had just come up.

A few moments later he was sipping his beer and checking out the Chief of Staff's derriere as she fluffed up a pillow on the broad couch before sitting down. She smiled at him, delicately sipped her wine.

"How long have you been in the Service, Tim?"

"Almost six years."

"You've risen quickly. The President thinks quite a lot of you. He's never forgotten that you saved his life."

"I appreciate that. I really do."

She took another sip of wine and ran her eyes over him. He sat erect; his obvious nervousness amused her. She finished her examination and came away very impressed. Her attention had not been lost on the young agent, who was now hiding his discomfort by examining the numerous paintings that adorned the walls.

"Nice stuff." He pointed at the artwork.

She smiled at him, watched him hurriedly gulp his beer. *Nice stuff.* She had been thinking the same thing.

"Let's go sit where it's more comfortable, Tim." Russell stood up and looked down at him. He was led from the living room through a long, narrow hallway and then through double doors into a large sitting room. The lights came on by themselves, and Collin noted that through another set of double doors the Chief of Staff's bed was clearly visible.

"Would you mind if I take a minute to change? I've been in this suit long enough."

Collin watched as she went into her bedroom. She did not close the doors all the way. A sliver of the room was visible from where he was sitting. He turned his head away, tried to focus all his attention on the scrolls and designs of an antique fireplace screen that would be seeing activity soon. He finished his beer and instantly wanted another one. He lay back in the thick cushions. He tried not to but he could hear every sound she made. Finally, he couldn't resist it. He turned his head and looked straight through the open doorway. With a pinch of regret he saw nothing. At first. Then she moved across the opening.

It was only a moment, as she lingered by the end of the bed, to pick up some article of clothing. Chief of Staff Gloria Russell parading naked in front of him sent a jolt through Collin, although he had been expecting it, or something close to it.

The night's agenda confirmed, Collin turned his head away, more slowly than he probably should have. He licked the top of the beer can, absorbing the last few drops of the amber liquid. He felt the butt of his new weapon dig against his chest. Normally the mass of metal felt comforting against his skin. Now it just hurt.

He wondered about fraternization rules. Members of the First Family had been known to become quite attached to their Secret Service agents. Over the years there had always been talk of fooling around, but the official policy was clear on that point. Were Collin discovered in this room with a naked Chief of Staff in her bedroom, his career would be short-lived.

He thought rapidly. He could leave right now, report in to Burton. But how would that look? Russell would deny it all. Collin would look like a fool, and his career would probably be over anyway. She had brought him here for a reason. She said the President needed his help. He wondered now who he would really be helping. And for the first time Agent Collin felt trapped. Trapped. Where his athleticism, his quick wits and his 9mm were useless to him. Intellectually he was no match for the woman. In the official power structure he was so far below her, it was like he stared up from an abyss with a telescope and still couldn't glimpse the bottom of her high heels. It promised to be a long night.

Walter Sullivan paced while Sandy Lord watched. A bottle of Scotch occupied a prominent position on the corner of Lord's desk. Outside, the darkness was marred by the dull glow of street lamps. The heat had returned for a short spell and Lord had ordered the air conditioning to remain on at Patton, Shaw for his very special visitor tonight. That visitor stopped his pacing and stared down the street where a half-dozen blocks away sat the familiar white building, home to Alan Richmond, and one of the keys to Sullivan and Lord's grand scheme. Sullivan, however, was not thinking about business tonight. Lord was. But he was far too cunning to show it. Tonight he was here for his friend. To listen to the grief, the outpouring, to let Sullivan mourn his little hooker. The quicker that was done, the sooner they could get down to what really mattered: the next deal.

"It was a beautiful service, people will remember it for a long time." Lord chose his words carefully. Walter Sullivan was an old friend, but it was a friendship built on an attorney-client relationship and thus its underpinning could experience some unexpected shifting. Sullivan was also the only person in Lord's acquaintance who made him nervous, where Lord knew he was never in complete control, that the man he was dealing with was at least his equal and probably more.

"Yes it was." Sullivan continued to look down the street. He believed that he had finally convinced the police that the one-way mirror was not connected to the crime. Whether they were completely convinced was another matter. In any event it had been quite an embarrassing moment for a man not accustomed to such. The detective, Sullivan couldn't remember his name, had not given Sullivan the respect he deserved and that had angered the older man. If anything, he had earned the respect of everyone. It did not help matters that Sullivan did not feel the least bit confident in the local police's abilities to find the persons responsible.

He shook his head as his thoughts returned to the mirror. At least it had not been disclosed to the press. That was attention Sullivan could not tolerate. The mirror had been Christine's idea. But he had to admit he had gone along with it. Now as he looked back, it seemed ludicrous. At first it had fascinated him, watching his wife with other men. He was beyond the age where he could satisfy her himself, but he could not reasonably deny her the physical pleasures that were beyond him. But it had all been absurd, including the marriage. He saw that now. Trying to recapture his youth. He should have known that nature bowed to no one, regardless of their monetary worth. He was embarrassed and he was angry. He finally turned to Lord.

"I'm not certain that I have confidence in the detective in charge. How can we get the federals involved?"

Lord put his glass down, lifted a cigar from a box hidden within the recesses of his desk and slowly unwrapped it.

"Homicide of a private citizen isn't grounds for a federal investigation."

"Richmond is getting involved."

"Fluff, if you ask me."

Sullivan shook his massive head. "No. He seemed genuinely concerned."

"Maybe. Don't count on that concern lingering for too long. He has a thousand cans of worms to handle."

"I want the people responsible for this caught, Sandy."

"I understand that, Walter. Of all people, I understand that. They will be. You have to be patient. These guys weren't nickel-and-dimers. They knew what they were doing. But everybody makes mistakes. They'll go to trial, mark my words."

"And then what? Life imprisonment, correct?" Sullivan said contemptuously.

"It's probably not going to be a capital murder case, so life is what they'll end up getting. But no chance of parole, Walter, believe me. They'll never breathe another drop of free air. And getting a little prick in the arm might seem real desirable after a few years of getting bent over every night."

Sullivan sat down and stared at his friend. Walter Sullivan wanted no part of any trial. Where all the details of the crime would be revealed. He winced at the thought of all of it being rehashed. Strangers knowing intimate details of his life and that of his deceased wife. He could not bear that. He just wanted the men caught. He would arrange the rest. Lord had said the Commonwealth of Virginia would imprison for life the persons responsible. Walter Sullivan decided right then and there that he would save the commonwealth the cost of that lengthy incarceration.

Russell curled up on the end of the couch, bare feet tucked under a loose-fitting cotton pullover that stopped slightly above her calves. Her ample cleavage peeked at him where the fabric suddenly dipped. Collin had fetched himself two more beers and poured her another glass of wine from the bottle he had brought with him. His head was now slightly warm, as though a small fire were burning inside. The necktie was now loosened, the jacket and gun lay on the opposite couch. She had fingered it as he had taken it off.

"It's so heavy."

"You get used to it." She did not ask the question he was usually confronted with. She knew he had killed someone.

"Would you really take a bullet for the President?" She looked at him through drooping eyelids. She had to remain focused, she kept telling herself. That had not stopped her from leading the young man to the very threshold of her bed. She felt a large measure of her control slipping away. With a masterful effort she started to regain it. What the hell was she doing? At a crisis point in her life and she was acting like a prostitute. She needn't approach the issue in this way. She knew that. The tugging she was feeling from another sector of her being was disrupting her decision-making processes. She could not allow that, not now.

She should go change again, retreat back to the living room, or perhaps to her study where the dark oak paneling and walls of books would quash the unsettling rumblings.

He eyed her steadily. "Yes."

She was about to get up but never made it.

"I'd take one for you too, Gloria."

"For me?" Her voice quavered. She looked at him again, her strategic plans forgotten, her eyes wide.

"Without thinking. Lot of Secret Service agents. Only one Chief of Staff. That's the way it works." He looked down and said quietly, "It's not a game, Gloria."

When he went again for more beer he noticed that she had moved close enough that her knee touched his thigh when he sat down. She stretched her legs out, rubbing against his, and then she rested them on the table across from them. The pullover had some-how worked itself up, revealing thighs that were full and creamy white; they were the legs of an older woman, and a damned attractive one. Collin's eyes moved slowly across the display of skin.

"You know I've always admired you. I mean all of the agents." She almost seemed embarrassed. "I know sometimes you get taken for granted. I want you to know that I appreciate you."

"It's a great job. Wouldn't trade it for anything." He chugged another beer, and felt better. His breathing relaxed.

She smiled at him. "I'm glad you came tonight."

"Anything to help, Gloria." His confidence level was going up as his alcohol intake increased. He finished the beer and she pointed with an unsteady finger to a stand of liquor over by the door. He mixed drinks for them, sat back down.

"I feel I can trust you, Tim."

"You can."

"I hope you don't take this the wrong way, but I don't feel that way with Burton."

"Bill's a top agent. The best."

She touched his arm, left it there.

"I didn't mean it that way. I know he's good. I just don't know about him sometimes. It's hard to explain. It's just an instinct on my part."

"You should trust your instincts. I do." He looked at her. She looked younger, much younger, like she should be graduating college, ready to take on the world.

"My instincts tell me that you're someone I can depend on, Tim."

"I am." He drained his drink.

"Always?"

He stared at her, touched his empty glass to hers. "Always."

His eyes were heavy now. He thought back to high school. After scoring the winning touchdown in the state championship, Cindy Purket had looked at him just like that. An all-giving look on her face.

He laid his hand on her thigh, rubbed it up and down. The flesh was just loose enough to be intensely womanly. She didn't resist but instead inched closer. Then his hand disappeared under the pullover, tracing over her still firm belly, just nicking the undersides of her breasts, and then returning into view. The other arm encircled her waist, drawing her closer to him; his hand dropped down to her bottom and gripped hard. She sucked in air and then let it out slowly, as she leaned into his shoulder. He felt her chest push into his arm, up and down. The floating mass was soft, and warm. She dropped her hand to his hardening crotch and squeezed, then lingered her mouth over his, slowly pulling back and looking at him, her eyelids moving up and down in slow rhythms.

She put her drink down, and slowly, almost teasingly, slid out of the pullover. He exploded against her, hands digging under the bra strap until he felt it give way and she poured out to him, his head buried in the loose mounds. Next, the last remaining piece of clothing, a pair of black lace panties, was ripped from her body; she smiled as it was sent sailing against the wall. Then she caught her breath as he lifted her effortlessly and carried her into the bedroom.

ELEVEN

The Jaguar drove slowly up the long drive, stopped, and two people got out.

Jack turned up the collar on his coat. The evening was brisk as rain-heavy clouds marched into the area.

Jennifer walked around the car and settled in next to him as they leaned against the luxury car.

Jack looked up at the place. Thick sheets of ivy swept across the top of the entrance. The house had a heavy substance to it, real and committed. Its occupants probably would absorb a good measure of that. He could use that in his life right now. He had to admit, it was beautiful. What was wrong with beautiful things anyway? Four hundred thou' as a partner. If he started bringing in other clients, who knew? Lord made five times that, two million dollars a year, and that was his base.

Compensation figures of partners were strictly confidential and were never discussed even under the most informal circumstances at the firm. However, Jack had guessed correctly on the computer password to the partner comp file. The code word was "greed." Some secretary must have laughed her ass off over that one.

Jack looked over a front lawn the size of a carrier flight deck. A vision galloped across. He looked at his fiancée.

"It has plenty of space to play touch football with the kids." He smiled.

"Yes, it does." She smiled back at him, kissed his cheek gently. She took his arm and encircled her waist with it.

Jack looked back at the mansion; soon to be his three-point-eight-million-dollar home. Jennifer continued to look at him, her smile broadening as she gripped his fingers. Her eyes seemed to glisten, even in the darkness.

As Jack continued to stare at the structure, he felt a rush of relief. This time he only saw windows.

At thirty-six thousand feet, Walter Sullivan leaned back in the deep softness of his cabin chair and glanced out the window of the 747 into the darkness. As they moved east to west, Sullivan was adding a number of hours to his day, but time zones had never bothered him. The older he became the less sleep he needed, and he had never needed very much to begin with.

The man sitting across from him took the opportunity to examine the older man closely. Sullivan was known throughout the world as a legitimate, although sometimes bullying, global businessman. Legitimate. That was the key word running itself through Michael McCarty's head. Legitimate businessmen typically had no need of, nor desire to speak with, gentlemen in McCarty's profession. But when one is alerted through the most discreet channels that one of the wealthiest men on earth desires a meeting with you, then you attend. McCarty had not become one of the world's foremost assassins because he particularly enjoyed the work. He particularly enjoyed the money and with it the luxuries that money inspired.

McCarty's added advantage was the fact that he appeared to be a businessman himself. Ivy League good looks, which wasn't too far afield, since he held a degree in international politics from Dartmouth. With his thick, wavy blond hair, broad shoulders and wrinkle-free face he could be the hard-charging entrepreneur on the way up or a film star at his peak. The fact that he killed people for a living, at a per-hit fee of in excess of one million dollars, did nothing to dampen his youthful enthusiasm or his love of life.

Sullivan finally looked at him. McCarty, despite an enormous confidence in his abilities and a supreme coolness under pressure, began to grow nervous under the billionaire's scrutiny. From one elite to another.

"I want you to kill someone for me," Sullivan said simply. "Unfortunately, at the present time, I do not know who that person is. But with any luck, one day I will. Until that time comes, I will place you on a retainer so that your services will always be available to me until such time as I need them."

McCarty smiled and shook his head. "You may be aware of my reputation, Mr. Sullivan. My services are already in great demand. My work carries me all over the world, as I'm sure you know. Were I to devote my full time to you until this opportunity arose, then I would be forgoing other work. I'm afraid my bank account, along with my reputation, would suffer."

Sullivan's reply was immediate. "One hundred thousand dollars a day until that opportunity arises, Mr. McCarty. When you successfully complete the task, double your usual fee. I can do nothing to preserve your reputation; however, I trust that the per diem arrangement will forestall any damage to your financial status."

McCarty's eyes widened just a bit and then he quickly regained his composure.

"I think that will be adequate, Mr. Sullivan."

"Of course you realize I am placing considerable

confidence not only in your skills at eliminating subjects, but also in your discretion."

McCarty hid his smile. He had been picked up in Sullivan's plane in Istanbul at midnight local time. The flight crew had no idea who he was. No one had ever identified him, thus someone recognizing him was not a concern. Sullivan meeting him in person eliminated one thing. An intermediary who would then have Sullivan in his control. McCarty, on the other hand, had no earthly reason to betray Sullivan and every motivation not to.

Sullivan continued, "You will receive particulars as they become available. You will assimilate yourself into the Washington, D.C., metropolitan area, although your task may take you anywhere in the world. I will need you to move on a moment's notice. You will make your location known to me at all times and will check in with me daily on secured communication lines that I will establish. You will pay your own expenses out of the per diem. A wire transfer will be set up to funnel the fee to an account of your choosing. My planes will be available to you if the need arises. Understood?"

McCarty nodded, a little put off by his client's series of commands. But then you didn't get to be a billionaire without being somewhat commanding, did you? On top of that McCarty had read about Christine Sullivan. Who the hell could blame the old man?

Sullivan pushed a button on the armrest of his chair.

"Thomas? How long until we're stateside?"

The voice was brisk and informed. "Five hours and fifteen minutes, Mr. Sullivan, if we maintain present air speed and altitude."

"Make sure that we do."

"Yes, sir."

Sullivan pressed another button and the cabin attendant appeared and efficiently served them the sort of dinner that McCarty had never had on a plane before. Sullivan said nothing to McCarty until the dinner was cleared and the younger man rose and was being directed to his sleeping quarters by the attendant. Registering on a sweep of Sullivan's hand, the attendant disappeared within the recesses of the aircraft.

"One more thing, Mr. McCarty. Have you ever failed on a mission?"

McCarty's eyes turned to slits as he stared back at his new employer. For the first time it was evident that the Ivy Leaguer was extremely dangerous.

"Once, Mr. Sullivan. The Israelis. Sometimes they seem more than human."

"Please don't make it twice. Thank you."

Seth Frank was roaming the halls of the Sullivan home. The yellow police lines were still up outside, fluttering softly in the increasing breeze and thickening bank of dark clouds that promised more heavy rain. Sullivan was staying at his Watergate penthouse downtown. His domestic staff were at their employer's residence on Fisher Island, Florida, catering to members of Sullivan's family. He had already interviewed each of them in person. They were being flown home shortly for more detailed questioning.

He took a moment to admire the surroundings. It was as though he were touring a museum. All that money. The place reeked of it, from the superlative antiques to the broadbrush paintings that casually hung everywhere, with real signatures at the bottom. Hell, everything in the house was an original.

He wandered into the kitchen and then into the dining room. The table resembled a bridge spanning

193

the pale blue rug spread over the refinished parquet flooring. His feet seemed to be sucked into the thick, heavy fibers. He sat down at the head of the table, his eyes constantly roaming. As far as he could tell nothing had happened in here. Time was slipping by and progress was not coming easily.

Outside, the sun momentarily pushed through the heavy clouds and Frank got his first break on the case. He wouldn't have noticed it if he hadn't been admiring the moldings around the ceiling. His father had been a carpenter. Joints smooth as a baby's cheek.

That's when he observed the rainbow dancing across the ceiling. As he admired the parallels of color, he began to wonder about its source, like the folklore of tracking the pot of gold at the end of the striped apparition. His eye scanned the room. It took him a few seconds, but then he had it. He quickly knelt down beside the table and peered under one of the legs. The table was a Sheraton, eighteenth century, which meant it was as heavy as a semi. It took him two tries, and perspiration broke across his forehead, a trickle entering his right eye and making him tear for a moment, but he finally managed to budge the table and pull it out.

He sat back down and looked at his new possession, maybe his little pot of gold. The little piece of silver-colored material acted as a barrier between the furniture to prevent the wet carpet from causing damage to wood or upholstery and also stopped leaching into the damp fibers. With the aid of sunlight, its reflective surface also made for a nice rainbow. He had had similar ones in his own house when his wife had gotten particularly nervous about a visit from her in-laws and decided some serious household cleaning had to be done.

He took out his notebook. The servants arrived at

Dulles at ten tomorrow morning. Frank doubted in this house if the small piece of foil he was holding would have been allowed to remain in its resting place for very long. It could be nothing. It could be everything. A perfect way to gauge the lay of the land. It would probably fall somewhere in between, if he were very, very lucky.

He hit the floor again and sniffed the carpet, ran his fingers through the fibers. The stuff they used nowadays, you could never tell. No odor, dried in a couple of hours. He would know soon enough how long it had been; if it could tell him anything. He could call Sullivan, but for some reason, he wanted to hear it from someone other than the master of the house. The old man was not high on the list of suspects, but Frank was smart enough to realize that Sullivan remained on that list. Whether his place descended or ascended depended on what Frank could find out today, tomorrow, next week. When you boiled it down, it was that simple. That was good, because up to now nothing about the death of Christine Sullivan had been simple. He wandered out of the room, thinking about the whimsical nature of rainbows and police investigations in general.

Burton scanned the crowd, Collin beside him. Alan Richmond made his way to the informal podium set up on the steps of the Middleton Courthouse, a broad block of mortar-smeared brick, stark white dentil moldings, weather-beaten cement steps and the ubiquitous American flag alongside its Virginia counterpart swooping and swirling in the morning breeze. Precisely at nine-thirty-five the President began to speak. Behind him stood the craggy and expressionless Walter Sullivan with the ponderous Herbert Sanderson Lord beside him.

Collin moved a little closer to the crowd of reporters at the bottom of the courthouse steps as they strained and positioned like opposing teams of basketball players waiting for the foul shot to swish or bang off the rim. He had left the Chief of Staff's home at three in the morning. What a night it had been. What a *week* it had been. As ruthless and unfeeling as Gloria Russell seemed in public life, Collin had seen another side of the woman, a side that he was strongly attracted to. It still seemed like a careless daydream. He had slept with the President's Chief of Staff. That simply did not happen. But it had happened to Agent Tim Collin. They had planned to see each other tonight as well. They had to be careful, but they were both cautious by nature. Where it would lead, Collin did not know.

Born and raised in Lawrence, Kansas, Collin had a good set of Midwestern values to fall back upon. You dated, fell in love, married and had four or five kids, strictly in that order. He didn't see that happening here. All he knew was he wanted to be with her again. He glanced across and eyed her where she stood behind and to the left of the President. Sunglasses on, wind lifting her hair slightly, she seemed in complete control of everything around her.

Burton had his eyes on the crowd, then glanced at his partner in time to see the latter's gaze riveted for an instant on the Chief of Staff. Burton frowned. Collin was a good agent who did his job well, maybe to the point of overzealousness. Not the first agent to suffer from that, and not necessarily a bad trait in their line of work. But you kept your eyes on the crowd, everything out *there*. What the hell was going on? Burton made a sideways glance at Russell, but she stared straight ahead, seemingly oblivious to the men assigned to protect her. Burton looked at Collin once more. The kid now scanned the crowd, changing his pace every now and then, left to right, right to left, sometimes up, occasionally he would stare straight ahead, no trace of a pattern a potential assailant could count on. But Burton could not forget the look he had given the Chief of Staff. Behind the sunglasses Burton had seen something he did not like.

Alan Richmond finished his speech by staring stonily out at the cloudless sky as the wind whipped through his perfectly styled hair. He seemed to be looking to God for help, but in actuality he was trying to remember if he was meeting the Japanese ambassador at two or three that afternoon. But his faraway, almost visionary look would carry well on the evening news.

On cue he snapped back to attention and turned to Walter Sullivan and gave the bereaved husband a hug befitting someone of his stature.

"God, I am so sorry, Walter. My deepest, deepest condolences. If there is anything, anything that I can do. You know that."

Sullivan held on to the hand that was offered to him, and his legs began to shake until two of his entourage invisibly supported him with a quick thrust of sinewy arms.

"Thank you, Mr. President."

"Alan, please, Walter. Friend to friend now."

"Thank you, Alan, you have no idea how much I appreciate your taking the time to do this. Christy would have been so moved by your words today."

Only Gloria Russell, who was watching the pair closely, noticed the slight twinge of a smirk at the corner of her boss's cheek. Then, in an instant it was gone.

"I know there are really no words I can say to do

justice to what you're feeling, Walter. It seems more and more that things in this world happen for no purpose. Except for her sudden illness, this never would've happened. I can't explain why things like this occur, no one can. But I want you to know that I am here for you, when you need me. Anytime, anyplace. We've been through so much together. And you've certainly helped me through some pretty rough times."

"Your friendship has always been important to me, Alan. I won't forget this."

Richmond slid an arm around the old man's shoulders. In the background microphones dangled on long poles. Like giant rods and reels, they surrounded the pair despite the collective efforts of the men's respective entourages.

"Walter, I'm going to get involved in this. I know some people will say it's not my job and in my position I can't become personally involved with anything. But goddammit, Walter, you're my friend and I'm not going to just let this slide away. The people responsible for this are going to pay."

The two men embraced once more as the photographers popped away. The twenty-foot antennas sprouting from the fleet of news trucks dutifully broadcast this tender moment to the world. Another example of President Alan Richmond being more than just a President. It made the White House PR staff giddy thinking about the initial pre-election polls.

The television channel-hopped from MTV to Grand Ole Opry to cartoons, to QVC to CNN to Pro Wrestling and then back to CNN. The man sat up in bed and put out his cigarette, laid the remote down. The President was giving a press conference. He looked stern and appropriately appalled at the abominable murder of Christine Sullivan, wife of billionaire Walter Sullivan, one of the President's closest friends, and its symbolism of the growing lawlessness in this country. Whether the President would have made the same pitch if the victim had been a poor black, Hispanic or Asian found with their throat cut in an alley in Southeast D.C. was never addressed. The President spoke in firm, crisp tones with the perfect trace of anger, of toughness. The violence must stop. The people must feel safe in their homes, or at their estates in this particular case. It was an impressive scene. A thoughtful and caring President.

The reporters were eating it up, asking all the right questions.

The television showed Chief of Staff Gloria Russell, dressed in black, nodding approvingly when the President hit key points in his views on crime and punishment. The police fraternity and AARP vote was locked up for the next election. Forty million votes, well worth the morning drive out.

She would not have been so happy if she knew who was watching them right this minute. Whose eyes bored into every inch of flesh on both her and the President's faces, as the memories of that night, never far from the surface, welled up like an oil fire spewing heat and potential destruction in all directions.

The flight to Barbados had been uneventful. The Airbus was a vast ship whose massive engines had effortlessly ripped the plane from the ground in San Juan, Puerto Rico, and in a few minutes they had hit their cruising altitude of 36,000 feet. The plane was packed, San Juan acting as a feeder for tourists bound for the clusters of islands that made up the Caribbean vacation strip. Passengers from Oregon and New York and all points in between looked at the wall of black clouds as the plane banked left and moved away from the remnants of an early-season tropical storm that had never hit hurricane status.

A metal stairway met them as they departed the aircraft. A car, tiny by American standards, shepherded five of them on the wrong side of the road as they left the airport and headed into Bridgetown, the capital of the former British colony, which had retained strong traces of its long colonialism in its speech, dress and mannerisms. In melodious tones the driver informed them of the many wonders of the tiny island, pointing out the pirate ship tour as the skull and crossbones ship pounded through still rough seas. On its deck, pale but reddening tourists were plied with rum punch in such levels that they would all be very drunk and/or very sick by the time they returned to the dock later that afternoon.

In the back seat two couples from Des Moines made excited plans in chirrupy patters of conversation. The older man who sat in the front seat staring out the windshield had his thoughts mired two thousand miles north. Once or twice he checked where they were headed, instinctively craving the lay of the land. The major landmarks were relatively few; the island was barely twenty-one miles long and fourteen miles across at its widest point. The near constant eighty-five-degree heat was ameliorated by the continual breeze, its sound eventually disappearing into one's subconscious but always nearby like a faded but still potent dream.

The hotel was an American standard Hilton built on a manmade beach that jutted out on one end of the island. Its staff was well-trained, courteous and more than willing to leave you alone if that was desired. While most of the guests gave themselves wholeheartedly to the pampering efforts, one patron shunned contact, leaving his room only to wander to isolated areas of the white beach or the mountainous Atlantic Ocean side of the island. The rest of the time was spent in his room, lights set low, TV on, room service trays littering the carpet and wicker furnishings.

On the first day there Luther had grabbed a cab from in front of the hotel and taken a ride north, almost to the edge of the ocean, where atop one of the island's numerous hills stood the Sullivan estate. Luther's selection of Barbados had not been arbitrary.

"You know Mr. Sullivan? He's not here. Went back to America." The cabbie's lyrical tones had brought Luther out of his trance. The massive iron gates at the bottom of the grassy hill hid a long, winding drive up to the mansion, which, with its salmon-colored stucco walls and eighteen-foot-high white marble columns, looked strangely appropriate in the lush greenery, like an enormous pink rose jutting out from the bushes.

"I've been to his place," Luther answered. "In the States."

The cabbie looked at him with new respect.

"Is anyone home? Any of the staff maybe?"

The man shook his head. "All gone. Dis morning."

Luther sat back in his seat. The reason was obvious. They had found the mistress of the house.

Luther spent the next several days on the broad white beaches watching cruise ships unload their population into the duty-free shops that littered the downtown area. Dreadlocked residents of the island made their rounds with their battered briefcases housing watches, perfumes and other counterfeit paraphernalia.

For five American dollars, you could watch an

islander cut up an aloe leaf and pour its rich liquid into a small glass bottle for use when the sun started to nip at tender white skin that had lain dormant and unblemished behind suits and blouses. Your own handwoven corn rows cost you forty dollars and took about an hour, and there were many women with flabby arms and thick, crumpled feet who patiently lay in the sand while this operation was performed upon them.

The island's beauty should have served to free Luther, to some degree, from his melancholy. And, finally, the warming sun, gentle breezes and low-key approach to life of the island populous had eroded his nervous agitation to where he occasionally smiled at a passerby, spoke monosyllables to the bartender and sipped his mixed drinks far into the night while lying on the beach, the surf pounding into the darkness and gently lifting him away from his nightmare. He planned to move on in a few days. Where to, he wasn't quite sure.

And then the channel-hopping stopped at the CNN broadcast and Luther, like a battered fish on an unbreakable line, was sent reeling toward what he had spent several thousand dollars and traveled several thousand miles trying to escape.

Russell stumbled out of bed and walked over to the bureau, fumbled for a pack of cigarettes.

"They'll cut ten years off your life." Collin rolled over and watched her naked machinations with amusement.

"This job's already done that." She lit up, inhaled deeply for several seconds, put the smoke out and climbed back in bed, snuggling butt-first to Collin, smiling contentedly as she was wrapped up in his long, muscular arms.

"The press conference went well, don't you

think?" She could feel him thinking it through. He was fairly transparent. Without the sunglasses they all were, she felt.

"As long as they don't find out what really happened."

She turned to face him, traced her finger along his neck, making a V against his smooth chest. Richmond's chest had been hairy, some of the tufts turning gray, curling at the edges. Collin's was like a baby's bottom, but she could feel the hard muscle beneath the skin. He could break her neck with no more than a passing motion. She wondered, briefly, how that would feel.

"You know we have a problem."

Collin almost laughed out loud. "Yeah, we've got some guy out there with the President's and a dead woman's prints and blood on a knife. That qualifies as a big problem I'd say."

"Why do you think he hasn't come forward?"

Collin shrugged. If he were the guy he would've disappeared. Taken the stash and gone. Millions of dollars. As loyal as Collin was, what he could do with that kind of money. He would disappear too. For a while. He looked at her. With that kind of money would she condescend to go with him? Then he turned his thoughts back to the discussion at hand. Maybe the guy was a member of the President's political party, maybe he had voted for him. In any event, why bring yourself that kind of trouble?

"Probably scared to," he finally replied.

"There are ways of doing it anonymously."

"Maybe the guy's not that sophisticated. Or maybe there's no profit in that. Or maybe he doesn't give a shit. Take your pick. If he was going to come forward, he probably would have. If he does, we'll sure know soon enough."

She sat up in bed.

"Tim, I'm really worried about this." The edge in her voice made him sit up too. "I made the decision to keep that letter opener as is. If the President were to find out . . ." She looked at him. He read the message in her eyes and stroked her hair and then cupped her cheek with his hand.

"He's not going to find out from me."

She smiled. "I know that, Tim, I really believe that. But if he, this person, were to somehow try to communicate with the President directly."

Collin looked puzzled. "Why would he do that?"

Russell shifted to the side of the bed, let her feet dangle several inches from the floor. For the first time Collin noticed the small reddish oval birthmark, half the size of a penny, at the base of her neck. Next he noticed that she was shivering, even though the room was warm.

"Why would he do that, Gloria?" Collin edged closer.

She spoke to the bedroom wall. "Has it occurred to you that that letter opener represents one of the most valuable objects in the world?" She turned to him, rubbed his hair, smiled at the vacant expression that was slowly coming to a conclusion.

"Blackmail?"

She nodded at him.

"How do you blackmail the goddamned President?"

She got up, threw a loose robe around her shoulders and poured another drink from the almost-empty decanter.

'Being President doesn't make you immune from blackmail attempts, Tim. Hell, it just gives you that much more to lose . . . or gain."

She slowly stirred her drink, sat down on a couch and tipped her glass back, the liquid warm and soothing going down. She had been drinking much more than usual lately. Not that her performance had been impaired, but she would have to watch it, especially at this level, at this critical point. But she decided she would watch it tomorrow. Tonight, with the weight of political disaster lurking above her shoulders, and a young, handsome man in her bed, she would drink. She felt fifteen years younger. Every passing moment with him made her feel more beautiful. She would not forget her primary goal, but who was to say she couldn't enjoy herself?

"What do you want me to do?" Collin looked at her.

Russell had been waiting for that. Her young, handsome Secret Service agent. A modern white knight like the kind she read about as a wide-eyed girl. She looked at him as the drink dangled from her fingers. She used her other hand to slowly pull off her robe and let it drop to the floor. There was time enough, especially for a thirty-seven-year-old woman who had never had a serious relationship with a man. Time enough for everything. The drink soothed away her fear, her paranoia. And with it her cautiousness. All of which she needed in abundance. But not tonight.

"There is something you can do for me. But I'll tell you in the morning." She smiled, lay back on the couch and put out her hand. Obediently he rose and went to her. A few moments later the only sounds were intermingled groans and the persistent squeaks of the overwrought couch.

A half-block down the street from Russell's home, Bill Burton sat in his wife's nondescript Bonneville and cradled a can of Diet Coke between his knees. Occasionally he would glance at the house that he had observed his partner entering at 12:14 A.M. and where he'd caught a glimpse of the Chief of Staff in attire that didn't indicate the visit was a business one. With his long-range lens he had gotten two pictures of that particular scene that Russell would have killed to get her hands on. The lights in the house had moved progressively from room to room until they reached the east side of the place, when all lights were dramatically extinguished.

Burton looked at the dormant taillights of his partner's car. The kid had made a mistake. Being here. This was a career ender, maybe for both him and Russell. Burton thought back to that night. Collin racing back to the house. Russell white as a sheet. Why? In all the confusion Burton had forgotten to ask. And then they were smashing through cornfields after someone who shouldn't have been there but sure as hell had been.

But Collin had gone back in that house for a reason. And Burton decided it was time he found out what that reason was. He had a dim feeling of a conspiracy slowly evolving. Since he had been excluded from participating, he naturally concluded that he was probably not intended to benefit from that conspiracy. Not for one moment did he believe that Russell was interested solely in what was behind his partner's zipper. She was not that type, not by a long shot. Everything she did had a purpose, an important purpose. A good fuck from a young buck was not nearly important enough.

Another two hours passed. Burton looked at his watch and then stiffened as he saw Collin open the front door, move slowly down the walk and get in his car. As he drove by, Burton ducked down in his seat, feeling slightly guilty at this surveillance of a fellow agent. He watched the wink of a turn signal as the Ford made its way out of the high-priced area.

Burton looked back up at the house. A light came on in what probably was the living room. It was late, but apparently the lady of the house was still going strong. Her stamina was legendary around the White House. Burton briefly wondered if she exhibited that same endurance between the sheets. Two minutes later the street was empty. The light in the house remained on.

TWELVE

The plane landed and thundered to a stop on the short strip of tarmac constituting National Airport's main runway, hit an immediate left a few hundred yards from the tiny inlet that accessed the Potomac for the swarms of weekend boat enthusiasts, and taxied to gate number nine. An airport security officer was answering questions from a group of anxious, camera-toting tourists and did not observe the man walking rapidly past him. Not that identification was going to be made anyway.

Luther's return trip had followed the circuity of his exit. A stopover in Miami, and then Dallas/Fort Worth.

He grabbed a cab and watched the south-moving rush-hour traffic on the George Washington Parkway as weary commuters threaded their way home. The skies promised more rain, and the wind whipped through the tree-lined parkway meandering lazily on its parallel course with the Potomac. Planes periodically rocketed into the air, banking left and rapidly disappearing into the clouds.

One more battle beckoned Luther. The image of a righteously indignant President Richmond pounding the lectern in his impassioned speech against violence, his smug Chief of Staff by his side, was the one constant in Luther's life now. The old, tired and fearful man who had fled the country was no longer tired, no longer fearful. The overriding guilt at allowing a young woman to die had been replaced with an overriding hate, an anger that surged through every nerve in his body. If he was to be, of sorts, Christine Sullivan's avenging angel, he would perform that task with every ounce of energy and every shred of ingenuity he had left.

Luther settled back into his seat, munched on some crackers saved from the plane trip, and wondered if Gloria Russell was any good at playing chicken.

Seth Frank glanced out the car window. His personal interviews of Walter Sullivan's household staff had revealed two things of interest, the first of which was the business enterprise Frank was now parked in front of; the second could keep. Housed in a long, gray concrete building in a heavy commercial area of Springfield just outside the Beltway, Metro Steam Cleaner's sign proclaimed that it had been in business since 1949. That was stability that meant nothing to Frank. A lot of long-standing legitimate businesses were now money-laundering fronts for organized crime, both Mafia, Chinese and America's own homegrown versions. And a carpet cleaner firm that catered to affluent homeowners was in a perfect position to scope alarm systems, cash and jewelry nests and patterns of behavior of the intended victims and their households. Whether he was dealing with a loner or an entire organization Frank didn't know. It was more likely that he was headed toward a dead end, but then you never knew. There were two patrol cars stationed three minutes away. Just in case. Frank got out of his car.

"That would have been Rogers, Budizinski and Jerome Pettis. Yep, August 30, nine A.M. Three floors. Damn house was so big, it took all day even with three guys." George Patterson consulted his record book while Frank's eyes took in the grimy office.

"Can I speak to them?"

"You can to Pettis. The other two are gone."

"Permanently?" Patterson nodded. "How long had they been with you?"

Patterson's eyes scanned his employment log. "Jerome's been with me five years. He's one of my best people. Rogers was about two months. I think he moved out of the area. Budizinski had been with us about four weeks."

"Pretty short stays."

"Hell, that's the nature of the business. Spend a thousand bucks training these guys and wham they're gone. It's not a career-type job, you know what I mean? It's hot, dirty work. And the pay ain't exactly going to put you on the Riviera, you hear what I'm saying?"

"You got addresses for them?" Frank took out his notebook.

"Well, like I said, Rogers moved. Pettis is in today, if you want to talk to him. He's got a job to do out in McLean in about a half hour. He's back loading his truck now."

"Who decides which crew goes to which house?"

"I do."

"All the time?"

Patterson hesitated. "Well, I got guys who specialize in different stuff."

"Who specializes in the high-dollar areas?"

"Jerome. Like I said, he's my best guy."

"How did the other two get assigned to him?"

"I don't know, we juggle stuff like that. Depends on who shows up for work sometimes."

"You remember any of those three being particularly interested in visiting the Sullivan place?"

Patterson shook his head.

210

"What about Budizinski? You got an address on him?"

Patterson consulted a notebook crammed with paper and wrote on a slip of paper. "It's over in Arlington. Don't know if he's still there."

"I'll want their employment file. Social Security numbers, birthdates, job history, all that stuff."

"Sally can get that for you. She's the gal up front."

"Thanks. You got photos of these guys?"

Patterson looked at Frank like he was nuts. "Are you kidding. This ain't the FBI, for crying out loud."

"Can you give me a description?" Frank asked patiently.

"I've got sixty-five employees and a turnover rate of over sixty percent. I usually don't even see the guy after he's hired. Everybody starts to look the same after a while anyway. Pettis'll remember."

"Anything else you think might help me?"

Patterson shook his head. "You think one of them might have killed that woman?"

Frank stood up and stretched. "I don't know. What do you think?"

"Hey, I get all kinds in here. Nothing surprises me anymore."

Frank turned to leave, then turned back. "Oh by the way, I'll want records of all homes and establishments cleaned by your firm in Middleton in the last two years."

Patterson exploded out of his chair. "What the fuck for?"

"You have the records?"

"Yeah, I got 'em."

"Good, let me know when they're ready. Have a good one."

Jerome Pettis was a tall, cadaverous black man in his

early forties with a perpetual cigarette hanging from his mouth. Frank watched admiringly as the man methodically loaded the heavy cleaning equipment with a practiced hand. His blue jumpsuit announced that he was a senior technician with Metro. He didn't look at Frank, kept his eyes on his work. All around them in the huge garage white vans were being similarly loaded. A couple of men stared over at Frank but quickly returned to their work.

"Mr. Patterson said you had some questions?"

Frank parked himself on the van's front bumper. "A few. You did a job at Walter Sullivan's home in Middleton on August 30 of this year."

Pettis's brow furrowed. "August? Hell, I do about four homes a day. I don't remember them cuz they aren't that memorable."

"This one took you all day. Big house out in Middleton. Rogers and Budizinski were with you."

Pettis smiled. "That's right. Biggest goddamned house I'd ever seen and I've seen some bad places, man."

Frank smiled back. "That's the same thing I thought when I saw it."

Pettis straightened up, relit his cigarette. "Problem was all that furniture. Had to move every damn piece, and some of that shit was heavy, heavy like they don't make no more."

"So you were there all day?" Frank hadn't meant the question to come out that way.

Pettis stiffened, sucked on his Camel and leaned against the door of the van. "So how come the cops are interested in how the carpets were cleaned?"

"Woman was murdered in the house. Apparently she mixed it up with some burglars. Don't you read the papers?"

"Just the sports. And you're wondering if I'm one of them dudes?"

212

"Not right now. I'm just collecting information. Everybody who was near that house recently interests me. I'll probably talk to the mailman next."

"You're funny for a cop. You think I killed her?"

"I think if you did, you're smart enough not to stick around here waiting for me to ring your doorbell. These two men who were with you, what can you tell me about them?"

Pettis finished his smoke and looked at Frank without answering. Frank started to close his notebook.

"You want a lawyer, Jerome?"

"Do I need one?"

"Not as far as I'm concerned, but it's not my call. I don't plan on pulling out my Miranda card if that's what you're worried about."

Pettis finally looked at the concrete floor, crushed out his cigarette, looked back at Frank. "Look, man, I've been with Mr. Patterson a long time. Come to work every day, do my job, take my paycheck and go home."

"Then it sounds like you have nothing to worry about."

"Right. Look, I did some stuff a while back. Did some time. You can pull it off your computers in five seconds. So I'm not gonna sit here and bullshit you, okay?"

"Okay."

"I've got four kids and no wife. I didn't break into that house and I didn't do anything to that woman."

"I believe you, Jerome. I'm a lot more interested in Rogers and Budizinski."

Pettis eyed the detective for several seconds. "Let's take a walk."

The two men left the garage and walked over to an ancient Buick as big as a boat that had more rust than metal. Pettis got inside. Frank followed.

"Big ears in the garage, you know?"

Frank nodded.

"Brian Rogers. Called him Slick cuz he was a good worker, picked up things fast."

"What'd he look like?"

"White guy about fifty, maybe older. Not too tall, five eight, maybe a buck fifty. Talkative. Worked hard."

"And Budizinski?"

"Buddy. Everybody here has a nickname. I'm Ton. For skele*ton*, you know." Frank smiled at that one. "He was a white guy too, a little bigger. Maybe a little older than Slick. He kept to himself. Did what he was told and nothing more."

"Which one did the master bedroom?"

"We all did. We had to lift the bed and the bureau. They weighed a couple tons each. Back still hurts." Jerome reached in the rear seat and pulled out a cooler. "No time for breakfast this morning," he explained as he pulled out a banana and an egg biscuit.

Frank shifted uncomfortably in the worn seat. A piece of metal jabbed into his back. The car reeked of cigarette smoke.

"Were either of them ever alone in the master bedroom or the house?"

"Always somebody in the house. Man had a lot of people working there. They coulda gone upstairs by themselves. I never kept a watch on them. Wasn't my job, you know?"

"How'd Rogers and Budizinski come to be working with you that day?"

Jerome thought for a moment. "I'm not sure, come to think of it. I know it was an early job. It might've just been they were the first ones here. Sometimes that's all it takes."

"So if they knew ahead of time you were going to

214

do a place like that early, and they got here before everyone else, they could hook on with you?"

"Yeah, I guess they could. Man, we just look for bodies, you know what I'm saying? Don't take no brain surgeon to do this shit."

"When was the last time you saw them?"

The other man scrunched up his face, bit into his banana.

"Couple of months ago, maybe longer. Buddy left first, never said why. Guys come and go all the time. I've been here longer than anybody except Mr. Patterson. Slick moved away, I think."

"Know where?"

"I remember him saying something about Kansas. Some construction work. He used to be a carpenter. Got laid off up here when commercial went belly up. Good with his hands."

Frank wrote this information down while Jerome finished his breakfast. They walked back to the garage together. Frank looked inside the van, at all the hoses, power handles, bottles and heavy cleaning equipment.

"This the van you used to do the Sullivan place?"

"This been my van for three years. Best one in the place."

"You keep the same equipment in the van?"

"Damn straight."

"Then you better get a new van for a while."

"What?" Jerome slowly climbed out of the driver's seat.

"I'll talk to Patterson. I'm impounding this one."

"You're shitting me."

"No, Jerome, I'm afraid I'm not."

"Walter, this is Jack Graham. Jack, Walter Sullivan." Sandy Lord sat down heavily in his chair. Jack shook hands with Sullivan and then the men sat around the

215

small table in conference room number five. It was eight o'clock in the morning and Jack had been in the office since six after pulling two all-nighters. He had already consumed three cups of coffee and proceeded to pour himself out a fourth from the silver coffee pot.

"Walter, I've told Jack about the Ukraine deal. We've gone over the structure. The Hill word looks real good. Richmond pushed all the right buttons. The Bear's dead. Kiev got the glass slipper. Your boy came through."

"He's one of my best friends. I expect that from my friends. But I thought we had enough lawyers on this deal. Padding the bill, Sandy?" Sullivan heaved himself up and looked out the window at the pristine early-morning sky that promised a beautiful fall day. Jack glanced sideways at the man as he made notes from the crash course on Sullivan's latest deal. Sullivan didn't look all that interested in completing the multibillion international monolith. Jack didn't know that the old man's thoughts hung back at a morgue in Virginia, remembering a face.

Jack had caught his breath when Lord had ceremoniously appointed him to play second chair to Lord on the biggest transaction currently going on in the firm, leapfrogging over several top partners and a host of associates senior to Jack. Hard feelings had already started to roll through the plush hallways. At this point Jack didn't care. They didn't have Ransome Baldwin as a client. Regardless of how he had gotten it, he had rain, substantial rain. He was tired of feeling guilty for his position. This was Lord's test case on Jack's abilities. He had as good as said it. Well, if he wanted the deal rammed through, Jack would deliver. Philosophical, politically correct ivory tower babble didn't cut it here. Only results.

216

"Jack is one of our best attorneys. He's also Baldwin's legal eagle."

Sullivan looked over at them. "Ransome Baldwin?"

Sullivan appraised Jack in a different light and then turned once more to the window.

"Our window of opportunity, however, is growing more narrow by the day," Lord continued. "We need to firm up the players and make sure Kiev knows what the hell they're supposed to do."

"Can't you handle it?"

Lord looked at Jack and then back at Sullivan. "Of course I can handle it, Walter, but don't assume you can abdicate right now. You still have a major role to play. You sold this deal. Your continued involvement is absolutely necessary from the point of view of all sides." Sullivan still did not stir. "Walter, this is the crowning glory of your career."

"That's what you said about the last one."

"Can I help it if you keep topping yourself?" Lord shot back.

Finally, almost imperceptibly, Sullivan smiled, for the first time since the telephone call from the States had come to shatter his life.

Lord relaxed a bit, looked over at Jack. They had rehearsed this next step several times.

"I'm recommending that you fly over there with Jack. Shake the right hands, pat the right shoulders, let them see you're still in control of this tiger. They need that. Capitalism is still a new game for them."

"And Jack's role?"

Lord motioned to Jack.

Jack stood up, went over to the window. "Mr. Sullivan, I've spent the last forty-eight hours learning every aspect of this deal. All the other lawyers here have just been working on a piece of it. Except for Sandy, I don't think there's anyone at the firm who knows what you want to accomplish better than I do."

Sullivan slowly turned to Jack. "That's a pretty big statement."

"Well, it's a pretty big deal, sir."

"So you know what I want to accomplish?"

"Yes, sir."

"Well, why don't you enlighten me as to what you think that is." Sullivan sat down, crossed his arms and stared expectantly up at Jack.

Jack didn't bother to swallow or catch his breath. "Ukraine has massive natural resources, all the things that heavy industry around the world use and want. The issue becomes how to get the resources out of Ukraine at minimal cost and minimal risk, considering the political situation over there."

Sullivan uncrossed his arms, sat up and sipped at his coffee.

Jack continued, "The hook is, you want Kiev to believe that the exports your company will be making will be matched by investments in Ukraine's future. A long-term investment, I gather, you do not want to commit to."

"I spent the bulk of my adult life being scared to death of the reds. I have about as much belief in perestroika and glasnost as I do in the tooth fairy. I consider it my patriotic duty to strip the communists of as much as I can. Leave them without the means to dominate the world, which is their long-term plan, despite this latest hiccup of democracy."

Jack said, "Exactly, sir. 'Strip' being the key word. Strip the carcass before it self-destructs . . . or attacks." Jack paused to check both men's reactions. Lord stared at the ceiling, his features unreadable.

Sullivan stirred. "Go on. You're getting to the interesting part."

"The interesting part is how to leverage the deal so

that Sullivan and Company has little or no downside exposure and the maximum upside potential. You'll either broker the deal or you'll buy direct from Ukraine and you'll sell to the multinationals. You sprinkle a little of those proceeds around in Ukraine."

"That's right. Eventually the country will be almost cleaned out, and I'll walk away with at least two billion net."

Jack again looked at Lord, who now sat straight in his chair, listening intently. This was the hook. Jack had thought of it only yesterday.

"But why not take from Ukraine what really makes them dangerous?" Jack paused. "And triple your net at the same time."

Sullivan stared intently at him. "How?"

"IRBMs. Intermediate-Range Ballistic Missiles. Ukraine has a shitload of them. And now that the '94 Nonproliferation Treaty fell apart, those nukes are a major headache for the West again."

"So what are you suggesting? That I buy the god-damn things? What the hell would I do with them?"

Jack watched Lord finally lean forward, then continued. "You buy them for bottom dollar, maybe a half-billion, using a portion of the proceeds from the raw materials sales. You will buy them using dollars, which can then be used by Ukraine to purchase other necessities in the world markets."

"Why bottom-dollar? Every Middle Eastern country will be bidding on them."

"But Ukraine can't sell to them. The G-7 countries would never allow it. If Ukraine did, they'd be cut out of the EU and other Western markets, and if that happens, they're dead."

"So I buy them and sell them to whom?"

Jack couldn't help but grin. "To us. The United States. Six billion is a conservative estimate on their

219

worth. Hell, the weapons-grade plutonium those babies contain is priceless. The rest of the G-7s would probably pitch in a few billion. It's your relationship with Kiev that makes this whole thing work. They look to you as their savior."

Sullivan looked stunned. He started to rise and then thought better of it. Even to him the amounts of money potentially out there were staggering. But he had enough money, more than enough. But to remove part of the nuclear equation from the collective miseries of the world . . .

"And this was whose idea?" Sullivan looked at Lord as he asked the question. Lord pointed at Jack.

Sullivan leaned back in his chair and looked up at the young man. Then he rose with a swiftness that startled Jack. The billionaire took Jack's hand in an iron grip. "You're going places, young man. Mind if I tag along?"

Lord beamed like a father. Jack couldn't stop smiling. He had started to forget what it was like to hit one out of the park.

After Sullivan departed, Jack and Sandy sat at the table.

Finally Sandy said, "I recognize it was not an easy assignment. How do you feel?"

Jack couldn't help but grin. "Like I just slept with the prettiest girl in high school, kind of tingling all over."

Lord laughed and stood up. "You'd better go home and get some rest. Sullivan's probably calling his pilot from the car. At least we got his mind off the bitch."

Jack didn't hear the last part as he quickly left the room. For now, for once in a long time, he felt good. No worries, just possibilities. Endless possibilities.

That night he sat up late telling a very enthusiastic

Jennifer Baldwin all about it. Afterward, over a very chilled bottle of champagne and a platter of oysters specially delivered to her townhouse, the couple had the most gratifying sex of their courtship. For once, the high ceilings and murals did not bother Jack. In fact, he was growing to like them.

THIRTEEN

The White House receives millions of pieces of nonofficial mail each year. Each item is carefully screened and appropriately processed, the whole task handled by an in-house staff with assistance and supervision by the Secret Service.

The two envelopes were addressed to Gloria Russell, which was somewhat unusual since most of this type of correspondence was addressed to the President or members of the First Family, or frequently the First Pet, which currently happened to be a golden retriever named Barney.

The handwriting on each was in block letters, the envelopes white and cheap and thus widely available. Russell got to them about twelve o'clock on a day that had been going pretty well up until then. Inside one was a single sheet of paper and inside the other was an item she had stared at for some minutes. Written on the paper, again in block letters, were the words:

> Question: What constitutes high crimes and misdemeanors? Answer: I don't think you want to find out. Valuable item available, more to follow, chief, signed not a secret admirer

Even though she had expected it, in fact had desperately wanted to receive it, she still could feel her heartbeat increase to where it pounded against the wall of her chest; her saliva dwindled down to where she reached for and gulped down a glass of water and repeated the procedure until she could hold the letter without shaking. Then she looked at the second item. A photograph. The sight of the letter opener had brought the nightmare events rushing back to her. She gripped the sides of her chair. Finally the attack subsided.

"At least he wants to deal." Collin put down the note and photo and returned to his chair. He noted the extreme pallor of the woman and wondered if she was tough enough to make it through this one.

"Maybe. It could also be a setup."

Collin shook his head. "Don't think so."

Russell sat back in her chair, rubbed at her temples, downed another Tylenol. "Why not?"

"Why set us up this way? In fact, why set us up at all? He's got the stuff to bury us. He wants money."

"He probably got millions from the Sullivan heist."

"Maybe. But we don't know how much of it was liquid. Maybe he stashed it and can't get back to it. Maybe he's just an extremely greedy person. World is full of those."

"I need a drink. Can you come over tonight?"

"The President is having dinner at the Canadian embassy."

"Shit. Can't you get someone to replace you?"

"Maybe, if you pulled some strings."

"Consider them pulled. How soon do you think we'll hear from him again?"

"He doesn't seem too anxious, although he might just be acting cautious. I would in his situation."

"Great. So I can smoke two packs of menthols a day until we hear from him. By then I'll be dead of lung cancer."

"If he wants money, what are you going to do?" he asked.

"Depending on how much he wants, it can be

accomplished without too much difficulty." She seemed calmer now.

Collin rose to go. "You're the boss."

"Tim?" Russell went over to him. "Hold me for a minute."

He felt her rub against his pistol as he gripped her.

"Tim, if it comes down to more than money. If we can't get it back."

Collin looked down at her.

"Then I'll take care of it, Gloria." He touched his fingers to her lips, turned and left.

Collin found Burton waiting in the hallway.

Burton looked the younger man up and down. "So how's she holding up?"

"All right." Collin continued to walk down the hallway, until Burton grabbed his arm, spun him around.

"What the fuck's going on, Tim?" Collin loosened his partner's grip.

"This isn't the time or the place, Bill."

"Well, tell me the time and the place, and I'll be there because we need to talk."

"What about?"

"You gonna fucking play stupid with me?" He roughly pulled Collin to a corner.

"I want you to think real clearly about that woman in there. She doesn't give a shit about you or me or anybody else. The only thing she cares about is saving her own little ass. I don't know what kind of story she's spinning on you, and I don't know what you two are cooking up, but I'm telling you to be careful. I don't want to see you throw everything away over her."

"I appreciate the concern but I know what I'm doing, Bill."

"Do you, Tim? Does fucking the Chief of Staff

come within the purview of a Secret Service agent's responsibilities? Why don't you show me where that is in the manual? I'd like to read it for myself. And while we're talking about it, why don't you enlighten me about what the hell we went back into that house for. Because we ain't got it, and I guess I know who does. My ass is on the line here too, Tim. If I'm going down I'd like to know why."

An aide passed by in the hallway and stared strangely at the two men. Burton smiled and nodded and then returned his attention to Collin.

"Come on, Tim, what the hell would you do if you were me?"

The young man looked at his friend and his face slowly relaxed from the hard line he normally wore while on duty. If he were in Burton's position what would he do? The answer was easy. He'd kick some ass until people started talking. Burton was his friend, had proven it time and again. What the man was saying about Russell was probably true. Collin's reasoning hadn't totally evaporated in the presence of silk lingerie.

"You got time for a cup of coffee, Bill?"

Frank walked down the two flights of stairs, turned right and opened the door to the crime lab. Small and in need of paint, the room was surprisingly well-organized due in large measure to the fact that Laura Simon was a very compulsive person. Frank imagined her home to be every bit as neat and well-kept despite the presence of two preschoolers that kept her sufficiently haggard. Around the room were stacked unused evidence kits with their unbroken orange seals creating a bit of color against the drab, chipping gray walls. Cardboard boxes, carefully labeled, were piled in another corner. In yet another corner was a small floor safe that held the few physical items requiring additional security measures. Next to it was a refrigerator that housed evidence requiring a temperature-controlled environment.

He watched her small back as it curved over a microscope at the far end of the room.

"You rang?" Frank leaned over. On the glass slide were small fragments of some substance. He couldn't imagine spending his days looking at microscopic pieces of who knew what, but he was also fully aware that what Laura Simon did was an enormously important contribution to the conviction process.

"Look at this." Simon motioned him over to the lens. Frank removed his eyeglasses, which he had forgotten were still on. He glanced down and then raised his head back up.

"Laura, you know I never know what I'm looking at. What is it?"

"It's a sample of carpet taken from the Sullivans' bedroom. We didn't get it on the initial search, picked it up later."

"So, what's significant about it?" Frank had learned to listen very attentively to this tech.

"The carpet in the bedroom is one of those very high-priced models that cost about two hundred dollars a square foot. The carpet just for the bedroom must have run them almost a quarter mil."

"Jesus Christ!" Frank popped another piece of gum in his mouth. Trying to quit smoking was rotting his teeth and adding to his waistline. "Two-fifty for something you walk on?"

"It's incredibly durable; you could roll a tank across it and it would just spring back. It's only been there about two years. They did a bunch of renovation back then."

"Renovation? The house is only a few years old."

"That's when the deceased married Walter Sullivan."

"Oh."

"Women like to make their own statement about those things, Seth. Actually, she had good taste in carpets."

"Okay, so where does her good taste get us?"

"Look at the fibers again."

Frank sighed but obeyed the request.

"You see at the very tips? Look at the cross section. They've been cut. Presumably with not very sharp scissors. The cut is pretty ragged, although like I said these fibers are like iron."

He looked at her. "Cut? Why would anyone do that? Where'd you find them?"

"These particular samples were found on the bed skirt. Whoever cut them probably wouldn't have noticed a few fibers clinging to his hand. Then he brushed against the skirt and there you are."

"You find a corresponding part on the carpet?"

"Yep. Right under the left side of the bed if you're looking toward it about ten centimeters away at a perpendicular angle. The cut was slight but verifiable."

Frank straightened back up and sat down on one of the stools next to Simon.

"That's not all, Seth. On one of the fragments I also found traces of a solvent. Like a stain remover."

"That might be from the recent carpet cleaning. Or maybe the maids spilled something."

Simon shook her head. "Uh-uh. The cleaning company uses a steam system. For spot cleaning they use a special organic-based solvent. I checked. This one is a petroleum-based, off-the-shelf cleaner. And the maids use the same cleanser as recommended by the manufacturer. It's an organic base too. They have a whole supply of it at the house. And the carpet is chemically treated to prevent stains from soaking in. Using a petroleum-based solvent probably made it worse. That's probably why they ended up snipping out pieces."

"So presumably the perp takes the fibers because they show something. Do they?"

"Not on the sample I got, but he might have cut around the area just to make sure he didn't miss anything and we got one of the clean specimens."

"What would be on the carpet that someone would go to the trouble of cutting one-centimeter fibers out? It must've been a pain in the ass."

Both Simon and Frank had the same thought and indeed had it for several moments.

"Blood," Simon said simply.

"And not the deceased's either. If I remember correctly, hers wasn't anywhere near that spot." Frank added, "I think you got one more test to run, Laura."

She hooked a kit off the wall. "I was just getting ready to go do it, thought I'd better buzz you first."

"Smart girl."

The drive out took thirty minutes. Frank rolled down his window and let the wind course over his face. It also helped dispel the cigarette smoke. Simon was constantly giving him a hard time about that.

The bedroom had remained sealed under Frank's orders.

Frank watched from the corner of Walter Sullivan's bedroom as Simon carefully mixed the bottles of chemicals and then poured the result into a plastic sprayer. Frank then helped her stuff towels under the door and tape brown packing paper to the windows. They closed the heavy drapes, cutting out virtually all traces of natural light.

Frank surveyed the room once again. He looked at the mirror, the bed, the window, the closets and then his eyes rested on the nightstand and at the gaping hole behind where the plaster had been removed. Then his eyes moved back to the picture. He picked it up. He was reminded again that Christine Sullivan had been a very beautiful woman, as far removed as one could get from the destroyed hulk he had viewed. In the photograph she was sitting in the chair beside the bed. The nightstand was clearly visible to her left. The corner of the bed made its way into the right side of the picture. Ironically so, considering all the use she had probably made of that particular vehicle. The springs were probably due for their sixty-thousand-mile checkup. After that, they probably wouldn't have much to do. He remembered the look on Walter Sullivan's face. Not much left there.

He put the photo down and continued to observe Simon's fluid movements. He glanced back at the photo, something bothering him, but whatever it was popped out of his head as quickly as it had sprung into it.

"What's that stuff called again, Laura?"

"Luminol. It's sold under a variety of names, but it's the same reagent stuff. I'm ready."

She positioned the bottle over the section of carpet where the fibers had been cut from.

"Good thing you don't have to pay for this carpet." The detective smiled at her.

Simon turned to look at him. "Wouldn't matter to me. I'd just declare bankruptcy. They could garnishee my wages from here until eternity. It's the poor person's great equalizer."

Frank hit the light, plunging the room into pitch-black darkness. Swishes of air were heard as Simon squeezed the trigger on the spray bottle. Almost immediately, like a mass of lightning bugs, a very small portion of the carpet started to glow a pale blue and then disappeared. Frank turned on the overhead light and looked at Simon.

"So we got somebody else's blood. Helluva pickup, Laura. Any way you can scrape up enough to analyze, get a blood type? DNA typing?"

Simon looked dubious. "We'll pull the carpet to see if any leaked through, but I doubt it. Not much soaks into a treated carpet. And any residue has been mixed with a lot of stuff. So don't count on it."

Frank thought out loud. "Okay, one perp wounded. Not a lot of blood, but some." He looked for confirmation from Simon on that point and received an affirmative nod of the head. "Wounded, but with what? She had nothing in her hand when we found her."

Simon read his mind. "And as sudden as her death was, we're probably talking cadaveric spasm. To get it out of her hand they would've almost had to break her fingers."

Frank finished the thought. "And there was no sign of that on the autopsy."

"Unless the impact of the slugs caused her hand to fly open."

"How often does that happen?"

"Once is enough for this case."

"Okay, let's assume she had a weapon, and now that weapon is missing. What kind of weapon might it have been?"

Simon considered this as she repacked her kit.

"You probably could rule out a gun; she should've been able to get a round off, and there were no powder burns on her hands. They couldn't have scraped those off without leaving a trail."

"Good. Plus there's no evidence she ever had a gun registered to her. And we've already confirmed that there are no guns in the house."

"So no gun. Maybe a knife then. Can't tell what kind of wound it made, but maybe a slash, probably superficial. The number of fibers that were snipped out was small, so we're not talking life-threatening."

"So she stabbed one of the perps, maybe in the arm or leg. Then they backed up and shot her? Or she stabbed as she was dying?" Frank corrected himself. "No. She died instantly. She stabs one of them in another room, runs in here and then gets shot. Standing over her, the wounded perp drips some blood."

"Except the vault's in here. The more likely scenario is that she surprised them in the act."

"Right, except remember the shots came from the doorway *into* the room. And fired *down*. Who surprised who? That's what keeps bugging the ever-loving shit out of me."

"So why take the knife, if that's what it was?"

"Cause it IDs somebody, somehow."

"Prints?" Simon's nostrils quivered as she thought of the physical evidence lurking out there.

Frank nodded. "That's how I read it."

"Was the last Mrs. Sullivan in the habit of keeping a knife with her?"

Frank responded by slapping his hand to his forehead so hard it made Simon wince. She watched as he rushed over to the nightstand and picked up the photo. He shook his head and handed it to her.

"There's your goddamned knife."

Simon looked at the photo. In it, resting on the nightstand was a long, leather-handled letter opener.

"The leather also explains the oily residue on the palms."

Frank paused at the front door on the way out. He looked at the security control panel, which had been restored to its operating condition. Then he broke into a smile as an elusive thought finally trickled to the surface.

"Laura, you got the fluorescent lamp in the trunk?"

"Yeah, why?"

"You mind getting it?"

Puzzled, Simon did so. She returned to the foyer and plugged it in.

"Shine it right on the number keys."

What was revealed under the fluorescent light made Frank smile again.

"Goddamn, that's good."

"What does it mean?" Simon looked at him, her brow furrowed.

"It means two things. First, we definitely got us somebody on the inside and, second, our perps are real creative."

Frank sat in the small interrogation room and decided against another cigarette and opted instead for a cherry Tums. He looked at the cinder block walls, cheap metal table and beat-up chairs and decided this was a very depressing place to be interrogated in. Which was good. Depressed people were vulnerable people, and vulnerable people, given the appropriate prodding, tended to want to talk. And Frank wanted to listen. He would listen all day.

The case was still extremely muddled, but certain elements were becoming clearer.

Buddy Budizinski still lived in Arlington and now worked at a car wash in Falls Church. He had admitted being in the Sullivan house, had read about the murder, but beyond that knew nothing. Frank tended to believe him. The man was not particularly bright, had no previous police record and had spent his adult life performing menial tasks for a living, no doubt compelled by his having finished only the fifth grade. His apartment was modest to the point of near poverty. Budizinski was a dead end.

Rogers, on the other hand, had produced a treasure trove. The Social Security number he had given on his employment application was real enough, only it belonged to a female State Department employee who had been assigned to Thailand for the last two years. He must have known the carpet cleaning company wouldn't have checked. What did they care? The address on the application was a motel in Beltsville, Maryland. No one by that name had registered at the motel in the last year and no one fitting Rogers's description had been seen there. The state of Kansas had no record of him. On top of that he had never cashed any of the payroll checks given to him by Metro. That in itself spoke volumes.

An artist's sketch based on Pettis's recollection was being made up down the hallway and would be distributed throughout the area.

Rogers was the guy, Frank could feel it. He had been in the house, and he had disappeared leaving behind a trail of false information. Simon was right this minute painstakingly examining Pettis's van in the hopes that Rogers's prints were still lurking somewhere within. They had no prints to match at the crime scene, but if they could ident Rogers, then dollars to donuts he had priors, and Frank's case would finally be forming. It would take a great leap forward if the person he was waiting for would decide to cooperate.

And Walter Sullivan had confirmed that an antique letter opener from his bedroom was indeed missing. Frank feverishly hoped to be able to lay his hands on that potential evidentiary gold mine. Frank had imparted his theory to Sullivan about his wife stabbing her attacker with that instrument. The old man hadn't seemed to register the information. Frank had briefly wondered if Sullivan was losing it.

The detective checked his list of employees at Sullivan's residence once more, although by now he knew them all by heart. There was only one he was really interested in.

The security company rep's statement kept coming back to him. The variations generated by fifteen digits to get a five-digit code in the correct sequence was impossible for a portable computer to crunch in the very brief time allowed, particularly if you factored in a less than blazing fast response from the security system's computer. In order to do it, you had to eliminate some of the possibles. How did you do that?

An examination of the keypad showed that a chemical – Frank couldn't remember the exact name although Simon had recognized it – which was revealed only under fluorescent light, had been applied to each of the number keys.

Frank leaned back and envisioned Walter Sullivan – or the butler, or whoever's job it was to set the alarm – going down and entering the code. The finger would hit the proper keys, five of them, and the alarm would be set. The person would walk away, completely unaware that he or she now had a small tracing of chemical, invisible to the naked eye, and odorless, on their finger. And, more important, they would be totally ignorant of the fact that they had just revealed the numbers comprising the security code. Under fluorescent light, the perps would be able to tell which numbers had been entered because the chemical would be smeared on those keys. With that information, it was up to the computer to deliver the correct sequence, which the security rep was certain it could do in the allotted time, once given the elimination of 99.9 percent of the possible combos.

Now the question remained: who had applied the chemical? Frank at first had considered that Rogers, or whatever his real name was, might have done it while at the house, but the facts against that conclusion were overwhelming. First, the house was always filled with people and to even the most unobservant a stranger lurking around an alarm panel would arouse suspicion. Second, the entry foyer was large and open and the most unsecluded spot in the house. Lastly, the application would take some time and care. And Rogers didn't have that luxury. Even the slightest suspicion, the most fleeting glance and his whole plan could be ruined. The person who had thought this one up was not the type to take that sort of risk. Rogers hadn't done it. Frank was pretty sure he knew who did.

Upon first glance, the woman appeared so thin as to convey the impression of emaciation perhaps due to cancer. On second glance, the good color in the cheeks, the light bone structure and the graceful way she moved led to the conclusion that she was very lean but otherwise healthy.

"Please sit down, Ms. Broome. I appreciate your coming down."

The woman nodded and slid into one of the seats. She wore a flowery skirt that ended midcalf. A single strand of large fake pearls encircled her neck. Her hair was tied in a neat bun; some of the strands at the top of her forehead were beginning to turn a silvery gray, like ink leaching onto paper. Going on the smooth skin and absence of wrinkles, Frank would have put her age at about thirty-nine. Actually she was some years older.

"I thought you were already done with me, Mr. Frank."

"Please call me Seth. You smoke?"

She shook her head.

"I've just got a few follow-up questions, routine. You're not the only one. I understand you're leaving Mr. Sullivan's employment?"

She noticeably swallowed, looked down and then back up. "I was close, so to speak, to Mrs. Sullivan.

235

It's hard now, you know . . ." Her voice trailed off.

"I know it is, I know it is. It was terrible, awful." Frank paused for a moment. "You've been with the Sullivans how long now?"

"A little over a year."

"You do the cleaning and . . .?"

"I help do the cleaning. There's four of us, Sally, Rebecca and me. Karen Taylor, she does the cooking. I also looked after Mrs. Sullivan's things for her too. Her clothes and what-not. I was sort of her assistant, I guess you could say. Mr. Sullivan had his own person, Richard."

"Would you like some coffee?"

Frank didn't wait for her to answer. He got up and opened the door to the interrogation room.

"Hey Molly, can you bring me a couple of javas?" He turned to Ms. Broome. "Black? Cream?"

"Black."

"Make it two pures, Molly, thanks."

He shut the door and sat back down.

"Damn chill in the air, I can't seem to stay warm." He tapped the rough wall. "This cinder block doesn't help much. So you were saying about Mrs. Sullivan?"

"She was really nice to me. I mean she would talk to me about things. She wasn't – she wasn't, you know, from that class of people, the upper class I guess you could say. She went to high school where I did right here in Middleton."

"And not too far apart in years I'm thinking."

His remark brought a smile to Wanda Broome's lips and a hand unconsciously moved to cajole back into place an invisible strand of hair.

"Further than I'd like to admit."

The door opened and their coffee was delivered. It was gratefully hot and fresh. Frank had not been lying about the chill.

"I won't say she fit in real well with all those types

of people, but she seemed to hold her own. She didn't take anything from anybody if you know what I mean."

Frank had reason to believe that was true. From all accounts the late Mrs. Sullivan had been a hellion in many respects.

"Would you say the relationship between the Sullivans was . . . good, bad, in between?"

She didn't hesitate. "Very good. Oh I know what people say about the age difference and all, but she was good for him, and he was good for her. I truly believe that. He loved her, I can tell you that. Maybe more like a father loves his daughter, but it was still love."

"And she him?"

Now there was perceptible hesitation. "You've got to understand that Christy Sullivan was a very young woman, maybe younger in a lot of ways than other women her age. Mr. Sullivan opened up a whole new world for her and—" She broke off, clearly unsure of how to continue.

Frank changed gears. "What about the vault in the bedroom? Who knew about it?"

"I don't know. I certainly didn't. I assume that Mr. and Mrs. Sullivan knew. Mr. Sullivan's valet, Richard, he may have known. But I'm not sure about that."

"So Christine Sullivan or her husband never indicated to you that there was a safe behind the mirror?"

"My goodness no. I was her friend of sorts, but I was still just an employee. And only with them a year. Mr. Sullivan never really spoke to me. I mean that's not the sort of thing you would tell someone like me, is it?"

"No, I guess not." Frank was certain she was lying, but he had been unable to unearth any evidence to the contrary. Christine Sullivan was the very type to show off her wealth to someone she could identify with, if only to show how far she had suddenly risen in the world.

"So you didn't know the mirror was a one-way looking into the bedroom?"

This time the woman showed visible surprise. Frank noticed a blush under the light application of makeup.

"Wanda, can I call you Wanda? Wanda, you understand, don't you, that the alarm system in the house was deactivated by the person who broke in? It was deactivated by the appropriate code being put in. Now, who set the alarm at night?"

"Richard did," she replied promptly. "Or sometimes Mr. Sullivan did it himself."

"So everyone in the house knew the code?"

"Oh no, of course not. Richard did. He's been with Mr. Sullivan for almost forty years. He was the only one other than the Sullivans who knew the code that I know of."

"Did you ever see him set the alarm?"

"I was usually already in bed when the system was set."

Frank stared at her. *I'll bet you were, Wanda, I'll bet you were.*

Wanda Broome's eyes widened. "You're, you're not suspecting that Richard had anything to do with it?"

"Well, Wanda, somehow, somebody who wasn't supposed to be able to, disarmed that alarm system. And naturally suspicion falls on anyone who had access to that code."

Wanda Broome looked like she might start to cry, then composed herself. "Richard is almost seventy years old."

"Then he's probably in need of a nice little nest

egg. You understand what I'm telling you is to be held in the strictest confidence of course?"

She nodded and at the same time wiped her nose. The coffee, untouched, was now sipped in quick little bursts.

Frank continued, "And until someone can explain to me how that security system was accessed, then I'm going to have to explore the avenues that make the most sense to me."

He continued to look at her. He had spent the past day finding out everything he could about Wanda Broome. It was a fairly average story except for one twist. She was forty-four years old, twice divorced with two grown children. She lived in the servants' wing with the rest of the in-house staff. About four miles away her mother, aged eighty-one, lived in a modest, somewhat run-down home, existing comfortably on Social Security and her husband's railroad pension. Broome had been employed by the Sullivans, as she said, for about a year, which was what initially had drawn Frank's attention: she was by far the newest member of the house's staff. That in itself didn't mean much, but by all accounts Sullivan treated his help very well, and there was something to be said for the loyalty of long-standing, well-paid employees. Wanda Broome looked like she could be very loyal too. The question was to whom?

The twist was that Wanda Broome had spent some time in prison, more than twenty years ago, for embezzlement when she had worked as a bookkeeper for a doctor in Pittsburgh. The other servants were squeaky-clean. So she was capable of breaking the law, and she had spent time on the inside. Her name back then had been Wanda Jackson. She had divorced Jackson when she got out, or rather he had dropped her. There was no record of arrest since then. With the name change and the conviction far in the past, if the Sullivans had done a background check, they might not have turned up anything, or maybe they didn't care. From all sources Wanda Broome had been an honest, hardworking citizen these last twenty years. Frank wondered what had changed that.

"Is there anything you can remember or think of that might help me, Wanda?" Frank tried to look as innocent as possible, opening his notebook and pretending to jot down some notes. If she were the inside person, the one thing he didn't want was Wanda running back to Rogers, which would result in his going even further underground. On the other hand, if he could get her to crumble, then she just might jump sides.

He envisioned her dusting the entrance hall. It would have been so easy, so easy to apply that chemical to the cloth, then casually brush it against the security panel. It would all look so natural, no one, even staring directly at her while she did it, would have given it a thought. Just a conscientious servant doing her job. Then sneaking down when everyone was asleep, a quick sweep of the light and her part was done.

Technically, she would probably be an accomplice to murder, since homicide was a reasonably likely result when you burglarized someone's home. But Frank was far less interested in sending Wanda Broome away for a large portion of the rest of her life than he was in bagging the trigger man. The woman sitting across from him had not concocted this plan, he believed. She had played a role, a small, albeit important role. Frank wanted the master of ceremonies. He would get the Commonwealth's Attorney to cut a deal with Wanda to accomplish that goal.

"Wanda?" Frank leaned across the table and

earnestly took one of her hands. "Can you think of anything else? Anything that will help me catch the person who murdered your friend?"

Frank finally received a small shake of the head in return and he leaned back. He hadn't expected much on this go-round, but he had made his point. The wall was beginning to crumble. She wouldn't warn the guy, Frank was certain of that. He was getting to Wanda Broome, little by little.

As he would discover, he had already gone too far.

FOURTEEN

Jack threw his carry-on into the corner, tossed his overcoat on the sofa and fought the impulse to pass out right there on the carpet. Ukraine and back in five days had been a killer. The seven-hour time difference had been bad enough, but for someone closing in on octogenarian status, Walter Sullivan had been indefatigable.

They had been whisked through the security checkpoints with the alacrity and respect Sullivan's wealth and reputation commanded. From that point forward a series of endless meetings had commenced. They toured manufacturing facilities, mining operations, office buildings, hospitals and then had been taken to dinner and gotten drunk with the Mayor of Kiev. The President of Ukraine had received them on the second day, and Sullivan had him eating out of his hand within the hour. Capitalism and entrepreneurship were respected above all else in the liberated republic and Sullivan was a capitalist with a capital *C*. Everyone wanted to talk to him, shake his hand, as if some of his money-making magic would rub off on them, producing untold wealth in a very short time.

The result had been more than they could have hoped for as the Ukrainians fell in line on the business deal with glowing praise for its vision. The pitch for dollars for nukes would come later at the appropriate time. Such an asset. An unnecessary asset that could be turned into liquidity.

Sullivan's retrofitted 747 had flown nonstop from Kiev to BWI and his limo had just dropped Jack off. He made his way into the kitchen. The only thing in the fridge was soured milk. The Ukrainian food had been good but was heavy, and after the first couple of days he only picked at his meals. And there had been way too much booze. Apparently business could not be conducted without it.

He rubbed his head, tussling with sleep deprivation of massive proportion. In fact he was too tired to sleep. But he was hungry. He checked his watch. His internal clock said it was almost eight A.M. His watch proclaimed that it was well after midnight. While D.C. was not the Big Apple in its ability to cater to any appetite or interest no matter the time of day or night, there were a few places where Jack could get some decent food on a weeknight despite the lateness of the hour. As he struggled into his overcoat, the phone rang. The machine was on. Jack started to go out, then hesitated. He listened to the perfunctory message followed by the beep.

"Jack?"

A voice swarmed up on him, from out of the past, like a ball held underwater until it's free and explodes to the surface. He snatched up the phone.

"Luther?"

The restaurant was hardly more than a hole in the wall, which made it one of Jack's favorites. Any reasonable concoction of food could be gotten there at any time, day or night. It was a place that Jennifer Baldwin would never set foot inside and one that he and Kate had frequented. A short time ago, the results of that comparison would have disturbed him, but he had made up his mind, and he didn't intend on revisiting the question. Life was not perfect, and you could spend your entire life waiting for that perfection. He was not going to do that.

Jack wolfed down scrambled eggs, bacon and four pieces of toast. The fresh coffee burned his throat going down. After five days of instant java and bottled water, it tasted wonderful.

Jack looked across at Luther, who sipped on his coffee and alternated between looking out the dirty plate-glass window onto the dark street and passing his eye around the small, grimy interior.

Jack put his coffee down. "You look tired."

"So do you, Jack."

"I've been out of the country."

"Me too."

That explained the condition of the yard and the mail. A needless worry. Jack pushed the plate away and waved for a refill on his coffee.

"I went by your place the other day."

"Why was that?"

Jack had expected the question. Luther Whitney had never taken anything other than the direct approach. But anticipation was one thing, having a ready answer another. Jack shrugged.

"I don't know. Just wanted to see you, I guess. It's been a while."

Luther nodded agreement.

"You seeing Kate again?"

Jack swallowed a mouthful of coffee before answering. His temples started to throb.

"No. Why?"

"I thought I saw you two together a while back."

"We sort of ran into each other. That's all."

Jack couldn't tell exactly, but Luther looked upset with that answer. He noticed Jack watching him closely, then smiled.

"Used to be, you were the only way I could find out if my little girl was doing okay. You were my pipeline of information, Jack."

"You ever consider just talking to her directly, Luther? You know that might be worth a shot. The years are going by."

Luther waved the suggestion off and stared out the window again.

Jack looked him over. The face was leaner than usual, the eyes puffy. There were more wrinkles on the forehead and around the eyes than Jack remembered. But it had been four years. Luther was at the age now where the onslaught of age hit you quickly, deterioration was more and more evident every day.

He caught himself staring into Luther's eyes. Those eyes had always fascinated Jack. Deep green, and large, like a woman's, they were supremely confident eyes. Like you see on pilots, an infinite calmness about life in general. Nothing rattled them. Jack had seen happiness in those eyes, when he and Kate announced their engagement, but more often he had seen sadness. And yet right beneath the surface Jack saw two things he had never seen in Luther Whitney's eyes before. He saw fear. And he saw hatred. And he wasn't sure which one bothered him the most.

"Luther, are you in trouble?"

Luther took out his wallet and, despite Jack's protests, paid for the food.

"Let's take a walk."

A taxi cab ride took them to the Mall and they walked in silence to a bench across from the Smithsonian castle. The chilly night air settled in on them and Jack pulled up the collar of his coat. Jack sat while Luther stood and lit a cigarette.

"That's new." Jack looked at the smoke curving up slowly in the clear night air.

"At my age who gives a shit?" Luther flung the match down and buried it in the dirt with his foot. He sat down.

"Jack, I want you to do me a favor."

"Okay."

"You haven't heard the favor yet." Luther suddenly stood up. "You mind walking? My joints are getting stiff."

They had passed the Washington Monument and were headed toward the Capitol when Luther broke the silence.

"I'm in kind of a jam, Jack. It's not so bad now, but I got a feeling it's going to get worse and that might happen sooner rather than later." Luther didn't look at him, he seemed to be staring ahead at the massive dome of the Capitol.

"I'm not sure how things are going to play out right now, but if it goes the way I think it's gonna go, then I'm going to need a lawyer, and I want you, Jack. I don't want no bullshitter and I don't want no baby lawyer. You're the best defense lawyer I've ever seen and I've seen a lot of them, up close and personal."

"I don't do that anymore, Luther. I push paper, do deals." It struck Jack at that moment that he was more a businessman than a lawyer. That thought was not an especially pleasing one.

Luther did not seem to hear him. "It won't be a freebie. I'll pay you. But I want someone I can trust, and you're the only one I trust, Jack." Luther stopped walking and turned to the younger man, waiting for an answer.

"Luther, you want to tell me what's going on?"

Luther shook his head vigorously. "Not unless I have to. That wouldn't do you or anybody else any good." He stared at Jack intently until it made him uncomfortable.

"I gotta tell you, Jack, if you're my lawyer on this, it's gonna get kinda hairy."

"What do you mean?"

"I mean people could get hurt on this one, Jack. Really hurt, like not-coming-back hurt."

Jack stopped walking. "If you've got some guys like that on your butt it might be better to cut a deal now, get immunity and disappear in a Witness Protection Program. Lots of people do. It's not an original idea."

Luther laughed out loud. Laughed until he choked and ended up doubled over, coughing up the little that was in his stomach. Jack helped him back up. He could feel the older man's limbs trembling. He did not realize they were trembling with rage. This outburst was so out of character for the man that Jack felt his flesh crawl. He realized he was perspiring despite watching his breath produce small clouds in the late-night chill.

Luther composed himself. He took a deep breath and looked almost embarrassed.

"Thanks for the advice, send me a bill. I gotta go."

"Go? Where the hell are you going? I want to know what's going on, Luther."

"If something should happen to me—"

"Goddammit, Luther, I'm growing real tired of this cloak-and-dagger shit."

Luther's eyes became slits. The confidence suddenly returned with a touch of ferocity. "Everything I do is for a reason, Jack. If I'm not telling you the whole scoop now you better believe it's for a goddamned good reason. You may not understand it now, but the way I'm doing it is to keep you as safe as I can. I wouldn't be involving you at all except I needed to know if you'd go to bat for me when and if I needed you. Because if you won't, forget this conversation ever happened, and forget you ever knew me."

"You can't be serious."

"Serious as shit, Jack."

247

The men stood looking at each other. The trees behind Luther's head had shed most of their leaves. Their bare branches reached to the skies, like bursts of dark lightning frozen in place.

"I'll be there, Luther." Luther's hand swiftly settled into Jack's and the next minute Luther Whitney disappeared into the shadows.

The cab dropped Jack off in front of the apartment building. The pay phone was right across the street. He paused for a moment, gathering energy and the nerve he would need for what he was about to do.

"Hello?" The voice was full of sleep.

"Kate?"

Jack counted the seconds until her mind cleared and identified the voice.

"Jesus Christ, Jack, do you know what time it is?"

"Can I come over?"

"No, you cannot come over. I thought we had settled all of this."

He paused, steeled himself. "It's not about that." He paused again. "It's about your father."

The extended silence was difficult to interpret.

"What about him?" The tone was not as cold as he would have thought.

"He's in trouble."

Now the familiar tone returned. "So? Why the hell does that still surprise you?"

"I mean he's in serious trouble. He just proceeded to scare the living shit out of me without really telling me anything."

"Jack, it's late and whatever my father is involved in—"

"Kate, he was scared, I mean really scared. So scared he threw up."

Again there was a long pause. Jack tracked her mental processes as she thought about the man they both knew so well. Luther Whitney scared? That didn't make sense. His line of work necessarily demanded someone with steel nerves. Not a violent person, his entire adult life had been spent right on the edge of danger.

She was terse. "Where are you?"

"Right across the street."

Jack looked up as he saw a slender figure move to a window of the building and look out. He waved.

The door opened to Jack's knock and he saw her retreating into the kitchen where he heard a pot clattering, water being poured and the gas on the stove being lit. He looked around the room, and then stood just inside the front door feeling a little foolish.

A minute later she walked back in. She had on a thick bathrobe that ended at her ankles. She was barefoot. Jack found himself staring at her feet. She followed his gaze and then looked at him. He jolted back.

"How's the ankle? Looks fine." He smiled.

She frowned and said tersely, "It's late, Jack. What about him?"

He moved into the tiny living room and sat down. She sat across from him.

"He called me up a couple hours ago. We grabbed some food at that little dive next to Eastern Market and then started walking. He told me he needed a favor. That he was in trouble. Serious trouble with some people who could do some permanent damage to him. Real permanent."

The tea kettle started whistling. She jumped up. He watched her go, the sight of her perfectly shaped derriere outlined against the bathrobe bringing back a flood of memories he wished would just leave him the hell alone. She came back with two cups of tea.

"What was the favor?" She sipped her tea. Jack left his where it was.

"He said he needed a lawyer. He *might* need a lawyer. Although things might turn out so he wouldn't. He wanted me to be that lawyer."

She put her tea down. "Is that it?"

"Isn't that enough?"

"Maybe for an honest, respectable person, but not for him."

"My God, Kate, the man was scared. I've never seen him scared before, have you?"

"I've seen all I need to see of him. He chose his lifestyle and now apparently it's catching up to him."

"He's your father for chrissakes."

"Jack, I don't want to have this conversation." She started to get up.

"What if something happens to him? Then what?"

She looked at him coldly. "Then it happens. That's not my problem."

Jack got up and started to leave. Then he turned back, his face red with anger. "I'll tell you how the funeral service goes. On second thought, what the hell would you care? I'll just make sure you get a copy of the death certificate for your scrapbook."

He didn't know she could move that quickly, but he would feel the slap for about a week, like someone had poured acid across his cheek, a truer description than he realized at the moment.

"How dare you?" Her eyes blazed at him as he slowly rubbed his face.

Then the tears erupted from her with so much force that they spilled onto the front of the robe.

He said quietly, as calmly as he could, "Don't shoot the messenger, Kate. I told Luther and I'm telling you, life is way too short for this crap. I lost both my parents a long time ago. Okay, you have reasons for not liking the guy, fine. That's up to you. But the old man loves you and cares about you and regardless of how you think he's screwed up your life you have to

250

respect that love. That's my advice to you, take it or leave it."

He moved toward the door but she again got there before him.

"You don't know anything about it."

"Fine, I don't know anything about it. Go back to bed, I'm sure you'll fall right asleep, nothing important on your mind."

She grabbed his coat with such force that she jerked him around, even though he outweighed her by eighty pounds.

"I was two years old when he went to prison for the last time. I was nine when he got out. Do you understand the incredible shame of a little girl whose dad is in prison? Whose dad *steals* other people's property for a living? When you had show-and-tell at school and the one kid's dad is a doctor and another's is a truck driver and it comes to your turn and the teacher looks down and tells the class that Katie's dad had to go away because he did something bad and then she'd skip to the next kid?

"He was never there for us. *Never!* Mom worried sick about him all the time. But she always kept the torch, right up until the end. She made it easy for him."

"She finally divorced him, Kate," Jack gently reminded her.

"Only because that was the only choice she had left. And right when she was just getting her life turned around, she finds a lump in her breast and in six months she's gone."

Kate leaned back against the wall. She looked so tired, it was painful to witness. "And you know what the really crazy thing is? She never once stopped loving him. After all the incredible shit he put her through." Kate shook her head, having a hard time believing the words she had just spoken.

251

She looked up at Jack, her chin trembling slightly.

"But that's okay, I have enough hate for both of us." She stared at him, a mixture of pride and righteousness on her features.

Jack didn't know if it was the complete exhaustion he was feeling or the fact that for so many years what he was about to say had been pent up inside him. Years of watching this charade. And brushing it aside in favor of the beauty and vivaciousness of the woman across from him. His vision of perfection.

"Is that your idea of justice, Kate? Enough hate balanced against enough love, and everything equals out?"

She stepped back. "What are you talking about?"

He moved forward as she continued to retreat into the small room. "I've listened to this goddamned martyrdom of yours until I'm sick of it. You think you're some perfect defender of the hurt and victimized. Nothing comes above that. Not you, not me, not your father. The only reason you're out there prosecuting every sonofabitch that comes into your sights is because your father hurt you. Every time you convict somebody that's another nail in your old man's heart."

Her hand flew to his face. He caught it, gripped it. "Your whole adult life has been spent getting back at him. For all the wrongs. For all the hurt. For never being there for you." He squeezed her hand until he heard her gasp. "Did you ever once stop to think that maybe you were never there for him?"

He let go of her hand as she stood there, staring at him, a look on her face he had never seen before.

"Do you understand that Luther loves you so much that he's never tried to contact you, never tried to be a part of your life, because he knows that's how you want it? His only child living a few miles away from him and he's completely cut out of her life. Did you ever think about how he feels? Did your hate ever let you do that?"

She didn't answer.

"Don't you ever wonder why your mother loved him? Is your picture of Luther Whitney so goddamned distorted that you can't see why she loved him?"

He grabbed her shoulders, shook her. "Does your goddamned hatred ever let you be compassionate? Does it ever let you love anything, Kate!"

He pushed her away. She stumbled backward, her eyes locked on his face.

He hesitated for a moment. "The fact is, lady, you don't deserve him." He paused and then decided to finish. "You don't deserve to be loved."

In one furious instant her teeth gnashed, her face contorted into rage. She screamed and flew at him, hammering her fists into his chest, slapping his face. He felt none of her blows as the tears slid down her cheeks.

Her assault stopped as quickly as it started. Her arms like lead, they clutched at his coat, holding on. That's when the heaves started and she sank to the floor, the tears bursting from her, the sobs echoing through the tiny space.

He lifted her up and placed her gently on the couch.

He knelt beside her, letting her cry, and she did so for a long time, her body repeatedly tensing and then going limp until he felt himself growing weak, his hands clammy. He finally wrapped his arms around her, laid his chest against her side. Her thin fingers clutched tightly to his coat as both their bodies shook together for a long time.

When it was over she sat up slowly, her face red, splotchy.

Jack stepped back.

She refused to look at him. "Get out, Jack."

"Kate—"

"Get *out!*" Despite her scream the voice was fragile, battered. She covered her face in her hands.

He turned and walked out the door. As he headed down the street he turned to look at her building. Her silhouette was framed in the window, looking out, but she wasn't looking at him. She was looking for something, he wasn't sure what. Probably she didn't even know. As he continued to watch, she turned from the window. A few moments later the light in her apartment went out.

Jack wiped at his eyes, turned and walked slowly down the street, heading home after one of the longest days he could ever remember.

"*Goddammit!* How long?" Seth Frank stood next to the car. It was not quite eight in the morning.

The young Fairfax County patrolman didn't know the significance of the event and was startled by the detective's outburst.

"We found her about an hour ago; an early-morning jogger saw the car, called it in."

Frank walked around the car and peered in from the passenger side. The face was peaceful, much different from the last corpse he had viewed. The long hair was undone, streamed down the sides of the car seat and flowed across the floorboard. Wanda Broome looked like she was asleep.

Three hours later the crime scene investigation was completed. Four pills had been found on the car seat. The autopsy would confirm that Wanda Broome had died from a massive overdose of digitalis, from a prescription she had filled for her mother but obviously had never delivered. She had been dead for about two hours when her body was discovered on the secluded dirt path that ran around a five-acre pond about eight miles from the Sullivan place just over the county line. The only other piece of tangible evidence was in a plastic bag that Frank was carrying back to headquarters after getting the okay from his sister jurisdiction. The note was on a piece of paper torn from a spiral ring notepad. The handwriting was a woman's, flowing and embellished. Wanda's last words had been a desperate plea for redemption. A shriek of guilt in four words.

I am so sorry.

Frank drove on past the rapidly fading foliage and misty swamp that paralleled the winding back road. He had fucked that one up royally. He never would have figured the woman for a suicide candidate. Wanda Broome's history pegged her as a survivor. Frank couldn't help but feel sorry for the woman, but also raged at her stupidity. He could've gotten her a deal, a sweetheart deal! Then he reflected on the fact that his instincts had been right on one count. Wanda Broome *had* been a very loyal person. She had been loyal to Christine Sullivan and could not live with the guilt that she had contributed, however unintentionally, to her death. An understandable, if regrettable, reaction. But with her gone, Frank's best, and perhaps only, opportunity to land the big fish had just died too.

The memory of Wanda Broome faded into the background as he focused on how to bring to justice a man who had now caused the death of two women.

"Damn, Tarr, was it today?" Jack looked at his client in the reception area of Patton, Shaw. The man looked as out of place as a junkyard mutt at a dog show.

"Ten-thirty. It's eleven-fifteen now, does that mean I get forty-five minutes free? By the way, you look like hell."

Jack looked down at his rumpled suit and put a hand through his unkempt hair. His internal clock was still on Ukraine time, and a sleepless night had not helped his appearance.

"Believe me, I look much better than I feel."

The two men shook hands. Tarr had dressed up for the meeting, which meant his jeans didn't have holes in them, and he wore socks with his tennis shoes. The corduroy jacket was a relic from the early 1970s, and the hair was its usual tangle of curls and mats.

"Hey, we can do it another day, Jack. Me, I understand hangovers."

"Not when you got all dressed up. Come on back. All I need is some grub. I'll take you to lunch and won't even bill you for the tab."

As the men walked down the hallway, Lucinda, prim and proper in keeping with the firm's image, breathed a sigh of relief. More than one Patton, Shaw partner had walked through her turf with absolute horror on their face at the sight of Tarr Crimson. Memos would fly this week.

"I'm sorry, Tarr, I'm running on about twelve cylinders lately." Jack tossed his overcoat over a chair and settled down miserably behind a stack of pink message slips about six inches high on his desk.

"Out of the country, so I heard. Hope it was someplace fun."

"It wasn't. How's business?"

"Booming. Pretty soon, you might be able to call me a legitimate client. Make your partners' stomachs feel a lot better when they see me sitting in the lobby."

"Screw 'em, Tarr, you pay your bills."

"Better to be a big client and pay some of your bills than a teeny client who pays all of his."

Jack smiled. "You got us all figured out, don't you?"

"Hey, man, you seen one algorithm, you've seen 'em all."

Jack opened Tarr's file and perused it quickly.

"We'll have your new S corp set up by tomorrow. Delaware incorporation with a qualification in the District. Right?"

Tarr nodded.

"How're you planning on capitalizing it?"

Tarr pulled out a legal pad. "I've got the list of potentials. Same as the last deal. Do I get a reduced rate?" Tarr smiled. He liked Jack, but business was business.

"Yeah, this time you won't pay for the learning curve of an overpriced and underinformed associate."

Both men smiled.

"I'll cut the bill to the bone, Tarr, just like always. What's the new company for, by the way?"

"Got the inside track on some new technology for surveillance work."

Jack looked up from his notes. "Surveillance? That's a little off the mark for you, isn't it?"

"Hey, you gotta go with the flow. Corporate business is down. But when one market dries up, being the good entrepreneur that I am, I look around for other opportunities. Surveillance for the private sector has always been hot. Now the new twist is big brother in the law enforcement arena."

"That's ironic for somebody who got thrown in jail in every major city in the country during the 1960s."

"Hey, those causes were good ones. But we all grow up."

"How does it work?"

"Two ways. First, low-level orbit satellites are downlinked to metropolitan police tracking stations. The birds have preprogrammed sweep sectors. They spot trouble and they send an almost instantaneous signal to the tracking station, giving precise incident information. It's real time for the cops. The second method involves placing military-style surveillance equipment, sensors and tracking devices on top of telephone poles, or underground with surface sensors or on the outside of buildings. Their exact locations will be classified, of course, but they'll be deployed in the worst crime areas. If something starts to go down, they'll call in the cavalry."

Jack shook his head. "I can think of a few civil rights that might be trampled."

"Tell me about it. But it's effective."

"Until the bad guys move."

"Kinda hard to outrun a satellite, Jack."

Jack shook his head and turned back to his file.

"Hey, how're the wedding plans coming?"

Jack looked up. "I don't know, I try to keep out of the way."

Tarr laughed. "Shit, Julie and I had a total of twenty bucks to get married on, including the honeymoon. We got a Justice of the Peace for ten dollars, bought a case of Michelob with the rest, and rode the Harley down to Miami and slept on the beach. Had a helluva good time."

Jack smiled, shook his head. "I think the Baldwins have something a little more formal in mind. Although your way sounds like a lot more fun to me."

Tarr looked at him quizzically, remembering something. "Hey, whatever happened to that gal you were dating when you were defending the criminal elements of this fair city? Kate, right?"

Jack looked down at his desk. "We decided to go our separate ways," he said quietly.

"Huh, I always thought you two made a nice-looking couple."

Jack looked across at him, licked his lips and then

closed his eyes for a moment before answering. "Well, sometimes looks can be deceiving."

Tarr studied his face. "You sure?"

"I'm sure."

After lunch and finishing up some overdue work, Jack returned half of his phone messages and decided to leave the rest until the following day. Looking out the window, he turned his thoughts fully to Luther Whitney. What he could be involved in, Jack could only guess. The most puzzling aspect was that Luther was a loner in private life and with his work. Back when he was with the PD, Jack had checked on some of Luther's priors. He worked alone. Even on the cases where he hadn't been arrested but had been questioned, there was never an issue of more than one person involved. Then who could these other people be? A fence Luther had somehow ripped off? But Luther had been in the business much too long to do something like that. It wasn't worth it. His victim perhaps? Maybe they couldn't prove Luther had committed the crime but nevertheless held a vendetta against him. But who held that sort of grudge for getting burglarized? Jack could understand if someone had been hurt or killed, but Luther was not capable of that.

He sat down at his small conference table and thought back for a moment to the night before with Kate. It had been the most painful experience of his life, even more so than when Kate had left him. But he had said what needed to be said.

He rubbed his eyes. At this moment in his life the Whitneys weren't especially welcome. But he had promised Luther. Why had he done that? He loosened his tie. At some point he would have to draw the line, or cut the cord, if only for his own mental well-being. Now he was hoping that his promised favor would never come due.

He went down and got a soda from the kitchen, sat back down at his desk and finished up the bills for last month. The firm was invoicing Baldwin Enterprises roughly three hundred thou' a month and the work was accelerating. While Jack had been gone, Jennifer had sent over two new matters that would occupy a regiment of associates for about six months. Jack quickly calculated his profit sharing for the quarter and whistled under his breath when he got an approximate. It was almost too easy.

Things were really improving between Jennifer and him. His brain told him not to screw that up. The organ in the center of his chest wasn't so sure, but he was thinking that his brain should start taking command of his life. It wasn't that their relationship had changed. It was only that his expectation of that relationship had. Was that a compromise on his part? Probably. But who said you could manage to get through life without compromise? Kate Whitney had tried and look what it had gotten her.

He phoned Jennifer's office, but she wasn't there. Gone for the day. He checked his watch. Five-thirty. When she wasn't traveling, Jennifer Baldwin rarely left the office before eight. Jack looked at his calendar. She was in town the whole week. When he had tried her from the airport last night there had been no answer either. He hoped nothing was wrong.

As he was contemplating leaving and heading over to her house, Dan Kirksen popped his head in.

"Could I trouble you for a minute, Jack?"

Jack hesitated. The little man and his bow ties irritated Jack, and he knew exactly why. Deferential as hell, Kirksen would have treated Jack like a piece of manure had he not controlled millions in business.

On top of that, Jack knew that Kirksen desperately wanted to treat him like a piece of shit anyway, and he hoped to accomplish that goal one day.

"I was thinking about heading out. I've been hitting it pretty heavy lately."

"I know." Kirksen smiled. "The whole firm's been talking about it. Sandy better watch out – by all accounts Walter Sullivan is very enamored with you."

Jack smiled to himself. Lord was the only person whom Kirksen wanted to kick in the ass more than Jack. Lord without Sullivan would be vulnerable. Jack could read all those thoughts as they passed behind the spectacles of the firm's managing partner.

"I don't think Sandy has anything to worry about."

"Of course not. It'll just take a few minutes. Conference room number one." Kirksen disappeared as quickly as he had appeared.

What the hell was all this about? Jack wondered. He grabbed his coat and walked down the hallway. As he passed a couple of fellow associates in the hallway, they gave him sidelong glances that only increased his puzzlement.

The sliding doors to the conference room were closed, which was unusual unless something was going on inside. Jack slid back one of the thick doors. The dark room confronting him exploded into bright light, and Jack looked on in amazement as the party came into focus. The banner on the far wall said it all: CONGRATULATIONS PARTNER!

Lord presided over the lavish affair of drinks and an expensive, catered spread. Jennifer was there, along with her father and mother.

"I am so proud of you, sweetie." She had already consumed several drinks and her soft eyes and gentle caresses told Jack things would only get better later that night.

261

"Well, we can thank your dad for this partnership."

"Uh-uh, lover. If you weren't doing a good job, Daddy would cut you loose in a New York minute. Give yourself some credit. You think Sandy Lord and Walter Sullivan are easy to please? Honey, you pleased Walter Sullivan, stunned him even, and there's only a handful of attorneys who have ever done that."

Jack swallowed the rest of his drink and contemplated that statement. It sounded plausible. He had scored big with Sullivan, and who was to say Ransome Baldwin wouldn't have taken his business elsewhere if Jack hadn't been up to the task?

"Maybe you're right."

"Of course I'm right, Jack. If this firm were a football team, you'd be MVP or rookie of the year, maybe both." Jennifer took another drink and slid her arm around Jack's waist.

"And on top of that, you can now afford to support me in the lifestyle I've grown accustomed to." She pinched his arm.

"Grown accustomed to. Right! Try, from birth." They stole a quick kiss.

"You'd better mingle, superstar." She pushed him away and went in search of her parents.

Jack looked around. Every person in this room was a millionaire. He was easily the poorest of them all, but his prospects probably surpassed all of theirs. His base income had just quadrupled. His profit sharing for the year would easily be double that. It occurred to him that he too was now, technically, a millionaire. Who would've thought it, when four years ago a million dollars seemed to be more money than existed on the planet?

He had not entered law to become rich. He had spent years working as hard as he ever had for what amounted to pennies. But he was entitled now, wasn't he? This was the typical American Dream, wasn't it? But what was it about that dream that made you feel guilty when you finally attained it?

He felt a big arm around his shoulder. He turned to look at Sandy Lord, red eyes and all staring at him.

"Surprised the hell out of you, didn't we?"

Jack had to agree with that. Sandy's breath was a mixture of hard liquor and roast beef. It reminded Jack of their very first encounter at Fillmore's, not a pleasant memory. He subtly distanced himself from his intoxicated partner.

"Look around this room, Jack. There's not a person here, with the possible exception of yours truly, who wouldn't love to be in your shoes."

"It seems a little overwhelming. It happened so fast." Jack was talking more to himself than to Lord.

"Hell, these things always do. For the fortunate few, wham, zero to the top in seconds. Improbable success is just that: improbable. But that's what makes it so damn satisfying. By the way, let me shake your hand for taking such good care of Walter."

"Pleasure, Sandy. I like the man."

"By the way, I'm having a little get-together at my place on Saturday. Some people are going to be there you should meet. See if you can persuade your extremely attractive Significant Other to attend. She might find some marketing opportunities. Girl's a natural hustler just like her daddy."

Jack shook the hand of every partner in the place, some more than once. By nine o'clock he and Jennifer were headed home in her company limo. By one o'clock they had already made love twice. By one-thirty Jennifer was sound asleep.

Jack wasn't.

He stood by the window looking out at the few stray snowflakes that had started to fall. An early

263

winter storm system had settled in over the area although accumulations were not supposed to be significant. Jack's thoughts were not on the weather, however. He looked over at Jennifer. She was dressed in a silk nightgown, nestled between satin sheets, in a bed the size of his apartment's bedroom. He looked up at his old friends the murals. Their new place was supposed to be ready by Christmas, although the very proper Baldwin family would never allow patent cohabitation until the vows were exchanged. The interiors were being redone under the sharp eye of his fiancée to suit their individual tastes and to boldly cast their own personal statement – whatever the hell that meant. As he studied the medieval faces on the ceiling it occurred to Jack that they were probably laughing at him.

He had just made partner in the most prestigious firm in town, was the toast of some of the most influential people you could imagine, every one of them eager to advance his already meteoric career even further. He had it all. From the beautiful princess, to the rich, old father-in-law, to the hallowed if utterly ruthless mentor, to serious bucks in the bank. With an army of the powerful right behind him and a truly limitless future, Jack never felt more alone than he did that night. And despite all his willpower, his thoughts continually turned to an old, frightened and angry man, and his emotionally spent daughter. With those twin beauties swirling in his head he silently watched the gentle fall of snowflakes until the softened edges of daybreak greeted him.

The old woman watched through the dusty Venetian blinds that covered the living room window as the dark sedan pulled into her driveway. The arthritis in both grossly swollen knees made getting up difficult, much less trying to move herself around. Her back was permanently bent and the lungs were dense and unforgiving after fifty years of tar and nicotine bombardment. She was counting down to the end; her body had carried her about as far as it could. Longer than her daughter's had.

She fingered the letter that she kept in the pocket of her old, pink dressing gown that failed to completely cover the red, blistered ankles. She figured they would show up sooner or later. After Wanda had come back from the police station, she knew it was a matter of time before something like this happened. The tears welled up in her eyes as she thought back to the last few weeks.

"It was my fault, Momma." Her daughter had sat in the tiny kitchen where, as a little girl, she had helped her mother bake cookies and can tomatoes and stringbeans harvested from the strip of garden out back. She had repeated those words over and over as she slumped forward on the table, her body convulsing with every word. Edwina had tried to reason with her daughter but she was not eloquent enough to dent the shroud of guilt that surrounded the slender woman who had started life as a roly-poly baby with thick dark hair and horseshoe legs. She had shown Wanda the letter but it had done no good. It was beyond the old woman to make her child understand.

Now she was gone and the police had come. And now Edwina had to do the right thing. And at eighty-one and God-fearing, Edwina was going to lie to the police, which was to her the only thing she could do.

"I'm sorry about your daughter, Mrs. Broome." Frank's words rang sincere to the old woman's ears. A trickle of a tear slipped down the deep crevices of her aged face.

The note Wanda had left behind was given to Edwina Broome and she looked at it through a thick magnifying glass that lay on the table within easy reach. She looked at the earnest face of the detective. "I can't imagine what she was thinking when she wrote this."

"You understand that a robbery took place at the Sullivan home? That Christine Sullivan was murdered by whoever it was that broke in?"

"I heard that on the television right after it happened. That was terrible. Terrible."

"Did your daughter ever talk to you about the incident?"

"Well of course she did. She was so upset by it all. She and Mrs. Sullivan got along real well, real well. It broke her up."

"Why do you think she took her own life?"

"If I could tell you, I would."

She let that ambiguous statement hang in front of Frank's face until he folded the paper back up.

"Did your daughter tell you anything about her work that might shed some light on the murder?"

"No. She liked her job pretty much. They treated her real well from what she said. Living in that big house, that's real nice."

"Mrs. Broome, I understand that Wanda was in trouble with the law a while back."

"A *long* while back, Detective. A *long* while back. And she lived a good life since then." Edwina Broome's eyes had narrowed, her lips set in a firm line, as she stared down Seth Frank.

"I'm sure she did," Frank added quickly. "Did Wanda bring anyone by to see you in the last few months. Someone you didn't know perhaps?"

Edwina shook her head. That much was the truth.

Frank eyed her for a long moment. The cataract-filled eyes stared straight back at him.

"I understand your daughter was out of the country when the incident happened?"

"Went down to that island with the Sullivans. They go every year I'm told."

"But Mrs. Sullivan didn't go."

"I suppose not, since she was murdered up here while they were down there, Detective."

Frank almost smiled. This old lady wasn't nearly as dumb as she was making out to be. "You wouldn't have any idea why Mrs. Sullivan didn't go? Something Wanda might have told you?"

Edwina shook her head, stroked a silver and white cat that jumped up on her lap.

"Well, thank you for talking to me. Again I'm sorry about your daughter."

"Thank you, I am too. Very sorry."

As she wrenched herself up to see him to the door, the letter fell out of her pocket. Her weary heart skipped a beat as Frank bent down, picked it up without glancing at it and handed it to her.

She watched him pull out of the driveway. She slowly eased herself back down in the chair by the fireplace and unfolded the letter.

It was in a man's hand she knew well: *I didn't do it. But you wouldn't believe me if I told you who did.*

For Edwina Broome that was all she needed to know. Luther Whitney had been a friend for a long time, and had only broken into that house because of Wanda. If the police caught up to him, it would not be with her assistance.

And what her friend had asked her to do she would. God help her, it was the only decent thing she could do.

Seth Frank and Bill ank's office and the sun was shook hands and sat down. They your seeing me, Seth." barely ittle unusual."

"Damn unusual if you ask me." Burton grinned. "Mind if I light one up?"

"How about I join you?" Both men pulled out their packs.

Burton bent his match forward as he settled back in his chair.

"I've been with the Service a long time and this is a first for me. But I can understand it. Old man Sullivan is one of the President's best friends. Helped get him started in politics. A real mentor. They both go way back. Just between you and me, I don't think the President actually wants us to do much more than give an impression of involvement. We are in no way looking to step on your toes."

"Not that you have jurisdiction to do that anyway."

"Exactly, Seth. Exactly. Hell, I was a state trooper for eight years. I know how police investigations go. The last thing you need is somebody else looking over your goddamned shoulder."

The wariness started to fade from Frank's eyes. An ex-state trooper turned Secret Service agent. This guy was really a career law enforcement person. In Frank's book you didn't get much better than that.

"So what's your proposal?"

"I see my role as an information pipeline to the President. Something breaks, you give me a call and I'll fill in the President. Then when he sees Walter Sullivan he can speak intelligently about the case. Believe me, it's not all smoke and mirrors. The President is genuinely concerned about the case." Burton smiled.

"And no interference from the feds? No second-guessing?"

"Hell, I'm not the FBI. It's at me as the civilian emissary of more than a professional courtesy real case. Look much

268

Frank looked around his office as he slowly absorbed the situation. Burton followed that gaze and tried to size up Frank as precisely as possible. Burton had known many detectives. Most had average capabilities, which, coupled with an exponentially increasing caseload, resulted in a very low arrest and much lower conviction rate. But he had checked out Seth Frank. The guy was former NYPD with a string of citations a mile long. Since his coming to Middleton County, there had not been one unsolved homicide. Not one. It was a rural county to be sure, but a one hundred percent solve rate was still pretty impressive. All those facts made Burton very comfortable. For although the President had requested that Burton keep in contact with the police in order to fulfill his pledge to Sullivan, Burton had his own reason for wanting access to the investigation.

"If something breaks really fast, I might not be able to apprise you right away."

"I'm not asking for miracles, Seth, just a little info when you get a chance. That's all." Burton stood up, crushing out his cigarette. "We got a deal?"

"I'll do my best, Bill."

"A man can't ask for more than that. So, you got any leads?"

Seth Frank shrugged. "Maybe. Might peter out, you never know. You know how that goes."

"Tell me about it." Burton started to leave and then looked back. "Hey, as some quid pro quo if you need any red tape cut during your investigation, access to databases, stuff like that, you let me know and your request gets a top priority. Here's my number."

Frank took the offered card. "I appreciate that, Bill."

Two hours later Seth Frank lifted up his phone and

nothing happened. No dial tone, no outside line. The phone company was called.

An hour later, Seth Frank again picked up his phone and the dial tone was there. The system was fixed. The phone closet was kept locked at all times, but even if someone had been able to look inside, the mass of lines and other equipment would have been indecipherable to the layperson. Not that the police force ordinarily worried about someone tapping their lines.

Bill Burton's lines of communication were open now, a lot wider than Seth Frank had ever dreamed they would be.

FIFTEEN

"I think it's a mistake, Alan. I think we should be distancing ourselves, not trying to take over the investigation." Russell stood next to the President's desk in the Oval Office.

Richmond was seated at the desk going over some recent health care legislation; a quagmire to say the least and not one he planned to expend much political capital on before the election.

"Gloria, get with the program, will you?" Richmond was preoccupied; well ahead in the polls, he thought the gap should be even greater. His anticipated opponent, Henry Jacobs, was short, and not particularly good-looking or a great speaker. His sole claim to fame was thirty years of toiling on behalf of the country's indigent and less fortunate. Consequently, he was a walking media disaster. In the age of sound bites and photo ops, being able to look and talk a big game was an absolute necessity. Jacobs was not even the best among a very weak group that had seen its two leading candidates knocked out over assorted scandals, sexually based and otherwise. All of which made Richmond wonder why his thirty-two-point lead in the polls wasn't fifty.

He finally turned to look at his Chief of Staff.

"Look, I promised Sullivan I'd keep on top of it. I said that to a goddamned national audience that got me a dozen points in the polls that apparently your well-oiled re-election team can't improve upon. Do

I need to go out and start a war to get the polls where they should be?"

"Alan, the election's in the bag; we both know that. But we have to play not to lose. We have to be careful. That person is still out there. What if he's caught?"

Exasperated, Richmond stood up. "Will you forget him! If you'd stop to think about it for a second, the fact that I have closely associated myself with the case takes away the only possible shred of credibility the guy might have had. If I hadn't publicly proclaimed my interest some nosy reporter might have pricked up his ears at an allegation that the President was somehow involved in the death of Christine Sullivan. But now that I've told the nation that I'm mad and determined to bring the perpetrator to justice, if the allegation is made, people will think the guy saw me on TV and he's a whacko."

Russell sat down in a chair. The problem was Richmond didn't have all the facts. If he knew about the letter opener would he have taken these same steps? If he knew about the note and photo Russell had received? She was withholding information from her boss, information that could ruin both of them, absolutely and completely.

As Russell walked down the hallway back to her office, she didn't notice Bill Burton staring at her from a passageway. The look was not one of affection, not anywhere close.

Stupid, stupid bitch. From where he was standing he could've popped three slugs into the back of her head. No sweat. His talk with Collin had cleared up the picture completely. If he had called the police that night, there would have been trouble, but not for him and Collin. The President and his skirted sidekick would've taken all the heat. The woman had snookered him. And now he was barely hanging on the edge of all that he had worked for, sweated for, taken bullets for.

He knew far better than Russell what they were all confronted with. And it was because of that knowledge that he had made his decision. It had not been an easy one, but it was the only one he could make. It was the reason he had visited Seth Frank. And it was also the reason he had had the detective's phone line tapped. Burton knew his course of action was probably a long shot, but they were all well outside the range of guarantees of any kind now. You just had to go with the cards you had and hope Lady Luck would smile on you at some point.

Again Burton shook with anger at the position the woman had put him in. The decision her stupidity had caused him to make. It was all he could do not to run down the stairs and break her neck. But he promised himself one thing. If he lived to do nothing else, he would ensure that this woman would suffer. He would rip her from the safe confines of her power career and hurl her right into the shit of reality – and he would enjoy every minute of it.

Gloria Russell checked her hair and lipstick in the mirror. She knew she was acting like a damned love-struck teenager, but there was something so naive and yet so masculine about Tim Collin that it was actually starting to distract her attention from her work, something that had never happened before. But it was a historical fact that men in power positions usually got some action on the side. Not an ardent feminist, Russell saw nothing wrong with emulating her male counterparts. As she saw it, it was just another perk of the position.

As she slipped out of her dress and underwear and

into her most transparent nightgown, she kept reminding herself of why she was seducing the younger man. She needed him for two reasons. One, he knew about her blunder with the letter opener and she needed absolute assurance that he keep quiet about that, and, second, she needed his help to get that piece of evidence back. Compelling, rational reasons and yet tonight, like all the nights before, they were the furthest things from her mind.

At that moment she felt she could fuck Tim Collin every night for the rest of her life and never tire of the feelings that flooded through her body after each encounter. Her brain could rationalize a thousand reasons why she should stop, but the remainder of her body was, for once, not listening.

The knock on the door came a little early. She finished primping her hair, quickly checked her makeup again, and then awkwardly slipped into her heels as she hurried down the hallway. She opened the front door and it felt like someone had plunged a knife between her breasts.

"What the hell are you doing here?"

Burton put one foot inside the half-opened door and one massive hand against the door itself.

"We need to talk."

Russell unconsciously checked behind him for the man she had expected to make love to her tonight.

Burton noted the glance. "Sorry, lover-boy ain't coming, Chief."

She tried to slam the door closed, but couldn't budge the two-hundred-and-forty-pound Burton an inch. With maddening ease he pushed open the door and went inside, shutting the door behind him.

He stood in the entranceway looking at the Chief of Staff, who was now desperately trying to understand what he was doing there at the same time she was trying to cover up strategic parts of her anatomy.

She was not succeeding with either.

"Get out, Burton! How dare you come barging in here? You're through."

Burton moved past her into the living room, barely brushing against her as he walked by.

"Either we talk here or we talk someplace else. It's up to you."

She followed him into the living room. "What the hell are you talking about? I told you to get out. You're forgetting your place in the official hierarchy, aren't you?"

He turned to face her. "You always answer the door dressed like that?" He could understand Collin's interest. The nightgown did nothing to hide the Chief of Staff's voluptuous figure. Who would've thought? He might have been aroused despite twenty-four years with the same woman and four children spawned from that marriage, except for the fact that he was absolutely repulsed by the half-naked woman standing across from him.

"Go to hell! Go straight to hell, Burton."

"That's probably where we're all going to end up, so why don't you go get on some clothes and then we're going to talk and then I'll leave. But until then I ain't going anywhere."

"Do you realize what you're doing? I can crush you."

"Right!" He pulled out the photos from his jacket pocket and tossed them down on the table. Russell tried to ignore them, but finally picked them up. She steadied her trembling legs by placing a hand on top of a table.

"You and Collin make a beautiful couple. You really do. I don't think the media will lose sight of that fact. Might make for an interesting movie of the week. What do you think? Chief of Staff gets brains screwed out by young Secret Service agent. You could call it *The Fuck Heard 'Round the World*. That's catchy, don't you think?"

She slapped him, as hard as she had ever slapped anyone. Pain shot through her arm. It had been like hitting a piece of wood. Burton took her hand and twisted it sideways until she screamed.

"Listen, lady, I know every fucking thing that's going on here. Everything. The letter opener. Who's got it. Most importantly, how he got it. And now this recent correspondence from our little larcenous voyeur. Now any way you cut it, we got us a big problem, and seeing that you've screwed everything up from the get-go, I think a change of command is in order. Now go get out of the hooker clothes, and come back in here. If you want me to save your horny little ass, you'll do exactly what I tell you to do. Do you understand? Because if you don't then I suggest we go have a little chat with the President. It's up to you, Chief!" Burton spat out the last word, communicating unequivocally his absolute disgust with her.

Burton slowly let go of her arm but still towered over her like a mountain. His massive bulk seemed to block out her ability to think. Russell gingerly rubbed her arm and almost timidly looked up at him as the hopelessness of her situation started to sink in.

She went immediately to the bathroom and threw up. It seemed like she was spending an increasing amount of her time doing that. The cold water on her face finally started to work through the throes of nausea until she was able to sit up and then walk slowly to her bedroom.

Her head spinning, she changed into long pants and a thick sweater, dropping the negligee on the bed, too ashamed to even look at it as the garment floated down; her dreams for a night of pleasure shattered with terrifying abruptness. She replaced her red stilettos with a pair of brown flats.

Patting her cheeks down as she sensed the rush of blood there, she felt like she had just been caught by her father with a boy's hands far up her dress. That event had actually occurred in her life and probably contributed to her absolute focus on her career to the detriment of everything else, so embarrassed had she been by the entire episode. Her father had called her a whore and beaten her so badly that she had missed a week of school. She had prayed her entire life that she would never feel such embarrassment again. Until tonight that prayer had been answered.

She forced herself to breathe regularly and when she went back into the living room she noted that Burton had taken his jacket off and a pot of coffee sat on the table. She eyed the thick holster with its deadly occupant.

"Cream and sugar, right?"

She managed to meet his gaze. "Yes."

He poured out the coffee and she sat down across from him.

She looked down at her cup. "How much did Ti . . . Collin tell you?"

"About the two of you? Nothing really. He's not the kind of guy who would. I think he's fallen for you pretty hard. You've fucked with his head and his heart. Nice going."

"You don't understand anything, do you?" She almost exploded out of her chair.

Burton was maddeningly calm. "I understand this much. We're about one inch from the edge of the cliff and where we're headed I can't even see the bottom. Frankly, I don't give a shit who you're sleeping with. That's not why I'm here."

Russell sat back down and forced herself to drink the coffee. Her stomach started to finally settle down.

Burton leaned across and held her arm as gently as he could. "Look, Ms. Russell. I'm not going to sit here and bullshit and tell you I'm here because I think the world of you and I want to get you out of a jam, and you don't have to pretend to love me either. But the way I look at it, like it or not, we're in this thing together. And the only way I see us making it through is to work as a team. That's the deal I'm offering." Burton sat back and watched her.

Russell put down her coffee and dabbed a napkin against her lips.

"All right."

Burton immediately leaned forward. "Just to recount, the letter opener still has both the President's and Christine Sullivan's prints on it. And their blood. Correct?"

"Yes."

"Any prosecutor would be salivating for that thing. We've got to get it back."

"We'll buy it. He wants to sell it. The next communication will tell us how much."

Burton shocked her for the second time. He tossed the envelope across.

"The guy's savvy, but at some point he has to tell us a drop point."

Russell took out the letter and read it. The writing was block print as before. The message was brief:

Coordinates coming soon. Recommend advance steps be taken for financial backing. For such prime property suggest mid seven figures. Would suggest consequences of default be considered thoroughly. Respond via Post personals if interested.

"He's got quite a writing style, doesn't he? Succinct, but he gets his point across." Burton poured another cup of coffee. Then he tossed across another photograph of what Russell was desperately hoping to retrieve.

"He sure likes to tease, doesn't he, Ms. Russell?"

"At least it sounds like he's ready to deal."

"We're talking some big bucks. You prepared for that?"

"Let me worry about that piece, Burton. Money won't be the problem." Her arrogance was returning just in time.

"Probably not," he agreed. "By the way, why the hell didn't you let Collin wipe that thing clean?"

"I don't have to answer that."

"No, actually you don't, *Madam* President."

Russell and Burton actually smiled at each other. Maybe she had been wrong. Burton was a pain in her ass, but he was cunning and careful. She realized now that she needed those qualities more than Collin's gallant naîveté even if it was accompanied by a fresh, hard body.

"There's one more piece to the puzzle, Chief."

"And that is?"

"When it comes time to kill this guy, are you gonna get squeamish on me?"

Russell choked on her coffee and Burton had to literally pound her on the back until she started breathing normally again.

"I guess that answers that."

"What the hell are you talking about, Burton — killing him?"

"You still don't understand what's going on here, do you? I thought you were some brilliant professor somewhere. Ivory towers ain't what they used to be, I guess. Or maybe you need a little dose of common sense. Let me explain this real simply for you. This guy was an eyewitness to the President trying to murder Christine Sullivan, Sullivan trying to return the favor, and me and Collin doing our job and taking her out before the President gets stuck like a side of beef. An eyewitness! Remember that term. Before I found out about this little piece of evidence you left behind, I figured our asses were cooked anyway. Guy leaks the story somehow, some way and it snowballs from there. Some things we just can't explain, right?

"But nothing happens and I figure maybe we all got lucky and this guy is too afraid to come forward. Now I find out about this blackmail shit and I ask myself what does that mean."

Burton looked questioningly at Russell.

She answered, "It means he wants money in exchange for the letter opener. It's his lottery. What else could it mean, Burton?"

Burton shook his head. "No, it means this guy is fucking with us. Playing mind games. It means we got an eyewitness out there who's getting a little daring, a little adventurous. On top of that it took a real professional to crack the Sullivan nest. So this guy is not the type who's gonna scare too easily."

"So? If we get back the letter opener aren't we home free?" Russell was dimly beginning to see what Burton was getting at, but it still wasn't clear.

"If he doesn't keep photos of it, which might end up on the front page of the *Post* any day now. An enlarged photo of the President's palm print on a letter opener that came from Christine Sullivan's bedroom on page one. Probably make for an interesting series of articles. Grounds enough for the papers to start digging around. Even the slightest hint of a connection between the President and Sullivan's murder and it's over. Sure, we can argue the guy's a whacko and the picture's a clever forgery, and maybe we'll succeed. But one of those photos showing up at the *Post* doesn't concern me half as much as our other problem."

"Which is?" Russell sat forward now, her voice low, almost husky, as something terrible was beginning to dawn on her.

"You seem to have forgotten that this guy saw everything we did that night. Everything. What we were wearing. Everybody's name. How we wiped the place clean, which I'm sure the police are still scratching their heads over. He can tell them how we arrived and how we left. He can tell them to check the President's arm for traces of a knife wound. He can tell them how we dug one slug out of the wall and where we were standing when we fired. He can tell them everything they want to know. And when he does, they'll at first think he knows all about the crime scene because he was there and was actually the trigger man. But then the cops will start to realize that this was more than a one-man show. They'll wonder how he knows all this other stuff. Some of which he couldn't have made up and which they can verify. They'll begin to wonder about all those little details that just don't make sense but that this guy can explain."

Russell stood up and went over to the bar and poured herself a Scotch. She poured one for Burton too. She thought about what Burton had said. The man *had* seen everything. Including her and an unconscious President having sex. Miserable, she pushed the thought from her mind.

"Why would he come forward after he'd been paid off?"

"Who says he actually has to come forward? Remember like you said that night? He could do it from a distance. Laugh all the way to the bank and take down an administration. Hell, he can write it all down and fax it to the cops. They'll have to investigate it and who's to say they won't find something? If they got any physical evidence from that bedroom, hair root, saliva, seminal fluid, all they need is a body to match it against. Before, there was no reason for them to look our way, but now, who the hell knows? You get a DNA match against Richmond, we're dead. Dead.

"And so what if the guy never comes forward voluntarily? The detective on the case is no bonehead. And my gut tells me that, given time, he's gonna find the sonofabitch. And a guy looking at life in prison or maybe the ultimate penalty will talk his head off, believe me. I've seen it happen too many times."

Russell felt a sudden chill. What Burton said made absolute sense. The President had sounded so convincing. Neither of them had even considered this line.

"Besides, I don't know about you, but I don't plan on spending the rest of my life looking over my shoulder waiting for that shoe to drop."

"But how can we find him?"

It amused Burton that the Chief of Staff had fallen in with his plans without much argument. The value of life apparently did not mean much to this woman when her personal well-being was threatened. He hadn't expected less.

"Before I knew about the letters, I thought we had no chance. But with blackmail, at some point you gotta have the payoff. And then he's vulnerable."

"But he'll just ask for a wire transfer. If what you say is true, this guy's too smart to be looking for a bag of money in a Dumpster. And we won't know where the letter opener will be until long after he's gone."

"Maybe, maybe not. You let me worry about that. What is imperative is that you string the guy along just a bit. If he wants the deal done in two days, you make it four. Whatever you put in the personals make it sincere. I'll leave that up to you, Professor.

But you've got to buy me some time." Burton got up. She grabbed his arm.

"What are you going to do?"

"The less you know about it the better. But you do understand that if the whole thing blows up, we all go down, including the President? There's nothing at this point I could or would do to prevent that. As far as I'm concerned you both deserve it."

"You don't sugarcoat things, do you?"

"Never found it useful." He put on his coat. "By the way, you realize that Richmond beat Christine Sullivan up bad, don't you? From the autopsy report it looks like he tried to turn her neck into a spaghetti loop."

"So I understand. Is that important to know?"

"You don't have any children, do you?"

Russell shook her head.

"I've got four. Two daughters, not much younger than Christine Sullivan. As a parent you think about things like that. Loved ones getting messed up by some asshole like that. Just wanted you to know the kind of guy our boss is. That is, if he ever gets frisky, you might want to think twice."

He left her sitting in the living room contemplating her wrecked life.

As he climbed into his car, he took a moment to light a cigarette. Burton had spent the last few days reviewing the preceding twenty years of his life. The price being paid to preserve those years was heading into the stratosphere. Was it worth it? Was he prepared to pay it? He could go to the cops. Tell them everything. His career would be over, of course. The police could get him on obstruction of justice, conspiracy to commit murder, maybe some bullshit manslaughter charge for popping Christine Sullivan and other assorted nickel-and-dime stuff. It would all add up, though. Even cutting a deal he was going to do some serious time. But he could do the time. He could also endure the scandal. All the shit the papers would write. He'd go down in history as a criminal. He'd be inextricably linked to the notoriously corrupt Richmond administration. And yet he could take that, if it came to it. What the hard-as-rock Bill Burton could not take was the look in his children's eyes. He would never again see pride and love. And the absolute and complete trust that their daddy, this big hulk of a man, was, indisputably, one of the good guys. That was something that was too tough even for him.

Those were the thoughts that had been racing through Burton's head ever since his talk with Collin. A part of him wished he hadn't asked. That he had never found out about the blackmail attempt. Because that had given him an opportunity. And opportunities were always accompanied by choices. Burton had finally made his. He wasn't proud of it. If things worked out according to plan, he would do his best to forget it had ever happened. If things didn't work out? Well, that was just too bad. But if he went down, so would everyone else.

That thought triggered another idea. Burton reached across and popped open the car's glove compartment. He pulled out a mini-cassette recorder and a handful of tapes. He looked back up at the house as he puffed on his cigarette.

He put the car in gear. As he passed Gloria Russell's house, he figured the lights there would remain on for a long time.

SIXTEEN

Laura Simon had just about given up hope of finding it.

The exterior and interior of the van had been minutely dusted and then fumed for prints. A special laser from the state police headquarters in Richmond had even been brought up, but every time they found a match, it was someone else's prints. Someone they could account for. She knew Pettis's prints by heart now. He was unfortunate enough to have all arches, one of the rarest of fingerprint compositions, as well as a tiny scar on his thumb that had in fact led to his arrest years earlier for grand-theft auto. Perps with scars across their fingertips were an ident tech's best friend.

Budizinski's prints had shown up once because he'd stuck his finger in a solvent and then pressed it against a piece of plywood kept in the back of the van, a print as perfect as if she had fingerprinted him herself.

All told, she had found fifty-three prints, but none were of any use to her. She sat in the middle of the van and glumly looked around its interior. She had gone over every spot where a print could reasonably be expected to exist. She had hit every nook and cranny of the vehicle with the handheld laser and was running out of ideas where else to look.

For the twentieth time she went through the motions of men loading the truck, driving it – the rearview mirror was an ideal spot for prints – moving the equipment, lifting the bottles of cleaners, dragging the hoses, opening and closing the doors. The difficulty of her task was increased by the fact that prints tended to disappear over time, depending on the surface containing them and the surrounding climate. Wet and warm were the best preservatives, dry and cool, the worst.

She opened the glove compartment and went through the contents again. Every item had already been inventoried and dusted. She idly flipped through the van's maintenance log. Purplish stains on the paper reminded her that the lab's stock of ninhydrin was low. The pages were well-worn although the van had had very few breakdowns the three years it had been in commission. Apparently the company believed in a rigorous maintenance program. Each entry was carefully noted, initialed and dated. The company had its own in-house maintenance crew.

As she scanned the pages, one entry caught her eye. All the other entries had been initialed by either a G. Henry or an H. Thomas, both mechanics employed by Metro. This entry had J.P. initialed beside it. Jerome Pettis. The entry indicated that the van had run low on oil and a couple of quarts had been added. All that was terribly unexciting except that the date was the day the Sullivan place had been cleaned.

Simon's breathing accelerated slightly as she crossed her fingers and got out of the van. She popped the hood and began looking at the engine. She shone her light around and within a minute she found it. An oily thumbprint that preened back at her from the side of the windshield washer fluid reservoir. Where someone would naturally rest their hand when they were applying leverage to open or close the oil cap. And a glance told her it wasn't Pettis's.

Nor was it either of the two mechanics. She grabbed a file card with Budizinski's prints on it. She was ninety-nine percent sure they weren't his and she turned out to be right. She carefully dusted and lifted the print, filled out a card and nearly ran the entire way to Frank's office. She found him with his hat and overcoat on, which he quickly removed.

"You're shitting me, Laura."

"You want to check with Pettis to see if he remembers Rogers adding the oil that day?"

Frank called the cleaning company, but Pettis had already gone for the night. Calls to his home went unanswered.

Simon looked at the lift card like it was the most precious jewel in the world. "Forget it. I'll run it through our files. Stay all night if I have to. We can get Fairfax to access the state police AFIS, our damn terminal's still down." Simon was referring to the Automated Fingerprint Identification System housed in Richmond, where latent prints found at crime scenes could be compared against the ones on the state's computerized database.

Frank thought for a moment. "I think I can do one better."

"How's that?"

Frank pulled a card out of his pocket, picked up the phone and dialed. He spoke into the phone. "Agent Bill Burton please."

Burton picked up Frank and they drove down together to the FBI's Hoover Building, located on Pennsylvania Avenue. Most tourists know the building as bulky and rather ugly and as a place not to miss on a visit to D.C. Housed here was the National Crime Information Center, a computerized information system operated by the FBI, consisting of fourteen centralized-distributed types of databases and two subsystems that constituted the world's largest collection of data on known criminals. The Automated Identification System (AIS) component of NCIC was a cop's best friend. With tens of millions of criminal print cards on file, Frank's chances of a hit were measurably increased.

After depositing the print with FBI technicians – who had clear instructions that this assignment was to be moved to as near the top of the pile as possible – Burton and Frank stood outside in the hallway nervously sipping coffee.

"This is gonna take a little while, Seth. The computer's gonna kick out a bunch of probables. The techs will still have to make the ident manually. I'll hang out and let you know as soon as a match comes back."

Frank checked his watch. His youngest was in a school play that started in forty minutes. Her role was only that of a vegetable, but was right now the most important thing on earth to his little girl.

"You sure?"

"Just leave me a number where I can reach you."

Frank did so and hurried out. The print could turn out to be nothing, a gas station attendant, but something told Frank that was not the case. Christine Sullivan had been dead a while now. Trails that cold usually stayed as cold as the victim resting six feet under, the longest six feet any of them would ever have to face. But a cold trail had suddenly turned blazing hot; whether it would flicker out remained to be seen. For now, Frank was going to enjoy the warmth. He smiled, and not just at the thought of his six-year-old running around dressed as a cucumber.

Burton stared after him, smiling for a very different reason. The FBI used a sensitivity and reliability factor in excess of ninety percent when processing latents through the AFIS. That meant that no more than two probables, and most likely only one, would be kicked out of the system. In addition, Burton had obtained a higher priority for the search than he had told Frank. All of which gained Burton time, precious time.

Later that night, Burton stared down at a name that was totally unfamiliar to him.

LUTHER ALBERT WHITNEY.

DOB 8/5/29. His Social Security number was also listed; the first three digits were 179, indicating it had been issued in Pennsylvania. Whitney's physical description was given as five foot eight, a buck sixty, with a two-inch scar on his left forearm. That comported with Pettis's description of Rogers.

Using NCIC's Triple I (Interstate Identification Index) database, Burton had also gotten a good snapshot of the man's past. The report listed three prior felony convictions for burglary. Whitney had records in three different states. He had done lengthy time, last coming out of prison in the mid-1970s. Nothing since then. At least nothing the authorities knew about. Burton had known men like that before. They were career guys who just kept getting better and better at their chosen profession. He was betting Whitney was one of those types.

One hitch, the last known address was in New York and was almost twenty years old.

Taking the point of least resistance, Burton walked down the hallway to a phone cubicle and grabbed up all the phone books for the area. He tried D.C. first; surprisingly it was a blank. Northern Virginia was next. There were three Luther Whitneys listed. His next phone call went to the Virginia State Police, where he had a longtime contact. Division of Motor Vehicles records were accessed by computer. Two of the Luther Whitneys were twenty-three and eighty-five years old respectively. However, Luther

Whitney of 1645 East Washington Avenue, Arlington, had been born on August 5, 1929, and his Social Security number, used in Virginia as the driver's license number, confirmed that he was the man. But was he Rogers? There was one way to find out.

Burton pulled out his notebook. Frank had been very courteous in letting Burton go through the investigation file. The phone rang three times and then Jerome Pettis answered. Vaguely identifying himself as being with Frank's office, Burton asked the question. Five long seconds followed while Burton tried to keep his nerves intact as he listened to the shallow breathing of the man on the other end of the line. The response was worth the short wait.

"Damn, that's right. Engine almost locked up. Somebody had left the oil cap loose. Got Rogers to do it cuz he was sitting on the case of oil we carry in the back."

Burton thanked him and hung up. He checked his watch. He still had time before he would have to leave Frank the message. Despite the mounting evidence, Burton still couldn't be absolutely certain Whitney had been the guy in the vault, but Burton's gut told him Whitney was the man. And although there was no way in hell Luther Whitney would have gone anywhere near his house after the murder, Burton wanted to get a better feel for the guy and maybe get some indication of where he'd gone. And the best way to do that was to check out where he lived. Before the cops did. He walked as quickly as he could to his car.

The weather had turned wet and cold again as Mother Nature toyed with the most powerful city on earth. The wipers flapped relentlessly across the windshield. Kate didn't exactly know why she was there. She had visited the place exactly once in all these years. And on that occasion she had sat out in the car while Jack had gone in to see him. To tell him that he and Luther's only child were getting married. Jack had insisted, despite her maintaining that the man wouldn't care. Apparently he had. He had come out on the front porch and looked at her, smiling, an awkward thrust to his body that proclaimed his hesitation in approaching her. Wanting to congratulate but not knowing exactly how, given their peculiar circumstances. He had shaken Jack's hand, pounded him on the back, then looked over at her as if for approval.

She had resolutely looked away, arms folded, until Jack had climbed back in and they had driven off. She had caught the reflection of the small figure in the side mirror as they pulled away. He looked much smaller than she remembered, almost tiny. In her mind her father would forever represent an enormous monolith of all that she resented and feared in the world, that filled all space around it and dragged one's breath away with its sheer, overpowering bulk. That creature obviously never existed, but she refused to admit that fact. But while she had not wanted to deal with that image ever again, she could not look away. For more than a minute as the car gathered speed her eyes dipped into the reflection of the man who had given her life and then taken it and her mother's away with brutal finality.

As the car pulled away he had continued to look at her, a mixture of sadness and resignation on his features that had surprised her. But she had rationalized it away, as another of his tricks to make her feel guilty. She could not attribute benign qualities to any of his actions. He was a thief. He had no regard for the law. A barbarian in a civilized society. There was no possible room in his shell for sincerity. Then they had turned the corner and his image had disappeared, like it had been on a string and was suddenly pulled away.

Kate pulled into the driveway. The house was pitch dark. As she sat there her headlights reflected off the rear of the car parked in front of her and the glare hurt her eyes. She switched off the lights, took a deep breath to steady her nerves and climbed out into the cold and wetness.

The previous snowfall had been light, and what little residue there was crunched under her feet as she made her way up to the front door. The temperature promised icy conditions developing overnight. She placed one hand against the side of his car to balance herself as she walked. Despite not expecting to find her father home, she had washed and styled her hair, was encased in one of her suits normally reserved for court and had actually applied more than a dab of makeup. She was successful, in her own way, and if chance brought them face-to-face, she wanted him to realize that despite his maltreatment she had not only survived, she had flourished.

The key was still where Jack had told her it was so many years ago. It had always seemed ironic to her that a consummate burglar should leave his own property so accessible. As she unlocked the door and slowly went inside, she did not notice the car that had pulled to a stop on the other side of the street or the driver who watched her intently, and who was already writing down her license plate number.

The house had the built-up musty odor of a long-abandoned place. She had occasionally imagined what the place would look like on the inside. She had figured it to be neat and orderly and she was not disappointed.

In the darkness she sat down in a chair in the living room, not realizing it was her father's favorite and totally unaware that Luther had unconsciously done the same thing when he had visited her apartment.

The photo was on the mantel. It must've been almost thirty years old. Kate, held in her mother's arms, was swaddled from head to toe, a few wisps of tar-colored hair visible from under the pink bonnet; she had been born with a remarkably thick head of hair. Her father, calm-faced and wearing a snap-brim, was standing next to mother and daughter, his muscular hand touching Kate's tiny outstretched fingers.

Kate's mother had kept that same photo on her dressing table until her death. Kate had thrown it away the day of the funeral, cursing the intimacy between father and daughter that the image displayed. She had hurled it away right after her father had come by the house where she had exploded at him with a fury, an outburst that became more and more out of control since its target did not respond, did not fight back, but stood there and accepted the barrage. And the quieter he had become, the more angry she became until she had slapped him, with both hands, until others had pulled her away and held her down. And only then did her father put his hat back on, lay the flowers he had brought down on the table and, with an inflamed face from her pounding and water-filled eyes, he had walked out the door, closing it quietly behind him.

And it occurred to Kate as she sat in her father's chair that he too had been grieving that day. Grieving for a woman he had presumably loved for a good portion of his life and who certainly had loved him. She felt a catch in her throat and rushed to forestall it with pressure from her fingers.

She got up and moved through the house, peering cautiously into each room and then backing away, growing more and more nervous as she penetrated further and further into her father's domain. The bedroom door was ajar, and she finally decided to push it open all the way. As she moved into the room, she risked turning on a light, and as her eyes adjusted to the exit from darkness they fell upon the nightstand and she drew nearer, finally sitting down on the bed.

The collection of photographs was, in essence, a small shrine to her. From the earliest age upward, her life was retold here. Each night as her father went to sleep, the last thing he saw was her. But what shocked her the most were the photos from later in life. Her graduation from college and law school. Her father had certainly not been invited to these events, but they were recorded here. None of the photos were posed. She was either walking or waving to someone or just standing there obviously unaware of the camera's presence. She moved on to the last photo. She was walking down the steps of the Alexandria Courthouse. Her first day in court, nervous as hell. A petty-misdemeanor case, General District Court Mickey Mouse stuff, but the big smile on her face proclaimed nothing less than absolute victory.

And she wondered how in the world she had never seen him. And then she wondered if she had but just would not admit it.

Her immediate reaction was anger. Her father had been spying on her all these years. All those special moments of her life. He had violated them. Violated her with his uninvited presence.

Her second reaction was more subtle. And as she felt it rising through her she abruptly jumped up from the bed and turned to flee the room.

That's when she thudded right into the big man standing there.

★

"Again, I'm sorry, ma'am, I didn't mean to startle you."

"Startle me? You scared the living hell out of me." Kate sat on the side of the bed, trying to regain her nerves, to stop shaking, but the chill in the house didn't help.

"Excuse me, but why is the Secret Service interested in my father?"

She looked at Bill Burton with something akin to fear in her eyes. At least he read it as fear. He had watched her in the bedroom, swiftly gauging her motives, her intent from her subtle body movements. A skill he had spent years developing, scanning endless crowds for the one or two true dangers that might be lurking there. His conclusions: estranged daughter and father. She had finally come looking for him. Things started to add up, and maybe in a very positive way for his purposes.

"We're not really, Ms. Whitney. But the police in Middleton County sure as hell are."

"Middleton?"

"Yes, ma'am. I'm sure you've read about the Christine Sullivan homicide." He let that statement hang out there to test her reaction. He got the expected one. Complete disbelief.

"You think my father had something to do with that?" It was a legitimately asked question. And not one framed particularly defensively. Burton deemed that significant and another positive for his plan, which had been forming the minute he'd laid eyes on her.

"The detective in charge of the case does. Apparently your father, as part of a carpet cleaning crew, and using a false name, was in the Sullivans' house a short time before the murder."

Kate caught her breath. Her father cleaning carpets? Of course, he had been casing the place.

Figuring its weaknesses, just like before. Nothing had changed. But murder?

"I can't believe he killed that woman."

"Right, but you can believe he was trying to burgle that house can't you, Ms. Whitney? I mean this isn't the first time, is it, or the second?"

Kate looked down at her hands. Finally she shook her head.

"People change, ma'am. I don't know how close you've been to your father lately" – Burton noted the small but discernible jerk in her expression – "but the evidence is pretty strong that he was involved somehow. And the woman is dead. You've probably gotten a conviction on less evidence that that."

Kate looked at him suspiciously. "How do you know about me?"

"I see a woman sneaking into the house of a man the police are looking for, I do what any law enforcement officer would do: I ran your license plate. Your reputation precedes you, Ms. Whitney. The state police think the world of you."

She looked around the room. "He's not here. It doesn't look like he's been here for a while."

"Yes, ma'am, I know. You wouldn't happen to know where he is, would you? He hasn't tried to contact you or anything?"

Kate thought of Jack and his late-night visitor. "No." The answer was quick, a little too quick for Burton's taste.

"It'll be better if he turns himself in, Ms. Whitney. You get some trigger-happy beat cop out there . . ." Burton expressively raised his eyebrows.

"I don't know where he is, Mr. Burton. My father and I . . . we haven't been close . . . for a long time."

"But you're here now and you knew where he kept the spare key."

Her voice rose an octave. "This is the first time I've stepped foot in this house."

Burton scrutinized her expression and decided she was telling the truth. Her unfamiliarity with the house had already led him pretty much to that conclusion, and also that she and her father were estranged.

"Is there any way you can get in touch with him?"

"Why? I really don't want to get involved in this, Mr. Burton."

"Well, I'm afraid you already are, to a degree. It'd be better if you'd cooperate."

Kate slung her purse over her arm and stood up.

"Listen, Agent Burton, you can't bluff me, I've been in the business too long. If the police want to waste their time questioning me, I'm in the phone book. The government phone book under Commonwealth's Attorney. See you around."

She headed for the door.

"Ms. Whitney?"

She whirled round, ready for some verbal sparring. Secret Service or not, she wasn't going to take any crap from this guy.

"If your father committed a crime, then he should be tried by a jury of his peers and convicted. If he's innocent, he goes free. That's how the system's supposed to work. You know that better than I do."

Kate was about to respond when her eye caught the photos. Her first day in court. It seemed a century ago and was, in a lot more ways than she could ever admit to herself. That smile, the pie-in-the-sky dreams everybody starts with, nothing less than perfection the only goal. She had dropped back to earth a long time ago.

Whatever barbed remark she was going to come back with had just escaped her, lost in the smile of a pretty young woman with a lot she wanted to do with her life.

Bill Burton watched her turn and leave. He looked over at the photos and then back at the empty doorway.

SEVENTEEN

"Shouldn't have fucking done that, Bill. You said you were not going to interfere in the investigation. Hell, I ought to throw your keester right in jail. That'd go over real well with your boss." Seth Frank slammed his desk drawer and stood up, eyes blazing at the big man.

Bill Burton stopped pacing and sat down. He had expected to take some lumps over this one.

"You're right, Seth. But Jesus I was a cop for a long time. You were unavailable, I go over there just to reconnoiter the place, I see some skirt slipping in. What would you have done?"

Frank didn't answer.

"Look, Seth, you can kick me in the ass, but I'm telling you, friend, this woman is our ace up the sleeve. With her we can nail this guy."

Frank's tensed face relaxed, his anger subsiding.

"What are you talking about?"

"The girl is his daughter. His friggin' daughter. In fact his only child. Luther Whitney is a three-time loser, a career crim who's apparently gotten better with age. His wife finally divorced him, right? Couldn't take it anymore. Then when she starts to get her life in order, she dies from breast cancer."

He paused.

Seth Frank was all attention now. "Go on."

"Kate Whitney is devastated by her mother's death. Her father's betrayal as she sees it. So devastated that she totally breaks off from him. Not

299

only that, she goes to law school and then goes to work as an Assistant Commonwealth's Attorney where she has the reputation of being one hard-assed prosecutor, especially for property-related crimes — burglary, theft, robbery. She goes for the max on all those guys. And usually gets it, I might add."

"Where the hell did you get all that info?"

"A few well-placed phone calls. People like to talk about other people's misery; it makes them feel their own life is somehow better when it usually isn't."

"So where does all this family turmoil get us?"

"Seth, look at the possibilities here. This girl hates her old man. Hates with a capital H underscored."

"So you want to use her to get to him. If they're estranged that badly, how do we do it?"

"That's the twist. By all accounts, all the hate and misery is on her side. Not his. He loves her. Loves her more than anything else. He's got a goddamned shrine to her in his bedroom. I'm telling you the guy is ripe for this."

"If, and it's still a big if in my mind, if she's willing to cooperate, how does she get in touch with him? He sure as hell isn't going to be hanging around his phone at home."

"No, but I bet he checks in for messages. You should see his house. This guy is very orderly, everything in its place, bills probably paid ahead of time. And he's got no idea we're on his ass. Not yet anyway. He probably checks his machine once or twice a day. Just in case."

"So she leaves him a message, arranges a meeting and we nail him?"

Burton stood back up, flushed two cigarettes from his pack and flipped one over to Frank. They both took a moment to light up.

"Personally, that's how I see it going down, Seth. Unless you got a better idea."

300

"We still have to convince her to do it. From what you said, she didn't seem too willing."

"I think you need to talk to her. Without me there. Maybe I came down a little too hard on her. I have a tendency to do that."

"I'll hit it first thing in the morning."

Frank put on his hat and coat and then paused.

"Look, I didn't mean to jump all over your butt, Bill."

Burton grinned. "Sure you did. I would've done the same thing if I were you."

"I appreciate the assistance."

"Anytime."

Seth started to walk out.

"Hey, Seth, little favor to an old-fart ex-cop."

"What's that?"

"Let me in on the kill. I wouldn't mind seeing his face when the hammer comes down."

"You got it. I'll call you after I talk to her. This cop's going home to his family. You should do the same, Bill."

"After I finish this smoke I'm outta here."

Frank left. Burton sat down, slowly finished his cigarette, then drowned it out in a half cup of coffee.

He could've withheld Whitney's name from Seth Frank. Told him there had been no match by the FBI. But that was too dangerous a game to play. If Frank ever found out, and the detective could through a myriad of independent channels, Burton would be stone-cold dead. Nothing could explain that deception other than the truth, which wasn't an option. Besides, Burton needed Frank to know Whitney's identity. The Secret Service agent's plan all along was to have the detective hunt the ex-con down. Find him, yes; arrest him, no.

Burton stood up, put on his coat. Luther Whitney. Wrong place, wrong time, wrong people.

Well, if it were any solace he wouldn't see it coming. He'd never even hear the shot. He'd be dead before the synapses could fire the impulse to his brain. Those were the breaks. Sometimes they went for you and sometimes against you. Now if he could only think of a way to leave the President and his Chief of Staff high and dry, he would've done a good day's work.

But that one, he was afraid, was beyond even him.

Collin parked his car down the street. The few remaining multicolored leaves gently cascaded down on him, nudged along by the breeze that lazily made its way past. He was dressed casually: jeans, cotton pullover and leather jacket. There was no bulge under his jacket. His hair was still damp from a hasty shower. His bare ankles protruded from his loafers. He looked like he should be heading to the college library for a late-night study session or hitting the party circuit after playing in the Saturday afternoon football game. As he made his way up to the house, he started getting nervous. It had surprised him, her phone call. She had sounded normal, there was no strain, no anger in her voice. Burton said she had taken it pretty well, considering. But he knew how abrasive Burton could be and that was why he was worried. Letting him keep Collin's appointment with the lady probably was not the smartest thing Collin had ever done. But the stakes were high. Burton had made him see that.

The door opened to his knock and he walked in. As he turned, the door closed and she was standing there. Smiling. Dressed in a sheer white negligee that was too short and too tight everywhere that counted, she stood tiptoe in her bare feet to kiss him gently on the lips. Then she took his hand and led him into the bedroom.

She motioned for him to lie down on the bed. Standing in front of him she undid the straps holding up the flimsy garment and let it drop to the floor. Next her underwear slid down her legs. He started to rise up, but she gently pushed him back down.

She slowly climbed on top of him, running her fingers through his hair. She slid a hand down to his erection and nicked at it through his jeans with the tip of her fingernail. He almost screamed as the confines of his pants became too painful. Again he tried to touch her but she held him down. She slid his belt off and then undid his pants. They dropped to the floor. Next she freed his explosion of flesh. It sprung up at her and she cradled it between her legs, squeezing it tightly between her thighs.

She dipped her mouth down to his and then nestled her lips against his ear.

"Tim, you want me, don't you? You want to fuck me so bad, don't you?"

He groaned and clutched at her buttocks, but she quickly moved his hands away.

"Don't you?"

"Yes."

"I wanted you so bad too, the other night. And then he showed up."

"I know, I'm sorry about that. We talked and—"

"I know, he told me. That you didn't say anything about us. That you were a gentleman."

"That part was none of his business."

"That's right, Tim. It was none of his business. And now you want to fuck me, don't you?"

"Jesus Christ yes, Gloria. Of course I do."

"So bad it hurts."

"It's killing me. It's goddamn killing me."

"You feel so good, Tim, God, you feel so good."

303

"Just wait, baby, just wait. You don't know what good is."

"I know, Tim. All I seem to think about is making love to you. You know that, don't you?"

"Yes." Collin was in so much pain now his eyes watered.

She licked at the drops, amused.

"And you're sure you want me? You're absolutely sure?"

"Yes!"

Collin felt it before his mind actually registered the fact. Like a blast of cold air.

"Get out." The words were spoken slowly, deliberately, as though practiced a number of times, to get just the right tone, the correct inflection; the speaker savoring each syllable. She climbed off him, taking care to apply enough force to his erection that he gasped for breath.

"Gloria—"

His jeans hit him in the face as he lay there. When he pulled them away and sat up, her body was covered in a thick, full-length robe.

"Get out of my house, Collin. Now."

He dressed quickly, embarrassed, as she stood there watching him. She followed him to the front door and as it opened and he stepped across the portal, she abruptly pushed him through and then slammed it behind him.

He looked back for a moment, wondering if she were laughing or crying behind the door or maybe displaying any emotion at all. He hadn't meant to hurt her. He had clearly embarrassed her. He shouldn't have done it that way. She had certainly paid him back for that embarrassment, bringing him to the threshold like that, manipulating him like some laboratory experiment and then bringing the curtain crashing down on top of him.

304

But as he walked to his car the memory of that look on her face made him relieved their brief relationship had ended.

For the first time since joining the Commonwealth's Attorney's office, Kate called in sick. Bedcovers pulled up to her chin, she sat propped up on pillows staring out at a bleak morning. Every time she had tried to get out of bed, the image of Bill Burton loomed up in front of her like a mass of sharp-edged granite, threatening to crush or impale her.

She slid down lower in the bed, sinking into the soft mattress like immersing herself in warm water, just below the surface where she could neither hear nor see anything that transpired around her.

They would be coming soon. Just like with her mother. All those years ago. People pushing their way in and firing off questions Kate's mother couldn't possibly answer. Looking for Luther.

She thought of Jack's outburst from the other night and tightly closed her eyes, trying to hurl those words away.

Goddamn him.

She was tired, more tired than any trial had ever made her. And he had done it to her, just like he had to her mother. Drawn her into the web even though she wanted no part of it, detested it, would destroy it if she could.

She sat up again, unable to breathe. She held her throat with her fingers, tightly, trying to prevent another attack. When it subsided, she turned over on her side and stared at the photo of her mother.

He was all she had left. She almost laughed. Luther Whitney was all the family she had left. God help her.

She lay on her back and waited. Waited for the knock at the door. From mother to daughter. It was her turn now.

At that moment, barely ten minutes away, Luther stared again at the old newspaper article. A cup of coffee sat near his elbow, forgotten. The small refrigerator hummed in the background. In the corner CNN droned on. Otherwise the room was absolutely quiet.

Wanda Broome had been a friend. A good friend. Ever since their accidental meeting in a Philadelphia halfway house after Luther's last prison term and Wanda's first and only. And now she was dead too. Had taken her own life, the newspaper article said, slumped over in the front seat of her car with a bunch of pills stuffed down her throat.

Luther had never operated in the mainstream, and yet, even to him, this was all a little much to take. It could have been some continuing nightmare except that every time he awoke and stared in the mirror, cold water dripping from features that grew more and more grizzled, more and more sunken with each passing day, he knew he was not going to wake up from this one.

What was ironic, in the shadow of Wanda's tragic death, was that the Sullivan job had been *her* idea. A miserable, terrible idea looking back, but one that had leapt from her surprisingly fertile mind. And an idea to which she had held doggedly, despite warnings from both Luther and her mother.

And they had planned it and he had done it. It was really that simple. And in the cold face of retrospection he had wanted to do it. It was a challenge, and a challenge combined with a huge payoff was too tough to resist.

How Wanda must have felt when Christine Sullivan hadn't gotten on that plane. And no way for her to let Luther know that the coast was not nearly so clear as they thought it would be.

She had been Christine Sullivan's friend. That part had been absolutely sincere. A last reminder of real people in the midst of the sybaritic life Walter Sullivan lived. Where everyone was not only beautiful, like Christine Sullivan was, but educated, well-connected and sophisticated, all things Christine Sullivan was not and never would be. And because of that burgeoning friendship Christine Sullivan had begun to tell Wanda things she shouldn't have, including, finally, the location and contents of the vault constructed behind a mirrored door.

Wanda was convinced that the Sullivans had so much, they couldn't possibly miss so little. The world did not work that way, Luther knew, and Wanda probably did too, but that didn't matter now.

After a lifetime of hardship, where money was always too scarce, Wanda had gone for her lottery win. Just like Christine Sullivan had, neither of them realizing just how high the price for such things really was.

Luther had flown to Barbados, would have gotten a message to Wanda there if she hadn't already left. He had sent the letter to her mother. Edwina would have shown it to her. But had she believed him? Even if she had, Christine Sullivan's life had still been sacrificed. Sacrificed, as Wanda would have seen it, to Wanda's greed and desire to have things she had no right to. Luther could almost see those thoughts running through his friend's mind as she drove out, alone, to that deserted spot; as she unscrewed the cap to get at those pills, as she drifted into permanent unconsciousness.

And he had not even been able to attend the funeral. He could not tell Edwina Broome how sorry he was, without risking getting her pulled into this nightmare. He had been as close to Edwina as he had to Wanda, in some ways even closer. He and Edwina had spent many nights trying to dissuade Wanda from her plan, to no avail. And only when it dawned on them that she would do it with or without Luther did Edwina ask Luther to take care of her daughter. Not let her go to prison again.

His eyes finally turned to the personals in the newspaper and it took him only a few seconds to find the one he was looking for. He did not smile when he read it. Like Bill Burton, Luther did not believe Gloria Russell had any redeeming qualities.

He hoped they believed this was only about money. He pulled out a piece of paper and began to write.

"Trace the account." Burton sat across from the Chief of Staff in her office. He sipped on a Diet Coke but wished for something stronger.

"I'm already doing that, Burton." Russell put her earring back on as she replaced the phone in its cradle.

Collin sat quietly in a corner. The Chief of Staff had not yet acknowledged his presence although he had walked in with Burton twenty minutes ago.

"When does he want the money again?" Burton looked at her.

"If a wire transfer does not reach the designated account by close of business, there will be no tomorrow for any of us." She swept her eyes across to Collin and then returned them to Burton.

"Shit." Burton stood up.

Russell glowered at him. "I thought you were taking care of this, Burton."

He ignored the stare. "How does he say he's going to work the drop?"

"As soon as the money is received he'll provide the location where the item will be."

"So we gotta trust him?"

"So it would seem."

"How does he know you've even gotten the letter yet?" Burton started to pace.

"It was in my mailbox this morning. My mail is delivered in the afternoon."

Burton collapsed in a chair. "Your fucking mailbox! You mean he was right outside your house?"

"I doubt if he would have allowed someone else to deliver this particular message."

"How'd you know to check the mailbox?"

"The flag was up." Russell almost smiled.

"This guy has got balls, I'll give him that, Chief."

"Apparently bigger ones than either of you." She concluded the statement by staring at Collin for a full minute. He cringed under the gaze, finally looking down at the floor.

Burton smiled to himself at the exchange. That was okay, the kid would thank him in a few weeks. For pulling him out of this black widow's web.

"Nothing really surprises me, Chief. Not anymore. How about you?" He looked at her and then at Collin.

Russell ignored the remark. "If the money is not transferred out, then we can expect him to go public somehow soon thereafter. What exactly are we going to do about it?"

The Chief of Staff's calm demeanor was no sham. She had decided that she was through crying, through vomiting every time she turned around, and that she had been hurt and embarrassed enough to last the rest of her life. Come what may, she felt almost numb to anything else. It felt surprisingly good.

"How much does he want?" Burton asked.

"Five million," she replied simply.

Burton went wide-eyed. "And you got that kind of money? Where?"

"That doesn't concern you."

"Does the President know?" Burton asked the question knowing full well the answer.

"Again, that doesn't concern you."

Burton didn't push it. What did he care anyway?

"Fair enough. Well, in answer to your question, we are doing something about it. If I were you I'd find a way to pull that money back somehow. Five million dollars isn't going to do much to someone not among the living."

"You can't kill what you can't find," Russell shot back.

"That's true, that's so true, Chief." Burton sat back and recounted his conversation with Seth Frank.

Kate was fully dressed when she answered the door, thinking, somehow, that if she were in her bathrobe the interview would endure longer, that she would appear more and more vulnerable as each question came her way. The last thing she wanted to appear was vulnerable, which was exactly how she felt.

"I'm not sure what you want from me."

"Some information, that's all, Ms. Whitney. I realize you're an officer of the court, and believe me, I hate to put you through this, but right now your father is my number-one suspect in a very high-profile case." Frank looked at her with a pair of earnest eyes.

They were sitting in the tiny living room. Frank had his notebook out. Kate sat erect on the edge of the couch trying to remain calm, although her fingers kept fluttering to her small chain necklace, twisting and turning it into small knots, tiny centers of bedlam.

"From what you've told me, Lieutenant, you don't have much. If I were the ACA on that case I don't think I'd even have enough to get an arrest warrant issued, much less a bill of indictment returned."

310

"Maybe, maybe not." Frank eyed the way she played with the chain. He wasn't really there to gather information. He probably knew more about her father than she did. But he had to ease her into the trap. Because, as he thought about it, that's what it was, a trap. For someone else. Besides, what did she care? It made his conscience feel better anyway, to think that she didn't really care at all.

Frank continued, "But I'll tell you some interesting coincidences. We have your father's print on a cleaning van that we *know* was at the Sullivan place a short time before the murder. The fact that we know he was in the house, and in the very bedroom where the crime was committed, a short time before. We have two eyewitnesses to that. And the fact that he used an alias and a false address and Social Security number when applying for the job. And the fact that he seems to have disappeared."

She looked at him. "He had priors. He probably didn't use his real info because he didn't think he'd get the job otherwise. You say he's disappeared. Did you ever think he just may have taken a trip? Even ex-cons go on vacation." Her instincts as a trial lawyer found her defending her father, an unbelievable thought. A sharp pain shot through her head. She rubbed at it distractedly.

"Another interesting discovery is that your father was good friends with Wanda Broome, Christine Sullivan's personal maid and confidante. I checked. Your father and Wanda Broome had the same parole officer back in Philly. According to certain sources, they've apparently kept in touch all these years. My bet is Wanda knew about the safe in the bedroom."

"So?"

"So I talked with Wanda Broome. It was obvious she knew more about the matter than she was letting on."

311

"So why aren't you talking to her instead of sitting here with me? Maybe she committed the crime herself."

"She was out of the country at the time, a hundred witnesses to that effect." Frank took a moment to clear his throat. "And I can't talk to her anymore because she committed suicide. Left behind a note that said she was sorry."

Kate stood up and looked blankly out the window. Bands of cold seemed to close around her.

Frank waited for some minutes, staring at her, wondering how she must feel, listening to the growing evidence against the man who had helped create her and then apparently abandoned her. Was there love left there? The detective hoped not. At least his professional side did. As a father of three, he wondered if that feeling could ever really be killed, despite the worst.

"Ms. Whitney, are you all right?"

Kate slowly turned away from the window. "Can we go out somewhere? I haven't eaten for a while and there's no food here."

They ended up at the same place Jack and Luther had met. Frank started to devour his food, but Kate touched nothing.

He looked across at her plate. "You picked the place, I figured you must like the food. You know, nothing personal, but you could stand to put on some weight."

Kate finally looked at him, a half-smile breaking through. "So you're a health consultant on the side?"

"I've got three daughters. My oldest is sixteen going on forty and she swears she's obese. I mean she probably goes one-ten and she's almost as tall as me. If she didn't have such rosy cheeks, I'd think she was anorexic. And my wife, Jesus, she's always on some diet or another. I mean, I think she looks great, but there must be some perfect shape out there that every woman strives for."

"Every woman except me."

"Eat your food. That's what I tell my daughters every day. *Eat.*"

Kate picked up her fork and managed to consume half her meal. As she sipped her tea and Frank fingered a big trough of coffee, they both settled themselves in as the discussion wound its way back to Luther Whitney.

"If you think you have enough to pick him up, why don't you?"

Frank shook his head, put down his coffee. "You were at his house. He's been gone for a while. Probably blew out right after it happened."

"If he did it. Your party bag is all circumstantial. That doesn't come close to being beyond a reasonable doubt, Lieutenant."

"Can I play straight with you, Kate? Can I call you Kate, by the way?"

She nodded.

Frank put his elbows on the table, stared across at her. "All bullshit outside, why do you find it so hard to believe that your old man popped this woman? He's been convicted of three prior felonies. The guy's apparently lived on the edge his whole life. He's been questioned in about a dozen other burglaries, but they couldn't pin anything on him. He's a career crim. You know the animal. Human life doesn't mean shit to them."

Kate finished sipping her tea before answering. A career criminal? Of course her father was that. She had no doubt he had continued to commit crimes all these years. It was in his damn blood apparently. Like a coke addict. Incurable.

"He doesn't kill people," she said quietly. "He may

313

steal from them, but he's never hurt anyone. It's not the way he does things."

What had Jack said specifically? Her father was scared. Terrified so badly he was sick to his stomach. The police had never scared her father. But if he *had* killed the woman? Perhaps just a reflex, the gun fired and the bullet ended Christine Sullivan's life. All that would have transpired in a matter of seconds. No time to think. Just to act. To prevent him from going to prison for good. It was all possible. If her father had killed the woman, he would be scared, he would be terrified, he *would* be sick.

Through all the pain, the most vivid memories she held of her father was his gentleness. His big hands encircling hers. He was quiet to the point of rudeness with most people. But with her he talked. To her, not above her, or below her as most adults managed to do. He would speak to her about things a little girl was interested in. Flowers and birds and the way the sky changed color all of a sudden. And about dresses and hair ribbons and wobbly teeth that she constantly fiddled with. They were brief but sincere moments, between a father and daughter, smashed between the sudden violence of convictions, of prison. But as she had grown up those talks somehow became gibberish, as the occupation of the man behind the funny faces and the big but gentle fingers came to dominate her life, her perspective of Luther Whitney.

How could she say that this man could not kill?

Frank watched the eyes as they blinked rapidly. There was a crack there. He could feel it.

Frank fingered his spoon as he scooped more sugar into his coffee. "So you're saying it's inconceivable that your father killed this woman? I thought you said the two of you hadn't really kept in touch?"

Kate jolted back from her musings. "I'm not saying it's inconceivable. I'm just saying . . ." She was really

314

blowing this. She had interviewed hundreds of witnesses and she couldn't remember one who had performed as badly as she was right now.

She hurriedly rummaged through her purse for her pack of Benson & Hedges. The sight of the cigarette made Frank reach for his pack of Juicy Fruit.

She blew the smoke away from him, eyed the gum. "Trying to quit too?" A flicker of amusement crossed her face.

"Trying and failing. You were saying?"

She slowly exhaled the smoke, willed her nerves to cease their cartwheels. "Like I told you, I haven't seen my father in years. We aren't close. It's possible that he could have killed the woman. Anything's possible. But that doesn't work in court. Evidence works in court. Period."

"And we're attempting to build a case against him."

"You have no tangible physical evidence tying him to the actual crime scene? No prints? No witnesses? Nothing like that?"

Frank hesitated, then decided to answer. "No."

"Have you been able to trace any of the stuff from the burglary to him?"

"Nothing's turned up."

"Ballistics?"

"Negative. One unusable slug and no gun."

Kate sat back in her chair, more comfortable as the conversation centered on a legal analysis of the case.

"That's all you've got?" Her eyes squinted at him.

He hesitated again, then shrugged. "That's it."

"Then you got nothing, Detective. Nothing!"

"I've got my instincts and my instincts tell me Luther Whitney was in the house that night and he was in that bedroom. Where he is now is what I want to know."

315

"I can't help you there. That's the same thing I told your buddy the other night."

"But you did go to his house that night. Why?"

Kate shrugged. She was determined not to mention her conversation with Jack. Was she withholding evidence? Maybe.

"I don't know." That, in part, was true.

"You strike me, Kate, as someone who always knows why she does something."

Jack's face flashed across her mind. She angrily pushed it out. "You'd be surprised, Lieutenant."

Frank ceremoniously closed his notebook and hunched forward.

"I really need your help."

"For what?"

"This is off the record, unofficial, whatever you want to call it. I'm more interested in results than in legal niceties."

"Funny thing to tell a state prosecutor."

"I'm not saying I don't play by the rules." Frank finally caved in and pulled out his cigarettes. "All I'm saying is I go for the point of least resistance when I can get it. Okay?"

"Okay."

"My information is that while you may not be wild about your father, he is still out there pining for you."

"Who told you that?"

"Jesus I'm a detective. True or not?"

"I don't know."

"Goddammit, Kate, don't play fucking games with me. True or not?"

She angrily stabbed out her cigarette. "True! Satisfied?"

"Not yet, but I'm getting there. I've got a plan to flush him out, and I'm looking for you to help me."

"I don't see that I'm in any position to help you."

Kate knew what was coming next. She could see it in Frank's eyes.

It took him ten minutes to lay out his plan. She refused three times. A half hour later they were still sitting at the table.

Frank leaned back in his chair and then abruptly lurched forward. "Look, Kate, if you don't do it, then we don't have a chance in hell of laying our hands on him. If it's like you say and we don't have a case, he goes free. But if he did do it, *and* we can prove it, then you've got to be the last goddamned person in the world that should tell me he should get away with it. Now, if you think I'm wrong about that, I'll drive you back to your place and forget I ever saw you, and your old man can go right on stealing . . . and maybe killing." He stared directly at her.

Her mouth opened but no words came out. Her eyes drifted over his shoulder where a misty image from the past beckoned to her, but then suddenly faded away.

At almost thirty years of age Kate Whitney was far removed from the toddler who giggled as her father twirled her through the air, or the little girl who divulged important secrets to her father she would tell no other. She was all grown up, a mature adult, out on her own for a long time now. On top of that she was an officer of the court, a state prosecutor sworn to uphold the law and the Constitution of the Commonwealth of Virginia. It was her job to ensure that persons who broke those laws were appropriately punished regardless of who they were and regardless of to whom they were related.

And then another image invaded her mind. Her mother watching the door, waiting for him to come home. Wondering if he were okay. Visiting him in prison, making up lists of things to talk to him about, making Kate dress up for those encounters, getting all excited as his release date came closer. As if he were some goddamned hero out saving the world instead of a thief. Jack's words came back to her, biting hard. He had called her entire life a lie. He expected her to have sympathy for a man who had abandoned her. As if Luther Whitney had been wronged instead of Kate. Well, Jack could go straight to hell. She thanked God she had decided against marrying him. A man who could say those awful things to her did not deserve her. But Luther Whitney deserved everything coming to him. Maybe he hadn't killed that woman. But maybe he had. It wasn't her job to make that decision. It was her job to make sure that decision had an opportunity to be made by men and women in a jury box. Her father belonged in prison anyway. At least there he could hurt no one else. There he could ruin no more lives.

And it was with that last thought that she agreed to help deliver her father into the hands of the police.

Frank felt a twinge of guilt as they got up to leave. He had not been entirely truthful with Kate Whitney. In fact, he had downright lied to her about the most critical piece of the case other than the million-dollar question of where Luther Whitney happened to be. He wasn't pleased with himself right now. Law enforcement people had to occasionally lie, just like everybody else. It didn't make it any easier to swallow, especially considering the recipient was someone the detective had instantly respected and now heavily pitied.

EIGHTEEN

K ate had placed the call that night; Frank had wanted to waste no time. The voice on the machine stunned her; it was the first time in years she had heard those tones. Calm, efficient, measured like the practiced stride of an infantryman. She actually began to tremble as the tone sounded and it took all her will to summon the simple words that were designed to trap him. She kept reminding herself how cunning he could be. She wanted to see him, wanted to talk to him. As soon as possible. She wondered if the wily old mind would smell a trap, and then she recalled their last face-to-face meeting, and she realized that he would never see it coming. He would never attribute deceit to the little girl who confided in him her most precious information. Even she had to give him that.

It was barely an hour later when the phone rang. As she reached out for it, she wished to God she had never agreed to Frank's request. Sitting in a restaurant hatching a plan to catch a suspected murderer was quite different from actually participating in a charade designed solely to deliver your father to the authorities.

"Katie." She sensed the slight break in the voice. A tinge of disbelief blended in.

"Hello, Dad." She was grateful that the words had come out on their own. At that moment she seemed incapable of articulating the simplest thought.

Her apartment was not good. He could understand

that. Too close, too personal. His place, she knew, would be unworkable for obvious reasons. They could meet on neutral grounds, he suggested. Of course they could. She wanted to talk, he certainly wanted to listen. Desperately wanted to listen.

A time was reached, tomorrow, four o'clock, at a small café near her office. At that time of day it would be empty, quiet; they could take their time. He would be there. She was sure nothing short of death would keep him away.

She hung up and called Frank. She gave him the time and the place. Listening to herself it finally dawned on her what she had just done. She could feel everything suddenly giving way and she could not stop it. She flung down the phone and burst into tears; so hard did her body convulse that she slumped to the floor, every muscle twitching, her moans filling the tiny apartment like helium into a balloon; it all threatened to violently explode.

Frank had stayed on the phone a second longer and wished he hadn't. He yelled into the phone but she could not hear him; not that it would have made a difference if she had. She was doing the right thing. She had nothing to be ashamed about, nothing to feel guilty about. When he finally gave up and cradled the receiver, his moment of euphoria at growing ever closer to his quarry was over like a flamed-out match.

So his question had been answered. She loved him still. That thought for Lieutenant Seth Frank was troubling but controllable. For Seth Frank, father of three, it made his eyes water and he suddenly didn't like his job very much anymore.

Burton hung up the phone. Detective Frank had been true to his promise to let the agent in on the kill.

Minutes later Burton was in Russell's office.

"I don't want to know how you're going to do it." Russell looked worried.

Burton smiled to himself. Getting squeamish, just like he predicted. Wanted the job done, just didn't want to get her pretty nails dirty.

"All you have to make sure you do is tell the President where it's going down. And then you make damn sure he tells Sullivan before the fact. He has *got* to do that."

Russell looked puzzled. "Why?"

"Let me worry about that. Just remember, do what I tell you." He was gone before Russell had a chance to explode at him.

"Are the police sure he's the one?" There was a hint of anxiousness in the President's voice as he looked up from his desk.

Russell, pacing the room, stopped to look at him. "Well, Alan, I'm assuming that if he weren't they wouldn't be going to all the trouble to arrest him."

"They've made mistakes before, Gloria."

"No argument there. Just like us all."

The President closed the binder he had been examining and stood up, surveyed the White House grounds from the window.

"So the man will shortly be in custody?" He turned to look at Russell.

"So it would seem."

"What's that supposed to mean?"

"Only that the best-laid plans sometimes go awry."

"Does Burton know?"

"Burton seems to have orchestrated the entire thing."

The President walked over to Russell; put his hand on her arm.

"What are you talking about?"

Russell relayed the events of the last few days to her

boss. The President rubbed his jaw. "What is Burton up to?" The question was said more to himself than to Russell.

"Why don't you buzz him and ask him yourself? The only point he was absolutely insistent on was your relaying the message to Sullivan."

"Sullivan? Why the hell would . . ." The President did not finish his thought. He rang for Burton but was told he had suddenly become ill and gone to the hospital.

The President's eyes bored into his Chief of Staff. "Is Burton going to do what I think he's going to do?"

"Depends on what you're thinking."

"Cut the games, Gloria. You know exactly what I mean."

"If you mean does Burton intend on making sure that this individual is never taken into custody, yes, that thought had crossed my mind."

The President fingered a heavy letter opener on his desk, sat down in his chair and faced out the window. Russell shuddered when she looked at it. She had thrown the one on her desk away.

"Alan? What do you want me to do?" She stared at the back of his head. He was the President and you had to sit and wait patiently, even if you wanted to reach across and throttle him.

Finally he swiveled around. The eyes were dark, cold and commanding. "Nothing. I want you to do nothing. I better get in touch with Sullivan. Give me the location and time again."

Russell thought the same thing she had earlier as she recounted the information. *Some friend.*

The President picked up his phone. Russell reached across and put her hand on top of his. "Alan, the reports said Christine Sullivan had bruises on her jaw and had been partially strangled."

322

The President didn't look up. "Oh really?"

"What exactly happened in that bedroom, Alan?"

"Well, from the small pieces I can remember she wanted to play a bit rougher than I did. The marks on her neck?" He paused and put down the phone. "Let's just put it this way: Christy was into a lot of kinky things, Gloria. Including sexual asphyxiation. You know, people get off when they're gasping for air and climaxing at the same time."

"I've heard of it, Alan, I just didn't think you'd be into something like that." Her tone was harsh.

The President snapped back: "Remember your place, Russell. I do not answer to you or anyone else for my actions."

She stepped back, and quickly said, "Of course, I'm sorry, Mr. President."

Richmond's face relaxed; he stood up and spread his arms resignedly. "I did it for Christy, Gloria, what can I say. Women sometimes have strange effects on men. I'm certainly not immune to it."

"So why did she try to kill you?"

"Like I said, she wanted to play rougher than I did. She was drunk and she just went out of control. Unfortunate, but those things happen."

Gloria looked past him out the window. The encounter with Christine Sullivan did not just "happen." The time and planning that had gone into that rendezvous had eventually taken on the elements of a full-blown election campaign. She shook her head as the images from that night poured back to her.

The President came up behind her, gripped her shoulders, turned her to him.

"It was an awful experience for everyone, Gloria. I certainly didn't want Christy to die. It was the last thing in the world I wanted. I went there to have a quiet, romantic evening with a very beautiful

323

woman. My God, I'm no monster." A disarming smile emerged across his face.

"I know that, Alan. It's just, all those women, all those times. Something bad was bound to happen."

The President shrugged. "Well, as I told you before, I'm not the first man to hold this office to engage in those types of extracurricular activities. Nor will I be the last." He cupped her chin in his hand. "You know the demands of the office I hold, Gloria, better than most. There's no other job like it in the world."

"I know the pressures are enormous. I realize that, Alan."

"That's right. It's a job that really requires more than is humanly possible to deliver. Sometimes you have to deal with that reality by relieving some of that pressure, from pulling yourself out from between the vise occasionally. How I deal with that pressure is important, because it dictates how well I can serve the people who have elected me, who have placed their trust in me."

He turned back to his desk. "And besides, enjoying the company of beautiful women is a relatively innocuous way of combating that stress."

Gloria stared angrily at his back. As if he expected her, of all people, to be swayed by the rhetoric, by a bullshit patriotic speech.

"It certainly wasn't innocuous for Christine Sullivan," she blurted out.

Richmond turned back to her; he was no longer smiling. "I really don't want to talk about this anymore, Gloria. What's past is past – start thinking about the future. Understand?"

She bowed her head in formal assent and stalked from the room.

The President again picked up the phone. He would deliver all the necessary details about the police sting to his good friend Walter Sullivan. The President smiled to himself as the call was being placed. It sounded like it wouldn't be long now. They were almost there. He could count on Burton. Count on him to do the right thing. For all of them.

Luther checked his watch. One o'clock. He showered, brushed his teeth and then trimmed his newly grown beard. He lingered over his hair until it met with his satisfaction. His face looked better today. The phone call from Kate had worked wonders. He had cradled the phone in his ear playing the message over and over again, just to hear the voice, the words he had never expected to hear again. He had risked going to a men's store downtown where he bought a new pair of slacks, sports coat and patent leathers. He had considered and then discarded the notion of a tie.

He tried on his new coat. It felt good. The pants were a little loose on him; he had lost weight. He would have to eat more. He might even start with buying his daughter an early dinner. If she'd let him. He'd have to think about that one; he didn't want to push it.

Jack! It must've been Jack. He had told her of their meeting. That her father had been in trouble. That was the connection. Of course! He had been stupid not to see it right away. But what did that mean? That she cared? He felt a tremble start in his neck and it ended at his knees. After all these years? He swore under his breath at the timing. The fucking timing! But he had made up his mind and nothing could change that decision now. Not even his little girl. Something terribly wrong had to be set right.

Luther was certain Richmond knew nothing about his correspondence with the Chief of Staff. Her only hope was to quietly buy back what Luther had and then make sure no one ever laid eyes on it again. Buy him off, hoping he'd disappear forever and the world would never know. He had verified that the money had arrived in the designated account. What happened to that money would be their first surprise.

The second surprise, though, would make them forget all about the first. And the best part was that Richmond would never see it coming. He seriously doubted that the President would actually do any time. But if this didn't meet the criteria for impeachment he didn't know what did. This made Watergate look like a third-grade prank. He wondered what impeached ex-Presidents did. Withered in the flames of their own destruction, he hoped.

Luther pulled the letter out of his pocket. He would arrange for her to receive it right about the time she'd be expecting the last set of instructions. The payoff. She would get her payoff. They all would. It was worth it, letting her squirm like he knew she had all this time.

No matter how often he tried he couldn't erase the memory of the woman's leisurely sexual encounter in the presence of a still warm body, as though the dead woman was a pile of trash, not to be bothered with. And then Richmond. The drunken, slobbering bastard! Again the visions made Luther seethe. He clenched his teeth, then abruptly smiled.

Whatever deal Jack could cut him he would take. Twenty years, ten years, ten days. He didn't care anymore. Fuck the President and everybody around him. Fuck the whole town, he was taking them down.

But first he was going to spend some time with his daughter. After that he really didn't care anymore.

As he walked over to the bed, Luther's body took a jolt. Something else had just occurred to him. Something that hurt, but which he could understand.

He sat on the bed and sipped a glass of water. If it were true could he really blame her? And besides, he could just kill two birds with one stone. As he lay back on the bed, it occurred to him that things that looked too good to be true usually were. Did he deserve any better from her? The answer was absolutely clear. He did not.

When the money transfer had reached District Bank, automatic prewire instructions kicked in and the funds were immediately transferred out of the account to five different area banks, each in the amount of one million dollars. From there the funds followed a circuitous route until the total sum was once again assembled in one place.

Russell, who had put a tracer on the flow of money from her end, would find out soon enough what had happened. She would not be particularly pleased about it. She would be far less pleased about the next message she received.

The Café Alonzo had been open about a year. It had the usual array of outdoor tables with colorful umbrellas in a small space on the sidewalk enclosed by a waist-high black iron railing. The coffee was varied and strong; the on-premises bakery was popular among the morning and lunch crowds. At five minutes to four only one person sat at the outdoor table. In the chilly air the umbrellas were collapsed down resembling a column of giant drinking straws.

The café was located in the ground floor of a modern office building. Two stories up hung a scaffolding. Three workers were replacing a glass panel that had cracked. The entire facade of the building consisted of mirrored panels that gave a complete image of the area directly opposite it. The panel was heavy and even the burly men struggled with the weight and bulk.

Kate bundled her coat around her and sipped her coffee. The afternoon sun was warming in spite of the chill, but it was fading rapidly. Long shadows had commenced to creep over the tables. She felt the rawness in her eyes as she squinted at the sun suspended directly over the tops of a number of dilapidated row houses that sat diagonally across the street from the café. They were destined for demolition to make room for the continued renovation of the area. She did not notice that the upper-story window on one of the row houses was now open. The row house next door had two windows smashed out. The front door on another was partially caved in.

Kate looked at her watch. She had been sitting there for approximately twenty minutes. Used to the frenetic pace of the prosecutor's office, the day had dragged interminably. She had no doubt there were dozens of police officers in the vicinity waiting to pounce once he walked up to her. Then she thought about it. Would they even have a chance to say anything to each other? What the hell could she say anyway? Hi Dad, you're busted? She rubbed her raw cheeks and waited. He would be there right at four. And it was too late for her to change any of it. Too damned late for anything. But she was doing the right thing, despite the guilt she was feeling, despite breaking down like that after calling the detective. She angrily squeezed her hands together. She was about to hand her father over to the police, and he deserved it. She was through debating it. She now just wanted it to be over.

McCarty did not like it. Not at all. His usual routine was to follow his target, sometimes for weeks, until the assassin understood the victim's patterns of behavior better than the victim did. It made the killing so much easier. The additional time also allowed McCarty to plan his escape, to allow for worst-case scenarios. He had none of those luxuries on this job. Sullivan's message had been terse. The man had already paid him an enormous sum on his per diem, with another two million to follow upon completion. Under any yardstick he had been compensated – now he had to deliver. Except for his first hit many years ago, McCarty could not remember being this nervous. It didn't help matters that the place was crawling with cops.

But he kept telling himself things would be okay. In the time he had, he had planned well. He had reconnoitered the area right after Sullivan's phone call. The row house idea had hit him immediately. It was really the only logical place. He had been here since four in the morning. The back door to the house opened into an alleyway. His rental car was parked at the curb. It would take him exactly fifteen seconds from the moment the shot was fired to drop his rifle, make his way down the stairs, out the door and into his car. He would be two miles away before the police even fully understood what had happened. A plane was leaving in forty-five minutes from a private airstrip ten miles north of Washington. Its destination was New York City. It would carry one passenger, and in a little over five hours McCarty would be a pampered passenger on board the Concorde as it descended into London.

He checked his rifle and scope for the tenth time, automatically flicking away a grain of dust on the barrel. A suppressor would have been nice, but he had yet to find one that worked on a rifle, especially one that was chambered with supersonic ammo as his weapon was. He would count on the confusion to mask the shot and his subsequent departure. He looked across the street and checked his watch. Almost time.

McCarty, while being a very accomplished killer, could not have possibly known that another rifle would be trained on his target's head. And behind that rifle would be a pair of eyes as sharp if not sharper than his own.

Tim Collin had qualified as an expert marksman in the Marine Corps, and his master sergeant had written in his evaluation that he had never seen a better shot. The focus of that accolade was now sighting through his scope; then he relaxed. Collin looked around the confines of the van he was in. Parked down the street on the curb opposite from the café, he had a straight shot to the target. He sighted through his rifle again, Kate Whitney appearing fleetingly in the crosshairs. Collin slid open the side window of the van. He was under shadow of the buildings behind him. No one could notice what he was doing. He also had the added advantage of knowing that Seth Frank and a contingent of county police were stationed to the right of the café while others were in the office building lobby where the café was located. Unmarked cars were stationed at various locations up and down the street. If Whitney ran he wouldn't get far. But then Collin knew the man wasn't going to run anywhere.

After the shot Collin would quickly disassemble the rifle and secrete it in the van, emerge with his sidearm and badge and join the other authorities in pondering what the hell had happened. No one would think to check a Secret Service van for the firearm or shooter who had just wasted their target.

Burton's plan made a lot of sense to the young agent. Collin had nothing against Luther Whitney but there was a lot more at stake than a sixty-six-year-old career criminal's life. A helluva lot more. Killing the old man was not something Collin was going to enjoy; in fact, he would do his best to forget it once done. But that was life. He was paid to do a job, had in fact sworn to do that job, above all else. Was he breaking the law? Technically he was committing murder. Realistically he was just doing what had to be done. He assumed the President knew about it; Gloria Russell knew about it; and Bill Burton, a man he respected more than anyone else, had instructed him to do it. Collin's training simply did not permit him to ignore those instructions. Besides, the old guy had broken into the place. He was going to do twenty years. He'd never make twenty years. Who wanted to be in prison at eighty years old? Collin was just saving him a lot of misery. Given those choices, Collin would've taken the round too.

Collin glanced up at the workmen on the scaffolding above the café as they struggled to right the replacement panel. One man grabbed the end of a rope connected to a block and tackle. Slowly the piece began to rise.

Kate looked up from studying her hands and her eyes locked on him.

He moved gracefully along the sidewalk. The fedora and muffler hid most of his features but the walk was unmistakable. Growing up she had always wanted to be able to glide along the ground like her father, so effortlessly, so confidently. She started to rise and thought better of it. Frank had not said at what point he would move in, but Kate didn't expect him to wait very long.

Luther stopped in front of the café and looked at her. He had not been this close to his daughter for over a decade, and he was a little unsure how to proceed. She felt his uncertainty and forced a smile to

331

her lips. He immediately went to her table and sat down, his back to the street. Despite the chill he took off his hat and put his sunglasses away in his pocket.

McCarty sighted through his rifle scope. The iron-gray hair came into focus and his finger flipped off the safety and then floated to the trigger.

Barely a hundred yards away, Collin was mirroring those actions. He was not as hurried as McCarty since he had the advantage of knowing when the police were going to move in.

McCarty's trigger finger crooked back. Earlier, he had noticed the workmen on the scaffolding once or twice but then had put them out of his mind. It was only the second mistake he had ever committed in his line of work.

The mirrored panel suddenly jerked upward as the rope was pulled down and the panel cocked in McCarty's direction. Catching the falling sun directly on its surface, the panel threw the reflection, red and glimmering, full in McCarty's eyes. Momentary pain shot through his pupils and his hand jerked involuntarily as the rifle fired. He cursed and flung down the gun. He made it to the back door five seconds ahead of schedule.

The bullet struck the umbrella pole and severed it before ricocheting off and imbedding into the concrete pavement. Both Kate and Luther went down, father instinctively shielding daughter. A few seconds later Seth Frank and a dozen uniforms, guns drawn, formed a semicircle around the pair, facing out, their eyes scanning every nook and cranny of the street.

"Shut this whole fucking area down," Frank screamed to the sergeant, who barked orders into his radio. Uniforms spread out, unmarked cars moved in.

The workmen stared down at the street, completely oblivious to the unwitting role they had played in the events unfolding below.

Luther was pulled up and handcuffed and the entire party hustled into the lobby of the office building. An excited Seth Frank stared at the man for one satisfying moment and then read him his rights. Luther looked across at his daughter. Kate at first could not meet his gaze, but then decided he at least deserved that. His words hurt her more than anything she had prepared for.

"Are you all right, Katie?"

She nodded and the tears started to pour, and this time, despite squeezing her throat in an iron grip, she could not stop them as she crumpled to the floor.

Bill Burton stood just inside the lobby doorway. When an astonished Collin came in, Burton's look threatened to disintegrate the younger man. That is until Collin whispered in his ear.

To his credit Burton assimilated the information rapidly and hit upon the truth a few seconds later. Sullivan had hired a hit man. The old man had actually done what Burton had intended to falsely set him up for.

The wily billionaire rose a notch in Burton's estimation.

Burton walked over to Frank.

Frank looked at him. "Any idea what the fuck that was all about?"

"Maybe," Burton answered back.

Burton turned around. For the first time he and Luther Whitney actually looked at each other. For Luther, memories of that night again came hurtling back to him. But he was calm, unruffled.

Burton had to admire that. But it also was a great source of concern for him. Whitney was obviously not overly distressed at being arrested. His eyes told

Burton – a man who had participated in literally thousands of arrests, which normally involved adults blubbering like babies – all he needed to know. The guy was planning to go to the cops all along. For what reason Burton was unsure and he really didn't care.

Burton continued to look at Luther while Frank checked in with his men. Then Burton looked over at the huddled mass in the corner. Luther had already struggled with his captors in an attempt to go to her, but they were having no part of it. A policewoman was making awkward efforts to console Kate but with little success. Traces of tears worked their way down the thick wrinkles in the old man's cheeks as he watched each sob wrack his little girl.

When he noticed Burton right at his elbow, Luther finally flashed fire at the man until Burton led the old man's eyes back over to Kate. The men's eyes locked again. Burton raised his eyebrows a notch and then settled them back down with the finality of a round being fired into Kate's head. Burton had stared down some of the worst criminals the area had to offer and his features could be menacing, but it was the absolute sincerity in those features that turned hardened men cold. Luther Whitney was no punk, that was easy enough to see. He was not one of the blubberers. But the wall of concrete that made up Luther Whitney's nerves had already started to crumble. It swiftly finished dissolving and the remnants trickled toward the sobbing woman in the corner.

Burton turned and walked out the door.

NINETEEN

Gloria Russell sat in her living room and held the epistle in her quavering hand. She looked at the clock. It had come right on time, via messenger; a turbaned older man in a beat-up Subaru. A Metro Rush Couriers logo on the passenger door. Thank you, ma'am. Say good-bye to your life. She had expected to finally have in her hand the key to wiping away all the nightmares she had suffered. All the risks she had taken.

The wind was starting to howl in the chimney. A cozy fire burned in the fireplace. The house was scrupulously clean thanks to the efforts of Mary, her part-time maid, who had just left. Russell was expected at Senator Richard Miles's home for dinner at eight. Miles was very important to her own personal political aspirations and he had started making all the right noises. Things had finally started to go right again. The momentum had shifted back to her. After all those torturous, humiliating moments. But now? But now?

She looked at the message again. The disbelief continued to sweep over her like an enormous fishing net, dragging her to the bottom, where she would remain.

Thanks for the charitable contribution. It will be greatly appreciated. Also appreciate the extra rope you just gave me to hang you. About that item we had discussed, it's no longer for sale. Now that I think

*about it, the cops will probably need it for the trial.
Oh, by the way, FUCK YOU!*

It was all she could do to stagger up. Extra rope? She couldn't think, she couldn't function. She first thought to call Burton, but then realized he would not be at the White House. Then it hit her. She raced to the TV. The six o'clock news was just recounting a late-breaking story. A daring police operation conducted jointly by the Middleton County Police Department and Alexandria City Police had netted a suspect in the Christine Sullivan murder case. A shot had been fired by an unknown gunman. The target was assumed to be the suspect.

Russell watched as footage from the Middleton police station was run. She saw Luther Whitney, staring straight ahead, not in any way attempting to hide his face, walk up the steps. He was far older than she had imagined he would be. He looked like a school principal. That was the man who had watched her . . . It never even occurred to her that Luther had been arrested for a crime she knew he had not committed. Not that that revelation would have prompted her to do anything. As the cameraman swung around, she glimpsed Bill Burton with Collin behind him as they stood listening to Detective Seth Frank make a statement to the press.

The goddamn incompetent bastards! He was in custody. He was in fucking custody and she had a message right there in her head that guaranteed the guy was going to make sure they were all brought down. She had trusted Burton and Collin, the President had trusted them, and they had failed, failed miserably. She could hardly believe how Burton could be standing there so calmly while their entire world was about to flame out, like a suddenly used-up star.

336

Her next thought surprised even her. She raced to the bathroom, tore open the medicine cabinet and grabbed the first bottle she saw. How many pills would be enough? Ten? A hundred?

She twisted at the cap but her shaking hands couldn't get it off. She continued to struggle; finally the pills spilled into the sink. She scooped up a handful and then stopped. In the mirror, her reflection stared back. For the first time she realized how much she had aged. The eyes were gaunt, her cheeks had caved in and her hair looked as if it were graying before her eyes.

She looked at the mass of green in her hand. She couldn't do it. Despite her world shattering in front of her, she could not do it. She flushed the pills, turned out the light. She telephoned the senator's office. Sickness would prevent her from attending. She had just lain down on the bed when the knock came.

At first it seemed like the distant beating of drums. Would they have a warrant? What did she have that could incriminate her? The note! She tore it out of her pocket and tossed it in the fireplace. As it ignited and a burst of flame sailed up the chimney, she smoothed down her dress, put on her pumps and walked out of the room.

For the second time a stab of pain seared her chest as her eyes fell upon Bill Burton at the front door. Without a word he walked in, threw off his coat and went straight to the liquor.

She slammed the door.

"Great job, Burton. Brilliant. You took care of everything beautifully. Where's your sidekick? Getting his damned eyes examined?"

Burton sat down with his drink. "Shut up and listen."

Ordinarily such a remark would have sent her off.

But his tone stopped her dead. She noted the holstered weapon. She suddenly realized she was surrounded by people carrying guns. They seemed to be everywhere. Shots were now being fired. She had thrown in her lot with some very dangerous people. She sat down and stared at him.

"Collin never fired his weapon."

"But—"

"But somebody did. I know that." He swallowed most of his drink. Russell thought about mixing herself one, but decided against it.

He looked at her. "Walter Sullivan. That sonofabitch. Richmond told him, right?"

Russell nodded. "You think Sullivan was behind this?"

"Who the fuck else could it be? He thinks the guy killed his wife. He has the money to hire the best shooters in the world. He was the only other person who knew exactly where it was going down." He looked at her and shook his head in disgust. "Don't be stupid, lady, we don't have time for stupid."

Burton stood up and paced.

Russell's thoughts went back to the TV. "But the man's in custody. He'll tell the police everything. I thought it was them at the door."

Burton stopped pacing. "The guy's going to say nothing to the police. At least for now."

"What are you talking about?"

"I'm talking about a man who will do anything so his little girl can keep on living."

"You, you threatened him?"

"I got my message across real clear."

"How do you know?"

"Eyes don't lie, lady. He knows the game. Talk and his daughter goes bye-bye."

"You, you wouldn't really—"

Burton reached down and grabbed the Chief of

Staff, effortlessly lifting her off the floor and holding her in midair so she was eye-level.

"I will kill any fucking person who is in a position to fuck with me, do you understand that?" His tone was chilling. He threw her back into the chair.

She stared up at him, the blood gone from her face, her eyes filled with terror.

Burton's face was crimson with fury. "You were the one who got me into this. I wanted to call the cops right from the get-go. I did my job. Maybe I killed the woman, but there ain't a jury in the world that would've found me guilty. But you sucker-punched me, lady, with all your global disaster talk and bullshit concern for the President, and stupid me, I fell for it. And right now I'm about one step away from pissing away twenty years of my life and I'm not happy about it. If you can't understand that, tough."

They sat without speaking for several minutes. Burton cradled his glass and studied the carpet, thinking intently. Russell kept one eye on him as she tried to stop shaking. She could not bring herself to tell Burton about the note she had received. What good would it do? For all she knew Bill Burton would pull out his gun and shoot her on the spot. The thought of violent death so close to her made her blood turn to ice.

Russell managed to sit back in her chair. A clock ticked in the background; it seemed to be counting down the last remaining moments of her life.

"You're sure he won't say anything?" She looked at Burton.

"I'm not sure of anything."

"But you said—"

"I said the guy will do anything to make sure his little girl doesn't get herself killed. If he takes that threat away, then we'll be waking up the next few years staring at the bottom of a bunk bed."

"But how can he take that threat away?"

"If I knew the answer to that, I wouldn't be so worried. But I can guarantee you that Luther Whitney is sitting in his cell block right now thinking of precisely how to do that."

"What can we do?"

He grabbed his coat and pulled her up roughly. "Come on, it's time to talk to Richmond."

Jack shuffled through his notes and then looked around the conference table. His transaction team consisted of four associates, three paralegals and two partners. Jack's coup with Sullivan had spread throughout the firm. Each of them looked at Jack with a mixture of awe, respect and a little fear.

"Sam, you'll coordinate the raw materials sales through Kiev. Our guy over there is a real hustler, plays close to the edge; keep an eye on him, but let him run with things."

Sam, a ten-year partner, snapped his briefcase shut. "You got it."

"Ben, I checked your report on the lobbying efforts. I agree, I think we should push hard on Foreign Relations, can't hurt to have them on our side." Jack flipped open another file.

"We've got approximately a month to get this operation up and running. Of chief concern is Ukraine's tenuous political status. If we're going to hit the brass ring we have to do it pretty quickly. The last thing we need is Russia annexing our client. Now I'd like to take a few minutes to go over—"

The door opened and Jack's secretary leaned in. She looked edgy.

"I'm terribly sorry to bother you."

"It's okay, Martha, what's up?"

"There's someone on the phone for you."

"I told Lucinda to hold my calls except for an

340

emergency. I'll get back to everybody tomorrow."

"I think this might be an emergency."

Jack swiveled around in his chair. "Who is it?"

"She said her name was Kate Whitney."

Five minutes later Jack was in his car: a brand-new copper-colored Lexus 300. His thoughts raced. Kate had been near hysterical. All he managed to understand was that Luther had been arrested. For what he didn't know.

Kate opened the door on the first knock and nearly collapsed into his arms. It was several minutes before she started breathing regularly.

"Kate, what is it? Where's Luther? What's he charged with?"

She looked at him, her cheeks so puffy and raw it looked like she'd been mugged.

When she finally managed to breathe the word out, Jack sat back stunned.

"Murder?" He looked around the room, his mind going too fast for him to register. "That's impossible. Who the hell is he supposed to have murdered?"

Kate sat up straight and pushed the hair out of her face. She looked directly at him. This time the words were clear, direct and cut into him like chunks of jagged glass.

"Christine Sullivan."

Frozen for a long moment, Jack exploded out of the chair. He looked down at her, tried to speak and found he couldn't. He staggered over to the window, threw it open and let the cold beat into him. His stomach churned pure acid; it reached up into his throat until he was barely able to push it back. His legs slowly regained their rigidity. He closed the window and sat back down next to her.

"What happened, Kate?"

She dabbed raw eyes with a ragged tissue. Her hair

was a mass of tangles. She had not taken off her overcoat. Her shoes lay next to the chair where she had kicked them off. She collected herself as best she could. She wiped a strand of hair from her mouth, and finally looked at him.

The words rolled out of her mouth in quiet bursts. "The police have him in custody. They, they think he broke into the Sullivans' home. No one was supposed to be there . . . But Christine Sullivan was." She paused and took a deep breath. "They think Luther shot her." As soon as she uttered those last words her eyes closed, the eyelids seemed to ram down by themselves under a terrible weight. She slowly shook her head, her forehead a stack of wrinkles as the throbbing pain clicked up a notch.

"That's crazy, Kate. Luther would never kill anybody."

"I don't know, Jack. I, I don't know what to think."

Jack stood up and took off his coat. He put a hand through his hair as he struggled to think. He looked down at her.

"How did you find out? How the hell did they catch him?"

In response, Kate's body shook. The pain seemed to be so strong as to be visible, hovering above before it plunged repeatedly into her lean frame. She took a moment to wipe her face with another tissue. It took her so long to turn to him, one inch at a time, that she seemed like an ancient grandmother. Her eyes were still closed, her breathing interrupted by gasps, as if the air was being trapped and was having to struggle mightily before escaping.

Finally her eyes opened. The lips moved but no words came out at first. Then she managed to say them, slowly, distinctly, as though she were forcing herself to absorb every blow that accompanied them as long as possible.

"I set him up."

Luther, dressed in an orange jail suit, sat in the same cinder block interrogation room that Wanda Broome had occupied. Seth Frank sat across from him watching him closely. Luther stared directly ahead. He wasn't zoned out. The guy was thinking about something.

Two other men came in. One carried a recorder that he placed in the middle of the table. He turned it on.

"You smoke?" Frank extended a cigarette. Luther accepted it and both men exhaled tiny clouds.

For the record, Frank repeated, verbatim, Luther's Miranda warning. There would be no procedural miscues on this one.

"So you understand your rights?"

Luther vaguely waved his cigarette in the air.

The guy was not what Frank had been expecting. His record was certainly a felonious one. Three priors, but the last twenty years were clean. That didn't mean much. But no assaults, no violent acts. That also didn't mean much, but there was something about the guy.

"I need a yes or no to that question."

"Yes."

"Okay. You understand that you've been arrested in connection with the murder of Christine Sullivan?"

"Yes."

"And you're sure you want to waive your right to have counsel present on your behalf? We can get a lawyer for you, or you can call your own."

"I'm sure."

"And you understand you do not have to make any

343

statement to the police? That any statement you make now can be used in evidence against you?"

"I understand."

Years of experience had taught Frank that confessions early on in the game could spell disaster for the prosecution. Even a confession given voluntarily could be shredded by the defense with the result often being that all evidence obtained through that confession was thrown out as tainted. The perp could have led you right to the goddamned body and the next day he walks free with his attorney smiling at you and hoping to God his client never shows up in his neighborhood. But Frank had his case. Whatever Whitney added to it was just gravy.

He focused intently on the prisoner. "Then I'd like to ask you some questions. Okay?"

"Fine."

Frank stated the month, day and year and time of day for the record and then asked Luther to state his full name. That was as far as they got. The door opened. A uniform leaned in.

"We got his lawyer outside."

Frank looked at Luther, turned off the recorder.

"What lawyer?"

Before Luther could answer, Jack burst past the officer and entered the room.

"Jack Graham, I'm the accused's attorney. Get that recorder out of here. I want to talk to my client alone, right now, gentlemen."

Luther stared at him. "Jack——" he began sharply.

"Shut up, Luther." Jack looked at the men. "Right now!"

The men began to clear the room. Frank and Jack did an eye-to-eye and then the door was closed. Jack put his briefcase down on the table but didn't sit.

"You want to tell me what the hell's going on?"

"Jack, you gotta keep out of this. I mean it."

344

"*You* came to me. *You* made me promise I'd be there for you. Well, goddammit, here I am."

"Great, you did your part, now you can go."

"Okay, I go, then what the hell do you do?"

"That doesn't concern you."

Jack leaned into his face. "What are you going to do?"

Luther's voice rose for the first time. "I'm pleading guilty! I did it."

"You killed her?"

Luther looked away.

"Did you kill Christine Sullivan?" Luther didn't answer. Jack grabbed him by the shoulder.

"Did you kill her?"

"Yes."

Jack scrutinized the face. Then grabbed his briefcase.

"I'm your lawyer whether you want me anymore or not. And until I figure out why you're lying to me don't even think about talking to the cops. If you do I'll have you declared insane."

"Jack, I appreciate what you're doing, but—"

"Look, Luther, Kate told me what happened, what she did and why she did it. But let me tell it to you straight. If you go down for this, your little girl is never going to recover. You hear me?"

Luther never finished what he was about to say. Suddenly the tiny room seemed about the size of a test tube. He never heard Jack leave. He sat there and stared straight ahead. For one of the few times in his life, he had no idea what he should do.

Jack approached the men standing in the hallway.

"Who's in charge?"

Frank looked at him. "Lieutenant Seth Frank."

"Fine, Lieutenant. Just for the record, my client doesn't waive his Miranda rights and you're not to attempt to talk to him outside of my presence. Understood?"

Frank folded his arms across his chest. "Okay."

"Who's the ACA handling this?"

"Assistant Commonwealth's Attorney George Gorelick."

"I'm assuming you got an indictment?"

Frank leaned forward. "Grand jury returned a true bill last week."

Jack put his coat on. "I'm sure they did."

"You can forget about bail, I guess you know that."

"Well, from what I've heard, I think he might be safer hanging with you guys. Keep an eye on him for me, will you?"

Jack handed his card to Frank and then walked purposefully down the hallway. At the parting remark, the smile faded from Frank's lips. He looked at the card and then toward the interrogation room and back at the rapidly disappearing defense counsel.

TWENTY

Kate had showered and changed. Her damp hair was swept straight back and hung loosely down to her shoulders. She wore a thick indigo blue V-neck sweater with white T-shirt underneath. The faded blue jeans hung loosely around her narrow hips. Thick wool socks covered her long feet. Jack watched those feet as they moved up and down, propelling their lithe owner about the room. She had recovered somewhat from earlier. But the horror was still lurking in her eyes. She seemed to be battling it with physical activity.

Jack cradled a glass of soda and sat back in the chair. His shoulders felt like a two-by-four. As if sensing that, Kate stopped pacing and started massaging.

"He didn't tell me they had an indictment." Kate's voice was angry.

"You really think cops are above using people to get what they want?" he shot back.

"I can see you're getting back into the defense attorney state of mind."

She really dug into his shoulders; it felt wonderful to him. Her wet hair dipped into his face as she bore down on the stiffest points. He closed his eyes. On the radio Billy Joel's "River of Dreams" was playing. What was his dream? Jack asked himself. The target seemed to keep jumping on him, like spots of sunlight you tried to chase down as a kid.

"How is he?" Kate's question jarred him back. He swallowed the rest of his drink.

"Confused. Screwed up. Nervous. All the things I never thought he could be. They found the rifle, by the way. Upper-story room of one of those old townhouses across the street. Whoever fired that bullet, they're long gone by now. That's for sure. Hell, I don't even think the cops care."

"When's the arraignment?"

"Day after tomorrow, ten o'clock." He arched his neck and gripped her hand. "They're going for capital murder, Kate."

She stopped massaging.

"That's bullshit. Homicide in the commission of a burglary is a class one felony, murder in the first degree, tops. Tell the ACA to check the statute."

"Hey, that's my line isn't it?" He tried to make her smile, but didn't succeed. "The commonwealth's theory is that he broke into the house and was in the middle of the burglary when she caught him in the act. They're using the evidence of physical violence – strangulation, beating and two shots to the head – to sever it from the act of burglary. They believe that takes it into the realm of a vile and depraved act. Plus they have the disappearance of Sullivan's jewelry. Murder in the commission of armed robbery equals capital murder."

Kate sat down and rubbed her thighs. She wore no makeup and had always been one of those women who didn't need to. The strain was telling though, especially in and under her eyes, in the slope of her shoulders.

"What do you know about Gorelick? He's going to be trying this sucker." Jack popped an ice cube in his mouth.

"He's an arrogant asshole, pompous, bigoted and a terrific trial lawyer."

"Great." Jack got up from his chair and sat down next to Kate. He took her ankle and rubbed it. She sunk down into the sofa and put her head back. It had always been that way with them, so relaxed, so comfortable in the company of each other, like the last four years had never happened.

"The evidence Frank told me he had wasn't even close to getting an indictment. I don't understand, Jack."

Jack slipped off her socks and rubbed her feet with both hands, feeling the fine, tiny bones. "The police got an anonymous tip on the license plate of a car seen near the Sullivan place on what was probably the night of the murder. It was traced to the D.C. impoundment lot on that night."

"So. The tip was wrong."

"No. Luther used to tell me how easy it was to pick up a car from the impoundment lot. Do a job and then return it."

Kate didn't look at him, she appeared to be studying the ceiling.

"Nice little chats you two used to have." Her tone held the familiar reproach.

"Come on, Kate."

"I'm sorry." Her voice was weary again.

"The police checked the floor matting. Rug fibers from the Sullivan bedroom were found there. Also present was a very peculiar soil mixture. Turns out that exact same soil mix was used by Sullivan's gardener in the cornfield next to the house. The soil was a special blend made up for Sullivan; you won't find that exact composition anywhere else. I had a chat with Gorelick. He's feeling pretty confident, I can tell you that. I haven't gotten the reports yet. I'll file my discovery motion tomorrow."

"Again, so what? How does that tie in to my father?"

"They got a search warrant for Luther's house and car. They found the same mixture on the floor mat in the car. And another sample on the living room rug."

Kate slowly opened her eyes. "He was in the house cleaning the damn carpets. He could've picked up the fibers then."

"And then he took a run through the cornfield? Come on."

"It could've been tracked in the house by somebody else and he stepped in it."

"That's what I would've argued except for one thing."

She sat up. "Which is?"

"Along with the fiber and dirt, they found a petroleum-based solvent. The police pulled traces of it out of the carpet during their investigation. They think the perp tried to clean some blood away, his blood. I'm sure they've got a handful of witnesses ready to swear that there was no such thing used on that carpet prior to or at the time the carpets were cleaned. Therefore Luther could've picked up traces of the carpet cleaner only if he had been in the house *after* that. Soil, fibers and carpet cleaner. There's your tie."

Kate slumped back down.

"On top of that they traced the hotel where Luther was staying in town. They found a fake passport and through that tracked Luther to Barbados. Two days after the murder he flew to Texas, then Miami and then on to the island. Looks like a fleeing suspect, doesn't it? They've got a sworn statement from a cab driver down there who drove Luther to Sullivan's place on the island. Luther made a reference to having been in Sullivan's place in Virginia. On top of that they've got witnesses who will testify that Luther and Wanda Broome were seen together several times prior to the murder. One woman, a close friend of Wanda's, will testify that Wanda told her she needed money, badly. And that Christine Sullivan had told

350

her about the safe. Which shows Wanda Broome had lied to the police."

"I can see why Gorelick was so free with the info. But it's still all circumstantial."

"No, Kate, it's a perfect example of a case with no home-run direct evidence linking Luther to the crime, but enough indirect stuff to where the jury will be thinking 'come on who are you kidding you did it you sonofabitch.'

"I'll deflect everywhere I can, but they've got some pretty heavy stones to hit us with. And if Gorelick can get in your Dad's priors, we might be finished."

"They're too old. Their prejudicial value far out-weighs their probative. He'll never get them in." Kate's words sounded more sure than she felt. After all, how could you be sure of anything?

The phone rang. She hesitated to answer it. "Does anyone know you're here?"

Jack shook his head.

She picked up the phone. "Hello?"

The voice on the other end was crisp, professional. "Ms. Whitney, Robert Gavin with the *Washington Post*. I wonder if I could ask you some questions about your father? I'd prefer to see you in person if that could be arranged."

"What do you want?"

"Come on, Ms. Whitney, your father is front-page news. You're a state prosecutor. There's a helluva story there if you ask me."

Kate hung up. Jack looked at her.

"What?"

"A reporter."

"Christ, they move fast."

She sat down again with a weariness that startled him. He went to her, took her hand.

Suddenly, she turned his face toward hers. She looked frightened. "Jack, you can't handle this case."

351

"The hell I can't. I'm an active member of the Virginia Bar. I've handled a half-dozen murder trials. I'm eminently qualified."

"I don't mean that. I know you're qualified. But Patton, Shaw doesn't do criminal defense work."

"So? You have to start somewhere."

"Jack, be serious. Sullivan is a huge client of theirs. *You've* worked for him. I read about it in *Legal Times*."

"There's no conflict there. There's nothing I've learned in my attorney-client relationship with Sullivan that could be used on this case. Besides, Sullivan's not on trial here. It's us against the state."

"Jack, they're not going to let you do this case."

"Fine, then I'll quit. Hang up my own shingle."

"You can't do that. You've got everything going for you right now. You can't mess that up. Not for this."

"Then for what? I know your old man didn't beat up a woman and then calmly blow her head off. He probably went to that house to burgle it, but he didn't kill anybody, that I know. But you want to know something else? I'm pretty damn sure he knows who killed her and that's what's got him scared to death. He saw something in that house, Kate. He saw *someone*."

Kate slowly let out her breath as the words sunk in.

Jack sighed and looked down at his feet.

He got up and put on his coat. He playfully pulled at her waistband. "When's the last time you actually had a meal?"

"I can't remember."

"I recall when you filled out those jeans in a way that was a little more aesthetically pleasing to the male eye."

She did smile that time. "Thanks a lot."

"It's not too late to work on it."

She looked around the four corners of her apartment. It held no appeal whatsoever.

"What did you have in mind?"

"Ribs, slaw and something stronger than Coke. Game?"

She didn't hesitate. "Let me get my coat."

Downstairs, Jack held open the door of the Lexus. He saw her studying every detail of the luxury car.

"I took your advice. Thought I'd start spending some of my hard-earned money." He had just climbed inside the car when the man appeared at the passenger door.

He wore a slouch hat and had a gray-trimmed beard and skinny mustache. His brown overcoat was buttoned up to his neck. He held a minicassette recorder in one hand, a press badge in the other.

"Bob Gavin, Ms. Whitney. I guess we got cut off before."

He looked across at Jack. His brow furrowed. "You're Jack Graham. Luther Whitney's attorney. I saw you at the station."

"Congratulations, Mr. Gavin, you've obviously got twenty-twenty vision and a very winning smile. Be seeing you."

Gavin clung to the car. "Wait a minute, c'mon just a minute. The public is entitled to hear about this case."

Jack started to say something, but Kate stopped him.

"They will, Mr. Gavin. That's what trials are for. I'm sure you'll have a front-row seat. Good-bye."

The Lexus pulled away. Gavin thought about making a run for his car but then decided not to. At forty-six, he and his soft and abused body were clearly in heart attack country. It was early in the game yet. He'd get to them sooner or later. He pulled up his collar against the wind and stalked off.

It was nearing midnight when the Lexus pulled up in front of Kate's apartment building.

"Are you really sure you want to do this, Jack?"

"Hell I never really liked the murals, Kate."

"What?"

"Get some sleep. We're both going to need it."

She put her hand on the door and then hesitated. She turned back and looked at him, nervously flicked her hair behind her ear. This time there was no pain in her eyes. It was something else, Jack couldn't quite put his finger on. Maybe relief?

"Jack, the things you said the other night."

He swallowed hard and gripped the steering wheel with both hands. He had been wondering when this was going to surface. "Kate, I've been thinking about that—"

She put a hand to his mouth. A small breath floated from her lips. "You were right, Jack . . . about a lot of things."

He watched her walk slowly inside and then he drove off.

When he got home his answering machine had run out of tape. The blinking message indicator was so full the light was reduced to one continuous crimson beacon. He decided to do the most sensible thing he could think of so he pretended they weren't there. Jack unplugged the phone, turned out the lights and tried to go to sleep.

It wasn't easy.

He had acted so confident in front of Kate. But who was he kidding? Taking on this case, by himself, without talking with anyone at Patton, Shaw was akin to professional suicide. But what good would talking have done? He knew what the answer would have been. Given the choice, his fellow partners would have slit their collective flabby wrists rather than taken on Luther Whitney as a client.

But he was a lawyer and Luther needed one. Major issues like this were never that simple, but that was why he fought so hard to keep things as black and white as possible. Good. Bad. Right. Wrong. It was not easy going for a lawyer perpetually trained to search for the gray in everything. An advocate of any position, just depended on who your client was, who was filling the meter on any given day.

Well, he had made his decision. An old friend was fighting for his life and he'd asked Jack to help him. It didn't matter to Jack that his client seemed to be growing unusually recalcitrant all of a sudden. Criminal defendants were seldom the most co-operative in the world. Well, Luther had asked for his help and he was sure as hell going to get it now. There was no gray in this issue anymore. There was no going back now.

TWENTY-ONE

Dan Kirksen opened the *Washington Post* and started to take a sip of his orange juice. It never reached his mouth. Gavin had managed to file a story on the Sullivan case consisting chiefly of the information that Jack Graham, newly ordained partner at Patton, Shaw & Lord, was the defendant's counsel. Kirksen immediately called Jack's home. There was no answer. He dressed, called for his car and at half past eight walked through the lobby of his firm. He passed Jack's old office where boxes and personal items were still clustered. Jack's new quarters were just down the hall from Lord's. A twenty-by-twenty beauty with a small wet bar, antique furnishings and a panoramic view of the city. Nicer than his, Kirksen recalled with a grimace.

The chair was swiveled around away from the doorway. Kirksen didn't bother to knock. He marched in and tossed the paper down on the desk.

Jack turned slowly around. He glanced at the paper.

"Well at least they got the firm's name spelled correctly. Great publicity. This could lead to some big ones."

Kirksen sat down without taking his eyes off Jack. He spoke slowly and deliberately, as though to a child. "Have you gone insane? We don't handle criminal defense work. We don't handle any litigation whatsoever." Kirksen stood up abruptly, his long forehead now a shiny pink, his diminutive body shaking with rage. "Particularly when this animal has murdered the wife of the firm's largest client," he said shrilly.

"Well, that's not entirely correct. We didn't handle criminal defense work but now we do. And I learned in law school that the accused is innocent until proven guilty, Dan. Maybe you forgot that." Smiling, Jack eyed Kirksen steadily. *Four million versus six hundred thou', pal. So back off, dickhead.*

Kirksen slowly shook his head and rolled his eyes. "Jack, maybe you don't fully understand the procedures we have in place at this firm before any new matter is undertaken. I'll have my secretary provide you with the pertinent provisions. In the meantime, take the necessary steps to have yourself and this firm taken off this matter immediately."

With a dismissive air, Kirksen turned to leave. Jack stood up.

"Listen, Dan, I took the case and I'm going to try it and I don't care what you or the firm's policy has to say about it. Close the door on your way out."

Kirksen turned around slowly and looked at Jack with intense brown eyes. "Jack, tread cautiously. I am the managing partner of this firm."

"I know you are, Dan. So you should be able to manage to close the goddamned door on your way out."

Without another word, Kirksen spun on his heel, shutting the door behind him.

The pounding in Jack's head finally subsided. He returned to his work. His papers were just about completed. He wanted to get them filed first thing before anyone could try to stop him. He printed out the documents, signed them and called the courier himself. That done he sat back in his chair. It was almost nine o'clock. He would have to get going, he was seeing Luther at ten. Jack's entire brain was

357

overflowing with questions to ask his client. And then he thought about that night. That chilly night on the Mall. The look in Luther's eyes. Jack could ask the questions, he just hoped he was ready to handle the answers.

He threw on his coat, and in another few minutes was in his car on his way to the Middleton County Jail.

Under the constitution of the Commonwealth of Virginia and its criminal procedure stature, the state must turn over to a defendant any exculpatory evidence. Failure to do so was a terrific way for an ACA to abruptly derail his or her career, not to mention getting a conviction thrown out and letting a defendant walk on appeal.

Those particular rules were giving Seth Frank a very large headache.

He sat in his office and thought about the prisoner sitting alone in a cell less than a minute's walk away. His calm and seemingly innocuous manner didn't trouble Frank. Some of the worst offenders he had ever arrested looked like they had stepped out of the church choir right after they had split open somebody's skull for a couple of laughs. Gorelick was putting together a good case, methodically collecting a bagful of little threads that when woven together in front of a jury would make a nice sturdy necktie for Luther Whitney to choke himself on. That also didn't trouble Frank.

What did trouble Frank was all the little things that still didn't add up. The wounds. Two guns. A bullet dug out of the wall. The place sanitized like an operating room. The fact that the guy was in Barbados and then came back. Luther Whitney was a pro. Frank had spent the better part of four days learning everything he could about Luther Albert

358

Whitney. He had pulled off a crackerjack crime that except for one glitch would probably have remained unsolved. Millions from his heist, a cold trail for the cops; he's out of the country, and the sonofabitch comes back. Professionals did not do those things. Frank would've understood him coming back because of his daughter, but Frank had checked with the airlines. Luther Whitney, traveling under an alias, had returned to the United States long before Frank had hatched his plot with Kate.

And the kicker was this: was he really supposed to believe that Luther Whitney had any reason on earth to check Christine Sullivan's vagina? And on top of that somebody had tried to kill the guy. This was one of the few times Frank actually had more questions *after* he had arrested his suspect than he had before taking his guy into custody.

He felt in his pocket for a cigarette. His gum stage had long since passed. He would try again next year. When he looked back up Bill Burton was standing in front of him.

"You understand, Seth, I can't prove anything but I'm just letting you know how I think it went down."

"And you're sure the President told Sullivan?"

Burton nodded, fiddled with an empty cup on Frank's desk. "I just came from meeting with him. I guess I should've told him to keep it mum. I'm sorry, Seth."

"Hell, he's the President, Bill. You gonna tell the President what to do?"

Burton shrugged. "So what do you think?"

"Makes sense. I'm not gonna let it lie, I can tell you that. If Sullivan was behind it I'll take him down too, I don't care what his justification was. That shot could've hit anybody."

"Well, knowing the way Sullivan probably operates, you ain't gonna find much. The shooter's probably on some island in the Pacific with a different face and a hundred people who'll swear he's never even been in the States."

Frank finished writing in his log book.

Burton studied him. "Get anything out of Whitney?"

"Right! His lawyer has him clammed shut."

Burton appeared nonchalant. "Who is he?"

"Jack Graham. Used to be with the Public Defenders Service in the District. Now he's a big-shot partner with some big-shot law firm. He's in with Whitney now."

"Any good?"

Frank twisted a swizzle stick into a triangle. "He knows what he's doing."

Burton stood up to go. "When's the arraignment?"

"Ten tomorrow."

"You taking Whitney over?"

"Yeah. You want to come along, Bill?"

Burton threw his hands over his ears. "I don't want to know anything about it."

"How come?"

"I don't want anything leaking back to Sullivan, that's how come."

"You don't think they'd try anything again?"

"The only thing I know is that I don't know the answer to that question and neither do you. If I were you I'd make some special arrangements."

Frank looked at him intently.

"Take care of our boy, Seth. He's got a date with the death chamber at Greensville."

Burton left.

Frank sat at his desk for some minutes. What Burton said made sense. Maybe they would try again. He picked up the phone, dialed a number and spoke for a bit and then hung up. He had taken all the precautions he could think of for transporting Luther. This time Frank was confident there would be no leak.

Jack left Luther sitting in the interrogation room and walked down the hallway to the coffee machine. In front of him was a big guy, nice suit and a graceful tilt to his body. The man turned around just as Jack passed him. They bumped.

"Sorry."

Jack rubbed his shoulder where the holstered gun had struck him.

"Forget it."

"You're Jack Graham, aren't you?"

"Depends on who wants to know." Jack sized the guy up; since he was carrying a gun he obviously wasn't a reporter. He was more like a cop. The way he held his hands, his fingers ready to move instantly. The way the eyes checked out every feature without seeming to.

"Bill Burton, United States Secret Service."

The men shook hands.

"I'm kind of the President's earpiece on this investigation."

Jack's eyes focused on Burton's features. "Right, the news conference. Well I guess your boss is pretty happy this morning."

"He would be if the rest of the world wasn't in such a godawful mess. About your guy, hey, my feeling is they're only guilty if the court says they are."

"I hear you. You want to be on my jury?"

Burton grinned. "Take it easy. Good talking to you."

Jack put the two cups of coffee down on the table and

looked at Luther. He sat down and looked at his empty legal pad.

"Luther, if you don't start saying something I'm going to have to just make it up as I go along."

Luther sipped the strong coffee, looked out the barred window at the single bare oak tree next to the station. A thick, wet snow was falling. The mercury was plunging and the streets were already a mess.

"What's to know, Jack? Cut me a deal, save everybody the hassle of a trial and let's get this over with."

"Maybe you don't understand, Luther. Here's their deal. *They* want to strap you onto a gurney, insert an IV into your arm, pump nasty little poisons into you and pretend you're a chemistry experiment. Or I think now the commonwealth actually gives the condemned a choice. So you can opt for having your brain fried in the electric chair. That's their deal."

Jack stood up and looked out the window. For a moment the flash of a blissful evening in front of a toasty fire in the huge mansion with the big front yard with little Jacks and Jennifers running around went through his head. He swallowed hard, shook his head clear and looked back at Luther.

"Do you hear what I'm saying?"

"I hear." Luther eyed Jack steadily for the first time.

"Luther, will you please tell me what happened? Maybe you were in that house, maybe you burgled the safe, but you will never, ever make me believe you had anything to do with that woman's death. I know you, Luther."

Luther smiled. "Do you, Jack? That's good, maybe you can tell me who I am one of these days."

Jack threw his pad in his briefcase and snapped it shut. "I'm going to plead you not guilty. Maybe you'll come around before we have to try this thing."

He paused and added quietly, "I hope you do."

He turned to leave. Luther's hand fell on Jack's shoulder. Jack turned back to see Luther's quivering face.

"Jack." He swallowed with difficulty, his tongue seemed as big as a fist. "If I could tell you I would. But that wouldn't do you or Kate or anybody else any good. I'm sorry."

"Kate? What are you talking about?"

"I'll see you, Jack." Luther turned and stared back out the window.

Jack looked at his friend, shook his head, and knocked for the guard.

The snow had changed from fat, sloppy flakes to pellets of ice that clattered against the broad windows like handfuls of slung gravel. Kirksen paid no attention to the weather but looked directly at Lord. The managing partner's bow tie was slightly askew. He noticed it in the reflection from the window and angrily straightened it. His long forehead was red with anger and indignation. The little fuck was going to get his. No one talked to him like that.

Sandy Lord studied the dark clusters making up the cityscape. A cigar smoldered in his right hand. His jacket was off and his immense belly touched the window. The twin streaks of his red suspenders jumped out from the background of his highly starched monogrammed white shirt. He peered intently out as a figure dashed across the street frantically chasing down a cab.

"He is undermining the relationship this firm, *you*, have with Walter Sullivan. I could only imagine what Walter must have thought when he read the paper this morning. His own firm, his own attorney actually representing this, this person. My God!"

Lord digested only a fraction of the little man's

speech. He hadn't heard from Sullivan for several days now. Calls to his office and home had gone unanswered. No one seemed to know where he was. That was not like his old friend, who kept himself in constant contact with an elite inner circle of which Sandy Lord was a longtime member.

"My suggestion, Sandy, is that we take immediate action against Graham. We can't let this lie. It would set a terrible precedent. I don't care if he has Baldwin as a client. Hell, Baldwin is an acquaintance of Walter's. He must be livid as well about this whole deplorable situation. We can convene a meeting of the management committee tonight. I don't think it will take long to arrive at a conclusion. Then——"

Lord finally held up one hand and cut off Kirksen's ramblings.

"I'll take care of it."

"But, Sandy, as managing partner I believe that——"

Lord turned to look at him. The red eyes on either side of the large and bulbous nose cut right into the slender frame.

"I said I'll handle it."

Lord turned to look back out the window. Kirksen's hurt pride was of absolutely no consequence to him. What concerned Lord was the fact that someone had tried to kill the man accused of murdering Christine Sullivan. And no one could reach Walter Sullivan.

Jack parked his car, looked across the street and closed his eyes. That didn't help since the vanity plates seemed to be imprinted on his brain. He jumped out of his car and dodged traffic as he made his way across the slippery street.

He inserted the key in the lock, took a quick breath, and turned the doorknob.

Jennifer sat in the small chair by the TV. Her short black skirt was matched by black heels and patterned black stockings. A white blouse was open at the collar where an emerald necklace fired dazzling color into the little room. A full-length sable was draped carefully on the sheet covering his ragged couch. She was clicking her nails against the TV set when he walked in. She looked at him without speaking. The thick ruby lips were set in a firm, vertical line.

"Hi, Jenn."

"You've certainly been a very busy boy the last twenty-four hours, Jack." She didn't smile, her nails continued to click.

"Gotta keep hustling, you know that."

He took off his coat, undid his tie and went into the kitchen for a beer. He re-emerged, and sat across from her on the couch.

"Hey, got a new piece of business today."

She reached in her handbag and tossed across the *Post*.

"I know."

He looked down at the headlines.

"Your firm won't let you do it."

"Too bad, I already did it."

"You know what I mean. What in God's name has gotten into you?"

"Jenn, I know the guy, okay? I know him, he's a friend of mine. I don't believe he killed the woman, and I'm going to defend him. Lawyers do that every day in every place where there are lawyers, and in this country that's basically everywhere."

She leaned forward. "It's Walter Sullivan, Jack. Think about what you're doing."

"I know it's Walter Sullivan, Jenn. What? Luther Whitney doesn't deserve a good defense because somebody *says* he killed Walter Sullivan's wife? Excuse me but exactly where is that written?"

"Walter Sullivan is your client."

"Luther Whitney is my friend and I've known him a lot longer than I've known Walter Sullivan."

"Jack, the man you're defending is a common criminal. He's been in and out of jails all his life."

"Actually he hasn't been in prison for over twenty years."

"He's a convicted felon."

"But he's never been convicted of murder," Jack fired back.

"Jack, there are more attorneys in this city than there are criminals. Why can't another lawyer handle it?"

Jack looked at his beer. "You want one?"

"Answer my question."

Jack stood up and hurled the beer bottle against the wall.

"Because he goddamn asked me!"

Jenn looked up at him, the frightened look that had crossed her face passing as soon as the glass fragments and beer hit the floor. She picked up her coat and put it on.

"You're making a huge mistake and I hope you come to your senses before you do *irreversible* damage. My father almost had a coronary when he read that story."

Jack put his hand on her shoulder, turned her face to his and said quietly, "Jenn, this is something I have to do. I would've hoped you could support me on this."

"Jack, why don't you stop drinking beer and start thinking about how you want to spend the rest of your life."

When the door closed behind her, Jack slumped against it, rubbing his head until he thought the skin would start to peel away under the pressure his fingers were exerting.

He watched from the tiny, dirty window as the vanity plates disappeared into the blur of snow. He sat down, looked at the headlines again.

Luther wanted to cut a deal but there was no deal to cut. The stage was set. Everyone wanted to see this trial. The TV news had given a detailed analysis of the case; Luther's photo must have been seen by several hundred million people. They already had public opinion polls about Luther's guilt or innocence, and he was running far behind in all of them. And Gorelick was licking his chops thinking that this was the vehicle to catapult him into the Attorney General's office in a few years. And in Virginia, Attorneys General often ran for, and won, the Governor's Mansion.

Short, balding, big-voiced, Gorelick was as deadly as a rattler on speed. Dirty tactics, questionable ethics, just waiting to bury the knife in your back at the first opportunity. That was George Gorelick. Jack knew he was in for a long, tough fight.

And Luther wasn't talking. He was scared. And what did Kate have to do with that fear? Nothing was adding up. And Jack was going to walk into court tomorrow and plead Luther not guilty when he had absolutely no way to prove that Luther wasn't. But proof was the state's job. The problem was they probably had just enough to put them over the top. Jack would peck and chip, but he had a three-time loser as a client, even though the record said Luther had remained clean for the last two decades. They wouldn't care about that. Why should they? His guy made for the perfect ending to a tragic story. A poster boy for the three-strikes rule. Three heavies and your life is over, starring Luther Whitney.

He tossed the newspaper across the room and cleaned up the broken glass and spilled beer. He rubbed the back of his neck, felt the underused muscles in his arms and went to his bedroom and changed into sweats.

The YMCA was ten minutes away. Amazingly Jack found a parking space right in front and went inside. The black sedan behind him wasn't as lucky. The driver had to circle the block several times and then pull down the street and park on the other side.

The driver wiped his passenger-side window clear and checked out the front of the Y. Then he made up his mind, climbed out of his car and ran to the steps. He looked around, glanced at the gleaming Lexus and then slowly walked inside.

Three pickup games later, the sweat was pouring down Jack's body. He sat down on the bench as the teenagers continued to run up and down the court with the inexhaustible energy of youth. Jack groaned as one of the lanky black kids dressed in loose gym shorts, tank shirt and oversized sneakers tossed the ball at him. He tossed it back.

"Hey man, you tired?"

"No, just old."

Jack stood up, rubbed the kinks out of his aching thighs and headed out.

As he was leaving the building he felt a hand on his shoulder.

Jack drove. He glanced at his new passenger.

Seth Frank looked over the interior of the Lexus. "I've heard great things about these cars. How much it run you, if you don't mind my asking?"

"Forty-nine-five, loaded."

"Like hell! I don't even come close to making that in a year."

"Neither did I until recently."

"Public defenders don't make the big bucks, I've heard."

"You heard right."

The men fell silent. Frank knew he was breaking more rules than they probably had written down and Jack knew that too.

Finally Jack looked at him. "Look, Lieutenant, I'm assuming you didn't just come out here to check my taste in automobiles. Is there something you want?"

"Gorelick's got a winning case against your guy."

"Maybe. Maybe not. I'm not throwing in the towel if that's what you're thinking."

"You pleading him not guilty?"

"No, I'm gonna drive him down to the Greensville Correctional Center and inject the shit into him myself. Next question."

Frank smiled. "Okay, I deserved that. I think you and I need to talk. Some things about this case don't add up. Maybe it helps or hurts your guy, I don't know. You willing to listen?"

"Okay, but don't think this flow of information is going to be a two-way street."

"I know a place where you can actually cut the meatloaf with a butter knife and the coffee's passable."

"Is it an out-of-the-way place? I don't think you'd look good in a deputy's uniform."

Frank looked over at him, grinning. "Next question."

Jack managed a smile and then drove home to change.

Jack ordered another cup of coffee while Frank played with his first. The meatloaf had been terrific and the place was so isolated, Jack wasn't even sure where they were. Rural, southern Maryland, he thought. He looked around at the few occupants of the rustic dining room. No one was paying them any undue attention. He turned back to his companion.

Frank looked at him in an amused fashion. "I

understand you and Kate Whitney had a thing going a while back."

"Did she tell you that?"

"Hell no. She came down to the station a few minutes after you left today. Her father wouldn't see her. I talked with her for a while. Told her I was sorry about how things had gone down."

Frank's eyes glistened for a moment and then he continued. "I shouldn't have done what I did, Jack. Using her to get to her old man. Nobody deserves that."

"It worked. Some people would say don't argue with success."

"Right. Well anyway the subject got around to you. I'm not so old yet that I can't see a gleam in a woman's eyes."

The waitress brought Jack's coffee. He sipped it. Both men looked out the window where the snow had finally stopped and the whole earth seemed to be covered with a soft, white blanket.

"Look, Jack, I know the case against Luther is just about all circumstantial. But that's sent plenty of people to jail."

"I'm not arguing with that."

"The truth is, Jack, there's an awful lot of shit that doesn't make any sense."

Jack put down his coffee and leaned forward.

"I'm listening."

Frank looked around the room and then back at Jack. "I know I'm taking a chance doing this, but I didn't become a cop to send people to jail for crimes they didn't commit. Plenty enough guilty people out there."

"So what doesn't add up?"

"You'll see some of it for yourself in the reports you'll get in your discovery, but the fact is I'm convinced Luther Whitney burgled that house and

I'm also convinced that he didn't kill Christine Sullivan. But—"

"But you think he saw who did."

Frank sat back in his chair and stared wide-eyed at Jack. "How long have you thought that?"

"Not long. Any ideas on the matter?"

"I'm thinking your guy almost got caught with his hand in the cookie jar and then had to actually hide in that cookie jar."

Jack looked puzzled. Frank took a few minutes to explain about the vault, the incongruity of the physical evidence and his own questions.

"So Luther's in the vault all this time watching whoever gets it on with Mrs. Sullivan. Then something happens and she gets popped. Then Luther watches whoever wipe away all traces."

"That's how I got it figured, Jack."

"So he doesn't go to the cops because he can't without incriminating himself."

"That explains a lot."

"Except who did it."

"The only obvious suspect is the husband, and I don't believe it was him."

Jack thought back to Walter Sullivan. "Agreed. So who's not so obvious?"

"Whoever she was meeting that night."

"From what you've told me about the deceased's sex life, that narrows it down to a couple million."

"I didn't say it would be easy."

"Well, my hunch is it's not some ordinary Joe."

"Why's that?"

Jack took a swallow of coffee and looked at his slice of apple pie. "Look, Lieutenant—"

"Make it Seth."

"Okay, Seth, I'm walking a fine line here. I hear where you're coming from and I appreciate the info. But . . ."

"But you're not absolutely sure you can trust me, and in any event, you don't want to say anything that might prejudice your client?"

"Something like that."

"Fair enough."

They paid the bill and left. Driving back, the snow started again with such velocity that the wipers were having a hard time keeping up.

Jack looked over at Frank, who stared straight ahead, lost in thought or maybe just waiting for Jack to start talking.

"Okay. I'll take the chance, I don't have a helluva lot to lose, do I?"

Frank continued to stare straight ahead. "Not that I can see."

"Let's assume for the moment that Luther was in the house and saw the woman murdered."

Frank looked over at Jack; there was relief in the detective's features.

"Okay."

"You've got to know Luther, know how he thinks, to understand how he would react to something like that. He's about as unshakable a person as I've ever met. And I know his record doesn't indicate it, but he's about as trustworthy and dependable as you can get. If I had kids and needed to leave them with someone I'd leave them with Luther because I know absolutely nothing bad would happen to them on his watch. He's incredibly capable. Luther sees everything. He's a control freak."

"Everything except his daughter leading him into a trap."

"Right, except for that. He wouldn't have seen that coming. Not in a million years."

"But I know the kind of guy you're talking about, Jack. Some of the guys I've busted, except for the little habit of taking other people's property, they're some of the most honorable people I've ever met."

"And if Luther saw this woman killed, I'm telling you he would've found some way to deliver the guy to the cops. He wouldn't have let it go. He just wouldn't!" Jack stared grimly out the window.

"Except?"

Jack looked over at him. "Except for a helluva good reason. Like maybe he knew the person or knew *of* him."

"You mean the kind of person people would have a hard time believing could do something like that so Luther figures why even bother?"

"There's more to it than that, Seth." Jack turned the corner and pulled up next to the YMCA. "I've never seen Luther scared before this all happened. And he's scared now. Terrified, in fact. He's resigned himself to take the rap for the whole thing and I don't know why. I mean he left the country for godsakes."

"And came back."

"Right, which I still cannot figure out. You have the date by the way?"

Frank flipped opened his notebook and told him the date.

"So what the hell happened after Christine Sullivan was killed and before then to get him to come back?"

Frank shook his head. "Could be anything."

"No, it was one thing and if we could find out what that was, we might be able to figure this whole thing out."

Frank put away his notebook, absently rubbed his hand across the dashboard.

Jack put the car in park and leaned back in his seat.

"And he's not just scared for himself. Somehow he's scared for Kate too."

Frank looked puzzled. "You think somebody threatened Kate?"

Jack shook his head. "No. She would've told me. I

think someone got the message to Luther that he either keeps quiet or else."

"You think the same people who tried to take him out?"

"Maybe. I don't know."

Frank made a fist with both hands and looked out the car window. He took a deep breath and looked back at Jack. "Look, you've got to get Luther to talk. If he can deliver us whoever did Christine Sullivan, I'll recommend probation and community service in return for his cooperation; he won't do any time. Hell, Sullivan would probably let him keep what he stole if we could nail the guy."

"Recommend?"

"Let's put it this way, I'll cram it down Gorelick's throat. Good enough?" Frank extended his hand.

Jack slowly took it, eyeing the policeman steadily. "Good enough."

Frank got out of the car and then poked his head back in. "For what it's worth, as far as I'm concerned, tonight never happened and everything you've said stays with me, no exceptions. Not even on the witness stand. I mean it."

"Thanks, Seth."

Seth Frank walked slowly back to his car as the Lexus pulled down the street, turned the corner and was gone.

He understood exactly the kind of guy Luther Whitney was. So what the hell could scare that kind of a guy so badly?

TWENTY-TWO

It was seven-thirty in the morning when Jack pulled into the parking lot of the Middleton police station. The morning had broken clear but bitterly cold. Amid a number of snow-covered police cars was a black sedan with a cold hood that told him Seth Frank was an early riser.

Luther looked different today; the orange prison clothes had been replaced with a brown two-piece suit, and his striped tie was conservative and professional. He could be an insurance salesman or a senior partner in a law firm, with his thick gray hair neatly trimmed, and the remnants of his island tan. Some defense attorneys saved the nice citizen clothes for the actual trial where the jury could see that the accused wasn't such a bad guy, just misunderstood. But Jack was going to insist on the suit throughout. It wasn't merely game playing; it was Jack's firm conviction that Luther didn't deserve to be paraded around in neon orange. He might be a criminal, but he wasn't the kind of criminal where if you got too close you might get a shiv in your ribs or find a set of criminally insane teeth on your throat. Those guys deserved to wear the orange if only to make sure you always knew where they were in proximity to everyone else.

Jack didn't bother to open his briefcase this time. The routine was familiar. The charges against Luther would be read to him. The judge would ask Luther if he understood the charges and then Jack would enter the plea. Then the judge would take them through the dog-and-pony show to determine if Luther understood what a plea of not guilty entailed, and whether Luther was satisfied with his legal representation. The only problem was Jack had a nagging feeling that Luther might tell him to go to hell right in front of the judge and plead himself guilty. That was not unprecedented. And who knew? The damn judge might just accept it. But the judge would most likely follow the book closely, since, in a capital murder case, any screw-up along the way could be grounds for appeal. And death penalty appeals tended to last forever anyway. Jack would just have to take his chances.

With any luck the entire proceeding would take all of five minutes. Then a trial date would be set and the real fun would begin.

Since the commonwealth had gotten an indictment against him, Luther wasn't entitled to a preliminary hearing. Not that having one would have done Jack any good, but he would've gotten a quick look at the commonwealth's case and a crack at some of their witnesses on cross although the circuit court judges were usually diligent in not letting defense counsel use the prelim as a fishing expedition.

He also could have waived the arraignment, but Jack's thinking was to let them work for everything. And he wanted Luther in open court, for all to see, and he wanted that not guilty plea heard loud and clear. And then he was going to hit Gorelick with a change of venue motion and get this case the hell out of Middleton County. With any luck Gorelick would get bumped for a new ACA and Mr. Future Attorney General could stew on that disappointment for a few decades. Then Jack was going to make Luther talk. Kate would be protected. Luther would spill his story and then the deal of the century would be cut.

Jack looked at Luther. "You look good."

Luther's mouth curled up more in a smirk than a smile.

"Kate would like to see you before the arraignment."

The response shot out of Luther's mouth. "No!"

"Why not? My God, Luther, you've wanted a relationship with her forever and now that she's finally willing to come around, you clam up. Damn, I don't understand you sometimes."

"I don't want her anywhere near me."

"Look, she's sorry about what she did. It tore her up. I'm telling you."

Luther swiveled his head around. "She thinks I'm mad at her?"

Jack sat down. For the first time he finally had Luther's attention. He should have tried this before.

"Of course she does. Why else won't you see her?"

Luther looked down at the plain, wooden table and shook his head in disgust.

"Tell her I'm not mad at her. She did the right thing. You tell her that."

"Why don't *you* tell her?"

Luther abruptly stood up and walked around the room. He stopped in front of Jack.

"This place has a lot of eyes, you hear me? You understand me? Somebody sees her in here with me, then somebody might think she knows something she doesn't. And believe me, that is not good."

"Who are you talking about?"

Luther sat back down. "Just tell her what I said. Tell her I love her and I always have and always will. You tell her that, Jack. No matter what."

"So you're saying this somebody might think you told me something even if you haven't?"

"I told you not to take this case, Jack, but you wouldn't listen."

377

Jack shrugged, flipped open his briefcase and took out a copy of the *Post*. "Check out the lead story."

Luther glanced down at the front page. Then he angrily threw the paper against the wall. "Fucking bastard! Fucking bastard!" The words exploded out of the old man's mouth.

The door to the room flew open and a beefy guard poked his head in, one hand on his standard issue. Jack motioned that it was all right and the guy slowly backed out, his eyes glued on Luther.

Jack went over and picked up the paper. The cover story had a photo of Luther taken outside the police station. The headline was in bold three-inch letters normally reserved for when the 'Skins won the Super Bowl: SULLIVAN MURDER SUSPECT ARRAIGNMENT TODAY. Jack scanned the rest of the front page. More killings in the former Soviet Union as ethnic cleansing continued. The Defense Department was preparing for another budget hit. Jack's eyes glanced over but did not really register on President Alan Richmond announcing his intent to take another stab at welfare reform and a picture of him at a children's center in impoverished Southeast D.C. that made for a nice photo op.

The smiling face had hit Luther right between the temples. Holding poor black babies for all the world to see. Fucking, lying asshole. The fist hit Christine Sullivan again and again and again. Blood flew into the air. The hands wrapped around her neck like a wily serpent, crushing life without a thought. Stealing life, that's what he had done. Kissing babies and killing women.

"Luther? Luther?" Jack gently laid a hand on Luther's shoulder. The old man's frame was quaking like an engine in dire need of a tune-up, threatening to fly apart, no longer able to confine itself within a quickly eroding shell. For a terrible moment Jack

378

wondered if Luther had killed the woman, if his old friend had perhaps gone over the edge. His fears were dispelled when Luther turned and looked at him. The calm had returned, the eyes were clear and focused once more.

"Just tell Kate what I said, Jack. And let's go get this over with."

The Middleton Courthouse had long been the centerpiece of the county. A hundred and ninety-five years old, it had survived the British in the War of 1812 and the Yankees and the Confederates in the War of Northern Aggression or the Civil War depending on what side of the Mason-Dixon the person you asked hailed from. A costly renovation in 1947 had given it new life and the good townspeople expected it to be around for their great-grandchildren to enjoy and occasionally go inside, hopefully for nothing more than a traffic ticket or a marriage license.

Where before it had stood alone at the end of the two-lane road that made up Middleton's business district, it now shared space with antique shops, restaurants, a grocery market, a huge bed-and-breakfast and a service station that was all-brick in keeping with the architectural tradition of the area. Huddled within walking distance was a row of offices where the shingles of many a respected county lawyer hung with simple grace.

Normally quiet except on Friday morning, which was motions day for the civil and criminal docket, the Middleton Courthouse now held a scene that would have caused the town's forefathers to do somersaults in their final resting places. At first glance one could almost imagine that the Rebels and the Union Blue had returned to settle, once and for all, the score.

Six television trucks with thick call letters

emblazoned on their white sides held forth directly in front of the courthouse steps. Their broadcast masts were already rising skyward. Crowds ten-deep pushed and prodded against the wall of sheriffs reinforced by grim members of the Virginia State Police who stared silently at the mass of reporters pushing pads, microphones and pens into their faces.

Fortunately, the courthouse had a side entrance, which was at this moment surrounded by a semicircle of police, riot guns and shields front and center, daring anyone to come near. The van carrying Luther would come here. Unfortunately, the courthouse did not have an inside garage. But the police still felt they had matters under control. Luther would only be exposed for a few seconds at most.

Across the street, rifle-toting police officers patrolled the sidewalks, eyes sweeping up and down, looking for the glint of metal, an open window that shouldn't be.

Jack looked out the small window of the courtroom that overlooked the street. The room was as large as an auditorium with a hand-carved bench that rose a full eight feet high and swept more than fifteen feet from end to end. The American and Virginia flags stood at attention on either side of the bench. A lone bailiff sat at a small table in front of the bench, a tug boat before the ocean liner.

Jack checked his watch, eyed the security forces in place, then looked at the crush of media. Reporters were a defense attorney's best friends or worst nightmare. A lot depended on what the reporters thought about a particular defendant and about a particular crime. A good reporter will cry loud and hard about his or her objectivity on a story at the same time they're trashing your client in the latest edition, long before any verdict is in. Women journalists tended to go easier on defendants accused of rape, as they tried to avoid even the appearance of gender-bias. For similar reasons, the men seemed to bend over backward for battered women who had finally struck back. Luther would have no such luck. Ex-cons who murder rich, young women would receive the battering rams of all wordsmiths involved, regardless of sex.

Jack had already received a dozen phone calls from Los Angeles-based production companies clamoring for Luther's story. Before the guy had even entered a plea. They wanted his story and would pay for it. Pay well. Maybe Jack should tell them yes, come on in, but only on one condition. If he tells you anything you have to let me in on it, 'cause right now man, I've got nothing. Zip.

He looked across the street. The armed guards gave him some comfort. Although there had been police everywhere last time and the shot was still fired. At least this time the police were forewarned. They had things pretty much under control. But they had not counted on one thing, and that one thing was now coming down the street.

Jack swung his head around as he watched the army of reporters and plain curious turn en masse and race to the motorcade. At first Jack thought it must be Walter Sullivan, until he saw the police motor-cyclists followed by the Secret Service vans and finally the twin American flags on the limo.

The army this man had brought with him dwarfed the one that was preparing to receive Luther Whitney.

He watched as Richmond exited the vehicle. Behind him stepped the agent he had talked to earlier. Burton. That was the guy's name. One tough, serious dude. His eyes swept the area like a radar beam. His hand within inches of the man, ready to pull him down in an instant. The Secret Service vans parked across the street. One pulled into an alleyway across from the courthouse and then Jack looked back at the President.

An impromptu podium was set up and Richmond began his own little news conference as cameras clicked and half a hundred grown adults with journalism degrees tried to push and pull past their neighbor. A few ordinary and saner citizens were hovering in the back, two with video cameras recording what to them was certainly a special moment.

Jack turned to find the bailiff, a granite wall of a black man, beside him.

"Been here twenty-seven years and never had the man out here before. Now he's been here twice in the same year. Go figure."

Jack smiled at him. "Well, if your friend had invested ten mil in your campaign you might be out here too."

"Lot of big boys against you."

"That's okay, I brought a big bat with me . . ."

"Samuel, Samuel Long."

"Jack Graham, Samuel."

"You gonna need it, Jack, hope you loaded it with lead."

"So what do you think, Samuel? My guy gonna get a fair shake in here?"

"You ask me that question two, three years ago I'd say yeah, damn straight you will. Yes sir." He looked out at the crush of people. "You ask me today, I say I don't know. I don't care what court you're in. Supreme Court, traffic court. Things are changing, man. Not just the courts either. Everything. Everybody. Whole goddamn world's changing and I just don't know anymore."

They both looked out the window again.

The door to the courtroom opened and Kate

entered. Instinctively, Jack turned around and looked at her. No courtroom attire today, she had on a black pleated skirt that tapered at the waist where a thin black belt encircled her. The blouse was simple and buttoned to the neck. Her hair was brushed back off her forehead and hung to her shoulders. Her cheeks were rosy from the bitter cold, a coat was draped over her arm.

They sat together at the counsel table. Samuel discreetly disappeared.

"It's almost time, Kate."

"I know."

"Listen, Kate, like I told you on the phone, it's not that he doesn't want to see you, he's afraid. He's afraid for you. The man loves you more than anything."

"Jack, if he doesn't start talking, you know what's going to happen."

"Maybe, but I've got some leads to go on. The state's case isn't as foolproof as everyone seems to think."

"How do you know that?"

"Trust me on that one. Did you see the President outside?"

"How could you miss him? It's okay with me though. No one paid a bit of attention to me walking in."

"He definitely relegates everybody else to wallflowers."

"Is he here yet?"

"Soon."

Kate opened her purse and fumbled for some gum. Jack smiled and pushed her quivering fingers out of the way and pulled the pack out for her.

"Couldn't I at least talk to him on the phone?"

"I'll see what I can do."

They both sat back and waited. Jack's hand slipped

over Kate's and they both looked up at the massive bench where in a few short minutes it would start. But for now they just waited. Together.

The white van rounded the corner, passed the semi-circle of police officers and came to a stop within a few feet of the side door. Seth Frank pulled up directly behind the van and got out, radio in hand. Two officers alighted from the van, scanned the area. This was good. The entire crowd was in the front gawking at the President. The officer in charge turned and nodded to another man inside the van. A few seconds later Luther Whitney, ankles and hands manacled, and his suit covered by a dark trench coat, emerged. His feet touched the ground and, with an officer in front and back, he started to make his way to the courthouse.

That's when the crowd hit the corner. They were following the President, who was purposefully striding down the sidewalk to where his limo was parked. As he passed the side of the courthouse, he looked up. As if sensing his presence, Luther, whose eyes had been pressed to the ground, also looked up. Their eyes locked for one terrible instant. The words escaped Luther's lips before he knew what was happening.

"Fucking bastard." It was said quietly, but each officer heard something, because they looked around as the President walked by a mere hundred feet away. They were surprised. And then their thoughts focused on one thing only.

Luther's knees buckled. At first both officers thought he was intentionally making their job harder until they saw the blood streaming down the side of his face. One of them shouted an expletive and grabbed Luther's arm. The other pulled his gun and swung it in wide arcs at where he thought the shot

384

had come from. The events that happened in the next few minutes seemed a blur to most people who were there. The sound of the shot was not entirely clear over the screams of the crowds. The Secret Service agents heard it, though. Burton had Richmond on the ground in a second. Twenty dark suits carrying automatic weapons made a human cocoon around them.

Seth Frank watched as the Secret Service van tore out of the alley and blocked off the now hysterical crowd from the President. One agent emerged wielding a machine gun and scanned the street, barking into a radio.

Frank directed his men to cover every square inch of the area; every intersection was cordoned off and a building-by-building search would commence. Truckloads of officers would arrive shortly, but somehow Frank knew it was too late.

In another second Frank was beside Luther. He looked on in disbelief as the blood drenched the snow, warming it into a sickening pool of crimson. An ambulance was called and would be there in minutes. But Frank also knew it was too late for ambulances. Luther's face had already gone white, the eyes stared blank, the fingers were curled tight. Luther Whitney had two new holes in his head and the damn round had put a hole in the van after exiting the man. Someone was taking no chances.

Frank closed the dead man's eyes and then looked around. The President was up and being hustled into his limo. In a few seconds the limo and the vans were gone. Reporters started to flock to the murder scene, but Frank motioned to his men and the journalists were met by a brick wall of infuriated and embarrassed police officers who brandished their batons and hoped somebody tried something.

Seth Frank looked down at the body. He took off

his jacket despite the cold and laid it across Luther's torso and face.

Jack had made it to the window a few seconds after the screams started. His pulse was off the chart and his forehead was suddenly drenched in sweat.

"Stay here, Kate." He looked at her. She was frozen, her face having already registered a fact that Jack hoped beyond hope wasn't true.

Samuel had emerged from the inner sanctum.

"What the hell's going on?"

"Samuel, keep an eye on her, please."

Samuel nodded and Jack hit the door running.

Outside there were more men with guns than Jack had ever seen outside of a Hollywood war flick. He ran to the side of the courthouse and was about to have his head cracked open by a two-hundred-and-fifty-pound baton-wielding trooper when Frank's voice boomed out.

Jack warily approached. Each of his steps in the tight-packed snow seemed to take a month. All eyes seemed to be on him. The crumpled figure under the coat. The blood soaking the once pristine snowfall. The anguished and at the same time disgusted look on Detective Seth Frank's features. He would remember each of these things for many sleepless nights, perhaps for the rest of his life.

When he finally crouched down beside his friend, he started to draw back the jacket but then stopped. He turned around and looked back from where he had just come. The sea of reporters had parted. Even the wall of cops had hinged back just enough to let her through.

Kate stood there for a long minute, no coat on, shivering in the wind that swept down through the funnel-like space between the buildings. She looked straight ahead, her eyes so focused they seemed to register on nothing and everything simultaneously.

386

Jack started to rise, to go to her, but his legs did not have the strength. Just a few minutes ago, juiced and prepared to do battle, mad as hell at his uncooperative client, now every scintilla of energy had been stripped from his being.

With Frank's help he rose on unsteady legs and went to her. For once in their lives, nosy reporters did not attempt to ask questions. Photographers seemingly forgot to take their requisite shots. As Kate knelt beside her father and gently laid her hand on his still shoulder, the only sounds were the wind and the distant whine of the approaching ambulance. For a couple of minutes the world had stopped right outside the Middleton County Courthouse.

As the limo whisked him back to town, Alan Richmond smoothed down his tie and poured a club soda. His thoughts ventured to the headlines that would drown the upcoming papers. The major news shows would be salivating for him, and he would milk it. He would continue on his normal schedule for the day. The rock-solid President. Shots fired around him and he doesn't flinch, goes on about the business of running the country, of *leading* the people. He could envision the polls. A good ten points at least. And it had all been too easy. When was he ever going to feel a real challenge?

Bill Burton looked over at the man as the limo neared the D.C. line. Luther Whitney had just caught the business end of the most deadly piece of ammo Collin could find to chamber his rifle with, and this guy was calmly sipping soda water. Burton felt sick to his stomach. And it still wasn't over. He could never in his wildest dreams put any of this behind him, but perhaps he could live the rest of his life as a free man. A man whose children respected him, even if he no longer respected himself.

As he continued to look at the President it occurred to Burton that the sonofabitch was proud of himself. He had seen such calmness before amidst extreme and calculated violence. No remorse because a human being's existence had just been sacrificed. Instead, a rush of euphoria. Of triumph. Burton thought back to the marks on Christine Sullivan's neck. To the busted jaw. To the ominous sounds he had heard from behind other bedroom doors. The Man of the People.

Burton thought back to the meeting with Richmond where he had filled in his boss on all the facts. Other than seeing Russell squirm it had not been a pleasant experience.

Richmond had stared at each of them. Burton and Russell sat side by side. Collin hovered next to the door. They were clustered in the First Family's private quarters. A component of the White House the eager public was never permitted to see. The rest of the First Family was on a brief holiday visiting relatives. It was best that way. The most important member of that family was not in a pleasant mood.

The President was, finally, fully cognizant of the facts, the most remarkable of which had been a letter opener bearing some particularly incriminating evidence, and which had ended up in the hands of their intrepid and felonious eyewitness. The blood had almost frozen in the President's veins when Burton had told him. As the words fell out of the agent's mouth, the President had swiveled his head in Russell's direction.

When Collin recounted Russell's instructions not to wipe the blade and handle clean, the President had stood up and hovered over his Chief of Staff, who had pushed herself so far back in her chair that she seemed to have become part of the fabric. His stare was crushing. She finally covered her eyes with her hand. The underarms of her blouse were soaked in perspiration. Her throat was devoid of saliva.

Richmond had sat back down and slowly crunched the ice from his cocktail and finally turned his gaze out the window. He was still dressed in a monkey suit from yet another engagement but the tie was undone. He was still looking out to nowhere when he spoke.

"How long, Burton?"

Burton stopped looking at the floor. "Who knows? Maybe forever."

"You know better than that. I want your professional assessment."

"Sooner rather than later. He's got a lawyer now. Somehow, some way the guy's gonna pop to somebody."

"Do we have any idea where 'it' is?"

Burton rubbed his hands together uneasily. "No, sir. The police searched his house, his car. If they had found the letter opener, I would've heard."

"But they know it's missing from Sullivan's house?"

Burton nodded. "The police realize it has significance. If it turns up they'll know what to do with it."

The President stood up and played his fingers across a particularly ugly gothic crystal collection of his wife's that was displayed on one of the tables. Next to them were photos of his family. He never actually registered their countenances. All he saw in their faces were the flames of his administration. His face seemed to redden before the invisible conflagration. History was in jeopardy of being rewritten and all because of a little smart bimbo and an overly ambitious and incredibly stupid Chief of Staff.

"Any idea who Sullivan employed?"

Burton again answered. Russell was no longer an equal. Collin was there only to be told what to do.

"Could be one of twenty or thirty high-priced hit men. Whoever it is he's long gone by now."

"But you've laid the mental trail with our friend the detective?"

"He knows that you 'innocently' told Walter Sullivan where and when. The guy's plenty smart enough to follow up on that."

The President abruptly picked up one of the crystal pieces and hurled it against the wall where it shattered, sending fragments all across the room; his face contorted into a mass of hate and anger that made even Burton shudder. "Dammit, if he hadn't missed, it would've been perfect."

Russell looked at the tiny shards of crystal on the carpet. That was her life. All those years of education, toiling, hundred-hour weeks. For this.

"The police are going to follow up with Sullivan. I made sure the detective on the case understood Sullivan's possible involvement." Burton continued, "But even though he's the most likely suspect, he'll deny everything. They won't be able to prove anything. I'm not sure where that gets us, sir."

Richmond strolled around the room. He could've been preparing for a speech or getting ready to shake hands with a troop of Boy Scouts from a Midwestern state. He was actually contemplating how to murder someone in a way that absolutely no blame, not even a hint of suspicion, would ever fall his way.

"What if he tried again? And this time succeeded."

Burton looked puzzled. "How do we control what Sullivan does?"

"By doing it ourselves."

No one said anything for a couple of minutes. Russell glanced incredulously at her boss. Her entire life had just gone straight to hell and now she was compelled to participate in a conspiracy to commit murder. She had felt emotionally numb since all of

390

this had started. She had been absolutely certain her situation could not get any worse. And she had been absolutely wrong about that.

Finally Burton ventured an analysis. "I'm not sure the police would believe Sullivan would be that crazy. He's gotta know they're on to him, but can't prove anything. If we pop Whitney, I'm not sure they'd look Sullivan's way."

The President stopped strolling. He stood directly in front of Burton. "So let the police reach that conclusion themselves, if they ever do."

The reality was that Richmond no longer needed Walter Sullivan to regain the White House. Perhaps more important, this was a perfect way to rid himself of the obligation to back Sullivan's Ukraine deal over Russia; a decision that was growing into more and more of a potential liability. If Sullivan were even remotely implicated in the death of his wife's killer, he would be doing no more global deals. Richmond's support would be discreetly withdrawn. Everyone who counted would understand that silent retreat.

"Alan, you want to set Sullivan up for a murder?" These were the first words Russell had spoken. Her face betrayed her complete astonishment.

He looked at her, with unconcealed contempt in his eyes.

"Alan, think about what you're saying. This is Walter Sullivan, this is not some two-bit crook no one gives a damn about."

Richmond smiled. Her stupidity amused him. She had seemed so bright, so incredibly capable when he first brought her on board. He had been wrong.

The President did some rough calculations. At best Sullivan had perhaps a twenty percent chance of going down for the killing. Given similar circumstances, Richmond would take those odds. Sullivan was a big boy, he could take care of himself. And if he faltered? Well, that was why they had prisons. He looked at Burton.

"Burton, do *you* understand?"

Burton didn't answer.

The President said sharply, "You were certainly prepared to kill the man before, Burton. As far as I can determine, the stakes haven't changed. In fact they're probably higher. For *all* of us. Do you understand, Burton?" Richmond paused for a moment, then repeated his question.

Burton finally looked up and said quietly, "I understand."

For the next two hours they laid their plans.

As the two Secret Service agents and Russell rose to leave, the President looked at her. "So tell me, Gloria, what happened to the money?"

Russell looked straight at him. "It was donated, anonymously, to the American Red Cross. I understand it was one of their biggest single contributions ever."

The door closed and the President had smiled. *Nice parting shot. Enjoy it, Luther Whitney. Enjoy it while you can, you insignificant little nothing.*

TWENTY-THREE

Walter Sullivan settled into his chair with a book but never opened it. His mind wandered back. Back to events that seemed more ethereal, more wholly unconnected to his person than anything else that had ever happened in his life. He had hired a man to kill. To kill someone who stood accused of murdering his wife. The job had been botched. A fact for which Sullivan was quietly thankful. For his grief had subsided enough to where he knew what he had attempted to do was wrong. A civilized society must follow certain procedures unless it were to become uncivilized. And no matter how painful it would be to him, he was a civilized man. He would follow the rules.

It was then that he looked down at the newspaper. Many days old now, its contents continued to beat incessantly into his head. The thick, dark headlines shone back at him on the white background of the page. As he turned his attention to it, distant suspicions in his mind were starting to crystallize. Walter Sullivan was not only a billionaire, he possessed a brilliant and perceptive mind. One that saw every detail along with every landscape.

Luther Whitney was dead. The police had no suspects. Sullivan had checked the obvious solution. McCarty had been in Hong Kong on the day in question. Sullivan's last directive to the man had indeed been heeded. Walter Sullivan had called off his hunt. But someone else had taken up the chase in his place.

And Walter Sullivan was the only person who knew that for a fact, other than his bungling assassin.

Sullivan looked at his old timepiece. It was barely seven in the morning and he had been up for four hours already. The twenty-four hours in a day meant little to him anymore. The older he grew, the less important became the parameters of time. Four o'clock in the morning could find him wide awake on a plane over the Pacific while two in the afternoon might be the halfway point in his sleep for the day.

There were many facts that he was sifting through, and his mind worked rapidly. A CAT scan done at his last physical evidenced a brain with the youth and vigor of a twenty-year-old. And that splendid mind was now working toward the few undeniable facts that were leading its owner to a conclusion that would amaze even him.

He picked up the phone on his desk and looked around the highly polished cherry paneling of his study as he dialed the number.

In a moment he had been put through to Seth Frank. Unimpressed with the man early on, Sullivan had grudgingly given him his due with the arrest of Luther Whitney. But now?

"Yes sir, Mr. Sullivan, what can I do for you?"

Sullivan cleared his throat. His voice had a humble note to it that was as far from his customary tone as was possible. Even Frank picked up on it.

"I had a question regarding the information I had given you earlier about Christy, um, Christine's sudden departure on the way to the airport for our trip to the estate in Barbados."

Frank sat up in his chair. "Did you remember something else?"

"Actually I wanted to verify whether I had given

you any reason for her not going on the trip."

"I'm afraid I don't understand."

"Well, I suppose my age is catching up with me. My bones aren't the only thing deteriorating I'm afraid, though I don't care to admit it to myself much less anyone else, Lieutenant. More to the point I thought I had told you she had taken ill and had to return home. I mean I *thought* that's what I had told you in any event."

Seth took a moment to pull his file, although he was certain of the answer. "You said she didn't give a reason, Mr. Sullivan. Just said she wasn't going, and you didn't push it."

"Ah. Well, I guess that settles that. Thank you, Lieutenant."

Frank stood up. One hand lifted a cup of coffee and then put it back down. "Wait a minute, Mr. Sullivan. Why would you think you had told me that your wife was sick? Was she sick?"

Sullivan paused before answering. "Actually no, Lieutenant Frank. She was remarkably healthy. To answer your question, I believe I thought I had told you differently because, to tell you the truth, aside from my occasional memory lapses, I think I've spent these last two months trying to convince myself that Christine staying behind was for some reason. Any reason, I guess."

"Sir?"

"To, in my own mind, justify what happened to her. To not let it be just a damn coincidence. I don't believe in fate, Lieutenant. For me, everything has a purpose. I suppose I wanted to convince myself that Christine's staying behind did too."

"Oh."

"I apologize if an old man's foolishness has caused you any unnecessary perplexity."

"Not at all, Mr. Sullivan."

When Frank hung up the phone he ended up staring at the wall for a good five minutes. Now what the hell had all that been about?

Following up on Bill Burton's suggestion, Frank had made discreet inquiries into Sullivan having possibly hired a contract killer to make sure his wife's presumed killer never stood trial. Those inquiries were going slow; one had to tread cautiously in these types of waters. Frank had a career to think about, a family to support, and men like Walter Sullivan had an army of very influential friends in government who could make the detective's professional life miserable.

The day after the slug had ended Luther Whitney's life, Seth Frank had made immediate inquiries as to Sullivan's whereabouts at the time although Frank was under no delusions that the old man had pulled the trigger on the cannon that had propelled Luther Whitney into the hereafter. But murder for hire was a particularly wicked deed, and although perhaps the detective could understand the billionaire's motivation, the fact was he had probably gunned down the wrong guy. This latest conversation with Sullivan left him with even more questions and no new answers.

Seth Frank sat down and wondered briefly if this nightmare of a case would ever leave his watch.

A half hour later Sullivan placed a call to a local television station of which he happened to own a controlling interest. His request was simple and to the point. In an hour a package was delivered to his front door. After one of the staff handed him the square box he ushered her out, shut and locked the door to the room he was in, and pressed a small lever on a portion of the wall. The small panel slid down silently, revealing a very sophisticated audiocassette tape deck. Behind most of this wall rested a cutting-edge home theater system that Christine Sullivan had seen in a magazine one day and simply had to have, although her tastes in video entertainment ventured from pornography to soap opera, neither of which in any way taxed the electronic muscle of this monolithic system.

Sullivan carefully unwrapped the audiocassette and placed it inside the tape deck; the door automatically closed and the tape began to play. Sullivan listened for a few moments. When he heard the words, no emotion was revealed on his intricate features. He had expected to hear what he had. He had outright lied to the detective. His memory was excellent. If only his sight were half as good. For he had indeed been a blind idiot to this reality. The emotion that finally penetrated the inscrutable line of his mouth and the deep gray of his introspective eyes was anger. Anger like he had not felt in a long time. Not even at Christy's death. A fury that would only be relieved through action. And Sullivan firmly believed that your first salvo should be your last because that meant that either you got them, or they got you, and he was not in the habit of losing.

The funeral was conducted in humble surroundings and with only three people other than the priest in attendance. It had taken the utmost secrecy to avoid the obvious assaults by the armies of journalists. Luther's casket was closed. The remains of violent trauma to the head was not the lasting impression loved ones typically wanted to carry away with them.

Neither the background of the deceased nor the means of his demise mattered the slightest to the man of God, and the service was appropriately reverent. The drive to the nearby cemetery was short as was the procession. Jack and Kate drove over together; behind them was Seth Frank. He had sat in the back of the church, awkward and uncomfortable. Jack had shaken his hand; Kate had refused to acknowledge him.

Jack leaned against his car and watched Kate as she sat in the fold-up metal chair next to the earthen pit that had just accepted her father. Jack looked around. This cemetery was not home to grandiose monuments of tribute. It was rare to see a grave marker sticking up, most were the in-the-dirt variety; a dark rectangle with its owner's name, dates of entry and exit from the living. A few said "in loving memory," most ventured no parting remarks.

Jack looked back at Kate and he saw Seth Frank start toward her, then the detective apparently thought better of his decision and made his way quietly over to the Lexus.

Frank took off his sunglasses. "Nice service."

Jack shrugged. "Nothing's really nice about getting killed." Though miles away from Kate's position on the issue, he had not entirely forgiven Frank for allowing Luther Whitney to die like that.

Frank fell silent, studied the finish on the sedan, drew out a cigarette, then changed his mind. He stuck his hands in his pockets and stared off.

He had attended Luther Whitney's autopsy. The transient cavitation had been immense. The shock waves had dissipated radially out from the bullet track to such an extent that fully half the man's brain had literally disintegrated. And it was no small wonder. The slug they'd dug out of the seat of the police van was an eye-popper. A .460 Magnum round. The Medical Examiner had told Frank that type of ammo was often used for sports hunting, big game in particular. And it was no wonder, since the round had slammed into Whitney with stopping power equal to over eight thousand pounds of energy. It was like someone had dropped a plane on the poor guy. Big game hunting. Frank shook his head wearily. And it had happened on his watch, right in front of him in fact. He would never forget that.

Frank looked over the green expanse of the final resting place for over twenty thousand dearly departed. Jack leaned back against the car and followed Frank's gaze.

"So any leads?"

The detective dug a toe in the dirt. "A few. None of them really going anywhere."

They both straightened up as Kate rose, laid a small arrangement of flowers on the mound of dirt, and then stood, staring off. The wind had died down, and although cold, the sun was bright and warming.

Jack buttoned his coat up. "So what now? Case closed? Nobody would blame you."

Frank smiled, decided he'd have that smoke after all. "Not by a fucking long shot, chief."

"So what are you gonna do?"

Kate turned and started to walk toward the car. Seth Frank put his hat back on, pulled out his car keys.

"Simple, find me a murderer."

"Kate, I know how you feel, but you have to believe me. He didn't blame you for anything. None of this was your fault. Like you said, you were pushed into the middle involuntarily. You didn't ask for any of this. Luther understood that."

They were in Jack's car driving back into the city. The sun was eye level and dropping perceptibly with each mile. They had sat in his car at the cemetery for almost two hours because she didn't want to leave. As though if she waited long enough he would climb out of his grave and join them.

She cracked the window and a narrow stream of air engulfed the interior, dispelling the new-car smell with the thick moistness that heralded another storm.

"Detective Frank hasn't given up on the case, Kate. He's still looking for Luther's killer."

She finally looked at him. "I really don't care what he says he's going to do." She touched her nose, which was red and swollen and hurt like hell.

"Come on, Kate. It's not like the guy wanted Luther to get shot."

"Oh really? A case full of holes that gets blown apart at trial leaving everyone involved, including the detective in charge, looking like complete idiots. Instead you have a corpse, and a closed case. Now tell me again what the master detective wants?"

Jack stopped for a red light and slumped back in his seat. He knew that Frank was shooting straight with him, but there was no way in hell he was going to convince Kate of that fact.

The light changed and he moved through traffic. He checked his watch. He had to get back to the office, assuming he had an office to go back to.

"Kate, I don't think you should be alone right now. How about I crash at your place for a few nights? You brew the coffee in the morning and I'll take care of the dinners. Deal?"

He had expected an immediate and negative response and had already prepared his rejoinder.

"Are you sure?"

Jack looked over at her, found wide, puffy eyes on him. Every nerve in her body seemed ready to scream. As he walked himself through the paces of what was, to both of them, a tragedy, he suddenly realized that he was still totally oblivious to the enormity of the pain and guilt she was experiencing. It stunned him, even more than the sound of the shot as he sat holding her hand. Knowing before their

400

fingers ever parted that Luther was dead.

"I'm sure."

That night he had just settled himself on the couch. The blanket was drawn up to his neck, his bulwark against the draft that hit him chest high from an invisible crevice in the window across from him. Then he heard a door squeak and she walked out of her bedroom. She wore the same robe as before, her hair drawn up tightly in a bun. Her face looked fresh and clean; only a slight red sheen hovering around her cheeks hinted at the internal trauma.

"Do you need anything?"

"I'm fine. This couch is a lot more comfortable than I thought it would be. I've still got the same one from our apartment in Charlottesville. I don't even think it has any springs left. I think they all retired."

She didn't smile, but she did sit down next to him.

When they had lived together she had taken a bath every night. Coming to bed she had smelled so good it had nearly driven him mad. Like the breath of a newborn, there was absolutely nothing imperfect about it. And she had played dumb for a while until he lay exhausted on top of her and she would smile a decidedly wicked little smile and stroke him and he would ruminate for several minutes on how it was so crystal-clear to him that women ruled the world.

He found his baser instincts creeping firmly ahead as she leaned her head against his shoulder. But her exhausted manner, her total apathy, swiftly quelled his secular inclinations and left him feeling more than a little guilty.

"I'm not sure I'm going to be very good company."

Had she sensed what he was feeling? How could she? Her mind, everything about her, must be a million miles away from this spot.

"Being entertained was not part of the deal. I can look after myself, Kate."

401

"I really appreciate your doing this."

"I can't think of anything more important."

She squeezed his hand. As she rose to go the flap on her robe came undone exposing more than just her long, slender legs and he was glad she would be in another room that night. His ruminations until the early-morning hours ran the gamut from visions of white knights with large dark spots disfiguring their pristine armor to idealistic lawyers who slept miserably alone.

On the third night he had settled in again on the couch. And, as before, she came out of her bedroom; the slight squeak made him lay down the magazine he was reading. But this time she did not go to the couch. He finally craned his neck around and found her watching him. She did not look apathetic tonight. And tonight she was not wearing the robe. She turned and went back inside her bedroom. The door stayed open.

For a moment he did nothing. Then he rose, went to the door and peered in. Through the darkness he could make out her form on the bed. The sheet was at the foot of the bed. The contours of her body, once as familiar to him as his own, confronted him. She looked at him. He could just make out the ovals of her eyes as they focused on him. She did not put out her hand for him; he recalled that she had never done that.

"Are you sure about this?" He felt compelled to ask it. He wanted no hurt feelings in the morning, no crushed, confused emotions.

For an answer she rose and pulled him to the bed. The mattress was firm, and warm where she had been. In another moment he was as naked as she. He instinctively traced the half-moon, moved his hand around the crooked mouth, which now touched his. Her eyes were open and this time, and it had been a long time, there were no tears, no swelling, just the look he had grown so used to, expected to have around forever. He slowly put his arms around her.

The home of Walter Sullivan had seen visiting dignitaries of incredibly high rank. But tonight was special even compared to past events.

Alan Richmond raised his glass of wine and gave a brief but eloquent toast to his host as the four other carefully selected couples clinked their glasses. The First Lady, radiant in a simple, black dress, ash blonde hair framing a sculpted face that had worn remarkably well over the years and made for delightful photo ops, smiled at the billionaire. Accustomed as she was to being surrounded by wealth and brains and refinement, she, like most people, was still in awe of Walter Sullivan and men like him, if only for their rarity on the planet.

Technically still in mourning, Sullivan was in a particularly gregarious mood. Over imported coffee in the spacious library the conversation ventured from global business opportunities, the latest maneuvering of the Federal Reserve Board, the 'Skins' chances against the Forty-niners that Sunday, to the election the following year. There were none in attendance who thought Alan Richmond would have a different occupation after the votes were counted.

Except for one person.

In saying his good-byes the President leaned into Walter Sullivan to embrace the older man and say a few private words. Sullivan smiled at the President's remarks. Then the old man stumbled slightly but righted himself by grasping the arms of the President.

After his guests had gone, Sullivan smoked a cigar in his study. As he moved to the window, the lights from the presidential motorcade quickly faded from view. In spite of himself, Sullivan had to smile. The image of the slight wince in the President's eye as Sullivan had gripped his forearm had made for a particularly victorious moment. A long shot, but sometimes long shots paid off. Detective Frank had been very open with the billionaire about the detective's theories regarding the case. One theory that had particularly interested Walter Sullivan was his wife having wounded her assailant with the letter opener, possibly in the leg or arm. It must have cut deeper than the police had thought. Possible nerve damage. A surface wound certainly would have had time to heal by now.

Sullivan slowly walked out of the study, turning off the light as he exited. President Alan Richmond had assuredly felt only a small pain when Sullivan's fingers had sunk into his flesh. But as with a heart attack, a small pain was so often followed by a much larger one. Sullivan smiled broadly as he considered the possibilities.

From atop the knoll Walter Sullivan stared at the little wooden house with the green tin roof. He pulled his muffler around his ears, steadied his weakened legs with a thick walking stick. The cold was bitter in the hills of Southwest Virginia this time of year and the forecast pointed unerringly to snow, and a lot of it.

He made his way down across the, for now, iron-hard ground. The house was in an excellent state of repair thanks to his limitless pocketbook and a deep sense of nostalgia that seemed to more and more consume him as he grew closer to becoming a thread of the past himself. Woodrow Wilson was in the White House and the earth was heavily into the First World War when Walter Patrick Sullivan had first seen the glimmer of light with the aid of a midwife and the grim determination of his mother, Millie, who had lost all three previous children, two in childbirth.

His father, a coal miner – it seems everyone's father was a coal miner in that part of Virginia back then – had lived until his son's twelfth birthday and then had abruptly expired from a series of maladies brought on by too much coal dust and too little rest. For years the future billionaire had watched his daddy stagger into the house, every muscle exhausted, the face as black as their big Labrador's coat, and collapse on the little bed in the back room. Too tired to eat, or play with the little boy who each day hoped for some attention but ended up getting none from a father whose perpetual weariness was so painful to witness.

His mother had lived long enough to see her off-spring become one of the richest men in the world, and her dutiful son had taken great pains to ensure that she had every comfort his immense resources could provide. For a tribute to his late father, he had purchased the mine that had killed him. Five million cash. He had paid a fifty-thousand-dollar bonus to every miner in the place and then he had, with great ceremony, shut it down.

He opened the door and went inside. The gas fireplace threw warmth into the room without the necessity of firewood. The pantry was stocked with enough food for the next six months. Here he was entirely self-sufficient. He never allowed anyone to stay here with him. This had been his homestead. All with the right to be here, with the exception of himself, were dead. He was alone and he wanted it that way.

The simple meal he prepared was lingered over while he stared moodily out the window where in the failing light he could just make out the circle of naked elms near the house; the branches waved to him with slow, melodic movements.

The interior of the house had not been returned to its original condition or configuration. This was his birthplace but it had not been a happy childhood amid poverty that threatened never to go away. The sense of urgency spawned from that time had served Sullivan well in his career, for it fueled him with a stamina, a resolve before which many an obstacle had wilted.

He cleaned the plates, and went into the small room that had once been his parents' bedroom. Now it contained a comfortable chair, a table and several bookcases that housed an extremely select collection of reading material. In the corner was a small cot, for the room also served as his sleeping chamber.

Sullivan picked up the sophisticated cellular phone that lay on the table. He dialed a number known only to a handful of people. A voice on the other line came on. Then Sullivan was put on hold for a moment before another voice came on.

"Goodness, Walter, I know you tend to keep odd hours, but you really should try to slow down a bit. Where are you?"

"You can't slow down at my age, Alan. If you do, you might not start back up again. I'd much rather explode in a fireball of activity than recede faintly into the mists. I hope I'm not disturbing something important."

"Nothing that can't wait. I'm getting better about prioritizing world crises. Was there something you needed?"

Sullivan took a moment to place a small recording device next to the receiver. One never knew.

"I only had one question, Alan." Sullivan paused. It occurred to him that he was enjoying this. Then he thought of Christy's face in the morgue and his face became grim.

"What's that?"

"Why did you wait so long to kill the man?"

In the silence that followed, Sullivan could hear the pattern of breathing on the other end of the phone. To his credit Alan Richmond did not start to hyperventilate; in fact, his breathing remained normal. Sullivan came away impressed and a little disappointed.

"Come again?"

"If your men had missed, you might be meeting with your attorney right now, planning your defense against impeachment. You must admit you cut it rather close."

"Walter, are you all right? Has something happened to you? Where are you?"

Sullivan held the receiver away from his ear for a moment. The phone had a scrambling device that made any possible tracing of his location impossible. If they were trying to lock in his position right now, as he was reasonably certain they were, they would be confronted with a dozen locations from which the call was supposedly originating, and not one of them anywhere near where he actually was. The device had cost him ten thousand dollars. But, then, it was only money. He smiled again. He could talk as long as he wanted.

"Actually I haven't felt this good in a long while."

"Walter, you're not making any sense. Who was killed?"

"You know, I wasn't all that surprised when Christy didn't want to go to Barbados. Honestly, I figured she wanted to stay behind and do some alley-catting with a few of the young men she had targeted over the summer. It was funny when she said she wasn't feeling well. I remember sitting in the limo and thinking what her excuse would be. She wasn't all that creative, poor girl. Her cough was particularly phony. I suppose in school she used the dog-ate-my-homework excuse with alarming regularity."

"Walt—"

"The odd thing was that when the police questioned me regarding why she hadn't come with me, I suddenly realized I couldn't tell them that Christy had claimed illness. You may recall that there were rumors of affairs floating in the papers about that time. I knew if I reported her not feeling well, coupled with her not joining me on the island, that the tabloids would soon have her pregnant with another man's child even if the autopsy confirmed otherwise. People love to assume the worst and the juiciest, Alan, you understand that. When you're impeached they'll assume the worst of you, of course. And deservedly so."

"Walter, will you please tell me where you are? You are obviously not feeling well."

"Would you like me to play the tape for you, Alan? The one from the press conference where you gave me that particularly moving line about things that happen that have no meaning. It was quite a nice thing to say. A private comment between old friends that was picked up by several TV and radio stations in the area but that never made the light of day. It's a tribute to your popularity, I suppose, that no one picked up on it. You were being so charming, so supportive, who cared if you said Christy was sick. And you did say that, Alan. You told me that if Christy hadn't gotten sick she wouldn't have been murdered. She would've gone with me to the island and she would be alive today.

"I was the only one Christy told about being sick, Alan. And as I said, I never even told the police. So how did you know?"

"You must have told me."

"I neither met nor spoke with you prior to the

408

press conference. That much is easily confirmed. My schedule is monitored by the minute. As President your whereabouts and communications are pretty much known at all times. I say pretty much, because on the night Christy was killed you were certainly not among your usual haunts. You happened to be in my house, and more to the point, in my bedroom. At the press conference we were surrounded by dozens of people at all times. Everything we said to each other is on tape somewhere. You didn't learn it from me."

"Walter, please tell me where you are. I want to help you through this."

"Christy was never really good at keeping things straight. She must have been so proud of her subterfuge with me. She probably bragged to you, didn't she? How she had snookered the old man? Because in fact my late wife was the only person in the world who could've told you that she had feigned illness. And you carelessly uttered those words to me. I don't know why it took me so long to arrive at the truth. I suppose I was so obsessed with finding Christy's killer that I accepted the burglary theory without question. Perhaps it was also subconscious self-denial. Because I was never wholly ignorant of Christy's desires for you. But I guess I just didn't want to believe you could do that to me. I should have assumed the worst in human nature and I would not have found myself disappointed. But as they say, better late than never."

"Walter, why did you call me?"

Sullivan's voice grew more quiet but lost none of its force, none of its intensity. "Because, you bastard, I wanted to be the one to tell you of your new future. It will involve lawyers and courts and more public exposure than even as President you ever dreamed was possible. Because I didn't want you to be wholly surprised when the police presented themselves on your doorstep. And most of all, I wanted you to know exactly who to thank for all of it."

The President's voice became tense. "Walter, if you want me to help you, I will. But I am the President of the United States. And although you are one of my oldest friends, I will not tolerate this type of accusation from you or anyone else."

"That's good, Alan. Very good. You discerned that I would be taping the conversation. Not that it matters." Sullivan paused for a moment, then continued. "My protégé, Alan. Taught you everything I knew, and you learned well. Well enough to hold the highest office in the land. Fortunately, your fall will also be the steepest."

"Walter, you've been under a lot of stress. For the last time, please get some help."

"Funny, Alan, that's precisely my advice to you."

Sullivan clicked off the phone and turned off the recorder. His heart was beating abnormally fast. He put one hand against his chest, forced himself to relax. A coronary was not going to be allowed. He was going to be around to see this one.

He looked out the window and then at the inside of the room. His little homestead. His father had died in this very room. Somehow, that thought was comforting to him.

He lay back in the chair and closed his eyes. In the morning he would call the police. He would tell them everything and he would give them the tape. Then he would sit back and watch. Even if they didn't convict Richmond, his career was over. Which was to say the man was as good as dead, professionally, spiritually, mentally. Who cared if his physical carcass lingered? So much the better. Sullivan smiled. He had sworn that he would avenge his wife's killer. And he had.

It was the sudden sensation of his hand rising from his side that brought his eyes open. And then his hand was being closed around a cold, hard object. It wasn't until the barrel touched the side of his head that he really reacted. And by then it was too late.

As the President looked at the phone receiver, he checked his watch. It would be over right about now. Sullivan had taught him well. Too well, as it had turned out, for the teacher. He had been almost certain Sullivan would contact him directly prior to announcing the President's culpability to the world. That had made it relatively simple. Richmond rose and headed upstairs to his private quarters. The thought of the late Walter Sullivan had already passed from his mind. It was not efficient or productive to linger over a vanquished foe. It only set you back for your next challenge. Sullivan had also taught him that.

In the twilight the younger man stared at the house. He had heard the shot, but his eyes never stopped staring at the dim light in the window.

Bill Burton rejoined Collin in a few seconds. He could not even look at his partner. Two trained and dedicated Secret Service agents, killers of young women and old men.

On the drive back, Burton sank back in his seat. It was finally over. Three people dead, counting Christine Sullivan. And why not count her? That's what had started this whole nightmare.

Burton looked down at his hand, still barely able to comprehend that it had just curled around the grip of a gun, forced a trigger back and ended a man's life. With his other hand Burton had taken the cassette recorder and the tape. They were in his pocket headed for the incinerator.

When he had checked the telephone tap and listened to Sullivan's phone conversation with Seth Frank, Burton had no idea what the old man was getting at with Christine Sullivan's "illness." But when he reported the information to the President, Richmond had looked out the window for some minutes, a shade paler than he had been when Burton had entered the room. Then he had phoned the White House Media Department. A few minutes later they had both listened to the tape from the first press conference on the Middleton Courthouse steps. To the President commiserating with his old friend, about the whimsical nature of life; how Christine Sullivan would still be alive if she hadn't taken ill. Having forgotten that Christine Sullivan had told him that on the day of her death. A fact that could be proven. A fact that could possibly topple all of them.

Burton had slumped back in his chair, stared at his boss, who silently looked at the tape as if he were trying to erase its words with his thoughts. Burton shook his head incredulously. Caught up in his own mushy rhetoric, just like a politician.

"What do we do now, Chief? Make a run for it on Air Force One?" Burton was only half-joking as he studied the carpet. He was too numb to even think anymore.

He looked up to find the President's eyes full upon him. "Walter Sullivan is the only living person, other than ourselves, who knows the significance of this information."

Burton rose from his chair and returned the stare. "My job doesn't include popping people just because you tell me to."

The President would not take his eyes from Burton's face. "Walter Sullivan is now a direct threat to us. He is also fucking with us and I don't like people fucking with me. Do you?"

"He's got a damned good reason to, don't you think?"

Richmond picked up a pen from his desk and twirled it between his fingers. "If Sullivan talks we lose everything. Everything." The President snapped his fingers. "Gone. Just like that. And I will do everything possible to avoid it happening."

Burton dropped into his chair, his belly suddenly on fire. "How do you know he hasn't already?"

"Because I know Walter," the President said simply. "He'll do it in his own way. And it will be spectacular. But deliberate. He is not a man who rushes into anything. But when he does act, the results will be swift and crushing."

"Great." Burton put his head in his hands, his mind whirling faster than he thought possible. Years of training had instilled in him an almost innate ability to process information instantly, think on his feet, act a fraction of a second before anyone else could. Now his brain was a muddle, like day-old coffee, thick and soupy; nothing was clear. He looked up.

"But killing the guy?"

"I can guarantee you that Walter Sullivan is right this minute plotting how best to destroy us. That type of action does not invoke sympathy from me."

The President leaned back in his chair. "Plainly and simply this man has decided to fight us. And one has to live with the consequences of one's decisions. Walter Sullivan knows that better than anyone alive." The President's eyes again lasered in on Burton's. "The question is, are we prepared to fight back?"

Collin and Burton had spent the last three days following Walter Sullivan. When the car had dropped him off in the middle of nowhere, Burton both couldn't believe his luck and experienced deep sadness for his target, now, truly, a sitting duck.

413

Husband and wife wiped out. As the car sped back to the Capital City, Burton unconsciously rubbed at his hand, trying to whittle away the filth he felt in every crevice. What turned his skin cold was the realization that he could never wipe away the feelings he was having, the reality of what he had done. The rock-bottom emotional barometer would be with him every minute of every day of the rest of his days. He had traded his life for another. Again. His back-bone, for so long a steel beam, had wilted to pitiful rubber. Life had given him the supreme challenge and he had failed.

He dug his fingers into the armrest and stared out the window into the darkness.

TWENTY-FOUR

The apparent suicide of Walter Sullivan rocked not only the community. The funeral was attended by the high and mighty from all over the world. In an appropriately solemn and lavish ceremony at Washington's St. Matthew's Cathedral, the man was eulogized by a half-dozen dignitaries. The most famous had gone on for a full twenty minutes about the great human being Walter Sullivan had been, and also about the great stress he had been under and how those under such strain sometimes do things they would otherwise never contemplate. When Alan Richmond had finished speaking, there was not a dry cheek in the place, and the tears that dampened his own face were seemingly genuine. He had always been impressed with his superb oratorical skills.

The long funeral procession streamed out, and, over three and one half hours later, ended at the tiny house where Walter Sullivan had begun, and ended, his life. As the limos scrambled for space on the narrow, snow-covered road, Walter Sullivan was carried down and interred next to his parents, on the little knoll where the view down the valley was by far the richest part of the place.

As the dirt covered the coffin, and the friends of Walter Sullivan made their way back to the realm of the living, Seth Frank studied every face. He watched as the President made his way back to his limo. Bill Burton saw him, registered surprise for an instant, and then nodded. Frank nodded back.

When all the mourners had gone, Frank turned his attention to the little house. The yellow police lines were still around the perimeter and two uniformed officers stood guard.

Frank walked over, flashed his badge and entered.

It seemed the height of irony that one of the wealthiest men in the world had chosen a place like this to die. Walter Sullivan had been a walking poster child for Horatio Alger tales. Frank admired a man who had risen in the world on his own merit, sheer guts and determination. Who wouldn't?

He looked again at the chair where the body had been found, the gun beside it. The weapon had been pressed against Sullivan's left temple. The stellate wound, large and ragged, had preceded the massive bursting fracture that had ended the man's life. The gun had fallen on the left side of the floor. The presence of the contact wound and powder burns on the deceased's palm had prompted the locals to file the case away as a suicide, the facts of which were simple and straightforward. A grieving Walter Sullivan had exacted revenge on his wife's killer and then taken his own life. His associates had confirmed that Sullivan had been out of touch for days, unusual for him. He rarely came to this retreat and whenever he did, someone knew his whereabouts. The newspaper found beside the body had proclaimed the death of his wife's suspected murderer. All the signs pointed to a man who had intended on ending his life.

What bothered Frank was one small fact that he had purposefully not shared with anyone. He had met Walter Sullivan the day he had come to the morgue. During that meeting, Sullivan had signed off on several forms related to the autopsy and an inventory of his wife's few possessions.

And Sullivan had signed those forms with his *right* hand.

It was inconclusive in itself. Sullivan could have held the gun in his left hand for any number of reasons. His fingerprints were on the gun clear as day, maybe too clear, Frank thought to himself.

The physical condition of the gun: it was untraceable; the serial numbers had been so expertly obliterated that even the scope couldn't pull up anything. A completely sterilized weapon. The kind you'd expect to find at a crime scene. But why would Walter Sullivan be concerned about anyone tracing a gun he was going to use to kill himself? The answer was he wouldn't. But again the fact was inconclusive since the person providing Sullivan with the weapon could have obtained it illegally, although Virginia was one of the easier states in which to purchase a handgun, much to the dismay of police departments in the northeast corridor of the country.

Frank finished with the interior and paced outside. The snow still lay thickly on the ground. Sullivan had been dead before the snow had started, the autopsy had confirmed that. It was fortunate that his people knew the location of the house. They had come looking for him and the body had been discovered within approximately twelve hours of death.

No, the snow would not help Frank. The entire place was so isolated there was no one even to ask if anything suspicious had been observed on the night of Sullivan's death.

His counterpart from the county sheriff's department climbed out of his car and hustled over to where Frank was standing. The man carried a file with some papers in it. He and Frank conversed for a few moments and then Frank thanked him, climbed in his car and drove off.

The autopsy report indicated that Walter Sullivan had died sometime between eleven P.M. and one o'clock in the morning. But at twelve-ten Walter Sullivan had called someone.

The hallways of PS&L were unsettlingly quiet. The capillaries of a thriving law practice are ringing phones, pealing faxes, mouths moving and keyboards clicking. Lucinda, even with the firm's individual direct-dialing lines, was normally the recipient of eight phone calls per minute. Today she leisurely read through *Vogue*. Most office doors were closed, shielding from view the intense and often emotional discussions going on among all but a handful of the firm's lawyers.

Sandy Lord's office door was not only closed, it was locked. The few partners with the temerity to attempt a knock on the thick portal were quickly on the biting end of an obscene verbal barrage from the room's lone and moody occupant.

He sat in his chair, shoeless feet on the polished desk, tieless, collar undone, unshaven, a nearly empty bottle of his strongest whiskey within easy reach. Sandy Lord's eyes were now mere blots of red. At the church he had used those eyes to stare long and hard at the shiny brass coffin containing Sullivan's body; essentially it contained both their earthly remains.

For many years Lord had anticipated Sullivan's demise and had, with the help of a dozen PS&L specialists, established an elaborate series of safeguards that included cultivation of a loyal contingent on the board of directors of the parent holding company of Sullivan Enterprises, all of which would ensure continual representation of the huge network of Sullivan entities far into the future by PS&L generally and by Lord in particular. Life would go on. The PS&L train would thrive with its chief diesel engine intact and even replenished. But an unexpected development had occurred.

That Sullivan's passing was inevitable, the financial markets understood. What the business and investment community apparently could not accept was the man's death, allegedly by his own hand, coupled with the increasing rumors that Sullivan had had his wife's alleged killer gunned down, something that once accomplished, had prompted him to put a bullet into his own brain. The market was not prepared for such revelations. A surprised market, some economists would predict, often reacts wildly and precipitately. Those economists were not disappointed. Shares of stock in Sullivan Enterprises plummeted sixty-one percent in value on the New York Stock Exchange the morning after his body was discovered, on the heaviest trading volume for a single stock in the last ten years.

With the stock selling a full six dollars a share below book value it had not taken long for the vultures to circle.

Centrus Corp.'s tender offer was, upon Lord's advice, rejected by the board of directors. However, all indications pointed to overwhelming acceptance of the offer by the shareholders, who had nervously watched as a large chunk of their investment had evaporated overnight. It was likely that the proxy battle would be complete and the takeover finalized in two months. Centrus's counsel, Rhoads, Director & Minor, was one of the largest law firms in the country, well-stocked in all areas of legal expertise.

The bottom line was clear. PS&L would not be needed. Its largest client, over twenty million dollars' worth, almost one-third of its legal business, would disappear. Already résumés were flying out of the firm. Practice groups were trying to cut deals with Rhoads, pleading their familiarity with Sullivan's business as a hedge against the dreaded and costly learning curve. Twenty percent of the heretofore loyal PS&L attorney ranks had submitted their resignation and there were no indications the tidal wave would subside anytime soon.

Lord's hand slowly meandered along his desk until the whiskey was tilted back and finished. He swiveled around, checked out the gloom of the winter's morning and had to smile to himself.

There was no deal awaiting him at Rhoads, Director & Minor and, thus, it had finally happened: Lord was vulnerable. He had seen clients bite the dust with alarming swiftness, especially in the last decade where you were a paper billionaire one minute and an impoverished felon the next. He had, though, never imagined that his own fall, if it ever came, would be as terrifyingly fast, as painfully complete.

That was the problem with an eight-figure gorilla of a client. It took all of your time and attention. Old clients dried up and died away. New clients were not cultivated. His complacency had come back to bite him right in the ass.

He calculated swiftly. Over the last twenty years he had netted roughly thirty million dollars. Unfortunately, he had managed somehow not only to spend the thirty mil but a good deal more than that. Over the years he had owned a string of luxurious homes, a vacation place in Hilton Head Island, a hideaway fuck nest in the Big Apple where he had taken his wedded prey. The luxury cars, the various collections that a man of taste and resources was supposed to accumulate, the small but select wine cellar, even his own helicopter – he had had all those things, but three divorces, none of them amicable, had deteriorated his asset base.

The residence he now had left was straight from the pages of *Architectural Digest* but its mortgage matched its stunning opulence stride for stride. And the thing he truly didn't have much of was cash.

Liquidity escaped him and at PS&L you ate what you killed and PS&L partners didn't tend to hunt in packs. That was why Lord's monthly draw was so much larger than everyone else's. That revised draw check would now barely cover his plastic bills; his monthly Am Ex alone routinely crept into the five-figure range.

He turned his now-racing gray cells for a moment to his non-Sullivan clients. A rough ballpark estimate gave him maybe a half-million in potential legal business at best, if he pumped them hard, made the circuit, which he didn't want to do, lacked any desire to do. That was beneath him now. Or it had been up until good old Walter had decided life just wasn't worth living despite his several billions. *Jesus Christ. All for a little dumbshit whore.*

Five hundred thou'! That was even less than the little prick Kirksen. Lord winced at that realization.

He wheeled around and studied the artwork on the far wall. Within the brush strokes of a minor nineteenth-century artist he found reason to smile once more. He had an option left to him. Though his biggest client had royally screwed up Lord's life, the rotund deal-maker had an asset left to mine. He punched his phone.

Fred Martin pushed the cart quickly down the hallway. Only his third day on the job, and his first delivering the mail to the firm's attorneys, Martin was anxious to complete his task quickly and accurately. One of ten gofers employed by the firm, Martin was already feeling pressure from his supervisor to pick up his pace. After banging the streets for four months with no weapons other than his B.A. in history from Georgetown, Martin had figured his only recourse was to attend law school. And what better place to plumb the possibilities of such a career than at one of

D.C.'s most prestigious? His endless trek of job interviews had convinced him that it was never too early to commence networking.

He consulted his map with the attorneys' names listed in each square representing that person's office. Martin had grabbed the map from on top of the desk in his cubicle, not noticing the updated version buried under a multinational transaction closing binder that rose five thousand pages high, the indexing and binding of which awaited him that afternoon.

As he rounded the corner he stopped and looked at the closed door. Everyone's door was closed today. He took the Federal Express package and checked the name on the map, and compared that to the scrawled handwriting on the packing label. It matched. He looked at the empty nameplate holder and his eyebrows converged in confusion.

He knocked, waited a moment, knocked again and then opened the door.

He looked around. The place was a mess. Boxes littered the floor, the furniture was in disarray. Some papers lay scattered on the desk. His first instinct was to check with his supervisor. Maybe there was a mistake. He looked at his watch. Already ten minutes late. He grabbed the phone, dialed his supervisor. No answer. Then he saw the photo of the woman on the desk. Tall, auburn-haired, very expensively dressed. Must be the man's office. Probably moving in. Who'd leave a looker like that behind? With that rationale established, Fred carefully laid the package on the desk chair, where it would be sure to be found. He closed the door on his way out.

"I'm sorry about Walter, Sandy. I really am." Jack checked the view across the cityscape. A penthouse apartment in Upper Northwest. The place must have been enormously expensive, and the dollars had continued to flow for the interior design. Everywhere Jack looked were original paintings, soft leather and sculptured stone. He reasoned that the world didn't have many Sandy Lords and they had to live somewhere.

Lord sat by the fire that popped pleasantly in the grate, a loose paisley robe covering his bulky frame, bare feet comforted in leather slippers. A cold rain fell against the broad expanse of windows. Jack drew closer to the fire, his mind appeared to crackle and jump like the flames; a loose ember hit the marble surround, flamed and then quickly disappeared. Jack cradled his drink and looked at his partner.

The phone call hadn't been totally unexpected. "We need to talk, Jack, the sooner the better for me. Not at the office."

When he arrived, Lord's aged valet had taken his coat and gloves and then inconspicuously receded into the farther reaches of the home.

The two men were in Lord's mahogany-paneled study, a luxuriously masculine retreat that Jack felt guiltily envious of. A glimmer of the large stone house briefly came into focus. It had a library, much like this. With an effort he focused on Lord's back.

"I'm kinda fucked, Jack." The first words out of Lord's mouth had the effect of making Jack want to smile. You had to appreciate the man's candor. But he caught himself. The tone in Lord's voice demanded a certain respect.

"The firm'll be okay, Sandy. We're not going to lose many more. So we sublease some space, it's no big deal."

Lord finally stood up and went straight to the well-fed bar in the corner. The shot glass was filled to the rim and downed in a well-practiced motion.

"Excuse me, Jack, maybe I'm not making myself

real clear here. The firm took a blow, but not one that'll send it down for the count. You're right, Patton, Shaw will weather this broadside. But what I'm talking about is whether Patton, Shaw and *Lord* will live to fight another day."

Lord lurched across the room and wearily plunged himself on the burgundy leather couch. Jack traced the column of brass nails as they marched across the outline of the heavy piece. He sipped his drink and studied the wide face. The eyes were narrow, no more than penny-wide slits really.

"You're the firm's leader, Sandy. I don't see that changing, even if your client base took a hit."

Lord groaned from his horizontal perch.

"A hit? A hit? I took a goddamned A-bomb, Jack, right up my ass. The heavyweight champion of the world couldn't have hit me any harder. I'm going down for the count. The buzzards they are a circling, and Lord he is the main course; the stuffed hog with the apple in the mouth and a bull's-eye on the butt."

"Kirksen?"

"Kirksen, Packard, Mullins, fucking Townsend. Keep counting, Jack, the list goes on until you get to the end of the partnership roll. I have, I must admit, a most unusual, hate-hate relationship with my partners."

"But not Graham, Sandy. Not with Graham."

Lord slowly edged himself up, perching on one flabby arm as he looked at Jack.

Jack wondered why he liked the man as much as he did. The answer probably lay somewhere in the lunch at Fillmore's way back when. No bullshit. A real-world baptism where the sting of words made your gut clench and your brain hammer out responses you'd never have the nerve to actually deliver. Now the man was in trouble. Jack had the means to protect him. Or maybe he did; his relationship with the Baldwins right now was far from solid.

"Sandy, if they want to get to you, they'll have to go through me first." There, he had said it. And he meant it. It was also true that Lord had given him his chance to shine with the big boys, thrown him right into the fire. But what other way would you know if you could actually pull it off or not? That experience was also worth something.

"The waters might get a little rocky for both of us, Jack."

"I'm a good swimmer, Sandy. Besides, don't look at this as purely altruistic. You're an investment of the firm in which I'm a partner. You're a top-grade rainmaker. You're down now, but you won't stay down. Five hundred bucks says within twelve months you're back in the number-one slot. I don't intend on letting an asset like that walk away."

"I won't forget this, Jack."

"I won't let you."

After Jack had left, Lord started to pour another drink but stopped. He looked down at his quivering hands and slowly put down the bottle and glass. He made it to the couch before his knees gave out. The federal-style mirror over the fireplace caught his image. It had been twenty years since a single tear had escaped the heavy face. That had been at his mother's passing. But now the outpourings were steadily coming on. He had cried for his friend, Walter Sullivan. For years Lord had duped himself into believing that the man meant nothing more to him than a solid-gold draw check each month. The price for that self-deception had come due at the funeral, where Lord had wept so hard that he had gone back to his car until it was time to go bury his friend.

Now he rubbed at the puffy cheeks once again, pushing away the salty liquid. Fucking young punk.

Lord had planned everything down to the last detail. His pitch would be perfect. He had envisioned every possible response except the one he had gotten. He had mistaken the younger man. Lord assumed that Jack would have done what Lord himself would have done: pressed for every advantage in exchange for the enormous favor being asked.

It wasn't only guilt that pulled at him. It was shame. He realized that as sickness enveloped him and he bent low over the thick, spongy carpet. Shame. He hadn't felt that one for a long time either. When the nausea subsided and he once again looked at the wreck in the mirror, Lord promised himself that he would not disappoint Jack. That he *would* rise back to the top. And he would not forget.

TWENTY-FIVE

Frank had never in his wildest fantasies expected to be sitting here. He looked around and quickly determined that it was indeed oval in shape. The furnishings tended to be solid, conservative, but with a splash of color here, a stripe there, a pair of expensive sneakers placed neatly on a lower shelf, that stated that the room's occupant was not nearly ready for retirement. Frank swallowed hard and willed himself to breathe normally. He was a veteran policeman and this was just another routine inquiry in a series of endless ones. He was just following up a lead, nothing more. A few minutes and he'd be out of here.

But then his brain reminded him that the person he was about to make inquiries of was the current President of the United States. As a new shock wave of nervousness rushed over him the door opened and he quickly stood, turned and stared for a long moment at the extended hand until his mind finally registered and he slowly moved his out to meet it.

'Thank you for coming down into my neck of the woods, Lieutenant."

"No trouble at all, sir. I mean you've got better things to do than sit in traffic. Although I guess you never really sit in traffic, do you, Mr. President?"

Richmond sat behind his desk and motioned for Frank to resume his seat. An impassive Bill Burton, invisible to Frank until that moment, closed the door and inclined his head toward the detective.

"My routes are pretty well laid out in advance, I'm afraid. It's true I don't end up in many traffic jams but it does stifle the hell out of spontaneity." The President grinned and Frank could feel his own mouth automatically turning up into a smile.

The President leaned forward and stared directly at him. He clasped his hands together, his brow wrinkled and he went from jovial to intensely serious in an instant.

"I want to thank you, Seth." He glanced at Burton. "Bill has told me how cooperative you were with the investigation of Christine Sullivan's death. I really appreciate that, Seth. Some officials would have been less than forthcoming or tried to turn it into a media circus for their own personal gain. I hoped for better from you and my expectations were exceeded. Again, thank you."

Frank glowed as though he had been awarded the fourth-grade spelling bee crown.

"It's terrible, you know. Tell me, have you learned of any connection between Walter's suicide and this criminal being gunned down?"

Frank shook the stars from his eyes and his pair of steady eyes came to rest on the chiseled features of the President.

"Come on, Lieutenant. I can tell you that all of official and unofficial Washington is right this very minute savagely attacking the issue of Walter Sullivan having hired an assassin to avenge his wife's death and then taking his own life in the aftermath. You can't stop people from gossiping. I would just like to know if your investigation has led to any fact to substantiate Walter having ordered the killing of his wife's murderer."

"I'm afraid that I really can't say one way or another, sir. I hope you understand, but this is an ongoing police investigation."

"Don't worry, Lieutenant, I'm not treading on your toes. But I can tell you that this has been a particularly distressing time for me. To think Walter Sullivan would end his own life. One of the most brilliant and resourceful men of his era, of any era."

"So I've heard an awful lot of people say."

"But just between you and me, knowing Walter as I did, it would not be out of the realm of possibility that he would have taken precise and concrete steps to have his wife's killer . . . dealt with."

"Alleged killer, Mr. President. Innocent until proven guilty."

The President looked at Burton. "But I was led to understand that your case was pretty much ironclad."

Seth Frank scratched his ear. "Some defense attorneys love ironclad cases, sir. See, you dump enough water on iron, it starts to rust and before you know it, you got holes everywhere."

"And this defense attorney was such a person?"

"And then some. I'm not a betting man, but I would've given us no more than a forty percent shot at getting a clean conviction. We were in for a real battle."

The President sat back as he absorbed this information and then looked back at Frank.

Frank finally noted the expression of expectancy on his face and flipped open his notebook. His heartbeat calmed down as he perused the familiar scribbles.

"Are you aware it was right before his death that Walter Sullivan called you here?"

"I know that I spoke with him. I was not aware that it immediately preceded his death, no."

"I guess I'm a little surprised that you didn't come forward with this information earlier."

The President's face fell. "I know. I guess I'm a little surprised myself. I suppose I believed I was shielding

429

Walter, or at least his memory, from further trauma. Although I knew the police would eventually discover the call was placed. I'm sorry, Lieutenant."

"I need to know the details of that phone conversation."

"Would you like something to drink, Seth?"

"A cup of coffee would be fine, thank you."

As if on cue, Burton picked up a phone in the corner and a minute later a silver-plated coffee tray was delivered in.

The steaming hot coffee was sipped; the President looked at his watch, then saw Frank staring at him.

"I'm sorry, Seth, I *am* treating your visit with the importance it deserves. However, I've got a congressional delegation coming to lunch in a few minutes and quite frankly I'm not looking forward to it. As funny as it sounds, I'm not particularly enamored of politicians."

"I understand. This will only take a few minutes. What was the purpose of the call?"

The President leaned back in his chair as if organizing his thoughts. "I would characterize the call as one of desperation. He was definitely not his usual self. He seemed unbalanced, out of control. For long periods of time he would say nothing. Very unlike the Walter Sullivan I knew."

"What did he talk about?"

"Everything, and nothing. Sometimes he just babbled. He talked about Christine's death. And then about the man, the man you arrested for the murder. How he hated him, how he had destroyed his life. It was truly awful to hear."

"What did you tell him?"

"Well, I kept asking him where he was. I wanted to find him, get him some help. But he wouldn't tell me. I'm not sure he heard a word I said, really, he was that distraught."

"So you think he sounded suicidal, sir?"

"I'm no psychiatrist, Lieutenant, but if I had to make a layman's guess about his mental state, yes, I would definitely say Walter Sullivan sounded suicidal that night. It's one of the few times during my presidency that I felt truly hopeless. Frankly, after the conversation I had with him, I was not surprised to learn that he was dead." Richmond glanced at Burton's impassive face, then looked at the detective. "That's also why I questioned you as to whether you had determined if there was any truth to the rumor that Walter had anything to do with this person being gunned down. After Walter's telephone call I have to admit that the thought certainly crossed my mind."

Frank looked over at Burton. "I suppose you don't have a recording of the conversation? I know that some of the communications here are recorded."

The President answered. "Sullivan called my private line, Lieutenant. It's a secure communication link and no recordings of conversations on that line are allowed."

"I see. Did he directly indicate to you that he was involved in the death of Luther Whitney?"

"Not directly, no. He obviously wasn't thinking clearly. But reading between the lines, the rage that I knew he was feeling – well, and I hate to make this statement of a man who's dead, I think it was pretty clear that he had had the man killed. I have no proof of that of course, but it was my strong impression."

Frank shook his head. "Pretty uncomfortable conversation to have."

"Yes, yes it was very uncomfortable. Now, Lieutenant, I'm afraid that official duty calls."

Frank didn't budge. "Why do you think he called you, sir? And at that time of night?"

The President sat back down, threw another quick glance at Burton. "Walter was one of my closest

431

personal friends. He kept odd hours, but then so do I. It would not be unusual for him to call at that hour. I hadn't heard very much from him for the last few months. As you know, he had been under a considerable personal strain. Walter was the sort to suffer in silence. Now Seth, if you will excuse me."

"It just strikes me as odd that out of all the people he could have called, he called you. I mean, the chances were pretty good that you wouldn't even be here. Presidents' travel schedules are pretty hectic. It makes me wonder what he was thinking."

The President leaned back, placed his fingers together, and studied the ceiling. *Cop wants to play games to show me how smart he is.* He looked back at Frank and smiled. "If I were a mind reader I wouldn't have to rely so heavily on the pollsters."

Frank smiled back. "I don't think you have to be telepathic to know you're going to be occupying that chair for another four years, sir."

"I appreciate that, Lieutenant. All I can tell you is that Walter called me. If he was planning on killing himself, who would he call? His family has been estranged from him since his marriage to Christine. He had many business acquaintances, but few people he would call true friends. Walter and I have known each other for years, and I considered him a surrogate father. I had taken a very active interest in the investigation of his wife's death, as you know. All of that together could explain why he wanted to talk to me, particularly if he was contemplating taking his life. That's really all I know. I'm sorry I can't be of more help."

The door opened. Frank did not see that it was in response to a tiny button on the underside of the President's desk.

The President looked at his secretary. "I'll be right there, Lois. Lieutenant, if there's anything I can do for you, you let Bill know. Please."

Frank closed his notebook. "Thank you, sir."

Richmond stared at the doorway after Frank had departed.

"What was the name of Whitney's attorney, Burton?"

Burton thought for a moment. "Graham. Jack Graham."

"The name sounds familiar."

"Works at Patton, Shaw. He's a partner there."

The President's eyes froze on the agent's face.

"What's the matter?"

"I'm not sure." Richmond unlocked a drawer in his desk and took out a notebook he had compiled on this little extracurricular matter. "Don't lose sight of the fact, Burton, that one very important piece of incriminating evidence, for which we happened to have paid five million dollars, has never turned up."

The President flipped through the pages of his notebook. There were numerous individuals involved, to various degrees, in their little drama. If Whitney had given his attorney the letter opener along with an account of what had happened, the whole world would've known by now. Richmond thought back to the awards ceremony for Ransome Baldwin at the White House. Graham was clearly no shrinking violet. Clearly he didn't have it. But then who, if anyone, would Whitney have given it to?

As his mind spun out neat blocks of analysis and possible scenarios, one name suddenly stood out at the President from within the lines of precise writing. One person who had never really been accounted for.

Jack cradled the carry-out in one arm, his briefcase in the other, and managed to wiggle the key out of his pocket. Before he could put it in the lock, though, the door opened.

Jack looked surprised. "I didn't expect you home yet."

"You didn't have to stop. I could've made something."

Jack went inside, dropped his briefcase on the coffee table and headed to the kitchen. Kate stared after him.

"Hey, you work all day too. Why should you have to cook?"

"Women do it every day, Jack. Just look around."

He emerged from the kitchen. "No argument there. You want sweet and sour or moo goo gai pan? I got extra spring rolls too."

"Whichever you don't want. I'm not that hungry really."

He withdrew and came back with two fully stocked plates.

"You know if you don't eat more you're going to blow away. I half feel like stuffing rocks in your pockets as it is now."

He sat cross-legged next to her on the floor. She picked at her plate while he devoured his.

"So how was work? You know you probably could have stood to take a few more days off. You're always pushing yourself too hard."

"Look who's talking." She picked up a spring roll and then put it back down.

He put down his fork and looked over at her.

"So I'm listening."

She pulled herself up onto the couch and sat there playing with her necklace. Still dressed in her work clothes, she looked exhausted, like a flower collapsed in the wind.

"I think a lot about what I did to Luther."

"Kate—"

"Jack, let me finish." Her voice snapped at him like a whip. In an instant her features relaxed. She continued more calmly. "I've come to decide that I'm never going to get over it, so I might as well accept that fact. Maybe what I did wasn't wrong for a lot of reasons. But it was definitely wrong for at least one reason. He was my father. As lame as that might sound, it should've been a good enough reason." She twisted her necklace some more until it congealed into a series of tiny clumps. "I think being a lawyer, at least the kind of lawyer I am, has made me become someone I don't really like a lot. That's not a real good revelation to arrive at when you're hitting thirty."

Jack reached out his hand to stop hers from shaking. She didn't move it. He could feel the blood pumping through the veins.

"With all that said, I think I'm due for a radical change. In my life, my career, everything."

"What are you talking about?" He got up and sat down beside her. His pulse had accelerated as he anticipated the line she was taking.

"I'm not going to be a prosecutor anymore, Jack. In fact I'm not going to be a lawyer anymore. I submitted my resignation this morning. I have to admit, they were pretty shocked. Told me to think about it. I told them I already had. As much as I'm going to."

The incredulity was stiff in his voice. "You quit your job? Jesus, Kate, you've put a helluva lot into your career. You can't just throw that away."

She suddenly rose and stood by the window, looking out.

"That's just it, Jack. I'm not throwing anything away. My memories of what I've done for the last four years add up to about a lifetime of horror films. That's not exactly what I had in mind sitting in Con

Law as a first-year debating grand principles of justice."

"Don't sell yourself short. The streets are a heckuva lot safer because of what you've done."

She turned to look at him. "I'm not even stemming the flow anymore. I got washed out to sea a long time ago."

"But what are you going to do? You're a lawyer."

"No. You're wrong. I've only been a lawyer a tiny fraction of my life. My life before that time I liked a whole lot better." She stopped and stared at him, her arms folded across her chest. "You made that very clear to me, Jack. I became a lawyer to pay back my father. Three years of school and four years of no life outside a courtroom is a pretty big price." A deep sigh emerged from her throat, her body teetered for a moment before she regained her composure. "Besides, I guess I really paid him back now."

"Kate, it wasn't your fault, none of it." His mouth stopped moving as she turned away from him.

Her next words rocked him.

"I'm going to move away, Jack. I'm not exactly sure where yet. I've got a little money saved. The Southwest sounds nice. Or maybe Colorado. I want as different from here as I can get. Maybe that's a start."

"Moving." Jack said the word more to himself than to her. "Moving." He repeated the word as if both trying to make it go away and trying to dissect and interpret it in a manner that was not as painful as it felt at the moment.

She looked down at her hands. "There's nothing keeping me here, Jack."

He looked at her and he more felt than heard the angry response rush past his lips.

"Goddamn you! How dare you say that?"

436

She finally looked at him. He could almost see the crack in her voice as she spoke. "I think you better leave."

Jack sat at his desk unwilling to face the mounds of work, the small mountain of pink messages, wondering if his life could possibly get any worse. That's when Dan Kirksen walked in. Jack inwardly groaned.

"Dan, I really don't—"

"You weren't at the partners meeting this morning."

"Well, no one told me we were having one."

"A memo was sent around, but then your office hours have been somewhat erratic of late." He looked disapprovingly at the shambles of Jack's desk. His own was unfailingly in pristine condition; more a testament to how little actual legal work he did than anything else.

"I'm here now."

"I understand you and Sandy met at his house."

Jack eyed him keenly. "I guess nothing's private anymore."

Kirksen flushed angrily. "Partnership matters should be discussed by the full partnership. What we don't need are factions developing that will decimate this firm any more than it already has been."

Jack almost laughed out loud. Dan Kirksen, the undisputed king of the faction-builders.

"I think we've seen the worst."

"Do you, Jack? Do you really?" Kirksen sneered. "I didn't know you had so much experience with this sort of thing."

"Well, if it bothers you so much, Dan, why don't you leave?"

The sneer quickly evaporated from the little man's face. "I've been with this firm for almost twenty years."

"Sounds like it's about time for a change then. Might do you good."

Kirksen sat down, removed a smudge from his glasses. "Piece of friendly advice, Jack. Don't throw your lot in with Sandy. If you do that, you'll be making a big mistake. He's through."

"Thanks for the advice."

"I'm serious, Jack, don't endanger your own position in some futile, however well-intentioned attempt to salvage him."

"Endanger my position? You mean the Baldwins' position, don't you?"

"They're your client . . . for now."

"Are you contemplating a change at the helm? If you are, good luck. You'd last about a minute."

Kirksen stood up. "Nothing is forever, Jack. Sandy Lord can tell you that as well as anybody. What goes around comes around. You can burn bridges in this town, you just have to make sure there's no one left alive on those bridges."

Jack came around the desk, towering over Kirksen. "Were you like this as a little boy, Dan, or did you just turn into a fungus during your adulthood?"

Kirksen smiled and started to leave. "Like I said, you never know, Jack. Client relationships are always so tenuous. Take yours, for example. It's primarily based on your future nuptials with Jennifer Ryce Baldwin. Now, if Ms. Baldwin happened to find out, for instance, that you had not been going home at night, but, instead, had been sharing quarters with a certain young woman, she might be less inclined to refer legal business to you, much less become your wife."

It only took an instant. Kirksen's back was flat against the wall and Jack was so close in his face the man's glasses were fogged.

"Don't do anything foolish, Jack. Regardless of

your status here, the partnership would not look kindly on a junior partner assaulting a senior one. We still have standards here at Patton, Shaw."

"Don't ever fuck with my life like that, Kirksen. Don't ever." Jack effortlessly threw him against the door and turned back to his desk.

Kirksen smoothed down his shirt and smiled to himself. So easily manipulated. The big, tall good-looking ones. As strong as mules and no smarter. About as sophisticated as a brick.

"You know, Jack, you should realize what you've gotten yourself into. For some reason you seem to implicitly trust Sandy Lord. Did he tell you the truth about Barry Alvis? Did he happen to do that, Jack?"

Jack turned slowly back around and stared dully at the man.

"Did he use the permanent-associate, no-rain-making-capabilities line? Or did he tell you Alvis had screwed up a big project?"

Jack continued to look at him.

Kirksen smiled triumphantly.

"One phone call, Jack. Daughter calls complaining that Mr. Alvis had inconvenienced her and her father. And Barry Alvis disappears. It's just the way the game works, Jack. Maybe you don't want to play that game. If you don't there's no one stopping *you* from leaving."

Kirksen had been crafting this strategy for a while now. With Sullivan gone, he could promise Baldwin that his work would be the firm's top priority, and Kirksen still had the core of one of the best army of attorneys in the city. And four million dollars of legal business coupled with his own existing business would make him the largest rainmaker at the place. And the name Kirksen would finally go on the door, in substitution for another that would be unceremoniously dropped.

The managing partner smiled at Jack. "You may not like me, Jack, but I'm telling you the truth. You're a big boy, it's up to you to deal with it."

Kirksen closed the door behind him.

Jack stood for a second longer and then collapsed back into his chair. He lunged forward, scattered his desk clear with quick, violent thrusts of his arms, and then slowly laid his head down on its surface.

TWENTY-SIX

Seth Frank looked at the old man. Short, with a soft felt cap covering his head, dressed in corduroy pants, a thick sweater and winter boots, the man looked both uncomfortable and greatly excited at being in the police station. In his hand was a rectangular object covered in brown paper.

"I'm not sure I understand, Mr. Flanders."

"You see I was out there. At the courthouse that day. You know, when the man got killed. Just went to see what all the fuss was about. Lived here all my life, nothing ever came close to that spectacle, I can tell you that."

"I can understand that," Frank said dryly.

"So anyway I had my new Camcorder, real nifty thing, got an image screen and all. Just hold, look at it and shoot. Great quality. So the wife said I should come down."

"That's terrific, Mr. Flanders. And the purpose of all this?" Frank looked at him inquiringly.

Realization spread over Flanders's features. "Oh. I'm sorry, Lieutenant. I'm standing here rambling, have a tendency to do that, just ask the missus. Retired for a year. Never talked much at work. Assembly line at a processing plant. Like to talk now. Listen too. Spend a lot of time down at that little café over behind the bank. Good coffee and the muffins are the real thing, no low-fat stuff."

Frank looked exasperated.

Flanders hurried on. "Well, I came down here to show you this. Give it to you, really. Kept a copy for myself of course." He handed across the package.

Frank opened it and looked at the videocassette. Flanders took off his cap, revealing a bald head with cottony tufts of hair clustered around his ears. He went on excitedly, "Got some really good shots, like I said. Like of the President and right when that fella was shot. Got all that. Jesus, did I. I was following the President, you see. Ran me right into all the fireworks."

Frank stared at the man.

"It's all there, Lieutenant. For what it's worth." He looked at his watch. "Huh. I gotta go. Late for my lunch. Wife doesn't like that." He turned to leave. Seth Frank stared down at the cassette.

"Oh, Lieutenant. One more thing."

"Yes?"

"If anything were to come from my tape, do you think they might use my name when they write about it?"

Frank shook his head. "Write about it?"

The old man looked excited. "Yeah. You know, the historians. They'd call it the Flanders Tape, wouldn't they, or something like that. The Flanders Video maybe. You know, like before."

Frank wearily rubbed his temples. "Like before?"

"Yeah, Lieutenant. You know, like Zapruder with Kennedy."

Frank's face finally sagged in recognition. "I'll be sure to let them know, Mr. Flanders. Just in case. For posterity."

"There you go." Flanders pointed a happy finger at him. "Posterity, I like that. Have a good one, Lieutenant."

"Alan?"

Richmond absently motioned for Russell to come in and then looked down once again at the notebook in front of him. Finished, he closed it and looked at his Chief of Staff; his stare was impassive.

Russell hesitated, studying the carpet, her hands clasped nervously in front of her. Then she hurried across the room and fell rather than sat in one of the chairs.

"I'm not sure what to say to you, Alan. I realize my behavior was inexcusable, absolutely inappropriate. If I could plead temporary insanity I would."

"So you're not going to attempt to explain it away as being somehow in my best interests?" Richmond sat back in his chair; his eyes remained on Russell.

"No, I'm not. I'm here to offer my resignation."

The President smiled. "Perhaps I did under-estimate you, Gloria."

He stood up, went around the desk and leaned against it, facing her. "On the contrary, your behavior was absolutely appropriate. If I had been in your position I would've done the same thing."

She looked up at him. Her face betrayed her astonishment. "Don't misunderstand me, I expect loyalty, Gloria, like any leader. I do not, however, expect human beings to be anything more than that, meaning human, with all their associated weaknesses and survival instincts. We are, after all, animals. I have attained my position in life by never losing sight of the fact that the most important person in the world is myself. Whatever the situation, whatever the obstacle, I have never, *never* lost sight of that one simple truism. What you did that night displays that you also share that belief."

"You know what I intended?"

"Of course I do. Gloria, I don't condemn you for taking a situation and attempting to maximize its beneficial effect on you. My God, that's the basis upon which this country and this city in particular are built."

"But when Burton told you—"

Richmond held up one hand. "I admit I felt certain emotions that night. Betrayal perhaps foremost among them. But in the time since, I have concluded that what you did evidenced strength, not weakness, of character."

Russell struggled to see where this was going. "Then may I correctly assume that you do not want my resignation?"

The President bent forward, took one of her hands. "I can't recall you ever mentioning the word, Gloria. I can't imagine breaking up our relationship after we've come to know each other so well. Shall we leave it at that?"

Russell rose to go. The President went back to his desk.

"Oh, Gloria. I do have a number of things I want to go over with you tonight. The family's out of town. So perhaps we can work in my private quarters."

Russell looked back at him.

"It might be a late night, Gloria. Better bring a change of clothes." The President didn't smile. His stare cut right through her, than he went back to his work.

Russell's hand trembled as she closed the door.

Jack pounded on the door so hard he could feel the thick, polished wood cut into his knuckles.

The housekeeper opened the door but Jack shot through before she could say a word.

Jennifer Baldwin swept down the curved staircase and into the marbled entrance foyer. Dressed in yet another expensive evening gown, her hair tumbled down her shoulders framing her significant cleavage. She was not smiling.

"Jack, what are you doing here?"

"I want to talk to you."

"Jack, I have plans. This will have to wait."

"*No!*" He grabbed her hand, looked around, pushed open a pair of carved doors and pulled her into the library, shutting the doors behind them.

She jerked her hand free. "Are you insane, Jack?"

He looked around the room with its huge bookcases and well-fed shelves of gilt-edged first editions. All for show, none of them had probably ever been opened. All for show.

"I've got one simple question for you to answer and then I'll leave."

"Jack—"

"*One question*. And then I'll leave."

She eyed him suspiciously, crossed her arms. "What is it?"

"Did you or did you not call my firm and tell them to fire Barry Alvis because he made me work the night we were at the White House?"

"Who told you that?"

"Just answer the question, Jenn."

"Jack, why is this so important to you?"

"So you did have him fired?"

"Jack, I want you to stop thinking about that and start realizing the kind of future we're going to have together. If we—"

"Answer the goddamned question!"

She exploded. "*Yes!* Yes, I had the little shit fired. So what? He deserved it. He treated you as an inferior. And he was dead wrong. He was nothing. He played with fire and he got burned and I don't feel the least bit sorry for him." She looked at him without a trace of remorse.

Having heard the answer he expected to hear, Jack sat down in a chair and stared at the massive desk at the other end of the room. The high-backed, leather

445

desk chair faced away from them. He looked at the original oils adorning the walls, the huge windows with perfectly pooled flowing drapes that probably cost more than he could even guess, the ornate woodwork, the omnipresent sculptures of metal and marble. The ceiling with yet another legion of medieval characters marching across it. The world of the Baldwins. Well, they were welcome to it. He slowly closed his eyes.

Jennifer swept back her hair, looked at him, more than a hint of anxiousness in her eyes. She vacillated for a moment and then went to him, knelt beside him, touched his shoulder. The scent of her perfumed body cascaded over him. She spoke low, close to his face. Her breath tickled his ear.

"Jack, I told you before, you don't have to put up with that sort of behavior. And now that this ridiculous murder case is out of the way we can go on with our lives. Our house is almost ready, it's gorgeous, it really is. And we have wedding plans to finalize. Sweetheart, now everything can go back to normal." She touched his face, turned it toward hers. She looked at him with her best pair of bedroom eyes and then she kissed him, long and deeply, letting her lips pull back slowly from his. Her eyes quickly searched his. She didn't find what she was looking for.

"You're right, Jenn. The ridiculous murder case is over. A man I respected and cared for got his brains blown apart. Case closed, time to move on. Got a fortune to build."

"You know what I mean. You never should have involved yourself in that thing in the first place. It wasn't your problem. If you would just open your eyes you'd realize that all of that was beneath you, Jack."

"And hardly convenient for you, right?"

Jack abruptly stood up. He was more exhausted than anything else.

"Have a great life, Jenn. I'd say I'd see you around but I really can't imagine that happening." He started to leave.

She grabbed his sleeve. "Jack, will you please tell me what I did that was so awful?"

He hesitated and then confronted her.

"The fact that you even have to ask. Jesus Christ!" He shook his head wearily. "You took a man's life, Jenn, a man you didn't even know, and you destroyed it. And why did you do that? Because something he did to me 'inconvenienced' you. So you took ten years' worth of a career and wiped it out. With one phone call. Never thinking about what it would do to him, his family. He could've blown his brains out, his wife could have divorced him for all you know. You didn't care about that. You probably never even thought about that. And the bottom line is I could never love, I could never spend my life with someone who could do something like that. If you can't understand that, if you really think what you did wasn't wrong, then that's all the more reason why we need to say good-bye right now. We might as well flesh out the irreconcilable differences *before* the wedding. Saves everybody a lot of time and trouble."

He turned the handle on the door and smiled. "Everybody I know would probably tell me how crazy I am for doing this. That you're the perfect woman, smart, rich, beautiful — and you are all of those things, Jenn. They'd say we'd have a perfect life together. That we'd have everything. How could we not be happy? But the thing is, I wouldn't make you happy because I don't care about the things you do. I don't care about the millions in legal business, or houses the size of apartment buildings or cars that cost a year's salary. I don't like this house, I don't like your lifestyle, I don't like your friends. And I guess the bottom line is, I don't like you. And right now I'm probably the only man on the planet who would say that. But I'm a pretty simple guy, Jenn, and the one thing I'd never do to you is lie. And let's face it, in a couple of days, about a dozen guys a lot better suited to you than Jack Graham are going to be knocking on your door. You won't be lonely."

He looked at her and felt a grimace of pain as he observed the absolute astonishment on her face.

"For what it's worth, anybody who asks, you dumped me. Not up to the Baldwin standard. Unworthy. Good-bye, Jenn."

She still stood there several minutes after he left. A series of emotions competed for space across her face, none, in the end, winning out. Finally she fled the room. The sounds of her high heels against the marble floor disappeared as she hurried up the carpeted stairs.

For a few seconds more the library was quiet. Then the desk chair swung around and Ransome Baldwin eyed the doorway where his daughter had been standing.

Jack checked the peephole, half-expecting to see Jennifer Baldwin standing there with a gun. His eyebrows raised a notch when he saw who it was.

Seth Frank walked in, shrugged off his coat, and looked around appreciatively at Jack's cluttered little apartment.

"Man, this brings back memories of another time in my life, I can tell you."

"Let me guess. Delta House '75. You were vice president in charge of bar operations."

Frank grinned. "Closer to the truth than I'd care to admit. Enjoy it while you can, my friend. Without meaning to sound politically incorrect, a good woman will not allow you to continue such an existence."

"Then I might be in luck."

Jack disappeared into the kitchen and came back with a brace of Sam Adamses.

They settled into the furniture with their drinks.

"Trouble in wedded-bliss-to-be-land, counselor?"

"On a scale of one to ten, a one or a ten depending on your perspective."

"Why am I thinking that it's not the Baldwin gal that's entirely gotten to you?"

"Don't you ever stop being a detective?"

"Not if I can help it. You want to talk about it?"

Jack shook his head. "I might bend your ear another night, but not tonight."

Frank shrugged. "Just let me know, I'll bring the beer."

Jack noticed the package on Frank's lap. "Present?"

Frank took out the tape. "I'm assuming you've got a VCR under some of this junk?"

As the video came on Frank looked at Jack.

"Jack, this is definitely not G-rated. And I'm telling you up front, it shows everything including what happened to Luther. You up to it?"

Jack paused for a moment. "You think we might see something in here that'll catch whoever did it?"

"That's what I'm hoping. You knew him a lot better than I did. Maybe you'll see something I don't."

"Then I'm up to it."

Even forewarned, Jack was not prepared. Frank watched him closely as the moment grew closer. When the shot rang out he saw Jack involuntarily jerk back, his eyes wide in horror.

Frank cut off the video. "Hang in there, I warned you." Jack was slumped over in his chair. His breathing was irregular, his forehead clammy. His entire body shuddered for an instant and then he slowly came around. He wiped his forehead.

"Jesus Christ!"

Flanders's passing remark to the Kennedy example had not been inappropriate. "We can stop right now, Jack."

Jack's lips set in a firm line. "The hell we can!"

Jack hit the rewind one more time. They had gone through the tape about a dozen times now. Watching his friend's head virtually explode was not getting any easier to watch. The only mitigating factor was that Jack's anger was increasing with each viewing.

Frank shook his head. "You know it's too bad the guy wasn't filming the other way. We might've gotten a flash from the shooter. I guess that would've been too easy. Hey, you got any coffee? I have a hard time thinking without caffeine."

"Got some pretty fresh stuff in the pot, you can bring me a cup. Dishes are over the sink."

When Frank returned with the steaming cups, Jack had rewound the tape to a demonstrative Alan Richmond saying his piece on the impromptu stage outside the courthouse.

"That guy's a dynamo."

Frank looked at the screen. "I met him the other day."

"Yeah? Me too. That was in my I'm-marrying-into-the-rich-and-famous-set days."

"What'd you think of the guy?"

Jack gulped his coffee, reached for a bag of peanut butter crackers that lay on the couch, offered one to Frank, who took it and then put his feet up on the rickety coffee table. The detective was slipping easily back into the less-structured domain of bachelorhood.

Jack shrugged. "I don't know. I mean, he's the President. I always thought he was presidential. What do you think of him?"

"Smart. Really smart. The kind of smart you want to be real careful not to get into a battle of wits with unless you're real sure about your own abilities."

"I guess it's a good thing he's on America's side."

"Yeah." Frank looked back at the screen. "So anything grab your eye?"

Jack punched a button on the remote. "One thing. Check this out." The video leapt forward. The figures jerked around like actors in a silent movie.

"Watch this."

The screen showed Luther stepping out of the van. His eyes were turned toward the ground; the manacles were obviously making it difficult for him to walk. Suddenly, a column of people moved into the video, led by the President. Luther was partially obscured. Jack froze the frame.

"Look."

Frank scrutinized the screen, absently munching peanut butter crackers and draining his coffee. He shook his head.

Jack looked at him. "Look at Luther's face. You can see it right between the suits. Look at his face."

Frank bent forward, almost touching the screen with his face. He recoiled, his eyes wide.

"Damn, looks like he's saying something."

"No, it looks like he's saying something to somebody."

Frank looked across at Jack. "You're saying he's recognized somebody, like maybe the guy who popped him?"

"Under the circumstances, I don't think he'd just be making casual conversation with some stranger."

Frank looked back at the screen, studying it intently. Finally he shook his head. "We're going to

451

need some special talents on this." He rose. "Come on."

Jack grabbed his coat. "Where to?"

Frank smiled as he rewound the tape and then put on his hat.

"Well, first I'm gonna buy us some dinner. I'm married, and I'm also older and fatter than you. Consequently, crackers for dinner don't cut it. Then we're going down to the station. I've got somebody I want you to meet."

Two hours later Seth Frank and Jack walked into the Middleton police station, their bellies lined with surf and turf and a couple slices of pecan pie. Laura Simon was in the lab; the equipment was already set up.

After introductions, Laura popped the tape in. The images sprung to life on a forty-six-inch screen in the corner of the lab. Frank fast-forwarded to the appropriate spot.

"There," Jack pointed. "Right there."

Frank froze the tape.

Laura sat at a keyboard and typed in a series of commands. On the screen, the part of the frame containing Luther's image was blocked out and then magnified in increasingly large degrees, like a balloon being blown up. This process continued until Luther's face seemed to span the entire forty-six inches.

"That's as far as I can take it." Laura spun her chair around and nodded to Frank. He pushed a button on the remote and the screen again came to life.

The audio was choppy; screams, shouts, traffic noise and the blended sounds of hundreds of people served to make what Luther was saying incomprehensible. They watched as his lips moved open and closed.

"He's pissed. Whatever he's saying he is not

452

happy." Frank pulled out a cigarette, got a dirty look from Simon and put it back in his pocket.

"Anybody read lips?" Laura looked at each of them.

Jack stared at the screen. What the hell was Luther saying? The look on his face. Jack had seen that once before, if he could only remember when. It had been recently, he was sure of it.

"You see something we don't?" Frank asked. Jack looked over to see Frank staring at him.

Jack shook his head, rubbed his face. "I don't know. There's something there, I just can't place it."

Frank nodded to Simon to cut off the equipment. He stood up and stretched. "Well, sleep on it. Anything comes to you, let me know. Thanks for coming in, Laura."

The two men walked out together. Frank glanced over at Jack, then reached across and felt behind his neck. "Jesus, you are a stress grenade ready to explode."

"Christ, I don't know why I should be. The woman I was supposed to marry I'm not, the woman I wanted to marry just told me to get out of her life, and I'm reasonably sure I'm not going to have a job in the morning. Oh, not to mention, someone murdered a person I cared a lot about and we're probably never going to find out who it is. Hell, my life couldn't get any more perfect, could it?"

"Well, maybe you're due for some good luck."

Jack unlocked his Lexus. "Yeah, hey if you know anyone who wants an almost-brand-new car, let me know."

Frank's eyes twinkled as he looked at Jack. "Sorry, nobody I know could afford it."

Jack smiled back. "Me either."

Driving back, Jack looked at his car clock. It was

almost midnight. He passed the offices of Patton, Shaw, looked up at the stretch of darkened offices and wheeled his car around, turning into the garage. He slid his security card in, waved to the security camera posted outside the garage door, and a few minutes later was in the elevator heading up.

He didn't know exactly why he was here. His days at Patton, Shaw were now clearly numbered. Without Baldwin as a client, Kirksen would ride him out on a rail. He felt a little sorry for Lord. He had promised the man protection. But he wasn't going to marry Jennifer Baldwin simply to ensure Lord's mammoth draw check. And the man had lied to him about Barry Alvis's departure from the firm. But Lord would land on his feet. Jack hadn't been kidding about his faith in the man's resiliency. A number of firms would snap him up in a New York minute. Lord's future was far more assured than Jack's.

The elevator doors opened and Jack stepped into the firm's lobby. The wall lights were on low and the shadowy effect would have been a little unnerving if he hadn't been so completely preoccupied with his thoughts. He walked down the hallway toward his office, stopped at the kitchen and grabbed a glass of soda. Ordinarily, even at midnight, there were a few people beating their brains out over some impossible deadline. Tonight there was only stone-cold silence.

Jack turned on his light and closed his office door. He looked around at the domain of his personal partnership. His kingdom, if only for another day. It was impressive. The furniture was tastefully expensive, the carpet and wall coverings luxurious. He went down his line of diplomas. Some hard-earned, others freebies that you got for just being a lawyer. He noticed that the scattered papers had been picked up, the work of the meticulous and sometimes overzealous cleaning crew who were used to attorney sloppiness and the occasional full-blown tantrum.

He sat down, leaned back in his chair. The soft leather was more comfortable than his bed. He could visualize Jennifer talking with her father. Ransome Baldwin's face would flame red at what he would perceive as an unforgivable insult to his precious little girl. The man would lift the phone tomorrow morning and Jack's corporate career would be over.

And Jack couldn't have cared less. His only regret was not instigating that result sooner. Hopefully PD would take him back. That was where he belonged anyway. No one could stop him from doing that. No, his real troubles had started when he had tried being something and someone he wasn't. He would never make that mistake again.

His attention shifted to Kate. Where would she go? Had she really been serious about quitting her job? Jack recalled the fatalistic look on her face and concluded that, yes, she had been quite serious. He had pleaded with her once more. Just like four years before. Pleaded with her not to go, not to leave his life again. But there was something there he could not break through. Maybe it was the enormous guilt she carried. Maybe she simply did not love him. Had he ever really addressed that possibility? The fact was he hadn't. Consciously had not. The possible answer scared the hell out of him. But what did it matter now?

Luther dead; Kate leaving. His life hadn't really changed all that much, despite all the recent activity. The Whitneys were finally, irreversibly, gone from him.

He looked at the pink pile of messages on his desk. All routine. Then he hit a button on his phone to check his voice mail, which he hadn't done in a couple of days. Patton, Shaw let their clients have their choice of the antiquated written phone message or the technologically advanced voice mail. The more demanding clients loved the latter. At least then they didn't have to wait to scream at you.

There were two calls from Tarr Crimson. He would find Tarr another lawyer. Patton, Shaw was too expensive for him anyway. There were several Baldwin-related matters. Right. Those could wait for the next guy Jennifer Baldwin set her laser sights on. The last message jolted him. It was a woman's voice. Small, hesitant, elderly, clearly uncomfortable with the concept of voice mail. Jack played it back again.

"Mr. Graham, you don't know me. My name is Edwina Broome. I was a friend of Luther Whitney." Broome? The name was familiar. The message continued. "Luther told me that if anything happened to him I was to wait a little bit and then I was to send the package on to you. He told me not to open it and I didn't. He said it was like a Pandora's box. If you looked you might get hurt. God rest his soul, he was a good man, Luther was. I hadn't heard from you, not that I expected to. But it just occurred to me that I should call and make sure that you got the thing. I've never had to send something like that before, over-night delivery they call it. And I think I did it right, but I don't know. If you didn't get it, please call me. Luther said it was very important. And Luther never said anything that wasn't true."

Jack listened to the phone number and wrote it down. He checked the time of the call. Yesterday morning. He quickly searched his office. There was no package lurking there. He jogged down the hallway to his secretary's workstation. There was no package there either. He went back to his office. *My God, a package from Luther. Edwina Broome?* He put his hand through his hair, assaulted his scalp, forced himself to think. Suddenly the name came to him. The mother of the woman who had killed herself.

456

Frank had told him about her. Luther's alleged partner.

Jack picked up the phone. It seemed to ring for an eternity.

"H–hello?" The voice was sleepy, distant.

"Mrs. Broome? This is Jack Graham. I'm sorry for calling you so late."

"Mr. Graham?" The voice was no longer sleepy. It was alert, sharp. Jack could almost envision her sitting up in bed, clutching at her nightgown, looking anxiously at the phone receiver.

"I'm sorry, I just got your message. I didn't get the package, Mrs. Broome. When did you send it?"

"Let me think for a minute." Jack could hear the labored breathing. "Why it was five days ago, counting today."

Jack thought furiously. "Do you have the receipt with a number on it?"

"The man gave me a piece of paper. I'll have to go get it."

"I'll wait."

He tapped his fingers against his desk, tried to stop his mind from flying apart. *Just hold on, Jack. Just hold on*.

"I've got it right here, Mr. Graham."

"Please call me Jack. Did you send it by Federal Express?"

"That's right. Yes."

"All right, what's the tracking number?"

"The what?"

"I'm sorry. The number on the upper-right-hand corner of the piece of paper. It should be a long series of numbers."

"Oh yes." She gave it to him. He scribbled the numbers down, read them back to her to confirm it. He also had her confirm the address of the law firm.

"Jack, is this very serious? I mean Luther dying the way he did and all."

"Has anyone called you, anyone you don't know? Besides me?"

"No."

"Well, if they do I want you to call Seth Frank, Middleton police department."

"I know him."

"He's a good guy, Mrs. Broome. You can trust him."

"All right, Jack."

He hung up and phoned Federal Express. He could hear the computer keys clicking on the other end of the line.

The female voice was professional and concise. "Yes, Mr. Graham, it was delivered at the law offices of Patton, Shaw & Lord on Thursday at ten-oh-two A.M. and signed for by a Ms. Lucinda Alvarez."

"Thank you. I guess it's around here somewhere." Bewildered, he was about to hang up.

"Has there been some special problem with this package delivery, Mr. Graham?"

Jack looked puzzled. "Special problem? No, why?"

"Well, when I pulled up the delivery history of this package it shows that we already had an inquiry about it earlier today."

Jack's whole body tensed. "Earlier today? What time?"

"Six-thirty P.M."

"Did they leave a name?"

"Well, that's the unusual part. According to my records, that person also identified himself as Jack Graham." Her tone made it clear she was far from certain of Jack's real identity.

Jack felt a chill invade every part of his body.

He slowly hung up the phone. Somebody else was very interested in this package, whatever it was. And someone knew it was coming to him. His hands were shaking as he picked up the phone again. He quickly dialed Seth Frank, but the detective had gone home. The person would not give out Frank's home phone, and Jack had left that number back at his apartment. After some prodding by Jack the person tried the detective's home, but there was no answer. He swore under his breath. A quick call to directory assistance was useless; the home number was nonpub.

Jack leaned back in his chair, the breaths coming a little more rapidly. He felt his chest where his heart suddenly threatened to explode through his shirt. He had always considered himself a possessor of above-average courage. Now he wasn't so sure.

He forced himself to focus. The package had been delivered. Lucinda had signed for it. The routine at Patton, Shaw was precise; mail was vitally important to law firms. All overnight packages would be given to the firm's in-house gofer team to be distributed with the day's other mail. They brought it around in a cart. They all knew where Jack's office was. Even if they didn't, the firm printed out a map that was routinely updated. So long as you used the correct map . . .

Jack raced to the door, flung it open and sprinted down the hallway. Completely unbeknownst to him, around the corner, in the opposite direction, a light had just come on in Sandy Lord's office.

Jack clicked on the light in his old office and the room quickly came into focus. He frantically searched the desktop, then pulled out the chair to sit down and his eyes came to rest on the package. Jack picked it up. He instinctively looked around, noted the open blinds and hurriedly shut them.

He read the package label: Edwina Broome to Jack Graham. This was it. The package was boxy, but light. It was a box within a box, that's what she had said. He started to open it, then stopped. They knew the package had been delivered here. *They?* That was the only label he could think to apply. If *they* knew the package was here, had in fact called about it this very day, what would they do? If whatever was inside was that important and it had already been opened, presumably they would already know about it. Since that hadn't happened, what would they do?

Jack sprinted back down the hallway to his office, the package held tightly under his arm. He flung on his coat, grabbed his car keys off his desk, almost knocking over his half-empty glass of soda, and turned to go out. He stopped cold.

A noise. He couldn't tell from where; the sound seemed to echo softly down the hallway, like water lapping through a tunnel. It wasn't the elevator. He was sure he would have heard the elevator. But would he really? It was a big place. The background noise produced by that mode of transportation was so everyday, would he have even noticed it? And he had been on the phone, all his attention had been so concentrated. The truth was he couldn't be sure. Besides it might just be one of the firm's attorneys, dropping in to work or pick up something. All his instincts told him that conclusion was the wrong one. But this was a secure building. But then again, how secure could any public building be? He softly closed his office door.

There it was again. His ears strained to pick up its location without success. Whoever it was, they were moving slowly, stealthily. No one who worked here would do that. He inched over to the wall and turned off the light, waited for an instant and then carefully opened the door.

He peered out. The hallway was clear. But for how long? His tactical problem was obvious. The firm's office space was configured such that if he started down one way he was more or less committed to that path. And he would be totally exposed, the hallways were absolutely devoid of furnishings. If he met whoever it was going that way, he wouldn't have a chance.

A practical consideration struck him and he looked around the darkness of his office. His gaze finally fell upon a heavy, granite paperweight, one of the many knickknacks he had received upon making partner. It could do some real damage if wielded properly. And Jack was confident he could do so. If he was going down he wouldn't make it easy for them. That fatalist approach helped to stiffen his resolve and he waited another few seconds before venturing out into the hallway, closing the door behind him. Whoever it was probably would have to make a door-to-door search to find his office.

He crouched low as he came to a corner. Now he desperately wished the office was in total darkness. He took a deep breath and peered around. The way was clear, at least for now. He thought quickly. If there was more than one intruder, they would probably split up, cut their search time in half. Would they even know if he was in the building? Maybe he had been followed here. That thought was especially troubling. They might even at this moment be circling him, coming from both ways.

The sounds were closer now. Footsteps – he could make out at least one pair. His hearing was now raised to its highest level of acuteness. He could almost make out the person's breathing, or at least he imagined he could. He had to make a choice. And his eyes finally fell upon something on the wall, something that gleamed back at him: the fire alarm.

As he was about to make a run for it, a leg came around the corner at the other end of the hallway. Jack jerked back, not waiting for the rest of the body to catch up with the limb. He walked as swiftly as he could in the opposite direction. He turned the corner, made his way down the hall, and came to a stairwell door. He jerked it open and a loud creak hit him full in the face.

He heard the sounds of running feet.

"Shit!" Jack slammed the door closed behind him and clattered down the stairs.

A man hurtled around the corner. A black ski mask covered his face. A pistol was in his right hand.

An office door opened and Sandy Lord, dressed in his undershirt, with his pants halfway off, stumbled out and accidentally plowed into the man. They went down hard. Lord's flailing hands instinctively gripped the mask, pulling it off.

Lord rolled to his knees, sucking in blood from his battered nose.

"What the goddamn hell is going on? Who the hell are you?" Lord angrily looked eye-to-eye with the man. Then Lord saw the gun and froze.

Tim Collin looked back at him, shaking his head half in disbelief, half in disgust. There was no way around it now. He raised his gun.

"Jesus Christ! Please no!" Lord wailed and fell back.

The gun fired and blood spurted from the very center of the undershirt. Lord gasped once, his eyes glazed and his body landed back against the door. It fell the rest of the way open to reveal the nearly naked figure of the young legislative liaison, who stared in shock at the dead lawyer. Collin swore under his breath. He looked at her. She knew what was coming, he could see it in the terror-filled eyes.

Wrong place, wrong time. Sorry lady.

His gun exploded a second time and the impact knocked her slender body back into the room. Her legs splayed, her fingers clenched, she stared blankly at the ceiling; her night of pleasure turned abruptly into her last night on earth.

Bill Burton ran up to his kneeling partner and surveyed the carnage with incredulity, which was quickly replaced with anger.

"Are you fucking crazy!" he exploded.

"They saw my face, what the hell was I supposed to do? Make them promise not to tell? Fuck it!"

Both men's nerves were at their breaking point. Collin gripped his gun hard.

"Where is he? Was it Graham?" Burton demanded.

"I think so. He went down the fire stairs."

"So he's gone."

Collin looked at him and then stood up. "Not yet. I didn't waste two people just so he could get away." He started to take off. Burton grabbed him.

"Give me your gun, Tim."

"Goddammit, Bill, are you nuts?"

Burton shook his head, pulled out his piece and handed it to him. He took Collin's weapon.

"Now go get him. I'll try to do some damage control here." Collin ran to the door and then disappeared down the stairs. Burton looked at the two dead bodies. He recognized Sandy Lord and sucked in his breath sharply. "Goddamn. Goddamn," he said again. He turned and went quickly to Jack's office. Trailing his sprinting partner, he had found it right at the moment the first shot rang out. He opened the door and turned on the light. He surveyed the interior quickly. The guy would have the package with him. That was clear. Richmond had been right about Edwina Broome's involvement. Whitney had entrusted her with the package. Shit, they had been so close. Who knew Graham or anybody else would be here this late?

He made another sweep of the room's contents with his eyes.

463

They went past and slowly came back to the desk. His plan came together in a few seconds. Finally, something might be going their way. He moved toward the desk.

Jack reached the first floor and yanked on the doorknob. It didn't budge. His heart sank. They had had trouble with this before. Routine fire drills and the doors had been locked. The building management said they had fixed the problem. Right! Only now their mistake could cost him his life. And not from any inferno.

He looked back up the stairs. They were coming fast, silence was no longer an issue. Jack raced back up the stairs to the second floor, prayed silently before he grabbed the knob and a rush of relief swept over him as it turned in his sweating hand. He turned the corner, hit the elevator bank, pushed the button. He checked his backside, ran to the far corner and crouched down out of sight.

Come on! He could hear the elevator heading up. But then an awful thought ran through his mind. Whoever was following him could be on that elevator. Could have figured what Jack would try to do and attempt to checkmate him.

The car halted on his floor. At the instant the doors opened Jack heard the fire door smash against the wall. He jumped for the car, slid in between the doors and crashed against the back of the elevator. He leapt up and hit the button for the garage.

Jack felt the presence immediately, the slightly elevated breathing. He saw a flash of black, then the gun. He hurled the paperweight, and threw himself into the corner.

He heard a grunt of pain as the doors finally closed.

He ran through the dark underground parking garage, found his car and a few moments later he was through the automatic door and hit the accelerator. The car raced up the street. Jack looked back. Nothing. He looked at himself in the mirror. His face was drenched with sweat. His entire body was one large knot. He rubbed his shoulder where he had slammed into the elevator wall. Jesus, that had been so close. So close.

As he drove he wondered where he could go. They knew him, knew all about him, it seemed. He clearly couldn't go home. Where then? The police? No. Not until he knew who was after him. Who had been able to kill Luther despite all the cops. Who seemed to always know what the cops knew. For tonight he would stay someplace in town. He had his credit cards. In the morning, first thing in the morning, he would hook up with Frank. Everything would be okay then. He eyed the box. But tonight he would see what had almost cost him his life.

Russell lay underneath the sheets. Richmond had just finished on top of her. And without a word he had climbed off and left the room, her sole purpose brutally fulfilled. She rubbed her wrists where he had clenched them. She could feel the abrasions. Her breasts hurt where he had mauled them. Burton's warning came back to her. Christine Sullivan, too, had been mangled, and not just by the agents' bullets.

She slowly moved her head back and forth, fought to hold back the tears. She had wanted this so badly. Had wanted Alan Richmond to make love to her; she had imagined it would be so romantic, so idyllic. Two intelligent, powerful and dynamic people. The perfect couple. How wonderful it should have been. And then the vision of the man startled her back to reality; pounding away at her, with no more emotion on his features than if he had been masturbating alone in the toilet with the latest *Penthouse*. He had never

465

even kissed her; had never even spoken. He had just pulled off her clothes as soon as she came in the bedroom, sunk his hardened flesh into her and now he was gone. It had all taken barely ten minutes. And now she was alone. *Chief of Staff! Chief Whore more like it.*

She wanted to scream out *I fucked you! You bastard! I fucked you in that room that night and there wasn't a damn thing you could do about it, you sonofabitch.*

Her tears wet the pillow and she cursed herself for breaking down and crying yet again. She had been so sure of her abilities, so confident that she could control him. God, she had been so wrong. The man had people killed. Walter Sullivan. *Walter Sullivan* had been killed, murdered, with the knowledge, indeed the blessing, of the President of the United States. When Richmond had told her she couldn't believe it. He said he wanted to keep her fully informed. Fully terrified was more like it. She had no idea what he was up to now. She was no longer a central part of this campaign and she thanked God that she wasn't.

She sat up in bed, pulled the ripped nightgown over her quivering body. Shame rocked her again, momentarily. Of course she was now his personal whore. And his consideration for that was his unspoken promise not to crush her. But was that all? Was that really all?

She huddled the blanket around her and looked into the darkness of the room. She was an accomplice. But she was also something more. She was a *witness*. Luther Whitney had also been a witness. And now he was dead. And Richmond had calmly ordered the execution of one of his oldest and dearest friends. If he could do that, what was her life worth? The answer to that question was shockingly clear.

She bit into her hand until it hurt. She looked at

the doorway through which he had disappeared. Was he in there – in the dark, listening – thinking about what to do with her? A cold shudder of fear grabbed her and did not leave. She was caught. For once in her life she had no options. She wasn't sure if she would even survive.

Jack dropped the box on the bed, took off his coat, looked out the window of his hotel room and then sat down. He was pretty sure he hadn't been followed. He had gotten out of the building so fast. He had remembered, at the last minute, to ditch his car. He didn't really know who was pursuing him, but he assumed they were sophisticated enough to trace his car's whereabouts.

He checked his watch. The cab had dropped him off at the hotel barely fifteen minutes ago. It was a nondescript place, a hotel where tourists on the cheap would stay and then wander around the city to get their fill of the country's history before heading back home. It was out of the way but then he wanted out of the way.

Jack looked at the box and then decided he had waited long enough. A few seconds later he had it open and was staring at the object inside the plastic bag.

A knife? He looked at it more closely. No, it was a letter opener, one of the old-fashioned kind. He held the bag by its ends and examined the object minutely. He wasn't a trained forensic specialist, and thus he didn't register that the black crustings on the handle and blade were actually very old, dried blood. Nor was he aware of the fingerprints that existed within the leather.

He lay the bag carefully down and leaned back in the chair. This had something to do with the woman's murder. Of that he was certain. But what?

He looked at it again. This was obviously an important piece of physical evidence. It hadn't been the murder weapon; Christine Sullivan had been shot. But Luther had thought it critically important.

Jack jerked straight up. Because it identified who had killed Christine Sullivan! He grabbed the bag and held it up to the light, his eyes searching every inch of space. Now he could dimly make them out, like a swirl of black threads. Prints. This had the person's fingerprints on it. Jack looked at the blade closely. Blood. On the handle too. It had to be. What had Frank said? He struggled to recall. Sullivan had possibly stabbed her attacker. In the arm or the leg with a letter opener, the one in the bedroom photo. At least, that was one of the detective's theories he had shared with Jack. What Jack held in his hand seemed to bear that analysis out.

He carefully placed the bag back into the box and slid it under the bed.

He went over to the window and again looked out. The wind had picked up. The cheap window rattled and shook.

If only Luther would have told him, confided in him. But he was scared for Kate. How had they made Luther believe Kate was in danger?

He thought back. Luther had received nothing while in prison, Jack was certain of that. So what then? Had whoever it was just walked up to Luther and told him flat out: talk and your daughter dies? How would they even know he had a daughter? The two hadn't been in the same room with each other for years.

Jack lay down on the bed, closed his eyes. No, he was wrong about that. There was one time when that would have been possible. The day they had arrested Luther. That would be the only time that father and daughter would have been together. It was possible that, without saying anything, someone could have made it crystal-clear to Luther, with just a look, nothing more. Jack had handled cases that had been dismissed because witnesses were afraid to testify. No one had ever said anything to them. It was solely intimidation by the unspoken word. A silent terror, there was nothing new about that.

So who would've been there to do that? To deliver the message that had made Luther shut up like his mouth was stapled closed? But the only people who were there, as far as Jack knew, were the cops. Unless it was the person who had taken a shot at Luther. But why would he hang around? How could that person just waltz into the place, walk up to Luther, make eye contact, without anyone becoming suspicious?

Jack's eyes shot open.

Unless that person were a cop. His immediate thought hit him hard in the chest.

Seth Frank.

He dismissed it quickly. There was no motive there, not a scintilla of motive. For the life of him he couldn't imagine the detective and Christine Sullivan in any type of tryst and that's what this boiled down to, didn't it? Sullivan's lover had killed her and Luther had seen the whole thing. It couldn't be Seth Frank. He hoped to God it wasn't Seth Frank because he was counting on the man to get him out of this mess. But what if tomorrow morning Jack would be delivering the very thing Frank had been desperately searching for? He could have dropped it, left the room, Luther comes out of his hiding place, picks it up and flees. It was possible. And the place sanitized so clean a pro had to be behind it. A pro. An experienced homicide detective who knew exactly how to cleanse a crime scene.

Jack shook his head. No! Dammit no! He had to believe in something, someone. It had to be something else. Someone else. It had to be. He was just tired. His attempts at deduction were becoming ludicrous. Seth Frank was no murderer.

He closed his eyes again. For now he believed he was safe. A few minutes later he fell into an uneasy sleep.

The morning was refreshingly cold, the close, trapped air expunged by the storm of the night before.

Jack was already up; he had slept in his clothes and they looked it. He washed his face in the small bathroom, smoothed down his hair, cut the light off and went back into the bedroom. He sat on the bed and looked at his watch. Frank would not be in yet, but it wouldn't be long now. He pulled the box from under the bed, laid it beside him. It felt like a time bomb next to him.

He flicked on the small color TV that sat in the corner of the room. The early-morning local news was on. The perky blonde, no doubt aided by substantial amounts of caffeine as she waited for her break into prime time, was recounting the top stories.

Jack expected to see the litany of various world trouble spots. The Middle East was good for at least a minute each morning. Maybe Southern California had had another quake. The President fighting the Congress.

But there was only one top story this morning. Jack leaned forward as a place he knew very well flashed across the screen.

Patton, Shaw & Lord. The lobby of PS&L. What was the woman saying? People dead? *Sandy Lord murdered?* Gunned down in his office? Jack leaped across the room and turned up the volume. He watched with increasing astonishment as twin gurneys were wheeled out of the building. A picture of Lord flashed into the upper-right-hand corner of the TV screen. His distinguished career was briefly recounted. But he was dead, unmistakably dead. In his office, someone had shot him.

Jack fell back on the bed. Sandy had been there last night? But who was the other person? The other one under that sheet? He didn't know. Couldn't know that. But he believed he knew what had happened. The man after him, the man with the gun. Lord must have run into him, somehow. They were after Jack and Lord had walked right into it.

He turned off the TV and went back into the bathroom and ran cold water over his face. His hands shook, his throat had dried up. He could not believe that this had all happened. So quickly. It had not been his fault, but Jack could not help feeling enormously guilty for his partner's death. Guilty, like Kate had felt. It was a crushing emotion.

He grabbed the phone and dialed.

Seth Frank had been at his office for an hour already. A contact from D.C. Homicide had tipped him to the twin slayings at the law firm. Frank had no idea if they were connected to Sullivan. But there was a common denominator. A common denominator that had given him a throbbing headache and it was barely seven in the morning.

His direct line rang. He picked it up, his eyebrows arched in semi-disbelief.

"Jack, where the hell are you?"

There was a hard edge in the detective's tone that Jack had not expected to hear.

"Good morning to you too."

"Jack, do you know what's happened?"

"I just saw it on the news. I was there last night, Seth. They were after me; I don't know exactly how but Sandy must've walked into it and they killed him."

471

"Who? Who killed him?"

"I don't know! I was at the office, I heard a noise. The next thing I know I'm being chased through the building by someone with a gun and I barely get out of there with my head intact. Do the police have any leads?"

Frank took a deep breath. The story sounded so fantastic. He believed in Jack, trusted him. But who could be absolutely certain about anyone these days?

"Seth? Seth?"

Frank bit on his nail, thinking furiously. Depending on what he did next one of two totally different events would take place. He momentarily thought of Kate Whitney. The trap he had laid for her and her father. He had still not gotten over that. He might be a cop, but he had been a human being long before that. He trusted he still had some decent human qualities left.

"Jack, the police do have one lead, a real good lead in fact."

"Okay, what is it?"

Frank paused, then said, "It's you, Jack. You're the lead. You're the guy the entire District police force is combing the city for right this very minute."

The phone slowly slid down from Jack's hand. The blood seemed to have ceased flowing through his body.

"Jack? Jack, goddammit talk to me." The words of the detective did not register.

Jack looked out the window. Out there were people who wanted to kill him and people who wanted to arrest him for murder.

"Jack!"

Finally, with an effort, Jack spoke. "I didn't kill anybody, Seth."

The words were spoken as though they were spilling down a drain, about to be washed away.

472

Frank heard what he desperately wanted to hear. It wasn't the words – guilty people almost always lied – it was the tone with which they were spoken. Despair, disbelief, horror all rolled into one.

"I believe you, Jack," Frank said quietly.

"What the hell's going on, Seth?"

"From what I've been told the cops have you on tape going into the garage at around midnight. Apparently Lord and a ladyfriend of his were there before you."

"I never saw them."

"Well, I'm not sure that you necessarily would have." He shook his head and continued. "Seems they were found not completely clothed, especially the woman. I guess they had just finished doing it when they bought it."

"Oh God!"

"And again they have you on the video blowing out of the garage apparently right after they were killed."

"But what about the gun? Did they find the gun?"

"They did. In a trash Dumpster inside the garage."

"And?"

"And your prints were on the gun, Jack. They were the only ones on the gun. After they saw you on the videotape, the D.C. cops accessed your finger-prints from the Virginia State Bar file. A nine-point hit I'm told."

Jack slumped down in the chair.

"I never touched any gun, Seth. Somebody tried to kill me and I ran. I hit the guy, with a paperweight I pulled off my desk. That's all I know." He paused. "What do I do now?"

Frank knew that question was coming. In all honesty he wasn't sure what to answer. Technically, the man he was speaking to was wanted for murder.

As a law enforcement officer, his action should have been absolutely clear, only it wasn't.

"Wherever you are I want you to stay put. I'm gonna check this out. But don't, under any circumstances, go anywhere. Call me back in three hours. Okay?"

Jack hung up and pondered the matter. The police wanted him for murdering two people. His fingerprints were all over a weapon he had never even touched. He was a fugitive from justice. He smiled wearily, then he stiffened slightly. A fugitive. And he had just hung up from talking to a policeman. Frank hadn't asked where he was. But they could have traced the call. They could have done that easily. Only Frank wouldn't do that. But then Jack thought about Kate.

Cops never told the whole truth. The detective had suckered Kate. Then he had felt sorry about it, or at least he had said he had.

A siren blared outside and Jack's heart stopped for an instant. He raced to the window and looked out but the patrol car kept on going until the flashing lights disappeared.

But they might be coming. They might be coming for him right now. He grabbed his coat and put it on. Then he looked down at the bed.

The box.

He had never even told Frank about the damned thing. The most important thing in his life last night, now it had taken a back seat to something else.

"Aren't you busy enough out there in the boonies?" Craig Miller was a D.C. homicide detective of long standing. Big, with thick, wavy black hair and a face that betrayed his love of fine whiskey. Frank had known him for years. Their relationship was one of friendship and the shared belief that murder must always be punished.

"Never too busy to come over to see if you ever got any good at this detective stuff," Frank replied, a wry grin on his face.

Miller smiled. They were in Jack's office. The crime unit was just finishing up.

Frank looked around the spacious interior. Jack was a long way from this kind of life now, he thought to himself.

Miller looked at him, a thought registering. "This Graham fellow, he was involved in the Sullivan case out your way, wasn't he?"

Frank nodded. "The suspect's defense counsel."

"That's right! Man, that's a pretty big swing. Defense counsel to future defendant." Miller smiled.

"Who found the bodies?"

"Housekeeper. She gets in around four in the morning."

"So any motive work its way through that big head of yours?"

Miller eyed his friend. "Come on. It's eight o'clock in the morning. You drove all the way in here from the middle of nowhere to pick my brain. What's up?"

Frank shrugged. "I don't know. I got to know the guy during the case. Surprised the shit out of me to see his face on the morning news. I don't know, it just stuck in my gut."

Miller eyed him closely for another few seconds and then decided not to pursue it.

"The motive, it seems, is pretty clear. Walter Sullivan was the deceased's biggest client. This fellow Graham, without talking to anybody at the firm, jumps in and represents the dude accused of murdering the guy's wife. That, obviously, didn't sit too well with Lord. Apparently, the two had a meeting at Lord's place. Maybe they tried to work things out, maybe they just made things worse."

"How'd you get all the inside scoop?"

"Managing partner of the place." Miller flipped open his notebook: "Daniel J. Kirksen. He was real helpful on all the background shit."

"So how does that lead to Graham coming in here to pop two people?"

"I didn't say it was premeditated. The video time tables show pretty clearly that the deceased was here several hours before Graham showed up."

"So?"

"So the two don't know the other's here, or maybe Graham sees Lord's office light on when he's driving by. It overlooks the street, it'd be easy enough to see someone in the office."

"Yeah, except if the man and woman were getting it on, I'm not sure they'd be showcasing it to the rest of the city. The blinds were probably down."

"Right, but come on, Lord wasn't in the best of shape so I doubt if they were doing it the whole time. In fact the office light was on when they were found and the blinds were partially open. Anyway, accidental or not, the two run into each other here. The argument is rekindled. The feelings accelerate, maybe threats are made. And bam. Heat of the moment. It could be it was Lord's gun. They struggle. Graham gets the piece away from the old guy. Shot's fired. Woman sees it all, she has to eat a round too. All over in a few seconds."

Frank shook his head. "Excuse me for saying so, Craig, but that sounds awfully farfetched."

"Oh yeah? Well we got the guy blowing out of here white as a sheet. The camera got a clear shot of him. I've seen it, there was no blood left in the guy's face, Seth, I'm telling you."

"How come Security didn't come and check things out then?"

Miller laughed. "Security? Shit. Half the time those guys aren't even looking at the monitors. They got a tape backup, you're lucky if they even review on any consistent basis. Let me tell you, it is not hard to get into one of these office buildings after hours."

"So maybe somebody did."

Miller shook his head, grinning. "Don't think so, Seth. That's your problem. You look for a complicated answer when the simple one's staring you in the face."

"So where did this gun mysteriously appear from?"

"A lot of people keep guns stashed in their office."

"A lot? Like how many is a lot, Craig?"

"You'd be surprised, Seth."

"Maybe I would!" Frank shot back.

Miller looked puzzled. "Why do you have such a bug up your ass about this?"

Frank didn't look at his friend. He stared over at the desk. "I don't know. Like I said, I got to know the guy. He didn't seem like the type. So his prints were on the weapon?"

"Two perfect hits. Right thumb and index. Never seen clearer ones."

Something in his friend's words jolted Frank. He was looking at the desk. The highly polished surface had been defaced. The small water ring was clearly visible.

"So where's the glass?"

"What's that?"

Frank pointed to the mark. "The glass that left that mark. Have you got it?"

Miller shrugged and then chuckled. "I haven't checked the dishwasher in the kitchen, if that's what you're asking. Be my guest."

Miller turned to sign off on a report. Frank took the opportunity to check out the desk more closely. In the middle of the desk was a slight dust ring.

Something had been there. Square in shape, about three inches across. The paperweight.

A few minutes later Seth Frank walked down the hallway. The gun had perfect prints on it. Too perfect more like it. Frank had also seen the weapon and the police report on it. A .44 caliber, serial numbers obliterated, untraceable. Just like the weapon found next to Walter Sullivan.

Frank had to allow himself a smile. He had been right in what he had done, or more accurately, what he had not done.

Jack Graham had been telling the truth. He hadn't killed anybody.

"You know, Burton, I'm becoming a little tired of having to devote so much time and attention to this matter. I *do* have a country to run in case you've forgotten." Richmond sat in a chair in the Oval Office in front of a blazing fire. His eyes were closed; his fingers formed a tight pyramid.

Before Burton could respond, the President continued. "Instead of having the object back safely in our possession, you have managed only to contribute two more entries to the city's homicide fiasco, and Whitney's defense attorney is out there somewhere with possibly the evidence to bury us all. I'm absolutely thrilled with the result."

"Graham's not going to the police, not unless he's real fond of prison food and wants a big, hairy man as his date for life." Burton stared down at the motionless President. The shit he, Burton, had gone through to save all their asses while this prize stayed safely behind the lines. And now he was criticizing. Like the veteran Secret Service agent had really enjoyed seeing two more innocent people die.

"I do congratulate you on that part. It showed quick thinking. However, I don't believe we can rely

478

on that as a long-term solution. If the police do take Graham into custody he'll certainly produce the letter opener, if he has it."

"But I bought us some time."

The President stood up, grabbed Burton's thick shoulders. "And in that time I know you will locate Jack Graham and persuade him that taking any action detrimental to our interests would not be in *his* best interests."

"Do you want me to tell him that before or after I put a bullet in his brain?"

The President smiled grimly. "I'll leave that to your professional judgment." He turned to his desk.

Burton stared at the President's back. For one instant Burton visualized pumping a round from his weapon into the base of the President's neck. Just end the bullshit right here and now. If anyone ever deserved it this guy did.

"Any idea where he might be, Burton?"

Burton shook his head. "No, but I've got a pretty reliable source." Burton didn't mention Jack's phone call to Seth Frank that morning. Sooner or later Jack would reveal his location to the detective. And then Burton would make his move.

Burton took a deep breath. If you loved a pressure-filled challenge it didn't get much better than this. It was the ninth inning, the home ream was up by one, there were two outs, one runner on, and a full count on the bruiser at the plate. Could Burton close it out or would they all watch as the white orb disappeared into the stands?

As Burton walked out the door, more than a small part of him hoped it was the latter.

Seth Frank was waiting at his desk, staring at the clock. As the second hand swept past the twelve the phone rang.

Jack sat in the phone booth. He thanked God it was as cold as it was outside. The heavy, hooded parka he had bought that morning fit right in with the bundled-up mass of humanity. And still he had the overwhelming impression that everyone seemed to be looking at him.

Frank picked up on the background noise. "Where the hell are you? I told you not to leave wherever you were staying."

Jack didn't respond right away.

"Jack?"

"Look, Seth, I'm not real good at being a sitting duck. And I'm not in a position where I can afford to completely rely on anyone. Understood?"

Frank started to make a protest, but then leaned back in his chair. The guy was right, flat-out right.

"Fair enough. Would you like to hear how they set you up?"

"I'm listening."

"You had a glass on your desk. Apparently you were drinking something. You remember that?"

"Yeah, Coke, so what?"

"So whoever was after you ran into Lord and the woman like you said and they had to be popped. You got away. They knew the garage video would have you leaving right about the time of the deaths. They lifted your prints off the glass and transferred them to the gun."

"You can do that?"

"You bet your ass, if you know what you're doing and you've got the right equipment, which they probably found in the supply room at your firm. If we had the glass we could show it was a forgery. Just as one person's prints are unique from another person's, your print on the gun couldn't match in every detail the print on the glass. Amount of pressure applied and so on."

480

"Do the D.C. cops buy that explanation?"

Frank almost laughed. "I wouldn't be counting on that, Jack. I really wouldn't. All they want to do is bring you in. They'll let other people worry about everything else."

"Great. So now what?"

"First things first. Why were they after you in the first place?"

Jack almost slapped himself. He looked down at the box.

"I got a special delivery from someone. Edwina Broome. It's something I think you'll get a real kick out of seeing."

Seth stood up, almost wishing he could reach through the phone and snatch it. "What is it?"

Jack told him.

Blood and prints. Simon would have a field day. "I can meet you anywhere, anytime."

Jack thought rapidly. Ironically, public places seemed to be more dangerous than private ones. "How about the Farragut West Metro station, 18th Street exit, around eleven tonight?"

Frank jotted the information down. "I'll be there."

Jack hung up the phone. He would be at the Metro station before the appointed time. Just in case. If he saw anything remotely suspicious he was going underground as far as he could. He checked his money. The dollars were dwindling. And his credit cards were out for now. He would risk hitting several ATM machines. That would net him a few hundred. That should be enough, for a while.

He exited the phone booth, checked the crowd. It was the typical hurried pace of Union Station. No one appeared the least bit interested in him. Jack jerked slightly. Coming his way were a pair of D.C. police officers. Jack stepped back into the phone booth until they passed.

He bought some burgers and fries at the food court and then grabbed a cab. Munching down while the cab took him through the city, Jack had a moment to reflect on his options. Once he got the letter opener to Frank would his troubles really end? Presumably the prints and blood would match up with the person in the Sullivan house that night. But then Jack's defense counsel mentality took over. And that mind-set told him there were clear, almost insurmountable obstacles in the path of such a pristine resolution.

First, the physical evidence may well be inconclusive. There may be no match because the person's DNA and prints may not be on file anywhere. Jack again remembered the look on Luther's face that night on the Mall. It was somebody important, somebody people knew. And that was another obstacle. If you made accusations against a person like that, you better make damn sure you could back it up or else your case would never see the light of day.

Second, they were looking at a mammoth chain-of-custody problem. Could they even prove the letter opener came from Sullivan's home? Sullivan was dead; the staff might not know for certain. Christine Sullivan had presumably handled it. Perhaps her killer had possessed it for a short period of time. Luther had kept it for a couple of months. Now Jack had it and would, hopefully, soon be passing it on to Seth Frank. It finally struck Jack.

The letter opener's evidentiary value was zilch. Even if they could find a match, a competent defense counsel would shred its admissibility. Hell, they probably wouldn't even get an indictment based on it. Tainted evidence was no evidence at all.

He stopped eating and lay back in the grimy vinyl seat.

But come on! They had tried to get it back! They had killed to get it back. They were prepared to kill

Jack to take possession of what he had. It must be important to them, deadly important. So regardless of its legal efficacy, it had value. And something valuable could be exploited. Maybe he had a chance.

It was ten o'clock when Jack hit the escalator heading down into the Farragut West Metro station. Part of the orange and blue lines on the Washington Metro-rail system, Farragut West was a very busy station during the day due to its close proximity to the downtown business area with its myriad law and accounting firms, trade associations and corporate offices. At ten o'clock in the evening, however, it was pretty much deserted.

Jack stepped off the escalator and surveyed the area. The underground Metro stations of the system were really huge tunnels with vaulted honeycombed ceilings and floors consisting of six-sided brick. A broad corridor lined with cigarette advertisements on one side and automated ticket machines on the other culminated in a kiosk that sat in the center of the aisle with the turnstiles flanking it on either side. A huge Metro map with its multicolored rail lines, and travel time and pricing information, stood against one wall next to the dual phone booths.

One bored Metro employee leaned back in his chair in the glass-enclosed kiosk. Jack looked around and eyed the clock atop the kiosk. Then he looked back toward the escalator and froze. Coming down the escalator was a police officer. Jack willed himself to turn as casually as possible and he passed along the wall until he reached the phone booth. He flattened himself against the back of the booth, hidden behind its barrier. He caught his breath and risked peering out. The officer approached the ticket machines, nodded to the Metro guy in the kiosk and looked around the perimeter of the station entrance. Jack drew back. He would wait. The guy would move on shortly; he had to.

Time passed. A loud voice interrupted Jack's thoughts. He looked out. Coming down the escalator was a man, obviously homeless. His clothing was in tatters, a thick bundled blanket slung over one shoulder. His beard and hair were matted and unkempt. His face weather-beaten and strained. It was cold outside. The warmth of the Metro stations was always a welcome haven for the homeless until they got run out. The iron gates at the top of the escalators were to keep just such people out.

Jack looked around. The police officer had disappeared. Perhaps to check out the train platforms, shoot the breeze with the kiosk guy. Jack looked in that direction. That man too had vanished.

Jack looked back at the homeless man, who was now crumpled in one corner, inventorying his meager belongings, rubbing ungloved hands back and forth, trying to work circulation into limbs stretched to their breaking point.

A pang of guilt hit Jack. The gauntlet of such people downtown was staggering. A generous person could empty their entire pockets in the span of one city block. Jack had done that, more than once.

He checked the area one more time. No one. Another train would not arrive for about fifteen minutes. He stepped out of the booth and looked directly across at the man. He didn't seem to see Jack; his attention was focused on his own little world far away from normal reality. But then Jack thought, his own reality was no longer normal, if it ever had been. Both he and the pathetic mass across from him were involved in their own peculiar struggles. And death could claim either of them, at any time. Except that Jack's demise would probably be somewhat more violent, somewhat more sudden. But maybe that was preferable to the lingering death awaiting the other.

He shook his head clear. Thoughts like that were doing him no good. If he were going to survive this he had to remain focused, he had to believe he would outlast the forces marshaled against him.

Jack started forward and then stopped. His blood pressure almost doubled; the sudden metabolic change he was experiencing left him light-headed.

The homeless man was wearing new shoes. Soft-soled, brown leathers, which probably cost over a hundred and fifty bucks. They were revealed from out of the mass of filthy clothing like a shiny blue diamond on a bed of white sand.

And now the man was looking up at him. The eyes locked on Jack's face. They were familiar. Beneath the depths of wrinkles, filthy hair and wind-burnt cheeks, he had seen those eyes before; he was sure of it. The man was now rising off the floor. He seemed to have much more energy than when he first staggered in.

Jack frantically looked around. The place was as empty as a tomb. His tomb. He looked back. The man had already started toward him. Jack backed up, clutching the box to his chest. He thought back to his narrow escape in the elevator. The gun. He would see that gun appearing soon. It would be pointed right at him.

Jack backed down the tunnel toward the kiosk. The man's hand was going underneath his coat, a torn and beaten behemoth that spilled its woolen guts with every step. Jack looked around. He heard approaching footsteps. He looked back at the man, deciding whether he should make a run for the train or not. Then he came into sight.

Jack almost screamed in relief.

The police officer rounded the corner. Jack ran to him, pointing back down the tunnel at the homeless man who now stood stockstill, in the middle of the corridor.

"That man, he's not a homeless person. He's an imposter." The chance of him being recognized by the cop had crossed Jack's mind although the young cop's features didn't betray any such realization.

"What?" The bewildered cop stared at Jack.

"Look at his shoes." Jack realized he was making little sense, but how could he when he couldn't tell the cop the whole story?

The cop looked down the tunnel, saw the homeless man standing there, his face turned into a grimace. In his confusion he retreated to the normal inquiry.

"Has he been bothering you, sir?"

Jack hesitated, then said, "Yes."

"Hey!" The cop shouted at the man.

Jack watched as the cop ran forward. The homeless man turned and fled. He made it to the escalator, but the up escalator wasn't working. He turned and raced down the tunnel, darted around a corner and disappeared, the cop right after him.

Now Jack was alone. He looked back at the kiosk. The Metro guy hadn't returned.

Jack jerked his head. He had heard something. Like a shout, of someone in pain, from where the two men had disappeared. He moved forward. As he did, the cop, slightly out of breath, came back around the corner. He looked at Jack, motioned him to come over with slow movements of his arm. The guy looked sick, like he had seen or done something that disgusted him.

Jack hustled up next to him.

The cop gulped in air. "Goddammit! I don't know what the hell's going on, buddy." The cop again struggled to catch his breath. He put one hand out against the wall to steady himself.

"Did you catch him?"

The cop nodded. "You were right."

"What happened?"

"Go see for yourself. I've gotta call this in." The cop straightened up and pointed a warning finger at Jack. "But you are not to leave. I'm not explaining this one by myself and it sounds like maybe you know a helluva lot more about this than you're letting on. Understood?"

Jack nodded quickly. The cop hurried off. Jack walked around the corner. Wait. The cop had told him to wait. Wait for them to arrest him. He should bolt now. But he couldn't. He had to see who it was. He was certain he knew the guy. He had to see.

Jack looked up ahead. This was a service way for Metro personnel and equipment. In the darkness, far down the tunnel, there was a large bundle of clothing. In the dim lighting Jack strained to see more clearly. As he moved closer he saw that it was indeed the homeless man. For a few moments Jack remained motionless. He wanted the cops to show up. It was so quiet, so dark. The bundle did not move. Jack couldn't hear any breathing. Was the guy dead? Had the cop needed to kill him?

Finally, Jack moved forward. He knelt beside the man. What an elaborate disguise. Jack moved his hand briefly across the matted hair. Even the pungent odor of the street person was authentic. And then Jack saw the stream of blood as it trickled down the side of the man's head. He moved the hair away. A cut was there, a deep one. That was the sound he had heard. There had been a struggle and the cop had hit him. It was over. They had tried to trick Jack and gotten tripped up. He wanted to remove the wig and other elements of disguise, to see who the hell his pursuers had been. But that would have to wait. Maybe it was good the police were now involved.

He would give them the letter opener. He'd take his chances with them.

He stood up, turned and watched the cop striding quickly up the corridor. Jack shook his head. What a surprise this guy was about to get. Chalk it up to being your lucky day, pal.

Jack moved toward the cop and then stopped as the 9mm swiftly came out of the holster.

The cop glared at him. "Mr. Graham."

Jack shrugged and smiled. The guy had finally identified him. "In the flesh." He held up the box. "I've got something for you."

"I know you do, Jack. And that's exactly what I want."

Tim Collin watched the smile fade from Jack's lips. His hand tightened on the trigger as he moved forward.

Seth Frank could feel his pulse quicken as he drew nearer to the station. Finally, he would have it. He could envision Laura Simon devouring the evidence like it was a slab of aged beef. And Frank was almost one hundred percent certain they would score a hit on some database, somewhere. And then the case would crack open like an egg hurled from the Empire State Building. And finally his questions, the nagging, nagging questions would be answered.

Jack looked at the face, absorbing every detail. Not that it would do him any good. He glanced over at the crumpled clothing on the floor, at the new shoes covering lifeless feet. Poor guy had probably wangled his first new pair of shoes in ages and now would never enjoy them.

Jack looked back at Collin and said angrily, "The guy's dead. You killed him,"

"Let me have the box, Jack."

"Who the hell are you?"

"That really doesn't matter, does it?" Collin flipped open a compartment on his belt and pulled out a suppressor that he quickly twirled onto the barrel of his gun.

Jack eyed the hardware pointed at his chest. He thought of the gurneys wheeling out Lord and the woman. His turn would come in tomorrow's paper. Jack Graham and a homeless man. Twin gurneys. Of course they'd work it so Jack would be blamed for having done in the poor, wretched street person. Jack Graham, from partner at Patton, Shaw to deceased mass murderer.

"It matters to me."

"So?" Collin moved forward, placed both hands on the butt of his weapon.

"Fuck you, take it!" Jack flung the box at Collin's head right as the muffled explosion occurred. A bullet tore through the edge of the box and imbedded itself in the concrete wall. In the same instant, Jack hurled himself forward and made impact. Collin was solid bone and muscle but so was Jack. And they were about the same size. Jack felt the man's breath driven completely from his body as Jack's shoulder connected right at the diaphragm. Instinctively, long-ago wrestling moves came flowing back to his limbs and Jack picked up and then body-slammed the agent into the unwelcoming arms of the brick floor. By the time Collin managed to stagger to his feet, Jack had already turned the corner.

Collin grabbed his gun and then the box. He stopped for an instant as sickness enveloped him. His head hurt from having struck the hard floor. He knelt down, fighting to regain his equilibrium. Jack was long gone, but at least he had it. Finally had it. Collin's fingers closed around the box.

Jack flew past the kiosk, hurdled the turnstiles,

raced down the escalator and across the train platform. He was vaguely aware of people staring. His hood had fallen off his head. His face was clearly exposed. There was a shout behind him. The kiosk guy. But Jack kept running and exited the station on the 17th Street side. He didn't think the man had been alone. And the last thing he needed was someone tailing him. But he doubted if they had both exits covered. They probably figured he wouldn't be leaving the station under his own power. His shoulder ached from his collision and his breath came in difficult gulps as the cold air burned his lungs. He was two blocks away before he stopped running. He wrapped his coat around himself tightly. And then he remembered. He looked down at his empty hands. The box! He had left the goddamned box behind. He slumped against the front glass of a darkened McDonald's.

A car's lights came down the road. Jack looked away from them and quickly moved around the corner. In a few minutes he hopped on a bus. To where he wasn't sure.

The car turned off L street and onto 19th. Seth Frank made his way up to Eye Street and then turned toward 18th. He parked on the corner across from the Metro station, got out of his car and went down the escalator.

Across the street, hidden behind a collection of trash cans, debris and metal fencing, the products of a massive demolition project, Bill Burton watched. Swearing under his breath, Burton put out his cigarette, checked the street, and made his way quickly across to the escalator.

As he got off the escalator, Frank looked around and checked the time. He wasn't as early as he thought he would be. His eyes fell upon a collection of junk that lay against one wall. Then his gaze drifted over to the unmanned kiosk. There was no one else around. It was quiet. Too quiet. Frank's danger radar instantly lit up. With an automatic motion he pulled his gun. His ears had pricked up at a sound that came from his right. He moved quickly down the corridor away from the turnstiles. There a darkened corridor awaited him. He peered around and at first saw nothing. Then as his eyes adjusted to the diminished light he saw two things. One was moving, one wasn't.

Frank stared as the man slowly rose to his feet. It wasn't Jack. The guy was in a uniform, a gun in one hand, a box in the other. Frank's fingers tightened on his own weapon, his eyes locked on the other man's weapon. Frank stealthily moved forward. He hadn't done this in a long time. The image of his wife and three daughters veered across his mind until he pushed it back out. He needed to concentrate.

He was finally close enough. He prayed his accelerated breathing would not betray him. He leveled his pistol at the broad back.

"Freeze! I'm a police officer."

The man did indeed stop all motion.

"Lay the gun down, butt first. I don't want to see your finger anywhere near the trigger or I'm gonna put a hole right in the back of your head. Do it. Now!"

The gun slowly went toward the floor. Frank watched its progression, inch by inch. Then his vision became blurry. Frank's head pounded, he staggered and then he slumped to the floor.

At the sound, Collin slowly looked around to see Bill Burton standing there, holding his pistol by the barrel. He looked down at Frank.

"Let's go, Tim."

Collin shakily got to his feet, looked at the fallen

officer and put his gun to Frank's head. Burton's massive hand stopped him.

"He's a cop. We don't kill cops. We're not killing *anybody* else, Tim." Burton stared down at his colleague. Discomforting thoughts flickered in and out of Burton's head at the calm and accepting manner in which the younger man had stepped into the role of conscienceless assassin.

Collin shrugged, put his gun away.

Burton took the box, looked down at the detective and then over at the other crumpled mass of humanity. He shook his head disdainfully and looked reproachfully at his partner.

Several minutes after they were gone, Seth Frank let out a loud groan, tried to rise and then floated back into unconsciousness.

TWENTY-SEVEN

K ate lay in bed but was as far from sleep as she could possibly be. The ceiling of her bedroom had been replaced with a torrent of images, each one more terrifying than its predecessor. She looked across at the small clock on the nightstand. Three o'clock in the morning. Her window shade was open enough to reveal the pitch-black darkness outside. She could hear the raindrops on the windowpane. Normally comforting, now they simply added to the relentless pounding in her head.

When the phone rang, at first, she didn't move. Her limbs seemed too heavy for her to even attempt to budge, as if each had simultaneously lost all circulation. For one terrible moment she thought she had suffered a stroke. Finally, on the fifth ring she managed to lift the receiver.

"Hello?" Her voice was shaky, one step from oblivion; her nerves completely spent.

"Kate. I need some help."

Four hours later they sat in the front of the little deli at Founder's Park, the site of their initial rendezvous after so many years apart. The weather had worsened into a hard, pelting snow that had made driving nearly impossible and walking only for the irrationally daring.

Jack looked across at her. The hooded parka was off, but a ski cap, a few days' worth of beard and a pair of thick glasses obscured his features to such a degree that Kate had to look twice before she recognized him.

"You're sure no one followed you?" He looked anxiously at her. A cup of steaming coffee partially clouded her line of vision, but she could see the strain on his face. It was clear he was near the breaking point.

"I did what you said. The subway, two cabs and a bus. If anyone kept up with me in this weather, they're not human."

Jack put his coffee down. "From what I've seen, they might not be."

He had not specifically identified the meeting place on the phone. He now assumed that they were listening to everything, to anyone connected to him. He had only mentioned the "usual" place, confident that Kate would understand, and she had. He looked out the window. Every passing face was a threat. He slid a copy of the *Post* across to her. The front page was revealing. Jack had shaken with anger when he had first read it.

Seth Frank was in a stable condition at George Washington University Hospital with a concussion. The homeless man, as yet unidentified, had not been so fortunate. And smack in the middle of the story was Jack Graham, a one-man crime wave. She looked up at him after reading the story.

"We need to keep moving." He looked at her, drained his coffee and then got up.

The cab dropped them off at Jack's motel on the outskirts of Alexandria's Old Town. His eyes looking left and right and then behind, they made their way to his room. After locking and bolting the door, he took off the ski cap and glasses.

"God, Jack, I'm so sorry you're involved in any of this." She shook; he could actually see her trembling from across the room. It took a moment for him to wrap his arms around her until he felt her body calm, relax. He looked at her.

"I got myself involved. Now I just need to get myself uninvolved." He attempted a smile, but it didn't dent the fear she was feeling for him; the awful dread that he might soon join her father.

"I left a dozen messages for you on your machine."

"I never thought to check, Kate." He took the next half hour to tell her the events of the last few days. Her eyes reflected the growing horror with each new revelation.

"My God!"

They were silent for a moment.

"Jack, do you have any idea who's behind all this?"

Jack shook his head; a small groan escaped his lips. "I've got a bunch of loose threads sliding around in my head but none of them have added up to spit so far. I'm hoping that status will change. Soon."

The finality with which the last word was spoken hit her like a sudden slap. His eyes told her. The message was clear. Despite the disguises, the elaborate travel safeguards, despite whatever innate ability he could bring to the battlefield, they would find him. Either the cops or whoever wanted to kill him. It was only a matter of time.

"But at least if they got what they wanted back?" Her voice drifted off. She looked at him, almost pleadingly.

He lay back on the bed, stretched exhausted limbs that didn't seem to belong to him any longer.

"That's not something I can really hang my hat on forever, Kate, is it?" He sat up and looked across the room. At the cheap picture of Jesus hanging on the wall. He would take a dose of divine intervention right now. A small miracle would do.

"But you didn't kill anyone, Jack. You told me

Frank's already figured that out. The D.C. cops will too."

"Will they? Frank knows me, Kate. He knows me and I could still hear the doubt in his voice at first. He picked up on the glass, but there's no evidence that anyone tampered with it or the gun. On the other hand there's clear, take-it-to-the-bank proof, pointing to me killing two people. Three if you count last night. My lawyer would recommend my negotiating a plea and hoping for twenty to life with the possibility of parole. I'd recommend it myself. If I go to trial I've got no shot. Just a bunch of speculation trying to tie Luther and Walter Sullivan and all the rest into some landscape of conspiracy of, you have to admit, mind-boggling proportions. The judge'll laugh my ass right out of court. The jury will never hear it. Really, there's nothing to hear."

He stood up and leaned against the wall, hands shoved in his pockets. He didn't look at her. Both his short- and long-term prospects had doomsday written all over them.

"I'll die an old man in prison, Kate. That is, if I make it to old age – which is a big question mark in itself."

She sat down on the bed, her hands in her lap. A gasp caught midway in her throar as the sheer hopelessness sank in, like a boulder dropped in deep, dark waters.

Seth Frank opened his eyes. At first nothing came into focus. What his brain registered resembled a large white canvas on which a few hundred gallons of black, white and gray paint had been poured to form a cloggy, mind-altering quagmire. After a few anxious moments, he was able to discern the outline of the hospital room in all its stark white, chrome and sharp angles. As he tried to sit up, a hand planted itself firmly against his shoulder.

"Uh-uh, Lieutenant. Not so fast."

Frank looked up into the face of Laura Simon. The smile did not entirely hide the worry lines around the eyes. Her sigh of relief was clearly audible.

"Your wife just left to check on the kids. She's been here all night. I told her as soon as she left you'd wake up."

"Where am I?"

"GW Hospital. I guess if you were gonna have your head pounded in, at least you picked a place close to a hospital." Simon continued to lean over the bed so Frank wouldn't have to turn his head. He stared up at her.

"Seth, do you remember what happened?"

Frank thought back to last night. Or was it last night?

"What day is it?"

"Thursday."

"So it happened last night?"

"Around eleven or so. At least they found you about then. And the other guy."

"Other guy?" Frank jerked his head around. Pain shot through his neck.

"Take it easy, Seth." Laura took a moment to prop a pillow next to Frank's head.

"There was another guy. Homeless. They haven't identified him yet. Same kind of blow to the back of the head. Probably died instantly. You were lucky."

Frank gingerly touched his throbbing temples. He didn't feel so lucky.

"Anybody else?"

"What?"

"Did they find anybody else?"

"Oh. No, but you're not going to believe this. You know the lawyer who watched the tape with us?"

Frank tensed. "Yeah, Jack Graham."

497

"Right. The guy kills two people at his law firm and then he's spotted running away from the Metro about the time you and the other guy get whacked. The guy's a walking nightmare. And he looked like a Mr. All-American."

"Have they found him yet? Jack? They're sure he got away?"

Laura looked at him strangely. "He got out of the Metro station if that's what you mean. But it's only a matter of time." She looked out the window, reached for her purse. "The D.C. cops want to talk with you as soon as you're able."

"I'm not sure how much help I can be. I don't remember all that much, Laura."

"Temporary amnesia. You'll probably get it back."

She put on her jacket. "I have to go. Somebody's got to keep Middleton County safe for the rich and famous while you're counting sheep in here." She smiled. "Don't make a habit out of this, Seth. We were really worried we might have to hire a new detective."

"Where would you find someone as nice as me?"

Laura laughed. "Your wife will be back in a few hours. You need to get some rest anyway." She turned to go to the door.

"By the way, Seth, what were you doing at the Farragut West Metro at that time of night?"

Frank didn't answer right away. He didn't have amnesia. He recalled the night's events clearly.

"Seth?"

"I'm not sure, Laura." He closed his eyes and then reopened them. "I just don't remember."

"Don't worry, it'll come back to you. In the meantime, they'll catch Graham. That'll probably clear everything up."

After Laura left, Frank did not rest. Jack was out there. And he had probably initially thought the detective had set him up, although if Jack had seen the paper he would know that the detective had walked blindly into the ambush that had been laid for the lawyer.

But they had the letter opener now. That's what was in that box. He was certain of it. And without that, what chance did they have of nailing these people?

Frank again tried to struggle up. There was an IV in his arm. The pressure on his brain caused him to immediately lie back down. He had to get out of here. And he had to get in touch with Jack. Right now he had no idea how he would accomplish either.

"You said you needed my help. What can I do?" Kate looked directly at Jack. There were no reservations on her features.

Jack sat on the bed next to her. He looked troubled. "I've got some real serious doubts about getting you anywhere near this. In fact, I'm wondering if calling you was the right thing to do."

"Jack, I've been surrounded by rapists, armed robbers and murderers for the last four years."

"I know that. But at least you knew who they were. This could be anybody. People are getting killed left and right, Kate. This is about as serious as it gets."

"I'm not leaving unless you let me help you."

Jack hesitated, his eyes turned away from hers.

"Jack, if you don't, then I'm going to turn you in. Better you take your chances with the cops."

He looked at her. "You'd do that, wouldn't you?"

"Damn straight I would. I'm breaking all the rules by being here with you now. If you let me in on it, then I forget all about seeing you today. If you don't . . ."

There was a look in her eyes that, despite all the

horrific possibilities he was contemplating, made him somehow feel fortunate to be here at this exact moment.

"Okay. You need to be my contact with Seth. Outside of you he's the only one I can trust."

"But you lost the package. How can he help?" Kate could not hide her dislike of the homicide detective.

Jack stood up and paced. Finally he stopped and looked down at her. "You know how your dad was a freak for control? Always have a backup plan?"

Kate said dryly, "I remember."

"Well, I'm counting on that quality."

"What are you talking about?"

"That Luther had a backup plan on this one."

She stared at him, open-mouthed.

"Mrs. Broome?"

The door opened another notch as Edwina Broome peered out.

"Yes?"

"My name is Kate Whitney. Luther Whitney was my father." Kate relaxed as the old woman greeted her with a smile. "I knew I'd seen you before. Luther was always showing pictures of you. You're even prettier than your photos."

"Thank you."

Edwina jerked the door open. "What am I thinking about. You must be freezing. Please come in."

Edwina led her into the small living room where a trio of felines were cloistered on various pieces of furniture.

"I just made some fresh tea, would you like some?"

Kate hesitated. Time was short. Then she looked around the narrow confines of the home. In the corner sat a battered upright piano, thick dust on the

500

wood. Kate looked at the woman's weakened eyes; the pleasures of a musical pastime had also been taken from her. Husband passed on, her only daughter dead. How many visitors could she possibly have?

"Thank you, I would."

Both women settled into the old but comfortable furniture. Kate sipped the strong tea and she began to thaw out. She brushed the hair out of her face and looked across at the elderly woman to find a pair of sad eyes upon her.

"I'm sorry about your daddy, Kate. I really am. I know you two had your differences. But Luther was as good a man as I've come across in my life."

Kate felt herself growing warmer. "Thank you. We both have had a lot to deal with in that regard."

Edwina's eyes drifted over to a small table next to the window. Kate followed the gaze. On the table numerous photographs displayed a small shrine to Wanda Broome; capturing her in happy times. She strongly resembled her mother.

A *shrine*. With a jolt Kate recalled her father's own collection of her personal triumphs.

"Yes indeed." Edwina was looking at her again.

Kate put down her tea. "Mrs. Broome, I hate to jump right into this, but the fact is I don't have much time."

The old woman leaned forward expectantly. "This is about Luther's death, and my daughter's too, isn't it?"

Kate looked surprised. "Why do you think that?"

Edwina leaned forward even more; her voice dropped to a whisper. "Because I know Luther didn't kill Mrs. Sullivan. I know it as if I'd seen it with my own eyes.

Kate looked puzzled. "Do you have any idea who—"

Edwina was already shaking her head sadly. "No. No, I don't."

"Well, how do you know my father didn't do it?"

Now there was definite hesitation. Edwina leaned back in her chair and closed her eyes. When she finally reopened them, Kate had not moved a muscle.

"You're Luther's daughter and I believe you should know the truth." She paused, took a sip of her tea, pressed her lips dry with a napkin and then settled back into her chair. A black Persian drifted across and promptly went to sleep in her lap. "I knew about your father. His past, so to speak. He and Wanda got to know each other. She got into trouble years back and Luther helped her, helped her get back on her feet and get settled into a respectable life. I will always be grateful to him for that. He was always there when Wanda or I needed anything. The fact is, Kate, your father would never have been in the house that night if it weren't for Wanda."

Edwina spoke for some minutes. When she had finished Kate sat back in her chair and realized she was holding her breath. She let out a loud gasp that seemed to echo around the room.

Edwina didn't say anything but continued to watch the young woman with her large sad eyes. Finally she stirred. A thickly wrinkled hand patted Kate's knee.

"Luther loved you, child. More than anything."

"I realize that."

Edwina slowly shook her head. "He never blamed you for the way you felt. In fact, he said you were entirely right to feel that way."

"He said that?"

"He was so proud of you, your being a lawyer and all. He used to say to me, 'My daughter is a lawyer and a damned fine one. Justice is what matters for her and she's right, dead right.'"

Kate's head began to swirl. She was feeling

emotions she was ill-equipped right now to deal with. She rubbed the back of her neck and took a moment to look outside. A black sedan pulled down the street and then disappeared. She quickly looked back at Edwina.

"Mrs. Broome, I appreciate your telling me these things. But I really came here for a specific reason. I need your help."

"I'll do whatever I can."

"My father sent you a package."

"Yes. And I sent it on to Mr. Graham, like Luther said to."

"Yes, I know. Jack got the package. But someone . . . someone took it away from him. Now we're wondering if my father sent you something else, something else that might help us?"

Edwina's eyes no longer looked sad. They had collected into twin masses of stark intensity. She looked over Kate's shoulder.

"Behind you, Kate, in the piano seat. The hymnal on the left."

Kate opened the piano seat and lifted out the hymnal. Inside the pages was a small packet. She looked down at it.

"Luther was the most prepared man I have ever met in my life. Said if anything went wrong with my sending the package that I was to send this to Mr. Graham. I was getting ready to do that when I heard about him on the TV. Am I right in thinking Mr. Graham didn't do any of the things they say he did?"

Kate nodded. "I wish everybody thought like you did."

She started to open the package.

Edwina's voice was sharp. "Don't do that, Kate. Your father said that only Mr. Jack Graham was to see what was inside of there. Only him. I think it best if we took him at his word."

Kate hesitated, fighting her natural curiosity, and then closed the package.

"Did he tell you anything else? Whether he knew who had killed Christine Sullivan?"

"He did know."

Kate looked at her sharply. "But he didn't say who?"

Edwina shook her head vigorously. "He did say one thing though."

"What was that?"

"He said if he told me who had done it, I wouldn't have believed him."

Kate sat back, thought for several anxious moments.

"What could he have meant by that?"

"Well, it surprised me, I can tell you that."

"Why? Why did that surprise you?"

"Because Luther was the most honest man I'd ever met. I would have believed anything he would have told me. Accepted it as the gospel."

"So whatever he saw, whoever he saw, must have been someone so unlikely as to be unbelievable. Even to you."

"Exactly. That's exactly what I thought too."

Kate rose to go. "Thank you, Mrs. Broome."

"Please call me Edwina. Funny name, but it's the only one I have."

Kate smiled. "After this is all over, Edwina, I . . . I'd like to come back and visit if you don't mind. Talk about things some more."

"I'd like nothing better. Being old has its good and bad. Being old and lonely is all bad."

Kate put on her coat and went to the door. She put the package safely in her purse.

"That should narrow your search shouldn't it, Kate?"

Kate turned around. "What?"

"Someone that unbelievable. Can't be too many of them around I wouldn't think."

The hospital security guard was tall, beefy and uncomfortable as hell.

"I don't exactly know what happened. I was gone maybe two, three minutes tops."

"You shouldn't have been away from your post at all, Monroe." The diminutive supervisor was in Monroe's face and the big man was sweating hard.

"Like I said, the lady asked for some help with a bag, so I helped her."

"What lady?"

"I told you, just some lady. Young, good-lookin', dressed real professional." The supervisor turned away, disgusted. He had no way of knowing the lady was Kate Whitney and that she and Seth Frank were already five blocks away in Kate's car.

"Does it hurt?" Kate looked at him, with not much sympathy in either her features or her voice.

Frank gingerly touched the bandages around his head. "You kidding? My six-year-old hits me harder." He looked around the interior of the car. "You got some smokes? Since when the hell are hospitals nonsmoking?"

She rummaged in her purse and flipped him an open pack.

He lit up and eyed her over the cloud of smoke. "By the way, nice job on the rent-a-cop. You should be in the movies."

"Great! I'm in the market for a career change."

"How's our boy?"

"Safe. For now. Let's keep him that way."

She turned the corner and looked hard at him.

"You know, it wasn't exactly my plan to let your old man buy it right in front of me."

505

"That's what Jack said."

"But you don't believe him?"

"What does it matter what I believe?"

"It does. It matters to me, Kate."

She stopped for a red light. "Okay. Let's put it this way. I'm coming around to the idea that you didn't want it to happen. Is that good enough?"

"No, but it'll do for now."

Jack turned the corner and tried to relax. The latest storm front had finally wearied of the Capital City, but although there no longer was any pelting icy rain, the thermometer had remained consistently in the twenties and the wind had returned with a vengeance. He blew on stiff fingers and rubbed sleep-deprived eyes. Against a drift of black sky, a sliver of moon hung, soft and luminous. Jack checked his surroundings. The building across the street was dark and empty. The structure he was standing in front of had closed its doors a long time ago. A few passersby braved the inclement conditions, but for large chunks of time Jack stood alone. Finally he took shelter inside the doorway of the building and waited.

Three blocks away a rusting cab pulled to the curb, the back door opened and a pair of low heels touched the cement sidewalk. The cab immediately pulled off and a moment later the street was silent again. Kate tugged her coat around her and hurried off. As she passed the next block, another car, lights out, turned the corner and drifted along in her wake. Her thoughts focused on the steps that lay ahead of her, Kate did not look back.

Jack saw her turn the corner. He looked in all directions before moving, a habit he had quickly cultivated and hoped he would be able to discard very soon. He moved quickly to meet her. The street was quiet. Neither Kate nor Jack saw the sedan's nose as it crept past the corner building's front. Inside, the driver zeroed in on the couple with a night-vision device the mail-order catalogue had trumpeted as being the very latest in Soviet technology. And although the former communists had no clue as to how to run a democratic, capitalist society, they did, for the most part, build sound military hardware.

"Jesus, you're freezing, how long have you been waiting?" Kate had touched Jack's hand and the icy feel had coursed through her entire body.

"Longer than I needed to. The motel room was shrinking on me. I just had to get out. I'm going to make a lousy prisoner. Well?"

Kate opened her purse. She had called Jack from a pay phone. She couldn't tell him what she had, only that she had something. Jack had agreed with Edwina Broome that if risks had to be taken, he would take more than anyone. Kate had already done enough.

Jack grasped the packet. It wasn't that difficult to discern what was contained inside. Photographs.

Thank God, Luther, you didn't disappoint.

"Are you okay?" Jack scrutinized her.

"I'm getting there."

"Where's Seth?"

"He's around. He'll drive me home."

They stared at each other. Jack knew that the best thing was to have Kate leave, maybe leave the country for a while, until this blew over or he was convicted of murder. If the latter, then her intention of starting over somewhere else was probably the best plan anyway.

But he didn't want her to leave.

"Thank you." The words seemed wholly inadequate, like she had just dropped off lunch for him, or picked up his dry cleaning.

"Jack, what are you going to do now?"

"I haven't thought it all through yet. But it's coming. I'm not going down without a fight."

"Yeah, but you don't even know who it is you're fighting. That's hardly fair."

"Who said it was supposed to be fair?"

He smiled at her as the wind kicked old newspapers down the street.

"You better get going. It's not that safe around here."

"I've got my pepper mace."

"Good girl."

She turned to leave, then clutched him by the arm.

"Jack, please be careful."

"I'm always careful. I'm a lawyer. CYA is SOP for us."

"Jack, I'm not kidding."

He shrugged, "I know. I promise I will be as careful as I can." As Jack said this he stepped toward Kate and took off his hood.

The night goggles fixated on Jack's exposed features and then they were lowered. Shaky hands picked up the car's cellular phone.

The two clung in an easy embrace. While Jack desperately wanted to kiss her, under the circumstances he settled for a soft brush of his lips against her neck. When they stepped back from each other, tears had begun to form in Kate's eyes. Jack turned and walked quickly away.

As Kate walked back down the street she didn't notice the car until it swerved across the street and almost ended up on the curb. She staggered back as the driver's side door flew open. In the background, the air had exploded with sirens, all coming toward her. Toward Jack. She instinctively looked behind her. There was no sign of him. When she turned back, she was staring into a pair of smug eyes, framed under bushy eyebrows.

"I thought our paths might cross again, Ms. Whitney."

Kate stared at the man, but recognition was not forthcoming.

He looked disappointed. "Bob Gavin. From the *Post*?"

She looked at his car. She had seen it before. On the street passing Edwina Broome's house.

"You've been following me."

"Yes, I have. Figured you'd eventually lead me to Graham."

"The police?" Her head jerked around as a squad car, siren blaring, tore down the street toward them. "You called them."

Gavin nodded, smiling. He was obviously pleased with himself.

"Now before the cops get here I think we can work a little deal. You give me an exclusive. The down and dirty on Jack Graham, and my story changes just enough so that instead of an accessory, you're just an innocent bystander in this whole mess."

Kate glared at the man, the rage within her, having been built up from a month of personal horrors, was near its exploding point. And Bob Gavin was standing directly over the epicenter.

Gavin looked around at the patrol car nearing them. In the background, two more squad cars were heading in their direction.

"Come on, Kate," he said urgently, "you don't have much time, You stay out of jail and I get my long-overdue Pulitzer and my fifteen minutes of fame. What's it gonna be?"

She gnashed her teeth, her response startlingly calm, as though she had practiced its delivery for months. "Pain, Mr. Gavin. Fifteen minutes of pain." As he stared at her, she pulled the palm-size canister,

509

pointed it directly at his face and squeezed the trigger. The pepper gas hit Gavin flush in the eyes and nose, marking his face with a red dye. By the time the cops exited their vehicle, Bob Gavin was on the pavement clutching at his face, trying unsuccessfully to tear his eyes out.

The first siren had sent Jack into a sprint down a side street.

He slid flat against a building sucking in air. His lungs ached, the cold tore at his face. The deserted nature of the area he was in had turned into a huge tactical disadvantage. He could keep moving, but he was like a black ant on a sheet of white paper. The sirens were coming so heavy now he couldn't ascertain from what direction.

Actually they were coming from all directions. And they were getting closer. He ran hard to the next corner, stopped and peered around. The view was not encouraging. His eyes fastened on a police blockade being set up at the end of the street. Their strategy was readily apparent. They knew his general coordinates. They would simply cordon off a wide radius and systematically close that radius in. They had the manpower and the time.

The one thing he did have was a good knowledge of the area he was in. Many of his PD clients had come from here. Their dreams set not on college, law school, good job, loving family and the suburban split-level but on how much cash they could generate from selling bags of crack, how they could survive one day at a time. Survival. It was a strong, human drive. Jack hoped his was strong enough.

As he flew down the alley, he had no idea what he would encounter, although he supposed the fierce weather had kept some of the local felons indoors. He almost laughed. Not one of his former partners at

Patton, Shaw would have come near this place, even with an armored battalion surrounding them. He might as well be running across the surface of Pluto.

He cleared the chain-link fence with one jump and landed slightly off-balance. As he put out his hand against the rugged brick wall to steady himself he heard two sounds. His own heavy breathing and the sound of running feet. Several pairs. He'd been spotted. They were homing in on him. Next the K-9's would be brought in and you didn't run away from the four-legged cops. He exploded out of the alley and made his way over to Indiana Avenue.

Jack veered down another street as the squeal of tires flew toward him. Even as he raced in the new direction, a new flank of pursuers rushed to greet him. It was only a matter of time now. He felt in his pocket for the packet. What could he do with it? He didn't trust anybody. Technically, an inventory of an arrestee's possessions taken from him would be made, with appropriate signatures and chain-of-custody safeguards, all of which meant nothing to Jack. Whoever could kill in the middle of hundreds of law officers and disappear without a trace could certainly manage to secure a prisoner's personal possessions from the D.C. Police Department. And what he had in his pocket was the only chance he had. D.C. didn't have the death penalty but life without parole wasn't any better and in a lot of ways seemed a helluva lot worse.

He raced in between two buildings, stumbled on some ice and plunged over a stack of garbage cans and hit the pavement hard. He picked himself up and half-rolled into the street, rubbing at his elbow. He could feel the burn, and there was a looseness in his knee that was a new sensation. As he stopped rolling, he managed to sit up, then froze.

A car's headlights were coming right for him. The

police bubble light blasted into his eyes as the wheels came within two inches of his head. He slumped back on the asphalt. He was too winded to even move.

The car door sprang open. Jack looked up, puzzled. It was the passenger door. Then the driver's door flew open. Big hands slid under his armpits.

"Goddammit, Jack, get your ass up."

Jack looked up at Seth Frank.

TWENTY-EIGHT

Bill Burton leaned his head into the Secret Service command post. Tim Collin sat at one of the desks going over a report.

"Come on, Tim."

Collin looked up, puzzled.

Burton said quietly, "They've got him cornered down near the courthouse. I want to be there. Just in case."

Seth Frank's sedan flew down the street, the blue bubble light commanding immediate respect from a traffic population unaccustomed to conveying any whatsoever to fellow motorists.

"Where's Kate?" Jack lay in the back seat, a blanket over him.

"Right now she's probably being read her rights. Then she's gonna get booked on a slew of accessory charges for helping you."

Jack sprung up. "We've gotta go back, Seth. I'll turn myself in. They'll let her go."

"Yeah, right."

"I'm not kidding, Seth." Jack was halfway over the front seat.

"I'm not either, Jack. You go back and turn yourself in, that'll do nothing to help Kate and it'll snuff out what little shot you've got to get your life back to reality."

"But Kate—"

"I'll take care of Kate. I've already called a buddy

at D.C. He'll be waiting for her. He's a good guy."

Jack slumped back down. "Shit."

Frank opened his window, reached out and flicked the bubble light off and tossed it on the seat beside him.

"What the hell happened?"

Frank looked in his rearview mirror. "I'm not sure. The best I can figure is that Kate picked up a tail somewhere. I was cruising the area. We were going to meet at the Convention Center after she made the drop with you. Heard over my police radio that you had been spotted. I followed the chase over the air-waves, tried to guess where you might go. Got lucky. When I saw you blow out of the alley, I couldn't believe it. Damn near ran you down. How's the body by the way?"

"Never better. I ought to do this crap once or twice a year just to keep me limber. Get ready for the Fleeing Felon Olympics."

Frank chuckled. "You're still alive and kicking, my friend. Count your blessings. So did you get any nice presents?"

Jack swore under his breath. He had been so busy running from the police that he had never even looked. He took out the packet.

"Got a light?"

Frank flicked on the dome light.

Jack flipped through the photographs.

Frank checked the mirror. "So what do we got?"

"Photos. Of the letter opener, knife, whatever the hell you want to call it."

"Huh. Not surprising I guess. Can you make out anything?"

Jack looked closely in the poor light. "Not really. You guys must have some gadget that'll do some good."

Frank sighed. "I gotta be straight with you, Jack,

514

unless there's something else we don't have much of a shot. Even if we can somehow pull something that looks like a print off there who's to say where it came from? And you can't do DNA testing on blood from a friggin' photograph, at least not that I'm aware of."

"I know that. I didn't spend four years as a defense counsel picking my ass."

Seth slowed the car down. They were on Pennsylvania Avenue and the traffic had grown heavier. "So what's your idea then?"

Jack rubbed back his hair, dug his fingers into his leg until the pain in his knee subsided and then lay down on the seat. "Whoever's behind all this wanted the letter opener back really bad. Enough to kill you, me, anybody else that got in the way. We're talking paranoia at its peak."

"Which fits in with our theory of some big shot with a lot to lose if this comes out. So? They got it back. Where does that leave us, Jack?"

"Luther didn't make these photos just in case something happened to the original article."

"What are you talking about?"

"He came back into the country, Seth, remember? We could never figure that one out."

Frank stopped at a red light. He turned around in his seat.

"Right. He came back. You think you know why?"

Jack carefully sat up in the back seat, keeping his head below the window line. "I think so. Remember I told you that Luther wasn't the kind of guy to let something like this lie. If he could he'd do something about it."

"But he did leave the country. At first."

"I know. Maybe that was his initial plan. Maybe that was his plan all along if the job had gone according to plan. But the fact is he came back.

515

Something made him change his mind and he came back. And he had these photographs." Jack spread them fanlike.

The light turned green and Frank started up again.

"I'm not getting this, Jack. If he wanted to nail the guy why not just send the stuff in to the police?"

"I think that was his plan, eventually. But he told Edwina Broome that if he told *her* who he had seen, she wouldn't have believed him. If even she, a close friend, wouldn't have believed his story, considering he'd have to admit to burglary to convince someone, he probably thought that his credibility was zip."

"Okay, so he has a credibility problem. Where do the photos come in?"

"Let's say you're doing a straight exchange. Cash for a certain item. What's the hardest part?"

Frank's reply was immediate. "The payoff. How to get your money without getting killed or caught. You can send instructions later on for the pickup of the item. It's getting the money that's tough. That's why the number of kidnappings have plummeted."

"So how would you do it?"

Frank thought for a moment. "Since we're talking about the payoff coming from people who ain't gonna bring in the police I'd go for speed. Take minimal personal risk, and give yourself time to run."

"How would you do that?"

"EFT. Electronic Fund Transfer. A wire. I was involved in a bank embezzlement case when I was in New York. Guy did it all through the wire transfer department at his own bank. You wouldn't believe the dollars that fly through those places on a daily basis. And you also wouldn't believe how much stuff gets lost in the shuffle. A smart perp could take a little chunk here and there and by the time they caught it, he'd be long gone. You send your wire instructions. The money is sent out. Only takes a few minutes.

516

Helluva lot better than rummaging through a Dumpster in a park where somebody can take a nice little bead on your head with a cannon."

"But the sender can presumably trace the wire."

"Sure. You have to identify the bank it's going to. ABA routing number, you have to have an account at the bank. All that shit."

"So, assuming the sender is sophisticated enough, they trace the wire. Then what?"

"Then they can follow the flow of money. They might be able to dig some info on the account. Although no one would be stupid enough to use their own name or Social Security number. Besides, a real smart guy like Whitney would probably have preset instructions in place. Once the funds hit the first bank, bam they get sent out to another place, and then another and another. At some point, the trail probably disappears. It's instant money after all. Immediately available funds."

"Fair enough. I'm betting Luther did something just like that."

Frank carefully scratched around the edges of his bandage. His hat was pulled down tight and the whole thing was greatly uncomfortable. "But what I can't figure is why do it at all. He didn't need the money after the Sullivan hit. He could've just stayed disappeared. Let the whole thing blow over. After a while they figure he's permanently retired. You don't bother me, I don't bother you."

"You're right. He could've done that. Retired. Given it up. But he came back, and more than that, he came back and apparently blackmailed whoever he saw kill Christine Sullivan. And if he presumably didn't do it for money, then why?"

The detective thought for a moment. "To make 'em sweat. To let them know he was out there. With the evidence to destroy them."

"But evidence he wasn't sure was enough."

"Because the perp was so respectable?"

"Right, so what would you do, given those facts?"

Frank pulled to the curb and put the car in park. He turned around. "I'd try to get something else on them. That's what I'd do."

"How? If you're blackmailing someone?"

Frank finally threw up his hands. "I give up."

"You said the wire transfer could be traced by the sender."

"So?"

"So, what about the other way? Receiver back up the line?"

"Goddamned stupid." Frank momentarily forgot his concussion and slapped his forehead. "Whitney put a tracer on the wire, going the other way. The person sending out the money thinks all along that they're playing cat and mouse with Whitney. They're the cat, he's the mouse. He's hiding, getting ready to run."

"Only Luther didn't mention the fact that he was into role reversal. That he was the cat and they were the mouse."

"And that tracer would eventually lead right to the bad guys, probably no matter how many shields you put up, if they thought to put up any at all. Every wire in this country has to go through the Federal Reserve. You get the wire reference number from the Fed or the sending bank's wire room, you got something to hang your hat on. Even if Whitney didn't trace it back, the fact that he received the money, a certain amount, is damaging enough. If he could give that info to the cops with the name of the sender and they check it out . . ."

Jack finished the detective's thought. "And suddenly the unbelievable becomes very believable. Wire transfers do not lie. Money was sent. If it was a lot of money like I'm sure it was here, then that cannot be explained away. That is pretty damn close to bull's-eye evidence. He set them up with their own payoff."

"I just thought of something else, Jack. If Whitney was building a case against these people, then he was eventually planning to go to the police. He was going to just walk in the door and deposit himself and his evidence."

Jack nodded. "That's why he needed me. Only they were quick enough to use Kate as a way to ensure his silence. Later they used a bullet to accomplish that."

"So he was going to turn himself in."

"Right."

Frank rubbed his jaw. "You know what I'm thinking?"

Jack answered immediately. "He saw it coming." The two men looked at each other.

Frank spoke first; the words came out low, almost hushed. "He knew Kate was a setup. And he went anyway. And I thought I was so fucking clever."

"Probably figured it was the only way he'd ever get to see her again."

"Shit. I know the guy stole for a living, but I gotta tell you, my respect for him grows by the second."

"I know what you mean."

Frank put the car back in gear and pulled off.

"Okay, again, where does all this conjecture leave us?"

Jack shook his head, lay back down. "I'm not sure."

"I mean so long as we don't have a clue as to who it is, I'm not sure what we can do."

Jack exploded back up. "But we do have clues." He sat back as though all his energy had suddenly evaporated after that one thrust. "I just can't make any sense out of them."

The men drove on in silence for a few minutes.

"Jack, I know this sounds funny coming from a policeman, but I think you might want to start considering getting the hell out of here. You got some bucks saved? Maybe *you* should retire early."

"And what, leave Kate swinging in the wind? If we don't nail these guys what is she looking at? Ten to fifteen as an accessory? I don't think so, Seth, not in a million years. They can fry my ass before I let that happen."

"You're right. Sorry I brought it up."

As Seth glanced in his mirror the car next to them tried to do a U-turn directly in front of them. Frank hit the brakes and his car spun sideways, crashing into the curb with a bone-crunching impact. The Kansas license plates on the vehicle that had nearly crashed into them quickly disappeared.

"Stupid tourists. Fucking bastards!" Frank gripped the steering wheel hard, his breath coming in gasps. The shoulder restraint had done its job, but it had dug deeply into his skin. His battered head pounded.

"*Fucking bastard!*" Frank yelled again to no one in particular. Then he remembered his passenger and looked anxiously in the back seat.

"Jack, Jack, you okay?"

Jack's face was pressed up against the door glass. He was conscious; in fact, his eyes were staring at something with great intensity.

"Jack?" Frank undid his seat belt and gripped him by the shoulder. "You okay? Jack!"

Jack looked at Frank and then back out the window. Frank wondered if the impact had relieved his friend of his senses. He automatically searched Jack's head for bruises until Jack's hand stopped him and pointed out the window. Frank looked out.

Even his hardened nerves took a jolt. The rear view of the White House filled his entire line of vision.

Jack's mind raced; images hurtled across like a video montage. The vision of the President pulling back from Jennifer Baldwin, complaining of tennis elbow. Only it had been inflicted with a certain letter opener that had started this whole crazy thing. The unusual interest taken by the President and the Secret Service in Christine Sullivan's murder. Alan Richmond's timely appearance at Luther's arraignment. *Led me right to him.* That's what the detective had said their videotaping citizen had reported. *Led me right to him.* It also explained killers who killed in the middle of an army of law enforcement officers and walked away. Who would stop a Secret Service agent protecting the President? No one. No wonder Luther felt no one would believe him. The President of the United States.

And there had been a significant event right before Luther had returned to the country. Alan Richmond had held a press conference where he had told the public how terrible he felt about the tragic murder of Christine Sullivan. He was probably fucking the man's wife and somehow she had gotten killed and this slimeball was gaining political dollars showing what a sensitive and good friend he was; a man who would get tough on crime. It had been a tour de force performance. And that was truly what it had been. Nothing about it had been true. It had been broadcast to the world. What would Luther have thought, seeing that? Jack believed he knew. That was why Luther had come back. To settle the score.

All the pieces had been dangling inside Jack's head just waiting for the right catalyst to come along.

Jack looked back once more at the catalyst.

Directly under the lamplight, Tim Collin again glanced down the street at the minor traffic mishap, but could make out no details in the oncoming swarm of car headlights. Next to him Bill Burton was

521

also peering out. Collin shrugged, and then rolled the window back up on the black sedan. Burton threw his bubble light on top of the car, hit his siren, quickly drove the car through the rear White House gate and tore off in the direction of D.C. Superior Court in pursuit of Jack.

Jack looked at Seth Frank and smiled grimly as he reflected on the detective's outburst. The same phrase had erupted from Luther's mouth, right before his life had ended. Jack finally remembered where he had heard it before. The hurled newspaper at the jail. The smiling President on the front page.

Outside the courthouse, staring right at the man. Those same words had exploded out, with all the fury and venom the old man could muster.

"*Fucking bastard*," Jack said.

Alan Richmond stood by the window and wondered if he was destined to be surrounded by incompetents. Gloria Russell sat dronelike in a chair across from him. He had bedded the woman a half-dozen times and now had completely lost interest. He would catapult her away when the time was right. His next administration would be comprised of a far more capable team. Underlings who would allow him to focus on his particular vision for the country. He had not sought the presidency to sweat the details.

"I see we haven't gained an inch in the polls." He didn't look at her; he anticipated her response.

"Does it really matter so much whether you win by sixty percent or seventy percent?"

He whirled around. "Yes," he hissed. "Yes, it god-damn does matter."

She bit her lip and retreated. "I'll step up the effort, Alan. Maybe we can pull a shutout in the Electoral College."

"At a minimum, we should be able to do that, Gloria."

She looked down. After the election, she would travel. Around the world. Where she knew no one and no one knew her. A fresh start. That was what she needed. Then everything would be okay.

"Well, at least our little problem is cleared up." He was looking at her, hands clasped behind his back. Tall, lean, impeccably dressed and groomed. He looked like the commander of an invincible armada. But then again history had proven that invincible armadas were far more vulnerable than people imagined.

"It's been disposed of?"

"No, Gloria, I have it in my desk – would you like to see it? Perhaps you might wish to abscond with it again." His air was so thick with condescension she felt the urgent need to bring their consultation to a close. She rose.

"Will there be anything else?"

He shook his head and returned to the window. She had just put her hand on the doorknob when it turned and opened.

"We've got a problem." Bill Burton looked at each of them.

"So what does he want?" The President looked down at the photograph Burton had handed him.

Burton replied quickly. "Note doesn't say. I can guess that the shape the guy's in with cops on his ass, he's looking for some quick funds."

The President looked pointedly at Russell. "I'm very puzzled as to how Jack Graham knew to send the photo here."

Burton picked up on the look from the President, and while the last thing he wanted was to defend Russell they had no time to misanalyze the situation.

"It's possible Whitney told him," Burton answered.

"If that's true, he waited a long time to dance with us," the President fired back.

"Whitney may not have told him directly. Graham could've figured it out for himself. Pieced things together."

The President tossed down the photo. Russell quickly averted her eyes. The mere sight of the letter opener had paralyzed her.

"Burton, how could this possibly be damaging to us?" The President stared at him, seemingly probing through the inner areas of the agent's mind.

Burton sat down, rubbed his jaw with the palm of his hand. "I've been thinking about that. It could be Graham's grasping at straws. He's in a pretty tight fix himself. And his lady friend is cooling her heels in the lockup right now. I'd chalk it up to him being desperate. He gets a sudden inspiration, puts two and two together and takes a flyer on sending us this, hoping it's worth it to us to pay his price, whatever it might be."

The President stood up and fingered his coffee cup. "Is there any way to find him? Quickly?"

"There are always ways. How fast I don't know."

"So if we ignore his communication?"

"He may do nothing, just hightail it and take his chances."

"But again we're confronted with the possibility of the police catching up to him—"

"And him spilling his guts," Burton finished the sentence. "Yeah, that's a possibility. A real possibility."

The President picked up the photo. "With only this to back up his story?" He looked incredulous. "Why bother?"

"It's not the incriminating value of what's in the photo *per se* that bothers me."

"What bothers you is that his accusations, coupled with whatever ideas or leads the police can develop from the photo, might make for some very uncomfortable questions."

"Something like that. Remember, it's the allegations that can kill you. You're up for re-election. He probably sees that as an ace for him. Bad press can be just as deadly to you right now."

The President pondered for a moment. Nothing, no one would interfere with his reelection. "Buying him off is no good, Burton. You know that. So long as Graham's around, he's dangerous." Richmond looked over at Russell, who had sat the entire time, hands in her lap, eyes pointed down. His eyes bored into her. *So weak.*

The President sat down at his desk and started to sift through some papers. He said dismissively, "Do it, Burton, and do it soon."

Frank looked at the wall clock, went over and shut his door and picked up the phone. His head still ached, but the doctors predicted a full recovery.

The phone was answered. "D.C. Executive Inn."

"Room 233 please."

"Just a moment."

The seconds dragged by and Frank started to get anxious. Jack was supposed to be in his room.

"Hello?"

"It's me."

"So how's life?"

"Better than yours, I bet."

"How's Kate?"

"She's out on bail. Got 'em to let her go into my custody."

"I'm sure she's thrilled."

"That wasn't the word I was thinking of. Look, it's getting close to shit-or-get-off-the-pot time. Take my advice and run like hell. You're wasting valuable time right now."

"But Kate—"

"Come on, Jack, they've got the testimony of one guy who was trying to hit her up for an exclusive. His word against hers. Nobody else even saw you. It's a slam dunk she'll beat that charge. A slam dunk. I've talked to the Assistant U.S. Attorney. He's looking seriously at dropping the whole case."

"I don't know."

"Goddammit, Jack. Kate is gonna come out of this a whole helluva lot better than you are if you don't start thinking about your future. You've got to get out of here. That's not just me talking. That's her too."

"Kate?"

"I saw her today. We don't agree on much, but on that we do."

Jack relaxed, then let out a heavy sigh. "Okay, so where do I go and how do I get there?"

"I get off duty at nine. At ten o'clock I'll be at your room. Have your bags packed. I'll take care of the rest. In the meantime, stay put."

Frank hung up the phone and took a deep breath. The chances he was taking. It was better not to think about them.

Jack checked his watch and looked at the single bag on the bed. He wouldn't be running with much. He looked at the TV set in the corner but there wouldn't be anything on he cared to watch. Suddenly thirsty, he pulled some change from his pocket, opened the door to his room and peered out. The drink machine was just down the hallway. He plopped on his baseball cap, donned his Coke-bottle glasses and slipped out. He didn't hear the door to the stairwell at the other end of the hallway open. He had also forgotten to lock his door.

When he slipped back in, it struck him that the light was off. He had left it on. As his hand hit the switch, the door was slammed shut behind him and he was thrown onto the bed. As he quickly rolled over and his eyes adjusted to the light, the two men came into focus. They were not wearing masks this time, which spoke volumes in itself.

Jack started to lunge forward but twin cannons met him halfway. He sat back down, scrutinized each of their faces.

"What a coincidence. I've already made each of your acquaintance, separately." He pointed at Collin. "You tried to blow my head off." He swiveled to Burton. "And you tried to blow smoke up my ass. And succeeded. Burton, right? Bill Burton. Always remember names." He looked at Collin. "Didn't catch yours though."

Collin looked at Burton, then stared back at Jack. "Secret Service Agent Tim Collin. You pack a nice little wallop, Jack. Must've played some ball back in school."

"Yeah, my shoulder still remembers you."

Burton sat down on the bed next to Jack.

Jack looked at him. "I thought I'd covered my tracks pretty good. I'm kind of surprised you found me."

Burton looked at the ceiling. "A little bird told us, Jack."

Jack looked over at Collin and then back at Burton. "Look, I'm heading out of town, and I'm not coming back. I don't think you guys need to add me to the body count."

Burton eyed the bag on the bed and then got up and slipped his gun back in its holster. Then he grabbed Jack and flung him up against the wall. The veteran agent left nothing unprobed by the time he had finished. Burton spent the next ten minutes

527

examining every inch of the room for listening devices and other items of interest, ending his search at Jack's bag. He pulled out the photos and examined them.

Satisfied, Burton secreted them in his inner coat pocket and smiled at Jack. "Excuse me, but in my line of work paranoia is part of the mentality." He sat back down. "I would like to know, Jack, why you sent that photo to the President."

Jack shrugged. "Well, since my life here happens to be over, I thought your boss might want to contribute to my going-away fund. You could've just wired the funds, like you did with Luther."

Collin grunted, shook his head and grinned. "The world doesn't work that way, Jack, sorry. You should've found another solution to your problem."

Jack shot back, "I guess I should've followed your example. Got a problem? Just kill it."

Collin's smile evaporated. His eyes glittered darkly at the lawyer.

Burton stood up and paced around the room. He pulled out a cigarette and then crunched it up and put it in his pocket. He turned to Jack and said quietly, "You should've just gotten the hell out of town, Jack. Maybe you would've made it."

"Not with you two on my butt."

Burton shrugged. "You never know."

"How do you know I haven't given one of those photos to the cops?"

Burton pulled out the photos and looked down at them. "Polaroid OneStep camera. The film comes in a standard pack of ten shots. Whitney sent two to Russell. You sent one to the President. There are seven left here. Sorry, Jack, nice try."

"I could've just told Seth Frank what I know."

Burton shook his head. "If you had I think my little bird would've told me. But if you want to insist on

528

the point we can just wait for the lieutenant to show up and join the party."

Jack burst up from the bed and launched himself toward the door. Right as he reached it, an iron fist slammed into his kidney. Jack crumpled to the floor. An instant later he was hustled up and thrown back on the bed.

Jack looked up into Collin's face.

"Now we're even, Jack."

Jack groaned and lay back on the bed, fighting the nausea the blow had caused. He sat back up, caught his breath as the pain subsided.

When Jack finally managed to look up, his eyes found Burton's face. Jack shook his head, the disbelief clear on his features.

Burton eyed Jack intently and said, "What?"

"I thought you were the good guys," Jack said quietly.

Burton said nothing for several long moments.

Collin's eyes went to the floor and stayed there.

Finally Burton answered, his voice faint, as if his larynx had suddenly collapsed. "So did I, Jack. So did I." He paused, swallowed painfully and went on. "I didn't ask for this problem. If Richmond could keep his dick in his pants none of this would've happened. But it did. And we had to fix it."

Burton stood up, looked at his watch. "I'm sorry about this, Jack. I really am. You probably think that's laughable but it's the way I really feel."

He looked at Collin and nodded. Collin motioned Jack to lie back on the bed.

"I hope the President appreciates what you're doing for him," Jack said bitterly.

Burton smiled ruefully. "Let's just say he expects it, Jack. Maybe they all do, in one way or another."

Jack slid slowly back and watched as the barrel moved closer and closer to his face. He could smell the metal. He could envision the smoke, the projectile racing out faster than any eye could follow.

Then the door to the room was hit with an enormous blow. Collin whirled around. The second blow crashed the portal inward and a half-dozen D.C. cops bulled in, guns drawn.

"Freeze. Everybody freeze. Guns on the floor. *Now.*"

Collin and Burton quickly put their guns down on the floor. Jack lay back on the bed, his eyes closed. He touched his chest where his heart threatened to explode.

Burton looked at the men in blue. "We're United States Secret Service. IDs in our right inner pockets. We've tracked this man down. He was making threats against the President. We were just about to take him into custody."

The cops warily pulled out the IDs and scrutinized them. Two other cops pulled Jack roughly up. One began to read him his rights. Handcuffs were placed on his wrists.

The IDs were given back.

"Well, Agent Burton, you're just gonna have to wait until we get done with Mr. Graham here. Murder takes a priority even over threatening the President. Might be a long wait unless this guy's got nine lives."

The cop looked at Jack and then down at the bag on the bed.

"Shoulda taken off when you had the chance, Graham. Sooner or later we were gonna get you." He motioned for his men to take Jack out.

He looked back at the bewildered agents and smiled broadly. "We got a tip he was here. Most tips are worth shit. This one might get me that promotion I'm sorely in need of. Have a good day, gentlemen. Say hello to the President for me."

They left with their prisoner. Burton looked at Collin, and then pulled out the photos. Now Graham had nothing. He could repeat everything they had just told him to the police and they'd just get him ready for the rubber room. Poor sonofabitch. A bullet would've been a lot better than where he was headed. The two agents picked up their hardware and left.

The room was silent. Ten minutes later the door to the adjoining room was eased open and a figure slipped into Jack's room. The corner TV was swiveled around and the back was eased off. The TV was remarkably real-looking and an absolute sham. Hands reached inside and the surveillance camera was swiftly and silently removed and the cabling was pushed through the wall until it disappeared from sight.

The figure opened the adjoining door and went back through. A recording machine sat on a table next to the wall. The cable was coiled up and deposited in a bag. The figure hit a button on the recording machine and the tape slid out.

Ten minutes later the man, carrying a large back-pack, walked out of the front door of the Executive Inn, turned left and walked to the end of the parking lot where a car was parked, its engine idling. Tarr Crimson passed the car, and casually tossed the tape through the open window and onto the front seat. Then he proceeded over to his Harley-Davidson 1200cc touring bike, the joy of his life, got on, fired it up and thundered off. Setting up the video system had been child's play. Voice-activated camera. Recording machine kicked on when the camera did. Your standard VHS tape. He didn't know what was on the tape, but it must be something pretty damn valuable. Jack had promised him a year's free legal services for doing it. As he hurtled along the high-way, Tarr smiled, remembering their last meeting where the lawyer had balked at the new age of surveillance technology.

Back in the parking lot, the car glided forward, one hand on the steering wheel, the other protectively around the tape. Seth Frank turned onto the main road. Not much of a moviegoer, this was one tape he was dying to watch.

Bill Burton sat in the small but cozy bedroom he had shared with his wife through the evolution of four beloved children. Twenty-four years together. They had made love countless times. In the corner by the window, Bill Burton had sat in a much worn rocker and fed his four offspring before reporting for early-morning shifts, allowing his exhausted wife a few minutes of much needed rest.

They had been good years. He had never made a lot of money, but that had never seemed to matter. His wife had gone back and finished her nursing degree after their youngest had entered high school. The added income had been nice, but it was good to see someone who had long sacrificed her personal goals to the needs of others to finally do something just for herself. All in all it had been a great life. A nice house in a quiet, picturesque neighborhood safe, so far, from the ever-expanding war zones around them. There would always be bad people. And there would always be people like Bill Burton to combat them. Or people like Burton had been.

He looked out the dormer window. Today was his day off. Dressed in jeans, bright red flannel shirt and Timberland boots, he could have easily passed as a burly lumberjack. His wife was unloading the car. Today was grocery shopping day. The same day for the last twenty years. He watched her figure admiringly as it bent low to pull out the bags. Chris, his fifteen-year-old, and Sidney, nineteen, long-legged and a real beauty, and in her sophomore year at Johns Hopkins, with her sights set on medical school, were helping their mother. His other two were out on their own and doing well. They occasionally called their old man for advice on buying a car or a house. Long-term career goals. And he loved every minute of it. He and his wife had hit four out of the park and it was a good feeling.

He sat down at the little desk in the corner, unlocked a drawer and pulled out the box. He lifted the top and stacked the five audiocassette tapes on top of the desk next to the letter he had written that morning. The name on the envelope was written in large, clear letters. "Seth Frank." Hell, he owed the guy.

Laughter floated up to him and he again went to the window. Sidney and Chris were now engaged in a pitched snowball battle with Sherry, his wife, caught in the middle. The smiles were big and the confrontation culminated in all of them landing in a heap next to the driveway.

He turned away from the window and did something he could never remember doing before. Through eight years as a cop, where tiny babies had expired in his arms, beaten to death by the ones who were supposed to love and protect them, through day after day of looking for the worst in humankind. The tears were salty. He didn't rub them away. They kept pouring. His family would be coming in soon. They were supposed to go out to dinner tonight. Ironically, today was Bill Burton's forty-fifth birthday.

He leaned across the desk, and with a quick motion, pulled the revolver from his holster. A snowball hit the window. They wanted their daddy to come join them.

I'm sorry. I love you. I wish I could be there. I'm sorry for all I've done. Please forgive your dad. Before he could lose his nerve he pushed the .357 as far down his throat as he could. It was cold and heavy. One of his gums started to bleed from a nick.

Bill Burton had done everything he could to ensure that no one would ever know the truth. He had committed crimes; he had killed an innocent person and had been involved in five other homicides. And now, seemingly in the clear, the horror behind him, after months of mounting disgust with what he had become, and after a sleepless night next to a woman he had loved with all his heart for over two decades, Bill Burton had realized that he could not accept what he had done, nor could he live with that knowledge.

The fact was that without self-respect, without his pride, his life was not worth living. And the unfailing love of his family did not help matters, it only made them worse. Because the object of that love, of that respect, knew that he deserved none of it.

He looked over at the stack of cassette tapes. His insurance policy. Now they would constitute his legacy, his own bizarre epitaph. And some good would come out of it. Thank God for that.

His lips curled into a barely perceptible smile. The Secret Service. Well, the secrets were going to fly now. He briefly thought of Alan Richmond and his eyes glistened. *Here's hoping for life without parole and you live to be a hundred, asshole.*

His finger tightened on the trigger.

Another snowball hit the window. Their voices drifted up to him. The tears started again as he thought of what he was leaving behind. "Goddammit." The word floated from his mouth, carrying with it more guilt, more anguish than he could ever hope to bear.

I'm sorry. Don't hate me. Please God don't hate me.

At the sound of the explosion, the playing stopped

as three pairs of eyes turned as one toward the house. In another minute they were inside. It only took one more minute for the screams to be heard. The quiet neighborhood was no more.

TWENTY-NINE

The knock on the door was unexpected. President Alan Richmond was in a tense conference with his Cabinet. The press had lately been lambasting the administration's domestic policies and he wanted to know why. Not that the actual policies themselves were of much interest to him. He was more concerned about the perception they conveyed. In the grand scheme of things perceptions were all that mattered. That was Politics 101.

"Who the hell are they?" The President looked angrily at the secretary. "Whoever they are, they're not on the list for today." He looked around the table. Hell, his Chief of Staff had not even bothered to show up for work today. Maybe she had done the smart thing and taken a bottle of pills. That would hurt him short-term, but he would work out an impressive spin on her suicide. Besides, she had been right about one thing: he was so far ahead in the polls, who cared?

The secretary timidly crept into the room. Her growing astonishment was evident. "It's a large group of men, Mr. President. Mr. Bayliss from the FBI, several policemen, and a gentleman from Virginia, he wouldn't give his name."

"The police? Tell them to leave and submit a request to see me. And tell Bayliss to call me tonight. He'd be cooling his heels in some Bureau outpost in the middle of nowhere if I hadn't pushed through his

536

nomination as Director. I will not tolerate this disrespect."

"They're most insistent, sir."

The President flushed red and stood up. "Tell them to get the hell out. I'm busy, you idiot."

The woman quickly retreated. Before she could reach the door, however, it had opened. Four Secret Service agents entered, Johnson and Varney among them, followed by a contingent of D.C. police, including Police Chief Nathan Brimmer, and FBI Director Donald Bayliss, a short, thickly built man in a double-breasted suit with a face whiter than the building he was now in.

Bringing up the rear, Seth Frank quietly closed the door. In his other hand he carried a plain brown briefcase. Richmond stared at each of them, his eyes finally coming to rest on the homicide detective.

"Detective Frank, right? In case you weren't aware you are interrupting a confidential Cabinet meeting. I'm going to have to ask you to leave." He looked across at the four agents, raised his eyebrows and cocked his head toward the door. The men stared back; they didn't budge.

Frank stepped forward. He quietly slipped a paper out of his coat, unfolded it and handed it to the President. Richmond looked down at it while his Cabinet watched in utter bewilderment. Richmond finally looked back at the detective.

"Is this some kind of joke?"

"That is a copy of an arrest warrant naming you on capital murder charges for crimes committed in the Commonwealth of Virginia. Chief Brimmer here has a similar arrest warrant for murder one accessory charges that will be brought against you in the District. That is, after the commonwealth finishes with you."

The President looked over at Brimmer, who met

537

his gaze and sternly nodded. There was a cold look in the lawman's eyes that told exactly how he felt about the Chief Executive.

"I'm the President of the United States. You can't serve me with anything unless it's coffee. Now get out." The President turned to go back to his chair.

"Technically that may be true. However, I don't really care. Once the impeachment process is complete you won't be President Alan Richmond, you'll just be Alan Richmond. And when that happens I'll be back. Count on it."

The President turned back around, his face bloodless. "Impeachment?"

Frank moved forward until he was eye-to-eye with the man. On any other occasion this would have triggered prompt action on the part of the Secret Service. Now, they simply stood motionless. It was impossible to tell that each one of them was inwardly reeling over the loss of a respected colleague. Johnson and Varney seethed at having been duped as to the events of that night at the Sullivan estate. And the man they blamed for it all was now crumpling in front of them.

Frank said, "Let's cut through the bullshit. We already have Tim Collin and Gloria Russell in custody. They've both waived right to counsel and each has given detailed depositions regarding all of the events involving the homicides of Christine Sullivan, Luther Whitney, Walter Sullivan and the two killings at Patton, Shaw. I believe they've already cut deals with the prosecutors, who are really only interested in you anyway. This case is a real career-builder for a prosecutor, let me tell you."

The President staggered back a step, then righted himself.

Frank opened the briefcase and pulled out a video-tape and five audiocassette tapes. "I'm sure your counsel will be interested to see these. The video is of Agents Burton and Collin when they attempted to murder Jack Graham. The tapes are of several meetings at which you were present and at which the plannings for the various crimes took place. Over six hours of testimony, Mr. President. Copies have been delivered to the Hill, the FBI, CIA, the *Post*, the Attorney General, White House counsel and anybody else I could think of – and no gaps on the tapes. Also included is the tape Walter Sullivan made of your telephone conversation on the night of his murder. It doesn't exactly coincide with the version you gave me. All compliments of Bill Burton. Said in his note he was cashing in his insurance policy."

"And where is Burton?" The President's voice was filled with rage.

"He was pronounced DOA at Fairfax Hospital at ten-thirty this morning. Self-inflicted gunshot wound."

Richmond barely made it to his chair. No one offered to assist him. He looked up at Frank.

"Anything else?"

"Yeah. Burton left behind one other paper. It's his proxy. For the next election. Sorry, but it seems you didn't get his vote."

One by one the Cabinet members got up and left. Fear of political suicide by association was alive and well in the Capital City. The lawmen and Secret Service agents followed. Only the President remained. His eyes stared blankly at the wall.

Seth Frank popped his head back in the door.

"Remember, be seeing you soon." He quietly closed the door.

EPILOGUE

The seasons of Washington followed a familiar pattern, and a bare week of spring with tolerable temperatures and humidity under fifty percent gave way abruptly to a meteoric thermometer and a humidity level that routinely delivered a full body shower whenever you walked outside. By July, the typical Washingtonian had adapted as much as they were ever going to, to air that was difficult to breathe and movements that were never slow enough to prevent a sudden burst of perspiration under one's clothing. But in all of that misery, the occasional evening was not ruined by the sudden materialization of a whipping, drenching thunderstorm with multiple branches of lightning that threatened to touch the earth with every explosion. Where the breeze was cool, the air sweet-smelling and the sky clear. Tonight was just such a night.

Jack sat on the edge of the pool set up on the building's roof. His khaki shorts revealed muscled, tanned legs, hairs curled by the sun. He was even leaner than before, all remnants of office-induced flab banished by months of physical exertion. Cords of well-toned muscle sat just beneath the surface of his white T-shirt. His hair was short, his face as brown as his legs. The water swished between his bare toes. He looked at the sky and breathed deeply. The place had been packed a mere three hours ago as office dwellers dragged tan-free, fleshy bodies to the replenishing powers of the warm waters. Now Jack sat alone. No

540

bed beckoned him. No ringing alarm would disturb his sleep the next morning.

The door to the pool opened with a slight squeak. Jack turned and saw the beige summer suit, wrinkled and uncomfortable-looking. The man carried a brown paper bag.

"Building super told me you were back." Seth Frank smiled. "Mind some company?"

"Not if you've got what I think you've got in that bag." Frank sat down in a web chair and tossed a beer to Jack. They dinked cans and each man took a long pull.

Frank looked around. "So how was wherever you were?"

"Not bad. It was good to get away. But it's also good to be back."

"This looks like a nice place to meditate."

"It gets crowded around seven for a couple of hours. Most of the other time it's pretty much like this."

Frank looked wistfully at the pool and then started to take off his shoes. "You mind?"

"Help yourself."

Frank rolled up his pants, curled his socks into his shoes and sat down next to Jack, letting his milky-white legs sink into the water up to his knees.

"Damn, that feels good. County detectives with three daughters and a mortgage out the ying-yang rarely come into contact with swimming pools."

"So I've heard."

Frank rubbed his calves and looked at his friend. "Hey, being a bum agrees with you. You might want to think about sticking with it."

"I am thinking about it. The idea gets more appealing every day."

Frank eyed the envelope next to Jack.

"Important?" He pointed at the paper.

Jack picked it up, briefly reread the contents. "Ransome Baldwin. Remember him?"

Frank nodded. "What, has he decided to sue you for dumping his baby?"

Jack shook his head and smiled. He finished his beer and fished in the bag and pulled out another cold one. He tossed a second one to Frank.

"You never know, I guess. The guy basically said I was too good for Jennifer. At least for right now. That she had a lot of growing up to do. He's sending her out on some missionary duties for the Baldwin Charitable Foundation for a year or so. He said if I ever needed anything to let him know. Hell, he even said that he admired and respected me."

Frank sipped his beer. "Damn. Doesn't get much better than that."

"Yes, it does. Baldwin made Barry Alvis his chief in-house counsel. Alvis was the guy Jenn got fired at Patton, Shaw. Alvis promptly walked into Dan Kirksen's office and pulled the entire account. I think Dan was last seen on the ledge of a very tall building."

"I read where the firm closed its doors."

"All the good lawyers got snapped up right away. The bad ones ought to try something else for a living. Space is already rented out. The whole firm gone, without a trace."

"Well, same thing happened to the dinosaurs. It's just taking a little longer with you attorney types." He punched Jack in the arm.

Jack laughed. "Thanks for coming and cheering me up."

"Hell, I wouldn't miss it."

Jack looked at him, his face clouded. "So what happened?"

"Don't tell me you still haven't been reading the papers?"

"Not for months. After the gauntlet of reporters,

542

talk show hosts, teams of independent prosecutors, Hollywood producers and your run-of-the-mill curious person I've had to deal with I never want to know anything about anything. I changed my phone number a dozen times and the bastards kept finding it. That's why the last two months have been so sweet. No one knew me from Adam."

Frank took a moment to collect his thoughts. "Well, let's see, Collin pled to conspiracy, two counts of second-degree murder, obstruction and a half-dozen assorted lesser included offenses. That was the D.C. stuff. I think the judge felt sorry for him. Collin was a Kansas farm boy, Marine, Secret Service agent. He was just following orders. Been doing that most of his life. I mean, the President tells you to do something, you do it. He got twenty to life, which if you ask me was a sweetheart deal, but he gave a full account to the prosecution team. Maybe it was worth it. He'll probably be out in time for his fiftieth birthday. The commonwealth decided not to prosecute in return for his cooperation against Richmond."

"What about Russell?"

Frank almost choked on his beer. "Jesus, did that woman spill her guts. They must have spent a fortune on court-reporting fees. She just wouldn't stop talking. She got the best deal of all. No prison time. Thousand hours of community time. Ten years' probation. For fucking conspiracy to commit murder. Can you believe that? Between you and me, I think she's right on the borderline sanity-wise anyway. They brought in a court-appointed shrink. I think she might spend a few years in an institution before she's ready to come out and play. But I gotta tell you, Richmond brutalized her. Emotionally and physically. If half of what she said was true, Jesus . . . Mind games from hell."

"So what about Richmond?"

"You really have been on Mars, haven't you? Trial of the millennium and you slept right through it."

"Somebody had to."

"He fought right to the end, I have to admit that. Must've spent every dime he had. The guy didn't do himself any good testifying I can tell you that. He was so damn arrogant, obviously lying out his ass. And they traced the money wire straight back to the White House. Russell had pulled it from a bunch of accounts but made the mistake of assembling the five mil into one account before she wired it. Probably afraid if all of the money didn't show up at the same time Luther would go to the cops. His plan worked, even if he wasn't around to see it. Richmond didn't have an answer for that or a lot of other things. They tore him up on cross. He brought in a Who's Who of American Greatness and it didn't help him one little bit, the sonofabitch. One dangerous and sick dude if you ask me."

"And he had the nuclear codes. Real nice. So what'd he get?"

Frank stared at the ripples in the water for a few moments before answering. "He got the death penalty, Jack."

Jack stared at him. "Bullshit. How'd they manage that?"

"A little tricky from a legal-technical point of view. They prosecuted him under the murder-for-hire statute. That's the only one where the trigger man rule doesn't apply."

"How the hell did they get murder for hire to stick?"

"They argued that Burton and Collin were paid subordinates whose only job was to do what the President told them to do. He ordered them to kill. Like a Mafia hitman on the payroll. It's a stretch, but

544

the jury returned the verdict and the sentence and the judge let it stand."

"Jesus Christ!"

"Hey, just because the guy was President doesn't mean he should be treated differently than anybody else. Hell, I don't know why we should be surprised at what happened. You know what kind of person it takes to run for President? Not normal. They could start out okay, but by the time they reach that level they've sold their soul to the devil so many times and stomped the guts out of enough people that they are definitely not like you and me, not even close."

Frank studied the depths of the pool, then finally stirred. "But they'll never execute him."

"Why not?"

"His lawyers will appeal, the ACLU will file, along with all the other death penalty opposers; you're gonna get *amicus* briefs from all over the planet. The guy took a tidal wave plunge on the popularity scale but he's still got some powerful friends. They'll find something wrong on the record. Besides, the country might agree on convicting the scumball. But I'm not sure the United States could actually execute some guy they elected to the presidency. Doesn't look real good from a global perspective either. Makes me feel kind of queasy too, although the asshole deserves it."

Jack scooped up handfuls of water and let the warm liquid run down his arms. He stared off into the night.

Frank looked keenly at Jack. "Not that some positives haven't come out of all this. Hell, Fairfax wants to make yours truly a division head. I've gotten offers from about a dozen cities to be their Chief of Police. The lead prosecutor on the Richmond case, they say, is a shoo-in for the AG slot next election."

The detective took a sip of beer. "What about you, Jack? You were the one who brought the guy down.

Setting up Burton and the President was your idea. Man, when I found my line was tapped, I thought my head was gonna explode. You were right though. So what do you get out of all this?"

Jack looked at his friend and said simply. "I'm alive. I'm not practicing rich-man law at Patton, Shaw and I'm not marrying Jennifer Baldwin. That's more than enough."

Frank studied the blue veins on his legs. "You heard from Kate?"

Jack took another swallow of beer before answering. "She's in Atlanta. At least she was last time she wrote."

"She gonna stick there?"

Jack shrugged. "She's not sure. Her letter wasn't all that clear." He paused. "Luther left her his house in his will."

"I'm surprised she'd take it. Ill-gotten gains and all that."

"Luther's father left it to him, bought and paid for. Luther knew his daughter. I think he wanted her to have. . . something. A home's not a bad place to start."

"Yeah? A home takes two if you ask me. And then some dirty diapers and infant formula to make it complete. Hell, Jack, you two were meant to be together. I'm telling you."

"I'm not sure that matters, Seth." He wiped off the thick droplets of water from his arms. "She's been through a lot. Maybe too much. I'm kind of connected to all the bad stuff. I really can't blame her for wanting to get away from it all. Wipe the slate clean."

"You weren't the problem, Jack. From what I saw everything else was."

Jack looked across at a helicopter roaring its way across the sky. "I'm a little tired of always being the one to make the first step, Seth, you know what I'm saying?"

"I guess."

Frank looked at his watch. Jack caught the movement. "Got somewhere to go?"

"I was just thinking we need something a lot stronger than beer. I know this nice little place out by Dulles. Rack of ribs long as my arm, two-pound corn-on-the-cobs and tequila till the sun comes up. And some not-so-bad-looking waitresses if you're so inclined, although being married I will only watch from a respectful distance while you make a complete fool of yourself. We take a cab home because we'll both be shit-faced and you crash at my place. What do you say?"

Jack grinned. "Can I get a rain check on that? It sounds good though."

"You sure?"

"I'm sure, Seth, thanks."

"You got it." Frank stood up, rolled down his pants and flopped across to put on his shoes and socks.

"Hey, how about Saturday you come out to my place? We're grilling, burgers, fries and dogs. Got tickets to Camden Yard too."

"You got a deal on that one."

Frank stood up and headed to the door. He looked back. "Hey, Jack, don't think too much, okay? Sometimes that's not real healthy."

Jack held up his can. "Thanks for the beer."

After Frank left, Jack lay back on the cement and stared at a sky that seemed filled with more stars than there were numbers. Sometimes he would awaken from a deep sleep and realize that he'd been dreaming about the most bizarre stuff. But what he'd been dreaming about had actually happened to him. It was not a pleasant feeling. And it only added to the confusion that, at his age, he hoped would have been long since eliminated from his life.

An hour-and-a-half plane ride due south was probably the surest answer to what ailed him. Kate Whitney may or may not come back. The only thing he felt sure about was that he could not go after her. That this time it would be her responsibility to return to his life. And it was not bitterness that made Jack feel such was imperative. Kate had to make up her own mind. About her life and how she wanted to spend it. The emotional trauma she had experienced with her father had been surpassed by the overwhelming guilt and grief she had endured at his death. The woman had a lot to think through. And she had made it very clear that she needed to undertake that exercise alone. And she was probably right.

He took off his shirt, slid into the water and did three quick laps. His arms cut powerfully through the water and then he pulled himself back up on the tiled apron. He grabbed his towel and wrapped it around his shoulders. The night air was cool and each droplet of water felt like a miniature air conditioner against his skin. He again looked at the sky. Not a mural in sight. But neither was Kate.

He was deciding whether to head back to his apartment for some sleep when he heard the door squeak open again. Frank must have forgotten something. He looked over. For a few seconds he couldn't move. He just sat there with the towel around his shoulders afraid to make a sound. That what was happening might not be real. Another dream that would flicker out with the sun's first rays. Finally he slowly got up, water dripping off him, and moved toward the door.

Down on the street, Seth Frank stood next to his car for a few moments admiring the simple beauty of the evening, sniffed the air that was more reminiscent of a wet spring than a humid summer. It wouldn't be that late when he got home. Maybe Mrs. Frank would like to hit the neighborhood Dairy Queen. Just the two of them. He'd heard some good reports about the butterscotch-dipped cone. That would finish off the day just fine. He climbed in his car.

As a father of three, Seth Frank knew what a wonderful and precious commodity life was. As a homicide detective he had learned how that precious commodity could be brutally ripped away. He looked up at the roof of the apartment building and smiled as he put the car in gear. But that was the great thing about being alive, he thought. Today might not be so good. But tomorrow, you got another chance to get it right.

AUTHOR'S NOTE

This novel is obviously a work of fiction and intends to be nothing more. It in no way implies that members of the United States Secret Service would do any of the acts attributed to the fictional agents in the novel. The agents in *Absolute Power* were good, loyal men put into an impossible situation. The decisions they made were decisions any one of us might have made if confronted with the total destruction of all we have worked for.

I cannot imagine a more difficult task than the one every Secret Service agent undertakes on any given day. Weeks, months, or years of tedium may, at any moment, be shattered by the actions of those who wish to harm, to kill. Secret Service agents seem, to me, to be the counterparts of football's unheralded offensive linemen. No one praises them when things go right, when the millions of logistical details making up their daily routines result in no assassination attempt, nothing newsworthy. But, of course, we do hear of them on the very rare occasion when something bad does happen. And Secret Service agents must live with that unfairness every day as they protect people whose political survival demands that they do things that make them, in essence, unprotectable. For this and many other reasons, the men and women of the United States Secret Service deserve the respect and admiration of every American. They certainly have mine.

David Baldacci
Washington, D.C.
January 1996

ACKNOWLEDGMENTS

Jennifer Karas, for being a terrific friend and avid supporter and for getting the ball rolling way back when. Karen Spiegel, my biggest fan on the West Coast, may there be many huge movies and small statuettes in your future. Jim and Everne Spiegel, for all their support and encouragement.

Aaron Priest, the man who plucked me from obscurity, my friend and agent for life, and a helluva nice guy on top of it. And his assistant, Lisa Vance, who diligently answers every one of my questions, no matter how off-the-wall. And to the Priest Agency's editor-in-residence, Frances Jalet-Miller, whose insights and thoughtful comments made me dig deeper into my characters and made the book far better in the process.

My editor, Maureen Egen, for making my freshman publication experience so painless and rewarding. And to Larry Kirshbaum, who saw something in the pages very late at night and changed my life forever.

Steven Wilmsen, a fellow writer, who well knows how hard it is, and who fed me good advice and tons of encouragement all along the way. Thank you, my friend.

Steve and Mary Jennings, for technical advice, legwork, and being the best friends anyone could hope for. Richard Marvin and Joe Barry, for technical advice on security systems.

And to Art, Lynette, Ronni, Scott, and Randy for all their love and support.

Here, the words really do fail me.